THE BEADS

A NOVEL

DAVID McCONNELL

ITNA

ITNA PRESS
Los Angeles, CA
www.itnapress.com

David McConnell. -- 1st ed.
ISBN 979-8-9882829-5-2

Library of Congress Control Number: 2024935614

The author would like to thank the International Writers' and Translators' Centre of Rhodes for their generous support during a key phase of this novel's development.

For Darrell Brownlow Crawford

SOCRATES: And which gods will you swear by?
Because, to begin with, 'gods' aren't a coin current with us.
STREPSIADES: Then what do you swear by?
By the iron money of Byzantium?

—ARISTOPHANES

. . . people are under the misapprehension that
the brain is situated in the head.
Nothing could be further from the truth.
It is carried by the wind from the Caspian Sea.

—GOGOL

PART ONE

1

FROM THE POOL came a strange, laryngeal thud. No more than that. Something had gone in. Even though he knew it was too dark to see, Darius slipped out of bed and pressed his forehead to the window screen. He smelled dust and the cool aluminum frame. Sometimes a dog jumped in. A messier splash. This sounded hardly bigger than a frog. But Darius was positive it was a person. Trodden water tickled the concrete and made the overflow baffle cluck. Hushed voices clinched it: angry (bare feet on sycamore litter), hysterical peep, groan (water too cold) and, "Get in!" "Sh!" A boy's mock-heroic yelp was followed by a great limp of a splash and the after-drizzle. A girl screamed shyly. The back yard lights came on.

Downstairs, Oliver was just as quick as Darius. Just as silent. Not timid, but indifferent, and too dignified, he'd skip the outraged property-owner's bluster. He'd let self-consciousness run its course. In the bloodless glare one girl held her forearms like double doors over her breasts. Teenaged buttocks flashed as white as a toad's belly, yet beautiful.

Sibilant strides wetted the asphalt drive. They slap-slapped to the front of the house. Laughter and car doors. The teenagers squealed away, probably to the Schwartzbaugh's pool, or the Aveni's. The water still moved. Darius stayed at the window. The scene ought to have been melancholy—him alone up there, them on a spree—but he didn't experience it that way. He felt an indescribable pleasure. Now that they were gone, he did. Wound up, his thoughts and heart raced. He pressed his cheek to the screen, which gave like soft cloth. Even the rubble of insects in the gutter of the window frame was spattered by the—call it *love* that gushed from him in pools-full.

Love? He had a strange understanding of things. For him, everything good in life only came into its own, was only pure, though faint, when time had stopped, as in the great rotunda of a library or in the secret trays of a fanatical collector or at a window or in the moment after someone has gone. He didn't belong with the teenagers, but right where he was. Because he was—this isn't quite exact, but close—eternal. A quality like antiquated fame. Fame in the dry, stopped time, outdated encyclopedia sense, which doesn't care how obscure one has become over the centuries. Darius was a boy a few years shy of puberty and in every way unknown.

Others had no idea he had the good fortune to be so illustrious, though occasionally, when they looked at him, or listened, their gaze paused as if they just made out something in him, something brightly lensed by the invisible grandeur of eternity. Darius hoped so anyway.

He was modest about his illustriousness. A lonely boy's fantasy. A sort of timidity, perhaps. In his memory he held the pallor of those buttocks as a collector would a rare bivalve, with studious and immobile zeal. The love, faint as it was, was almost too strong to bear. Now the memory would last forever. Darius had, or was convinced he had, consecrated it to eternity.

He was fortunate in another way, too. Rich in the conventional way, as you could tell by a glance at the house, the pool, the showy luxury of his father Oliver's silk dressing gown or the opulent brocade curtain Oliver held aside with a finger. You could tell, but Darius was still too young for this *real* wealth to have much meaning to him. Oddly enough, his delusory wealth, his wealth of time, was far more vivid.

If he really thought about it, really exercised his memory, he'd have to say his illustrious quality went back several years to the time he decided to live in his own underground. His parents indulged him. They let him move down to the basement for a while. The basement of the house was enormous. Storage rooms, a vast laundry with a mangle, an ancient coal room, terrifying as an oubliette, a modern boiler room, a labyrinth of slatted closets filled with garden things and broken beach umbrellas and shelves lined with dusty jars of peaches in brandy.

Darius set up in the largest of the closets, which was littered with desiccated daffodil bulbs and seemed the most burrow-like. In another of the closets was an antique spool bed, which was pulled out and assembled for him. Oliver came down every night to check on his son. The elfin tinkle of his martini was at odds with the weary shuffle of his slippers on the gray wooden treads of the basement stairs. Darius could tell his mother had ordered Oliver to the basement, but once downstairs his father made the best of it. His smile wasn't too pained. And however long this life underground lasted—a few days? A week? Not a month; memory was unclear—Darius and Oliver seemed, to Darius, utterly complicit, almost like one person.

Here, memory was vaguer. What did they do? Darius seemed to recall they spoke in a foreign language. Maybe Oliver would pronounce the words, half distracted, and Darius would repeat them fervently. As if from a great distance, Oliver might smile and nod, only occasionally taking the trouble to correct the boy, more often making a "that's close enough" twitch of his eyebrows as he wet his lips in his martini. The glassy man's invisible attention, nervous as a fly on a window, was unbearably exciting to Darius, who remembered having to keep himself from thrashing under the covers out of pure high spirits. If he were able to stay perfectly motionless, Oliver might talk to him as he would to an adult when a conversation's going nowhere. "This bed you've got here used to belong to the man who had the house before us. Colin Vail, peculiar, artist type, one of those stories—"

He wouldn't tell the story. He'd look at Darius for a long moment and then wink.

On the subject of Colin Vail, Darius's memory became frankly fantastic. Did his father really come to the basement sometimes and carry the boy into a second closet? There, piled helter-skelter like grave goods, were shabby cardboard models of houses and villages, boxes of absurd objects. Trial-sized bottles of Prell and Mardi Gras beads had been glued into place in a shallow frame covered with bright yellow feathers. On the one hand, it was impossible. On the other hand, Darius had the unshakeable notion, almost a memory, that his father and he had made these things together. That this was their workshop. And that these objects were a playful and secret form of art entirely unlike the masterpieces of the world above. It was a real memory. But everything in that storage room had supposedly been created by this other person, Colin Vail.

Several years later, the man's sister showed up. Darius didn't remember her except as a tall woman with a clarion, haughty voice unlike his mother's whisper. His mother, who hated the basement, stayed upstairs. Oliver led the sister to the storage room. She peered in. She looked a little angry at the contents. Her hand brushed the mere thought of dust from her backside. Oliver eyed her. Emotions were charged, and Darius was careful to efface himself.

"Oh, and Cassie, there's an old bed we set up for the boy," Oliver said with an unctuous chuckle as if being a father embarrassed him. "Freak of fancy. Got it into his head to sleep down here."

They trooped over to the burrow-like closet. The bed was still there, forlorn without its mattress. Along the slats sprouted the velvety gray buds of insect chrysalides. The sister made a face. "It's something he's attached to?"

Oliver shrugged. Darius felt their attention turn to him. His answer was going to be momentous. He said, "Yes. I'm sorry."

The sister shrugged in turn. "No, that's fine. Who cares? It's yours." She looked back at the bed with an overbred flicker of a smile and sighed. Darius was certain he'd taken something precious from her. That the loss would be with her always. It was hard to keep himself from saying, "I've changed my mind. You can have it." But he remained silent. Soon afterwards, two workmen came to empty the closet of Colin Vail's creations. They took everything off in a van. Everything except the bed, which was cleaned up and put in an attic maid's room. By that time it was Darius' whim to live in the highest place in the house instead of the lowest.

These memories were uncertain and remote. The only evidence of Colin Vail's existence, of the treasure chamber of private art, which Darius and his father had actually made themselves, the only evidence that Darius had lived in the basement or spoken a secret language with Oliver, was the bed. It was still in his room under the eaves, and he slept in it every night. And when he had that sense of his illustriousness, of his former fame, as he did when he watched the naked teenagers in the pool and understood that time operated differently for him than it did for them, which is to say it didn't really operate at all for him—though the intuition didn't come to him in the form of articulate ideas like "immortality," "fame," or "eternity" any more than ideas of "food" or "beauty" would come to an albatross noticing the scaly glimmer of a flying fish hundreds of feet below—when this exaltation came over him and he wondered, "How did I end up like this?" he supposed it might have had something to do with his artistic work in the night with Oliver long ago and underground.

Private mythologies like this are incredibly hard to shake. Rather than checking things against his parents' memories, Darius kept it all to himself. Oliver didn't seem like the kind of magical personage who would make art or speak an unknown language. Not anymore anyway. There were no more periods of complicity between father and son, if there had ever been one. His father seemed perpetually fogged by adult concerns. His twitchy attention migrated over Darius in wintrier and wearier haste. Once or twice a year the name "Colin Vail" might be mentioned. Contentedly Darius narrowed his eyes and thought, *Ah so!* He felt in no hurry to ask questions.

Darius had recognized a couple of the teenagers from that flying pool party. Perhaps his mother was the first to mention it a month or so later—a horrible car accident on a treacherous hill before the turn-off to the Lawrence Academy upper school. A boy was killed. Everybody knew him. White pants sagging to his hips, he'd worked at the club snack bar, but he wasn't just a local kid. He was a Lawrence student. People knew his parents. The thing was tragic. Darius didn't recognize the boy's name. He made the connection later, one morning when he studied his father studying the newspaper. A halftone of a long-haired blond shifted back and forth in front of him. Button-down shirt and leather choker, three-quarter "casual" school profile, raffish smile. The dead boy. The boy who'd also taken a midnight dip in the Van Nest pool. The nakedness, the slapping feet and laughter and, especially, the squeal of the car, all came back to Darius. "Nude," he mouthed. A chill rose from the undersides of his thighs, through his armpits to the nape of his neck. A corner of his father's broadsheet wilted.

Distinctly Darius said, "Nudalia sexalia runawayedia wetten."

He got no response for a long time. Oliver folded and refolded the paper into fussy quarters and mumbled, "If that's supposed to be French, we'd better fire the David creature."

"It's not French. I'm thinking about that boy who was killed." Darius was careful not to sound emotional in the least. But replaying the living memory of the boy was like being hit in the belly.

Oliver wrestled with the paper. The dead boy faced him now instead of Darius. Oliver looked like he thought the boy a fool. Yet he managed a chilly sort of compassion as his reading glasses winked up and down the yearbook photo. "Well, that is sad. Pathetic."

"He came over here one time."

"I don't think so," Oliver said. He checked the surname. "We don't know them."

"I invited him over."

"You did?"

"We swam."

"No, you didn't. This boy was older than you. You've only had that Barry what's-his-name over."

"No. I'm serious. He came over to swim."

His father looked at him with a touch of eternity-lensed intensity. Darius had the pleasant sensation of being recognized. He felt something unpleasant as well. He couldn't put his finger on it. Oliver may have been experiencing the strange distaste certain grownups can't suppress when they see children playing at unearned experience. He asked, "Are you pretending? Don't pretend all over somebody else's tragedy, Darius. That's a trashy thing to do. You don't even know what it's like to lose somebody."

"I'm not pretending. He came over to swim."

The death was big news at school. There was a moment of silence. The kids excitedly acted stunned and woeful. But was it all an act? A gruesome detail stuck in Darius' mind. Apparently the body had been so mangled that, with the long blond hair, no one could tell at first whether the victim was a boy or a girl. That sort of unrecognizability, which seemed like complete and eternal anonymity, spooked Darius. In his view, that was more "death" than death was. Just like his eternity was more "life" than life.

When he came home, he took candle stubs from a kitchen drawer and ran up to his room. He was going to pray, see if he could get in touch with the world beyond, which was as familiar—through masterpieces and memories—as it was unverified. He had a lot of love stored up for the blond boy. He dressed himself in a ratty old satin comforter. In his closet, he bowed his head three times and solemnly shook a heavy chain hanging from the ceiling. The jingle was meant to be a sonorous knell. He burst through the bamboo curtain hanging across the closet doorway. With stately tread he marched around the spool bed and knelt by the open window. He jammed the candle stubs into the aluminum runners of the window screen frame. The air was just still enough to light the wicks. But when Darius took his cupped palm away the flames shrank to tremulous, imagination-thin drops of light. *If they go out, there's no life after death. Everything I believe is a dream.*

2

FORMER LEFTIST DREAMER Jane Brzostovsky taught ten-year-old boys. She was popular, and during the school year, about every month, she was invited to dinner by one or another of them. The invitations, enchanting displays of nymphal upper crust manners, didn't enchant her. Not at first. Coming from a job at an urban school where the custom didn't exist, she found the invitations made her uneasy, mistrustful even. The dinners were awkward. Once she'd eaten with her student and two Filipina housekeepers in the kitchen, while the parents (Dairy Queen franchisee and pharmaceutical sector analyst) dined alone in state. That comic book gazillionaire behavior was laughable but turned out to be unique.

Eventually Jane found a way to enjoy herself. She looked at the evenings as an education. Seeing the domestic worlds of her little men added psychological color to the forces of history she still often thought about. Careful not to be too well-mannered and careful not to gawp, she discovered the exotic gentility wasn't utterly irresistible. Observing "the help" was a nice corrective. They were either morose and perfunctory or ashimmer with the cynicism of slaves in Plautus. It was all new to her. A real education for a Queens girl whose father had wept at the clarity when he first read Thorstein Veblen. Or so he now claimed, a tearful, repetitive old man. Now his only pleasure was the occasional knock-down drag-out with Jane about how even what was left of the Left in 1983 supinely equated Ronald Reagan (Reagan*ism*, God forgive us) with society in its natural state. Social Darwinism. Father and daughter agreed. It only sounded like they were arguing.

However ambivalent she was about fraternizing with the rich, New York (she refused to say "Harlem") was finished for Jane. For five years she taught at a private school in a crumbling brownstone. One student and his whole makeshift family were blown to pieces in a gas explosion in their homestead across the river in the Bronx. Jane went to the homegoing service. That finished it for her. An insane minister sing-songed over a cluster of tiny white caskets piled with candy, cards, and droopy flower shop leftovers. The minister said he could hear choruses of angel children hollering welcome to the family in heaven: "Rakeef! Devon! Devon, get over here!" Jane realized that everyone believed this, truly believed it with doomed soft-headedness. They could smell the grass of heaven. She had to leave.

But the pretty world she'd entered concealed a much worse sin. She was no Thorstein Veblen, and anyway this sin was inconspicuous, exceedingly difficult to make out. After many months, however, with an excitement that felt wonderfully uncouth, Jane hit on it. The training in irony. That was it. That, she decided, was the spring of sin.

She saw it often and everywhere. On the patio of the Westerbrook Club's poolside snack bar. Tables of tanned children laughed with precocious knowingness about a TV show, an acquaintance or anything or nothing at all. A plastic "brass" plaque was glued to the wall of the snack bar above a raucous table. *Todd McCormick 1966-1983 We Miss You, Skeetch.* The shine hadn't come off the plaque yet, and a keychain with a plastic *E.T.* figurine hung precariously from one corner. This was a grave offering from an eleven-year-old girl. The children's attention turned to the figurine. Laughter exploded. Overhearing them, the mothers at the next table chuckled fondly. One of them dropped a lemon wedge on her napkin with an iced teaspoon and an air of infallibility. To Jane she explained, "We don't like *E.T.* anymore."

As if Jane couldn't gather that from the woman's son, who was leaning toward their table now to crack, "Mom, *please*! We've *got* to see *E.T.* for like the fiftieth time!" Laughter re-exploded.

The boy plucked the keychain from the plaque and made it hop into a friend's boat of French fries. "E.T. phone French fry! Please," he droned in a nasal voice.

Like any late twentieth century intellectual would, Jane tried to sort through the semantic feedback. A little boy parroted grown-up cynicism in order to ironize other little children innocently enamored of a *faux naïf* fable. She recoiled from the conceptual rococo. She fixed on the disdain. Cruelty—oppression, really—subtilized. She was too cautious not to question her own Reformation ferocity. Wasn't it a little much for her to bandy about the word "sin"?

No. Her paranoia was the blood drawn by their invisible weapons. It seemed sweet of them to invite her to Westerbrook. But once here she felt a bit like a paid companion, a ladies' maid, a babysitter. She couldn't think her way out of continual, faint resentment. When she tried to finesse it, adopt their sweetness, their "Belgian" shoes, their trumpeting laughter, her submission only felt more complete. Revolt against their little nothing airs was impossible.

Among these women, who'd endured lifelong training, all the heavy-handedness of irony had vanished. In fact, one and all, they'd forgotten their early lives as worms. Their creamy friendliness, their little frownlets of concern, as eloquent as cling wrap, were, to them, anything but the global falsehood Jane thought screamingly obvious. With an insistence that didn't strike them as suspicious in the least, they liked to murmur the name of their sort—"nice people." Sometimes they whispered the two words bare of any context at all! This time, into the aimless silence following the children's laughter, one of the women even piped, "I thought *E.T.* was a *nice* movie. A tiny bit gross in parts, but I like it when good triumphs." Her defiance sounded proud but little-girly. Yet with perfect distinctness, Jane understood her to mean the opposite of what she said: "Really, the movie was worthless, and I like it when evil triumphs!" It was one of those truths only hysterics can perceive, but no less true for that.

Gazing tranquilly at the splashed-in pool, another woman, Sohaila Van Nest, whispered, "I never see movies." Her conversation often wilted back on itself like this, hardly conversation at all. Highly articulate breathing, perhaps. But she snagged everyone's attention. Sohaila was an anomaly. Foreign. Her black bathing suit was rhinestone-encrusted. Huge sunglasses, like split black melons, didn't quite hide the tips of painted eyebrows. Had she been American, they would have thought her trashy, a tart, but, because she was foreign, even the ballsy garden club women accepted Sohaila's whispery manner, garish makeup and languid deportment. In fact, her unplaceable accent and exotic hauteur had a strong fairy tale allure for them. This was years before trashiness became a universal affectation, even among WASPs.

Her presence at the club today partly accounted for the long silences. Almost like suitors, the chummy women hunted for common ground. Sighs and mild exclamations about the weather kept the conversation going. One boxy wife chuffed, "You should be *in* movies, Sohaila! Doesn't she look like Sophia Loren? I've always thought so."

Sohaila smiled at the noises of assent. "But I always hated being so dark." Long fingernails kicked at her black hair. "You'll think I'm—do you know I was blond once? Like you." She nodded at the women, all of them. "So silly! Like a dancer! For me, I mean."

"This gang's not as blond as you think," one woman brayed.

"You remember Jeanette Paul when Barry was young!"

"Can you imagine?"

Clipped laughter yielded to an enjoyable tension. Looks were exchanged. "She's right over there," someone sang in a teensy whisper.

The boxy wife glanced at Jane. Leaning forward, she planted her chin on her fists. Her bathing suit straps fell from her shoulders like spent petals. "For years and years and years she's dyed poor Barry's hair the same color as her own. Right from the start, I imagine. Just so people would think it was natural. Hers, that is. But the thing was—years ago no one lightened or had streaks like we do now and the dye was *so* cheap. Barry lived in the pool, and, of course, the chlorine turned his hair green. Bright green. Nothing could have been more obvious."

"I mean, really! Who cares? I tint my hair! So what!"

"The woman's deeply, deeply unsure of herself."

"That's nothing." The iced tea spoon lady pursed her lips.

"Ah, well—" the boxy wife cautioned. She fussed with her straps.

Several of the group leaned back in their chairs. The tension abated.

"Darius doesn't look like me," Sohaila observed. Her accent was at its strongest when she pronounced her son's name. She said, almost, "Dah-li-*ush*," though the rest of the world pronounced it the ordinary American way. Unless she was present, when they avoided using his name at all.

"For obvious reasons! Adoption's a different case."

"She's talking up Bea Sayles," said a woman who was keeping tabs on Jeanette. "By the wee-wee pool." Even from a distance Bea Sayles's friendly squint looked besieged. She was mechanically dipping her youngest son, Ross, in the baby pool. "I should go rescue her."

"Bea can handle herself."

"To be blond they would think—" Sohaila said ethereally. "Almost—you were a concubine." Jane Brzostovsky looked at Sohaila skeptically. Could the woman be such an airhead? All jewels and rouge? Without seeming overly stiff, the other women managed not to laugh at the unusual word, though one of them turned it over softly. "Concubine."

Sohaila's son, Darius, was one of Jane's students. Something of a child dandy. Jane wondered if it wasn't the mother's influence. The boy had a penchant for wildly floral shirts. And too tight white pants that made him look like a sexualized clothespin, skinny with an overlarge head. Jane found him a little displeasing. He didn't strike her as boyish enough.

Darius was neat and prompt. He arrived early in homeroom and sat quietly while the other boys played chess or flicked triangular paper footballs across their desks. Sometimes he made a flowery gesture to himself before recomposing his hands on the glazed plywood.

In Jane's opinion, he was mostly dull and inhibited, but every so often he spoke at length in class. On these occasions he was riveting and made no sense at all. He'd twitch and flinch at the loud ticking of the clock as the words poured out. He only became still when he leered at a patch of the acoustical tile ceiling. "Sharks are animals! Sharks are *animals*! You look at them, and they have these major senses we don't have. And they're *animals*, so—also, the fishermen don't know about the cancer cure thing!"

Waving for his attention, Jane put in, "Are you saying they'd be more careful not to overfish sharks? Our speaker made the point that even though sharks are dangerous, they may benefit us." Jane knew the sense she tried to make for Darius wouldn't penetrate.

The student who'd just given his homeroom speech on sharks and who was still jumpy and flushed in patches squealed, "Yeah, because of what *I* just said—the cartilage!"

"No, no," Darius groaned. "Because sharks are animals!" His gaze made an appealing but haughty sweep of his audience before drifting to the ceiling again like oracular smoke. He made a passionate gesture with one arm in a way that caused giggles. He seemed not to hear them. "This, *this* is not what they see!"

Jane began to wonder whether this time he was making sense a bit too sophisticated for his age. Then she heard, "They're as scared of *us* as we are of them!" An age-appropriate banality.

But then, "I have a tooth from an extinct shark two-thousand-feet-long." Snorts of disbelief and *no ways* went unnoticed. "I threw it in our pool. I won't say why." Was it a contentless compulsion to perform? Gibberish rhetoric, in a manner of speaking? "I know he loved his tooth." Much laughter. And Darius laughed too, as if for a moment allowing this was all a joke. The moment passed. "But he's an animal—was. You guys might be useful for cancer, too. You could be! *This*!" Thrillingly he seized the homeroom speaker's hand and tried to hold it up. But the boy shook his arm free with a stormy look and blocked-sinus wheezing. Darius talked on. What could one say?

When the boy finally wound down and the bell rang, Jane reminded him to stay after class to discuss his own speech, next on the schedule. Darius sat, crossed his legs tightly and put a jaunty hand on his hip. He looked exhilarated, proud, which somehow annoyed Jane. The truth was, she disliked him. He was spoiled. Unseriousness bubbled up, like that moment of laughter today, even when passion had seized him. Most ironic and maddening of all, he adored her. She was his favorite teacher. He took her winces, her reserve, her dutiful encouragement as a sort of hilarious flirtation. She sighed. "Maybe you should think about doing a follow-up, more on sharks, since you feel so strongly."

"I'm doing it on the Borgia family," he said, an eyebrow raised. He'd moved to the desk closest to hers. "They've probably never heard of them." He chucked his head at the empty room.

"Darius, don't be so arrogant. You come off looking foolish. I'd wager some of them have heard of the Borgias."

He smiled at her, an oddly prying expression, and repeated "*Foolish?*"

"I only mean it takes a lot of hard work to do well and—to explain your thoughts clearly. I do get a sense that you have something to say sometimes. But let's get on with it. What about the Borgias?"

"Well, the Pope had a homosexual incest relationship with his nephew, who was really his son."

"I think there was a lot of nasty gossip about the Borgias. I mean—a very evil family."

"And the son was in love with his sister."

"I don't think you need to be—sensationalistic in your speech."

Again he raised an eyebrow at her.

"Darius, do you know what all that's about?"

"Of course."

"What?"

"Sex. The Borgias, you mean?"

"I don't know if that would be such an appropriate thing to dwell on. Maybe if you talked about the dark side of the Renaissance."

"You want me to hide the truth?" he asked in a most insinuating tone.

Jane made a face at the window. Outside, healthy-minded boys were playing flag football, plastic streamers, red and blue, dancing from their narrow hips.

"Don't look out the window on me," Darius said, outrageously, baselessly intimate.

"Darius!" Jane snapped. "A little respect!"

His face went slack. She closed and rolled her eyes briefly, causing herself an invigorating pain. The boy's ignorance didn't make him any more endearing. He had no clue about her real feelings. She glimpsed a vast rather than a poignant vulnerability in his shock. As vast and empty as the mother's glorious vacuity behind the intergalactic darkness of her sunglasses. The family resemblance startled Jane and frightened her a little. These people were deeply odd as well as dull. It wasn't a matter of colorful eccentricity.

Her heart sank when a chastened Darius frowned and asked, "I was wondering, if you feel like it, if you want to come over to my house for dinner."

"Does your mother know about this?"

"Of course," he mewed awkwardly, frowning harder. Then his lips made a nonsensical pout. His shyness was as unreal, as random as his arrogance, though perhaps it took more out of him. Jane knew she couldn't hold him responsible for not expressing his emotions clearly—he was only a boy—but her sense of being manipulated was overwhelming.

She said, "Well, let's have your phone number, so I can call and check. But yes, in principle, I'd love to come over. And we'll have your outline by Monday, and just remember—heavy on the politics, light on the sex. There're some things you have to—know more about before you can talk."

In the teacher's lounge she reported his infuriating reply. "He said, 'I know all.' What is it about that kid?"

Her much older colleague was a history teacher with a reduced schedule of classes. Jane had a soft spot for him, a mildly daft old boy from another era. He was looking dolefully at the discolored bottom of a glass coffee pot. His face was crumpled as if education, far from being an easy life for the unambitious, were uniquely exposed to time's bad weather. "You don't like him," he rumbled gently. "It happens." The faucet spattered the front of his pants. He moderated the flow.

"No. It's a little different. He gets to me. I'm talking about him now, and that actually annoys me. I'm usually curious about the kids, but he makes me not want to ask questions. I resent being interested. And it's not as if I know all about him or understand him. He's talented and smart but hardly outstanding. It's more his manner. A sort of negative star power."

"He was quiet with me. Had him in New Jersey History. Average and shy I always gathered."

"Well, it may be he has a crush in my case. But that's not what gets to me. It's—you want to shake him and say, *Connect, for God's sake!*"

"*Only connect*," the old man quoted stagily. "Hmm." He brushed at himself, looking hapless and incontinent. Tall and stooped, he wore a formless blazer. It hung like saddlebags, the gaping pockets full of quizzes folded lengthwise. "And so you must go to dinner, to dinner with the king! The board should be excellent," he said hopefully.

"About the last thing I care about. Fancy food." Jane crossed her arms stubbornly. "Could it be rivalry? Jealousy? Because he's rich? But all these kids are rich."

"The family's intriguing, Ms. Brzostovsky." He enjoyed pronouncing her name. "But you're not going to like them, I'm afraid."

"No, I know. I know already. He takes after that geisha of a mother of his—spacey."

"That can't be. He's adopted."

"Oh! Oh, damn. Was I supposed to know? I knew about the Baker boy. Does he know himself?"

"I'd imagine so."

"Funny, maybe that's what got him on the Borgias. Nephews who turn out to be sons. But, you see—even with something like that—I should feel more compassionate than I do. It's what I was saying about his mother. Not that they look alike but that they were disconnected in the same way, and that's upbringing."

At that, with a magical ping, the coffee began to piss itself into the dirty pot. The old teacher contentedly murmured, "Lifesblood! Yes, the mother, well—but I was thinking more particularly of the father with whom I've had a bit more interaction.

You won't care for him. Not a pushover like me." He winked amiably. "Very grand in his origins. We were doing a unit on the Puritans, and Darius brought in a manuscript letter from Cotton Mather. The real thing, written to one of the father's ancestors, I believe, and surprisingly toadying. He counsels *reflection* or something, if I recall."

"Aha! All right," Jane smirked. "The WASP with the exotic wife." The corners of her mouth curled tighter.

"But he can be—and this is between you and me, my dear—he can be quite sinister."

"The WASP with the exotic wife," Jane repeated in a heavier rhythm.

"Oh. I see what you mean." An old WASP himself, he looked hurt for a moment. He could see her lack of expression was meant as apology. "All *I* meant is the man can be ill-mannered."

"Wonderful! He said something in particular?"

"No-o-o," the history teacher said thoughtfully. He made sure the coffee maker's parts were in place. The drizzle was slowly lowering in pitch. "No. We've had dealings. We're both alumni. Darius is a legacy, of course. No, it's simply that he can be brusque. Snide, even. You don't know where you stand with him. Not my idea of the good old, none-too-bright WASP at any rate." He chuckled to gloss over a deception. He touched the side of the coffee pot with a finger. The heat made his hand jump, and the quizzes were jostled from one pocket and fell.

Only the month before, the aging history teacher had talked Oliver Van Nest into contributing five thousand dollars to help rebuild Lawrence Academy's upper school gymnasium, destroyed by arson. In the course of head-shaking over the unidentified firebug, Oliver muttered, "A sick kid. Or a communist like that Reichstag business." Then he remarked that Stern's *Hitler Diaries* might clear up some of the "tremendous confusion about those so-called death camps." Holocaust denial wasn't yet the notorious cottage industry it soon became. The old man had never heard of such a thing. He didn't know what to make of Oliver's remark. But he decided he wasn't going to tattle about it now. A mote of an incident, it was still radioactive. And he wasn't going to ruin Jane Brzostovsky's dinner.

The old man was suddenly unhappy. Mere secondary school historian that he was, he was aware his silence, even now, here in New Jersey, could be construed as complicity, albeit remote, in millions of deaths. "In silence, like fetal sharks, complicity devours civility," he intoned or, maybe, quoted mysteriously.

The coffee maker puttered and hissed now that the water had run through. Steam belched from the top, and the machine sighed like a luxuriating dragon. The fragrance of the coffee provided the history teacher no *oomph*, given his dreary consciousness of mass murder.

3

THE VAN NEST place was a Tudor style proto-McMansion, circa 1925. The massively gabled house had patinated somehow over the years until it almost looked like a real dwelling in its gloomy copse behind a vast front lawn. Huge rhododendrons clogged the narrow path to an unused front door, so Jane entered through the kitchen with a twinge of irritated pride. Over the door leading to the rest of the house a now-defunct register used to inform the servants where they were needed. Arrows cocked permanently to "Front Drawing Room" and "5th Guest Bed." made desuetude look like an Agatha Christie plot. Jane sized things up with distaste, all but ready to be shown to dinner in the nursery.

But the dining room table was set for the right number, four, plus one extra. The extra place was taken by a nervous, dwarfish young man who held his shoulders askew. He was Darius's French tutor, David Caperini. David had joined the household when Princeton, where he was an occasional graduate student of some kind, came into session. Employing him was Sohaila's inspiration. As a girl in north-eastern Iran, she'd had French tutors, a scatter-brained Armenian couple she'd adored. Jane doubted anyone adored David. Darius had never mentioned his tutor and ignored him throughout dinner.

But David was sociable. He greeted Jane with ridiculous joviality. "Ah, the—the celebrated, the swooned-over Ms.—uh—Ms. B!" She gave him a thin smile. Though he talked more than anyone during dinner, everything he said had a strange rhythm, a submissive scurrying-out-of-sight. When he wasn't talking, his fingers twitched and his shoulders jerked.

They dined by candlelight. Dishes were carried from the kitchen by a maid or housekeeper, who was as lethargic and careless as an embittered Denny's waitress. Though the places were set with paper napkins and everyday stainless, the regal china must have cost a fortune. The first few times Jane glanced at Oliver at the head of the table, she thought, "Heinrich Himmler." (Ironically, given the Holocaust denial secret.) It was simply the caricatural pairing of a receding chin and old-fashioned wire-rims. Maybe Oliver's preppy blue Oxford looked vaguely uniform-like, as well. Quirkily he fastened the top button. Jane wondered if the blue shirt hid a skin condition. Oliver was silent at first. Rude. He flared his nostrils. He sat perfectly still and seemed to count something by means of the nostril-flarings. Or he looked like a lizard, motionless except for its reptilian dewlap flexing.

He wasn't utterly rude. With an elaborate contortion he held his cigarette halfway behind his chair so as not to cause offense. At intervals the arm came flying around, and he energetically flicked the cigarette in the region of a dainty crystal and silver ashtray. The ashes flew everywhere. Onto his own plate and that of his son. The arm was then politely dislocated again. He set down his fork and used that hand to slick back the hair mostly absent from his bulbous forehead. Picking up the fork again, he made an idle gesture with it but still didn't say anything.

She had plenty of opportunity, but Jane gave up hunting for the right moment to unload the comments she'd prepared about Darius's progress in school. There was something odd, willed almost, about the awkwardness. It couldn't be made better by ordinary efforts at chit-chat. Sohaila wore a drowsy smile. Her painted cat eyes wandered the room, maybe judging the effect of this or that detail of the décor.

"And I—I—he told me the whole yellow rain chemical warfare to-do is going to collapse now, because he—he—Mikelson and they found out it was—of all things—bee pollen. Which I must—doesn't sound entirely convincing? Somewhat mysterious when it's so—so—dreamlike. No? Really—giant swarms of honeybees letting loose a—a golden shower? Really?" David maladroitly bumped the forks and knives of his place setting and repositioned them helter-skelter. Tiredly Jane counted the number of forks and courses.

Oliver snorted at what David had said. And Darius mouthed, "Golden shower." Exactly as the Westerbrook woman had whispered, "Concubine."

"Does the pollen drop off them when they fly or when they land?" Sohaila asked.

Jane pointed her chin toward David in a semblance of interest and was startled when he winked. Unless it was a big twitch.

"It falls from their leg hairs," he explained delicately. "In the air. And—and the mycotoxin, which—which they—they thought—wrongly apparently—"

The moment after she vowed not to speak, Jane weighed in. "A chemical attack wouldn't surprise me. They like playing games with the media. Consider the source." She went on broadly, "Is anything Al Haig has ever said *not* disinformation?" At that she was able to stop herself.

Interrupted, David twitched even more. He seemed to shrink in his seat slightly as if he thought Jane had done something naughty and might be punished. He shot her a private look. Jane wondered if it weren't a nerdy come-on of some kind. Except that he was obviously gay. Maybe he was why Darius was so screwy. Possibilities of abuse drifted through her mind like mass murder.

Oliver was staring at her. The instant Jane noticed, his gaze buzzed off. She thought to dilate soberly, "On the other hand, we have to be so careful when it comes to chemical weapons."

"Why?" Oliver whispered under his breath to a vacant corner of the room. The too soft word came bracketed by a sniffle and wasn't clearly part of the conversation. Everyone felt safe ignoring him.

By now Jane had gotten used to uncomfortable student/family dinners like this—the pressure to make a good impression, to praise the boy, to be polite without going overboard. Tonight, strangely, the discomfort was different. The oddity of the Van Nest *ménage* undermined intimidation. Oliver's childish silence,

David's absurd flirty glances. She felt none of her usual Belgian Shoes inhibition, and in fact she'd slipped them off under the table and was cracking her toes on the carpet. But rather than enjoying a sense of liberty, she was wary, afraid of herself almost. Before she'd finished her first glass of wine, outlandish ejaculations like "Faggot!" (to David) and "Nazi" (to Oliver) darted through her mind tauntingly like minnows.

Expecting a contemptuous basso, Jane was surprised when Oliver finally did speak aloud. His voice was thin and high and wavered unsurely. He said, "I don't believe a word they say. Any of them."

David's mouth formed a stagey O of alarm. Jane was surprised herself. Here was a Lawrence parent who wasn't giving Reagan the usual comfy benefit of the doubt. Unlikely he held any progressive opinions allied to her own, though.

"Consider the source," Jane said quickly. "Who made the original yellow rain accusation? Who but General 'I'm-in-control-of-the-White-House' Al Haig?" From the corner of her eye she could see David had raised his glass to her. Thinking she hadn't noticed his toast, he leaned forward to tickle the back of her hand with a forefinger. She flashed him a chilly smile and pulled her hand away with a shiver.

A vulpine half-smile spread on Oliver's face, and he closed his eyes in, it seemed, intense pleasure. His arm swung around, and he scattered ashes vigorously, muttering, "Yellow rain! Yellow rain! What crap!"

A titter escaped David, because he'd been thinking that yellow rain *was* bee crap in a sense. Jane suppressed a smile for a different reason. Oliver looked like he was making a chemical attack on his own dinner table with his flailing cigarette. Humor is better the closer it is to unfunny, and Oliver was unfunny. Not a man to be teased, however ripe for it.

"What kind of a chemical attack is it if nobody dies?" Sohaila wondered. "I haven't heard that people died. Did people die?"

"I think there were, besides—besides health problems, some people—did—" David managed to squeeze elaborate hesitations into the most hurried remarks.

Oliver didn't let him finish. "Of course not," he lashed out. "Even if people did die, how would they know what they died *of*—with all the—crap that's been dropped on these countries?"

"Regular bullets kill so many more," Sohaila said with feeling. "And landmines!"

"Exactly the point!" Oliver agreed harshly. He wasn't at all unsure of himself, despite the reedy voice. "This isn't about chemical whatever. It's about truth. About truth." An ironical smile ghosted his face, too fleeting for Jane to be certain it had been there at all. "These—assholes are drunk on what they think is secret knowledge. They're as ignorant as we are when it comes down to it. I know. I've been in government."

Jane frowned. Oliver was going off on a tangent. Curiously she probed, "But it seems the issue here is a conscious U.S. propaganda attack against the Soviet Union." She tacked on, "Right?" But she didn't come off sounding politely uncertain as she'd meant to do. Everybody was silent. Jane was afraid she'd gone too far.

"Think so?" Oliver mumbled at last. He shrugged impolitely. "Point is, when they do get these chemical weapons up to speed, there won't be any *maybe-maybe-who-knows-I'm-not-sure*. Scads and swathes'll be dead. Just like that! Scads and swathes of 'em. Everybody'll know it. And that'll be good. I mean, obviously bad. But long-term, not-obviously, in the way of very bad things, it'll be good. We'll know the truth and what they're capable of."

No one said anything for a while. "Uh—uh—" David began. "Mr. Van Nest has a theory that—that—that the convenience and lethality of weapons—no?—that it gives—that there's a paradoxical civilizing—"

"That it forces us to be aware. To think. March of civilization blah-blah." Oliver impatiently fed him the line.

"So you believe in progress?" Jane couldn't help teasing as if his argument were tantamount to believing the earth is flat.

"Oh, Mr.—believes many—thinks about these—things in a—well, he *experiments* with ideas." David looked at Jane too meaningfully. His tone of voice was indulgent to Oliver, yet also insulting. Jane wouldn't have been surprised to see him fired on the spot. She didn't dare say a word herself. The wrinkled green leather of five aged dining room chairs creaked in unison. Strangely Oliver was perfectly complacent. David swabbed the sweaty rings under his eyes with his fingertips and addressed his employer. "Remind me to give you a fascinating J.B.S. Haldane article. Along these–lines. Chemical–after the Mustard–in World War One." Now he sounded prudently sincere.

During this whole conversation, which held little interest for him, Darius couldn't sit still. The seat of his chair made a continual breathy squeaking. He ate and, at the same time, methodically cleaned his father's ashes from his plate with the tip of an index finger. The ashes that landed in his food didn't seem to bother him. Only the flakes that dirtied the gilt-edged porcelain.

When the housekeeper came from the kitchen to clear the plates, conversation about yellow rain was abandoned. Morose, slatternly, the woman's limping trips around the table filled Jane with an inward cacophony of anger and self-contempt, all the more unbearable because she somehow looked like she was *in it with them*.

David asked Darius in a cloying tone, "Are you enjoying having Ms.–*Ms. B*, all right if I call you–too?–with–having her here with us?"

"I'm going to marry her," Darius raved promptly. A grin, cute but sour, appeared on his face and vanished. His fingers touched Jane's shoulder like swarming butterflies. She'd felt them several times already this evening and tried not to flinch.

David's mouth made the O again, humorous this time. He laughed by tipping his head absurdly from side to side. His skin was dusky in the candlelight. Maybe a blush lingering after the *faux pas* with Oliver, or, Jane suddenly guessed, he was drunk.

"You'll have to earn a tremendous lot of money to support a grown-up woman," Sohaila commented.

Darius turned to Jane. "Are you OK with that? I mean, I'm sure you want to marry me. Obviously! I have everything."

"That's fine, Darius," Jane said. "Is that how we should pronounce it?" she asked the table as a diversion. Sohaila shrugged.

Under his breath, Oliver muttered, "We only learned later on what a big ghetto name it was. We'd never have chosen it."

"It's a popular Black person's name," Sohaila explained innocently. "For me, it was just Persian."

"Uh, marriage?" Darius insisted.

Finally Jane laughed a little to hide her annoyance. "That's fine."

"All settled!" Darius piped, crossing his arms and his legs.

Jane didn't want to look at him but did. Starred by candlelight his eyes seemed impossibly haughty. She wanted to feel warmth instead of simmering dislike, but these people hardly merited consideration. Unless Darius alone deserved it. A boy, still. She forced a smile. This shred of a kindly thought brought her enormous relief. Even before coming she'd known she would find his situation more pitiable than anything. Her anger suddenly rose up against the so-called grown-up desires—the personal indiscipline!—that led a couple like the Van Nests to adopt a child. The selfishness!

Oliver left the table without a word, only sneaking a last glance at Jane. Below the neck, she was almost certain. David bowed when he got up, shook her hand. His grip mixed twitch and mannered politeness. His lips moved but only garbled formulae came out. All the while his gaze implored her—it could have meant anything.

Darius pushed him aside and begged Jane to visit his bedroom. Infuriatingly Sohaila waved them off. She drifted across a cavernous entry hall into the unlit front drawing room as imperturbably as a tiny planet jostled out of orbit. Jane followed the *châtelaine's* gray figure until it disappeared. No light came on in the living room. Only tiny red, green and slowly blinking lights of electronics shone in the pitch darkness.

Darius reached for Jane's hand to lead her upstairs. She ran her other palm along the oak banister, smearing David's sweat on it. The foot-wide banister made her hand feel childishly small. The uprights were roughly carved telamones, their original bad taste intact. Jane managed to grumble something cheerful enough to Darius as she followed him up the shallow steps.

"I do love you," he laughed, sprinting ahead. "Adore you!" he added with somewhat stronger but seemingly arbitrary irony. He sang out nonsense syllables in a demented falsetto. She looked down at David, who'd reappeared at the foot of the stairs. He gave her a twiddly wave.

Darius was lost to sight. The stairs kept switching back, slightly less grand after each turning. Jane said, not loudly, "Darius, I can't follow if I don't know where you're going." He returned at a run. His arms flailed. He grabbed her hand again.

"Here," Darius announced. He was so overwrought he buried his face in his hands. They stood in the open doorway of a book-lined gable room. A tiny room. A former maid's room packed with scuffed family furniture, castoffs. Everything was old. The worn cloth-bound books must have belonged to a grandparent at least. A gray window fan, possibly as old as the house, thrummed in a cage of zig-zag wire covered in oily dust. This loud, dismal fan produced a weak current of air in which strands of a bamboo curtain clacked gently in the doorframe of a huge walk-in closet. The closet was nearly as big as the room.

The woodwork was painted the same functional gray as the fan. But its matte surface looked dry and porous like whitewash. The non-fan window was open. Jane looked down a steep roof at a swimming pool, black as petroleum. Darius was humming-moaning. Through the shimmying bamboo strands Jane could make out more furniture in the closet, and a grim-looking steel chain threaded with plastic roses hung from a hook in the ceiling.

"That's my closet. I guess I could show you."

"No, Darius. I don't want to be—"

"No, that's OK," he said bravely. He strode across the room and pulled the curtain aside.

"Darius, I don't want to," Jane let out. But she couldn't not see the sloping walls he'd painted in garish acrylics. Starbursts, hearts, *Peace* and *Love* in a pillowy sixties lettering. The bizarre chain of roses was inexplicable, but Jane refused to ask about it.

"I painted all that when I was a kid," Darius said. "I know it's stupid." He was nervously gathering the strands of the bamboo curtain into a huge chirruping cable.

"We all—" Jane began seriously. "It's not stupid at all. Peace and love? Come on!"

"No. It is. I mean I did it as a joke, of course." He was tugging a little too hard on the bamboo curtain. The flimsy tension rod popped from the top of the doorframe. Darius flinched. His hands covered his head. Yellow trickles of bamboo sluiced over him.

"That's embarrassing," he announced. He was blushing and wore a pouty, angry expression. Mock-dignified, he undraped himself and kicked at the bamboo on the floor. His pique suddenly disappeared. "That reminds me! I used to *wear* this thing! I just remembered. Maybe when I lived in the basement. I wonder how I did that?" He tried pulling the woody curtain around his shoulders like a cloak. One hand pinned it around his neck. With the other hand he flounced the cloth of bamboo and gestured sacredly. "I thought it made me look like some weird kind of priest. Or king. This is pretty good. Better than my other cape."

"Darius. What are you doing?"

"What?"

"Why don't we hang that back up? Straighten up in here?"

"Why? Someone else will take care of it. Let Tina do it. We don't have to do anything." He said this so provocatively Jane averted her eyes. Tina was the limping housekeeper. Darius let the bamboo cape clatter from his shoulders. He fixed on Jane's throat and whispered, "Tina is my *slave*." His hand at once covered his mouth and he guffawed, because, even for his family, that was going a little far. He leapt onto his bed wailing, "I'm sorry! I'm sorry! Here," he tried distracting her. "This is my bed.

"Darius." She said it without indulgence. She turned her back on him. "I'm going down."

David stood in the doorway, quite clearly glassy-eyed and flushed in the full light. "I thought I heard a—Darius—a big clatter. Having a—a tantrum or something?" He said it with what he meant to sound like fond irony.

"Shut up!" Darius muttered.

"Just the bead curtain," Jane said. "I'm going down."

Darius refused to see them downstairs, so David and Jane descended flight after flight in silence. David lagged and made several conversation-broaching noises, but Jane tried to keep the pace up. Coming to the last flight David finally spat out, "You know—you know—they've closed up shop. Gone to bed. The Van Nests. They won't—no need to say goodbye."

"Really?"

"Nightcap?" He finally produced his fuddy-duddy invitation. "A strange family."

"Clearly. Does he see somebody?"

"Ritalin, I think. The tantrums are real, by the way. He's been known to topple a whole bookshelf—why I came up—just kicked it over." David smiled. "You know what makes them like this, don't you?" he whispered. "It's just the money."

"Probably. Ultimately, yes, I'm sure that's it," Jane said warily. She didn't really want to befriend David. His expression begged her to speak, however, so she went ahead. "Is he really as awful as he seems?"

"Oliver? Yes. He'll—well, he'll say anything. All to—just anything for—shock effect."

"He doesn't believe in that poison gas scads-and-swathes'll-be-dead-and-it's-somehow-good theory?"

David shrugged. "Probably not. Low-grade self-entertainment, I'd say." He looked around before trailing off in the smallest whisper possible, "But racist, anti-Semite, all that seems pretty authentic—"

Darius went down to his parents' bedroom to say goodnight. Propped up by pillows, they lay on either side of a room-sized bed. Oliver sipped a beer. He was studying an inflammatory flyer about a Chinese restaurant boycott (Jade Tree on the Bowery), which someone had handed to him in the city. The boycott seemed to be about employee working conditions. A pouting lower lip made his chin vanish entirely. *The Wall Street Journal* waited its turn propped against yellowish knees.

Sohaila wasn't concentrating on her magazine. She kept thinking she heard music. She was certain she hadn't left the CD player on downstairs, and even if she had, she couldn't be hearing it up here. The illusion was interesting. Each phrase of the music was new, unknown but somehow remembered. She turned the glossy pages of *Metropolitan Home* from time to time, but she was trying to listen straight through. The music was brilliant, a little like Debussy.

His parents' symmetry on the bed pleased Darius. He knelt exactly between them, salaamed and rested his cheek on the down comforter. He faced his father for three beats, then he turned his head and faced his mother for three beats. He asked whether they'd enjoyed the evening. His father's soprano grunt was quick. Sohaila lagged. "Very nice!" After a voluptuous pause, she asked, "Why are you turning your head?"

"I have to. Do you like her? I'm going to marry her." He only mouthed the cute joke now, neither offering nor finding any humor in it. He seemed dulled.

"Well, I don't know if she's the best person for you."

"You don't like her? But I love her. She's my favorite teacher."

"I don't know if I think she cares about you in the way a really nice and loving person should—someone you'd want to marry."

Darius's head shot up. Then he mechanically recommenced turning his head on the comforter, one beat per side now. "Mom, I'm madly, madly, madly, madly, in love, with, her."

"Oho! You are, are you?" She smiled finely.

Oliver turned his head. He directed a very unpleasant expression at their two-thirds of the bed. He tugged the comforter slightly from under Darius's knees. The newspaper fell from his lap, and he snatched it up irritably. He slapped the salmon-colored boycott flyer to his bedside table, muttered "Fuckers!" This was followed by a strange peep of laughter.

Unperturbed Sohaila said, "Dah-li-*ush*? You know your little friend Barry?"

"Uh-huh. What about him?"

"The little blond boy."

"Not little, Mom. Bigger than me."

"Oh, you know the one, though. Your friend, right? You want to know something? He isn't blond. Not really."

Darius's head shot up.

"Maybe I shouldn't say. You mustn't tell. It's interesting, though, isn't it?"

Darius turned his head trying to think of a response. He stopped after a moment, settling on, "Yes, he is."

"No. He's not blond. His mother dyes his hair to be like hers. Like if I dyed your hair black. Would you like that?"

"I'm not sure," Darius said. "I don't think so."

"Not that it matters. He looks good as a blond boy, don't you think?"

"I guess." Darius frowned.

4

IN HIS LAWRENCE Academy homeroom, Darius, who'd been unusually quiet for several days, seemed on the verge of talking to the ceiling tiles. Jane Brzostovsky deliberately overlooked his waving arm, nearly double-jointed with yearning. At intervals a grainy, silvery thunder of cheering came through the open windows from the middle school playing field. "I know everybody wants to get out, so I'll try to wrap up," Jane said.

"I have something to *say*," Darius blurted out.

"Not sure we have time, Darius." Jane tried to sound offhand. She snuck a glance.

Darius looked betrayed, his brow pinched. In a snide tone of voice, he addressed the class. "She just doesn't want you to hear the true thing that will go against her small-minded—"

"Hey! Watch it! I don't like the sound—"

"Of course, she doesn't. She's—"

Jane grabbed his upper arm and flung open the classroom door. She dragged Darius into the hall. The other students, vocalizing like monkeys, peered after them.

The door had revolved on its hinges and struck the outer wall. The pewter glare from a glass pane shuddered on the tile floor, and an aqueous clangor reechoed up and down the hall. Jane's muscles felt like frothed milk, her eyes actually hurt in their sockets—she was so enraged. Darius' head rolled with flower-like indifference. "You've been wanting to touch me for a long time, haven't you, babe?" he said. She struck him with the flat of her hand. A light blow, the out-of-control controlled, almost symbolic, but still. His expression wrinkled up.

"And all of you, shut up," Jane snapped at the murmuring class.

The slap could have been a serious matter. Jane dutifully reported it to the head of school. Without exactly spelling it out in their discussion, the head of school and the Lawrence Board chair settled on a course of inaction, not even a phone call to the Van Nests. This risky calculation paid off, because Darius never did tell his parents that he'd been hit.

Jane felt an irritable sort of remorse. From that moment on, her patience with Darius was fantastic. This withering patience, even more than the slap, cooled his ardor for a while. Yet on a deeper level he didn't seem to register how much he was saddened by the apparent failure of their relationship. And while she rather enjoyed her own self-control, Jane had no idea how much he was saddened either. There was no sign of it. Perky with nonsense, chatty and outrageous, his personality was more haphazard than ever.

Maybe Jane wouldn't have been so hard on him, maybe she would have kept the horrendous parents more compassionately in mind, if only Darius weren't best friends with Barry Paul. Barry was Jane's favorite student by far. She had a full blown, frankly erotic, crush on him. It was parenthetic and humorous, of course—doll-sized—like Oliver's gassed millions or her own inward class turmoil about the Van Nest's housekeeper, Tina. Seeing the two boys together drove her crazy.

And they were almost always together. Inseparable from the start of the year. Jane, who'd kept a close eye on Barry since her first days at Lawrence, had completely missed the moment the friendship suddenly sprang into existence. It happened with kid-like abruptness. It was, she supposed, very pure, very beautiful and very mysterious. At least on Barry's side. Her flicker of jealousy was quite funny to her.

Next to Barry, who was husky, Darius looked svelte and crafty. With Barry, he was uncharacteristically self-effacing. Chin scratching his clavicle with feline strokes, he'd eye his friend and whatever his friend was eyeing. If he craved attention, a rapid whisper passed his lips. Then, as soon as Barry turned to him, frank and grinning and, for some reason, amazed at what he'd heard, Darius' fingers squirmed. They formed a white-knuckled spider on the white denim stretched tightly across his thigh. He smiled and seemed to recede again.

Now that Jane knew Barry's hair was dyed it was obvious. The eyebrows were a few shades too dark. She almost laughed. Self-deprecating amusement bubbled up in her, becoming more abundant affection for Barry, then diffuse happiness, then a barely visible smile.

Barry was considered mature for his age. As far as anyone could tell, he was unharmed by a dreadful mother and a wan, negligible father. He had a strange charisma of utter normality. Jane often tried pinning it down. The universal mistake people made—this was Jane talking to herself—was thinking that the quality didn't actually belong to him. People thought *they* were content, *they* were having a good day, *they* were interesting, *their* personality was bearable, even admirable, whenever they had some little dealing with Barry. And everyone did feel this way. Jane tried to make out it was her absurd crush talking, but she really believed Barry's appeal was widespread. It wasn't just her. Since he wasn't memorably beautiful and never said anything a suburban New Jersey boy wouldn't say, he was able to go about his business in the healthful anonymity that suited him. His star power was slow-acting, even subterranean. Jane invariably laughed it all off but sometimes failed. In subtle stages, she'd given up the notion that this quality Barry had might not be objective. Everybody knew it *and* it was a secret. Like naïve maps that place the Garden of Eden exactly here, so many miles northwest of Ur, her possible fulfillment seemed to be local, tangible, the fragrance of sour candy on this one boy's breath.

Barry's eyes were set wide. He squeezed the right one closed when he didn't understand something—often enough. In repose his mouth looked horizontal, grim and almost countrified, but it was always moving. He was an avid, poor skateboarder. He tied a spare wheel truck to the flap of his backpack as a sort of tradesman's token. He had no particular passion for any of his classes, though he liked the biology unit of Science best. The hair at his ankles and a straggly patch above his huge, red-eyed death's head belt buckle were thickening prematurely, which made him seem secretly manly, despite a beardless baby face.

Even at eleven, a year older than most of the boys in his class, he was lumbering. He was too big to have a mischief-maker's appeal. And since he was bigger in body, when he got in trouble the trouble seemed a bigger deal than it was. He was caught shoplifting *Rock Climber Magazine* from a 7-Eleven. There were frequent successful thefts, as well.

Barry and Darius couldn't answer the question about how their friendship had started any more than Jane could. They didn't notice they were particularly friends at all, until she smirked at them one time. "You're as thick as thieves, you two." Several other adults dropped similar aren't-you-cute comments. Which made friendship feel unpleasant, but the boys had to admit, they were always together. Other kids were matter of fact. If they wanted to know what Darius thought about something, they asked Barry. And vice versa. They addressed the two, even when one of them wasn't around, as "you guys." A wag wrote a poem about them: "Very hilarious/Are Barry and Darius."

The boys even traveled together. When she heard about this trip after the fact, Jane experienced an operatic jealousy. The emotion shocked her. *Ah, perfido!* It was torture how each boy came to her to report happily about spring break. And even worse torture hearing herself needle them about it over several days like some—well, some Claggart. Needle them and at the same time probe for more and more detail.

Barry had a cousin, a freshman at Rutgers. Pressured by his mother, this boy invited Barry to tag along on spring break. The cousin rented a clapboard house in Bel-Mar with ten schoolmates. Because parts of explanations were omitted and because the Jersey Shore was so close and because "cousin" sounded perfectly all right and the cousin's mother confirmed everything, Darius was allowed to go. Jeanette, who savored the connection to a schoolmate's rich parents. As for the cousin, he reconciled himself to the company of children for two contradictory reasons. He intended to use the boys the way a lady-killer uses a puppy. And he planned to enjoy a sincere and sentimental pantomime of fatherhood, surprisingly common among teenagers.

Like most New Jersey shore towns Bel-Mar was built along the narrow beach in ribbons, boardwalk, traffic-congested street, bars and surf shops facing the Atlantic, then a quieter strip of modest summer houses.

The world is marvelous when a mob of doting teenagers seems grown-up. Adulthood looks unbearably beautiful and energetic and free. To Barry and Darius Bel-Mar didn't seem anything like the drunken madhouse locals grumbled about. They were often so happy they panted when they talked. The first day they decided to speak as loudly as possible.

"SHAKE IT, DARE!"

"I AM, BARE." Darius turned to a voluptuous girl in a green bikini and purple kimono. She was the only one who was up at that hour. She'd fixed cereal for them and fumbled with a cigarette now. "Should I help clean up?" Darius asked her.

"Uh, no," she answered, unsure about letting them run off to the beach on their own. But Barry was so determined.

"I GOT YOUR TOWEL, DARE!"

"COMING! WEAPONS?"

"GOT 'EM."

The girl made an expression like *Yikes!* With a discreet finger she tucked away a few black pubic hairs showing at the top of a bikini-strangled thigh. Pulling her kimono over her lap, she blew an uninhaled mouthful of smoke away from Darius and through the screen door. From the humid dimness deeper in the house a mucous-y, male voice said, not unkindly, "Get out or shut the fuck up."

On the beach Barry shouted, "SEE THAT OUT THERE?"

"NO. WHERE? WHAT?"

"THE BOAT UNDER THE BANNER-TOWER. HURRY! UNDER THE TAIL OF THE BANNER—'QRL EASY-*PISSING* MUSIC' I THOUGHT IT SAID!" A bleating biplane with a trailing yellow radio-station ad indeed appeared to overfly a distant ship.

Darius laughed, gripped his belly. His too-large mirrored sunglasses, already askew, slipped off when he bent forward. "OK, YEAH. I SEE IT. SO?"

"ILLEGAL DUMPING. THAT'S WHAT HE'S DOING." Barry shrugged and pretended to inject his forearm with a hypodermic, by which he meant the ship was probably dumping infected needles along with its illegal trash. Darius squinted at the horizon. He couldn't see that the ship was dumping anything, illegal or not. "CAPITALIST *SCUM*!" Barry screamed.

"Hey!" a stranger in headphones barked.

Barry and Darius gave one another a long look. Barry arched his back, thrummed his belly like a duffer but deftly lifted his towel to his hand with a foot. "THINK WE CAN PIPE DOWN, DARE?"

"I DON'T THINK SO. THIS IS JUST THE WAY WE TALK." Darius cringed a little at his own outrageousness.

"WE JUST TALK THIS WAY?"

"YU-U-U-U-UP!" Darius screamed. He covered his mouth with both hands.

The stranger pulled off his earphones and feinted to get up. The boys ran down the beach. Half an hour later they were still escaping the man in fantasy. Darius pretended that the reverse of the Bel-Mar Daily beach tag safety-pinned to the hip of his Speedos was a video screen. He sat on the gritty boardwalk and pulled his towel over his head. One of the stranger's earphones was a camera (planted earlier) and Darius could observe the man's thoughts on the screen. "SHIT! HE'S COMING!" He scrambled to his feet and shoved Barry in the small of his back. The boardwalk boards made cooing thuds as they trotted off toward the bridge that led to Avon-by-the-Sea and Bradley Beach.

Fantasy was only tolerable to Barry. He enjoyed Darius's knack for it like he enjoyed watching movies. But left to his own devices he preferred talking with the teenagers. When the older boys exchanged meaningful glances about something he didn't understand yet, he took it good-naturedly.

He was fascinated by work. He pestered a pizza boy with questions about hours and wages. Though the pizza boy was standoffish at first, he let himself be drawn out. He scratched flour from the messy scar of a patched cleft lip. He was vague about his recent discharge from the navy, said he'd passed his GED. Barry listened with an expression so adult that the drink straw in the corner of his mouth looked like a gangster's cigarette. Somehow he'd gotten the navy boy thinking about his life.

Like an uncle slightly out of true, the boy fumbled in return, "What do you kids think you want to do, be, whatever?"

Barry and Darius answered at the same time. Darius said, "Actor, I guess." Barry's response was a question: "You ever put stuff on the pizza if the guy that ordered it's a real jerk?"

Darius had long had an inkling that his friend was a few levels more mature than he was himself. In an occasional funk he would narrow his eyes and dismiss Barry as painfully normal—boring, even. But the normality exerted a powerful fascination. Barry—maybe all normal boys—seemed hurtling and unprotected in a way that caused a familiar tenderness to well up in Darius. As if he and Barry and the dead boy Todd McCormick, for that matter, were all on a pool party spree, splashing and ducking, and Darius suddenly needed everything to stop. To be up in his attic window again. His grandiose tenderness, not unlike his secret and illustrious eternity, made Darius feel as if he had lived as fully as a grizzled warrior king already. The condescending emotion bore no similarity to his hilarious beach tag/video screen or earphone/thought camera, but they were basically both play-acting.

He must have been feeling homesick, because on the last day exactly that flying pool party anxiety came over him. The two boys and six half-naked teenagers piled into a car and sped off. Racing and bucking in traffic, they were driving who knew where. Everybody talked at once. Darius was queasy.

Toward the Atlantic, freighters and Jupiter pricked the lavender evening as white glimmers. The car was full of scent. The crammed bodies touched with secret alertness. Frightened, exhilarated, saliva sluicing along his inner cheeks and past his molars, Darius sat dumb among these extraordinary strangers. Even Barry was a stranger. Where were they going? Anything might happen.

They pulled up alongside the big park in Spring Lake, safe and sound. A band was playing under a panoply of Irish flags. An upstanding crowd of picnickers was scattered across the lawn. Pulling on T-shirts, the teenagers formed a sheepish group and ogled the clarinetist, their friend.

Barry and Darius ambled down to the pond. Their approach seemed to bump two swans onto the black water. The boys sat brushing the day's feather-shaped patches of sand from their skin. Darius made Barry hold his hand an inch from the skin of his thigh, not touching it. "My soul," he explained. "It got so hot today it's leaving my body. Feel it? Let's—yup. You're losing yours, too."

"Bullshit—Shit, I am!" Barry tried to sound amused, to play along.

"What'll you do without a soul?" Darius sighed. His tone wasn't so broad now.

Barry smiled. "I guess we'll go to Hell." He threw a dried pea of excrement at the swans. A gluttonous carp made rings in the water.

"But you have to *have* a soul to go to Hell," Darius countered.

"Oh, right. Well, I guess, maybe, we'll be like wandering souls. And our bodies will be like zombies. Maybe something like that."

"Whoa, Bare! Your foot!" Darius pointed.

Barry examined a black crust between his toes and along the edge of his scuffed left foot—dried blood. His sole was still wet with it. He recalled wincing on a broken cockle shell at some point that afternoon. Strangely, he'd felt no pain whatsoever, then or now, though at times he'd vaguely noticed something slick like mud underfoot. The wound was too horrible and painful looking to waste. "Oh, yeah. No big deal." Barry raised his chin and shrugged in contentment.

He garnered a satisfying expression of awe from Darius, who wondered, "You want to wash it?"

"Not in there! I just threw a swan turd in there."

"Really? These things are—?" Darius stirred the pellets with a stick. "I think I know a big secret of yours," he said. "You dye your hair."

Barry paused only a second. "I don't. My mom does. That's not *my* secret. You and me are blood brothers, so I tell you everything. But the reason you don't know that is cause it's not mine to tell." He tipped his head in consideration. "You shouldn't tell anybody else, though. My mom would probably fucking kill me if she thought everybody knew. She's such a bitch."

"Barry! Don't say that!" Darius whispered back in shock.

That evening Barry made a big deal about his injured foot. He was mewled over by two teenaged girls. They bandaged the wound, and the elaborate bandage caused him such pride that he started limping and kept it up till he went to bed.

5

IN THEIR BONES, many of the teachers at Lawrence Academy had a fatal conviction that adulthood was an isometric mapping of the shoulder-high personalities of middle school, or all but. With fair confidence they picked out the lawyers and the screw-ups.

Sexuality was a more interesting guessing game. No longer a subject too delicate even to think about, bets were only taken in short odds cases like Darius Van Nest. No one wanted to consult openly the handful of teachers one assumed had an eye for those things. After all, who wants to know? Ostentatious shrugs stood for tolerance. Barry and Darius were subject to a bit of speculation. Among fellow students, paradoxically, the couple got only friendly, *pro forma* attacks such as "You two faggots." Alone, Darius might have had to toss his head in bullied isolation.

Their friendship wasn't exactly erotic. They got into an argument about whose scrotum looked more like supermarket chicken skin. The issue had to be settled. Barry treated the comparison as a grave exercise, while Darius smirked. At Barry's direction off came their pants, and they kneaded their balls, pulling the skin over their knuckles like cling wrap. Barry's scrotum was bumpier and more chicken-like, they decided, holding them side by side under the bathroom light. Stiffening penises got knocked out of the way, dumb-seeming as puppies on Christmas morning. Wryly, Barry strangled his with one hand and knocked against Darius's in a meditative rhythm. The boys gradually lost both smiles and gravity, and they ended up just observing, or even just counting the beat, so inexpressive were their lowered faces.

A few days after their trip to the beach they'd gotten filthy setting up an "animatronic" (not really, but still Disney-inspired) zombie experience behind Barry's garage. Jeanette ordered them to shower. Barry sat on the edge of the tub examining his foot. For almost a week he'd carefully preserved the flirty dressing the teenaged girls had given his foot in Bel-Mar. Now, finally, he tugged off the zombie bandages. He picked curiously at the ring-straked gauze underneath, red, brown and yellow. "Hey!" he said crossly, noticing Darius. Darius had turned shyly toward the corner of the bathroom to peel off his underwear. "Don't do that," Barry said. He really seemed angry. "We should just strip down and jump in the shower. I think that's more normal, if you're buddies." For some reason Barry was offended by Darius's shyness. Maybe it made them seem less close. Or he was concerned for his friend: maybe he hated seeing Darius give in to unhealthy habits of mind.

Once, they were sitting together on Darius's bed. Barry was losing a game of *Stratego* through sheer indifference. Darius didn't want to go outdoors, so he tried to keep interest alive by talking. The bedroom's antiquated gray fan was making lopsided white noise. The strands of the bamboo curtain swayed and pecked.

Seeing it through the eyes of the guest he was hoping to entertain, Darius was aware of something dreary and prison-like about his bedroom. He couldn't love it as he usually did. Hypnotized by the boredom of the ticking bamboo and the beating fan he self-consciously stopped talking in the middle of a sentence. His mouth hung open. He felt the rigid panic that occasionally overcame him when he would focus on the fact that none of his relationships was quite real. He was adopted. All connections, from the very first, were based on words not reality. Even this one with his blood brother was unreal. Children may be more subject to these unnamable key changes of consciousness than grownups. Darius went from chattering to faint in an instant. "You ever worry we don't really exist, Bare?"

"No," Barry said.

With uncharacteristic boldness Darius then asked, "Do you ever like getting stuff stuck up your butt? 'Cause I actually do sometimes. Like when I was a kid I knew I was supposed to hate wedgies but I kind of liked them." It felt odd to be sitting there after saying this. He listened to the fan and gently pressed the fanged general token against his knee.

Barry seemed to stop what he was doing, though he'd been perfectly still. His smile looked a little like pleasure, a little like mocking cruelty withheld. "Hadn't really thought about it," he shrugged finally.

"Oh." Darius jerked his shoulders, which made Colin Vail's loose-jointed old spool bed creak for a surprisingly long time. "It's weird, I guess."

One weekend morning the two boys had been on the phone for what felt like hours. It got to the point where they were just breathing to each other and going about their business. Barry was particularly bored, which made him cranky. He threw out, "You know, Jeanette told me Ms. B is a chimo." He'd started calling his mother by her first name, and Darius was imitating him with Oliver.

"What's a chimo?"

"Child molester."

"Yeah?" Darius had taken the phone into a remote attic storage room to rummage through the contents of a junked mahogany sideboard. Inside, the shelves were heaped with countless pouches of soft silver cloth which made gong-like whispers when disturbed. Most of the old silver in the bags was tarnished iridescent black. Under the heap of bags were bundles of ancient family letters, some containing disturbing, beribboned curls of hair. Darius thought his friend was saying that Jane Brzostovsky was a child *beater*. He made himself sound supremely skeptical. "Yeah, I don't think so." He remembered her slap but couldn't call that abuse exactly.

"She asked me if I woke up sticky yet."

"What? Sticky?"

"Right, and then she laughs like she was only being funny. Weird-funny."

"What does that mean?"

"I told Jeanette, and she said, 'That bitch sounds like a fucking chimo!'"

"Barry! Shh!" Darius was shocked. "Don't say that." He opened a manila envelope full of old travel guides and spilled them onto his lap. Dresden decked out with swastikas. "Oh man! You won't believe what I just found. Hitler stuff! Bare?"

"Yeah?"

"You doing anything? I had this idea earlier. You want to come over and help me with it?"

Actually, Darius had had the idea a long time ago. The travel folders just reminded him. After leafing through an old guidebook to Ravenna once, he had conceived of a life-sized portrait of Barry, a dazzling, gold-encrusted mosaic with soulful brown eyes. His plan had been to create this portrait on the wall of his closet alongside Peace and Love. In addition to the mosaic portrait, the closet would eventually be embellished with a dome and a skylight, a far-fetched renovation which meant the whole project had stalled in the world of fantasy.

The return of this vision energized Darius. As soon as he got off the phone with Barry he started hunting for materials for the portrait. Under the rose-threaded chain in the closet Darius laid out colored felt highlighters and Elmer's glue. Downstairs, he found a huge carton of beads belonging to his father.

Beading was a recent fad of Oliver's. With a rich man's lightning enthusiasm, Oliver had ordered huge quantities of beads from a catalogue. Many of them were gold-filled according to the packages, and Darius figured they might work as *tesserae* for his mosaic.

He drew a rough outline of Barry wearing a Byzantine tunic on a bare patch of wall in the closet. Impatiently he smeared glue at the wrist of the garment and began pressing beads against the wall. They fell, danced like millet and were lost under a dresser. At best they slid out of position. He used more glue, set a number of beads in place and pressed his palm over them.

He was standing like this, waiting for the glue to dry, when David Caperini made a meek noise of greeting from the bedroom door. "In here," Darius called.

Pulling bamboo strands apart with two forefingers, David poked his head in the closet. "*Eh bien, tu es là. Tu t'amuse bien?*" Darius looked like he was just standing there, leaning against the wall. David's gaze roamed over the glue, the markers, and the drawn-on wall, pausing at the big carton. A few tattered copies of *Bead and Button* were tucked in amongst the plastic boxes and glassine bags.

"Yes? *Bahnjheur Daveed,*" Darius drawled indifferently. "*Cahnmahn-tallay-voo? Moi*—OK."

The bamboo curtain chattered when David shivered for no reason. "*Très bien merci. Alors, qu'est-ce qu'on fabrique ici?*"

Darius rolled his eyes. At random he tried, "Mmm—*Je pense-le gâteau*—"

"*Mais tu fais pas de la cuisine dans le dressing?*"

Darius frowned. Hearing only David's cute surprise, he said, "*Non! Je suis* NOT—what you think I am!"

"*Mais j'ai rien dit!*"

"*Oui–Moi–*"

"*Écoute, tu fais ce qui te plaît. Á mon avis, t'es garçon adorable. Je ne dirais jamais que ça.*"

"OK. OK. Shut up."

"Darius, I—I wasn't saying you were anything. I was only asking what you were up to."

"Oh. I'm working on this thing." With a squint of pain for drama's sake, Darius gingerly lifted his hand from the wall. Surprisingly, the beads held. But they were dull with smeared glue and disappointingly unlike his mosaic vision.

Standing back to judge his work, Darius pensively looped the steel chain around his shoulders. He wrapped the end around his neck a second time, dislodging a plastic rose. The chain was cold, but the weight felt good. Darius noticed David's eyes boring into him and asked in a sassy tone, "Uh—*yes?*"

"Oh, it's a—uh—what?—a sort of *mosaïque?*"

"Yes, it's supposed to be a *mose-eye-eek*. But it's actually crappy for now."

David's head disappeared. Letting the chain fall with a tinkling thud and more dropped roses, Darius followed him out of the closet.

David perched on the creaky spool bed and, using both hands, seemed to start squeezing something out of one thigh.

Darius wrinkled his nose. "Are you trying to *talk* to me? What are you doing up here?"

"No, not at all," David said. Both his hands batted the air dismissively, then rushed back to his thigh.

"You wanted to tell me my parents have screwed me up, right?"

"God, no. No." David tried to laugh.

Darius frowned and picked at a whorled skin of dried glue on his palm. Unlike some children—Barry, for example—Darius didn't believe adults knew things children didn't. He was the egotistical cat convinced its owners are also cats.

David had slipped his hand under his collar placket to massage his neck. "You know, I wasn't always the happiest kid in the world my—myself—"

Playing it for comedy, Darius sniffled. "At least I have my pills. Bummer for you, though."

"I had to lie on my back in bed for a year!" When Darius didn't respond with anything more than a frown, David made a dotty *pshew!* of laughter and pretended to shoot himself in the head.

"What are you talking about?"

David patted the bed next to him. It was an invitation for Darius to sit. The bed creaked. When the boy didn't budge, David pretended he was brushing at the comforter.

"*On est fort sadique*," he whispered mysteriously. "Where's your friend?"

"*Oui, oui-oui-oui*!" Darius interrupted. "*Non, non-non-non*! What are you talking about? Are you talking about Barry? He's coming over in a minute."

Smiling bleakly, David reached out to massage Darius's shoulder.

Darius squinched his face, "Uh—David. This might be a little bit—uh, chimo—child abuse." He was joking, but the earnest look that had crossed David's face disturbed him.

David released his grip, leaned back and slapped his thighs. Blandly hysterical laughter trailed off in absurd grown-up artificiality. "Oh-ho-ho-ho-ho!"

Darius raised his eyebrows. The way their two gazes met, neither had the remotest idea what the other was thinking. The not knowing was, on David's side, fascinating, heartbreaking.

With a head-clearing twitch, David announced, "Really, I came—Your father needs his—he was looking for his beading things." He nodded toward the closet.

"Why didn't you tell me? Is he mad?"

"*Pas de tout*, I don't think."

"*Pas de tout. Oui, oui-oui-oui*," Darius mocked in irritation. He immediately dragged the big box from the closet, the bamboo strands trailing over it. Still angry at David, who was hanging his head wearily, he lashed out. "You know, I saw you put those big folder things in your car. From *our* basement! And all that stuff down there is supposed to be *mine*." He wasn't expecting the cartoonish look of horror that appeared on David's face. Colin Vail's bed started creaking. "Sorry!" Darius piped airily. "I'm only teasing. It's not a big deal." David stuttered something.

Darius manhandled the heavy box of beads down five flights of stairs. He kicked it noisily across each carpeted landing and through the front hall. His father wasn't, after all, angry. He sat on a petit point footstool in the sprawling front drawing room.

A new silk dressing gown with the Barney's tag still attached by a plastic loop hung open, showing a wrinkled chest like softening cream paint. Oliver held a cigarette and a threaded needle aloft with surgical fastidiousness. He crooked his leg and pulled a plastic beading tray across the carpet toward him with a yellow-callused toe. The beading tray was indented with looping troughs, and the troughs were marked off in numbered segments. He said, "Oh, here we are," and nodded for Darius to push the carton of beads next to the tray. He looked back at Sohaila. He said, "I don't know." Sohaila was modeling one of his necklaces, a jade spider web bedewed with gold. "Does it swoop too low here? Or is it just the neckline of that thing you've got on?"

"It feels a little low," Sohaila whispered. "The color is good for me, though. What do I have—? Autumn—winter coloring? I don't remember."

Oliver stood up. Moving behind her, he shortened the strand at the nape of her neck and cocked his head.

Sohaila smiled at Darius. "Do you remember what you were?"

"Same as you," he said, though he didn't remember. "Can I ever use some of those, Dad?"

Oliver didn't answer. Sohaila asked, "What were you doing, darling?"

"Just this art thing."

"He's an indoor boy," Oliver observed. His tone was objective, more narrator than father. "I hate it," he concluded mildly about the necklace. "Somehow the overall shape is wrong for you. I thought *big* would work." As if reconsidering, he tugged a bit more at the necklace. "Ah, well!" he sighed. "Thanks for trying it on."

Sohaila smiled thinly, looking somewhere far off, as Oliver kissed her cheek with extreme primness. Oliver posed his hand on her shoulder for this dainty embrace, and as he did so he slyly pressed the needle still in his right hand into her shoulder.

Sohaila spun out of his arms with a cry of pain. "Oliver!" Her body shuddered and she tossed her hair in rage. After a moment, she shook her head again like a tormented animal. She massaged the pricked shoulder. She repeated her inarticulate cry several times as surprise burned off. *Auch! Auch! Auch!* She leveled a vengeful stare at Oliver. But something about her rapid recovery suggested Oliver's behavior wasn't totally unexpected. The extravagant, practiced frown Darius forced onto his brow made it look like he too had witnessed this sort of thing before.

"Sorry! I didn't—" Oliver blustered with the flimsiest air of innocence.

Sohaila's lips moved a moment before she said anything. "Oliver, really—!" she began with utter contempt. She took her hand from the hurt shoulder. A drop of blood had formed a streak, an angry red *accent grave*. She touched it with her fingertip. She examined her palm. "You're exactly like—"

"Like what?" Oliver whimpered.

"I don't know!" she shouted, though not very loudly. "Like a torturer—*Savak*! Really, you are. Like a—a goon."

"That's outrageous!" Oliver roared with a perverse sort of amusement.

"You're a torturer. You're like *Savak*."

Oliver turned to Darius with a comical madman's expression. Then, all reasonableness, he mused, "If I converted, I think I'd have the right to multiple wives. Four, to be precise. That would be nice. Wouldn't you like four mothers?"

"Oh, Oliver," Sohaila said with disgust.

"As long as I'm equitable and can afford to take care of them, which, of course, I can."

"Please, take all the wives you like. You've become a freak." She glanced at Darius and stopped herself. "You're not the person I married."

Darius echoed his mother's contempt. "What are you talking about, Oliver?"

Oliver suddenly growled and lunged at Darius in play. Darius flinched but held his ground. Full of dignity, he said, "Barry's coming over."

Eyeing her shoulder with teary, glittering concern Sohaila hurried from the room. Darius turned his back on his father and started to walk out, too. But slowly. He took only tiny, five-inch steps as a pure provocation. Given the size of the room this exit took a long time. He was still walking out long after Sohaila had washed her hand and shoulder, long after Oliver, with peculiar sighing groans, took his seat on the *petit point* stool again and started digging through the carton of beads.

Oliver spoke up at last. "You're not going to get very far at that rate." Darius took six more meticulous baby steps, and Oliver went on briskly, "I am sorry, Darius, but there're a lot of things going on you don't understand. I certainly have *not* left your mother high and dry. Foreigners—something you might want to watch out for—sometimes revert to being foreigners even after years living—" Darius started humming to drown out his father's words. He kept making baby steps.

He still hadn't made it out of the room when Tina shepherded Barry into the front hall. "Dare, honey, your friend's called for you."

Darius ended his enraged baby-stepping with full strides. There was no way to hide that his eyes were as glittery as Sohaila's had been. He turned it into drama. He raised his face to a huge cast iron lantern hanging from the hall's ribbed ceiling. He flung out an arm like a child Cicero and cried, "Barry, thank God! Jeez. What a day! You wouldn't believe the day I've been having. This place is a madhouse."

6

THE NEXT SCHOOL year Jane Brzostovsky noticed that Barry and Darius weren't so much of an item anymore. She couldn't celebrate her hero's liberation, because the change had come about too subtly. Nothing like the I-can't-see-you shunning she'd observed sometimes.

Freedom may indeed have been the issue for Barry. His love for Darius didn't lessen, but he liked other people, too. And he preferred practicing skateboarding with a gang of them to sitting in Darius's bedroom with just Darius.

The friendship may have run its course for now. Or perhaps a budding class consciousness figured into it. For Barry, skateboarding with friends had an egalitarian, comradely feel. Darius's tyrannical control of their schedule was tiresome. And Barry thought it bizarre and snobbish when Darius claimed to be "like three-hundredth in line to be *Shah*. The king of Persia, the king of *kings*. Because my mom's a *Qajar*!" When it came to the old dynastic name he pronounced *Farsi* carefully, unlike French, and with the heaviest possible aspiration.

Barry closed his right eye in displeasure. "The Palahvis are peasants!" Darius whispered fanatically.

Darius was only too aware that he wasn't, strictly speaking, a *Qajar* himself. Any more than he was a Van Nest. His aristocratic passions probably originated as a secret anxiety about his adoption. A similar deep-seated case of nerves kept him from reacting too much to Oliver's finicky spasms of cruelty. He could baby step or pout for an hour. But that was it. He preferred dwelling on the mythic, half-remembered period when his father and he were in cahoots in the basement. Cataclysmic changes, like replacement wives or an unrewarding adoptee's expulsion from the family didn't seem inconceivable under Oliver's regime of whims and distorted emotions. Out of caution, Darius forgave.

Barry Paul's gang of skateboarding friends was slightly older. He got in some trouble with them—a marijuana thing blown out of all proportion in his and Jeanette's opinion. Even so, he was hauled before a dour juvenile referee who put him on probation. She also ordered him to write a personal statement for a court psychologist and a letter of regret to her. "What's to keep me from just writing whatever? Whatever you want to hear?" Barry asked.

"'Whatever you want to hear, *ma'am.*' Kiddo, you're in no position to be snippy."

Barry frowned, insulted. "Whatever, *ma'am*. I wasn't trying to be snippy. Just wondering."

"'Just wondering, ma'am.'"

He got Jane to help him write the statement and letter, and thinking of the snippy judge, he told her, "Let's be extra polite. Her and me, we didn't jibe. She said she was this close to sending me to juvie."

Although Jane knew that this was untrue, a sort of twisted boasting—she could hear it in his voice—she fretted indulgently, "Oh, Barry, I really don't think that'll happen, do you?"

They were meeting in a small ground floor office in the 1967 wing of the Lawrence middle school building. Any teacher could use the room, ducking into it to scribble quizzes, assemble model molecules, or meet with students, though the space was almost too cozy for two. The desk and woodwork were blond, the door turquoise-painted steel. Jane and Barry had to sit on the same side of the desk. Her fingers were poised over a word processor. A stuck-looking aluminum crank window gave onto a claustrophobic woodland view made up entirely of saplings. Barry, whose chair was leaning against the wall at first, let it land softly on four legs. He slouched luxuriantly. He could just reach the desk with one elbow. When Jane looked down at him, she glimpsed a khaki thickness against his inner thigh.

She looked away, of course. She glanced out at the woods as if hunting for a word. She felt an ardent embarrassment for Barry. You couldn't be a teacher and not pick up on the humiliation boys feel when that kind of thing happened. Though Barry didn't seem too embarrassed.

When Jane glanced back, the boy was looking at her candidly. "What if we say I want to be a lawyer? Is that too suck-up? Or—you know—inappropriate?"

"A lie?" Jane looked out the window. "No. No, it's—whatever—what about—what if we just make it *wants to go to college* for now?" she murmured. She was thinking she'd been wrong. It was a *trompe l'oeil* fold of cloth or who knew what? She typed for a moment.

"Darius said he wanted to be an actor."

"We're not writing about him," Jane said. With a peculiar motion of her head, she dragged her gaze from the window, across her lap, across the floor, to Barry's lap, up the turquoise door to a small square of chicken-wire glass in its middle. Not exactly sly, but she was *not* mistaken.

Barry shifted wonderingly in his seat as he commented, "But he's a great guy. You never got him. Shy, you know? Sometimes I wish we were more friends like last year, but he's a loner."

"Are you—enemies, then, or...?"

He made a shocked sound. "No. Nothing like that. Come on!" He arched his back. His fists reached for the ceiling briefly. He closed his eyes and deflated. "I didn't sleep so well last night."

Jane got a good view when his eyes closed. The bowed thickness shifted unmistakably. Barry even scratched at it with an ultra-quick peck of a forefinger. It was, to say the absolute minimum, man-sized. Jane looked out the window and answered him a little sharply. "Barry, look, this is important. Please, take this seriously.

"Yeah, yeah, I am. Don't worry. But I really think that *ma'am* judge might be out to get me. Nothing like this would ever happen to Darius."

"Barry, wake up! You've got *so* much more going for you than—Darius Van Whoever-he-thinks-he-is." She dared to lay three fingers encouragingly on his knee, though she didn't look at him when she did and lifted them at once.

"I only meant cause he's rich," Barry whispered.

Jane brought her hands together in bony prayer and kicked her wheeled chair as far from Barry as she could get. Not more than a foot. The back of her chair butted the powdery aluminum window crank.

This was a terrible problem. Jane crossed her legs. She turned back to the keyboard but only scrabbled her painted nails on the desk to either side of it. The immediate problem was that Barry's lap wasn't part of a *private* fantasy suddenly. Unless this was a dream.

He appeared to notice something odd and looked at her. Really looked at her. Even before he said what he said, she snorted self-consciously. He said, "You don't look like you used to."

"Same me," she said in quiet hysteria. "Let's get back to it."

"I think you dress different. Like this whole year you dress different than you did last year."

"*Differently*, but I'm not sure what you're talking about." She did know. She'd started to use a flashy, child-friendly coral nail polish. She was certain Barry would never be able to figure it out. He was a kid, for God's sake. She had to be creating everything on her side. This was some erotic Turing-test confusion.

"Well, like those," he said uncannily. He nodded at her black stockings.

"This is just a French style. Tights."

"And that stuff," he said unerringly.

She wiggled her fingertips. She softly clapped several times. "OK, OK, OK, Barry. Let's get back to it, please." She looked at her watch for effect. She had the fluttery idea that he didn't care in the least about the thing in his pants. That he was aware she'd noticed and didn't care about that, either. Or that he did care, but not in an embarrassed way.

He continued to behave as matter-of-factly as ever. He crossed his arms and pushed out his lower lip. He scratched the inner corner of an eye. The two of them did some work. They composed sentences about Barry's earnest desire to learn, to get into a good college, to find gainful employment that would also benefit society. Jane continued stealing glances as Barry rattled on or yawned or stretched. The thing never changed. She knew what everyone knows about the vigor of youth, but she began to wonder if it was just the way he was permanently. In other words, maybe the lump was soft instead of hard. She thought she'd have noticed before now, but things change. Especially at his age. Barry could have suddenly grown up to be all *shower* and no *grower*. Honestly, if that was the case, he had, almost, a deformity. She began to wonder whether she could contrive to touch it. No matter how minuscule the office was, that was going to be hard—difficult.

She dwelt on the challenge for a moment. Though the situation was serious, she turned it over with much of her former broad humor about the crush. She never imagined she might actually follow through and touch him. She never guessed her fugitive hilarity was precisely the lead-in to trying.

She barely listened as Barry somehow talked his way back to the Van Nest family, Sohaila this time. "I always really liked her. A lot. I was sort of jealous of Dare. His mom's got this thing—like kind of a serene thing, you know what I mean?"

Jane wasn't typing this, of course. They'd more or less finished the personal statement. The letter of regret would be easier. Jane's fingers crooked on the desk in typing position. She stared right through the word processor. Rays of afternoon sun and the blond wood made for dreamlike fumes of honeyed light in the room.

Barry went on in bland innocence. "You want to know something really weird? I mean completely weird. Dare's mom has a boyfriend and his dad doesn't care about it. The guy comes over for dinner with them all the time. He's called Stan. So it's like all three of them together at the table every night. Four with the French teacher guy. At first they thought he—Dare's dad—was going to marry a bunch of wives like a Mormon but then they realized he wasn't into sex, like he's a neuter."

"See if I can get this open," Jane turned to the window. Barry's obvious tall tale about the Van Nests sluiced over her without effect. She gripped the chalky old aluminum crank. She threw the weight of her shoulders back and forth. Staring at the oxidized frame with a trace of wildness, she hit the window with the heel of her hand. "Won't work, I guess," she breathed mildly.

She formed a comical plan. She'd pull the completed statement from the word processor. With a casual flourish—*There-you-go!*—she'd press the sheet to Barry's lap. Her fingertips would feel him ever so slightly through paper and khaki. Then she'd know for sure. Turning back from the window, she took the paper from the word processor. It needed three yanks, and the sheet was a little crumpled.

The plan failed in every particular. There was no ever-so-slightly when she pressed the damaged sheet into Barry's lap. He jerked in his seat at the firm pressure of her hand. Impulsively her fingers pursued as his lap recoiled. They pressed, almost a grip, almost a squeeze. She pulled her hand back, crossed her arms and dropped her chin in thought. "There you go! Personal statement." Barry wore an expression of amused shock.

It was hard. It was hard for Jane to look at him now. She'd seen an expression cross his face, a knowing expression. And even now, the way his brown eyes glowed, the way the corners of his mouth squinched tightly and the down-dusted-doughy pallor of his beardless cheeks pinkened. There'd been neither embarrassment nor unawareness all along.

Not knowing what to say, he stretched a bit, shifted in his seat, more luxuriantly this time, making everything even more obvious. It was now clear to Jane that a portion of his restlessness had been deliberate display. She could see it in his face, and she felt angry, scammed, anything but the instigator. Very sharply she addressed the edge of the desk, "I think we can get to the rest another time. Your regret statement. That should be pretty simple. You could do it on your own." She motioned for him to clear the way to the turquoise door. He didn't move. She frowned in irritation.

"Uh—a minute?" His gaze fell to his lap briefly, brows rising. His knees yawned farther apart by an inch. "Could be a challenge for me to walk around." He snickered. "If you know what I mean."

7

THE RUNNEL-SCORED GRAVEL drive had never been refreshed or black-topped. Barry and another boy were hired to spread the lunar gray gravel as evenly as possible, pulling the largest rocks to the edges to form a rough curb. Barry was issued a real antique of a rake. The haft bulged and tapered slightly in a quaint effort at ergonomics. The stony polish of the old wood started raising blisters at once.

The Paul family lived exactly where a concrete sidewalk ended. To the east were more aging suburban bungalows like theirs, neat but almost abject in their mid-century modesty. Jane Brzostovsky lived in one several blocks closer to Lawrence Academy and Princeton but still in that fancy zip code's catchment for lower income households. To the west, after the sidewalk came to an abrupt weedy end in front of the Paul house, a fragment of countryside remained, including this Victorian farmhouse with its gray gravel drive. The new owner was standing with Barry's mother, Jeanette, in front of her place. She wore a resting expression of unpleasantness as he explained how car tires kicked up the dust of the drive, leaving the vehicles, including his Jaguar, coated in powder. He was going to have to go with asphalt in the end, though he hoped that wouldn't look too citified. Jeanette eyed Barry and the other boy intently, not out of interest but to discourage the boring neighbor.

Barry raked. He rewrapped his blisters with his T-shirt and kept raking. The other boy, a skateboarding friend, also shirtless, was shirking. He had Barry stop to observe a cute trick he liked to perform. His flat belly appeared organless, but he was able to distend it until it looked like he was eight months pregnant. He did this several times, making a great descending wave of his gut. The driveway owner turned to Jeanette with an indulgent smile. She ignored him.

The gritty noise the two boys were making might have been the quintessential sound of labor. Barry's pants and the lawn next to the drive whitened like the neighbor's Jaguar under groggy plumes of dust raised by the rakes. These low clouds floated toward the Paul house. Jeanette waved a hand in front of her face though they came nowhere near her. She gave the neighbor an annoyed up-and-down.

From the corner of his eye, Barry saw her turn when his father, Lynn, came out of the house. The screen door closed behind him with a wiry noise. He raised his foot as if it had been sticking to the welcome mat and toppled off the brick front stoop sprawling on all fours on the lawn. The neighbor had lurched toward him as if to help but stopped because Jeanette had failed to make the slightest move. She turned back to the raking boys.

Lynn was slow to gather his wits, unsteady about standing up. When he finally did, he massaged his sore elbows. He squinted at his son and the other boy as he moved toward them.

Barry guessed Lynn was drunk from the sticky-stepping way he pretended to concentrate on them. Jeanette and the neighbor followed him with, respectively, a narrow gaze and a frown. Eyelids half-closed, Lynn came up to Barry and the other boy. "Hard at work!" he whispered. "Here you are, hard at work."

Lynn noticed grass stains on the knees of his pants. He picked at the cloth and shook it slightly. "Now," he said. "Now. What?" He winced, looking up. "Oh, I mean the..." He chucked his head toward the weeds and Queen Anne's lace where the sidewalk ended. It seemed too bright for him outside. "No, we got a—that's prime territory for ticks—you got to police yourself everywhere after you walk in the woods or the—" He shook a hand, a languid rag, at the Queen Anne's lace. "Or the scrub. Especially your pubes. It's—" His forefinger tapped under one eye to indicate a careful examination for ticks.

Barry made a know-nothing face.

"Oh, yeah," said the flat-bellied boy. "We had a couple of people around here who got it. Uh, last year. Lyme disease."

Barry kept standing impassively. The other boy politely searched his forearms for ticks.

"You remember, Barry. You got to be careful, man. Those buggers are tiny. Those ticks." Lynn half-sneezed and scratched at the inside of one nostril with his thumbnail, prompting another ticklish snort.

"Who got sick?' Barry asked. Over by his own house his mother was leaning in toward the dull neighbor to whisper something. She produced a tart laugh and reentered her house, hips swaying, head shaking. The neighbor started walking toward them reluctantly.

Lynn waved his hand in the general direction of the Atlantic. "Some people living back there. A couple of women with dogs."

Barry began, "I don't want to sound like recalcitrant or anything, Lynn—" He gave the vocabulary word paternal emphasis.

Lynn cut him off, "Doesn't matter if you don't remember them. Just so you check your fucking pubes for ticks." The neighbor hovered behind Lynn.

"OK, we'll check. We'll check." Barry held a palm up to his father.

Lynn stared at the boy's blistered palm. His eyelids were half-shut again. "What happened?" he asked softly, not really asking.

"What happened to *me*?"

"Yeah, look." He pointed at Barry's palm. The blister had broken. A wrinkled flap of skin, awash in clear ichor, stuck to the raw wound in the center of Barry's palm.

Barry shrugged.

"Did you fall? *I* fell?" Lynn whispered. It seemed he was trying to remember. He looked down at his knees.

"No, it just happened," Barry said. "I didn't fall. I guess it's more like stigmata."

"Hey, Lynn," the neighbor finally touched Lynn's shoulder, causing the disoriented man to flinch.

"Look what happened." Lynn tried grabbing Barry's injured hand. He missed. "You got hurt, baby," he whispered.

"Maybe I should wash it?"

"Yeah, go on in and wash," the neighbor suggested. "You guys can get back to it later. Or some other time. I'll give you an hour on the clock for today."

By evening a few fireflies started to pulse in the shadows, though the treetops were golden still and the sky luminous blue. Barry practiced bike riding with no hands. He passed Jane Brzostovsky sitting on her front step holding a glass of whiskey. Teacher student meetings weren't uncommon in fine weather. Barry lived outdoors, and Jane enjoyed subtly blasting teacher etiquette by appearing in public with alcohol or sunbathing. She wondered whether seeing Barry so often as a real person, as a neighborhood kid, hadn't helped her crush along at first. But this time she stiffened and set her glass by her hip.

Since Barry had had good luck being nursed in Bel-Mar, he pulled up and showed her his blistered palms. He'd washed them at the neighbor's, but they were dirty again from the bike's black foam handlebars, which he kept having to grab when the bike wobbled. He was oblivious to the possibility of awkwardness between them. Jane seemed confused. "Do you want me to do something, Barry? You *are* a mess," she admitted, nodding at his white-powdered pant legs. "Here. Come in for a minute," she ordered. In the bathroom she splashed hydrogen peroxide on his palms. She handed him a wad of toilet paper and left him. She topped off her drink in the dining room.

"Your parents know what you're up to?" Jane demanded rather harshly. The whiskey bottle set off a glockenspiel riff when she replaced it among several others.

"They're in the middle of a big standoff. I'll probably have to fix a French bread pizza later."

"What's the problem with them?"

"I think they hate each other," Barry said equably. "He's an alcoholic," he added with a smile at Jane's whiskey.

Jane rounded on him. After an odd gulp of a pause, she said, "Listen. I don't know if I want you tracking dirt all over the house. Let me run those through the wash. It'll be twenty minutes."

She washed his pants. She tossed him a thin blanket to wrap around him like a sarong. Barry smiled at how her body jerked stiffly as she crammed the pants in the washer. His own hands had a tremor until he bunched the blanket at his waist.

"OK. Off you go and lie down while these finish. On the couch in there, I mean," she ordered. He obeyed. She sat in the kitchen by herself, glaring at the telephone. Her heart was pounding. Slight stabbing pains came out of nowhere in her thigh and an ankle. Sharp as they were, the pains were also teasing, messages from her poltergeist mind. Silent as a ghost, she got up and stood behind the half-open door to the dusk-charged living room. She crossed her arms. At length she forefingered the door ajar. She sidled into the room and stood on the far side of the threshold for a long time.

"I'm not asleep, you know." Barry said. "I'm not going to. It's way too early. Before dinner even. You didn't really expect me to go to bed?" Confusion about Jane's twitchiness in the shadows made him frown, but he acted at his ease, stilling his hands by clasping them behind his head. "What are you doing?" he asked.

Jane sighed a tragic, operatic sigh. "What do you mean *What am I doing?* I'm standing right here. Waiting for the wash to end." She pinched the knurled switch of a table lamp. It was loose and ratcheted *on–off–on–off–on*. She took funereal steps into the room.

She posed a hip on the couch arm, then slipped softly onto the cushion next to Barry's feet. Trembling but without touching him she slanted sideways, her fingers dragging her long arm along the back of the couch. A few inches, and decades, between them, her shoulders and side were in awful pain, tensed despite the languorous posture. The trembling got worse if she tried to relax her muscles. Her eyes had adjusted to the light, so she closed them.

She squinted at Barry. In the slowest of slow-motion, Jane pinched a corner of the blanket at Barry's shoulder. Just as slowly, she dragged it off him and kicked it to the floor. "I don't know," Barry said. He meant to sound amused, ironic, poised.

But the strangled syllables came out tiny. His puppy-large hands joined over his white briefs.

Her squint fluttered as if the luster of his skin were blinding. Flawless and white as a new baseball, his chest, belly, thighs, glared at her. This close, he even had a scent like nothing Jane had ever smelled. He shifted so the front of his briefs was better hidden, shyly turning his buttocks partway toward her looming arm and despairing expression. The white cotton twisted over his hip and the crest of ilium. Her eyes closed again. Despite his wiggling, the hidden part wasn't so hidden. In an eyelash-barred brightness Jane could see the untimely, expected swelling of the cotton fabric behind his hands. Barry attempted a wisecracking whisper again, "Mmm. I really don't know." Mirroring her, he shut his eyes, crumpled them tightly in the way of children. Jane's hand fell between the couch's back and his unbreathing torso. On its back, the hand inched under Barry. He seemed unable to move himself until, suddenly lighter than air, his hip rose and let her hand slip underneath.

A moment later—or so it seemed—Jane was back across the room shutting the lamp off. She folded her arms. She stared at the blanket she'd left trailing in front of the couch. She bent and dragged it toward her by one corner. The tense way she held her neck was killing her. She wrapped the blanket around her shoulders in a vaguely ecclesiastical fashion.

8

CASSIE'S FRIENDS DIDN'T know what to make of it when, with a queenly chuck of the chin, she barked, "My father! What a killingly dull *New* Canaan WASP he was!" Or when she complained about a week with friends at the Manasota Beach Club in Florida, "What a WASP-y crowd! And all so old! Help!" She was always happy to get back to New York, where the woman she was—Park Avenue, rangy, impatient, snippy—was as likely to be a laborious act as to be, like her, the real thing, a self-caricature. The possibility of being seen as a fake was liberating. She loved to dress. Tonight she wore the pieces of two different Chanel suits in the blown-up houndstooth popular at the time, the Reagan twilight, and Kenneth Lane "pearls" the size of finch eggs. She'd added a red sash around her middle tied like a cummerbund. Somehow it worked.

Darius trailed his father into Cassie's apartment, glum-looking and sickly-skinny in over-sized prep school shirt and khakis. His palpable unhappiness was perfectly familiar to Cassie. He was such a type: spoiled but miserable, heart already burned to ashes. And since she rarely saw anyone truly young, she also thought with a pang, *God, I must look freakishly old!*

Cassie always pretended to be in the middle of some little chore when guests arrived. She thought it put them at ease and was chic, besides. This time she was carrying a stack of yellowed newspapers she'd dug out of a basket by the fireplace. She meant to run them out to the pantry and replace them with new ones. Instead, she let them thump to the floor and put her hands on her hips exclaiming, "Darius! There you are! You don't remember when we met a thousand years ago. Honestly, seeing you walk in, Darius, I realize this place is way too neat. I had a horrible vision of my Dad's place in *New* Canaan. What a bore he was!"

"Let's mess up!" Oliver seconded with a wooden jollity that made Darius cringe.

"Oliver! *Mwah*!" Cassie briskly mocked *bisoux*. She kicked the newspapers aside. "Mmm. That feels good. I'd like to give a swift kick to all those *fucking*—" she whisper-mouthed the words, so she would be easy to understand: "*Tilted-Arc*-haters downtown—did you read about that, Oliver? An office worker *vote*?! I'm a horrible, horrible talent snob," she informed Darius. "Sorry! You'll have to get used to it."

None of them knew how this meeting would turn out. Their nervousness had a strange, high polish. Even Darius's downheartedness was polished. His uncanny youth drove Cassie a little wild with unease. A panicky suggestion about games came out and was immediately dismissed. Her bony hands knocked the Chanel jacket open and kneaded her red-wrapped loins. So as not to seem condescending, she offered the boy "the hard stuff."

Oliver nudged him. "Go on! Pretend I'm not here."

Unhappily, Cassie fixed an extremely weak vodka-cranberry-soda and two strong on-the-rocks martinis. "I can't believe I don't have any Coke," she muttered in self-reproach. "Or anything good at all."

Darius perched on Cassie's Knole settee, as silent and watchful as a praying mantis. He wiped his glass on his knee, leaving behind a dark crescent.

He was a different boy than he'd been a few years earlier. First, at home, had come the great—*glaciation*, he liked to think of it. Both parents and his mother's friend, Stan, inserted himself into the New Jersey household long before. Third Form, as they affected to call it (at Choate in Wallingford, Connecticut), had come as a shock to Darius. No longer master of a huge, solitary kingdom in the form of that fake Tudor New Jersey mansion, he was obliged to pay constant attention to his fellow Choaties. Though Darius was accustomed to his father's singular and refined brutality, he was not used to a mob of boys squirming like a brood of puppies. Constantly snapping with their milk teeth. He greeted the psychological cacophony with narrow-eyed standoffish-ness, which any grown-up could have told him was a poor choice.

At Choate, Darius let slip to fellow Third-Formers that he'd spent the summer in the hospital, because—his poise was fantastic—doctors had found cancer in his spleen. He had perhaps four years to live, no more. It wasn't true, needless to say, but he wanted a dark story as a kind of shield, the darker the better. Eyeing a concerned English teacher meaningfully, he answered the teacher's prompt by saying the single word that best described him was "evanescence."

The teacher pointed out that "evanescence" was usually a general noun. "Exactly," Darius crowed. "I am a general noun." The teacher was relieved to learn the cancer rumor was untrue, but alarmed by a short story Darius wrote in which the characters ended up in a bloody heap of severed heads and limbs. Darius preened about his alliterative prose style, an awkward pastiche of E. A. Poe, or, more precisely, Vincent Price. As to the content—the disturbing blood and gore—Darius gave a pert shrug. Nevertheless, he drank in the teacher's attention. He was too voracious for love not to take a little worry as an opportunity, but it turned out his teacher didn't like him *enough*. He had private conferences with other students and liked them, too. To be treated in so unexceptional a way could barely stir the ashes remaining of Darius's heart. It almost angered him.

> **Life Sliced** by Darius Van Nest
> Damon knew from the inexperient days of his infancy that his parents, the notorious Orville and the lovely Sheba, would forever be useless to him [...]

Darius was at an age when the powers of expression are at low ebb. The spontaneous, ponderably quirky things children say are plumped into the tedious opinions of adolescence. From a later essay: *The ordeal in Viet Nam taught us that every people must be allowed to choose their own system of government.* Choaties and teachers alike were bored by Darius's emotional aperçu that unilateral disarmament would end war. To him the idea was fresh. "What are they going to do with an army if we refuse to fight them?" Darius was all enthusiasm, truly moved by this dream of peace. Another student brayed, "Uh, exterminate us? That's just *What if they had a war and nobody came?* Passive resistance. What bull! Sorry, Sir."

Cassie Vail was wrong to think Darius might find her tiresome and too tidy. Despite his appearance, Darius found everything about this weekend with his father a marvel. He was thrilled to get away from the tension at Choate to spend a few days in New York, where he planned to live one day. He became fuddy-duddy with excitement on the train down from Wallingford, checking over and over the contents of his backpack, his ticket, his money. The leafless woods streamed past like a venous fog. He nervously curled his long hair behind his ears.

His father's sudden friendship with Cassie Vail was also momentous for Darius. It proved the skein of time *did* wind back on itself as he believed. The tangle of life *did* have a pattern. Cassie Vail was the woman who'd long ago come to pick up her brother's things at the New Jersey house. It was she who'd allowed him to keep the artist's bed. This visit was a wormhole to the mythic period of his life. He was only surprised that Cassie was alive at all, given how much time had passed. And she was still so young!

Oliver was making a museum-goer's round of Cassie's living room, eyeing the walls, even sidling behind the down-at-heel velvet settee to examine the bookshelves. He approved of the old money decor. Sohaila had a Persian infatuation with the gilded.

Oliver appreciated the pictures and book titles for about five seconds each, making meaningless grimaces. In front of a little Lyonel Feininger he started rubbing the flats of his hands together vigorously. "Now, I think this is really good. I like it." His body pirouetted jerkily to take a large tumbler from Cassie. The awkwardness meant Oliver was on his best behavior. Darius found it worrisome to see his father so out of practice. Cassie, on the other hand, dazzled the boy with her urbanity. He remembered her being scarily severe, but that must have been the slashing *hauteur* of her tone of voice, obvious even when she was self-deprecating. "What an idiot I always am. No Coke! I'm so sorry, Darius."

Darius tried exhaling the fuel taste of his drink discreetly. A splash of vodka had ruined it. Cassie sat aslant in the corner of the settee, arms and legs tightly crossed, listening to Oliver raptly but glancing at Darius. The volume of their conversation dropped. Darius took that to mean he was free to look around now.

He examined the model of an incomprehensible building which had been placed on a tall white column, basically the featureless rectangular prism museums use for statues or antique vases. Darius had never seen one in a regular home. Similar models were placed on bookshelves and several hung on the walls like reliefs. Oliver hadn't given any of them even a full five seconds.

Admittedly, the models looked cheap and poorly made. Mostly cardboard. They sported bridges that went nowhere and arches that supported nothing but a glued strip of paper, a cryptic sentence cut from some book or magazine. Other sentences ran up stairways. Many of the rooms were also pasted with collages of pictures and words. Through one tiny doorway Darius glimpsed a blue marble. Dusty plastic flowers and cheap necklaces, a fork, a matchbook, a glass microscope slide ornamented the rooves.

Oliver's indulgent chuckle rose from his subdued conversation with Cassie. He slouched on the lolling tongue of a stuffed chair, the shoulders of his blazer canting up, which made him look shriveled. He rested his lips on steepled hands. Outside, an idle-orchestra patter of car horns gave the muffled room an air of waiting-to-begin. Oliver was smiling smugly. He had been talking about the Nazis again. Darius tried not to listen.

Cassie loosened her knotted body slightly and drew herself back to mark a change of subject. "You ever think of taking a place in town again, Oliver? That would be fun."

"I was—uh—never a city person—" He took off his glasses and twiddled them, frowning and doing something rabbity with his mouth. "Darius says he is."

Cassie said, "I can't imagine having a big old house. Apartments are simple. They free you up to think about other things—other than the furnace. It's easier to travel."

"Mm. Mm. Mm," Oliver said. His mind had blanked as far as chit-chat went. Saying something more about the Nazis wouldn't do. Annoyance made him argumentative. "Grass, I suppose. Nice-*ish*. You don't have that. Play on the lawn—red rover, red rover—kids—you liked it, didn't you, Darius? But. Yes. I do see how one could—you know, on the other hand, sometimes I think, as this one grows up and gets more on his own, I might even enjoy being in the thick of things. Like you said. *Pied-à-terre*. Certainly with—" He'd been about to say, "the way things are with Sohaila." His expression became unpleasant.

"Let me get you another drinky-poo, Darius," Cassie barked. "Maybe just the cranberry this time." She lowered her chin to examine him across the room even though she wasn't wearing her reading glasses. "Getting a kick out of that thing?"

Darius was bending over the model to look inside, his long hair hanging to one side. "Yes!"

"Fantastic name: *Darius*. Darlin', can I get you another something to drink?"

"No. Thank you, though. Very much," Darius said.

"Though if you live in the city, you have to listen to constant special pleading by all your Jew friends," Oliver murmured softly enough the other two could both ignore him.

"You know what those are, Darius? Did you ever tell him much about Colin?" Cassie asked Oliver.

"Mmph?" He feigned a start and looked at Darius. "No. Oh, we mentioned him—just in outline, because of the—" He drew a finger across his neck. "Depressing story."

Cassie stilled. She looked more bewildered than angry. Oliver couldn't have meant to refer to her brother's suicide just now with that cutesy throat-cutting gesture!

But he had. Flustered, aware he'd misstepped, Oliver muttered under his breath, "Hang it!" This time the words barely passed his lips, too soft to be heard but outrageously offensive if they had been. "Hang it" was a correction. Colin hadn't cut his throat. He'd hanged himself in the front hall of the Tudor monstrosity in New Jersey. Oliver rushed on. "Those could've come from our basement, right?"

Cassie drawled, "No. Not those. There were never any models in your basement (*his*). Or maybe there were a few incomplete things. I can't remember. The Madonna was there. Those models, I've had them since before he died. He gave me most of them. Honestly, I considered them pretty foolish at first. I had to be educated." Cassie strode over to Darius. She clasped her arms almost girlishly behind her back. "Those were all made by my brother, Colin, who used to live in your house. You knew he was an artist? I guess he claimed *architect*, but that was a pose. He never built anything. They're all fantasies. He wanted people to think he was all bougie not bohemian. Opposite of most rich kids. You like them?"

"This one, especially," Darius answered.

Oliver knuckled his nose, sniffling and blowing roughly out his nostrils. The sound was too self-absorbed to be mocking laughter repressed.

"You've got a bed of his, remember?" Cassie said.

"Of course!" Darius said.

"You would have liked him," she said. "He's become a tiny bit famous lately. If you're interested."

Darius nodded.

"OK. Well, here's a catalogue." She tipped an oversized paperback from the bookshelf. Tickling the cover, she said, "This one gives you an idea. They're made-up buildings. That one you've been looking at is called *The Battle of Desires and Bitternesses*."

"*The Battle?*" Darius frowned.

"I know. And it's *BitternessES*," Cassie shrugged, tossing the book on a chair, not insisting. "I guess we're supposed to think about it." She took his glass.

Darius blurted, "But they're sort of—" He hadn't thought of anything they were like. He only wanted to express enthusiasm. "I do like them. All the eyes!" *The Battle of Desires and Bitternesses* was a cluster of Japanese-seeming pavilions linked by unlikely aqueducts. The interior surfaces of the pavilions were plastered with tiny images of eyes, apparently clipped from magazines.

Cassie sighed, "He's an oddball." She drawled, "Joseph Cornell is someone they compare him to. Although Colin was doing this much later, sixties, seventies. But unfortunately—well, Colin probably had too much money to function as an artist in the usual way."

"And then *it* happened!" Oliver lowed from across the room. "The terrible—oh, forget it!"

As soon as Cassie had gone to the kitchen, Oliver leapt up and crossed the room toward Darius and the model. He tottered unsteadily, because he was massaging a tendon in his neck, playing it *molto vibrato* as he walked. "I think my collagen is starting to degenerate," he tossed off. Looming over Darius he said, in the nasty whisper that was his most intimate tone, "Isn't sociable chitter-chattering the most enervating—?"

Darius pored over *The Battle of Desires and Bitternesses*, ignoring him.

Not offended, pleased, if anything, Oliver commented, "You're ignoring us."

"No. I just like this. It's cool."

Oliver heard a clank from the kitchen, an oven rack, maybe. A warm, muddy, spicy odor made him imagine some South Asian dish he wouldn't like. His fingers idly hunted bristle on his chin. "You and I both have large heads. Which is interesting. A pure coincidence."

"We're both smart," Darius murmured absently.

"Speaking of large heads. They were suggesting to your mother—and she mentioned to me—somebody at school or somewhere was talking about your seeing a shrink—talk therapy—personally I never wanted them to get near me. They probably thought I was ripe to stick a pin in the old voices and hallucinations, but I would never stand for that." He chuckled.

"Dad!" Darius' body stiffened.

"Is that a *No Thanks*? Well. Nothing to be embarrassed about." When Darius didn't reply for a long time, Oliver commented, "It's not real architecture, you know. It's all sort of a fanciful. Personally—"

"I really like it in a weird way. You know if they explain anywhere about the symbolism or whatever?" Darius pointed his chin at the catalogue.

"Nothing *to* explain. There's no key. That's how they decide it's art. Not very well-made, if you ask me. I remember him. Big hulking fellow, hunched up, and he mumbled, which I can't stand. When you leaned in, you could hear he had a very fancy, English-y way of talking, which a lot of people used to have in New York—nice people—my parents!—though you don't hear it so much anymore."

"Who cares if he mumbled?"

"He ended up hanging himself in our front hall. I don't think we ever told you that. Sohaila must've thought it was too spooky and depressing for a kid. I would have told you. Just so you knew the kind of man he was."

"Don't be heartless."

"I'm not saying anything against him, boy. But who knows what to make of all this? Kind of artsy-mumbly. Glorified model train town, if you ask me. Whatever happened to that Lionel outfit we got for you? That was fun."

"Dad, I think this is great," Darius insisted with a flicker of temper. "It's got—it's full of contumely." Darius *did* know what this word meant, more or less.

"Contumely? Contumely! Where'd you get that? My lord, you sound like one of them. I see that smile! Contumely! Or is *contumaciousness* better? Probably more modern."

"All true art is contumacious," Darius intoned.

"Contumely would have to do with the Bitterness part, I suppose. *BitternessES*." Oliver lowered his voice, "Though really he was a Caspar Milquetoast, no matter how hulking he was, the poor guy. Colin. Cassie got the balls in the family. Colin must've been more than a little—uh—disappointed in things. No career. Never did much with his life. It's nice, though, he had friends to underwrite a show—and this *festschrift*, memorial thingy—" He waved his hand down at the catalogue. "If it turns out you're homosexual, I strongly advise trying to take the dominant role in the proceeding. Try to be the top. You'll have a much happier life, I can promise you." Slicking his pate with an odd smile, he left for the kitchen. Darius froze, his cheeks flaming. Even after Oliver was gone he didn't move. He had to remain perfectly still for a good long time to ensure remarks like that would pass through him harmlessly, unconsidered almost.

Again Darius walked around Colin Vail's *The Battle of Desires and Bitternesses*. He was trying to understand both this work and art in general, to feel them as deeply as possible. But he sensed he was forcing things. He wanted to love art but only seemed able to, in a sense, press himself against it. The same had happened years ago when he tried praying for an obvious miracle or an immediate response from God, or when he tried seeing ghosts in attic windows or communicating with spirits in darkened mirrors. None of that had ever worked, of course.

Also, his back was pricking. His back was to the kitchen door. Were they kissing in there? Old faces like that pressing into one another? Or were they talking about him. Or Sohaila? Or Stan? Or Colin? His attention to the art was becoming intermittent, which seemed lazy. Art's breath of eternity was turning into a yawn. He had a sudden, extremely painful awareness that a gray, everyday blah was the true stuff of his life.

In the kitchen, bent over, Cassie directed a hostile simper at the oven window. She straightened. "Not too much longer, Oliver. Oh. Here, why not let me? The icemaker has a personality, unfortunately." Gingerly, she edged between Oliver and the refrigerator. The machine wheezed ice cubes at her special touch. "We're going to end up getting smashed." She turned and gave Oliver the glass. They stood barely a foot apart. "Oliver?"

He fingered aside her houndstooth lapel and touched her nipple through the blouse. He pressed carefully, trying to invert it.

"You don't believe all that—"

"What?"

Cassie rolled her eyes. "You know what I mean. That holocaust business. That Nazi stuff. It makes you sound—"

"What?" Oliver took a moment to switch tracks. "Oh, of course. I do. What could be more plausible? They snatch an old geezer—mental defective certainly—have him potter around *Spandau* for decades. Decades! And no interviews in all that time? No interviews at all? No one ever talks to him? Fascinating. And now he's dead, so we have to take it on faith that everything happened exactly like they say. Shouldn't I be able to talk freely? I hate how no inquiry is allowed anymore. It's all manipulation and no—no—listen, I hate to be a bore, but I need a cigarette. If you like I can try blowing it out the window."

Cassie reached into a cabinet for a monogrammed shell of crystal. When it hit the counter with an angry-sounding shock, she whispered, "Sorry. That slipped. I'm fine if you smoke."

The cigarette end bobbed in the flame as Oliver mumbled. "Secret history of that Armenian genocide hasn't disappeared. There's no keeping the truth down. That was the opposite situation. *Really happened* versus *didn't*. You wouldn't think there could be so much *Rashomon* about genocide. And you know what? That's because there ain't!"

Cassie didn't want to argue. She wanted him to stop. She interrupted, "Darius is so lovely." She finished their third round of drinks. "Take this fresh one, Ollie. Your lemon looks like it has some brown I-don't-know-what on it." He took the fresh lemon slice and dropped his bad one into her palm. With a pained-looking, lop-sided squint, hunching his shoulders mischievously, he lightly clinked Cassie's raised glass with his own. Very lightly, almost not at all. His long-fingered hands held his glass and cigarette in greedy proximity to his mouth. He smiled, childishly satisfied now. Both sipped.

Cassie immediately set her glass down. Pulling on hen-and-rooster oven mitts, though nothing was due out of the oven right away, Cassie rebelled. "But he does show—Darius does—how you're not the *most* reliable reporter in the world. Honestly, I expected a brat. He's shy!"

"What? Oh. First impressions. You have to look past the surface. I see what you mean, but—take my word for it—he has these passive, orphan-boy resources. I'm utterly under his thumb, truth to tell. Even this visit."

"Orphan-boy! Oliver!"

Oliver smiled behind a thicket of fingers and smoke.

"Oh, you're not—"

He stubbed out his smile. "I *am* serious. Just because I have a wry manner, I get no credit for my simple truthfulness. I know Darius quite well as a matter of fact and—" He stopped. "*Although!*—and you're the first person I've ever told this, so shhh!—when Sohaila got him home the first time, I had a powerful nudge-it-out-of-the-nest reaction. Intense! That kid ain't mine!" He chuckled. "No *Darius* used to be a fine name until it got taken over by the blacks. Luckily, the rejection panic didn't last. I warmed up to him."

"I didn't mean anything," Cassie apologized. "I was only wondering—but the two of you ought to be allies! With adoption, I would think some of the awful parts of family don't apply. No?"

"He's been colonized by his mother. And the boyfriend. Stan. Maybe my fault, because I keep those two underfoot in New Jersey. But it's perfectly natural for him to be close to the mother at his age. I couldn't care in the slightest."

"I think he's smitten with *you*. Or whatever the word would be."

This thought brought Oliver unexpected pleasure. He repressed any sign of it. He took a puff and exhaled. Was it a bit pushy of Cassie to start interpreting somebody she'd just met? He looked down his nose at the ashtray, clubbed its edge daintily. "You're nice to have us over," he monotoned dismissively. "Adds a third factor to the equation. When it's just him and me, what am I supposed to say? *You have a thousand demerits. You're fucking up at school?* That's so prep school predictable. We all know that story, and it's a bore. Maybe a shrink *would* help. Oh—something humorous, speaking of smitten. Yesterday we went to some idiotic ladies' place for lunch. They had a fruity Filipino—I guess—waiter there, and, you know, I really think he assumed Darius and I were—well, that Darius was my catamite. Surprised myself that I was actually a touch ill-at-ease about it. Maybe because his hair's gotten so long. And there's no resemblance at all, naturally."

"Don't harp on that," Cassie whispered.

Oliver ignored her. "Waiters should be old men. I'll say that for the *Veau d'Or*. It's sad when you think about it: that old waiters are so rare nowadays—or father and son eating together—that people would think *that* first thing. Pedophile. Glad I'm not his age, getting hit on. It's a magnet if you're sullen acting like he is." Behind the lenses of his glasses, his eyes flicked about.

In the living room Darius stood by a tall window. Though aglitter with city lights, the black glass was also smeared with indoor reflections, including the little ones of Cassie and Oliver just entering the room. The boy kept his hands in his pockets. He turned to them. "Don't you think this weekend feels like the dark ages? Like we're the most obscure and forgettable people who ever lived? Like peasants. Suddenly I feel that way. Or like we're driving together on the Jersey shore." He freed one hand and dragged it through his hair, an elegant motion.

"See?" Oliver said to Cassie as his son's hand wafted down and snuck back into a pocket. "What was I just talking about? You're a languorous creature, boy. You're no peasant. More like the designer type."

"I know," Darius admitted glumly.

"Darlin'!" Cassie exclaimed. "That's a wonderful thing. And we aren't peasants. You're not. None of us! You're memorable." *Yikes!* she thought. *Peasants of the dark ages?* Were the father and son both deranged? Darius let his head fell forward tragically, and two wings of silky hair slipped from behind his ears folding closed against his cheeks.

Oliver observed, "Now he looks like a fallen angel boy. He's meek, but he manages these domineering scenes. You'd be surprised."

9

FROM THE START, Darius was alert to Choate's swank reputation. He had a nose for status. Oliver's curtness on the phone impressed him. Clearly, his father outranked the third form dean. "Darius is going to be staying on a day or two longer. I'm keeping him down for a bit of family business. I'll send him back up on Wednesday."

Darius knew his father only wanted impersonal company for a few more days in New York. Even a child attendant would work. That didn't keep the boy from imagining real "family business" might be in store. The hours sitting in the dim hotel room, until Oliver rose at ten, were made interesting, even suspenseful, by exercises of imagination. Darius had never spent time alone with his father. And observing Oliver closely really did absorb him. The way his father slept in the ashen light of the curtained hotel room, hands praying under his slumped cheek, hopeless and suppliant like one of those plaster Pompeiians, more model than man—was poignant to Darius and filled him with adult-like pity. Even his father's ugliness was touching when he was asleep. Oliver wasn't the type to snore aggressively, to fling out hairy legs and work-tanned forearms. It might have been nice to be adopted by that kind of a man, a yeomanly man, and Darius did grieve for that obvious missed chance sometimes, wishing he had a completely different life. But the imaginary father and the grief were both a little maudlin and erotic. When you're ignored, almost anything can take on the semblance of love, even pity, so seeing Oliver's pathetic side was incredibly sweet for Darius.

Rather than a gruff, fly-fishing, tough guy of a father, his real one was a Rubik's Cube, a seemingly trivial plastic puzzle with all the infinities of thought and mathematics swirling behind it.

Poised as he'd been with the powers at Choate, Oliver was stymied by a Broadway ticket broker. Their phone call devolved into lofty bickering. Going to the theater was cancelled when Oliver hung up and remarked, more bewildered than angry, "Well, we won't do *that*." He proved inept at arranging anything. The museum they wandered to at noon on Monday was closed. At loose ends, they dawdled in Central Park. A twitchy sneer directed at Darius was the only sign that Oliver was aware of a failure. And he soon reminisced contentedly to himself about who used to live in which buildings. Now and then he glanced blankly at Darius as if at a limb asleep, not a son. For his part, Darius was too uncertain of his father to make suggestions. Footsore and famished by dinnertime, they ended up at the overfamiliar *Veau d'Or* again.

Nothing Darius watched his father do seemed quite right. It ran deeper than worldly incompetence, quirky facial expressions and the wrong tone of voice. After lunch at a midtown diner the next day Oliver stopped Darius from taking a pastel mint from a huge snifter by the cash register. He gave a warning jerk of his head. "Not a good idea." The cashier was watching him and raised her threaded eyebrows indifferently. When they were on the sidewalk, Oliver explained, "Some sly customer could easily have dropped something in the bowl, laced it with something—people really do appalling things like that. Sadistic at a remove. And if I'm not mistaken some poisons look like chalk, so there's no way to tell." Evil dangled bizarrely over them in the sunshine, while Oliver fogged his glasses with breath and rubbed at them with a shirttail, then it was forgotten.

No family business came up. The aimless, indelible two days slipped away. On Wednesday morning, Oliver took Darius to Grand Central for the train back to Connecticut. He waved at the ceiling and droned with tour guide dullness, "These constellations are painted on backward."

They'd come an hour too early for an express. At the ticket window Oliver discovered he had no money to buy Darius a ticket. Darius fished a crumpled twenty from his jeans. A sibilant order from his father made him stuff it back in. "Don't flash your money!" Something somewhere in the room's monumental dimness snagged Oliver's attention. His head cocked like a dog's. "And let's not use credit," he mused. Turning back to the clerk he said, "I'll draw a bit of cash and be back in two shakes."

Riding the escalator to the cash machine, Oliver imparted the following lesson. "Be tremendously careful, Darius, whom you give your credit cards to. I hardly use them. Emergency only. You can be followed. All sorts of information is transferred and stored. And we can't have that." As cheery as teaching this lesson seemed to make him, Oliver was irritable again as soon as he paid for the ticket. "I think that's gone way up again."

They sat on one of the great wooden benches in the waiting room, Oliver crossed his legs several ways. Full of filial discomfort, Darius studied the down-at-heels magnificence of Vanderbilt Hall. His head dropped back and he imagined this was his own private room. The quintuple-coffered ceiling, the obsessive acanthus leaves, the marble, the over-the-top imperial ornament—it was exactly his style. Dirty, prison-like grilles darkened the five huge windows. The immense space was almost as dim as a basement. Louche types, none with suitcases or even briefcases, idled in front of walls of yellowed tan marble, or shuttled in and out of the building under a shallow arch with the legend, 42ND STREET BUSES AND TAXIS. Something about the acoustics, the dim swimming pool murmur half-metamorphosed into choir, overwhelmed his puny fantasy of ownership, and Darius remembered—suddenly quite clearly—teenagers and a pool party and one of them dying and himself as lonely as a galaxy. This useless loneliness was his true inheritance, he supposed. Over them lapped the wobbly, aquatic clamor of voices: "...heat up that slice...for a copy of the *Journal*...run to the men's room..."

Oliver gave every sign of his usual inattention, so Darius was surprised when his father said something that sounded like he'd been reading his mind. "I hate that I'm always drowning in feelings. Useless. I hope you're not like that. Maybe it's because travel always feels forlorn. People like us should probably call it forlorn-*ing*." His nose hitched at his glasses when he tilted his head back to squint at the gloomy iron chandeliers. "If we happen to be at all alike, that is." The older man heaved a summing-up sigh. "You do seem almost sad. Did you have a good time?"

"All right," Darius said, cautiously mundane.

"Was there something you wanted to do that we didn't get to?"

"No."

"What did you enjoy best?"

"I don't know."

"Did you like Cassie?"

"Yeah, pretty much."

"Just that?"

"No, I liked her."

"Did you fall in love with her? Will we have to fight it out, you and me?"

Darius ignored the half-hearted provocation. Conversationally he said, "I wanted to talk more with her about—" He was unaccountably tremulous, liable to tears, even. He forced it out, "—you know—Colin, who used to own our house. Her brother. The artist guy."

"Colin! Colin?" All bland surprise, Oliver looked down at Darius for the first time. "Huh. That's interesting. He was nothing special, really. Not that—"

Darius nudged the dirty sleeve of a drinking straw on the marble floor with his sneaker toe. "I liked that thing of his."

"Why on earth?"

But Darius only shrugged. He stretched to push the strip of paper even further out of reach, and his crotch rose from the bench.

"Do that and you'll get all these men eyeing you," Oliver commented. It wasn't a complaint or a warning.

Darius settled back on the honeyed wood and looked around. An alert, pot-bellied man had paused by the passage to the men's room, his eyes on Darius. Another man with an overcareful coif and a slippery gaze had been standing there for quite a while. They looked normal to Darius.

As always in those days, the homeless were everywhere as well—reclining on the other benches, dozing on the marble floors. Human heaps of rags from a differently colored universe, they didn't seem to have bodies or heads, much less eyes. Was Oliver talking about them? Sometimes something glittered in the muddy folds. Were they watching?

Oliver's chin did thoughtful calisthenics, rising, crumpling. "You know," he said. "I could get that *Battle of* whatsit artwork. Hardly know what to call it. If it's something you want."

Darius opened his mouth in wild, orphan-boy gratitude, an expression which, though real, felt fake, so he was glad Oliver didn't look at him. He suppressed the expression. "Yeah! Yes," he was explicit.

"I could give it to you. Cassie has started to be a good friend." The offer appeared to embarrass him. He hurried on, "Do you know what I'm doing right now?"

Darius shook his head. He said *No* when Oliver still wouldn't look at him.

"I'm counting the money in my wallet. What I just got from the cash machine. You really have to be careful about flashing money." He looked around the room to demonstrate alertness. "I have a very sensitive thumb. Maybe beading helps. Anyway, you can learn to do it like this with your hand in your pocket, without ever taking the wallet out or opening it. It's a rough count, but still..." Soft, demented laughter bubbled from his chest. It sounded not unlike quiet sobs.

"What's so funny?"

Oliver smiled mischievously to himself and squinched his eyes closed. "How much? How much? How much? I find I have—*a lot*," he enunciated. "Rather a lot! Should I tell you?"

"I think so," Darius smiled.

"Without being specific—" His usual glumness reasserted itself. "I have rather a lot of money." He looked at Darius narrowly. "Not what I just took out, of course. I don't mean that."

"We're rich?"

"That would be understating it," Oliver murmured, hardly moving his lips. "If I wanted to, I could corner the market on—

let's see—teapots. Quite possibly, I could afford to buy every single teapot in the world. How's that for a shocker? Including the gold and silver ones! But hear what I'm going to tell you, boy. This is a big secret. Got to be. Really, a total secret. Here—" He shifted on the bench, turning toward Darius like the most indulgent teacher. "Now. Let's be very grown-up and serious. You know, naturally, between your mother and me—it's become something of a disaster. That happens. Just so you know—because I suppose you're old enough—the two of us, your mother and I, have a sort of a deal. According to this deal, she takes care of you financially—everything—school, whatever. In return, I give her—have already given her—a somewhat vast sum, and we're quits. I let her and even that Stan creature of hers, camp out in the New Jersey house with me, even though it must make me look like a perfectly sad and indulgent cuckold and a sorry fool. In fact, I gave her the fucking house, too. But, fool or not, we must never care what other people think about us. So. So, anyway, your mother's entirely responsible for you. She has a house and we're square. But I'm telling you this secret. Tremendous secret. That I, Oliver, have *rather* more than *everyone* believes. It's quite clever." He cocked his head at the ceiling. "Secrets *are* like Midas and the reeds, aren't they? Midas in more ways than one. Ha! I'm talking about teapot money! And one day—who knows?" He crossed his arms tightly. A gloomy expression tried to reassert itself.

Darius didn't entirely understand what his father was saying. "Is teapot money billions?"

Oliver put a finger to his lip. "Zillions! But hush about it!"

If this was family business, and it was, it didn't sound dramatically unlike Oliver's usual raving. Darius wasn't even sure he'd grasped the essential point, though he had. "You mean you have a lot more than you told mom?"

Oliver nodded.

"Is that allowed?"

"I'm letting them live together! In my own house with me! *Ex-my house*. But still." Oliver savored the argument. "Seems to me they have nothing to complain of."

"But now that you told me, what's to keep me from telling them—her, I mean?"

"Even if you did, they have no argument. It's all locked up in lawyer language, the hardest substance known to man." Oliver winked. He looked drowsy with pleasure. His eyes fell closed. He was silent a long time before adding crisply, "But you won't. Think about it, and you'll realize why. You won't say anything."

Darius did think. The first reason that came to him was sentimental. He thought his father was saying, in a harsh way, "I know how much, in spite of yourself, you love me, and you would never do anything that went against my wishes. You've promised to keep my secret." This reason had the ring of truth.

But Oliver meant nothing of the kind. For Oliver, conceiving himself the object of anyone's love was as unlikely a mental experience as he could possibly have. He was making a threat. Or, since the whole delicious plot he'd concocted, while real—he was indeed cheating his wife in divorce—had a slight disjunct from reality, like a contact lens knocked afloat on an eye, it was as if he were merely playing when he made the awful threat of disinheritance. Perhaps, he was so rich whatever he played at shaded into truth. Darius would keep silent about Oliver's hidden riches, because only if he did, would a fantastic windfall eventually come to him. In fact, given the familiar air of madman's fantasy, the entire secret was soon discounted in Darius's mind. He was much more excited about *The Battle of Desires and Bitternesses*.

Oliver thought he'd been brutally clear about the threat of disinheritance. So much so that he felt in his throat the faint pressure of a sob of a fossil emotion. He let his palms fall to his thighs and announced, "Enough of all this dirty talk about you-know-what. It's good, though." His smile was a little ghastly. His long-fingered hand rose, but at the last moment, he couldn't bring himself to ruffle Darius's hair. His hand plucked strangely at the faded, curling collar of the boy's polo shirt. "Good to chat away and—uh—confide. Whatever. I'll be off. Your train's in twenty minutes."

10

MOST TUESDAYS BEA Sayles came into the city for a session with her psychotherapist. That taken care of, she met up with Cassie Vail, an old Miss Porter's classmate. Companionably, each felt a hint of pity for the other's path in life. Cassie, the Manhattanite, was unmarried. Enough said. Bea came from an old Catholic family with a wonderful compound on the water in Noroton, Connecticut. They lived off ground rent from the ATT building and a few other ancient plots of land downtown. So, lots of money and history. But Bea had ended up with a philandering lawyer who made her live at *his* family's place in New Jersey. Out there all she had for friends were the awful, suburban Westerbrook crowd. And she wasn't skinny anymore.

Cassie often had tickets to a Met blockbuster, and they would spend an hour poring over Carolingian illuminated manuscripts or Italian parade armor before having a late lunch/early dinner at a perfectly ordinary diner on Madison Avenue. A paunchy Albanian, tipsy with fatigue after a long day, greeted them. "My lovely ladies!" His slightly demented gaze wandered over the floor and the greasy ceiling, but he deftly twirled menus into their hands with the flair of an illusionist. Cassie fretted whether "no mayo" was registering in his brown-eyed inattention. But at the perfect moment he focused and gave her a smug wink. Mostly a lunch place, The New Amity Restaurant was empty at five, except for three exhausted Dutch tourists studying their menus with funereal expressions.

"Maybe people are too much for him. He's been holed up in New Jersey an awfully long time," Cassie said. "I knew him for years when we were younger and he just never registered. A dreary loner, I thought. Nelson talked about an imperious streak—always shutting people down in conversation—expecting everyone to listen to him like footmen. Total dominance is still his thing. It seems. Even with the boy, for heaven's sake."

"So male," Bea murmured. "That's where we have to watch out, Cassie. I see it in you. I really do. You get all—" Pursing her mouth, she made a kewpie doll expression of tractability that caused Cassie to shout with laughter and breathe, "I don't!"

"*Yes, you do*! And you have to watch out, because it just isn't *you*. Not at all."

"I'm almost mad at him for upsetting my life like this. I was in a nice, spinsterish state. Really more content than I'd been in years. Doing things!"

"I'd hardly have called you a spinster," Bea flattered.

"Sweetheart!" Cassie shrugged urbanely. The Albanian swirled their iced tea glasses to the table as they watched in silence. He plucked straws from a sheaf in his vest pocket and, with another magical flourish, laid them across the mouths of the glasses, totally absorbed in his artistry.

"But I was getting used to my life. And then I just determined—I determined—I determined to spend time with this man. It was perfectly willful. It wasn't about love, of course. It's just that he's interesting. Clubbable. Makes me sound awful, I suppose. But it's nice to go out as a couple. And it's nice when the man can pay his own way. *More than*, in his case. But—well, now I can't stop. Which I know is the worst possible sign. I'm walking off a cliff. There's some kind of not-love emotion involved. Oh! And I've got rabbits running over my grave just talking about it." Her shiver resolved in a visible twitch of her shoulders.

"That *might* be a good sign," Bea said doubtfully. She'd always disliked Oliver Van Nest. The soon-to-be-ex-wife was some kind of tony foreign bimbo. She knew them a little from afar. Cassie was shaking her head in despair. Bea's chin jutted. "Poor baby! I hate to see you go through this. What are the rules of the road?

You have to have a frank conversation. Get it all on the table. If he won't bring it up himself—"

"It's as if I'm going at it on two levels. I don't mean I'm ambivalent. My two levels are—well, number one: my usual cool fifty-something-year-old self. Her assessment is we can go to some benefits, and maybe there'll be a bit of money and companionship. Even travel. And *then*, level two: there's this on-tenterhooks, afraid-to-speak-up, teen-agery, bad-man-obsessed me. Maybe I never got it out of my system when I was supposed to. Honestly, he can be a bit of a freak."

"He's freaky?"

"No. No, I'm exaggerating." Cassie thought about Oliver doubting Rudolf Hess had ever existed. And the Holocaust business. She knew exactly how awful she wanted her plight to sound, so she tucked those items away. "Though his interestingness is, I have to say, and it's the same with the boy—a little bit crazy, I do find it exciting. Like living with an artist, though he's the opposite of the artist type. Except for his beads." She posed her forearm to display a massive bracelet of loops and loops and loops of tiny black beads. Oliver had strung it for her. After hanging a moment, the bracelet's riotous ropes of caviar galumphed from her bony wrist almost to the crook of her elbow.

Bea didn't have much of a reaction, aesthetic or otherwise. "I thought he was the type who spends all of his time on his investments." Self-consciously she added, "I wish Preston would get into that. Spend time at the house."

Cassie admitted, "Actually, No. He has bankers—trust people—who take care of everything. I don't get the feeling he's much of a businessman himself. I mean, he reads the statements, probably. And keeps up." She hid the arm with the bracelet in her lap. "But—and you must know this—anybody who had *anything* in the market over the past twenty years, they're rich as Croesus now. You didn't have to do a thing. I liked buying art unfortunately."

Bea had indeed seen her fortune blow up since Reagan, but so much of it was roped-off in complicated generation-skipping trusts, it didn't feel like real money. She fixed her gaze on a yellowing blue photograph of Santorini. "Did someone tell me he was CIA a long time ago? Back when it was all gentlemanly?"

"That would be exciting." Cassie was surprised. "But I wouldn't think of Oliver and 'security clearance,' not in the same breath."

"You were the one who said he was exciting. Exciting how? Like exciting—sexually?"

Cassie was casual, "Hah! No. That's not really part of it."

"Nothing, huh?"

"Well—" She thought of his bizarre touches. She shrugged.

"Things are allowed to be slow," Bea reassured her.

"Right. Slow," Cassie echoed.

"On the other hand, for women there's also that awful allure and suffering of not being touched. *Not* something you want to get into. I've talked about it with Dr. Berman."

"I'm too old for that. It isn't that anyway."

"The kid *was* adopted."

"Bea! Oliver's not a eunuch. Supposedly the reason they had to adopt wasn't on his side anyway." Visibly, Cassie debated saying more. The story sounded so implausible—implausible coming from Oliver, at any rate. "I have an inkling from what he's told me that it was *her* who insisted on adopting Darius back when. *Her* who couldn't have kids. He hinted that she had some strange ovarian I-don't-know-what. Supposedly her ovaries don't work except to produce huge, huge—*excessive*—*abnormal*—amounts of estrogen. Which means—" A laugh escaped her. "She's—I guess—more of a woman. Her skin glows, and she has this intense sex appeal men pick up on. It makes her ultra-feminine, except, of course, she can't have children, or couldn't. Does that sound at all plausible?"

"My God!" Bea stared, delighted. "I think her skin *did* glow. I used to see her at Westerbrook. Big glasses like Jackie Onassis."

"For whatever it's worth," Cassie shrugged.

"But that means—it's flattering! That means you're the successor to the Iranian Venus! Unless it's just coconut oil or something."

The two women cackled. The laughter sputtered back and forth in girlish colloquy. "Ishtar!" They howled. They tried to eat, but laughed. Their eyes teared up from the scratch of dry toast in their throats. On the heels of laughter, however, a wounded expression came over Cassie's face. Ironing her paper napkin against her thigh, she let drop, "I haven't told you the worst."

"What?" Bea asked in the smallest possible voice.

"I bought–" Embarrassment stole Cassie's breath. The bracelet reappeared with a rustle. Her forefinger pressed a crumb of bacon. "I've bought him a very, very extravagant present. A way-too-much, way-too-soon sort of a thing."

"Why on earth–?"

"And it's beyond my means."

"Oh, Cassie! How far?"

"Very far," she said.

"You have to take it back! Whatever it is."

"I'm not going to. I'm going to give it to him." She broke the crumb of bacon with determined pressure.

"Are you sure?"

"I'm sure. Oddly enough." She gave Madison Avenue a look, her deep-seated hauteur peeping out, directed at nothing in particular. "A couple of days before the boy came down from Choate, Oliver and I stopped by the Carl Hagen gallery? Well, Oliver admired this *trompe l'oeil* thing–"

"Cassie! You're off your rocker."

"It feels right. It feels splashy. I want to be splashy for a change. I'm sick and tired of–"

"But it's too forceful. You'll jinx it or scare him away."

"No. That's just it. I have an intuition it's right. I think he'll be touched. He's insanely rich. Or so they say. Why is money always rumors?" she laughed. "But rich people feel deprived because everybody tells them they're not supposed to want anything. Well, for heaven's sake, Bea, everybody *wants*. And, *I* want to make him think of me. In a big way."

"I don't know–how could you even afford something like that?" Bea fretted.

"I couldn't. Carl said he'd take something of mine, one of Colin's things, in trade. So really it cost nothing–"

"You actually did a deal with Carl? Carl himself? That's so high-powered somehow! Cassie, I love that." Bea crossed her arms in admiration.

"I just asked him."

"But it's so sophisticated. I love that. I would never have dared bring it up. People always look at me and think 'retail' or 'Short Hills Mall' or something. Mom was never that way, but I am. I think you're a marvel. Of course, the other part—with Oliver—a present like that—you're also totally insane."

"Jibbering! Whoo-hoo!"

Bea said carefully, "You do know they're only separated? Oliver and the Iranian Venus?"

"Oh, of course."

"And that they still live together? I'm just making sure. Since you do know, I wish you'd please tell me what the story is. They're separated and together *and* another man moved into the house?"

"Stan, yes, the other man." Cassie waved away old news.

"What on earth is that about? That's exciting, I suppose. In a sex comedy way."

"No, it's just a convenience. Oliver and I have talked about it." They hadn't, really. "I mean, everybody involved is grown up. It's just a kind of overlap while people are divorcing and rearranging themselves. Oliver doesn't seem to care in the least about Stan. Or her at this point. Admittedly, it's awkward in a gossipy, suburban sort of a way, but isn't the place enormous?"

"It certainly is," Bea said, a little wounded, feeling that Cassie had lashed out by using the word *suburban*.

11

OLIVER CAME BACK into the city a month later. He saw his dermatologist about a keratinous something on his forehead. He met with a portly, throat-clearing banker at the Hell's Kitchen offices of a private trust company—the Van Nest *family* bank, as they called it. The fact that the offices looked like a fly-by-night travel agency bothered him not at all. Oliver was considering moving the business to Philadelphia anyway, because New York was getting too expensive.

He was invited to dinner again at Cassie's. Cassie bought cold salmon this time. She was taken up with her plan to give him the *trompe l'oeil* painting. Buying the dinner at a *traiteur* and serving it from the cartons, opting to wear blue jeans and an untucked white blouse, downplayed the munificent ceremony of the gift.

On entering, Oliver clasped his hands in front of his belly loosely as if accepting congratulations on a sermon. Cassie's *mwah* was awkwardly thwarted by his posture. His distracted babble of pleasantries was almost too soft to hear. "Well! Didn't notice this rug last time." He narrated his slightest actions. "Drink the drink. Take a couple paces and sit down—here or here? Do you—? Well, here, then. And try one of these rice crackers wrapped in—seaweed, it looks to me. Sort of a papery taste. Not peppery, ha!"

At length Oliver looked at Cassie with extreme gravity. "No," he seemed to disagree with everything he'd just said, even with the way he'd behaved for most of his life. "I'm thinking. I had a drink before coming over here and was thinking about the boy. What you said."

"What I said?"

"Last time I brought him down to the city—the only time, to be honest—I started to have a little talk about money with him," he continued slyly. "And I found—I found I was quite moved by—well—everything you said about him. That is, I noticed I wasn't thinking, *Oh, this is a terrible chore—weekend in the city—father, son.*"

Cassie felt a flicker of unease. When Oliver had been quiet for a long time, she tried changing the subject gently. "Am I crazy or did someone tell me you used to have something to do with government? The CIA? That can't be right, can it?"

"Yes. Oh, yes, yes, yes. How I met Sohaila, actually. Bombay. Not something I can talk about, of course, but there it is." He sounded like a terrible liar. Like he was riding the opportune story as a surfer catches a wave.

Cassie's skin crawled. Trying not to sound skeptical, she asked, "You met in Bombay? Mumbai, I guess we have to say now."

"Right. Her family was exiled by the Shah. They were quite grand and made the Shah nervous politically. This was long before any of that later business—revolution, Khomeini, what have you. But that's beside the point. What was I—? Oh. It occurred to me I'm not the best father-professor-teacher in the world. I mean to say I *could* do it, and rather brilliantly, but I don't. I'm talking about the boy. Because I've never thought it's right to impose your way on others. Nothing outrages me more, speaking for myself. So I don't do it. But because Darius seems fairly well screwed up in a rich boy sort of a way, I thought maybe I should tell him being rich isn't so bad. *If* it isn't, that is to say. This all came from what you recommended."

Left an opening, Cassie started weakly, "I'm not sure—I wouldn't like to think I was butting in."

"But you said I shouldn't treat him like an orphan boy. I should spoil him."

"I did?" She recouped. "Well. Clearly the key is being kind. But also getting the privileged kid to have a sense of responsibility towards others. Make it clear the whole thing—money—just depends on luck. Which—I've found—" she slowed. "Well, a lot of rich people don't seem to believe that in their hearts. They think they deserve it. Even if they learn how to say, *I'm just lucky*. You know—to make themselves sound good." She eyed Oliver nervously, "You know—*Ha, ha, it's all dumb luck. I'm just like you. But I'm lucky.*'"

"You are?"

"No. I mean that's what they say. Or they learn to say it without truly believing it in their hearts. Often. I don't mean to say I'm *lucky* myself."

"You're not lucky?"

"No. Wait. What are we talking about? Of course I'm lucky, but I'm not rich. Not *rich* rich." She waved at her sumptuous apartment irritably. "Weren't we talking about money?"

"Ah. So you think with Darius the idea should be, *Don't spoil him!* Chores, job, not getting anything he wants. Discipline."

"Well, no. Of course we spoil people we love. But you have to give a kid a keen sense of... of the difficult position of others in the world."

Oliver made a fish-lipped show of consideration. "I hope I didn't do everything backwards. What I wanted to convey to Darius—last time, when I began having that money talk with him, well, I wanted to show him I was generous, I think. I was tough on him as usual—but not in my usual hands off way—and I found he responded. I thought he was quite touched as a matter of fact." Oliver, a creature of fantastic reticence, thought any confidence, any secret shared, was a sign of love. And because the secret he'd imparted to Darius involved money, the greatest form of information possible, the love had to be greater, too, overwhelming. Oliver believed even his bizarre threat of disinheritance bound him to his son like the perfect kiss or like the shared ordeals of brothers in arms.

Cassie broke off the strange conversation and excused herself. She went to the kitchen to pour a second round of drinks. She'd put the open cartons of salmon and tomato salad on Majolica serving platters. The expectant array looked forlorn. The gloss on the dill sauce had clouded. Her plan was going awry.

Not only the timing but the emotions were all wrong. She fixed the drinks mechanically. She searched herself for the best possible of a small clutter of emotions.

Oliver was chuckling complacently to himself when Cassie returned. "Funny to talk family with you. Feels like we ought to be beyond that."

Cassie frowned.

"I know you think I keep a very odd household. Sohaila and Stan in there."

"Frankly, yes."

"I could even bring you into it if I wanted."

"No," Cassie laughed. "No."

"It's separate apartments in a manner of speaking. And Stan is contemptible, which helps."

"But doesn't it bother you sometimes?"

Unlike himself, Oliver was thoughtful. "Maybe it's just the way I am. Passive, fatalistic, shut down. All that probably helped when I was in the spy biz," he joked. "But that's not my focus anymore."

"Oliver," Cassie breathed with real uneasiness.

"Cassie, now it seems a lot—too much—to ask, but I had in mind—part of the reason I wanted to talk about all that with the boy—"

Cassie's cheeks grew hot. Haughtily her finger stroked the inner corner of one eye. Was she wiping away or inducing a tear?

"I was thinking, because, as you've hinted, I'm too hard on Darius."

"No," she whispered.

"Well, I am. And I was thinking I might want to get him a little something he loved, really loved. I was maybe tough on him about the money, and, I don't know, carrot and stick is the idea. So I was thinking—something he loved—why not that artwork he flipped for, Colin's thing, the *Battle of* I'm-not-sure-what? *Amertume?* And *Hopes?*"

"Oliver. I don't have it. I don't have it anymore." She blushed even more intensely. She averted her gaze. She smiled stiffly through the tender concussion of a wave of drunkenness.

"I'd want to pay," he murmured, fascinated by how hard it was to ask for something.

"No, Oliver. I don't have it."

"No, that's fine." He frowned curiously at his failure.

Cassie gestured across the room. "Look!" The white prism on which the *Battle of Desires and Bitternesses* had been sitting last time was bare. She stood. "Come. I'll show you. This is the most hideous irony. I've got—" She stopped herself from swaying. "Oliver?"

Giving him the painting was anything but splashy. Cassie was at sea emotionally, but she didn't think generosity was one of the emotions. She forced a smile as small and precise as the clear-eyed disquiet she couldn't ignore. Even with all the other emotions in her, she couldn't ignore this small disquiet. She'd meant to take Oliver's hand, so hers rose. It wilted back to the thigh of her jeans when he failed to take it.

"Are you all right?" Oliver asked, confused. His glasses had slipped to the tip of his nose. He looked back at the painting, staring vacantly, his mouth unclosed like a carp.

"A little present *I* got for *you*," Cassie explained. "Nothing, really."

Mouth still agape, Oliver put his hands on his hips in polite astonishment. "Oh, Cassie! Cassie, my goodness!"

She tittered in agony. It seemed the whole thing might work for a moment. Or at least not be a disaster. He was evidently touched.

"I'm—" A hand patted his belly. He let out a happy fragment of a sob. But he also frowned, shaking his head. He reached out to touch her shoulder but missed, stroking the lightly perfumed bedroom air.

She'd expected him to be tight as a drum when it came to thanks. She tipped her head to look at him.

"This means a great deal to me." His voice was momentous, low and slow.

Cassie spun the black bracelet on her wrist. "Not something I made, but—you see, I traded the other for it—the *Battle*—absurd irony, if it turns out that's what you really wanted."

Oliver picked up the small painting. He held it at arm's length—surprisingly possessive about it already, Cassie thought. He marched a few steps and rested the painting gently on a slipper chair. Turning back, he made good on stroking her shoulder. The ceremoniousness of his movements was peculiar, as if he'd blocked the scene the day before and was a terrible actor, besides. "You're tired of all my blah-blah about Darius, aren't you?" He gave her a yellow-toothed grin, unsettling at this point.

"I meant to wait till after dinner. Are you hungry?" Cassie asked evasively. He'd embraced her. He was abnormally shy physically, always twiddling at the back of her neck or poking her in the nipple and then no more. But now he held her in a vise grip. He kissed her on the lips: peck, peck, peck. Peck, peck. Peck.

"You, madame, are delicious." He swatted a cheerful rhythm on her buttocks.

Cassie let out a virginal peep. Then a more surprised one at the sudden, lewd wetness on her neck. It tickled. He smelled of smoke and salt, low tide almost. Her hands faintly bongoed a response on his lower back. It was uncomfortable the way he was squeezing her.

He threw her to the bed and came tumbling atop her with a gruesome, "Ha ha." It hurt. For a moment they were all middle-aged bracings and knocked elbows until he got her in his grip again.

His ashy breath wheezed over her. He shook her roughly, playing at tiger seizing fawn. Cassie's disquiet had exploded. The scene was disgusting. She hated Oliver, at least for the moment, and she experimented with a few seconds of laxness, a feint with escape as its object. Oliver knocked his hips against her, uninhibited and inept. He worked his fleshy, loose-seeming erection against her thigh. Though his glasses were unhooked from one ear, he smiled directly at her, yellow, proud, blind, humping.

12

IT DIDN'T HAPPEN often, but when Jane Brzostovsky and Barry Paul had sex, her eyes closed, his didn't. She could only bring herself to look at him in partial glimpses from under an arm, over a pillow. Or her eyes, precisely when she'd averted them in shame, caught a close-up of her woodland-creature's pudendum. Unlike her own bushy blur, his was flat and pale. Like grass crushed under a lost sandal for a month, the hair clung to a slight puckering of his abdomen, obscuring nothing. Only a tiny Hitlerian patch had gone dark. Directly under that, the plumbing hung out abruptly. A chrome sink trap couldn't have looked more bare. The lumpy cravat of scrotum did nothing to dress things up. Its ruddy crinkles were also bare. It too sprang from his smooth abdomen with a pipe fitting's abruptness. Then Jane would shut her eyes again. The idiocy of this pastoral peek-a-boo threatened to wake her from her dream. She couldn't let that happen. As if he were a minor deity whose beauty teetered between enchanting and grotesque, she pretended that, as a mere mortal, her risk was blindness, but it was death.

She knew they'd have to stop. She'd leave her job. She'd ask to teach third-graders or much older students at the upper school. Because she was so weak, yet so arrogant, instead of simply stopping, she thought she'd cleverly arrange for it to be impossible. It was all flailing. She wondered aloud to a colleague whether less mothering and more teaching might prolong her career. She brought up the time she'd slapped Darius Van Nest. "Could I be burning out already? I certainly don't want that."

Her efforts proved hopeless when Satan personally got involved, whispering mischief into Jeanette Paul's ear.

Jeanette called, begging Jane to start seeing *more* of her son outside of school. Apparently the chimo joke from years before had been, on balance, more joke and less gimlet-eyed intuition. Jeanette wanted Jane to tutor Barry. "You're the only one I know who lives close enough." In case that sounded like she cared about convenience most, Jeanette wheedled, "I really think you're the one teacher he responds to. He's told me that. I swear. He says, *I love her. I just love her*." Barry had never said anything of the kind, but Jane's heart fluttered despite her recognizing a lie. "It would mean so much to him. He's such a dope," Jeanette pleaded.

Jane said she'd call back. She had to play at reluctance at least. The handy extra pay enticed her, not the sinister convenience, she told herself. She shook her head in rough scorn after hanging up. She pretended to be repelled that Barry had used that word, love. If he'd used it. This was not love. She wasn't naïve. She slapped her hands together hard to make her palms sting. She noticed the dim, cold self that turns up when passions are playing out. The mind lurks in the wings like the star's accountant with a backstage pass.

Jane began to tutor Barry on Saturdays. Their sessions weren't the orgies some might imagine. Having engineered the delicious teacher-student premise, the great Pornographer moved elsewhere—on to pizza delivery boys and run-of-the-mill adulteries. This teacher and this student really studied. Jane taught at the kitchen counter with Jekyll-like civility. On warm September days, she and Barry met in the front yard and were full of innocent waves for the elderly neighbor who clapped feebly to scare off a housecat stalking songbirds.

When they met indoors, Jane was inhumanly patient with Barry's flirting, which was sexual in a formal sense only. Among children, imitation precedes feeling. The tickling of his sneaker toe under the table, the sudden bouts of exhaustion when his head and arms fell to the counter and his overgrown child's fingers accidentally brushed her shoulder or trapped her hand—all of that made him seem more like a restless kid than a seducer.

He was pushy and humorous, pumping his eyebrows when an obstreperous erection showed. It didn't seem to involve desire in the least. Only rarely, when Jane misted over, did she respond to his fidgeting, usher them away from the kitchen counter, slow things down until they got to real sex. At times like that he acted shell-shocked, awed by her methodical step-by-step.

A little experience seemed to go a long way with Barry. What he was after, or what he played at being after, was still a bit much for him. He wasn't panting constantly for a roll in the hay. Maybe Jane's game of indirection, of warm and cool, wasn't that different from what it always feels like to be a child, and Barry assumed this affair was the natural sequel to childhood.

The dislikeable mother, Jeanette, stopped in for chats at first. Her casual falsity was breathtaking. She let slip, "He didn't want to do it! As usual he fought me and fought me. I told him, *Barry, don't be an idiot like you always are. This is your favorite teacher! Or was. And she's nicely offered—*" Barry shrugged hugely and gave Jane, blushing with shame, a raffish smile. "Furthermore," Jeanette waved the envelope of cash aggressively in front of Barry's nose. Then, all demure sweetness, she presented it to Jane, "I really wonder if this idiot's even worth it."

The first time they really had sex, Jane had no greater inspiration—no thoughts in her head at all, really—than to heave the mannequin Barry into position with her hands. Her hands were more aware of what was going on than she was. They did the bulk of the work. Propped on his elbows, he got to work, swaybacked, arrhythmic, eyes closed. After a while he stopped. He rolled off her. With a pleased grin, he wiped his brow and lithely sat cross-legged. He flipped at the erection still rising behind his ankles. It was as stiff as ever, gleaming and full of promise, not fatigue. Barry made an uncertain stab at humor, "Boing, Boing." He seemed to feel the same friendly companionship for it as he did for Jane. "That was—amazing." He lowered his voice, certainly quoting some joke or movie. Jane didn't dare suggest they go on. The boy seemed not to realize there was more to it. Was he too embarrassed? The next few times sex ended with the same childish and abrupt change of subject. Since he never made the first move (beyond his general, constant flirtatiousness) Jane was confused by the decisive yet inconclusive way he kept breaking it off.

Then Jane grasped something awful. He was so painfully innocent that he thought of nocturnal emission as a rude mess. He knew of no connection between his own splurting at midnight, asleep in his bed, and what it was he and Jane had started to do in hers. He knew nothing!

Barry could have lived with sex or without it. But now that it was happening to him, now that Jane was making him happy on the whole and he was getting all the adoring attention he could want, he tried to reimagine it as something he'd pursued. Though he had no gift for fantasy, he came up with an enjoyable way to think of their relationship. He adopted a cool, James-Bond-like persona. In bed he made odd facial expressions, amused or supercilious, which mystified Jane but were supposed to drive her wild. When given an opening, he stroked Jane's chin with avuncular tolerance. "Yo, bitch."

When he started opening his eyes during sex, there was a lot for him to admire. The breasts with their forbidden, V-shaped pallor lurched in drunken, separable ways. Their sponginess needed so much restraint that it worked on his nerves. Even the slightest touch sometimes made her cringe. And the miraculous tubular muscle her hand usually had to lead him to!—when he did look at it for the first time, leaf upon leaf upon leaf parting, until she had him just graze the Jack-in-the-pulpit with his callused forefinger, he wore no expression at all, his heart in his throat. The thing was like some minute dungeonmaster secreted behind pink curtains that were half-animal, half-fluid. He tried raising his chin to give her a taste of Bond-like arrogance, but he couldn't stop staring. He was under her power. He couldn't conceive the extent of her power. After pulling his hand back, he reached out again, covering the apex of her legs with his palm as if to calm his mind. For a moment his eyes rested on the blue ink stamp on the back of his hand, leftover from admission to Frightmare Asylum, a Halloween attraction. His mind couldn't take in so much detail all at once. Or he was so young he didn't know the words for the details he did see. Which is probably the same thing.

To a surprising degree Jane was still his teacher. She refused to "play" at anything for Barry. He got no *Miss Moneypenny* or *Mrs. Robinson*. She calmly stared at him across the kitchen table's piles of dog-eared worksheets, until she was sure he really didn't know whether a comma was needed before a prepositional phrase. "It's not. Generally, the fewer commas the better," she smiled. In bed, with the very same calm, she'd pull his hand away. "Don't be a brute with a girl's clit, Barry." The uniform matter-of-factness went over well with her student and lover.

As long as it was tutoring, as long as they only met in the parallel world of her house, Jane could bear it. Not that the situation didn't take a toll. She had occasional attacks of nerves. She had an ominous bout of hilarity when she and Barry once opened her front door and startled Lynn Paul standing right there. He drifted inside as Jane and Barry retreated. He wangled a cocktail, pretending to solicit the teacher's thoughts about school board elections. The truth seemed to be *right there* on the surface, obvious to anybody. Apparently, it wasn't.

But school was a problem. Jane was in a constant agony of indigestion, waspishness and gloom. She mistrusted herself. She self-psychologized wildly. Another teacher commiserated with her about having a tough year. Was Jane trying to get caught despite herself? She skydived from unconsciousness to panic, from passion to unawareness.

Barry was insufferable. She tried to walk past him in the hall. "Yo, B! That Coke for me?" His insolent komminess caused no particular surprise with the other kids. But Jane's grip made her Diet Coke can emit an aluminum *ribbet* of annoyance. She said, "Mister Paul," in a wry and severe singsong and swept past. She told herself Barry was an incautious ass. She tried to disparage him. He wasn't even attractive compared to the obvious standouts. The standouts left her cold.

Then again, she and Barry might cross paths at school and it would be just them. Alone together at the end of the day, reduced to black flickers in the consuming glare of an over-waxed floor, like wisps of soot in a candle flame, they shared a gaze neither could actually see. Only a voice, Jane reminded him gravely, "Barry, I have *total* confidence in you." The way he nodded in the dazzle could have been manly. His smile, too faint or unclear to be cruel, struck her as impossibly sexual. Appalled, rapturous, she worried he could hear her heart kettle-drumming through her blouse, or see it. The over-stretched collar of his navy T-shirt was washed out in the glare and hung like a lasso around his neck. His messy, stripped and dyed blond hair caught the silver light like a staticky glory. He looked more apparition than real, and it was easy for Jane to return to her dream world for an hour.

The following summer Jane took a cruise of the Chilean fjords by herself. Life-vested, she was shuttled by Zodiac to a briny crag colonized by seals. She ignored the Iowa retirees in the boat with her, even the handsome guide. She studied the seals. What *animals* animals were! This wasn't a virtuous nature show. The seals stank. They bleated. They farted. They fought. They bled. Long yellow fingernails twisted over their flippers. But all around, the crushing sublimity of the fjord remained somehow unaffected by their uncleanness or their crimes against each other. Since this lonely trip was a trip away from Barry, Jane couldn't help holding up her own crime in comparison. Strange to say, seeing how it, too, had no impact at all on the sublime inattention of Nature and Time made her guilt seem *less* pardonable to her than ever before. Judge and criminal both existed in a single vessel.

A few days after she got back, Jane heard Barry rustling in the lilacs outside. He was hiding his bike from neighbors, a pretty much pointless habit from the early days. She opened the door and backed up without greeting him on the stoop. Also an old habit. She sat him down on the couch next to her, and his knees fell apart in the cocky way he had, though he could tell it wasn't going to be that kind of a visit. And if it had been, oddly, a breath of shyness would have come over him.

Jane addressed something they'd never mentioned before. "Our—friendship, Barry. You know, people don't think it's OK. They really don't."

He asked how dumb did she think he was. Of *course* he knew that.

"No, Barry, if this happened in—I don't know—in China, and someone found out, they might whatever-they-do—execute us, cut off our heads. I don't mean to be terrifying, but on the other hand, of course, if we were in a different time and place, like Rome, ancient Rome, I guess, maybe it wouldn't be a big deal at all. But we are where we are, right?"

He gave her a shrug. He looked off. Jane had a horrible reminiscence of justifying a failing grade to another student.

"We know we have to stop. Absolutely stop. Don't we?" Jane collapsed against the couch pillow with a sigh of regret and unpleasant clarity. Barry crossed his arms. He uncrossed them. For a second she thought he was going to hit her. Then she smiled at her ridiculous alarm. She'd relaxed again completely when his hand floated toward her as if involuntarily. He pinched her thigh as hard as he could, a strange, witchy or infantile punishment that made her jerk away. It really hurt. She shrank against the cushion, so shocked she couldn't not laugh and frown. She rubbed the sore spot. She looked at him. "Barry! What's that about?"

"Nothing." He pouted but raised his chin, Mussolini for an instant. His eyes—Jane stared with incomprehension—watered up. "You're done with your toy, so you throw it away."

Jane couldn't speak. The idea that he had feelings, or such strong feelings, had never occurred to her. He was a kid. A nauseating pang of guilt came when her heart and stomach spasmed at once. Might he betray her in anger? Was that something electrical with her heart, a palpitation? But his grief was sure to blow off in an afternoon. He was a kid. Besides, he was the one who cheerfully switched moods on *her*, who played Boing Boing, who got under *her* skin in the Lawrence halls. She was the only one of them with a full set of adult emotions in play.

His eyes narrowed. Tears bulged like glass matchsticks. He was a child. She felt an iota of anger and tried to crush the feeling, all feeling, because wasn't it intolerably selfish of her, an adult, to think she was the one who was going to suffer?

13

WHEN SHE'D LOOKED over the sublime fjord and it dawned on her that the world is indifferent to crime, Jane had experienced a subtle form of growing up, a summer change of heart. For her students, two years, a season, or even a month involved shocking transformation. They re-costumed themselves, became hairy or gangly or sullen, slouching, flamboyant, impenetrable. The young grew and weathered at the same time. By the time Jane ended things with Barry Paul, he too had changed. The difference had made her uneasy with the lines she'd prepared. Partly she had to remind herself he was still a child, because on seeing him, his being bigger, greasier-haired, lower-voiced and more tender made their whole secret history seem not quite so bad (and his pinch much stranger). But exactly their sort of relationship had become public in several recent cases. And had not been shrugged off by the world. Even in *Tierra del Fuego* she'd spotted the scandalous headline "*Mujer Monstruo de Maine–Maestra-Súcubo acecha en el aula!*" tucked into that handsome guide's orange backpack the day they toured a former prison camp near Ushuaia.

Darius Van Nest left Choate under a cloud, drug use or Bartlebyism. Jane heard he was coming back to Lawrence Academy. When she actually saw him in the first day rabble, his transformation was astonishing. She realized she'd been hoping time and trouble might have tempered him. After all, it wasn't his fault that godawful people had once upon a time pointed at him in an orphanage or in a cryoservices catalogue or wherever.

Since change was inevitable, why couldn't he have become modest and amiable by now? But the only thing that hadn't changed at all was the flood of dislike Jane felt when she saw him.

His face had thinned, his features becoming dark, sensual and accusing. His head was still overlarge. His body was easily a foot taller and looked emaciated, almost anorexic, in the baggy clothes he wore. Half-laced yellow work boots had been repaired with duct tape. Jane felt a touch of middle-class contempt for that lordly affectation of squalor. The unbuttoned cuffs and collar of his white dress shirt, impeccably laundered, had a paradoxical dandyism about them.

Darius stood unnaturally erect as Jane critiqued him from afar. He looked like he thought he was enduring fascinated examination from all sides, Jane thought sourly. Maybe tony Choate lingered in his deportment and his fashions. His meek superciliousness repelled her.

Jane turned away. She couldn't approach him and hoped he wouldn't see her in the thronged hall. A second later, he was in front of her, taller than she was and a bit too close. Long, glossy lashes curved back on themselves and almost touched his skin. He tucked a stringy lock of hair behind his ear. The effeminate gesture caused the cuff of his shirt to gape like a lily. But in a manly, if over-precise, voice he said, "Nice to see a familiar face."

Jane welcomed him back. Briskness covered her distaste.

He made a mildly ironic comment about being forgotten over the past years. His vocabulary was a touch overblown. His flower-petal cheeks and the blackheads nestled along the crease of his nostril made the middle-aged refinement of his manners feel like a bad school play.

His irony annoyed her, but somehow he got her to respond in kind. "Fear not, Mr. Van Nest. We've read your transcripts. We know all about you. I hope you appreciate we're giving you a second chance."

Darius nodded uncomprehendingly. The idea that readmission to Lawrence was a chance or a privilege or important to his future or even particularly notable, had never occurred to him and meant nothing. "Naturally," he murmured. "And I have to say—" The old knowing, presumptuous, too-intimate smile appeared. What gave him the right to stand so close? "I'm looking forward to many a long talk with you." Pathetically sincere, he added, "I really am. I've missed our—"

"Why rehash the past?" Jane blurted out. She feared a long first conversation with Darius would necessarily be all about Barry. Was her coldness lingering jealousy?

Darius stared at her blankly. Jane asked herself if Barry had let something slip over the summer. Maybe an investigative poise was hiding a millimeter under the surface of this arrogant kid's blank expression. He was imitating the false innocence of the detective, the eyebrow raised just before the truth is unsheathed with steely certainty. Maybe Darius was going to seduce that dope Barry and find out. Jane would more than pay for slapping him after all. "Any time, Darius, any time," she said with what sounded like villainous bravado.

By now Jane Brzostovsky should have been aware of her blind spot. She had no idea what went on in the hearts of young men. Darius wasn't out to destroy her. He still loved her. Or he still liked her very much in a way that made a self-conscious frost of poise settle on him whenever he came into her office. His remarks gleamed with ludicrous pomp and frigid curlicues of Vincent-Pricean diction. He crossed his legs and canted his hips in the chair. The toe of a yellow work boot tipped up and down with cavalier elegance. A few weeks into the semester, he drawled apropos of nothing, "Might I ask whether you're surprised?"

Jane leaned back. Head tilted, withdrawing behind crossed arms, she asked, "Surprised by what, Darius?"

"Surprised by—" He made a flowery, dilatory gesture.

Jane swiveled, her eye panning across the Lego bonsai Barry had given her, many of its tiny plastic blossoms dropped or missing by now. A second squint at her color-blocked schedule taped to the wall wasn't a big enough hint for Darius to cut things short.

"Well, by me. By what I look like. You certainly haven't changed in the minutest degree. As lovely as ever."

"What a crock! Obviously not what you came to talk to me about, Darius." She made her bark of laughter raucous. She had a weary inkling that Darius was leading up to some kind of I-think-I-may-be-gay admission. That could easily take him weeks or months or forever.

"I just have to learn to trust you again. We both do. Aren't we heading in that direction?" Darius looked unhappy about sounding earnest.

Jane gave her forehead a headachey massage and grimaced, guilt and annoyance in perfect balance.

Darius continued with his pushy visits. And she continued with her taut smiles. Polished eccentricity was the least appealing form of nervousness to Jane. Darius managed to be peremptory as well. "I need you to look at something."

"What?"

"And I want to talk about it with you."

"What?" Reluctantly Jane backed into her office.

After his usual dithering small talk, he opened a beribboned cardboard folder that he'd posed on his knees. With a forefinger he centered a large, brightly colored square of origami paper on one face of the open folder. Having gone through these preliminaries with trembling hands, he immediately began reciting, "*Love I do him? Fell I waste it was too or?–*"

"Darius, what is this? If we're going to discuss poetry–"

"But this is important."

"Why don't you ask me to read it when I actually have time?"

"Please. It's incredibly short and important. Yes, a poem. '*–breast apple fresh her kissed I and love made we after, tears her to said I go must I. House my dark into backwards walked I. Eyes mine from streamed blood of years. Fell I? Love I do him? Death in avails nothing–*'" He stopped. The origami paper made a faint skitching under his fingers. He had raised his eyes to her knees. His mouth was open, but his breath was gone. His whole face flushed, ears to clavicle, an all-encompassing blush, unlike the small red flags that showed on Barry's camellia-white cheeks sometimes–after sex.

With an impatient sigh, bouncing a pencil by its eraser on the desk, yet as kindly as possible Jane wondered, "Darius, do you want to tell me something that might be clearer in a more prosaic form? Not that that doesn't sound nice. Rhythmic. And I get the backwards syntax, I think."

"Inverted," he corrected her in a pitiful voice.

"Ah," she breathed. Tensing her buttocks she allowed the spring of her office chair to straighten her up. "And I hear some waffling as to gender."

His face shot up. He told her, "I'm not saying I'm a pederast. The author isn't. Is that what you were thinking? That's not what this is about at all. And anyway the reality of sex is far, far more complicated in my experience," he said with abrupt condescension.

"But. Well for one thing, I'm not sure I buy the author's experience in that department. I wasn't trying to over-analyze. But you did tell me this was important to you personally." Bemused and at a loss now, because he had seemed so obviously on the brink, Jane could only shrug.

"You know, *all* need not be read personally," Darius informed her. "Anyway, love isn't important? Art isn't important?" A fragment of a knowing smile perked on his lips, despite his redness. Jane readied herself for hostile irony, but he said, "I mean this could be about you as easily as me, not so? That's assuming it's even a personal lyric. Maybe it is. Maybe it isn't. I think part of the reason I've always—felt fondly toward you is that I think we're a lot alike on an emotional level. A lot."

Jane felt like snapping, *not in the least*, but settled for a hollow, "I'm not a poet."

"Nor am I. But, for people like us, aren't there some experiences in life that—you'll have to admit there are—that seem to come from a—parallel universe of—more intense experience? And they need to be expressed. They have to come out."

Come out? A slip in phrasing? What a jumble. He couldn't be suggesting this was really about her. She'd long ago gotten Barry to swear he would never gossip with Darius. "Darius, I don't have any idea what you're talking about. I'm a working-class girl from Queens. I'm not a poet. I'm sorry. And I'm not sure we're that alike. I really don't know what you're talking about."

"I think you do," he insisted. He composed his hands atop the now-closed folder. Jane's heart raced. She leaned her chair back so slowly the spring creaked. Though still blushing, frowning at his lap, Darius still seemed like the glibbest of detectives on TV. His gaze flashed up at her for a second. Were his eyes wet from the rawness of reciting his poem? "I think you do know what it's about and I think we do share an important experience." Did Darius know about Jane and Barry?

Darius had no idea what effect he was having on his teacher. For him all this was badinage, even the weepy embarrassment. This wasn't a conversation about anything definitely real. "I think you do know what I'm saying," he repeated, looking up at her in the most challenging way.

Sometime after this meeting Jane crooked her finger at Barry Paul as he shuffled past in the hall and gave him a stern nod. She led him into her office. She was more nervous than he'd ever seen her. She held her hands in isometric prayer. She made them bob mechanically in his direction.

"I don't want you having anything to do with Darius Van Nest," she announced in a strident whisper.

"What are you talking about?" Barry asked, astonished. "We're not—what gives you the right anyway, you know?"

"Look. What can I say? This is not about me or anything—us-related. I don't want to alarm you about him—or make wild accusations, but that's beside the point. Let me just say I think he could influence you in ways you wouldn't like. We have his transcript and we know there was some drug use at boarding school." Barry snorted in laughter. She held a hand up. "It may sound old-fashioned but the power rich kids have—have you ever heard the expression *the primrose path*?"

"No. I'm totally laughing," he said. "If anything, I'm much more—"

"*Please!* Would you just keep an eye out for him," she whispered sharply.

"What's wrong with you?"

"Nothing!"

"I've never told anyone anything, if that's what you think."

She begged him, "You mustn't, *mustn't* tell anyone, Barry. I hate it, of course, but that's how it is. But that's not what this is about."

"You think he wants to give me a blow job?"

Jane looked at him in shock. His instincts stunned her.

Barry shook his head. "No, you just think I'll end up being a loudmouth asshole about *you*. You think I'm such a—"

Now her own eyes were wet with confusion. Their liaison was one of those things, thoughtlessly begun, that hobbles you for life. The law expects you to recognize snares before they come along, but you never do. Once the snare is tripped, the sentence has already begun. "For now, anyway, be careful with Darius. You're the one I care about," she added in a soothing tone they both found unpleasant.

Barry frowned at her. He mustered a chilly expression. She was obviously freaking out because she couldn't make him go away or put him back in his box. "I'm not a thing," he said.

So why was her incredible, deceitful feebleness still arousing to him? His heart pounded. His muscles released his expression, and his brown eyes took on a wounded clarity. He had to turn his head to the side—pure melodrama—so looking at her wouldn't put him under her power. He jumped when he felt her hand on his thigh. "What are you doing?" he asked with a child's helpless shock, not quite pushing her away.

She leaned forward to smell his hair. Barry was making a panicky noise, a droning in his chest. "We're in school," he warned. "What are you doing?"

"Nothing," she whispered. "I'm sorry. I'm not doing anything. I'm not doing anything." She lifted her crippled-seeming fingers from his leg.

Infuriated, he watched her notice how the crotch of his pants had inflated. He crossed his arms over his belly. "I really can't believe you!"

Jane glanced up at the little square windowpane in her door. Every so often someone peered through it to check if she was in. "People are blind to what's going on in the world around them," she philosophized. "You have to know something to notice it."

"I have to go." Barry stood and turned his back on her. He remained motionless in front of the door for a time, explaining bitterly at last, "I'm waiting for it to go down."

...

Jane needn't have felt jealous or fretted about Darius. Barry and he weren't able to restart their friendship. It hadn't ended, but they couldn't help noticing how unalike they were as types go. Barry now had too many friends who wouldn't naturally get along with Darius, and Darius didn't naturally get along with anybody. Still, neither of them forgot their old intimacy. They felt a puppy nostalgia whenever they spotted one another across a sea of other students. The nostalgia was surprisingly sharp for people so young.

Even when they exchanged mere passing up-nods, their gazes twined. Darius thought Barry's eyes betrayed a strange, limpid but manly surrender, something he'd never seen in another person. Barry realized his haughty, biddable old friend wasn't the most easygoing person. But when he thought about Darius more closely, Barry's interest in the life and friends he himself was choosing trickled away temporarily, as if he registered a faint vestige of a heroic alternate life with Darius. Neither could make sense of it, but they relished their separation, the feeling of elevation tinged with sorrow.

Smoking wasn't allowed at Lawrence, but the stunted woods outside the main classroom building were, by tacit agreement, not policed. Paths weren't needed. The woods were sparse as well as stunted. For early December the trees seemed over-garnished with shriveled, ashy leaves. Students walked until they couldn't be seen from the school, which meant everyone ended up at the same slight dip in the ground. They called it a ravine. At the bottom, the earth was polished, saplings were broken or stripped, and beer cans had weathered almost to bare aluminum.

Barry and Darius happened to meet at the smoking spot out in the woods. By way of greeting Darius indulged his habit of world narration (you-me-here). Barry reminisced about something or other, then a slavish bit of flattery from Darius interrupted everything. "I can really see you becoming the head of some big corporation or a famous politician."

Barry smirked and shook his head at the ground. "Oh, buddy—man—" He couldn't respond to the absurdity. "You're killing me." Barry was almost as tall as the trees. He hid his cigarette in the meaty hollow of his palm. To exhale, his cheeks puffed like a Botticelli west wind, and his jet of smoke ruffled into the low azure sky.

A third boy, a handsome, taciturn friend of Barry's named Dean crouched, head bowed, wrists dangling over his knees. He came alive to suck at his cigarette, snorted the smoke out in laughter at Darius, then wilted again. It wasn't hurtful laughter, more like an older brother's distracted mockery.

A girl none of them knew blundered into their midst. She rubbed her bright magenta hands and shrugged hello. She seemed to be going for a neo-seventies look in huge clogs and a furry-lapelled yellow jacket. She fussed through her leather shoulder bag for Newports.

She begged a light and eyed Darius critically when he proffered his mini-Bic lighter.

The tip of her cigarette bobbing up and down in the flame she commented cynically about the school literary magazine. "You see that *Ovum* piece of shit came out? I swear every kid in this hellhole thinks they're some fucking Allen Ginsberg." Eyes pinched almost shut over her Newport, she went from incurably bitter to ecstatically sensual with one inhale.

"I actually have a poem in it," Darius smiled. "Not that I disagree with you, really."

"Ouch," Dean said in the seemingly relaxed silence that followed.

"Ouch," Barry laughed.

"Sorry. That sounded so..." the girl sounded like it was hard for her to apologize. She tapped her Newport in an unwoodsy way.

"Please." Darius shrugged.

"It hurts him because it's a love poem. Darius is in love with Barry," Dean said without raising his head.

The girl looked uncertain and sniffed. She blew on her fingers.

As if ironically, Darius said, "Yes. As you can see, I'm madly in love with him." He was smiling.

Still crumpled next to her mouth, one of the girl's pink-blue fingers pointed. "Oh, you're Barry. Yeah that's what I thought."

Nothing felt especially awkward, but Barry changed the subject anyway. "You see much of Ms. B this year?"

He was asking Darius, but the girl exclaimed, "Ukh, yes, I have her in English. You guys aren't fans of hers, are you? I'm only asking cause our class decided like she's some kind of bitch underneath it all. Even though everybody loves her. Maybe it's us. I don't trust the ones everybody else *loves. L-U-V.*"

"It's not you," Dean confirmed.

Darius decided not to say he was indeed a fan of hers, because he didn't want to come off as contrary. "I guess I see her," he admitted to Barry. "I don't have any classes with her, though."

"She's out to get you, man," Barry said to Darius. He started chuckling.

"I'm not out to get him," the girl complained.

"Ms. B," Dean corrected.

"Out to get me?" Darius frowned.

With smoky words, the girl said, "See now, this is good information. Kind of what we thought. She's got this tight-lipped thing going on like she wants to be tough. But think about it. What does it do to you if you spend your whole life with kids, you know? It's some kind of power trip."

"Tough?" Darius wondered scornfully. "What are you talking about? She's a sweetheart."

Dean squinted in pain at the word "sweetheart." "Don't say *sweetheart.* It sounds so gay."

Barry kept laughing about Ms. B. "She's got your number, Dare. She's out to get you."

"I never thought of her as tough," Darius repeated.

"Who cares?" Dean said.

"Really, she's out to get you," Barry said. "You want to know what she said? She warned me to watch out for you. *Barry, watch out for that Darius Van Nest!*" He couldn't imitate Jane, so he made himself sound generically shrill and stern.

"Wait, that's not *out to get me,* Barry," Darius argued.

"See, but that's sort of—I don't know—" the girl mused in a whisper.

"You're saying she told *you* to watch out for *me*? Right?" Darius was flummoxed. "Isn't that *nice*?" He shrugged indifferently for show, then started kicking a maple sapling. Its few crisped ochre leaves shuddered. "She means, because—what?—she doesn't think I can handle myself here? New kid on the block? That's weird."

"No," Barry insisted. "No, man. Not watch-out-for-you-take-*care*-of-you. Watch-out-for-you, because she thinks you're *evil*. Like you're a bad influence on me or something. I don't know." He couldn't help laughing at the expression of shock on Darius' face. Everyone laughed, in fact.

"On you! Me?" Darius said.

"I know," Barry confirmed the crazy misreading of their relationship.

"Obviously, she's not your friend, either," the girl said. "Really, these teachers spend all their time with kids, so in this sick way they end up more childish than we are. Not that we're not pathetic, loser kids with no idea what it's really like out there in the world."

14

DARIUS WAITED MONTHS but Barry's *watch-out-for-Darius* remark was still nagging at him just before Christmas break. Finally, slyly, he asked Jane whether she observed anything dark or evil in his personality. Jane's lips worked in a way that could have meant yes, but she said, "Of course not. You're too innocent to be evil." Darius persisted with his questions—me, me, me, she noticed—like every emotionally stunted rich kid. It sounded to Jane like someone had accused him of being evil. Somehow Barry came into it which aroused her suspicions. She became more inward, more distracted, more self-interrogating and even more clipped in her responses to Master Van *Needy*.

The weather had gotten cold. It had already snowed. Tonight was clear, though. A huge pink sun cast a glow over everything, wrong-seeming because it was warm to the eye. Pink snow and golden-quoined Georgian brick façades shone on the west-facing houses along the Van Nests' street. Darius snapped tiny icicles from the gutter of his personal school bus shelter, built by a gardener long ago and never really used. Everything was so quiet and empty he might have been the last person left on earth—and it was more enjoyable than lonely! Time itself felt like it was winding down.

Darius remembered being drawn to the evil Borgias as a child and wondered if that meant something. Maybe he had a tendency to darkness and had never noticed it. This was a surprisingly disturbing thought. And surprisingly surprising.

He'd always been in trouble at Choate, racking up a fantastic tally of demerits for going on strike in various classes. If that wasn't exactly evil, he'd also been called up twice before the somber-faced cherubs of the Student Judiciary Committee (for dorm burglary and vandalism). His concerned English teacher had noticed how the blood and gore continued in his writing even after *Life Sliced.* And now Sohaila complained that he was always gloomy, though he suspected, in her case, it was her own guilty fretting. The New Jersey household had an outlandish, depressive atmosphere with ignored son, deranged father, mother and mother's lover, all living together for years at this point.

Stunned to hear from Barry an hour ago, Darius had come down to wait at foot of the drive, the midpoint between his house and normalcy. He didn't want Barry to drive up and see the single garland of aqua lights Sohaila and Stan had strung over a bay window of that bloated, embarrassing Tudor monstrosity.

At the Paul house earlier that afternoon, a friend of Barry's had showed in a Malibu with an untalkative girlfriend. The three decided on an evening together. They practiced spinning out in the snow of an empty church parking lot. Barry suggested they invite Darius along.

On the way over, Barry, who happened to be at the wheel, made a skidding detour down Jane Brzostovsky's snow-muted street. Emboldened by his companions and weed and a novel car, he skied the Malibu to a stop in front of Jane's pinkened concrete stoop. The entry had been kicked free of snow, not shoveled. He started a merry honking.

Jane opened the door, rebounded inside to get her Chilean vacation parka and strode toward Barry, stalked rather. A ridge of snow fell when the driver's side window glided down. "Hi!"

Jane's lips compressed. Without using words at all, she made it plain she was furious. Animal hums or snorts accompanied her fierce get-out-of-that-car gesticulations. She squinted impatiently at the puttering elbow of exhaust rising from the tailpipe of the rusty Malibu. After she'd drawn him aside, she hissed, "What the hell is this, Barry? Who's in there?"

"Just friends."

"Great. Who?"

"No one. We were going to pick up Darius and hang out."

"Oh, that's lovely. Bring 'em all by. Get a load of the teacher I fucked."

Aghast with pot-headed slowness, Barry whispered, "That's not what I was doing!"

"Oh, really? As a matter of fact, we need to talk, Barry. I don't know how you want to handle it with your gang here. But I can't stand this anymore."

"Gang?"

"Come in. I'm getting cold."

"Wait a second. What do you mean? Talk about what? I'm supposed to be doing something."

"Hanging out? Please, come in. Now," Jane said frigidly. Her lips were nearly white.

With a put-upon sigh, Barry turned and called, "Go ahead, you guys!"

A townie scrambled across the front seat. He stuck his head and a shoulder out the driver's side window. "Huh?"

"I said *go!* I can't go. I can't go. I'm staying."

Jane snorted at the loudness of their voices. Everything in her life was teetering. She turned her back ostentatiously and yanked the parka tight. Barry explained to his friends how to find the Van Nest house where Darius would be waiting.

"You want me to come back in a while?" the townie asked.

"Maybe. I'll call Darius."

Jane laughed bitterly, softly.

"No," Barry said. "Just forget about it. I can't go tonight. Not yet. I'll see you later."

"How are you going to get home?"

"Just go!"

The townie was perfectly OK picking up a stranger, whose fancy bus shelter and driveway he eyed appreciatively. Darius was full of mild-mannered hesitation, which the townie found amusing. Jittering in the driver's seat, he ad-libbed cajoling arguments and promised they'd pick up Barry later. "Hi," the girl peeped when Darius got in. Darius sat in the back and watched them. The townie was a touch manic, which made the drive frightening at first. The girlfriend got a tiny ruby-barreled pipe of strong weed going.

Though Darius couldn't understand much that was said in the front seat, he kept *right-right-ing* and smiling agreeably. The girl smooched the little pipe's mouthpiece and shrank against her side of the car, so the smoke silently splashed against the glass. She was leaning as far as she could from the townie, but from the way she kept looking at him, glancing haughtily down her nose at his thigh, tugging on her bangs, snickering rudely when the back seat guy (Darius) said anything—from these clues Darius guessed at an intense, unhappy infatuation, which he was alarmed to recognize and identify with completely.

When a seed in the pipe popped, burping red sparks, they all laughed immoderately. Darius handed the pipe back to the front seat. He sank into a silence almost as deep as the girlfriend's, cheerfully lethargic, a vision of black woods purling alongside the car.

They ended up at a large park. They lowered a chain which blocked the snaking main road, plowed at some point but snowed under again. The townie eventually swerved onto a different snow-shrouded surface. Lawn or road or bike path, it hadn't been plowed at all. The Malibu handled the terrain better than expected, and they made it through a treeless opening in the woods to a dilapidated picnic shed, which the townie tried to set afire with his disposable lighter and hanks of vinyl torn from the back seat of the car. Stolen, the townie confided rather shyly. Darius was enjoying feeling less and less scared of him, but the townie's wild sense of fun also had his stomach in knots.

When the sun was gone, the frigid night felt as alert as the inside of a kettle drum. Silence twisted off the snowy squeak of their steps. The coughing of their lighters and their stupid remarks fell quietly dead in the vast, cramped-sounding park. They listened to their bodies' noises, to their heartbeats, which thrummed like a downpour thanks to drugs and the seething of blood in their ears

Later, the townie tried backing out at speed. Almost at once the Malibu slipped out of its wheel tracks. It fishtailed slowly, tires spinning, and lodged askew three feet from the original path. The tires beat up a froth of mud and snow. The woozy boys tried pushing the car while the girl took the wheel. They were outraged and laughing and a little worried. The car slithered a foot or two farther from the path and stuck fast.

All three went off to gather brush to wedge under the rear tires for traction. They tore branches from smaller trees and discovered several dead logs outlined under a pristine layer of snow. They uprooted an entire bush. Loaded like peasants, they trudged back to the car in single file. They didn't talk. They were caught up in the sensual mixture of exertion and drugs.

Inward-looking as they were, they were slow to register a man standing by the Malibu. He jingled and held a high-powered flashlight. Though dim behind the foggy glare, they could see he was wearing a uniform. Everything about the drug-addled scene was strange. Was the man speaking to them or singing in a lovely baritone? When the light glared from side to side across their faces, the kids saw the black pallor of a ghost horse looming directly behind him. Shaking its head, its snout jerked up. Its tackle jingled. It blubbered a puff of breath at the stars with velvet nostrils.

The ranger pointed his flashlight where he wanted them to drop their branches. He'd already laid a field-testing kit on the hood of the Malibu. Letting go of his branches, the townie ran. His running turned into a high-stepping waddle when he got to patches of deeper snow. He hit an open ridge, where the snow had drifted away and rimed straw showed through. He hit his stride. He headed for the woods, away from all paths.

The ranger was slow to react. He muttered in annoyance. He bobbled the flashlight. Darius felt the glare of it on his cheek. His eyes squinted shut. He thought he heard a terse question or two. "You OK? Don't you move, you hear me?" And the ranger pressed the reins of his gorgeous, half-real horse into Darius's hands. Hips clattering with the implements of his trade, the ranger jogged after the townie for a short distance. Stretching her neck, the ghost horse tested the firmness of Darius's grip on the reins. She lowered her eye to him, as bulbous and black as the night. Their breath misted together in a hay-scented cloud.

Evidently the ranger didn't want to leave his horse for long. He returned. Neither Darius nor the girlfriend betrayed the townie car thief, but they were arrested themselves. Parents were called.

At exactly the moment the ghost horse chucked her head at the night sky, Barry Paul was stalking Jane Brzostovsky's living room in his underwear. He felt betrayed. He paced with a bouncy bowleggedness and threw his arms in the air like an angry basketball coach. But he wasn't trying to look funny. He really was angry. His pacing came to a stop when he noticed a wet spot darkening the front of his jockey shorts. He pinched it between thumb and forefinger, slimy rather than wet. Therefore from sex, not from peeing afterward. He started pacing again, wiping his fingertips on his belly, then on the small of his back.

Jane was wrapped in her comforter, curled in a stuffed chair. It bothered her how withdrawn she was. She was exhausted almost beyond feeling. Not that she didn't have compassion for Barry, but it was hard to watch him like this. For herself: nothing, not even regret just at the moment.

She said, "Of course I knew—I should have known—sex would make you think what I said earlier didn't hold anymore. I'm sorry. It's shameless the way I keep putting so much pressure on you, Barry. But, among many other problems, the age thing is impossible. It's sad, but it's real, and insurmountable, and I'm just—I just let myself pretend sometimes. I'm sorry. You've got to understand, or at least trust me that we have to, have to, *have* to do something to get out of this, and—"

"You were just—" Punching the air, he cut her off. "You were just willing to do anything to weasel it out of me. Did I talk to anybody? Did I tell Darius about it? That's the only thing you cared about."

"No. They were two separate issues. Yes, I wanted to know. Yes, maybe I had a panic attack about it. That's why I made you stay. But—and I know it's unfair of me to claim this and it excuses nothing—but, Barry, with you I'm helpless. I just let it happen without thinking of you. Or thinking of anything."

"I don't believe you."

"Well, look, have I asked you what you and Darius did talk about in the end? No. Am I asking now? No. I don't care anymore. Because I can't help seeing there's something much more important we have to address."

In a dull, defeated tone, Barry mumbled, "Of course, I didn't tell him. I never told anybody anything."

Her relief sickened her. She opened her mouth. Then she turned to the window. Or rather to the cadaverous blur of herself on the glossy blackness. She could make out the faint, cheesy odor from his sneakers, which he'd self-consciously left at the foot of the stairs so they wouldn't offend her.

"What'd he even say that made you think—"

"Oh, Barry. It doesn't matter."

"It does. If you want me to fuck up my life to solve *your* problem, I'd like to know what started the whole thing."

"Nobody wants you to fuck up your life, Barry. We just have to find a way of dealing with this finally and absolutely. My only idea for how to do that is what I was talking about before. But my idea did not, did *not*, come about just because Darius talked to me. Even if I did flip out and get angry at you."

"And then seduced me. I didn't want to have sex."

"I know."

"This time. And now you're throwing me out like—like Trotsky." He made a grousing sigh.

"Barry, I'm not sending you into exile. We can talk about it. It's just an idea. Mexico was only a for-example."

He flopped onto the couch and complained, "Just tell me what he said."

"Oh, Barry it was nothing. He asked whether it was true that I didn't like him. Or if I thought he was evil."

"You don't like him."

"I've never said that."

"Well, but what did you two say about me?"

"Oh—"

"Say! Tell me!"

"He asked—was it true that I'd asked you, Barry, to watch out for him? And he told me he thought I had it backwards. He said you influenced him more than he did you."

"I don't think that's true."

"Oh, Barry, who cares? It was just the same maundering, self-conscious, me, me, me whining that he's always done. It's what he's all about. *Am I evil?!*" she scoffed.

"See, I told you, you didn't like him."

"He's just a child. A kid still. I'm sure he'll grow up."

"So, what do you want me to do? What am I supposed to do?"

"I haven't really thought the whole thing through," she admitted bitterly. "It's probably a crazy idea. And you're right. Maybe it is unfair. The idea was that if I left suddenly, it would look strange. Everyone would ask questions."

"I wouldn't tell."

"I know, Barry, but people may have noticed something. I don't know. It would open up a whole can of worms, because it would look strange for me to disappear. People would wonder. But then I thought if *you* went off for a while. Not forever. You wouldn't be fucking up your life or anything of the sort. And I'm perfectly confident you can handle yourself. But if *you* went off for a while. Then, say, at the end of the school year, you come back, and by that time I'm gone. I can tell them I burned out. But it would look more normal for me to leave at the end of the year, easier to find another job. I could drop hints about being tired. People will have forgotten that you left. No one will make the connection. And then you can come back and start again at school, and it'll just be this blip for you. This tiny blip."

"But where do I go? How am I supposed to live?"

"I have money." She lost her composure. Out of nowhere a wracking sob burst from her chest. She belched and panted for breath. A sore, hiccuppy flexion paralyzed her abdominal muscles for a while. She pulled the comforter to her jaw. Her hands smarmed her face, the nails pricking a nostril and an eyelid. Where did this ocean of grief come from? And where were the tears? Nothing trickled between her fingers. When poor Barry got up and tried to reassure her, stroke her hair with awkward manliness, she shoved him away. She shoved him roughly, though not as roughly as she wanted. She held back, because in some recess of herself she knew that, even at her weakest, even grief-stricken, she had much more power than was right.

After phone calls from a ranger's station outside Camden, Darius and the girl were picked up by the girl's tight-lipped father, a former Navy Seal. He assumed Darius was the instigator, basically a rapist, a case of mistaken identity that should have been laughable. In seething silence the not-so-old soldier dropped Darius off at home. Though a lot had happened, it wasn't late, only midnight or one.

Darius came in the front door. In the tiled vestibule, he kicked off his boots. In the extravagant heat, snow had melted from the laces and the duct-taped seams. Stray clots of snow dropped from his wet socks as he padded into the front hall. Overhead, the big lantern cast a yolky blur of light, its lowest setting. As always Darius registered that this was where Colin Vail had hanged himself, and as always, without real thought, like telling the rosary, he ran through the possible mechanics of that confounding suicide. Had the rope been tied to the lantern or to the wrought iron ring above or to the balustrade of the landing? How long was it? Had Colin jumped or lowered himself? The idea of a counterweight was absurd.

Plaster ribbed arches intersected over the lantern and were supported by oaken corbels carved with the Wales, Medici, Bourbon and Barberini crests as if the pudgy industrialist who built the place had planned on a renaissance summit meeting. Could the corbels have supported a rope? Koechlin's dreamy *Nuits Persanes* blasted from the front drawing room. Sohaila had turned up the volume of the CD in order to blot out everything.

Darius spotted her partway up the stairs, hugging her knees. She was hardly larger than the banister telamones. She wore a satin robe the color of skin, collar and cuffs embroidered in gold. She slapped her hand to the banister and pressed herself to her feet. She came downstairs heavily. Making a tense, snaky, after-you gesture with her forearm, she ushered Darius through the front drawing room. *Les Nuits Persanes* swelled and subsided.

At the far end of the room, past a shallow Tudor arch, was a further large sitting area. In enfilade beyond that was yet another room, a library, which was now outfitted as a bedroom. This apartment was Sohaila and Stan's realm. The door to the library/bedroom was open, and Darius could see, as if through the wrong end of a telescope, Stan propped up in bed reading. Even in miniature, Stan's Mephistophelean Van Dyke and flyaway, mad professor hair were unmistakable. The bedroom was bright, and Stan probably couldn't see them in the dimness. He shook a fingertip in his ear with violent unselfconsciousness.

Sohaila sat on an upholstered bench outside the door. She couldn't bring herself to look at Darius. Her gaze wandered the floor, the chair legs, his floppy socks. "Dah-li-*ush*," she kept repeating his name. "I'm so mad," she whispered.

She wasn't wearing makeup, and half-erased, she didn't resemble Sophia Loren or herself. Her suffering anonymity was impossibly poignant for Darius.

The arrest was meaningless to him. And it should have been meaningless to her. He tried explaining it. "Listen, Mom, I promise you this was a nothing—truly no big deal." He couldn't fathom his mother's particular bleakness. He hated the spacey music.

She opened her mouth and stopped, as if she remembered only her first language tonight. She leaned forward and tugged a rumpled Kilim flat on the beige carpet. "You would say that," she whispered. "Nothing touches you. *A nothing, Mom*," she muttered in a mocking singsong. "It's a nothing, Mom!"

"Can we turn the music down?" he complained.

"I need it on." Her eyes glittered over tightly crossed arms. She briefly uncrossed them to touch the top of her forehead, a tragic gesture from antiquity or from beyond the Caucasus. She said, "I know you hate this life of ours. And so do I." She stood up and turned her back on Darius. Now she was looking into the bedroom at Stan, who couldn't see her and wasn't looking back.

Darius's childish American crime made her own crime all the more obvious to Sohaila. She felt an antique self-disgust about divorce, adultery, concubinage, even about the unnaturalness of adoption. The steps leading her to this emotional midnight looked shallow, despicable, un-Islamic. Oliver's blandishments, her taste for sybaritic tranquility, Stan's protective energy. Poor Darius, a whim of her husband's originally (each of them believed adopting a child had been the other's idea) would end up being destroyed.

Without turning around, she said, "You can't imagine what it's like having a foreigner for a son. I don't ever understand. I don't ever understand." A sob or chill caused a long tremor. Her spine and shoulders moved under the satin. Sohaila despised her own luxurious sense of guilt, her inability to act even the tiniest bit American. "I don't understand you at all," she repeated as monotonously as Koechlin.

Darius, petrified by his mother's anguish, finally came up with words that were particularly American and inadequate. "Mom, Mom—Jesus, this is really not serious. I'm not involved in anything you need to worry about. I'm telling you."

Sohaila looked past him through the front drawing room, back into the front hall where she'd glimpsed Oliver. She made a minuscule noise of revulsion. "I know. I know. I love you," she sighed. "Now you have to talk to your father. Or he'll talk to you, of course." She lifted a rigid, recurved palm, touching but not cupping, her son's cheek, a final, exotic gesture before she returned to her bedroom.

Oliver stood on the hall threshold, backlit by the yolky lantern, his drink tinkling in a languid grip. "Don't get down here much," he said when Darius came to him. He seemed perfectly calm. Before Sohaila had quite closed her door, he waved and called, "Yoo-hoo, Stan." The tiny figure in the bed leaned forward and squinted. The door closed.

Oliver sat on an Elizabethan-ish side chair in the hall and crossed his legs briskly. He rested the musical highball glass on his knee with an odd sprightliness. He seemed cheerful. "Can we turn that off?"

"Mom wants it on. I think it helps her sleep."

Oliver peered across the hall threshold at the stereo-CD set up and more generally at the recently redecorated drawing room. "They've made a mess in there, haven't they?" He made a face. "Not my style at all."

"She's so upset." Darius breathed. "It's like I died."

"You fucked up. Arrested." Oliver snorted. "But I'm not sure—" He interrupted himself with a bland noise of disgust. "*Euch*, I loathe big speakers and TVs, all that techno—more suited to a bachelor pad in a high-rise, if you ask me. But all this is more your mother than it is Stan." He waved at the drawing room décor professorially. "Look at that mirror. Iranians are obsessed with gold. This isn't Stan's taste. He's a Slavic peasant. That's an odd thing about your mother. She sort of *yields* her way into getting her way. An enviable trait, I guess, as far as it goes, but then the man always goes crazy in the end. I used to have quite a lot of trouble—" his tone changed to one of suggestive amusement. "—exercising my rights."

"Dad." Darius's eyes fell closed.

"What? You think I'm going to bawl you out for this? *Undignified* is probably what we should call it. The Choate what-all was much more serious. Not that I was immoderately angry about that, was I?" His gaze jumped around the hall and back toward the drawing room. Horny and yellow, his bare foot wagged with adolescent energy.

"Dad—"

"I rarely worry about your behavior. Maybe not at all. Drugs? Look!" He held up his drink for a second. "Go out. Have fun. You and I have a deal. You'd never damage our relationship. Your mother doesn't know that. I think you even love me. We both know what you're probably after in the long run." He smiled. The glass was tinkling very loudly on his shaking knee. "It's comforting. Like a pact."

Darius argued irritably, "We don't have a pact, Oliver. What are you talking about?"

"Yes, we do. We both know what you're waiting for. And why you'll always be an obedient bad boy. It doesn't matter if you give your mother and me trouble along the way. In fact, I'm often glad I decided to let her get you in the first place. Does that surprise you?"

Oliver's cryptic remark stopped Darius cold. "*Get me*? Like—an espresso machine? And I know you're talking about money and your secret stash." Almost involuntarily, Darius had lowered his voice. He glanced up at the lantern. Still seated, Oliver followed his gaze dumbly.

During all these years the notion of Oliver's fantastic wealth had come to seem more like his mother's dreamy Qajar connection to the Peacock throne, a fantasy. He knew his family were what most people considered rich. But that was it. Oliver's jiggling gaiety tonight didn't make vast secret wealth seem any more plausible. Nevertheless, Darius was shocked to notice his father's face drop from the lantern wearing an extremely crafty expression. Darius seemed to snap the pieces together in his mind: it all might, *might*, be true. His sudden silence was humiliating.

"I see you see," Oliver chortled.

"Dad, watch the glass."

"Ah," Oliver said. He screwed his giddy mood tighter by a turn. He crowed, "All part of the plan! All part of the plan!" He waved an arm around, perhaps gesturing at everything, the house, his hidden piles of gold. He particularly wiggled his fingers toward the drawing room and Sohaila and Stan's door beyond. The manic hand returned to his thigh with a slap. With a little twist of his other wrist, he emptied his glass on the front hall rug. He looked blankly at the dark splotch flecked with ice. "Don't tell me to watch my glass," he argued dully. "Marking my territory," he explained.

"You told me you gave the house to mom." Darius made an appeasing sort of a challenge. Then he looked scared.

"And I did." Oliver sobered up a bit. He waved away Darius's sudden alarm. "Oh, come on. Don't nursemaid me. It's a little vodka and ice water. No stain. I'm just playing." Unable to suppress the insane change of subject, he lowered his voice and went on. "You know, Darius, I've never understood why everybody thinks *Mutually Assured Destruction* is a crazy system. I mean, why do they think that's such a bad way to live with nukes, if you have to live with nukes? It always seemed perfectly sensible to me. That's the way people really do deal with each other most of the time, isn't it? As long as everybody does the right thing and behaves, everybody else withholds their terrible power."

15

BARRY PAUL'S DISAPPEARANCE got surprisingly little attention. The school authorities and certain teachers checked and rechecked with the parents. Their skeletal explanation sounded odd but nothing to fuss about: their son had moved in with relatives out of state. Some paperwork had to be taken care of. A small portion of the tuition was eventually refunded. People whispered about Jeanette being a vicious mother and Lynn an alcoholic father and supposed they'd figured the whole thing out.

Despite the moribund state of their friendship, Darius missed Barry terribly. The only uncomplicated fondness he'd ever felt was finished. He moped and reminisced sadly about the wild night in the stolen Malibu with the townie and his girlfriend, a joyful experience. It had been a valedictory gift from Barry. Not something he could ever reproduce on his own. Feeling diminished, he returned to his affectless and boring routine.

A few weeks after Barry vanished, Sohaila round-abouted to Darius, "Darling, you know—" She was trying to snap a CD onto its jewel box spool with a refined grimace. Her hands seemed almost too weak. Stan took the CD and box from her and squeezed them together. Uninvolved except for his usual remote, ironical grin and close attention to Sohaila, Stan perched himself on the arm of a couch. Sohaila continued, "The fact is I don't actually know Jeanette Paul. I doubt I've met her even once. And if your father dragged me to some school thing and I *did* meet her, I can't remember. I'm sorry. That's the truth. I don't know what to say to her."

Uncomprehending, Darius frowned.

In a faint Romanian accent, Stan put in cheerfully, "She's social climbing. She wants to be your friend."

"I don't think so. Who am I? She isn't even particularly friendly." Sohaila shrugged. Jeanette had been hounding her with phone calls, by steps more confiding, about her "Barry disaster."

"But why would she be calling you?" Darius asked.

Sohaila made an expression of confusion. "Oh, Dah-li-ush! I somehow thought you knew about it or that you'd talked to her already. It's difficult for me to put together what she says. She was talking about you. You and Barry."

Sohaila and Darius were both startled by a satanic yelp from Stan. "She rattles!" he exclaimed. That lofty, ironical grin reappeared as he waited for their complete attention. Traian (Stan's real name) had a Slavic eye for melodramatic clandestinity and lies. After waiting long seconds, he revealed, "She also tried talking to me. She thought I was the butler. Probably. But her theory is that you, Darius, gave Barry a large amount of money, and he's run away with it. Also, you, Darius, know where he is! She *thinks*." Stan's lulling accent was always pleasing no matter what.

"That's ridiculous," Darius said. "First of all, I don't have any money. Second of all I've barely talked to him all year."

"Oh, I'm relieved," Sohaila sighed. "Not that I didn't trust you."

"I didn't," Stan accused matter-of-factly. He smiled. He wasn't shy about terrible teeth. "Until I realized this woman is insane and dangerous. Rattle, rattle, rattle. I put her rattling all together. I think Barry came up with the idea to go away himself and told the evil parents what they had to say to the school to get back their tuition money or locker deposit. And you see what that means, of course. The parents have no idea where he is or how he's supporting himself. Everything they've been saying is a scam to get the tuition money back."

"Not necessarily," Sohaila cautioned.

"That almost sounds like her," Darius admitted. "Mercenary. But—"

"You see!" Stan crossed his arms triumphantly.

Darius called the Paul home. Lynn handed him off to Jeanette immediately. Jeanette's condescending politeness was as precise as tweezers. Darius stammered that he was as much in the dark about where Barry was and what he was doing as everyone else. He hadn't been involved. "Of course, of course," Jeanette murmured. "That's what your mother's friend told me. You have to understand, Lynn and I were desperate when I called at first. You and Barry were always so cute together. I only wish you were his best friend still. You could have kept him from going off like a blockhead. But don't worry. Lynn and I have a notion what it was all about now," she lied convincingly. "And it's nothing too serious. A private thing with some family members. Out of state. We were just a teensy-weensy bit upset at first. Your beautiful mother was so generous and so..."

In the late spring, Darius had to appear in juvenile court about his marijuana charge and "unauthorized use of a vehicle." Sohaila insisted on a lawyer. Darius ended up over-represented by a Manhattan law partner, an old Yale classmate of Oliver's. The lawyer seemed to enjoy the trip to New Jersey as a sort of professional bagatelle. Darius found him terrifyingly cheerful and glamorous.

From the outset, Oliver was in poor form. He was twitchy, unsteady, silent. If necessary, he uttered a single perfunctory syllable when the lawyer reminisced about something. Listening, walking and talking all at the same time seemed beyond his mincing powers of attention. After the three of them met at a bar called *Schooners*, they strolled toward Juvenile Hall, Darius a step behind the two older men. The lawyer wasn't put off by Oliver's strange distraction. He chatted on, every so often turning around to fix Darius with an ironical, picket fence of a smile that seemed to say, "Let's be wolves and hunt the weak together." He was able to bring out a hint of savage humor to things that weren't so funny on the surface—like the time he and Oliver as young Yalies had seen a man's brain propelled from his skull after a seemingly minor car accident. "Yah," Oliver remembered.

Darius was smitten by the lawyer's insinuating heartlessness. In the gentler female world of family, suburbia, and school he'd never met anyone like him. Darius couldn't help sounding eager: "My dad never told me that about the brain! You never told me that!"

Oliver fell behind without their noticing. Even in a small city like Camden, people handed out flyers or cards or special offer coupons on the sidewalks, a kind of ultra-local advertising important before email. The flyers were offered with a card dealer's flick of the wrist and rapidly disappeared if someone was just blundering past or was a bad prospect. So men wouldn't get sale offers for women's shoes, women wouldn't get two-for-one drinks at a topless bar, kids wouldn't get ads for bulk office supplies and aging businessmen wouldn't get notices for a local club's 60s night. Oliver hated—really hated—having any of this ephemera withheld from him, as if he were being kept from a secret. When Darius and the lawyer noticed they'd lost him, they saw him half a block backstabbing his open palm at a teenager with lime handouts. With ill grace, the kid finally handed one to Oliver, who folded it in half, then in sharp quarters and eighths. Darius couldn't think of anything mitigating to say to the lawyer. "Dad likes to be in the know," he tried.

Inside the courthouse, the lawyer swung into action. He clapped every shoulder in sight. Darius was dazzled. Everyone knew the man. He buttonholed a judge, leaning into her body with a cozy respect that seemed to delight her just because it was transparently false. He whispered a word or two, shrugged intimately about some other case or scandal, then laughed at a brilliant joke she hadn't made. Off she went, unresentfully seduced.

Pin-striped rubber runners hushed the green marble. The anthropology of the visit was riveting to Darius. Court was full of caricatures he recognized from TV: the smartly dressed clerks, the obese mothers of wayward sons, the sons themselves, the fatigued, slouchy public defenders, the occasional peacock of a cop flashing his gold bracelet and finely honed rudeness. His cloistered ignorance was inexcusable, but Darius looked at everyone as if famished. In the same way the lawyer's savage curiosity or the raw friendliness of that townie car thief (who was nowhere to be seen today, of course) charmed him, the sheer density of personality was delightful. It didn't matter that almost everyone here was miserable or tense, lives hanging in the balance or crushed by routine, Darius could hardly keep himself from laughing in twisted pleasure.

Oliver's behavior started to become a problem. The crowd agitated him. He flinched from passing strangers. Abandoning his bland syllables of attentiveness, he muttered snippets of commentary. "She's a fat one. He's got to be a killer. Ugly mug."

The lawyer jovially warned him off criticism. "Oliver, don't incite the natives, for Chrissakes. We want to act like sweethearts."

"They can't hear."

The elevator faltered and wobbled on the way up like a loose clapper in the shaft. Oliver began patting both his thighs and humming aloud. Oliver had always been claustrophobic, but Darius had never seen him suffer like this.

In alarm, Darius gripped his father's forearm and whispered, "Hey." The soothing instinct, Darius realized, might have been the first time he'd ever initiated physical contact with his father. Even stranger, Oliver didn't shake him off for a moment.

Darius looked at the lawyer, who smiled reassuringly. "I think your father hates the courts. Like any sensible person. Otherwise he would've been a lawyer like me. But the law's all bullshit talk. And Oliver likes the truth. Right, Ol?" He clapped Oliver's shoulder. "More of a history/natural sciences sort of a mind," he finished, sounding frankly worried.

"Ha, ha, ha," Oliver said in an artificial voice. "Ha, ha, ha," he echoed himself softly.

The family and juvenile courtrooms were basically just offices. The momentous pantomime of the law took place without robes or stately wood paneling. The bailiff was a balding gent in a mustard polo shirt, and the beeper on his sagging belt didn't give him much in the way of official gravitas. He came into the teeming hall and droned names from his list in a high tenor. The crowd shifted. The disorderly rank of Eames-y plastic shell chairs creaked, or the chrome legs shrilled against the marble. Only the wait was momentous.

Darius was called in for a preliminary interview with a psychologist. Then a wait. Then Oliver was called in. Then they waited. Then both were called in together for a chat about drugs (No), sports (No), and chores like mowing the lawn ("I have pretty bad allergies." "We have a gardener.")

After another wait in the hall, the lawyer jumped up and had a chummy word with an official he saw walking past. They waited some more. Oliver sank into psychic dormancy. His eyes squinted shut. From time to time his fingers felt for the beating of his heart under his jacket lapel, or checked on the lime flyer in his pocket.

Darius didn't mind the waiting at all. Shifting his chair slightly, he could look out a window, across a dismal courtyard and into another wing of the building, its windows severely grated—juvenile detention, the lawyer explained off-handedly.

Darius studied the windows and the boys, mostly flickers, beyond them. He could sometimes make out the bright jumpers, tattooed hands and necks, a scarred pallor, or an all-over Italianate posture he recognized from his earliest leafings through *Masterpieces of World Art*.

The idea of people in cages, now that he saw it in actuality, stirred him in a way he barely comprehended. He wasn't so stupid that he didn't recognize something was off about the interest he felt. He liked the fact that the boys were in cages as much as he liked anything else about them. Why this was so, he conjectured, was either that he sympathized with evil or that he had great compassion. Evil, more likely. Spying on them over there felt as bad as it did wonderful.

The moment of truth was cursory. The psychologist who'd asked about drugs, sports and chores stepped in to give Darius a thumbnail treatment for the judge: "Definitely not an organizer. Not someone to stir up trouble. I feel Darius is more of a follower or a loner." This deflating opinion was quite painful. When he had an opportunity, the lawyer leaned intimately toward the referee's steel desk. He dropped a legal term or two into a commonsensical-sounding murmur. He said *sir* often. He sat back obediently at the right moment. And at exactly the right moment, he cajoled, "Come on. Kids get in trouble." He mentioned that Darius had been trusted with the horse. He alluded to a probable cause ambiguity about the ranger's search for drugs. Darius was dazzled. Afterward, they had to wait again in the marble hall.

The lawyer asked Oliver if he was feeling all right. Oliver put him off with a terse shake of his head. He didn't open his eyes. Darius tried to ignore the lawyer's concern. This wait seemed especially long. Between the alluring flickers of the inmates and the lawyer's sophisticated, man's man harshness, Darius was in heaven. "What did the brain actually look like?" he asked.

"A dollop of gray jelly. Just sitting there on the asphalt," said the lawyer with warm gruesomeness.

Darius still thought, as children do, that the world is tamer and better regulated than it really is. He enjoyed the strange liberty of laughing at the poor dead idiot who'd lost his brain. He even leaned forward in vulpine excitement. "You know, a guy hanged himself in our front hall," he whispered. "I swear." The lawyer gave him the same formal attention he'd have given a judge. Darius went on, "I didn't see it, but Dad knows about it." A puppy-like mewl of assent or pain came out of Oliver. "He was an artist. He owned the house before Dad," Darius hurried on. "I don't think anybody ever knew why he did it, did they, Dad? Dad knows his sister pretty well."

The lawyer remembered the story. He turned to Oliver. "I think someone mentioned you were seeing a bit of Cassie, Ol."

Oliver managed, "Nnnnn—"

"I'm not sure if they're still—" Darius warned.

"Well, that was a grotesque, tragic business with her brother." The lawyer's compassion sounded entirely conventional, so he added a hard-hearted chuckle for Darius' benefit. He grinned and twinkled at the boy. "In the midst of life we are in death. Ever feel like the place is haunted?"

Darius shook his head.

The lawyer scanned the rabble around them with cool pity and returned his gaze to Darius whispering, "We are rams, and they are sheep." His look of fraternity soothed Darius, who hadn't liked being pegged as a "follower" by the insulting psychologist.

"I've always thought it was amazing," Darius said, returning to the Colin Vail story. "I slept in his bed growing up! Amazing in a creepy way, I guess," he added weakly. "But when I look up in our hall I can't figure it out, because he couldn't have done it from the lantern. Maybe from one of the bannisters?" Darius realized the lawyer couldn't see the architectural details of their front hall or imagine the perverse difficulty of trying to hang oneself there. "Dad, you never knew, did you?" he asked, more as a conversational fade-out. He wasn't expecting his father to respond, and Oliver didn't.

A spell of probation was the verdict, delivered after a stern lecture against thuggee and dacoity. The lawyer and Darius were both pleased. A youthful error dispatched. Lessons learned. Darius didn't even have to write a personal statement. Oliver patted his pockets for the lime flyer. The lawyer went off to Manhattan never to be seen again.

The pressure to behave well had suddenly lifted from Oliver. During the drive home, he started acting, frankly, like a lunatic. He bobbed violently over the steering wheel. He tried to yank the wheel from the steering column. His lips compressed in fury. He snorted until a glistening needle of mucus materialized on the back of his hand. He looked back and forth between that glinting needle and the road ahead for a long time. "We were never really friends." Oliver meant the lawyer. Darius said nothing. His father's behavior was far too disturbing to be all about a phony old friendship. Or about anything, really. The thread of mucus went dull under an increasing overcast, Oliver finally slapped at it like a mosquito. "I hated that," he hissed.

"I did too. A wasted day," Darius agreed. "I completely get that it was too much for you, for me, for—and my fault. I get that too."

"No!" Oliver's head jerked negatively. He was in a rage, but the rage wasn't directed at Darius until he barked a sidelong, "How would I know that? How he hanged himself? I wasn't there! You think I spent all these years mapping it out?"

"Of course not. I was just talking. Sorry."

With relief, Darius felt his father's anger passing on from him like a sweeping lighthouse beam.

"I can't stand having it thrown in our faces what a pointless life we lead!" He paused contemptuously. "I lead!"

After they'd drawn onto the highway, it started to rain, lightly at first. Large drops fragmenting on the windshield looked like the glass paw prints of some tiny animal. There got to be a lot of these tracks, up and down across the glass, back and forth. They turned prismatic when the sun peeked through clouds. Oliver didn't turn the windshield wipers on, even after Darius pointed out it was getting hard to see.

Oliver began pumping the accelerator slightly. The car sped up and lagged in a queasy rhythm. Keeping to this variable speed, Oliver passed more timid drivers. Darius was getting nervous. Instead of complaining, he repeated the only explanation he could think of. "You've been under a lot of pressure. This didn't help. I'm really sorry."

Oliver interrupted his bobbing just long enough to say, "No! Are you crazy? What do you mean, *pressure?*"

"I'm talking about the situation at the house, I guess. Obviously."

"Oh, that!" Oliver exclaimed in a comical way, his voice light suddenly like sunshine in vinegar.

"Dad, please, could we just—turn on the wipers."

"No! If you concentrate on shape—and momentum—it's kind of like a video game."

"Dad, we can't see a thing." Through the windshield other cars appeared to be warped and speckled blurs of burgundy or black. When they passed a white van, Darius made out an alarmed face turning to look at them. "Dad, this is way too fast. Let's get off, please," he said quietly.

Oliver pumped the accelerator some more. At this speed the engine was too slow to react. His fists turned the wheel back and forth in a kind of tantrum. The car lurched. The burgundy and marl blurs dropped behind them with an audible lowering of pitch. Their own tires made screeches, left and right. The engine wheezed, and a jack or tire iron tumbled in the trunk.

Bracing his feet in terror, Darius pressed himself against the seat's back. As unprovocatively as possible, he reached over and twisted the wipers on. The right-hand blinker came on, too. He left it, saying nothing.

They made it off the highway in one piece. The blinker stopped by itself. Things seemed a little calmer. They drove a mile or two in tense silence. Then just as Oliver started his back-and-forth with the steering wheel again, he braked. The car slid onto the berm and crashed nose-first into a locust tree. The tree was ancient and had grown so close to the road its roots had raised the pavement. A known hazard apparently, red and white chevrons had been painted on its trunk at some point. Before the crash Oliver managed to slow the car to about ten miles-per-hour. Even so, the air bags exploded. Their deployment had the shocking as well as the physical effect of a punch in the face.

Time recommenced slowly—reproachfully—as if, unlike Oliver, it had gently braked at an intersection like a proper driver. The car was centered perfectly against the trunk. The engine was still running. The white bag at Oliver's chin had mostly deflated. When Darius patted his own down, curlets of a chemical-scented white smoke came out. The same smoke had risen from Oliver's bag but didn't last long enough to suggest a fire. It wasn't smoke. The bags were packed in talc which had gotten all over Darius's hair and fingertips. He expelled talc or nitrogen from his nose with repeated snorting.

Unbuckled, Darius found himself almost unable to stand next to the car. He seemed to lag behind himself. He'd uttered a curse and now said something he could hardly hear about his door still working.

From his side, the car didn't look too bad at all. The grille was dented in a V, and a raised ridge ran down the center of the hood. But the hood hadn't popped. The fender appeared—somehow off. Shards of transparent and amber plastic littered the berm. Darius remembered the soprano shattering and the metallic baritone occurring at once like a crude demonstration of stereophony. He leaned on the top of his door. His legs trembled, which made him think of cartoon knock-knees, and he laughed when he couldn't make them stop. He felt needle-like twinges in his racing heart. His cheek was sore. The bag had socked Darius before he'd been able to react or raise his hands.

While he was still gripping the door, the whole car shifted back a few inches. To avoid getting caught or crushed by the open side door, Darius jumped back into his seat, a cringing tumble, really.

Incredibly, Oliver had put the still-running car in reverse. A patch of white talc on his flushed cheek, he flattened his air bag by rubbing his forearm up and down against the wheel. He didn't appear disconcerted in the least. The accident seemed barely to have interrupted his train of thought. Darius squawked, "*No!*" but pulled his door closed anyway when Oliver shifted into drive. Darius sat in rigid terror as if the vehicle could blow up now. It lumbered back over the root-crumpled asphalt and gained speed.

"Dad, you've got to stop," Darius said in a sort of hysterical calm. He tasted talc on his lips. The car pulled left rhythmically. Something was being lathed against a front tire. Oliver continued to the house as if nothing had happened. He parked and walked to the kitchen door as usual, Darius trailing in a legless stupor.

Father and son paused inside the door. The atmosphere in the kitchen was strained in a way that had nothing to do with car accidents. The whole household was there. The broad-shouldered housekeeper Tina rinsed something in the sink, her back to the room. A thin old man was standing with a mug of coffee or tea. Oliver thought he recognized him but not well enough not to treat him like a stranger. Sohaila and Stan both noticed that Oliver and Darius were inexplicably disheveled. They said nothing about it as if to avoid causing embarrassment in front of the visitor.

With an air of forced pleasantness, Sohaila stood at a counter stirring a batch of hummingbird nectar—red sugar water. At the far end of the counter, a small TV jigged from shot to shot on mute. No one was watching. Stan sat at the kitchen table. In front of him were spread the parts of the hummingbird feeder: glass vials, metal rods, a big plastic sunflower with a hole for a vial in each petal. A finger with a dirty nail pinned down the crumpled instructions for assembly.

Stan looked the most serene and was, perhaps, even genuinely pleased to see Oliver and Darius. The sun hit his handsome face and unwashed hair making him look like a hero of the Danubian hinterland, all gallantry and failure. "Ah! The master of our house," he greeted Oliver.

"Sorry I've burst in on you," said the old man. "Now I really do feel this was ill-timed."

Sohaila warned her ex-husband, "Our guest is visiting from Lawrence Academy." Darius had never seen the man at school. "And everything is my fault, because I told him you'd be right back." She paused pointedly. "Like a ditz." This word, so carefully pronounced, only made her sound more foreign and more refined. "Mr.—"

"Drinkwater," the old man put in.

"—works in development?" Sohaila sounded politely unsure.

"Board, actually. Though it amounts to the same thing. More's the pity. Good to see you, Oliver." He raised his cup and chuckled before setting it down on the counter. "I honestly thought I'd called you and set up a chat. But it looks like I was a complete surprise—very graciously received by your wife—" he blustered on.

"No," Oliver ordered. "You should stay, Drinkwater. We were longer than expected—car trouble. And it's ex-wife. You've been living under a rock?"

Stan raised an eyebrow at Oliver's accommodating snarl.

"Oh, of course," Drinkwater apologized. He opened his mouth but thought better of going on.

Sohaila interrogated Darius with a stare. Her stare became more and more probing until Darius breathed (about his court appearance, not the crash), "Everything's fine."

Sohaila reached out to brush something from his hair and pat his shoulder. "Did you fall?"

The housekeeper dried her hands on a rag and slapped it across the edge of the stainless sink. When she turned, she surveyed the room yet somehow avoided everyone's eyes at the same time. To get out, she navigated among them at a half-crouch like a polite moviegoer.

"I come to call on a friend, but it's also all about money," the old man joked. "I guess we're not quite tax collectors yet, but almost as bad. Isn't that so?" The man's hands and face were liver-spotted. Milky spittle was drying at the corners of his mouth despite the tea or coffee, which he must have sipped through the glistening midpoint of his lips. An ex-ambassador, he was considered a trophy member of the Lawrence Board. "Course it's all highly important. Are you sure, Oliver, I never rang to set us up for—?"

Oliver peered at Drinkwater, apparently making an effort to recognize him. Instead, he snapped, "Did anybody get him more coffee?"

"Not allowed, not allowed. Regrettably." The old man held up two tremulous hands. He greeted Darius, "My goodness, my goodness, my goodness. Mr. Van Nest the younger. Now you have a special sort of a connection with our Ms. Brzostovsky, don't you? I don't mean a crush!" Drinkwater smiled. He looked grateful for his flicker of memory. Everyone else in the room was stunned a stranger would know a detail like that. "Pity she seems a bit ill-at-ease among us sometimes. Takes time to acclimate. Gifted teacher, very gifted, of course." He shrugged. "Did she take it badly, I wonder? That student of hers leaving?"

"No. Well, I don't really know. I didn't have her this past year."

Stan shifted impatiently. "So. What's the verdict? All's well that ends well?" he asked Oliver. Sohaila minutely, crossly, shook her head at her paramour. He was always too blatant.

"Are we doing something later?" Darius asked about possible dinner plans. He was anxious to get to his room. Stan was looking at him now, so he answered him aloud, even loudly, "Fine. Everything was fine."

The housekeeper looked back in at the door, and Sohaila exclaimed, "Poor you! This is impossible. I'm sure you can't get anything done in here with all of us—with all this—" She flung her hand dismissively at the unassembled hummingbird feeder. "Come on, let's—" she urged.

Mr. Drinkwater made an obedient shuffle, but no one else budged. Stan watched Oliver, who, Darius noticed with alarm, had begun patting his thighs.

The Romanian asked, "Not driven mad by this morning's duties, Oliver?"

"Oh, please," Sohaila laughed uneasily. "Everything went well, I'm sure."

With a light in his eyes Stan asked, "Did you two get in a fight?"

"Fight!" Mr. Drinkwater exclaimed in humorous alarm.

And Sohaila whispered dismissively, "Fight!"

Oliver rolled his eyes, fixing them over the kitchen door on the non-functioning bank of arrows now forever pointing servants to the absurd "Front Drawing Room." His show of patience looked difficult for him. He grumbled, "Don't irritate me. I'll be busy. I'm giving all my money away."

"Oho!" Mr. Drinkwater cooed. But he was frowning in concern. With surprise, he watched Stan lean forward in his chair and pluck the lime flyer from the side pocket of Oliver's jacket. Drinkwater's hand rose to draw gunk from the corners of his mouth nervously.

A minute clap of paper sounded as Stan shook open the folded sheet. "What's this?" He pinched the lime paper by its corners and read, "'RAVE!!!! TONIGHT 11 till 4EVER AFTER.' This must be yours, Oliver. A note to self, maybe?"

"Ah," said Mr. Drinkwater. Then he closed his mouth, and his cheeks ballooned as if he were literally swallowing a remark. Self-effacingly, he looked at the floor.

"A rave is a dance, Stan. Even I know that," Sohaila said briskly. "Come in, come in, Tina! We're sorry. We'll all be getting out." She made a complicated Thai dance-like gesture of come-in and right-this-way.

To Drinkwater who wasn't looking at him, Stan lowered his Van Dyke confidentially. "He collects huge quantities of these." He waved the green paper. "Usually it's just *Buy one, get one free!* A key concept in this country. Even for someone like Oliver."

Oliver took the flyer languidly proffered and refolded it. "As you know better than anyone, two for one is always my deal."

Nothing sounded triumphant about this come-back. Oliver seemed confused, in fact.

But Stan spilled his ironical smile into his lap and said, "That's very good, Oliver. That's very good."

"If no one needs me..." Darius touched his cheek gingerly. "I'm going up to my room."

"Everything went well!" Sohaila affirmed.

"What? Darius, yes, goodbye," Mr. Drinkwater said. "Oh, Darius, I meant to tell you, you know, your father and I—he ever tell you?—we were both in The Gridiron. That's not football. Old style social club we used to have for Lawrence graduates. (St. Lawrence on the gridiron.) It kind of fell off, but now there's talk about starting it up again, if you ever have any interest."

Oliver obviously hadn't recognized Drinkwater as an old classmate. The expression of confusion that drifted across Oliver's face made Darius worry about a minor stroke or dementia, a consequence of the accident, or of quietly drinking his evenings away for as long as Darius could remember.

When he was trudging upstairs alone Darius felt a retrospective shock over the crash. The trembling restarted in his limbs, faintly this time. He imagined the Oliver situation getting so bad his mother would be forced to do something. With real alarm he understood immediately the doer could never be Sohaila. It would have to be him. The notion of taking care of his father was a total blank. Darius thought of himself as the least decisive person in the world, a follower, so what kind of authority would he have, anyway? He had no power to think. He jogged up the last flight to his room, got his shoes and clothes off and pulled on sweatpants. He could smell the chemical airbag odor on his pants and dress shirt before he threw them in the closet. Darius had junked the bamboo curtain and put a real door on the closet long before. His murals and beaded patches of glue still decorated the walls in there, however, and the chain still hung from the ceiling.

Thinking rationally may be especially difficult in the room one grew up in. Even ignored, the objects around Darius were balky with significance. The emanations as heavy as a narcotic.

Looking in a mirror, he prodded his cheek. It was red, a touch swollen, but no bruise showed yet. He tried desperately to think in that momentous, hopeless way people do sometimes: *right now, I must come up with a solution! Now!* His effort resembled how he'd tried to get close to art once upon a time—pushing himself with nearly physical concentration up to the imagined boundary between *here* and grace. He was heading toward the same or some other boundary right now, close to thinking something tremendously important.

People say age adds depth to our understanding of the world. A better way of putting it is that age adds layers and layers of surface. Which is the same thing, of course, except that most people can't hold more than that single layer in mind at the same time. Darius was as close to deep understanding as he could get. But "deep" was a useless sort of a surface thing to him, a feeling. Nothing had changed since he'd stared at the *Battle of Desires and Bitternesses* at Cassie's apartment, feeling exquisite pain that he couldn't get close enough to the art in it.

The vestige of terror after the car accident, the tremulous fatigue in his muscles, were powerfully erotic, strange to say. But Darius kept trying to think. It seemed all-important not to give up and masturbate. This thought he was after, if postponed, might have to be postponed forever. He stood at his window looking down at the pool. Pool-gazing was his characteristic behavior, the area by the window his typical habitat, where he was likeliest to forget himself, evanesce or become pure thought.

Leaning forward, Darius pressed a difficult-to-ignore erection against the windowsill. The pressure was slightly gratifying but also slightly hostile to himself. He still wanted to make the final push across *some* boundary to *some* unreal and eternal world of order. But he was sure he was going to break down and masturbate soon. Not that he'd feel the least bit guilty about it ordinarily. He loved the closed-door *bizarrerie* of beating off. The cool weight of the chain around his neck. But right now, perversely, he was after something else. His thoughts attacked the obdurate *thought* he was after like projectiles of ribbon.

The longer he stood there, the more his mental world fragmented. Boredom, exhaustion, indiscipline, sexual feeling, hammered his consciousness to pieces, insisted he wake up from thinking altogether, and he knew when that happened he was going to feel like a failure. He reached into his sweatpants and idly grasped the handle of himself. His fingers compared the spongy underside to the girder-like top. Now sensation had almost completely overridden thought. He was starting to see the trees, to feel the heavenly leaf-scented breeze through the distended black window screen. The antique fan was off, so he could hear the crepitation of sycamore branches, a sound he'd grown up with, and the whispery thud of a nut falling to the lawn. Past a steep slope of chipped plum and gray roof slates, the swimming pool glowed in the middle of the lawn, as still and perfect seeming as the eternal thought he was trying to dream up.

The wrecked car was hauled off, a new one appeared. The impossible, triangular situation Oliver had engineered at the house dragged on. Oliver himself withdrew upstairs more. Stan became a little freer downstairs. What should have been a single scene of sex comedy surprise—*you're in bed with my wife!*—was prolonged for years. Eternalized, it became the institution of the family.

"Dah-li-*ush*!" Sohaila called. He jogged to the house and found his mother's arms crossed. "A collect call. I took it. I don't know why," she commented. She'd gotten a tiny bit waspish with Darius lately. He suspected she was disappointed by his depression, which she read as lack of enterprise. He hung about the house, full of a diffuse unhappiness, secretly clinging to Oliver and Sohaila, and even Stan, as another looming, planless summer commenced.

He blundered past her. "I'll take it in the basement!" He thundered down the stairs into his old outlandish private world amid cool odors of mildew and laundry detergent. "Hello?"

He'd spooked a house centipede, which purled off in silence across stained concrete and into a drain. He caught Barry Paul's name. He arranged his breath. He held the phone with the tense concentration it takes to remember a dream.

Barry was perfectly casual about his disappearance. Darius detonated with lame exclamations, repeated them, interrupted himself. Their former conversational rhythm was completely broken. Barry would have passed over the subject of his absence entirely, but old rumors about where he'd gone and what he'd done made him laugh. "Yes! True!" Darius panted in pleasure. He thought of telling Barry more—about the night the Malibu got stuck and about his arrest and sort-of trial and probation, all of which he was a little proud of. He was, for some reason, nervous when Barry started taking the reins of the call. But it was Barry's call, and Darius had to risk listening.

"Darius, man. The thing is, you've got to loan me some money. Can you do that, buddy? It's a lot. A grand."

"I don't have it, Barry. I don't, but—"

"Shit."

"But I can get it. I'm sure I can," Darius insisted. The loveless subject of loveless money made his insides lurch for a second. But his surprise and unworthy doubt were easy to quash. Darius didn't ask what the loan was for. He didn't even allow himself to ask where Barry was calling from.

As Barry rambled on, avoiding any satisfactory explanations, Darius was leafing madly through his own story. Caught up in this urgent form of self-consciousness, Darius hoped to prolong the baritone scintillation of Barry's voice or his own purely physical response to it. Darius shut his eyes in enjoyment and pain. He leafed through the book of himself wildly, backward and forward.

In haste, Barry dismissed his own recent experiences. "The truth is just boring. It's embarrassing, even. Except for this girl." Darius felt his cheeks warm. "But she's the whole problem now. She's why I need the money. She's in a motel at the moment."

"Oh. So, it's for the motel bill?" Darius hurried to add, "Not that I care."

"No, no," Barry was saying. "It's much worse than that. Shit! It's fucked up." As a mere change of subject, he asked, "Whatever happened to Ms. B?"

"She left right after you."

"End of the year?"

"No. Closer to the same time. Months. She just went off. People wondered, as a matter of fact."

"What? Like there was a connection?"

"To what? You? No. They thought it was weird is all. She quit, I guess. She disappeared. They were angry. Some of her students—" Darius gulped as an irrelevant detail came to him. "—I think she was tutoring them for the SATs, and she just abandoned them. They were crying all over the place. But why is—are you in trouble?"

Barry laughed and pressed on. "The best would be if you don't mind racking up a cash advance—"

"What?"

"On your credit card."

"I don't really have one."

"What! Are you fucking with me? The rich kid doesn't have a credit card? Man, what's going on?"

"I have one, but it's just for emergencies. I mean, all the charges show up on my parents' bill. My mom's. I don't even know where it is. But I do have a checking account."

"A check wouldn't be so good. Maybe a money order?"

"What's that? How do I do that?"

"Take it out at the ATM and go to the post office—or you could have the bank do a teller's check maybe." Barry sounded unsure about that method. Darius listened intently to Barry's breathing. A shifting, staticky sound came through, too loud to be stubble. "You know, buddy, it's sad we weren't more friends the past couple of years. You know what I mean? This last part wouldn't have been so shitty."

"You mean—now? Asking me for help?"

"No, of course not. No. I'm talking about the last part of the year. How it was so shitty. It would have been nice to see you more is all."

"That's what your mother told me when I called. I called her. Have you? You've been in town?"

Barry snorted—his entire ambiguous response. After a moment, he waxed nostalgic, "I loved how you always had us do the strangest things. Like, you were my most creative friend. You were the best."

"No, I'm not. I didn't. It doesn't matter."

"The money's for this girl's abortion," Barry said.

"Oh." Partly because he was adopted, Darius liked to avoid the subject of abortion. On the one hand he resented the foolishness of his birth mother, who must have been too silly or holy to have a fetus sensibly taken care of, and he hoped he hadn't inherited that trait! On the other hand, he couldn't really consider her silly, holy foolishness worse than the alternative: his own personal and eternal non-being. "Oh."

"Yeah." Barry's murmur sidled past the politics of abortion.

"I'm not against it, obviously," Darius assured him. He was obscurely offended.

"No. I wasn't saying that." Things had gotten awkward fast. "It's just...I wanted to talk about how we used to have good times." Barry was stolidly nostalgic, like someone who rarely experienced emotions but found they were nice now that he'd tried one.

"Well, let's figure the money out," Darius said warmly. "I didn't mean to make you feel bad about that other stuff. Or about the money, of course. At all. I didn't mean to make you feel bad about anything at all."

Darius had to beg the money from Sohaila. He told her it was for Barry, but he was discreet about the reason. He used "motel bill" as the excuse.

She grumbled pleasantly about the money to prolong negotiation. Having Darius suppliant instead of remote was sweet, and she wanted to linger over it. She was confounded that he couldn't answer questions about Barry's disappearance. "I don't see why you couldn't find out more. A *girl*. What does that mean? Was it *Romeo and Juliet*? What will they do when they move out of the motel? I know you were excited to hear from him, but you should've asked about more than just the money, no?" Sohaila rarely asked questions herself. She wasn't incurious, exactly, but she sometimes enjoyed the placidity of not knowing things. Even as she reproached Darius for not asking more questions, she seemed to smile about the enduring mystery of it all.

PART TWO

16

DAVID CAPERINI, EX-FRENCH tutor, was the son of a Princeton professor whose life's work was a mind-numbing concordance of *The Faerie Queen*. David had been expected to do something in the academic line. He was physically tremulous, precociously a heavy drinker and could be fawning and evasive in argument. But he balked at things like final exams, requisite credits and graduation. In fact, he had trouble finishing anything, even his brilliant midnight conversations with friends. Fueled by beer and braininess, they lasted until total exhaustion set in at dawn. David had ended up unemployed in his late twenties without any laurels or prospects whatsoever. "Pity our ambition didn't trickle down to the next generation, thine or mine," was his father's jowly aside to a fellow academic who had a similarly wayward son. David considered himself a writer. He had a sixty-page manuscript proving it, but he was now writing almost nothing at all.

As a boy, David had the bad luck to have a slight spinal deformity, which left him on the short side. One futile treatment kept him flat on his back in a brace for a year. Since he couldn't raise his head, he'd used prismatic glasses to read. That year of voracious inactivity set the tone for his life. To this day, he nervously dipped into everything from Kant to *Aquaman* to *Vanity Fair*. Time, whole days or months, lurched past. He felt a sickroom inability to concentrate on anything more involved than forewords and afterwords, lists, a bit of critical apparatus, liner notes, glossaries, squibs and droll literary gewgaws of the Punch-

New Yorker variety. Aphoristic Pascal was his current enthusiasm. Reading him kept his French up.

After leaving the Van Nest household, David found work at a New York non-profit. The organization provided living wills and lawyer-vetted DNR orders to anxious older people all over the country. The mailroom where the wills were put in envelopes and addressed was called "Fulfillment." The head of Fulfillment was a woman, single and surprisingly young, who had decided to start a family *in vitro* without the active involvement of men. She now had an eighteen-month-old. Intrigued by her co-worker's erudite tameness, she invited him to move into her tiny Tudor City studio to form some kind of relationship. David agreed. Now, while his partner was at the office, David watched over the baby and tried to write. As always he read snatches of this and that. A stack of books and magazines rose every day next to the padded play cage.

When Jane Brzostovsky ran into David again in New York, she sized him up and decided he was her fated companion, at least for the present. He could be both a friend and more punishment, a reminder of how far she'd fallen. Like the head of Fulfillment, except not amorously, Jane judged David to be indefinably masochistic, bully-able yet astute, socially passive. When he could get away from the Tudor City apartment and the baby, David would go along with Jane to see any movie or gallery show she liked. They gossiped about the Van Nests and Lawrence Academy at first. Jane dragged him to bars, paying for his time with drinks. After a banal first meeting at a Columbia University watering hole, they saw each other constantly for weeks. David teased her that his hard-working partner was getting jealous. One groggy pre-dawn, he asked Jane to marry him but backed down immediately. He pretended he'd been joking.

Jane called David on one of those summer Sundays when so little is going on in New York that the natural world almost shows through like an underpainting. The sumac trees nod, and huge red-brown dragonflies slalom in from the Hudson so fast their flight appears to hang in the air behind them for a second like string. If the buildings and pavement could go just a little transparent, the silence increase just a notch, the underground streams rise out of the storm drains—the original *Mannahatta*, the world of the Lenape, seemed ready to snap into focus, their canoes gliding below Riverside Park.

Jane had chosen *Poco Loco*, a Mexican restaurant popular with doughy young corporate types, who were working at the New York office for a year before transferring back to Dallas. For Jane's purposes, it was as obscure as it was popular. Being seen with David in front of real New Yorkers somehow embarrassed her. *Poco Loco* was like meeting at a provincial mall.

They had to wait outside for a table. David was agitated. He rooted something out of his eternal plastic bag full of newspapers and magazines. *The New York Post.* The paper was damp from the sweat of his palms, and the outer page tore softly when his forefinger prodded it.

David started telling Jane about a column by a conservative pundit he'd found a perverse way to admire. The syndicated blowhard wrote philistine op-eds foreshadowing the hammy politics of Newt Gingrich. The current column recounted a story about a teacher fired for using the word "niggardly." Students didn't recognize the word but protested racism. "Can you believe that?" David chuckled at the column title, *Three Syllables, Sounds like Racism.*

Jane was meant to laugh. Was David twitting her? He knew her politics. "To me," Jane said. "That's just some piggish white guy claiming black people are dumb. I hear him saying—"

"No! It's about the ignorance. Their completely impoverished vocabulary!"

"Come on. Who cares?" Jane scoffed. "How important is *niggardly*? Do we even need it?"

David's mouth hung open as if *niggardly* was *Amen.*

Jane suspected a catastrophic depression was coming for David. She'd seen it looming from the moment they reconnected. The Tudor City setup was unsustainable. Jane found it hard to believe David didn't see the falsity of the relationship himself. Of course, her own self-ignorance when it came to Barry Paul had been virtuosic. But this was different. Maybe David just wasn't as smart as he'd seemed at the Van Nest's table. Or did screaming babies really oxidize intelligence as she'd always suspected?

After a handful of visits Jane had observed that David wasn't much of a father figure. Holding a glass of scotch in one hand, he inattentively tried to quiet the baby with a fistful of colored pencils. The baby knocked the rainbow kindling from his hand with several uncoordinated slaps. Without lowering his eyes from the ceiling David finished his witty story about Darius Van Nest, the closet mosaicist. The story was only slightly embellished.

Today, David brought up a conversation he and Jane had had months ago. He got excited. "Don't you even remember?" he cried, red-faced. Jane, exactly like the blowhard columnist, had said something scathing about political correctness. He quoted her. How did he remember these things? Making an effort to be no more argumentative than a drifting leaf, Jane pointed out they hadn't been talking about *niggardly*.

Animated, David said he wanted to write an article *elaborating* how the left-right divide was a *mirage*, because here, among *many* examples, was something *you yourself* said that's perfectly in line with the thoughts of a *notorious* conservative. His emphasis made Jane wince. She couldn't help eyeing the slab-like bros in off-duty golf shirts. They were also waiting for brunch tables. Were they listening to this raving? "Why not do an article like you said—get it out of your system?" Jane agreed softly.

"Ha!" David scoffed. "Maybe if the *milieu* of influence weren't so closed!" he challenged bitterly. "You haven't tried publishing anything lately."

People kept entering *Poco Loco* and coming back out to wait amidst the growing crowd. David continued his stuttering tirade about how the world works, how you had to know people. Rhetorical questions were posed, grabbed out of the air and flung to the gum-spotted concrete. Fate, it seemed, had chosen Jane as company for self-repressed David at the very moment of his breakdown.

Condensation dripped onto Jane's scalp from an air conditioner hose overhead. When she shifted, David flared, "Stop—

stop moving away from me!" She'd never seen him so aggressive. His domineering spasms were usually comical, if she noticed them at all. Other people really were eavesdropping now, whispering intermittently in sham conversations of their own. David said, "It just bugs me that everything has to be so false. Why—I don't know why people can't—whatever happened to criticism? Why is it always bad to be critical? Why can't people say something is—well—shit, if it is? If they think it is?"

Jane hummed in a soothing pretense of engagement which caused David's eyes to narrow.

In the brick wall next to her, the kitchen's gray metal street door squealed open. One of the dishwashers appeared. He balanced on the doorway's raised threshold on the balls of his feet and propped the door open with an elbow while he lit a cigarette.

"What are you thinking, Jane?" David demanded. "And the worst—well, I think the worst is in friendship. When friends don't tell each other what they really think. Fuck irony!" he exclaimed.

Jane's embarrassed casting about must have made their conversation seem slightly public, open to anyone, so the dishwasher smiled cheerily at them. Jane smiled back. The dishwasher kept butting the door open with his shoulder or elbow. He blew smoke upward and out like a fountain. Whenever the door fell back against his shoulder, the jet of smoke flinched from his lips.

Jane tried changing the subject. "Except for this place, the city's completely empty. Why do they all come here?" She fanned her chin. "Balmy. Wouldn't it be better to be lonely on a beach—I mean, on a lonely beach somewhere?" She was half-addressing the dishwasher.

Peculiarly, David asked, "Have you ever stolen anything?"

"What?"

The dishwasher spoke up. "You got that. About the beach. I like to be at the beach today."

David decided to conceal his rage. He put on a wooden grimace and echoed, "She got that right. That's for sure, man."

Still, tipping playfully on the balls of his feet, the dishwasher ignored David and addressed Jane. "We got the best beaches in my country, Mexico. You ever been?"

"Of course," Jane said, friendly but brisk. She couldn't tell whether the dishwasher was a jerk. She mentioned getting lost at a teocalli as a child and being afraid the feathered priests would find and gut her. "A few years ago I was in Chile. Now that was beautiful. The fjord country." She mused aloud, "That's what New York reminded me of today. Strange to say."

The dishwasher said, "We're a very ancient people. Most people don't know that stuff like what you said. Teotihuacan, our capital, was the largest city in the world."

Jane stared at him. Her gaze must have loitered on his face too long, because his dark eyes appeared in an odd way to hunch expectantly. He was about to say something more when David's hand touched Jane's shoulder. She hated it when David touched her. A table had opened up.

Once they were seated, David began complaining about the world again. He even pulled his much-underlined copy of Pascal from his filthy plastic bag. He opened the book on her plate and translated a passage about untruthfulness word for word.

Jane simpered and asked after the baby.

David said, "We're a bit worried. He hasn't grown for a while, but that doesn't—it doesn't mean a thing, because they grow in spurts—very normal. Supposedly."

"Ah."

"We took him to a party, and I think—I think he'll be a great socialite. Much better than either of us at it. He was so at ease—letting people pick him up and crawling around their legs." David suddenly asked, "Am I being hostile? About what I was talking about before? Tell me if I am, because I've heard—some people have said I've been a bully lately."

"Just depressed or something. But who knows?"

"Wow. *Depressed.* Tell me. Because I don't see how talking about things—I mean, don't you want people to be honest with you?"

She eyed him. "Sometimes I want them to be—yeah—a certain way."

"What do you mean *depressed*? I don't feel depressed. Fed—fed up with bullshit maybe. Anyway, what do I—I don't have anything to be depressed about." He looked at her sharply. "For god's—don't try that still-in-the-closet bullshit. I'm sick of that from people—always." New acquaintances often assumed David was gay.

"Did I ever? I wouldn't. And as a matter of fact, I get it, too, sometimes. But I didn't mean to suggest your behavior cancelled everything you said. About the world being difficult. The no day job and the whole apartment-kid situation is enough to drive anybody—"

"What?" He wasn't listening.

Thudding hollowly, the kitchen door swung open. Two fast-moving waiters, tall and short, passed through it, one into, one out of a cloud of steam. Both were holding oval platters which swung high when their bodies briefly twined together. Then a brown hand stopped the door. The dishwasher peered out, looking for Jane. She was careful not to return his gaze, but she felt it when his eyes found her. Even from the corner of her eye, she could tell he was more beautiful than he'd seemed outside, his face glazed almost to tears by the mizzling kitchen steam. The door fell closed, equal parts blow and sigh.

"Explain to me what you're worried about again," Jane asked David.

"I don't know," he groaned. "I just hate the idea—money's become—money's become this huge problem. I hate it. I can't stand having low, normal problems." He glanced at Jane to see how this was going over. "I was always afraid I'd turn out to be—I think I might be a failure."

"Way too young still. Come on. And I doubt you have to worry about turning out at all," Jane said drily. "Ever. Sorry."

"Is that a gay crack?"

"Oh, please!"

"No, but I did have this one idea. To do with money. It was something I thought we could talk about."

She guessed he was going to ask her for a loan. It was something he'd do.

"I'm—what I asked before—I've actually done that."

"What?"

"What I said. What I said when we were outside. I told you I've stolen something."

"I thought you were asking me if I had."

"Whatever. I stole something from the Van Nests. Sort of. It was a—it *is* a serious—anyway, this is absolutely—you can't—confidential."

"Of course," Jane said, compressing her mouth in a teacherly way.

"Do you know Colin Vail?"

"Maybe."

"An artist."

"No, then. I don't think so. May have heard the name."

"Anyway, he was from a very grand old New York family, and he had the house that—later the Van Nests bought it from him—or after he died—I'm not sure. It's a little weird him owning that hideous place. Because he was sort of a cousin to the Pop movement. When I was staying there—I took—well, I took a box of his drawings. Left in the basement." He became his old, obsequious self, chuckling with shame, leaning back for the waiter to set down his quesadilla.

Jane wondered noncommittally, "Are they worth a lot?"

"There's a—you'd be surprised. Amazed. There's a revival—"

"Problem solved for you."

"No, because the thing is—the catalogue says—supposedly he didn't do any drawings. More like assemblages were his thing—and these would be the only—which would make them even more valuable."

"Are you sure they're his?"

"Oh, definitely—but I would need to get them authenticated."

"That's a problem."

"Well, yes. Because his sister—Colin Vail's—is still alive. He's dead—killed himself—but she's alive and has a ton of his work, and she's started riding this revival. So she would be one obvious expert—the best one, really, in terms of money—her imprimatur. But I could never go to her myself. Do you get it? She knows the Van Nests. Or they know her. So it would be—*Where did these come from? And who did you say you were?*–and obviously I worked there. Everybody knows. Or what if she recognized them? On top of that I think, there's a remote chance Darius would remember I might have taken the box to my car one time. But you're in a completely different position. You've never had anything to do with any of them. Except one teacher dinner, right?"

"No. I'm sorry, David."

"But I–"

"I could never do that for you. If that's what you mean. Take them to the sister for you."

David was stymied. "I didn't–" he tried. His leg had started bouncing so violently that when his knee accidentally hit the underside of the table, everything jumped. He looked around wildly.

"I don't mean that I'm Ms. Virtuous," Jane allowed, wondering if she was about to confess her own crime. She felt her brain make a dizzy quarter turn. Vision went shadowy for a bare second. The moment hadn't been well-prepared, though for a long time Jane had probably needed to tell somebody else–somebody a little sleazy–what had happened between her and Barry.

Why now? Like snow slumping from a fir branch, the indelible words came out, "I even had a thing with a very young student of mine one time." She immediately feared telling David every detail.

David was hardly able to weasel the bare facts out of her. "How old?"

"Same age as Darius. But completely mature, of course. No, a little older, I think." She laughed at her defensiveness. David being weaselly, not entirely trustworthy, felt just right to her. This was a jailhouse friendship, low punishment. But she didn't want to risk telling him too much. Surely David had seen or met Barry, so no names.

Now two people knew. The other was far more unlikely than David Caperini. Oliver's friend Mr. Drinkwater, the ex-ambassador on the Lawrence Academy board, put it together one day with a breathtaking guess. A week or so after he'd made his fundraising call on the Van Nests, Drinkwater still mulled over his pleasant feat of memory in the family's kitchen. He could see their amazed faces. It was such a tiny thing, but he was proud of his enduring sharpness. Ms. Brzostovsky and Darius. Darius had a crush on loveable, popular Ms. Brzostovsky. After the tenth time the little triumph flitted through his mind—Ms. Brzostovsky and Darius—another presence joined them. The boy who'd disappeared. His memories of that boy intersected and braided into his memories of the other two, and the shocking idea came to him.

"Ms. B," Drinkwater quavered. His craggy finger rose to stop her in a hall at Lawrence. "Ms. Brzostovsky. Please. No, right here. Yes. So." He crooked the finger and had her follow him outside. She was irritated. Being led to a surprise was the form of passivity she most disliked. Drinkwater stopped in a courtyard formed by wings of the administration building. He looked around him, making sure they were alone. He bent his head tragically. At their feet, a dusty puddle covered the rectangular basin of a defunct fountain. Hairy with floating seed husks and shreds of glinting cobweb the black water reflected their heads, the overarching trees and sky.

"So! Yes! I have a notion things may have gotten out of line? The board had several talks about our missing student a little while back. Barry Paul. It was a poser for us all—what really happened. The parents, too. No, no!" Jane had gone sunburn red. Her eyes filled with tears. She was confirming everything before he even finished. Drinkwater hurried. He didn't want her to speak. Returning his gaze to the motionless puddle of water he tried to be firm. The wrinkled pouches of his cheeks wobbled when he clenched his jaw. "Far out of line, and I really—really, I'm going to ask—I think you might need to break camp. Strike the tent. Sooner the better. I think you really must, because otherwise, I have a duty to the school and—of course... I'm sorry. There." His hand reached out to her upper arm to steady her. She really looked ready to topple over.

Jane wasn't grateful in the least for Drinkwater's discretion. His misplaced kindliness itself irritated her. She wasn't blind. She could see. This was a kindly man. So what was off about him? Did some types of innocence call for harshness in response? Should she have tried to lie? "Bug off, you're mistaken." *That,*

Jane, is your usual impulse, isn't it? Treating innocence roughly? But what if it was how she was made? A born teacher, molding, demanding, controlling, caressing, punishing. And what about men like Drinkwater? If kindliness was just his species, what credit did he deserve for it? She pretended she'd have preferred shackles, a noose and snare drums, but she wouldn't have, of course.

That her fucking a kid was the ultimate cause of Drinkwater's awkward courtliness by the fountain made Jane's muscles tense in anger for months. She didn't *hate* innocence and kindliness. But she could never find her way to them. Her ecstatic crime and the tormenting guilt about it didn't lie at opposite poles of the moral universe after all. They were the same. Sin-guilt was apparently a continuum like space-time, and innocence and kindliness were inaccessible for her outside the cone of her experience.

David Caperini looked frustrated that Jane had burdened him with something so momentous. He frowned. He pouted. He tried to absorb a story that, for the time being, was mostly dead weight.

"Because you confessed to me, I confess to you, I guess." Jane sounded sheepish. With a sidelong glance, she chased the dishwasher back through the kitchen door where he'd appeared again, clumsy and persistent.

"But we never finished what we were saying about the drawings." David emerged from calculating bemusement.

"What?"

"Let's think about it some more." Sounding reasonable, he continued, "My situation wouldn't—except for the not-enough money—it wouldn't hurt so much if I had a little emotional support. But nobody cares about straight families anymore. Not that we're a family. I'm more like the babysitter. But you should hear what he says about us—my dad. And my mom never calls. Neither of them ever asks me any questions. Or only, *If you're gay, we don't care.*"

"They say that?"

"Well, not in so many words. No. But a lot of people have that attitude. Why do they all think I would care in this day and age? That's the last thing worrying me. Maybe the problem is I'm *so* relaxed about the gay stuff. I mean, I wish I *was* gay. Everybody would be—*Oh you poor baby–!*"

"I don't think it can be that easy."

"It is! Or if I was a transvestite. I wish I *was*. I love transvestites, transexuals, whatever. I wish I was a screaming fruitcake! Nobody believes—nobody believes you are what you are if you're not something unbelievable. Everybody's—"

"Poor baby. Things would be so much more complicated, David, if you were a transvestite. Or transexual." Jane felt oddly deflated that her Barry news hadn't held its ground.

"I could make money performing," David joked hysterically before going all at once sour, pettish. "I don't want to talk to you about any of this. We have to go back to the Colin Vail drawings."

"No."

"Yes, because like you said: You confess, I confess. What you just told me changes everything. It means we're in it together in a way and we can help each other, right?" He stopped her before she could answer. "Wait! Listen. What you said is important. I don't want to sound like I wasn't following you. But you should know I don't blame you either."

Jane felt herself going heavy and small.

"But now I just—I think—based on what we've talked about—what *you've* just told me you did that's sort of worse than what I did—sorry!—now we each know something, and it would be—it's in our own interests that no one ever learns—" He raised his eyebrows to complete the proposition. He pursed his mouth with contrasting primness. Under the table his palms ran slowly down his thighs, half-childish, half-lewd. It took Jane quite a while to understand him. He was threatening to betray her over Barry Paul, if she didn't help him with the Vail drawings.

The plot was too outlandish for her not to doubt her understanding. No. Jane looked at David's empty bottle of Corona. "Are you drunk?" she asked mildly.

It may have been the shortest blackmail plot in history, though probably not the least serious. David's eyes winced closed. His head fell back then forward. He started stroking his chest and belly. "I'm sorry. I'm sorry. It's just that—Jane, I'm so desperate," he mewled fluently.

"Listen," Jane said. "Forgetting about whatever insane threat just popped out of your mouth—"

"No threat! No threat. Come on. Don't!"

"—I'm thinking you should pay attention to this depression. You're wrong about no one caring. Think about Prozac or even psychotherapy."

"How would I ever pay?" He snorted.

He really didn't have any money. That simple truth made Jane reconsider his seriousness. She wondered if him wanting to blackmail her wasn't an absurdity after all. It sounded like a joke. But that's the way real crime usually sounds at first. In her experience, anyway. That, in turn, reminded her how vulnerable she was. Truly vulnerable. Someone would say something one day. When she was in her seventies, perhaps, the way it was happening with decrepit bishops and coaches. She started to get terribly scared for herself. This sometimes happened nowadays.

"Clinics? Or I'm supposed to get a pity shrink?" David moaned. The thought was outrageous to him. "Maybe I should be daycare-ized. Yeah, put me in Davey Day Care, why not?"

"I'm not surprised you react that way."

"This is—"

"OK. OK. Forget it. It just occurred to me. Because I was worried."

"I don't seem that bad, do I?"

"No. Of course not," she lied.

17

JANE APPROVED. A RUN-DOWN New York bar, mid-afternoon—early mid-afternoon at that. Near the door, a well-dressed young alcoholic put away shots, furtive and efficient. A tobacco-stained graybeard at the deep end of the bar kept scratching under a Stars-and-Stripes necktie he wore as a headband. One couple was almost lost in shadow in the back. The girl, in tears maybe, bent over her knees. She looked sickened by something her boyfriend had told her. The boy was torturing a matchbook, staring at it with clockmaker's concentration and an air of contempt. Jane sat at the bar.

Her elbows rose weightlessly when the bartender wiped the gouged wood before setting down a beer for her. The wood was just as sticky after a pass of his rag.

Jane had to wait a long time as usual. The Stars-and-Stripes codger exploded in argument with the bartender. His outburst turned into laughter. The boy in the back whispered tensely to his matches. Jane nursed her beer but was almost finished by the time Raimundo appeared, scrupulously neat, smelling of verbena and himself. His weighty hand, plaster at the cuticle of the thumb, skittered over the placket of a denim shirt, an orator's dignified hand-on-heart. He said, "I don't like this place so much." The plaster on his thumbnail meant he'd been doing construction instead of manning the industrial dishwasher at *Poco Loco*.

"I was just thinking it's nice. Unpretentious."

"The rich girls always love trashy."

She laughed happily at this crazy mistake, which he liked to insist on. Dutifully she repeated, "I'm not rich at all. I'm poor. I'm from Queens."

To order, he held up two fingers in the slightly showoffy way he had. The bartender brought two beers, wiped and set them down. Raimundo appeared satisfied, happy to be with her, to complain, to be served promptly. He swung around on the barstool and slouched back against the bar on his elbows. His hand tolled lightly against her shoulder, then grasped it for a moment, feeling the material. "That's soft. But look at these lights." He nodded at the cheap string of Christmas lights kinked across walnut-stained plywood. "That's like in Mexico. That's like what the poor people put up."

"Who cares?"

He shrugged. Then he insisted, "No. Me. I like clean. In fact, I like to have a bar one day which would have—mmm—like diffused light, little spotlights. Everything glass. Maybe with light under here." He spun back around and tapped the underside of the bar. "You ever been to Miami? Everything is very well designed." He gave his fingertips a Sicilian kiss. "Very clean. Very nice people. Look, nobody's happy here."

"I am."

"Mm." He grinned, nuzzled, kissed her. Despite herself, she stiffened, twittered. He could veer to the physical so suddenly. He flung a loose hand at the room, which meant, "Who cares what we do here?" He slumped and stuck out his lower lip. Then unslumped and crowded her again. "I wanna come to your place."

"What? No conversation? No night on the town?"

"You never like it. What? You like to now? OK, me, too. Let's go," he countered.

"I don't like going out. You're right. I'm too old. Or just not into it at the moment."

"I am. The bar I'd like to have—you ever see that Captain Morgan ad in the subway—with all these friends? A big poster of everybody being friendly?"

"Maybe. On the subway car?"

"No. Station." He smiled, paused, then barreled ahead. Even if she thought him fatuous, he took the risk. "No. I know it's stupid. But I imagine my bar is like that. With everybody very happy. Dressed very elegant. Very elegant place."

"I thought you wanted to do more contracting. You said you wanted to incorporate—licensed, bonded, the whole shebang." She made a face because she heard teacher in her voice, high school career counselor. Sudden as faintness, she relished intensely the obscurity of this bar. Of him. Of her. No one would ever look for her here. No one would ever guess she had anything to do with this man.

Raimundo noticed the startling gravity of her expression. "That's right," he admitted. "Maybe I would like to have the bar in the long term. Because I know how I can build it myself." He was wondering if her expression meant she was lonely or bored with him and longed for someone more intellectual, more aggressive, passionate about politics, like a romantic trade union organizer. "Look, my mom was just a party girl in Mexico. Me too. I gotta tell her some time you never go out, you always talk politics and you hate fun. She'd like you a lot more."

"That would impress her?"

"Yeah, she'd say, Good, Rai, you're getting serious."

"I'm not really political. Not anymore. How could I be? I'm American. America has no politics."

He opened his mouth.

"If you want a bar, you should do it. I'm all for doing what you want now. You know, unless it hurts somebody else."

He shrugged as if he wasn't serious about the bar.

"And I don't hate fun. If you're wondering what I was thinking about a second ago, I was trying to decide if we were in love."

He made a comic expression of surprise. "This you never decide."

"Oh, really?" she disagreed.

"What do you think, then?"

"Are we in love?"

"It's something," he negotiated. "In a way," he allowed.

"Have you had sex with other women since we've known each other?"

He merely smiled, though he hadn't.

"I could've, too, I suppose. But I haven't. And I hadn't for a very long time before you. I do feel tender about you. Especially when you have nightmares."

"I don't have nightmares." He did. The few times they'd fallen asleep together, he invariably started mouthing words in the most pathetic voice. They didn't even sound Spanish.

"Whatever. I do feel tender. But it was a huge mistake us going over to see your mother."

"She never said you were too old for me."

"But she did say—well, it's sort of plausible what she said. It's been making me depressed. I hate being forced to think what other people are thinking." Raimundo's mother had given Jane a look like she was an erotic tourist who couldn't afford airfare. She'd told Rai Jane was slumming. "You know what I mean, don't you? It *is* plausible, what she said."

He was visibly uncomfortable. "I should never told you."

"Not that I think she's right, but how can I know?"

"You just know."

"No, I don't! It's like being raped, isn't it? People looking at something you thought you were doing for your own reasons and calling it whatever they want. I thought I liked you—but no, according to your mom it's *erotic tourist*. You were supposed to be *my* thing—this was our thing, I mean." She stopped when he sighed. "I'm sorry, Rai. Look at how hurt I was by her."

"Why'd you want to go meet her, my mom?"

"I just did. I wanted to be up front."

"Why do you care what she thinks?"

"I just do." She almost asked him, "Don't you?" But she could see the subject was making him unhappy.

He smiled and slyly interposed. "I do love you, I think. Because you have perfect tits, you know that?"

Her horsey guffaw startled him. "My best feature."

"Yeah, yeah, they're not too big but perfect, you know that?" He'd slotted one of his big knees between hers. Careful as a seamstress he pulled the hem of her green silk skirt over it. He leaned forward to whisper something. She felt the side of her face bathed in a murmuring cloud of beer, verbena and thoracic heat turned into words. "It's good we don't see each other too much or I'd never stop fucking you. I'd do no work. When I see you, I think I cannot be at rest till I fuck you."

"Well, I like fucking you, too," she answered matter-of-factly, which made him smile and shake his head a little at their conjoined lap.

They did end up at her apartment. And though they fell into a long embrace as soon as the door closed, they broke it off. Raimundo walked around the studio trying light switches, none of which worked.

From the kitchen, Jane exclaimed *à la Mexicaine*, "Ai! The freezer melted all over everything." Raimundo could hear tinkling steps as she hopped through a vast puddle of water on the floor. She slipped two beers from the dark refrigerator as quickly as possible and slammed the door shut. She tinkled back to him.

"What's going on?"

Jane explained, "They shut off the electricity. Not really my fault. The idiot I'm subletting from was supposed to pay the bill. Plus—" She lit a cigarette. She'd started smoking again. "Con Ed treats you like some naughty high school kid. They want you to go down to their office and grovel. It's insulting. And then they try to charge this outrageous penalty. I'm not going to pay for someone else's mistake."

He gave her a look. She was sounding arrogant. In the streetlight that barred the studio, his head hung forward slightly with a calm stare like a tiger's.

She argued, "No. I'm *not* a snotty rich girl. And, you're right, it would be a thousand times worse for somebody with no recourse, no money at all, but I don't really have money, either."

"It's harder for them, because those people don't mean to forget to pay the bill. They're just stupid."

She didn't catch his smile and protested, "What, do you think I let this happen on purpose? I didn't. She was supposed to be paying the bills, remember. I didn't do this on purpose."

"Partly it must be the way you like everything that's trashy. So you trash this place. Even me, you think I'm this trashy, macho—and you're only using me to crush you."

Jane laughed. "Are you smiling? You'd better be."

When he moved to show her he was, the shadows of the blinds moved across his body like a dancer's tights being tugged on. They both wore this same sensual cloth of shadow and streetlight. Jane turned on a crank portable radio her father had given her in case of nuclear winter. The charge was nearly gone already, and she didn't feel like cranking. Faint music settled behind static. The static, or the vaguely familiar tune she thought she recognized from a long time ago, made the lightless assignation feel even more obscure than the bar had.

"You want me to do your favorite thing?" Raimundo asked.

"What? Oh! Yes, I do." She set her bottle on the floor next to the futon and flung herself down, corpse-straight and fully clothed.

Raimundo dropped to his knees. Slowly he lowered his body onto hers, transferring his weight little by little. His tiger face gleamed. Jane closed her eyes, enjoying the pressure. He quoted his romantic line again. "You're just using me to crush you."

With the little breath she could draw, she peeped, "Yes."

18

A MONTH OR TWO later Raimundo and Jane were about to run into each other on a thronged sidewalk below Union Square. Each had spotted the other when they were still almost a full block apart. As they got closer, though their eyes locked, and curious, involuntary smiles appeared on their faces, it seemed they were actually strangers. What could they possibly have to do with each other? It was disconcerting to surface from public solitude like this. Their intriguing unalikeness didn't pop and hiss when they came together like acid-plus-base, but they cautiously avoided kissing or even touching.

Raimundo was carrying a brown paper bag too tiny for any purchase Jane could imagine. She got the upward half of a nod and gave him an indecipherable wave with her right hand down by her hip. They laughed. Jane indicated the subway entrance. "I have to go in two seconds." Still, she strolled a ways in Raimundo's direction before coming to a stop.

Raimundo held up the tiny bag. "I'm putting a new carpet in my mom's apartment." When he shook the bag, carpet tacks jingled like jewelry. "My mom wanted this gray industrial style. It's fairly cool."

Their glances kept catching on passersby. Both felt a touch proud, because each was happy to see the other's desirability stand up in a crowd. Partly for this audience of strangers, Jane seized on wild confession, exclaiming, "I was starting my life of crime this morning, but it seems like I'm having problems with my accomplice. Or rather he's having some issues that need to be smoothed over." She narrowed her eyes. "What? No, not you! Rai! Ha! Never you. I'm talking about that semi-friend of mine, David. You've met. I think he was there the day I met you."

Raimundo formed a sly limp wrist as a question.

"Rai," she scolded. "That's never been decided. And actually I think he's *not* gay. Just one of those newt-like low testosterone types." She laughed in surprise at this slashing caricature. Where had she gotten it? "You'd have a problem with that, incidentally?"

"No, no. They're everywhere. Me, I don't care."

"You must get harassed all the time. You have such a great ass. And you're awfully pretty with those pink lips."

His cheeks darkened. His embarrassment seemed to delight him. "Hey, watch that!" He laughed and mimed punching her shoulder with a meaty fist. "What makes him a criminal? What makes *you* a criminal?"

"Ah!"

"What crime you planning?"

"Oh, just your average forgery/fraud. No. I'm kidding. He said he was depressed. Some huge psychodrama is brewing with the woman he lives with and her kid. I'm his only regular friend, sad to say." She shuddered. Out of the blue, she begged Raimundo, "Why don't you come? Please?"

"To him? No. I got to—" He held up the bag of tacks.

"Please, Rai. I never ask anything. I don't want to see him alone. What if he goes crazy and tries to assault me? He did ask me to marry him one time. He's unstable."

Raimundo resembled a bull, considering. "You serious? That little guy scares you?"

"Disturbs. You know how some depressed people feel like they're drowning and they might drag you down, too? It's harsh, I guess."

"That's supposed to make me want to go?"

"Please."

"Can we work?"

"Work on what?"

"*Wark.* Can we *wark?*"

"What–?" Furiously he raised his foot and pointed at it. She cried, "Oh, walk! Walk. No, he lives at Tudor City. But we can take the express. What? No, I swear. I just couldn't understand what you were saying. That was all."

The stiff flat of his palm caressed her cheek, a pantomime of a slap. People glanced over. Jane didn't love the joke violence but felt she should hate it even more than she did. He was clearly well-brought up, but playacting violence was a constant tic of his. She was grateful he was coming, though, so she didn't feel obliged to challenge him this time. Her annoyance may have showed. He laughed at her expression and pantomimed cringing from her attack. "Yeah, watch it," she said. "I've been known to slap little children."

The décor of the tiny Tudor City studio where David Caperini was living combined disarray and obsessed storage. Steel shelves ran floor to ceiling against three walls. These were densely packed with boxes, stools, scuba masks, winter clothes, broken lamps, Tonka toys. What gaps remained were tightly stuffed with empty fast-food cups and clamshells, crumpled Kleenex, painted river stones, rubber-banded bank statements. The whole had a jumbled neatness about it like an outcropping of fossiliferous rock. Identical clear plastic boxes lined the floors at the foot of the shelves. They were stuffed with baby things, hats, board games, cheap plastic earrings (hoops and triangles) a rubble of crumpled acrylic paint tubes, empty prescription bottles. Atop the boxes rose stacks of books and magazines. A bed and furniture were just emergent from throws and comforters, shawls and pillows. The padded play cage was empty.

David was obviously displeased to see Raimundo. He made an effort to withhold an ingratiating greeting and almost succeeded. He apologized for his rudeness before being rude, but he did finally manage it. He avoided meeting their eyes and crossed his legs tightly in the apartment's only undraped piece of furniture, a tan corduroy wing chair. A castoff from his father's Princeton office, it was ink-stained and the left wing flapped when touched.

David answered Jane's nervous, chatty questions with monosyllables. Stubbornly he looked out the window at a dismal view of tar-papered rooves under an ashen sky. He was pretending Raimundo didn't exist. A red filigree of capillaries showed at the glinting corners of his eyes.

Jane's not-so-secret shrugs of incomprehension and eyerolls did nothing to put Raimundo more at ease. He'd broken a sweat. The atmosphere felt asthmatic, lukewarm despite an air conditioner. Jane had been exactly right. This was like drowning. He would be dragged under. He could almost feel the manic order and disorder of the apartment tighten around his shoulders and belly like Lilliputian cables.

"Where's the baby?" Jane asked.

"He's with my wife," David harrumphed, looking at her for the first time, a flat stare.

"What? Wife?"

"Oh, didn't I mention it? You haven't called for a while. Yeah we got married, and it lasted—" He looked at his wrist where he didn't wear a watch. "Three days, it would be, as of last night. So three and a half."

David's angry gravity couldn't keep Jane from one obvious cough of laughter. The whole thing was too strange. "You got married? And it's already over? What about—?"

"You had your chance. I wanted to marry *her*." David produced a gruesome smile and addressed Raimundo, or the shelves behind him. "But it looks like she was lucky she didn't. It seems—it seems I'm not very—not very easy to live with."

"What!?" Jane demanded. "You weren't serious, David. He was never serious!"

Raimundo's heart started racing.

Jane barked, "Are you saying she just left or something? With the baby?"

"Not just. Last night. It's been building up, I guess."

Raimundo and Jane glared at each other. He couldn't have looked more put-upon or she more abject. David caught the stare and turned, chin up, to the window again. "Sorry—sorry to inflict this on you," he told Raimundo with the politesse of the damned.

Raimundo uttered a soft, animalistic syllable and tipped his head toward the bathroom door. "You mind?"

"Please. Just jiggle the—the flush thing until it catches."

"My God! David, I had no idea," Jane breathed. "What happened?"

"She says I attacked her. She claims I hit her, and she says she absolutely refuses to stand for any violence. Because of her father or something." Bitterly he explained, "She claims he hit her too. And her father's best friend used to feel her up or something." Jane couldn't think of a word to say. David hissed, "But *nobody ever believes her*, supposedly. Of course. Actually, I'm not sure I do."

"David," Jane said gravely.

"Oh, shut up! I didn't hit her. I mean, maybe—I was just—I got so frustrated, I grabbed her by the arm. That was it."

"Oh, David. No, of course you didn't. I mean, I know you." She couldn't help doubting him, though usually she was as quick to doubt the victim's tales of abuse as he was. So, for the moment Jane doubted everything. She could hear the torrent of Raimundo's urine, seemingly inches away. She had to close her eyes to concentrate on judging David, who'd tried to blackmail her, after all, and was generally a dodgy person. But violent? If Raimundo had meant to efface himself by vanishing into the slightly less storage-packed bathroom, it wasn't working. His *basso* burbling out-puttered the wan air conditioner. It filled the room with noise and prompted a hysterically magnified thought-picture of his penis.

David smiled wryly at the sound. "Small apartment."

"I don't know what to say. Your family? Do they know about this?"

"She's probably there now. For all I know. They feel sorry for her getting stuck with me."

"What?"

They heard a boulder being moved in the bathroom.

David looked annoyed. "Hey!" he called. "Just—just jiggle the thing, and it'll—it'll work!"

"I'm fixing it," Raimundo muttered through the wall.

David's eyes closed in a ladylike pique. His words quietly goose-stepped, "It needs this plastic piece."

"He's a contractor," Jane explained. "He knows this stuff. He really knows what he's doing."

"I thought he washed dishes," David muttered insultingly, the first indication that he recognized Raimundo.

After a moment, they heard a perky-sounding flush. Unruffled as a surgeon, Raimundo emerged and announced in a quadruply strong accent, "Now I work. Bye, Jane. Now I'm going to do my mama's carpet." He didn't sound like he was losing his English, so much as recoiling from it.

"Thanks for the toilet. I think." David wore an ungrateful frown. He stuttered less the bitchier he got.

Raimundo ignored him and motioned Jane into the hall. Not for a hug goodbye. He was stony, unforgiving. "I don't ever wanna meet any more of your friends."

"That's mean," Jane whispered, pounding his chest once, light as a feather. Raimundo gave no quarter. His hands ran over her body lasciviously when they kissed. This caused Jane to shiver out of his arms. She stamped her foot in girlish frustration. Raimundo tipped her a cocky wave from the elevator. He was deliberately playing the jerk.

Jane was a hair less compassionate with David after Raimundo had gone. "We're going to have to go someplace I can smoke."

"You can smoke here. As long as the baby's not around," he trumped her. "I don't—feel like going out."

She sighed, unwilling to commit to the draped bed or the ottoman, if that's what it was. She jerked open a window in a brown aluminum frame. With a few pulls and shoves it rose fully, and she rested her hip on the sill. She used a dry Popeye's cup as an ashtray.

After rising to punch off the air conditioner with frugal resentment, David shrank into his chair again. "I'm glad he left."

Jane mumbled, "I just bumped into him. I couldn't not bring him. Sorry."

David's eyebrows rose. "Am I right, he worked at that Mexican place? And now you're in a relationship—or something with him? I didn't know that's who you meant when you said *Raimundo*."

"Does that matter?"

"I find it interesting you would bring him. It's revealing. A glabrous cheek, I noticed, which should probably be a danger signal for you."

Jane didn't get how snarky this jibe was at first. She misremembered what *glabrous* meant and thought David was talking about the *color* of Raimundo's skin. "I think the question is about you and your bizarre marriage. Is it for real or is this some freaky performance piece?"

"You bring a young, handsome—*young* guy to meet somebody who asked you to—who wanted you to marry him. Seriously? You do that even after you called this morning and that person made it perfectly clear that he was feeling—I don't know—depressed? But I'm the one putting on a performance piece?"

"You said you were depressed. I admit it. But I had no idea what had happened. And don't pretend you were ever serious about marrying me, David. I don't even know how serious all of this really is with—"

"My wife?"

"Stop! Do you think this is recoverable?"

"I don't think so. And no. The problem isn't just her and me. It's bigger. I probably said OK to getting married because I'm sick of being such a side issue in everybody's lives. You know, my father—my father told me—as if he's being nice—he said he was considering putting aside some money for the baby. It's not even my fucking baby! *Thanks, Dad! How prudent! How dynastic!* I feel like my fate is in the hands of incompetents. My dad is like a baby himself. Money is his toy. He would never trust *me* with a penny!"

"David."

"I swear they have more respect for that drooling shit-tube! Can you believe it? I'm sure she went out there. She took the baby to Princeton to be with my family!"

"You're really angry," Jane noted gently.

"Of course I am. I have no money, no prospect of any money, except for those fucking drawings. And I guess—I guess I'm a wife-beater. What do I do?" He shook his hand at a paisley-covered surface on which lay a very pale manuscript. It was twenty pages or so—printed until the ink ran out. "Everyone thinks my stuff is shit. And he says—my dad—he's putting aside money for a kid he's met maybe two times. And I'm supposed to be grateful? *Thanks for keeping the money from irresponsible me, Dad.* Because—because he thinks I'll drink through it. Or I'm sneaky. That was always their word. *Don't be sneaky, David!*"

Jane raised her eyebrows. She followed a flight of pigeons spooked when a cable guy a few buildings over dropped a tarpapered roof hatch behind him. "Listen, David. With families. We've just got to lead our own lives."

"Right. That's easy for you to say. You rely on yourself. You're like a man—the way you run through your bimbo boyfriends. I've got—I've got my whole family conspiring—against me—and you can go, *Oh, maybe I fucked up some underage kid? Well, I'll pop a Prozac*. That's what you—you're the one who told me. Go on Prozac. See a shrink." He blanched. "I'm sorry! I'm mad about—about the drawings, still. I guess."

Jane sighed, too hurt to be angry, unsure how to tackle this. "First of all—I mean, what's the problem right now? If you're right that she went out to Princeton, what would she be talking about with your parents?"

"Who?" David's gaze flashed keenly. His expression made it plain. He'd suddenly realized that Jane couldn't remember the name of his head of Fulfillment, his wife. Jane tensed aggressively and looked him even harder in the eyes. But David looked down, deciding he couldn't afford to blow up at the last person willing to endure him. He answered softly, "She'll tell them I'm a wife-beater!"

"No. Come on, David. That's the whole story? There's something you've wanted to talk to me about for a long time. I just haven't been picking up on it."

"I doubt you could understand. I can't understand. She—she thinks I'm overbearing."

"Really? I always assumed—you made it sounded like she's much more—"

"I know. Ha-ha! She's the one wearing the pants, really. Everything gets done her way. Then it's me—sissy boy parasite—*I'm* the one who's violent and uncontrollable. Probably because I really need to—want to be some—he-man's bitch. Deep down," he snorted contemptuously. "I'm supposed to be gay, remember?"

"Look at your situation, though. You're living in this tiny room. The pressure of dealing with a baby. It's inevitable people are going to fight, isn't it? Isn't that part of marriage under the circumstances?"

"But what can I do now?" he whimpered. "She—she—won't talk to me. Like my parents—she has this way of—she just cuts you off."

"She won't discuss it?"

"No. That's the whole point. That's why she left. Because she says I always twist discussions my way. So there was no point in talking anymore."

"Well, you can't do anything. You have to take care of yourself and wait for her to make a move."

"But that's unfair. I'm left in the position of—in everybody's eyes—it looks like I'm the wife-beater. And I can't say anything about it. I'm not allowed to respond. It would be different if I could appear suddenly with a huge pot of money from the Vail drawings." He sniffled.

"Does she know you have those?"

"Why did you call this morning? You never call me anymore."

"No reason. I admit I've been a little worried. But it had nothing to do with changing my mind about your drawings. What I meant was, if she knows about the drawings, she might tell your parents. Then—"

"She doesn't know I have them. Or what they are." Emotion draining, he eyed her. Then a wave of frustration crashed over him. "See, this all so unfair! Everybody else decides who I am. *You can't handle money, little boy*. I'm a fag. I'm a fuck-up drunk. And this is going to be the worst. You're a woman, so you don't understand. I have no say. Now I'm the wife-beater. I'm beginning to doubt it myself. Am I violent?"

"Nobody ever hit anybody in your family, did they? It's an inherited thing. You're under pressure is all."

"Have you ever hit anybody?"

"No," she lied. Her finger brushed at a tickling on her cheek. Funny, she'd just been thinking about the time she slapped Darius Van Nest.

"But maybe there was some secret violence in the past, and it's coming out in me because I've sunk so low—socially. My dad is insanely systematic. Isn't that a kind of violence? Kind of—ingrown?"

"That's crazy, David."

"No one talks." He hopped in his seat. The corduroy wing fluttered. "So—so—I start thinking things like that! Jesus! Even—look at your expression, will you!" he demanded with a hint of a sob. "You look like you're scared of me! I can tell you're thinking, *Who knows what he's capable of?*"

One stormy afternoon a couple of weeks later, Jane's apartment seemed to be rising—rising straight up in the air—so much water was sheeting down the windowpanes. The wind spit rain through gaps in the frames, and the droplets caused a spider plant's leaves to nod on their stems. The old futon had been unfolded. Jane and Raimundo lay naked on the dirty canvas.

Raimundo was peaceably describing the décor of his mother's apartment, on which he worked when other contractor jobs were lacking. They'd turned the volume down on a trash talk show but still occasionally heard the mob-like audience jeer or applaud over the thrumming rain.

Jane was listening to this awful human noise and may have sounded uninterested when Raimundo described shelf brackets designed to look like little outcroppings of crystal. So, he inquired calmly, "You think my taste is not so great."

"That's not true."

Without taking offense, he pressed her. "Yeah. When you say *I like that song* or *I like that shirt you're wearing,* it's not really true."

"Of course, it is, Rai. And even if it wasn't, or if I didn't like that stuff, what would it matter? It's just taste. There are more important things."

"Maybe. Or it could be that you're intimidated by the world, and it makes you go for everything low. What you *think* is low."

The way he looked at her was something of a challenge. As if his brown eyes dared her to call him a wetback or worse.

"I'm friends with you because I want to be," Jane said levelly. She turned away and leaned back against his terra cotta shins, nicked pink in quite a few places. She felt his broad feet wriggle under her buttocks. When she didn't say any more, she sensed that he shrugged. "You know more about me than anyone," she argued disingenuously.

He was silent.

"You know, a guy tried picking me up—not bad-looking or a creep. I told him I was in love with someone else. Maybe not that word, but I told him about you. I think it was clear."

His silence may have been a tease. Or proof that she truly was, in the final analysis, alone with him. She turned her head and caught his mischievous smile, reassuring in a way.

He sighed—for himself, from the sound of it. His knees parted, and he tried to pull her back between his legs. His great fingers looked monstrous to her, ugly, for an instant. "Ai," he grunted when he found her immoveable. "Getting a little fat?"

She brayed in delight. "Nice try. One-twenty-three! Saggy maybe. Crepey-skinned, a little."

"One-twenty-three? You sure about that? You know, it's not bad for the woman to get a little voluptuous."

"You're the big elephant." She reached around the small of her back and tweaked his trunk.

"Ai!"

With a playful scream, she jumped up. "No, Rai!" She was marvelously, helplessly happy—almost as if she'd never experienced happiness before. She tottered on the futon, put her arms out for balance. The happiness only lasted a second or two. "Here. Let me read you something weird. This is a case where I really need to know what you think."

Lifting a messy stack of bills from a dresser, she smiled when Raimundo remarked, "Mm. Nice ass, but I'm telling you, it's starting to jiggle."

From a thick envelope under the bills, she slid several carefully folded pages. She jumped back on the futon. Standing over him, she touched his cheek with her finger and said admiringly, "Glabrous-cheeked boy!"

He knew what she meant. "I've always had lots of hair down here, but nothing up here. You mind if I can never grow a beard?"

She fell to her knees and pushed Raimundo's legs together, shutting a casual erection behind his muscular thighs, which, unlike his cheek, had a dense pelisse of black hair. She settled against his shins again. Unfolding the pages, she felt a flicker of nervousness for some reason. "Letter from David Caperini. See, it's all decorated." She wagged the first sheet over her shoulder for him to see.

"No. Come on. Let me see." He grabbed her wrist. He examined the letter for a long time.

"I feel like I'm drowning," Jane said idly about the rain. Still, Raimundo held her wrist and studied the letter. She was as nervous, almost, as David himself would have been. "Or like a deep-sea diver coming up. I'll get the bends."

Each of the letter's paragraphs was framed by colored pencil foliage from which peeped mournful faces and humping putti.

"Shit," Raimundo said. "This is amazing. Really excellent, I think."

"Really? I don't know. I'm not crazy about that cartoony style," Jane groused, still nervous. "It's good, I suppose."

"No, it's definitely good," Raimundo said. "Come on."

"I guess so, but listen. Blah, blah, blah. He begins with some irrelevant stuff. Then he says, 'But now I don't mind the marriage and everything flying to pieces. Maybe everything else will fly apart too, including the vicious and humiliating resentment I feel toward dad, and even toward that unhappy mouse/phantom, mom. Her for not having any strength. Him for being an asshole. Both of them for not being rich like the Van Nests. That, honestly, feels to me like pure stupidity on their part, which is totally unfair, but there it is. I hate them both for damaging me beyond repair. But I've decided there's no point in suppressing the constant burning envy I feel toward anyone who knows how to function in the world, even you, sometimes. Let me be calcined to dust! Knowing the way I am, you'll laugh, but this raging, shifting, unstable condition in which I no longer have the power to think makes me feel naïve, defenseless and morally brutal. All in a good sense, if you can imagine.'"

Raimundo whistled. "This is crazy. I don't get any of this. He says he can't think, but it's all thinking. Thinking that doesn't make sense."

Jane raised her eyebrows. She didn't turn to look at Raimundo. She seemed to agree but was trying to keep from influencing her consultant. He started cuddling her wearily. His hands crept up and weighed her breasts. She said, "Wait. End of page one. It gets better. 'I'm so tired of being steamrollered by the ideas other people have about me. When you bring one of your 'hunks' by, I–' That's you, Rai. He puts *hunks* in ironic quotes and underlines it." Raimundo's forehead landed in his palm. "'–I know I'm meant to admit to being just an asexual clown, not a real man. (Even if you don't think you intend it, you do.) But all that stops if I'm nothing but ashes. This is nothing new, you and I have often discussed it: who are we when all our delusions and rote habits are destroyed? I hope you understand the note of pride I feel that, even while I may be burning and fragmenting and flying apart, certain things remain constant, namely the deep nothingness that precedes being. This sense of atomized peace and alienation from myself, from my friends and my so-called family tells me something breathtakingly deep and true about myself–'"

"Jane, please. Come on," Raimundo begged.

"No, this is the part I really wanted to read. Last page. Buck up. '–about myself. I'm not pompous enough to make outsized claims, and I have nothing but pity for childish and spasmodic arrogance (e.g. Darius V. N.), but this is more than colossal presumption on my part. I'm coming to recognize that if anyone gets the dust version of me, the worthless me, it's you. Not just in the clichéd sense of now you know I'm a sneaky little pilferer, because we exchanged confessions. But also in the sense that, as dust, you and I necessarily disbelieve in affective links between people or anywhere in Nature at all, except as human narrative constructs to give the purely aesthetic clockwork of life a moral air. In connection with gli disegni di Vail which we discussed, I understand your knee-jerk reaction was that it would be wrong to profit. Entitlement is currently a swear word, but my true feeling is that Vail's memory and gli disegni are, in every important sense, yours. This certainty trumps career, rights, economics, law, even the cold emotion that links us. Your 'baby clock' indifference has always fascinated me, and I wonder if that's how you choose to burn, if that self-imposed sterility is your way of reducing yourself to dust. I think you realize you're also a deceiver, like me, and that, unless recognized by someone, you will inevitably be alone. Like me. My proposal, not just about selling gli disegni but the original proposal, i.e. marriage, was, is, and always will be serious. David.'"

The rain had slowed some. After Jane fell silent, its pelting sounded weary and cross. "See, he asked me to marry him," she explained. "That's what I wanted you to hear. There was a lot in there you wouldn't get—*gli disegni* are these drawings, a long story—but the main thing was he asked me to marry him. Married with a kid, and he's asking to marry me!" This big punch line came out flat. Reading the letter had been more painful, less funny, than she'd expected. Raimundo was running his beardless cheek along her shoulder with distracting tenderness. She stood it as long as she could, even pretending to rub back a little. Then she pushed him away.

She stood up and crossed her arms, throwing the letter to the floor in irritation. She stood at the window which was trembling in the frame whenever the wind gusted. "We know this isn't for the long term."

"What do you want me to say about it? What am I supposed to say about that thing?" he complained.

"Not the fucking letter. I'm sorry, Rai. Not the letter. I hate the way he thinks, though. Just having those thoughts run around inside me—" She shuddered.

"Don't let them get in there."

"I'm not talking about that, Rai. I'm not talking about the letter when I say this isn't going to work for very long. I just suddenly *know*. This isn't going to work. We should probably start getting ready to break up. You and me." She found it hard to believe that ten minutes ago she'd been, for a moment, as happy as she ever remembered.

Raimundo stood up, nearly stumbling on the thick futon as if on a quaking bog. His expression was scared.

Jane couldn't help smiling wryly at his nodding satyr-like tumescence. "What's that about?"

"What do you think?" he demanded with perfect gravity. In truth, he was almost as surprised as she was. Here he was, shocked, or quite possibly even crushed by her words, and the thing raged on. He seemed to be lugging it around the room with a strange, ecstatic resignation that couldn't have been entirely sexual. Maybe it wasn't sexual at all.

"Now I've said it," Jane said regretfully. "And I guess I meant it. But I'm just sorry and regretful and feeling miserable. I suppose I am a deceiver. That's what you said at first."

"You're completely messed up," he said affectionately. "I'm much more together than you. I think you're the one who gets nightmares. Not me."

"I meant it, Rai. I'm sorry. If I were a teenager, I'd tell you—well, I'm sorry to tell you even what I *would* tell you—it's just as scummy—but if I were a teen-ager, I'd say, *I do love you. I only hate the way I am.* And—I guess, *I wish I were dead.*" At that, his mouth hung open a moment. "I'm sorry," she said in a slightly different tone, looking down at his body. Abruptly she asked, sounding matter of fact and not at all humorous, "Isn't that distracting for you?"

He shrugged. He plodded across the bed to embrace her, penis bobbing. It was sandwiched between their bellies like a leaf spring. Though he was exceedingly gentle, he could feel her displeasure.

"Something's getting between us," Jane said. Now she *was* joking, but in an exhausted, unfunny way. She'd gone limp in his arms. He looked down at her with a childish, fostering frown. She answered him almost sharply, "Yes, Rai, I *do*. I do want to fuck. The only problem is, I also mean what I say."

He didn't want to be put off. Passively, she let herself be lowered to her knees, then to her back on the futon. Sex in this condition felt ceremonial, a communicant's visit to the whore of

Babylon's temple-top boudoir, awkward, passionate, static. In the faintest voice, she whispered a theoretical protest, "No contraception." Her head fell to the side.

He continued in the most tentative way, perversely slow almost.

"Rai, I think you think because we're upset, you have to be gentle. You don't. Just the opposite."

"What?" he murmured.

"Here." She took his hand and forced a pantomime slap across her cheek. There was something off about it. For him, anyway. He slowed and stopped and broke it off.

Raimundo thought about pretending to go for contraception. That was too involved. He just wanted to stop now. Jane reacted to his breaking off as if it were exactly what she expected. She gave his back a brisk, teacherly rub when he stood up. With lilting steps, he padded across the floor to the bathroom, his penis, stiff as ever, bobbing with the rhythm of a blind man's cane. His arousal felt as perfunctory as isometrics. Really, he was on the verge of tears. The whole thing was so confusing and sad for him that he forced himself not to look back at her from the bathroom door.

Her hands were laced behind her head. Her feet yawned, toes outward. A hint of inflamed color split the shadow between her legs, where the hair was slicked apart. She reached down. The heel of her palm rubbed at an itch in her tangled *mons*, a casual thump. She stretched her arms. She sighed. She slapped the canvas on either side of her in a silly rhythm. Her breasts jiggled and swirled flat like eggs.

19

LOADING DOCKS, BIG boxes of painted steel tread plate, squat in front of many of the old manufacturing buildings in Tribeca and Soho. A handsome, severe-looking young man, Alan Wilkinson, often sat on the one in front of his building. It was painted fawn brown to match the nattily restored structure behind it. Atop a row of brown cast iron columns, fresh gilding read, *Mohawk Electrical Supply Co.* This was the home of a famous interior architect. The architect was in Paris for the summer visiting his friend, Andrée Putman, and putting finishing touches on former TV star Susan Dey's apartment. What Alan was doing living in the man's Tribeca place was anybody's guess. Alan was mysterious about what he did. Though a graduate student in the Philosophy of Mathematics there, he was rarely seen uptown at Columbia. No one knew where his money came from, whether he was actually a student, if he ever worked, or why he would enjoy chatting for hours with a freshman he'd met on campus the year before, Darius Van Nest. Darius didn't think Alan was gay. The architect obviously was—just look at his furniture. And Alan definitely had one foot in the city's glamorous gay circles. He'd played Darius flirty messages David Hockney left on his answering machine. But Darius had a feeling Alan was mostly trading on his good looks and charm—an old-fashioned, tweedy, Keynesian, public charm built of well-turned anecdotes and a vast stock of witticisms.

Darius approached from Canal Street. His grin felt as stiff as putty. Alan acknowledged him with a fractional nod and an inviting, scornful chuckle. Even the slight emotion of greeting embarrassed him. He sat on the brown loading dock with indoorsy unease. He cadged a cigarette. A cigarette break was the excuse for most of their meetings that summer. Alan wasn't allowed to smoke in the interior architect's place. In fact, he hardly smoked and never carried cigarettes. So Darius took an hour-long subway trip from Inwood to offer up one of his own Marlboros. They would smoke and talk on the loading dock.

Almost at once Alan embarked on a clever story about "Van" Quine, and Darius tried to glean from his amused tolerance exactly what Alan felt about the philosopher. Condescending affection, Darius decided—the same feeling Alan expressed, even more strongly, when he talked about Bertrand Russell. Wittgenstein made him frown slightly, as if the duty of admiring such a peculiar genius were irritating. Nietzsche, he dismissed, "Really just psychological poetry, don't you think?" And he was wholly dismissive of anyone French later than, say, Voltaire. This was a wonderfully intimate, impressionistic way for Darius to pick up a little philosophy.

Not that Darius was shy about unpacking his own ideas, such as they were. Alan listened with the cool patience of a Ms. Brzostovsky. He pointed out that Darius's slashing reductivism wasn't as scientific as Darius liked to think. He fondly accused Darius of being an Intuitionist. With evident distaste, he quoted the first principle of Intuitionism, *The perception of a move of time may be described as the falling apart of a life moment into two distinct things, one of which gives way to the other, but is retained in memory. If the twoity thus born is divested of all quality, it passes into the empty form of the common substratum of all twoities. And it is this common substratum, this empty form, which is the basic intuition of mathematics.* "Yes!" Darius exclaimed.

"It's Jan Brouwer. And you don't want to go that route." Darius asked why not. "Besides him being odious—misogynist, anti-Semite, borderline fascist—it's just uninteresting. Nothing comes of it. It's a mathematical cul-de-sac. Most thinking people would say it's the sort of *truth* that, even if it is true—well, basically, *so what!*"

With more pleasure, Alan tore open the empty Marlboro box and on the blank interior sketched a proof of the infinite density of the number line. Darius held his cigarette for him while he drew. Although he was mostly unconscious of Alan's good looks, or of his physical presence at all, Darius always became giddy, almost drunk on the gorgeous abstractions Alan talked about. They made his chest tighten.

The number line got them onto time, which Alan delighted in proving, as philosophers can, was *unreal*. Darius insisted that there had to be an instant of fundamental tininess, and that these instants had to be *out there*—for real in the real world—strung like beads. Alan argued that there wasn't any real framework on which reality could hang. There were no passing instants in the void, only worldly things changing, which gave the impression of instant following instant, that is, of time.

The way they talked, the fuddy-duddy pomposity of their turns of phrase, was saved because they were young and good-looking. They sat on the loading dock with a slight all-over awkwardness as if they didn't know what to do with having bodies. Their high-flown periphrases and nerdy point/counterpoint couldn't possibly have sounded right before they reached age sixty, if ever. But they were young. Even Alan, who downed a bottle of claret every night, would, after spending all day studying or thinking or writing, go out in a T-shirt and gym shorts and start running up Greenwich Street, block after block, just to clear his head.

Darius had changed in the unreal passage of time. His head was still big. But his features had equalized. He'd grown into dramatic, faintly Tatar or Semitic, good looks, as if he carried a trace of his mother's blood after all. His body had continued to lengthen. But he remained gawky, and his awkwardness suggested an insanely well-defended virginity—which is to say, it suggested *sex*, the last thing Darius intended.

In little Duane Park across the street from the Mohawk Electrical Supply Co., nine dusty sycamores were as still as cut flowers. A policeman in jodhpurs sat on a roan, which stamped twice and scratched a fetlock. A building was being restored on the far side of the park. While Darius and Alan talked, the illusion of time was marked by the rattle of debris falling through a six-story chute of nested blue cones. The shirtless workers, all brown originally, were matte white with plaster dust.

Darius tried, "Maybe we'll get a place together this coming year. I could see that. Somewhere close to Columbia." He felt he was just talking, not making a firm proposal. "I'm tired of Inwood. My sublet's not as nice as yours." He turned his head fractionally to indicate the slender colonnade behind them.

Alan raised his eyebrows. This was his resting expression of attenuated amusement. Judiciously, he answered, "That's an attractive concept. Regrettably, I already made a commitment to Tom Samuels. He's gotten a place on Claremont Avenue."

"Ah, are you two...?" Darius asked delicately. His hand loosely shuttled between their chests to mean love, or anything like it.

"Uh, no," Alan said with a pitying simper. "I realize he's considered a famous beauty. But no."

"I was only thinking it might be convenient. For our studies." Darius meant the torn cigarette pack. "Sharing an apartment could enable our eternal, elevated dialogue."

"More *Stoa* or *Garden*?"

"Oh, Epicurus, definitely," Darius said. "I'm an entirely sensual creature."

"That would be nice. Awfully appealing. As a matter of fact, Tom's always been, in a manner of speaking, oriented toward the gutter, so a loftier atmosphere has a lot of appeal."

Chatty suddenly, Darius said, "Well, it's too bad you can't. I don't know what to do then. I'm being pursued by that guy, Ali."

Alan's expression was discreetly inquiring.

"He thinks I should join St. Anthony's. Or even live with him. I was looking for a good excuse to say no."

"Who is this Ali character?"

"Oh, I thought everyone knew him at Columbia. A very elegant—Kuwaiti, maybe? I've gone to a party or two with him. He must be forty or something. A big mystery. You know, one of those types who haunt colleges. Hard to imagine they're students. I think he just rifles the student directory. Preying on freshman, probably. Sort of like you, come to think of it. But talking with him isn't as interesting. He kept following me around last year and finally just introduced himself. He stares at me like he's got handcuffs in his briefcase."

After the academic year began, Darius found himself observing Alan and Tom Samuels from afar, not sure whether he felt jealousy or what. They were giving a campus tour to Alan's Tribeca architect—a frizzy gray-haired man wearing a green woolen cape, though it wasn't cold. They'd paused by the statue of *Alma Mater* to take in the view down the steps. Black-eyed and dashing, a little cruel, even wearing tweed, Alan's face was wine-flushed. He squinted in the bright September light. He seemed to look down his nose at the teeming quadrangle. Tom, by his side, truly was a beauty. He wore a seventies disco revival outfit and stood with a Bronzino kink in his lumbar spine. Silky hair bothered his right eye picturesquely. He kept nodding coyly into the hand that rose to deal with it, feigning attention as Alan smirked his way through, probably, some ingratiating Evelyn Waugh anecdote. The architect threw his head back in laughter and swished his cloak from his shoulders.

Darius had been able to escape Ali's clutches. He re-upped his sublet in Inwood, the remote northern panhandle of Manhattan. He started joining Alan for cigarette breaks at Tom's Claremont apartment, a much shorter trip than Tribeca. Tom always happened to be out. Who knew where? With hustlers. Or tied up (literally) for the weekend at an art dealer's place on Fire Island. Darius was curious about the absent roommate, though Alan sounded bored with him. Maybe they'd been boyfriends briefly. Perhaps that had been Alan's one indulgence in that direction.

Alan once gave Darius a supercilious tour of Tom's desk. He may have wanted to observe Tom through fresh eyes. A row of clipped newspaper photographs was stuck along the wall over the desk. An incorrigible aesthete, Tom had used unusually stylish pushpins with tiny striped resistors for heads. Apparently he had a fascination for cute murderers. Wearing a smile of worldly and accepting distaste, Alan flicked at a halftone of Paul Cox, a blackout killer well-known at the time. To tell the truth, Darius found the whole thing unsettling—not the murderers themselves but

Tom's preoccupation with them. He asked Alan about each picture, drawing the moment out, just because the thing was unpleasant, curious.

"And who's this one?" At the end of the row a strapping Latino boy looked down at his lap. The older woman with him glared at the camera with hostility.

"Uh, that's Raimundo Azil. With his mother."

"Who did he kill? Or they?"

"No one. He's not a true member of the set of cute murderers. It's an old picture, I think. Maybe his brother was murdered by the Sinaloa cartel and he witnessed it? I can't remember exactly."

"Never heard of him," Darius said with a touch of Oliver's brusque finality. Though Raimundo was cute.

"Of course—let's—" Gallantly, Alan made an ushering motion toward his room, his unmade bed. "Sheet's a bit gamey, I'm afraid. But I don't understand it either. I think Tom has an empathic deficit, but that may be common among very good-looking people."

"I *may* have an empathic deficit, myself," Darius ruminated with naïve self-absorption, causing Alan to smile. Darius lowered himself to the edge of the bed, deep in thought, eyes straying back through the door to the cute murderers. He was remembering his old fascination for the juveniles locked up in that Camden courthouse. Was that so different? He was certainly a little bit gay himself. Not committed like Tom, maybe more experimental.

"I wouldn't say so. Though you'd obviously be an exception to the good-looking rule." Alan remained standing with public-seeming awkwardness. He wiggled his hands, only to the knuckles, into the front pockets of his jeans.

"Thank you," Darius said with a strange blush. "How was his brother killed?"

Alan spun and glanced out of the room at the cute murderers. "Oh, pretty distasteful, I'm sure. You'll have to ask Tom some time. He loves talking about them. We were at a dinner the other night and he put everyone off their feed with one of them." His chuckle was as polished as a pundit's on TV. (As a matter of fact, Alan had had lunch the day before with a scout from the *PBS Newshour*. "A miserable showing," he reported suavely.) "Tom has a weakness for anything gruesome. He noticed—which is actually somewhat clever—that all these methods of butchering people are named after clothing—the necktie in Colombia. Necklace in South Africa. Sierra Leone—short sleeves or long sleeves."

Darius laughed. The mere linguistic observation pleased him. "Excellent."

"Hmm. You do have a cold streak, yourself, don't you?"

"I'm not as good-looking as Tom, though. By far."

"I suppose he's got a conventional something or other. Surprised you would go for it."

Darius gave him a dignified little frown of incomprehension. What was Alan talking about? *Go for?*

"I would have thought, with your *recherché* tastes—"

Flattered, Darius grinned, "Which tastes?"

"Oh, I was thinking Raymond Roussel, Oulipo. And who was the American artist no one ever heard of?"

"Colin Vail. But those aren't people. Those are artistic tastes. Am I *recherché* with people? I mean, I can see as well as anyone that Tom is incredibly handsome, but that doesn't mean—well, I'm not sure what you meant. Do I seem to go for him?"

Alan considered a long time. "For some reason," he said slowly. "I think it would make me exceedingly unhappy if you ever had sex with him."

Astonished, Darius didn't know what to say. The turn in the conversation stunned him. "I—why would I ever, remotely, think of that?"

"Right, it probably wouldn't work," Alan said, flustered, but comfortably so. "That's what I've been imagining. That you were more *catcher* than *pitcher*." He pronounced the words with overbred archness.

Darius was visibly taken aback again. His mouth hung open in a way that made Alan laugh. "*Catcher*?" Darius repeated with matronly shock, to idiotic effect.

"Oh, sorry! Was that too—?" Alan seemed amused, pleased even, by his own slight embarrassment. "Maybe it's not the right moment. After that ugly talk about murderers. People get spooked. And I think I didn't explain it well anyway. Because what I've really decided is it would make *me* deeply unhappy, if you and I *didn't*. I've been hoping that might be the drift of all this. You and me." Alan made the same small shuttling gesture with his hand that Darius had made to ask about anything romantic or sexual between Alan and Tom.

A long pause intervened during which time, if real at all, shifted speeds or stopped and restarted.

Darius couldn't have been as gobsmacked as he felt. But our minds are so easy to trick. Since the language wasn't entirely explicit, he wasn't sure he'd actually caught on. At the same time he was obviously catching on, because his heart raced and he seemed to lack oxygen. And he was a catcher, right? The less self-conscious Darius—the one who was obviously catching on—lowered his eyes to the floor. For the first time in ten thousand years this other Darius spoke, "All right. I guess. That would be OK with me. Definitely." It was as simple as that.

"Oh, good." Alan patted his tummy contentedly.

"What? You mean, right now?" Getting no response but raised eyebrows, Darius let his right hand touch the gamey sheet.

Alan was a gentlemanly seducer. Darius was corpse-like, though this wasn't even the first time he'd been fucked. That had happened at Choate with presexual matter-of-factness—my turn, your turn—with a pot-smoking misfit from Allentown, PA. This was different, clearly gay. Alan used hair gel from atop his dresser. "A serviceable colloid," he explained. And one that spared him the indignity of buying louche commercial lube. The condom was opened with as much furtive romance as a packet of Sweet'N'Low. Sex was intensely pleasurable and over quickly.

After his corpse-like performance, Darius became frisky, a monkey—childish in a way he would never want anyone to observe—ever. The giddy behavior was disgusting to him, but he couldn't help himself. He felt a pet-like freedom touching Alan's body. While Alan lay there in masculine torpor, Darius cupped his broad feet, stroked his thighs and his chest. When a placid, disapproving frown crossed Alan's face, Darius pouted, "I'm allowed!" And he frolicked all the more but hated it. He hoped his silliness this afternoon would be obliterated from the permanent record of himself.

Alan mentioned that he needed to do a little work. Darius, he said, was free to lounge around. He left the younger man in bed. This grown-up and abrupt treatment of sex was new to Darius, but he said nothing. He lay perfectly still. His body felt strange, as if a hound had been baying inside him and his hindgut still echoed with the sound. Only his eyes moved, touching every object in the room, roaming, touching more. He was at an extraordinary pitch of emotion. He felt an ecstatic sense of defeat, which it never occurred to him not to identify with homosexuality. Like Alan scribbling one of his incessant truth tables, Darius coldly entered several facts about himself into the cells. Not only was he homosexual, he was also a catcher, a bottom. And since humiliation and getting fucked were more or less the same thing, he must also be a masochist. Oh, and a *follower*. Yet somehow all this wasn't wholly awful. Though in his present condition, he wasn't able to categorize or judge anything the way he usually could.

His gaze slurred across the floor to a photography book propped against the baseboard. The cover looked a little like Ansel Adams but that was probably too mainstream a taste for the Alan/Tom household. The glazed paper of the dust jacket was torn in places. The corners curled. It bore a dirty orange 50% off sticker. Despite all that, the image of a snowy mountain peak gleamed majestically. On one side of the mountain, the snow was blinding. On the other, a jagged black shadow ran down its flank. Darius drew an obscure lesson from the contrast. Nature had its arrangements of light and darkness, sun and planet, against which there was no appeal. *A common substratum of all twoities*. His old visit to juvenile hall had, perhaps, introduced him to a remote projection of this possibly cruel fatality. Now Darius knew he was a creature of shadow. He wasn't unhappy, though. More crushed and exalted.

Because Darius assumed his own masochism was inevitable, then so was Alan's sadism. A laughable delusion followed on the heels of his truth-tabulations about his sexuality. Darius started scanning the room again and half-expected to notice instruments of torture lying casually amongst the ordinary objects. Broken squash racket? Whom did Alan beat with that? And Alan really was mysterious. It was the most carefully curated aspect of his character. Could he be in the set of cute murderers himself? Darius wondered. Emotion made it seem almost plausible that, instead of "studying," Alan had gone to another room to prepare knives or ropes. Darius ignored the fact that a cute murderer wouldn't have been so correct about using a condom.

Love is commonly described as a feeling. This is comical, but anyone who knows is forbidden to laugh. His education was laughable, his ignorance to weep over, but it is our duty to forgive Darius when he confused emotion with love. When he failed to notice his complete ignorance about his ruthless Apollo, Alan. Or when, in the fever of feeling, he assumed Alan and he were bound tightly together from this day on.

He was surprised no major changes came about between them. They got together often enough, had sex quite a few times. But an overall suspense lingered, which Darius supposed was a part of love he couldn't account for. He'd have to get used to it.

Inevitably a worldly template for being gay came crashing down on him out of the blue sky. That he had always known was the first certainty. His friendship with Barry Paul was sanctified and promoted to love retroactively. Stan's smirk when presenting him a print of Gerôme's *Pollice Verso* one birthday years ago was seen for the hint it was. His dire fascination for the imprisoned boys in Camden was easily explained, too. Even his uncanny sympathy for Colin Vail seemed born of an affinity too deep to be called taste. But this new way of looking at things wasn't simply happy, headlong puzzle-solving. His doggedness in wrestling down plain awareness for so many years frightened him. How could he have been so severe? Looking at things through new eyes did anything but prove to him the reality of change, however. He'd uncovered a deeper layer of the immutable. That was all.

Darius started going downtown to gay bars with Alan and Tom and their friends. Even the famous architect would put in an appearance. Reassured by their air of superiority, Darius stuck close to his gang. They were far too grand to play at introducing him to the mores of gay subculture. Gay graybacks in the provinces may have done that still, but these brilliant New York friends were only slumming. They were too elevated to be part of any subculture.

Life in Inwood was listless and vacant, not at all the life one hopes for in a great metropolis. So, Darius spent as much time as he could at Alan and Tom's Claremont Avenue place. The poisoned syrup smell of roach spray hanging in the pink terrazzo lobby became the way marker of a strange, ungraspable mood. During long evenings at the apartment, Alan practiced his anecdotes. Darius leafed through the gay rags rolled into sweaty batons that others had carried back from bars. In public he wouldn't touch these free magazines or even deign to look at the slumping stacks of them in bar vestibules. Tom, if he was there, presided with an indecipherable smile. He crossed his legs and leaned back against his desk under the murderers as gingerly as he'd lean on an umbrella. Virile, voluptuous thighs squeezed his hand. He had the sort of Praxitelean body that, no matter how languidly disposed, doesn't look effeminate.

Darius was never asked to stay the night when Tom was home. Which Darius found strange, because he was the boyfriend and Tom was only the roommate. Alan wouldn't suffer questions, however. And Darius wasn't in the habit of asking them. From Sohaila, he'd adopted that perverse pleasure of not knowing things. Even so, he'd nose around if Alan left him alone in the apartment. That's how he found a drawer full of papers in Alan's dresser. Witticisms, anecdotes, definitions and quotations were all scribbled down and stored in a shifting heap of scratchpad paper, Post-It Notes and torn napkins. Here was the first principle of Intuitionism written out in skipping ball point with the annotation, "Luitzen Egbertus Jan Brouwer—finally uninteresting—nothing evolves from it—mathematical cul-de-sac—" Darius, who felt the self should be extemporaneous, couldn't have been more shocked by the mess of notes. Because here was Alan's software. The material of his personality. After that, Darius eyed Alan when he was speaking and wondered how much of it was memorized, diligently prepared, and therefore unreal.

He kept the discovery secret. He husbanded it, because maybe it was a useful mote of power.

Darius considered Alan mysterious but didn't realize he was almost as mysterious himself. He never recounted stories about his childhood. Alan's minimal curiosity about him made this less noticeable. But even Alan had once exclaimed, "Do you even *have* parents? It's hard to imagine." Something kept Darius from confiding. With a nervous discretion so total it looked sinister, Darius buried the basic facts about himself. For instance, he never told Alan that his father was probably mentally ill. Or that his father had invited his mother's lover to live with them in a perverse *ménage* in New Jersey. Or that he'd been in love once before, his boyish love for Barry Paul. Or—above all—that he was adopted. He wasn't forgetful of these facts, of course. In Alan's presence, they'd sometimes catch light in the front of his mind. He would almost read them off out loud like lines on a teleprompter. But then adoption, or whatever it was, would wink into shadow. With an interior shrug, Darius said nothing. The fact about himself was rejected not as too charged but as irrelevant.

When sophomore year was well under way sometime in late November, Sohaila came into the city for an appointment with her gynecologist. She insisted it was nothing. She'd grown almost mistrustful of Darius in recent years. She feared questions. She seemed evasive and shy with him.

La Côte Basque was the obvious rich person's place she'd chosen for lunch. At every table, women had the shrink-wrapped look of surgery. Men wore Palm Beach blazers and strange suntans. Sohaila offered Darius both cheeks to kiss. Then she fussed unduly with the complicated drapery of her neckline, tiny, stressed dimples appearing in her cheeks.

After two salads arrived, and they'd begun shifting the lettuce about with their forks, Sohaila spoke up as if lightly diverting the conversation, except there hadn't been any conversation. "Dahli-*ush*, I wanted to mention, your father has finally moved out." Her strange lack of emphasis was meant to make Darius think Oliver's moving out had been an issue for a long time. "I have the information for you in a minute." She gestured at her purse on the banquette next to her, inattentively striking it, so the golden chain links of the strap trickled like a startled viper. Darius was quick. He caught the chain with a finger and passed it back to her. "You can try calling him, when—when you like," she finished, heaping the metal purse-strap back in place on the seat next to her.

"When did this happen?" Darius kept himself from sounding shocked. He didn't want her to freeze up.

"It had to eventually, no?"

"But where to?"

"I've got it for you." She struggled not to sound annoyed. She forced her voice to rise airily, "The city."

"Here?"

"Yes, yes. Downtown."

"Dad is living downtown? Here?" Darius was incredulous. He couldn't keep it out of his voice.

Sohaila seized on his tone to snap, "Yes. He's living downtown. So what? You live—wherever you live. I live in the house. So, now we know."

"Inwood. I live in Inwood."

"Fine. Inwood, then."

"But what do we know? What are you talking about—*Now we know?*"

"Nothing. Nothing, Dah-li-*ush*." She feigned exhaustion. "I just wanted to let you know. I feel—good about it."

"But when did he go? I never heard anything about this."

"Oh, Dah-li-*ush*. When? A while ago. I don't remember. What does it matter?" She was especially evasive.

"Please, tell me when."

"A few months. Perhaps. Honestly, I'm not sure."

Darius was surprised by how unhappy this detail made him. That so great a change had been made without him ever knowing. "You couldn't have told me earlier?" The last time he'd been to the house had been in August. Oliver hadn't appeared, but that by itself wasn't unusual anymore. He'd last seen his father five months ago. "Was he there in August?"

No was the clear but unspoken answer. "Dah-li-*ush*," Sohaila sounded pained. She recited an evidently prepared remark. "We weren't sure at first what his plan was."

"Whether he was gone?" Darius had lost his self-control and was sounding petulant.

Sohaila did her best to act tough-minded. "Also, listen. You've struck out on your own. So have I. You don't live there anymore, and there's a lot about my life you don't—" She was starting to sound harsh to her own ear. "Look. We didn't know what he was up to. Do you notice it never occurs to you to blame *him*? Has he ever let you—or anyone—know what he's up to?"

"I'm not blaming. You mean he left without a word?"

"Yes!" she exclaimed. But there was a reedy evasiveness even in this.

"He's been here all this time?"

"But Dah-li-*ush*. When have you ever seen much of him? Believe me, believe me, I know it's crushing. Of all people, I do know this. It's terribly sad he's gotten the way he has, but what can either of us do but get on with our lives?"

"We could try to help him," Darius protested childishly.

"Yes. It's nice to say," Sohaila admitted. "But when you have no idea how to reach him? When you have no idea if he's alive or dead for months?" The stressed dimples appeared. She was annoyed with herself for letting the cat out of the bag.

Darius absorbed this. Sohaila had been trying to protect him. She used the tines of her fork to make cross-hatching in the pollen-colored dressing on a tomato. Oliver had likely vanished. It may have taken all this time to track him down. Darius could understand his mother's discomfort. She would have felt she'd misplaced her ex-husband. Hateful and difficult as he was, Oliver still engendered a woeful sense of responsibility in Sohaila and Darius.

"How did you find out where he'd gone?"

Sohaila looked miserable that he'd gotten to the stratum of her real unhappiness. Her heavily lined eyes gave him the steady, challenging look that fortune-tellers sometimes have when they look up from their knitting or from a small TV and out the plate glass of a red-curtained storefront.

"Mom, I'm not trying to take you apart," Darius said sensitively. "And if I ask about the doctor's appointment, it's just out of concern. I don't want to get anything on you. The truth is we hardly ever see each other alone anymore."

"Dah-li-*ush*. I know." She was exhausted and shy. "The doctor—it's a feminine thing and not serious. I promise. No. And, as a matter of fact, Stan hired a person. A private detective. I don't know how these things work. Apparently it's very simple."

"Ah." Gently, Darius pressed, "You were in touch with him, then? Finally? Dad."

"Yes. It's the reason I say you might have trouble. He's got a machine and you call many times before he might get back to you. Then again, you could have less trouble than I did."

"Is he seeing anybody at all? Any human contact?"

"How would I know?" she asked. Then she said certainly, "No. I don't think so. But in the city, you can feel like you're seeing people," she added hopefully. With the fanatical daintiness that soothed her, she cut her tomato in minute pieces. As she ate these, the muscles of her face didn't move at all. Finished, she posed her knife and fork on the edge of the plate. She cocked her head at the abundant remains of the salad. "I always believed it was a cultural difference with us. Many years I believed that. Not that he was anywhere near as bad in the old days. This is almost funny, but what did I know? Everything was so strange to me. And dreary! Americans hate colors. There were no colors anywhere. All the houses were white and gray. Which, by the way, is why it was such a tremendous pleasure when Stan took me to Bermuda. Pink! But up here—" She shuddered. "And Oliver I thought was just—American. Now I know it wasn't like that at all. But he was severe and impressive like the houses. I assumed I wouldn't have to think for myself. This is a sick desire Muslim—perhaps all—women deal with. But then maybe you understand," she finished with a slight chill. A month before, Darius had dutifully, and very formally, told her he was gay. After an immense pause, she'd commented politely that that must give him a great understanding of all people, both women and men. The subject had never come up again. Now, she murmured, "*Death and The Maiden*. Who can be playing that here?"

"I don't think there's any music. I don't hear anything."

She shrugged in embarrassment and seized her quilted black leather purse. With a sly look at the other diners, she took an envelope from it, which she handed to Darius.

Darius glanced inside, saw what it was but not how much. Thirty hundred-dollar bills, he counted later. His face crumpled with pity at her ineptness. He posed the envelope against a water glass. "Mom—"

"Take it! Take it!" Sohaila's eyes flashed. "Don't be foolish!"

"Mom. We're not living in some—caravan—" He stopped. Oliver used to tease her about her tribal streak.

"Dah-li-*ush*! Look where we are! I'm no *mush khour*! I don't wear my—gold coins strung around my neck. Really! You're foolish. Take it, will you? It should be yours. I found an old checking account I can still write checks on. I think your father's forgotten all about it, so I take a little here and there. I may not be as smart as you'd like, but I've got sense. Take it and save it. It's real money. This is sensible. I know about the world."

20

IMMEDIATELY AFTER LUNCH Darius tried phoning the number Sohaila had given him. He didn't have a cell phone at that time so, like a bee, he had to keep visiting pay phones on the street until he found one that still worked. Each ring had its own discrete emotion, from the second, when he particularly hoped Oliver would pick up, to the fifth, when he despaired and the answering machine answered. Darius hung up as fast as he could. He didn't want a messageless hiss to betray him, and he thought it might. But his reflexes were too slow. The phone kept his quarter. Upset because of his father, he called the operator and complained imperiously about the mechanical theft. He sounded demented, a righteous monster, but he couldn't help himself. He wanted his quarter back. Seething, he debated going straight to Oliver's address on Cedar Street, which wasn't merely downtown but in the financial district, well below Chambers Street and near the very toe of Manhattan, a neighborhood Darius had hardly ever visited. But he was wary of being turned away.

He took the A train uptown. The rocking of the car and the considerate aloofness of the passengers, which can look unfriendly but is actually a very democratic and sociable public behavior, soothed him slightly. On impulse, he hopped off at 125th Street, well before Inwood. The whole spindly station, on high trestles over the street, trembled when the train jerked back into motion. The railing under his forearms stilled. Darius was leaning there to calm himself further, gazing across the boxy, drab cityscape of Harlem.

His idea was to visit Alan Wilkinson, spend the afternoon, then all night, with him. Until then, he'd refrained from ever visiting Alan unannounced (which was onerous, because Darius was still so young that all appointments and pre-arrangements felt constraining). Today a sense of emergency made dropping in seem all right. He climbed Broadway toward Columbia. He broke a sweat. He always walked fast, and it was sunny and warm for November.

The building on Claremont had a grand buff-colored portico. The lower third of the four granite columns had been painted battleship gray. The inevitable modern brown aluminum door and window frames showed the building had been updated on the cheap. A steel panel of apartment buzzers was as dense as a bingo card. Darius pressed 2F and stared through the plate glass at the pink terrazzo, a 1940s update. He caught the faint whiff of roach spray, even from outside. He ignored a weak, mysterious hesitation.

When he heard hallooing, Darius backed off the front steps. Alan was leaning out a window directly above the pediment, peering over an abatis of metal prongs set up against pigeons. He chuckled when he saw Darius and commented, "That's bold of you."

It wasn't promising that Alan would mention this first thing. "I had an inspiration to talk with you." Darius tried to sound humorous and relaxed.

"Ah." Alan didn't move.

Darius stared at him, then looked up and down the deserted avenue, astonished to be kept waiting.

"You're passing through the neighborhood?" Alan asked.

"In a manner of speaking. Do you mind opening up?"

"Right, right," Alan grimaced, submitting to good form. "I'll buzz you. But wait in the lobby. I'll come down." His head bobbed, and he disappeared.

Darius waited in uncertainty in the cloying atmosphere of the lobby. Why couldn't he come up? When Alan pushed open the elevator door with its single round porthole, at least he was smiling. He made a surprised face at the unpleasant smell, but he did that every time he was in the lobby with another person. His pale, blue-striped Oxford was untucked. His hands were in his pockets to the knuckles. He indicated the front door with an elbow, then looked down to glimpse the watch on his wrist in passing. "Go for a walk?" He led them up Claremont and over to Riverside Park, moving with the peppy stiffness of a young academic in the flower of unused strength.

The witty story Alan told about Sidney Morgenbesser increased Darius's uncertainty. Darius wasn't able to get a word in for a long time. He'd been expecting flashes of intimacy or tenderness. He'd expected them to converse with simple directness. He'd expected all that, even though nothing like it had ever happened before with Alan. Darius bowed his head. Alan's story seemed to be crowding him into self-examination. He did notice Alan's eyes roll toward him once in a horsey, affrighted way, as if at a dropped match on a bed of pine needles.

Darius disliked a virginal meekness he was powerless to repress in Alan's company. "I keep thinking," Darius mused when he had the chance, sounding obligingly inhibited, "There must be mental states it would be mistaken to characterize as thought."

Alan shot back, "Of course. Ninety-nine percent of what takes place in the mind isn't thinking."

"Oh." Darius paused. "To me it was a new—or the idea had special significance—"

They were coming down Riverside Drive's great promenade, which overlooks the park atop battlements. The sun made the sycamore colonnade's vault of still-yellow leaves glow like burning paper. More leaves made an airy clatter at their feet. Between breaks in the trees the Hudson River appeared as a painful white blaze. Only the roar of the invisible West Side Highway had to be edited out—or particularly attended to.

A confession came out of Darius at long last. "My father—there's a difficult situation going on with my father." Dry as the ochre leaves his feet scattered, Darius made this awesome announcement as mere explanatory matter. He rushed to get to a more abstract point. "He used to be obsessed with beading—my father, which sounds weird—*is*—and even as a kid I remember wondering, *what can he possibly be thinking about?* Because, really, doing that must have been like counting. Just counting all the time. The lowest form of math. Like Intuitionism. You said it was uninteresting. But can you imagine spending your life counting—like—counting sheep? Which of course you do—"

"Right."

"—to fill your mind when you want to *sleep*—to stop thinking."

"Is this what you needed to tell me?"

"No. I'm just talking. It's whatever comes into my mind," Darius said truthfully. "I suppose I was having a bad day somehow. My mother gave me some money."

"Isn't unhappiness an inappropriate reaction to windfall profit? I suppose your charm is your inversion of—"

"What do I invert?" Darius asked, greedy for an answer. "Or do you mean I am an invert, which of course—" Then, feeling the remark was perfectly at random, he threw out, "Is this love?"

The question had a faint resonance, as if the future had flicked at it to make it ring like a wine glass. Darius was surprised when, in the present, he saw Alan's face change. The change of expression showed that Alan, at any rate, thought they'd come to the difficult, substantive part of the conversation. Gravely, he said, "I seem to have a surfeit of opportunity in that area. Just at the moment. With you and Tom."

"Oh, really? But if you know what *you* want—" Again, he was surprised when Alan's face looked like he was hearing something infinitely remote from what was intended. Airily, Darius went on, as if hazarding a mildly funny comment. "I mean I feel attached to you—"

Alan made the whispery puff of laughter that well-behaved people produce to stopper a flash of cruel annoyance. "Sometimes opting for a less than optimal—"

"I think we're a lot alike, and I feel attached to you."

Wintry, abstract, Alan observed, "Love is almost always unequal, isn't it? Besides being non-commutative—"

With effort Darius interrupted. "But, you know, I didn't really even realize there was an issue like this—" His thin-fingered hand shunted vaguely between them, his usual denotation of love. "—between you and *Tom*. You and *me*—maybe, *maybe*. *Perhaps*."

"I think things were probably somewhat up in the air with Tom when you and I met. But he's been finding it rather confusing to have you come by the apartment so much, though it's added-value, in a manner of speaking, for our sex life. Just having you around livens things up."

"Oh, that's why I couldn't come up. He's there." Darius sounded happy to have the little mystery cleared up.

"No. No, actually. He's not. But I made him a sort of promise."

Darius frowned in perfect confusion. "A *promise*. That's so—abstract. That's nothing." He murmured, but he felt his earlier anger coming back. It wasn't directed at Alan, but at the idea that a promise, a word, something with no physical reality, could be a bar to him. He was maddened in the way criminals must be when the verdict goes against them. The law looks like weak stuff, invisible conventions, an elaborate play of whim, or the secret language of inimical persons. Not like something that should have any impact on personal desire or personal freedom.

"Is it that we're alike?" Darius asked.

"I don't think we're alike."

Darius couldn't decide which felt worse, not being with the person he loved or being doomed to be unlike him.

After a long tutelage in self-control, it hardly registered with Darius that Alan and he no longer had sex and that he never went to the Claremont apartment anymore, never saw Tom Samuels. Darius had such a feeble perception of time passing that he almost thought it had always been like this. Time was unreal. He could wander to a different spot in time whenever he wished, out of sight of the place he'd been before. He did once come upon Tom browsing eight or so early disco records laid out on a peddler's blanket on Broadway. He went over to him and noted quizzically, "We never see each other anymore." It wasn't that Darius was demonstrating insane self-control, as Tom might have thought. The beautiful boy pulled his hair aside to eye Darius as he would look at a door through which *someone* was expected to come at any moment. But just then Darius didn't know why he and Tom never saw each other. He couldn't help looking Tom up and down, thinking he'd like to start seeing more of him. Or, since getting to know someone involves a notion of time passing, that he'd like to be the type of person who got along easily with Tom. And too bad he wasn't.

21

DARIUS DRIFTED THROUGH his next year at Columbia. He completely misunderstood the attentions of successive suitors. Their friendships just seemed weird to him. When someone appealed to him clearly enough for him to act, a sudden mute fixation made it impossible to talk. He figured out how to go to gay bars on his own. And he and Alan still enjoyed witty dinners together at whatever restaurant was the most talked about and the most difficult to get into.

Darius's mediocrity in classes led to a half-resigned expectation he'd end up at a law school somewhere. He had no more positive goal, but he dreaded the bizarre, luxurious unemployment of Oliver. In all this time, he never saw his father, though both were living on the same small island. He got through to him by phone a handful of times. They made plans that went nowhere. Darius walked by the building on Cedar Street a few times a year, thinking he might see Oliver in the neighborhood, but he never did. It wasn't until Darius's last year of school began that he finally contrived to meet his father briefly.

Sohaila had called Darius. Her we're-both-on-our-own-now voice was even crisper than usual. She asked Darius to dinner at the New Jersey house. He could spend the night if he wanted. The occasion for the invitation sounded innocent enough. Rolf, the son of a beloved family friend, was visiting from Paris. He was seven years older than Darius but that was close enough. Sohaila made her invitation with a greater than usual frost of pleasantries. She refused to beg a favor, though if Darius came, it would make entertaining Rolf a lot easier. When Darius asked if something was wrong, Sohaila said *No* guardedly. Darius was left to wonder what she was hiding during his train trip to New Jersey.

When he walked in, Sohaila was at the kitchen sink rinsing a vase for a bunch of anemones. She gave Darius a weak, staticky smile at first. She glanced at Stan who was slouching against the counter. His mouth opened to say something. He thought better of it and merely smiled. He returned to contemplating the pretzel sticks in his palm.

Sohaila decided to make a show of enthusiasm. She shook her hands and gave Darius a light, wristy embrace, keeping her damp hands off his shirt. When Darius asked about Rolf, Sohaila shrugged. "He was resting earlier, I think." She glanced at the defunct bell register. The cockeyed arrows pointed to the same quaintly labeled rooms they'd pointed to for decades, including Rolf's room: *Guestroom No. 2*.

Stan slapped his hands together and began chafing them as if literally trying to kindle good cheer. "What has our metropolitan scholar to teach us about? What great new dance performance must we all rush to?" For a moment, he held Darius's gaze with playfully aggressive intensity. He sounded as sarcastic as ever, but he, too, was avoiding some subject.

"Dah-li-*ush*. Could you–?" Sohaila asked nervously. She tugged the lavender-patterned paper from under the anemones and slid it across the counter toward Darius. He disposed of it for her. He smelled his hands after crumpling the paper into the garbage. His mother measured the thick flower stems against the vase.

Stan said, "We've had shocking news."

"Stan, please. Not right away."

Uncharacteristically tractable, Stan straightened and made a curious, antique bow. He wasn't being ironical about it. His hands mimicked a wave of emotion coming from his breast, and he apologized, "I'm always, *Out with it!* For So, there's the perfect moment."

"Nothing to do with Dad?" Darius asked in alarm. The other two exchanged a look, before Sohaila said *No* and Stan commented with a creeping half-shrug.

"Oliver is fine as far as I know," Sohaila said, clearly displeased about being cornered.

"The *not fine* is on our side," Stan said gravely. "I'm sorry." He promptly retracted the remark. He pressed his lips together.

Sohaila asked, "What do these look like? Are they too—?" She stepped back. The anemones lolled against the rim of a celadon vase like queasy ferry passengers.

"I like them like that," Darius said.

With energy, Sohaila lifted the flowers from the vase to trim the stems more. She looked crushed that she'd done such a poor job at first.

"Remember, So," Stan said gently. "This is not a little tiny thing. Not a little emotional poke in the eye. We've discussed this. It's monstrous, because it has a major impact on our life. Real harm."

"What are you talking about?" Darius asked.

Sohaila set down her shears and the flowers. She covered her face with one hand. She gripped her elbow with the other. She wasn't crying. She even peeked through her fingers at the kitchen door, not wanting to be surprised by Rolf. She seemed to smell the life-fragrance of the flowers on her fingers, the same way Darius had. She closed her eyes. Her hand fell. She looked at Stan, helplessly giving him permission.

"Your father cheated your mother in a particularly outrageous way," Stan said. He eyed Darius.

Dabbing a tear or eyeliner with her littlest finger, Sohaila made a sighing noise, as if she wanted to moderate Stan's harshness.

"Completely illegal," he insisted. "And showing a certain cruelty I think you're familiar with in him."

"He's a fantasist," Darius breathed. He felt horribly guilty. He worried instantly about looking like he was lying for some reason. He was impressed by Stan's barbarous gravity. The way the Romanian doffed irony or donned earnestness so completely made Darius feel, vaguely, that he was up against someone both powerful and sincere.

"You didn't know about this, Dah-li-*ush*?" Sohaila pleaded.

"Of course not," Darius assured both of them a touch evenly.

Nodding toward a plastic hamper by the basement door, Sohaila warned them about the housekeeper. "Tina's going to be up and down with laundry. We shouldn't bother her. Can't we go to the living room, Stan?"

All three of them walked through the hall to the front drawing room with their arms tightly folded. They said nothing but drifted to a stop near the room's midway point, next to a huge armorial fireplace. Sohaila chose a few lamps to switch on. Hurrying their discussion at the same time she flower-arranged the lighting, she whispered, "I don't know when Rolf will be coming down. Any minute, I imagine."

"I've never heard about any beloved family friend from Europe. I thought you and Dad had barely any friends." Darius felt Stan's gaze on him.

"Rolf's family, his father, was an enormous help to us in Mumbai. To me and Oliver. When I left Iran for good." She turned off one of the lamps, leaving three lit. She stationed herself so she could see into the front hall and to the foot of the stairs. Past the hall on the other side, a table set for four glittered in the murk of the dining room like the flank of a dozing silver-scaled dragon. "This is all so—" Sohaila returned to the issue at hand. "Who knows? Who knows what to do?"

"What's—?"

"Your father seems to have an enormous—"

"And Dah-li-*ush*!" Sohaila interrupted. "Why couldn't you tell us you knew Ali?" She lashed out.

"What?"

"Ach! He knows you. From Columbia."

"Ali? The Kuwaiti guy? But he—"

"Yes, you see who I mean now. You know him. I knew he was Arab, but that's all."

"No, I haven't seen him in years. He tried to get me to join St. Anthony's. What does he have to do with any of this?"

"There are two things we found out," Stan stopped Sohaila. "Ali works for a group called *Ta'aleem,* run by a guy Sohaila knew, an Iranian from the Old Westbury crowd. Sohaila introduced this Iranian friend to Oliver many years ago."

"Not really a friend. It was only because it was a charity," Sohaila explained. "*Ta'aleem* is a charity. For the Palestinian thing."

Stan shrugged. "Anyway, Ali came by—"

"Here?"

"—or rather the Iranian called and told us to talk to him, so Ali came by and said Oliver used to give a large amount of money every year to *Ta'aleem.* But now he's stopped. Naturally, they were wondering why and couldn't get in touch with him any more than we could."

"And I knew nothing about this. Nothing about the money he was giving. Nothing at all," Sohaila said.

"Yes. But Ali told us—do you know about this?—that the money Oliver gave always came in the form of a check from—Mather Capital." Stan dramatized, "What?" He paused for effect. "What is this? A company? A private equity firm, it turns out. Do you know what that is? I didn't. I'd never heard the term *private equity firm.* I thought Sohaila must know about Mather Capital, because of the divorce. But she didn't either. So what is it? Why don't we know about it? Is it big? Is it all Oliver? *Yes* and *yes,* it turns out. Mather Capital is even important enough to be a partner with the Abu Dhabi Investment Authority in certain things. But who runs it, since Oliver obviously can't be. This, even my investigator has been unable to find out!"

"You know what this sounds like, you two," Darius said drily.

"We're *not* attacking," Sohaila snapped, anger and reproach making her choose an odd word. *Attack.* "Stan's mother in Bucharest has just found out she has cancer!"

"No, no, let's—that's a different issue, So. No emotional pleading. This is legal fairness we're concerned about." Stan hurried on in a snaky, calming whisper, trying to stage-manage the conversation. "But did *you* know about Mather Capital?"

"Come on! I've never heard of it. I don't care about any of that."

"Never heard of it," Stan echoed.

"Dah-li-*ush*!" Sohaila barked. "Dah-li-*ush*, I don't have money! *You* don't! Forget about what this place looks like. I spend everything I have. And a lot of it—a *lot* of it—on you."

Stan said, "So if the case is that Oliver had—who knows?—which he never told anybody about. If it was secret at the time of the divorce... Well, this is a lawsuit. I'm sorry. A very important one."

"Stan," Sohaila said, near tears. He put his arm around her, something he'd never done before in Darius's presence.

Darius wrestled to conceal different kinds of surprise. Oliver's old boasting about his immeasurable wealth might not have been the early sign of mental illness he'd assumed. Or not that alone. He remembered his father talking at Grand Central. He remembered Oliver's crackpot scheming against Sohaila and Stan but only as a kind of rant. Feeling he shouldn't be, Darius was just as surprised as they were.

Darius was equally surprised by the news about Ali. The plump Arab's suave interest in him had been romantic, the docile and unambitious sexual attraction young people tolerate in someone a couple of decades older. As passing as their Columbia acquaintance had been, Darius now felt tricked. It stung that Ali had all along been fund raising as much as he'd been infatuated. Darius was better prepared to be betrayed on a grand scale by Alan than he was to be fooled by Ali.

"No one's talking about suing," Sohaila sighed, massaging her clavicles.

"Not yet."

"I want you to talk to him, Dah-li-*ush*, if you possibly, possibly can. I know it's hard. But, you see, I can't. Not about this. Obviously he's arranged it so I'm supposed to come crying and begging to him." The muscles of her face deformed. Darius thought she was about to sob. But her painted expression resolved into ghastly delight. She cried out, "Rolf, darling! Rolf! Rolf! We're here, all of us!"

An incredibly tall man, all long arms and legs, rounded the great newel post at the foot of the stairs. He crossed the hall toward them and became a lanky shadow for a long time before the three little lamps showed his boyishly correct gray jacket, a touch short in the sleeves, wide, deeply colored lips smiling in perfect confidence, and blue eyes.

The change of gears had been so brutal for Sohaila that she let out a giggle. She fanned her throat and exclaimed naughtily, "You are so, *so* tall, Rolf!"

Rolf's smile lasted longer than it should have.

Sohaila was quick to apologize. "Oh, you must be so completely bored to hear it. Everyone tells you, of course."

Rolf's smile dragged on expressively.

"Darling Rolf, I have no drinks or anything ready yet. I'm sorry. This is my Dah-li-*ush*, in any case. This is Rolf, whose father—*so* gracious to Oliver and me." Her ingénue fluttering made Darius think for the first time, with sudden gloom, that she was old.

At dinner, Rolf picked up that something was amiss with his hosts. Since he was extraordinarily well-mannered, a diplomat's son, he labored to keep the conversation afloat with non-controversial observations about the United States. It was his first visit. His opinions were so non-controversial that Darius began to wonder if he might actually hate America.

While they were still at the table, Tina came in to say she was going home. She said there was still a load of laundry in the dryer, though, she mentioned pointedly, she'd already taken out Rolf's shirts and *panties*. They heard her slam the door. They listened to the hoarse cough of her Cadillac in the drive. They remained silent until Stan apologized to Rolf, "It's not you. She doesn't like me. And through me, she doesn't like anything European, not even the underwear."

"Ah," Rolf said, lofty and vague, his smile reforming like a careful measure of oil. He was finding the dinner odd.

"Not true. Not true," Sohaila said. Her delay was so strange, none of them knew what she was talking about at first. One of her ears was cocked to a new favorite, Enescu's *Romanian Rhapsodies*, in honor of Stan. She'd switched it on before leaving the drawing room. When she saw them all looking bewildered, she explained. "That she doesn't love you, Stan. That's not true. She loves all of us—and we love her, of course."

The dinner's only excitement came when Rolf learned that the house had once belonged to Colin Vail. He'd heard of him and was clearly an admirer. "Vail is almost like Pierre Klossowski—not their work so much, but as cultural figures. They're so deeply peculiar. Anti-popular. And probably much more appreciated in Europe, I think. Especially now. They adore Vail in Paris." Darius had never imagined that Colin Vail might be known outside of the United States. The weedy power of culture to spread impressed him. He had always assumed Vail was a wholly private taste, a man doomed to being forgotten as an artist. Now his idol had an entirely independent existence through Rolf and Europe.

Immediately after dinner, Darius called his father's number from the basement. He left a message saying it was important they meet soon. That much he'd tried before. He had to call many more times and leave many more messages over the next weeks. At first he kept second-guessing his tone of voice, his choice of words. When, inexplicably, he got the living person, Oliver sounded appallingly normal. It threw Darius into confusion for a minute. What happened to the incommunicado for years, the fantastic scheme to defraud Sohaila? Darius peremptorily announced a meeting. "I've decided I have to stop by your place. Afternoon, because I know you prefer it. Three, I guess. We have to talk about some things. And this is—sort of—required." He wasn't at all sure it would work.

The visit was set for a Saturday. The Friday evening before, Darius went out with friends, an unexpectedly fun-loving Barnard girl and her taciturn African lover of the moment. As they all danced to an Angolan band at a rock club downtown, the African and Darius were slowly crowded from the girl's vicinity by a group of husky Greeks. She seemed happy enough, so they sipped beers on the sidelines. Watching her dance and watching the milky glitter of the African's eye following her, Darius had the idea to use her power with straight men for his own purposes. He'd ask her to come with him the following afternoon. Her presence might make it more difficult to talk to Oliver about money, and in truth Darius didn't know the girl that well. But he had an intuition laying a virgin on his father's altar could be just the thing. Oliver used to be well-behaved around Cassie.

Oliver's apartment was in a neighborhood of skyscrapers built atop a seventeenth century village. The shadowy streets were barely wide enough for the modern mercantile bustle of hawkers and deliveries. On top of that, day-workers sheep-dogged the sidewalk crowds with petitions for Greenpeace and Planned Parenthood. Box trucks teetered half off the curb. People sidled between truck tires and storefronts. An *Office Furniture Giant* truck had pulled up to the diminutive back entrance of a huge office tower. Its crew shoved plastic-wrapped desk chairs down the truck's welt-covered loading ramp. With each slide, the chair casters brayed like an elephant trumpeting in pain. Everything about the neighborhood (except the flyers) made Darius think, *Oliver must hate this*.

The building on Cedar Street was a nineteenth-century spice warehouse. A discounter of adding machines and electronics shops owned the place through the sixties. Urban pioneers started living there in the seventies and eighties.

His companion had no idea how momentous this visit was for Darius. As they walked, she idled by store windows, disparaged the beetling masses who hold regular jobs and, after they got inside the building, pursed her lips at a long wait in front of the blank steel apartment door. She spotted a man who looked like a super at the end of the long hall. With the egalitarian brusqueness New Yorkers like to have on hand, she cried, "Hey! Hey! You know if this guy in?"

"He's in," Darius whispered tautly. He wasn't sure they'd get an answer.

The door opened with a loud unsticking noise, as if it had been painted shut. "Darius," Oliver enunciated slowly in a macabre voice. He sounded a little comical, a little threatening. Patches of seborrheic dermatitis reddened the sides of his nose. A torturer's amusement lighted his eyes. But the instant Oliver caught sight of the girl, his expression died. Whatever little scene he may have prepared for Darius was aborted. Discountenanced, he hunted for a normal-sounding greeting. "Ah! Ah-ah! How d'ye do, then? Uh. Darius?" He finished severely. Darius introduced the girl.

Oliver's expression kept changing. Originally willful tics had turned into a neurological jumble. He'd lost weight. Sagging cheeks had slightly altered the line of his jaw and chin. He'd shaved but had missed a large patch of several days' growth which looked like gray toothbrush bristle. He was dressed as a penitent or prisoner in a yellowing white button-down and beltless gray slacks. He wore white socks, but no shoes. Though he was acting as poised as he could possibly manage, his intense awkwardness made it seem Darius and his friend had, in some hallucinatory fashion, blundered into his weird internal privacy, the mind-realm ruled by this homunculus Oliver. The sprinkler pipes and capped gaslight lines were his paint-crusted neurons. The steel shutters at the front of the loft were his eyelids seen from the inside.

A previous owner had built a kitchen and a tiny bedroom out of unfinished plasterboard. These rooms huddled along one wall like a shepherd's hut in a ruined basilica. Next to them was a small arrangement of chairs, couch, table and lamp. Apart from this furniture, the vast space was barren, lacking anything to look at besides populations of dust bunnies along the baseboards. The room was too dim to show much color, but ruby red pellets gleamed here and there in a grid of sprinklers hanging from the pressed-tin ceiling. These pellets held open the jaws of the sprinkler heads and were ready to fail in a fire. The setup conjured a powerful atmosphere of contingency for anybody living underneath.

The girl perched gingerly on the couch, her head turning everywhere in the cavernous space. She exclaimed that it was a *fabulous, fantastic apartment!*

Obviously unaccustomed to people, Oliver took his chair, and stroked his shirt front and crossed and recrossed his legs, each time flashing them detailed black footprints on the soles of his white socks.

He continued to make odd facial expressions, and his hands kept stiffening. His fingers were crooked awry when he gestured to Darius. "Sit down! Since you're here. Since you're here. Sit down. You might as well." Between agonized glances around him, Darius's eyes drilled his own crossed forearms.

Oliver's head lolled back. He appeared to count the red sprinkler jewels for a spell. He stroked his chin. He found the spot of stubble. He addressed the girl, "I don't have—much of a bar here. You'll forgive. As this one should have known. So."

Her perky response that she didn't need anything led to silence. She wasn't stupid, and about now she realized exactly how she'd been used. She didn't resent it. It was hard not to feel compassion for Darius when you understood the situation. In full, polite control of herself, she mentioned she'd be going on to Century 21 to shop for sweaters in a moment. "I wish we could call them jumpers like the Brits. So much cuter."

Gratefully, Darius breathed, "I'll follow you down in a few minutes."

Oliver's watery gaze prowled the girl's bust. "Well," he said. His hands clapped his knees as if they'd been sitting there for hours. He did it again.

"Maybe we could use a little light on the subject," the girl said boldly.

"Ah! This—uh—" Oliver's fingers lightly plucked the long chain of an earthenware lamp on the table next to him. "—this—uh—you know for a long time I thought this was a whispering device." He pinched the minuscule bell at the end of the chain. "Not listening. Whispering. So silly." He was admitting the silliness mostly for the benefit of his rational guests. "No. Ho-ho-ho!" His mouth stopped at the last O. His look of naughty boy alarm was comical.

His manner kept hitting two or three notes at once. Darius and the girl each started looking at him and wondering, was this play-acting or had he utterly lost the knack for natural behavior? What he'd done to his life wasn't acting. Furthermore, anyone would have sensed that the same self-conscious question was coursing through his own mind. For instance, after touching the chain, he made several more weird hand gestures, deploying them, as it were, to test his autonomy.

"What have you been up—how's it going?" Darius got out in a husky relic of his usual voice. An excess of nerves kept him from waiting for an answer, "I've been—we were out dancing last night." Darius was already so tense he could barely move. Gathering any information for Sohaila and Stan looked to be impossible.

Oliver rose. "I've got to see about something, before we—uh—" He disappeared into the sheetrock kitchen where he rattled around a bit.

"Sorry!" Darius mouthed to the girl.

She shrugged. She smiled forgivingly, only tipping her head to mean Oliver was a piece of work. To pretend nothing was wrong wouldn't be friendly in this case.

"I wish I hadn't come. I'm sorry I brought you," Darius whispered.

The girl's eye caught the bar of light along the hinge side of the kitchen door. The light twizzled with shadow like a spiraling barber pole. Dim as the apartment was, she thought she saw a blush-colored something, which had to be the tip of Oliver's nose or his inflamed cheek. With a marked movement of her eyes she warned Darius that his father was spying on them. When he turned to look, they heard a little thud in the kitchen.

Once the girl had departed to shop for winter sweaters, the silence wound around Darius's chest like a boa. The easiest way to speak was to look at the floor and imagine himself alone. "Mom found out about your big plan. And Stan."

Oliver didn't understand.

Yearning toward the ceiling, Darius explained, "About your money. This Mather Capital thing."

"Oh, that's not true. None of that's true." Did this statement have the bored certainty of a well-disguised lie?

Darius was able to glance at his father. The older man appeared drowsy, eyes shut. "Uh. I'm talking about the stuff you told me a long time ago. You said you did have—"

"That was just a story," Oliver interrupted. "That was all just made up."

Darius nearly believed him for several seconds. He frowned. "But wait. It is true. Because Stan found out about it. I don't want you to get upset, but Stan had somebody look into it. I think." Worried about Oliver's reaction, Darius added, in a tone of confidential disdain, "He's so over-dramatic. Only he would do something like that—hire somebody." Oliver's eyes fluttered open, then closed again. Seriously, Darius said, "It was real, though. I remember how you talked about it. It was a big deal for you. Me, too. You described the whole scheme, and it turned out just the way you said it would. Sort of amazing."

"There wasn't any scheme."

"I was supposed to keep the secret. And then I would get everything. Or something. Someday."

The naturalness of his father's chuckle filled him with doubt. "No, boy. I'm sorry."

"OK," Darius said. A little strength was coming to him. "Let me put it this way. Mom has absolutely no money. It's not a joke. I've been taking way too much. She's had to pay for Columbia this whole time, and she isn't doing it with income. She doesn't know anything about money. Neither does Stan. So they're running through whatever you gave her. If I wanted to go somewhere—I don't know—take some time off to travel—I mean, she'd want me to, but she'd have to pay. And Stan's mother is sick apparently. I don't know if that costs a lot in Romania, but I don't think he's qualified to do anything here. If I had money, or if I was going to get any, I'd want mom to have it now."

This got raised eyebrows from Oliver. Darius's hopes soared. Then Oliver said stubbornly, "*Mather Capital* doesn't exist. What a name! I must have been joking. That's the kind of man I am."

Instead of responding to this or sticking with his mission on behalf of Sohaila and Stan, Darius blurted out, "What do you do here?" For the first time, their eyes met briefly. Oliver didn't say anything. The hissing stillness of the loft filled Darius's mind. The background had become the foreground. Darius had a despairing pang of certainty that his life would never fit into a cogent narrative. All of its great moments, like this one, were only the shadows of real incidents. Fearless at last, he commented, "This is insane. I don't know what I'm doing here. I don't even know if it was a good thing you finally opened the door."

"Finally?" Oliver asked. He seemed not to understand. Darius wondered whether Oliver's sense of time wasn't so altered that the old man actually believed there had been no incommunicado for years, that he was only getting around to talking with Darius in the ordinary course of time. Oliver flicked at the metal lamp chain, had it trickle over his fingertips. He smiled as if preparing one of his old, cruel lies. "But I assumed you were like Cassie. You didn't want to see anything more of me." He pouted. "Because I was too—loathsome and cold—and deceptive—and upsettingly odd—and an antisemite and a racist."

In the days after the visit, Darius was overwhelmed by a sense of filial responsibility he knew he could never rise to. Sohaila and Stan weren't happy with his report. He couldn't get them to appreciate how difficult it had been talking with Oliver. And now Oliver had no one left in his life except his son. The idea of educational travel—Tunis? Rome?—was just Darius imagining escape.

Sohaila and Stan nagged him into trying one more time with Oliver. It didn't go any better. Oliver met with him but refused to let him in the apartment this time. The half rejection reminded Darius of Alan Wilkinson. Oliver wore a preposterous pair of electric green Crocs, and father and son went downstairs to walk around the block together. The streets were so busy Oliver needed all his concentration to control his sparrow-like jitters. He wasn't able to talk at all, except for a disagreeable hum that came out of him with machine monotony. A brute in a hardhat dropped one of the metal leaves of a store's bulkhead basement doors. At the great bang, Oliver rounded on him and swatted the ConEd patch on the man's breast pocket. In a sinister voice, he hissed, "Fucking idiot! What? Do you not see me here? Am I invisible?" Darius's look of horror was just enough to calm the man. Not such a brute after all. He brushed at his chest. "Better keep your geezer locked up. I feel for you, man."

22

IN THE SUMMER of 1997, the ancient Khmer ruler Jayawarman VII lorded it over Paris in a manner of speaking. Carvings, statues, lingams, lintels, friezes, steles, betyl-stones of all kinds had been imported for an encyclopedic show of Khmer art at the *Grand Palais*. When his escape from Oliver, Alan, Sohaila and Stan ended in France, Darius attended the Khmer show. He found it difficult to enjoy. Droning AC recycled discreet farts and opinions through the underventilated galleries. The jostling crowd had trouble putting up with itself.

Outdoors, his optic nerve crazed by the relentless and humbling grandeur of the city, Darius couldn't stop noticing the one person who saw none of it—because his eyes were closed. This was Jayawarman VII. The man's stone portrait appeared everywhere on banners advertising the Khmer show. Evidently awake, the fact that Jayawarman shut his eyes wherever he went in the beautiful capitol was quite attention-getting. Eyes closed, lips flexing imperceptibly in enlightenment—a peace too awesome to call contentment, much less a smile—the portrait was conventionally Buddhist in type, though clearly a masterpiece.

Darius didn't think Jayawarman disliked Paris. He wasn't inclined to argue, "Open your eyes, old man!" Nor was it a matter of eastern and western art contending, though the meditative banner and the rearing golden Pegasi of the *Pont Alexandre III* made for a nice contrast. Realism, Darius decided, was what it was all about. The key to the eerie realism of the Khmer head, conventional or not, was in the closed eyes. Any sculpture of a figure asleep, say, a Psyche or an Adonis—Darius couldn't call one to mind—might have the same hypnotic power. Sculptures with open eyes, of which there was a superabundance in Paris, were just sculptures in the end. Some were realistic illusions in stone or bronze, some were less so.

Close the eyes, however, and something strange happened. The viewer no longer has to pretend the statue is thinking or feeling or experiencing any mental activity whatsoever. No more than the actual stone thinks. Suddenly stone isn't just illusionistic, not just an apt medium to represent an unconscious figure or an aristocratic bonze's disciplined emptying of his mind. Thoughtlessness and stone are, to all intents and purposes, one thing. The realism of Jayawarman VII's portrait didn't grip Darius. A frisson of actuality did. A *frisson*—he loved mouthing the word on the street in the slight verbal drunkenness he'd felt since arriving.

Like Jayawarman VII, Darius hadn't come to Paris to see Paris. He hadn't come to see Jayawarman. The Khmer show was just a foretaste. If someone in Tunis or in Rome had been enthusiastic enough to arrange a retrospective of Colin Vail's work, he would have gone there. But it was going to be in Paris, so he landed in Paris when he fled college, America, father. The show was due to be mounted that fall in an undistinguished Left Bank gallery.

Darius was letting Sohaila and Stan and a few friends think he was dallying in the way of many young people whose parents finance a year of drift. Had he told anyone he thought his secret purpose in coming was to genuflect at the temple of an obscure American artist, Colin Vail, they might have been charmed or impressed. The pursuit looked wonderfully romantic. In a certain light he could see the romance himself. But he told no one. He feared the reactions of other people would throw an uncomfortable shadow of comedy—or bullshit—on his most solemn beliefs. And make it clear this was all about Oliver.

He had to do some groundwork. Of the Paris connections he scraped together, Cassie Vail passed along the most glamorous name, the dealer and collector who was organizing the Vail show. She knew the man. Before leaving, Darius had labored for days over a light sounding note. Cassie shot back a scrawl on stationery headed *Cassandra Vail Fine Art*. She gave him the gallerist's name, plus one or two others. She added, "Darius! Lovely! Lovely to hear! Often so sorry things ended not as smoothly as they might have with your father and me. Always feel the deepest concern and fondness for him. But where on earth is he? Please inform. Can I help? Also, come to see me when you're back from Paris. Wanted to go desperately myself, but a beau has hip surgery scheduled. Much love!"

His early French lessons with David Caperini had inoculated Darius against corny Parisian daydreams. He expected to hate the museum city, a good place for art of the closed up and put away sort. The city fairly sweated eternity. Darius had never seen anything like it. And in spite of himself he started to love the trickle of life still flowing through endless channels of Lutetian limestone (all subtly golden now that the nineteenth-century gray had been sand-blasted away).

Every day, fascinating generalizations rose like morning mist from the inconceivably detailed foreignness of packages, matchbooks, plugs, switches, everything. It wasn't a new land, it was a new way of thinking. Here idleness was almost esteemed. It was heaven for a dropout. Loafers in cafés were treated respectfully as if they might be geniuses, ministers-in-exile or terrorists, not mere wastrels like Darius. The deadly infection of American vim and entrepreneurialism had already taken hold. But coming from the United States, Darius didn't notice it so much.

Darius lived at the Hotel Moderne, a two-star place a block from the *Jardins du Luxembourg*. A futuristic armoire of black laminated particleboard loomed over the bed on which he reviewed his daily hoard of scribbled phrases and museum postcards. He masturbated constantly, not as considerate as he could have been of the Styrofoam ceiling tiles or chocolate velveteen curtains, easy targets for ejaculations of wild loneliness. At first he thought the narrow-eyed hotel proprietress had no taste. Then the generalization came to him that black plastic furniture and a chocolate color scheme were typically French.

His most welcoming connection was Rolf, the family friend, German but living in Paris and the one who'd told Darius about the Vail show in the first place. He was the first person Darius called. Rolf cut through his pretense of casualness. "Thank God, an American! You wouldn't believe the French shit I've been putting up with. My roommate Roger-Pôl wants his crush to move in. This snooty Mauritanian prince. I hate aristocrats. And I certainly don't want one living in my home!" He didn't sound like the ultra-polite houseguest he'd been. He wanted to meet at once.

Darius arrived first at a sprawling café at the Bastille. A thousand iterations of the same gorgeous but drab French boy hunched at the tables, morose, regal. All of them had rested an elbow on the orb of a motorcycle helmet and held the liquid scepter of a *panaché* in one hand. Rolf, when he came, stood out, to say the least. The good boy gray jacket was gone. He wasn't at all the houseguest he'd been. Nearly seven feet, he was dressed in an orange shirt and orange and green camouflage pants. A maroon chiffon scarf was wrapped tightly around his great columnar neck. He flipped up the clip-on shades of his clunky glasses and scanned the crowd like an orange lighthouse. Darius raised an arm. Rolf's smile of perfect confidence was the same as before.

Brisk, kind and, as the son of diplomats, an experienced traveler himself, Rolf knew what a newcomer needed. In moments he was writing names, phone numbers, restaurant addresses on the backs of old notes to himself, which he reread and summarily scored through, all the while debating aloud with himself. "There are many good things still. I don't want to sound like I'm dissing Paris. *Enfin*, I was a little blue-eyed when I first came to the *Beaux Arts*—that was a long time ago—am I, what, seven years older than you?—anyway, in German, we have this expression, *blue-eyed*. It's the same in English, no? Sort of—*innocent*. But I may be coming to the end of my time here. Perhaps." He took out cigarettes.

"*Dommage*." Darius hoped this chirrup had an air of fluency.

"*Pourquoi ça?*"

"Well," Darius retreated to English. "Just things ending. I hate that."

Darius was glad of the thick glasses and the gargantuan fingers continually pushing them back up Rolf's nose, because they slightly interfered with the almost bruising blue-eyed smile Rolf kept lowering on him. "Don't say that," the German murmured paternally. "Look at us!"

After many more smiles, Rolf invited Darius to come shopping with him and to drop by the apartment after. Darius agreed readily, thinking it would seal their acquaintance better than a quick cup of coffee could. Rolf smiled again, his eyes detonating with generous satisfaction. Kindness certainly lay at the bottom of Rolf's behavior, but what most impressed Darius was the perfection of his manners. The orange was as carefully chosen as the gray had been. These smiles, the sparks in his eyes, were all controlled, deliberate, detached. Not false, surely, but not spontaneous, either. After all, Rolf *was* still the perfect houseguest.

Rolf was leaving the next day with some friends to drive to his family's summer home on *Lago Maggiore* (the Swiss, not the Italian side). After the idiomatic "summer home" came out, Rolf paused. He plucked the cigarette from his wide mouth with a considering pop. He corrected himself. "It's a little *rustico*. A beautiful place, but just a shack, a nothing."

"A cottage?"

"Yes. Not a summer home. A cottage, that's it." The well-bred deprecation made Darius smile. Against a background of unremitting strangeness, this fugitive quirk of personality stood out. Something he'd thought American or his own was reproduced exactly in Europe. "*Enfin*! That's why I have to shop. We need food to eat in the car. It's faster if we don't stop during the drive."

"A road trip."

"Yes. A road trip. Exactly." He stubbed out his cigarette and eyed Darius. "But not long. I mean the trip is long, but I'm not away long. After a week or ten days, I come back. We'll see each other." It wasn't a question.

"Yes," Darius answered.

When they left, the German threaded his way amongst the tables of French boys with the necessary elegance of the enormous or the orange. Outside, he flung his terrifying hand toward Jayawarman VII, whose banner bellied gently on a lamp post. "Have you seen this?" He bent intimately toward Darius. "Fantastic. *Fantastique. Sauf la publique.* These blockbusters *à l'Américain*. Disgusting. Your country has a lot to answer for, you know." He teased so gently it was like a caress.

They went to a *Prisunic*. Rolf chose a plastic tablet of salami, a plastic-wrapped baguette and even, bashfully, *les chips*. A messy bin of cheap, picked-through Camemberts made him sigh. "And your mother? She's well?" he drawled politely. For the first time, he seemed to slow down some, though he kept unscrewing Camembert cartons to prod and sniff them.

"She's fine."

"She lives in that house, that large, large house. A mansion, really. I got lost going to the bathroom."

"Yes. With Stan. Not exactly a *rustico*."

"The Romanian. An interesting *ménage*. I have to say I found it—well—"

"Please. You can't say anything that would offend me."

"They didn't strike me as completely—oriented, those two."

"They're foreigners there. Now that I'm here I'm beginning to see what it's like. The language thing is incredibly tiring. But you're also right. My family is not well-oriented. I have a feeling you are, though. My parents met your family in India, right?"

"In Mumbai. Not too long after I was born, I think. I was born in Afghanistan. What I remember about Mumbai is the towers of the dead. Very moving, as a matter in fact. The vultures started going extinct, so the bodies in the towers, instead of being eaten—sky burial—they just rotted. My mother became very involved in a foundation to save the vultures. That has nothing to do with your parents, though. How did they meet?"

"I'm asking you. I don't know. Only that your parents helped mine."

"The only thing I know is that my father was stationed there somewhat before the revolution in Iran. Was your father—I don't know this—in the CIA or with the State Department? Maybe you don't know. *Bref*, my father introduced yours to this group of Iranian exiles, among them your mother. I think there *was* some

Zoroastrian connection. Not sky burials. Maybe the Zoroastrians wanted to help the Iranian exiles, but then they got angry when they found out the Iranians were just a bunch of Muslims. I don't know exactly."

"That sounds like your father introduced my parents to each other."

"Perhaps."

"I think my grandfather was CIA—or OSS?—but not my father. At least that's what my mother told me once. You have to understand, my father lies sometimes. He'll claim he did what *his* father actually did. Or even random things. He's the least oriented of all of us." A tone of wistfulness eked through.

"But you're—if I understand it—not to pry..."

"Yes. I'm adopted. Not from anywhere exciting. Just New Jersey." Fearing he sounded forlorn, Darius began to boast. "My mom was—well, you hate it, but—she was a little like your friend's crush, Moktar."

"Ah, yes. Our prince. But he's Mauritanian, not Iranian. There's a big difference."

"You said he was an exile."

"Yes. He's living on a tiny government subsidy. But I don't *hate*—you have to understand. My own family—oh forget it, forget it!" He put his hands on his hips and laughed into the bin of Camemberts. "I'm enjoying talking. I talk too much. I must be starved for American company."

"You have an exaggerated opinion of Americans."

"Darius—" Rolf gave up and took a doubtful Camembert. He led Darius into a narrow aisle of fruit juices in foil bricks. Darius felt a heavy smile coming to rest on him and raised his eyes to it. "I have something to ask, but I don't want to offend you," Rolf began.

"Please. You can't."

"But I want to be clear—"

"You can't offend me, I mean. Go ahead."

"I just want to ask *en passant*—purely *en passant*, you understand... No. Let me say this about me instead. Ever since *L'Ecole des Beaux Arts*, or forever, really, people think I'm gay."

Darius could see the *but* coming. "Oh." He felt an automatic sensation of disappointment. Annoyance, too, because he was sure he hadn't been thinking along those lines. "That's not a problem, or—an issue. Really, I hadn't even thought—"

"*Tant mieux*. Well. There we are, then. I am. Them thinking it taught me in a way."

"Wait! You are? I'm confused."

"I wanted to ask so I wouldn't be thinking about it for ten days in my *rustico*."

"Ask *me*, you mean?"

"Yes."

They checked out without saying anything more. On the street, Darius took it up again. "Well, yes. *Yes* is the answer to what you were asking. But why? Did we ever talk about that before, you and I?"

"No. I only wanted to be clear."

"But you thought you had to ask *me*. Not that I care if anybody thinks that about me. Or if I give off—"

"You sound French. They're so extremely self-conscious. They hate getting cornered into their identity. They always have to be general. Then they all end up exactly the same, like those scooter boys at the café. But, no. You don't give off *le parfum gai*, if that's what you mean. It's only—you remember when we had dinner with your mother in New Jersey?"

"Of course," Darius said.

"You talked a lot about another boy."

"I did?"

"Yes. A mathematician. So I assumed—it just struck me that way very clearly."

"But that had been over—that hadn't been going on for a long time at that point." Darius frowned. They passed an African in a green jumpsuit who shunted soaked rags along a streaming gutter with his green plastic besom.

"Yes, well. Things are slow in life, no? Even me." He looked down and gestured at himself so the bag of groceries swung like a pendulum. "It's taken me so long—all my life—to become—" When Darius looked at him and suggested "Orange?" the

German howled with laughter. Though even that was controlled. "*Précisément*! I have become orange. Finally!"

"And do you have a mathematician friend?" The din of voices and traffic seemed to increase in volume. Even the car horns had accents.

"Ah. No." Rolf smiled.

When his mathematician, Alan Wilkinson, came to Paris for a fall visit and suggested an evening together, Darius was quick to take him up on it, happy to assume the role of helpful local connection for a change. Alan was freelancing for the review pages of the *New Republic* and half-regretfully laying the groundwork for a chatty career as an intellectual journalist. He lived on a pittance from his family in Virginia and a stipend from his frizzy-haired architect friend.

Timing was the critical issue of the evening. The plan was to meet a famous actress, in town to shoot a celebrity blue jeans commercial. The actress was dining early (jet-lag) with the books editor of *Vogue* and the Brazilian director hired to shoot her commercial. Meanwhile, Alan, Darius and the director's gay brother's close gay friend (but not lover) were having a drink at the Café Beaubourg. In fact, they were waiting for the actress to finish dinner. Then her party would meet up with the director's gay brother, a runway model. The gay model brother would then call his close gay friend to tell him whether they were moving on to the actress' suite at L'Hotel or to the Brazilian director's girlfriend's Gare du Nord photography studio, in which case Alan, Darius and the close gay friend would pop by and meet the actress. And they could retail a story about her over future drinks as they waited on future celebrities. It wasn't much, but in the seller's market for celebrity stories, it was worth cooling their heels for an hour or two. Alan had also dangled a possible meeting with Gore Vidal.

The conversation at the Café Beaubourg was heightened by anticipation, but they didn't talk about the actress. In truth, they weren't much interested in her. The close gay friend sat forward in a self-consciously masculine posture, elbows on knees. His hands loosely hoarded a whiskey on the low cocktail table. He was fascinated by Alan, who was acting a touch disdainful as usual. Alan often inspired a kind of contentious fascination.

"I like stupid," the close friend said, describing his ideal lover. He had a bookish, hatchet face with sinewy temples, and a receding chin that shouted meekness. But he wasn't at all meek, apparently. He had a boxer's aggressive jitters, which is to say everywhere but in his eyes. His stubbly red jaw looked swarthy in the streetlight coming through the window. "A stupid boy, mouth hanging open. That's perfect." His proud grin looked both menacing and weak. "Tristão and I had a brief thing at first. But even though he's a model, he wasn't stupid enough."

Alan looked like he would rather have been anywhere else. The scheme to meet the actress embarrassed both him and Darius, though they were resigned to its importance. With a sigh, Alan inquired, "You hold that interior experience does or doesn't exist without the ability to put it into words?"

"Oh, it does," the close friend answered quickly. He reconsidered. "In a way, it does. It's more—abstract for them."

Eyeing his drink lest it spill, Alan slowly shot the cuff of one arm. Darius studied him, making low observations about Alan's ultra-American style—saggy blazer, button-down, cuffed pants. Clothes got Darius remembering bodies and Alan's surprisingly muscular back. This erotic thought rumbled like the Métro passing underneath them.

Alan drawled, "You impute interior life to them based on their behavior? Or are you universalizing from your own inner experience?"

The close friend grinned again, clearly enjoying someone he considered up to his level. "There's not much behavior to observe. They're always wearing headphones. They're dreaming of becoming DJ's. There's a total intellectual silence. Being with them is like going to a carnal library. Sh!" He eyed Darius briefly as if pointing to a *for-example*.

Unwillingly, Alan chuckled and drew back his head, a withdrawing mannerism of his whenever he laughed.

Darius whispered, "I always hide being in love. You can hide lots of things." The close friend paid no attention to Alan's loyal sidekick. His beady-eyed stare never left Alan.

Outside, under the streetlight, Jayawarman VII looked like he'd closed his eyes in relief at the early-dinner ebbing of tourists. The cobblestones were wet. Since it hadn't rained, Darius's gaze ran along the pavement till he saw a green sprinkler truck lumbering toward the Boulevard de Sebastopol trailing a glittering bustle of spray.

The good friend was happy he'd made Alan chuckle. He let drop, "I'm a complete top. I wonder if that doesn't privilege my own inner experience over the beloved's? We're like two paintings, me and this kid from the Ardennes I'm seeing now, or at any rate our inner lives are. I'm representational, highly realistic, and he's an abstraction, messy—I don't know—de Kooning?"

Alan shrugged. "But the kid has to be a lot better looking."

The good friend smiled, pugnaciously immobile. Still staring at Alan, he took the tiny straw from his whiskey and stroked it dry. "Like de Kooning—or like nonsense. Like that ridiculous Colin Vail."

With a slight motion of his head, Alan looked to Darius for comment.

"I grew up sleeping in his bed," Darius explained. He laughed at how that sounded. "I mean, not with—"

The good friend's eyebrows flexed dismissively. "I'm going to the Vail *vernissage* in a couple of days," he interrupted. "So we'll see." He avoided argument, yielding to Kant's insight that judgments of taste are necessarily both universal and unjustifiable. Darius, who smiled submissively, understood that principle too. Therefore he and the good friend subtly hated each other.

They actually did meet that famous actress in the end. She was amazingly nice and tiny. Her inviting smile made everyone feel famous along with her. But the earlier part of the evening—with Alan and the good friend—had made more of an impression on Darius. It left him miserable for some reason, and prey to weird fantasies of violence. The fantasies didn't upset him. In the narrow case of violence, he had no trouble distinguishing the reality of the mind from the reality of the world. What was unexpected was so intense a rebellion against his settled self-image as a receding, masochist bottom. The fantasies felt like products of Oliver's sick imagination. He half-wondered whether a similar inner rebellion had been what drove Oliver mad.

23

OF COURSE, DARIUS had also gotten an invitation to the Vail *vernissage*. He didn't go. It wasn't about avoiding the good friend. The show was too important to him. He wanted to be alone with his master. Vail was someone in whose home he'd spent his whole life. Every time he entered or left it, he'd passed Vail's suicide spot and tried to figure out how it was done. He didn't want to suffer through a simpering evening of *Ça j'adore* and *voici les recoins de l'imaginaire étrangement évertés*.

In momentous solitude, he pushed at the gallery's glass door. The glassy reflected sky warped, but the door was locked. Darius frowned. He watched the swatch of sky wobble and still, blue enough to merit a sob of gratitude in other circumstances. Beyond the azure, a streaky shadow gestured at him. The door made a flatulent buzzing and Darius pushed it open. Cassie's gallerist friend wasn't there, only a well-dressed peon and an intense hush. The main room was filled with large, late Sam Francis paintings in screaming California colors. Darius thought he had the wrong gallery for a second. "Colleen Velle?" he asked the peon and was waved toward three smaller rooms.

Everything was there. A smile feathered his lips. He began with one of the six extant versions of *The Battle of Desires and Bitternesses*. This wasn't the one that had been meant for him. But it, too, was dusty and woebegone, especially in contrast to the gallery's spic-and-span whiteness. Blobs of glue showed. Corners of the cut-out magazine eyes along the pavilion interiors were unstuck and curling. The very shoddiness somehow added a tragic, human element that a critic had once insisted was missing from Vail's fantasies. One after another, the assemblages seemed to fit back into him like old pieces of himself, both necessary and useless.

He felt disappointment, too. Even before he'd finished looking, he sensed a purpose that had been driving him for a long time was now extinct. "Where do I go from here?" was the gist of it. Darius paused in the center of the third and largest room. He turned around. This room was full of drawings. A hygrograph sat on a white shelf. The pen had ceased recording on a roll of graph paper, its scratchy purple line about half complete. The cylinder had paused, or else the instrument was only there for show. The silence here was even deeper than it had been in the front room. Darius examined the hygrograph as if it were an unknown Vail work before glancing around him at the drawings again.

Over the years, Darius had become a bit of an expert on Vail. He knew the catalogue. He'd read all the books and articles. He looked down at the glossy page he'd taken from the peon's desk on his way in. Turning to the English side of it, he read that the drawings were from the "collection of a gentleman." There was no more information on them. If they were for sale, the prices weren't listed.

His slight confusion, the affront to his expertise, was the smallest part of the strange mental state Darius found himself in. As far as he knew, no Vail drawings existed. He frowned extravagantly. He thought the drawings were Vail-like at least. Several of them included small, skewed sketches of other works by Vail. Here was the early Madonna with Prell bottles and Mardi Gras beads which Darius had just looked at in the other room. Which he remembered from the basement in New Jersey. Here was a sketch of *The Battle of Desires and Bitternesses* from overhead. But recognizing bits and pieces didn't make Darius believe any of the drawings were authentic. He was positive they weren't.

He didn't know what to call his state of mind. Not *déjà vu*. He had no memory of the drawings. None at all. At the same time, he thought he'd seen them before. What's more—though memory still wasn't involved—he could pick out with some confidence—here, here, here, here, here—a typical spastic line in pencil, tiaras with clumsy lozenge-shaped jewels and circular pearls, several awkward princesses in hoop skirts, their hair worn in a sixties flip—things had been his own particular artistic specialty as a child. Darius himself had defaced or collaborated on these drawings. They must have come from the New Jersey house.

Disoriented, his body didn't seem to know what emotion it was going for. Doubting everything for a moment, his where-do-I-go-from-here hollowness returned along with anxiety that this whole journey to Paris was an oxbow in his life, an empty gesture, and that the true, unbearable pull on his life was coming from elsewhere. No, he was right. A workman must have taken them. Or Oliver. Stan? Not the housekeeper. Not Sohaila obviously. He remembered nothing.

Darius asked Rolf to come with him on a return visit to the show. Rolf was delighted to spend the day with his American friend. And when they got to the gallery, he was content to be watched closely as he examined the works on view. He smiled at Darius frequently, meaningfully, but said nothing about Vail or the work until he'd looked at everything. He sighed. "I'm asking myself, *Is it a young taste*? Some are still marvelous—the Madonna. But I'm a tiny bit let down. All of them together, they're somehow less than I'd hoped."

"What about the drawings?"

"Yes. I've never seen those. They're strange. Almost like Basquiat. You know how he always has those men wearing crowns. And they're sort of childish and disordered like him. But not as convincing."

Darius was about to tell Rolf about recognizing his own work. He knew it would sound deranged, and he wasn't sure he could convince Rolf that something was odd about the drawings. That Darius really had been involved. That they'd come from his basement. But the argument felt like too much trouble or too intimate a truth was involved. Anyway, he had no plans to expose the drawings, if they even needed to be exposed. Why would he? Instead, he retold Rolf about the bed and the basement and growing up with the afterimage of a suicide-by-hanging in his front hall. They strolled east along the quays, then up toward the Bastille along the wall of the great Caserne. Rolf said, for his part, he remembered nothing of Afghanistan but that his father had always talked about the fields of mustard. And hippies. And he said he wanted to go back to visit the Buddhas of Bamiyan.

Darius saw the Vail show once more before it ended. That evening he ate alone. Around one a.m., he found himself stir-crazy and unable to sleep in his room at the Moderne. So he went to Le Trap to stare at California porn videos looping on a monitor over the bar. Immobile, staring, he got drunk so slowly he didn't notice.

Le Trap was a backroom bar on rue Jacob. Almost a sex club initially, the place had become a relic with the advent of AIDS. For now it endured, though it would close within the year. This being Paris, the possibility of actual death may have amped up the intense and decadent erotic electricity of the place. Apologizing for his French, Darius chatted with several people. A bear in a harness was unexpectedly genteel. A handsome blond had a Marquis de Something about him. His pallid skin resembled wax run under a broiler briefly. The resulting slippage didn't look like age so much as melt. He was older but not *old.* He pinched Darius's nipple very hard, eliciting shocked laughter, which was somehow also cozy. Darius thought he asked the bear, *Can you believe this guy?* Maybe he shot him an appalled side-eye instead of using words. Anyway, the bear looked unhappy for him and wore a censorious expression. Darius frowned back aggressively, and patted the blond sadist on his back as if to say, *Don't worry about him, you're OK in my book.*

By three or four, when he set off for the Moderne, his brain wasn't functioning in the usual way. The drunkenness had gone underground in him. He felt almost sober, but in a very muddy way. He thought it might just be some momentous gassy belch building inside him. At first his thoughts wouldn't stop. He couldn't put a brake to his mind's harassing riot of imagery, the sort that can give anybody an intimation of insanity. For one thing, he wasn't sure whether he'd left Le Trap with the marquis or not. He'd intended to or wanted to or imagined doing so. But once he was on the street, the presence walking next to him didn't have the solidity of a person. He didn't think they were talking. His busy thoughts started going dark then restarting at full speed, which made it seem he was repeatedly waking up a little farther along on his walk. That was confusing. He was too nervous to turn to glance at his invisible companion. The *Marquis's* footsteps might have been his own, echoing on the stony, deserted streets.

In his room, he undressed and staggered. More moments pattered out of existence like the centimes that sprayed from his pockets when he dug out his keys and wallet. "Ding, ding, ding," he spoke for them, because they landed on carpet and hadn't made a peep. "Whoa, big guy!" He felt over-full as if he'd been eating foam. He found himself masturbating on the bed. He heard a voice repeating something, but that didn't make him stop in shame or cover up. His hearing was peculiar. That he could be unconscious, sexual, and sick simultaneously—triple-bodied like Geryon—fascinated him. His mind churned on. He rolled over on the bed as if pretending to be a couple. Almost without him noticing, sperm from one of his bodies arced out, the usual youthful explosion onto the chocolate curtains. The most comical of body fluids, it made great white clown tears. A glyphic thought, *sadness*, came to Darius as he stared at the tears. He mouthed, "I'm so aggrieved you're here."

The intermittent darknesses went on and on. Spent penis in his fist, he felt the last oozing of semen separate like salad dressing, the watery part trickling off his abdomen. Then darkness. He was unable to move. The marquis in his black T-shirt detached himself from the curtain. He was standing over Darius.

This had to be a waking REM state, Darius figured. He couldn't raise his arm or open his fist to take the Oscar statuette that the famous actress and Jayawarman VII were trying to hand him. It's heavy! Whoa, really incredibly heavy! REM state, maybe, but Darius also felt a sort of unconsciousness paradoxically keeping him from sleep. Perhaps he got his fingers to twitch like a half-crushed ant. He probably had a fever. He went dark again.

With the worst headache of his life, Darius awoke to an interior debate. He held himself impossibly still in the bed. The stillness was so perfect his body couldn't sense anything for certain. Feelings of illness or pain might be imaginary. He avoided deep breaths. But his heart raced. His thoughts toggled from one position to the other. No one had been with him in his room last night. Yes, the marquis really had been here and had—sort of—raped him. He remembered nothing. But then he argued to himself that he hadn't remembered the Vail drawings, and he certainly hadn't been drugged during his childhood. Eventually, when he allowed himself the first slight motion, sensations throughout his body forced him to abandon the innocent alternative. He was bitterly angry, overwhelmed by screaming anger as he pried himself from the bed and staggered to the commode to piss in clench-jawed silence. All grim resignation. He drank from the faucet until he regurgitated water and bile. He swore. After the toilet, the bidet, then the shower.

It so happened that Iran got into the World Cup that year. In exile, Reza Pahlavi published some palaver about the team's achievement in the *International Herald Tribune*. Darius showed the vacuous article to Rolf and said, more in sorrow than in anger, "They're not really a good family, you know. The Pahlavis. *Arrivistes*." He shrugged. He couldn't have been more transparent.

Darius noticed he'd begun to sound a touch bitchy or bitter sometimes. This darker shading of his manners didn't seem to have anything to do with his most recent aristocratic encounter with the marquis. Indeed Darius refused to search for interior transformation, or for possible deep feelings in himself at all.

With a repressed smile, Rolf indulged what he took to be Darius's New World snobbery about the Pahlavis. He concluded that Darius somehow felt his adoption made him inadequate. As a matter of irony, it now came out that Rolf was, properly speaking, the Graf von Hartzfeldt-Trachtenberg. (And that wasn't even the good side of the family.) His mother's Swabian ancestors had been Crusaders. Rolf's real name wasn't Rolf. It was Rudolfus. He kept all of this secret as part of his arduous effort to become orange.

Darius couldn't conceive of hating being a count, or a marquis for that matter. But he pretended to act embarrassed by his enthusiasm for aristocracy. Rolf cast him a jaded look and explained how obsequious grade school teachers had tried to drill into him the importance of his heritage. They chalked his full name and title across the blackboard for the whole class to read. His younger brother, in contrast, had terrorized fellow eight-year-olds with regal threats of torture or decapitation. "Rolf, honestly, that's probably healthier," Darius told him. "I bet I would have done the same."

Darius had been able to truss up the memory of rape in his mind. This wasn't entirely unlike extinguishing consciousness of Alan Wilkinson's rejection in New York. Of course, he was terrified for his health at first, until a blood test came out negative for HIV. And he supposed he was feeling the inevitable self-dislike. But the testing, the hatred, guilt and vengeful fantasies all transpired in perfect darkness, quarantined from the tick-tock of the world and, nearly, from personal awareness. But he no longer spent the occasional evening prowling the bowels of the mall at Les Halles for Arab hustlers as he'd done at first. He put an end to that life. He even indulged in a kind of Magdalene sobriety.

With rigor, he embraced fond daytime life with Rolf. Between them, a freshet of bright talk about art and politics burbled continually. Rolf took the liberal side. Darius liked the brutal, libertarian slant. As fascism was politics aestheticized, his libertarianism was politics made psychological. He wasn't thinking about the social contract. Or people's lives. Or other people.

Darius and Rolf's slashing critiques of art aligned much better. They started to see each other almost every day. The days themselves got longer. Sex, eventually, was pastel for Darius. More intense for Rolf, perhaps.

Rolf had finished his studies at the Beaux Arts. While Darius was content to drift, his friend made elaborate plans and junked them time and again. He wanted to leave Paris. He wanted to move to New York. With his thoughtless, tender availability, Darius was holding him back. Rolf's roommates, Roger-Pôl and Moktar, on the other hand, were goading him to leave if only to escape the drama of their tedious, ever-thwarted love affair. Moktar was straight. Roger-Pôl was a chivalrous fantasist.

An ocean apart from Sohaila and Stan and Oliver, Darius wasn't so far from them at all. He tolerated Sohaila's embarrassing construction that he was "trying to find himself." Real orphan though he was, the great cord of his life ran straight back, taut as ever, to Oliver and to Oliver's pot of gold and to the *Qajar* daydream, never sufficiently put to bed.

During his years in Paris, Darius tried the Cedar Street place by phone and by letter several times. He talked to his mother weekly. Sohaila began to doubt Oliver's fortune, a relief for her. "He never sees bankers. He has no office. You know what he's like. It doesn't seem plausible." But slowly, money started becoming a problem for her. The sums involved were large—insurance, taxes on the house, so it was hard to see trouble coming. The absurd warren of savings and checking accounts and money market funds in which she kept the money Oliver had settled on her was as difficult to navigate as ever, but happy discoveries were becoming rare. Unlike Sohaila, Stan didn't want to give up on the pursuit. His investigator claimed he'd unearthed filings on Mather Capital. So the firm at least existed.

Stan found work as a nurse/phlebotomist at a clinic for the blind. During one three-way call on Sohaila's birthday, he dominated the conversation. He'd discovered the key to the American work ethic, he said. "I think no other eastern European will understand this. It's sinister really. It's all about schizophrenia. You must act cheerful and humble, but you must also foster ruthlessness in your heart. Europeans naïvely think Americans really are naïve, but they're not. Nor are they exactly deceivers. What they are is *deliberately* insane."

24

THE FOLLOWING FALL, Stan called Darius and announced, with obscure laughter, that he was in Paris. He'd picked up his mother in Romania and brought her here to visit a specialist. She was ailing. The tourists had tapered off. Paris had a stretch of fine, warm fall weather to enjoy. Stan was oddly cagey about the hotel he and his mother were staying at ("a place of no character"), but he picked tony, two-star La Guirlande de Julie on Place des Vosges for dinner.

Stan intercepted Darius under the arcade where the restaurant had tables set up. It was the last gasp of summer before everything moved indoors. He looked scruffier than Darius remembered, more the wild-eyed revolutionary, not someone you'd want sticking you with needles unless you were blind. Black and gray hairs straggled down his hollow cheeks and throat as if the old Van Dyke had started to metastasize. After a fanatical smile of greeting, he confided, "I have serious news, Darius. But not for right away. Come."

"Stan!" Darius protested. The last thing he wanted was Carpathian drama. But he followed.

Despite the warmth, a strong wind was rising. Many of the diners who'd taken tables outdoors looked like they regretted it. Stan threaded his way through the crowd with absurd bows to strangers. Darius wondered whether his outgoing flourishes meant he was nervous. Once, Stan paused, leaned back and whispered loudly, "If you talk English, they think you're rich. We can behave as badly as we like." Darius had been in Paris long enough to know nearly all the diners around them spoke English. Half of them were probably well-behaved Americans.

"Shut up," Darius breathed. He was about to complain about the "serious news" tease, when Stan pointed to their table, the most tucked-away. A dowdy, grim-looking woman in a gray suit raised her eyes. Evidently Stan's mother. Her sharp-browed makeup job didn't fit her lumpish face. Nor did the too-tight suit fit her body. But she seemed to have a firm idea of how one turns oneself out in Paris. Her smile was mousey, dangerous, unfelt and vanished quickly after introductions had been pantomimed. She lowered her eyes. She patted one of the chairs. When Darius made a move toward it, her plump, pointy-fingered hand waved him away. Stan grinned in delight. "My mother," he announced to the restaurant at large and took the seat she'd reserved for him.

Stan seemed to find perverse pleasure in the awkwardness of his mother's presence. At the same time, he ignored her. He draped a pink napkin across his lap with giddy grandiosity. Chin up, he surveyed the crowd, though the other tables were largely blocked by one of the arcade piers. Whenever a strong gust of wind swept past, a general clattering arose as diners flinched to pin down linen, scarves, *l'addition* and hair.

Notwithstanding possible job-induced weight loss and red-rimmed eyes, Stan looked immensely satisfied. "A fancy-fancy place," he judged, rubbing thumb and fingertips together. "You see how I treat you, Darius? For you—anything!"

"Who knew you were so—" Darius began, in spite of himself. He held back for the old woman's sake, though it looked like she didn't speak English. His snarky tone of voice was a recent acquisition. Every time he heard it coming out of him, he wondered what disappointment was turning his manners so bitter.

"That I was so—?" Stan wondered, enjoying being needled and needling. "That such *largesse* runs in my veins?" He pronounced *largesse* with a strong French accent. "Darius, I do know one thing. I know that you think your mother and I are greedy. I know this. Principally, you think it of me!" Dramatically, he splayed the fingers of one hand across his shirtfront. "It's not true. I don't understand why Americans must always laugh when anyone dares to claim, *It's not about the money*. I have no idea of this, because—"

"Stan, do you think this is the right moment?"

Feigning to look around him for eavesdroppers, Stan leaned back expansively and went on. "Because it's never about money. How can it be? What's money? Money's nothing." His expression became kind for a moment. "I'll tell you something. Your mother loves your father. I have no worry saying this myself. Notice, I say *loves*, present tense."

"Stan, come on—"

"Of course, she did love him. Exotic, stern. You don't think of that, do you? That we of the exotic east could find the WASP exotic? But even now, she loves—"

"Stan, let's not talk about this right now." Darius looked pointedly at Stan's mother. Facetious though his tone was, all dark, half-swallowed vowels, Stan was serving up the only subject that mattered, the one Darius had tried to avoid all this time. Anything to do with his father had a premium reality that made the rest of his life look like a silly, dusty, glue-spotted Vail assemblage, or something equally airy-fairy.

Stan leaned across the table toward Darius. "She can't hear a word we say." His foreknuckle chucked her tenderly on a jowl. Her gaze wandered back to the table. Her unpleasant smile returned for a moment. Then she looked out at the park again with its chess-like array of pollarded trees. Only the far corner of the *Place* glowed with a farewell polygon of yellow sunlight. The old woman carefully pulled a gray lock from the corner of her mouth. "She's almost totally deaf. Especially in this wind." Stan smiled. To prove his point, he visibly tried to think of something appalling to say and came up with "vulva," which he pronounced loudly and distinctly. (That got a glance and raised eyebrows from an English-speaking diner.)

"All right. Then, what's the news?" Darius challenged him.

"No, Darius. This is too serious for right away," Stan replied, and he really did look serious. "Let us enjoy the fading glory of Western culture!"

"Fading? Paris has never been more beautiful or more put together. Everybody says it."

"You see. It's too much. It burns the most brightly at the very last moment. When all the fuel is spent."

The wind had blown a corner of the tablecloth over their butter plates and wine glasses. Tugging it back into place, Darius shrugged. "How's Mom?"

"As beautiful and as tender, as loving and—" Stan rhapsodized, looking at his own mother. She was watching the pollards, which shuddered like tuning forks as ochre dust devils ran among them. "You know, we went to Colorado, your mother and I. I saw a lovely thing. At this same hour, sunset, a doe disappearing—just walking, not running—dapple, dapple, dapple into a grove of aspen. I said, *That deer reminds me of you, dear.* She's always so lovely and elusive, your mother. Never alarm, never loss of dignity. Though she has been very wounded—more than you can know by—ah, well."

He talked all through dinner. But he didn't return to Sohaila or Oliver. As each dish was served, he took one studious, supercritical bite. He did the same with Darius's dishes, and with his mother's for whom he'd ordered. But after the one bite, he devoured everything on his plate with happy *gourmandise*. Still, he talked, assaulting the table with emphatic fingers and elbows. The table kept tipping.

Darius kept a footman-like eye on everything. He saved a Bordeaux glass when the wind nearly toppled it. He tried to keep the flouncing tablecloth in order with his hands and knees. The wind had gotten much worse. One party relocated inside, and others were hurrying to finish. Great helices of dust, as tall as the trees, rose from the park's earthen walkways. At the same time an unusual smattering of stars had come out in the almost ultramarine darkness directly overhead.

As Stan talked on and on, Darius was irritated by what seemed Stan's chattering obliviousness to Place des Vosges, Paris, himself, the whole world. But he finally caught the Romanian's eyes and realized Stan was actually observing—silently, as it were—even while he was emitting great plumes of speech to rival the plumes of dust in the park. Stan was smiling at Darius as if he knew all about the boy's martyred self-control, knees pinning the tablecloth, a toe against the tipping table leg. Stan became even more uproarious and needling. He didn't seem to mean any of it unkindly.

Stan came back to the eternal subject, pouting into the dregs of his Graves. "Your father is a remarkable man, do you know this?" His knife went vertical. "I have a theory. My theory is that Oliver began to lose his mind on purpose. On purpose! Then later, sadly, it got away from him. On purpose. Why would he do this? Because he was a searcher. As you are. Searching for—mmm—meaning, basic things, all that. His life had no needs or desires. It lacked them so completely, his only option was to begin thinking boldly in outlandish ways. To look where no one would look. *Ta-da*! It sounds banal. Almost, but it isn't."

Darius listened, his toe flexing against the table leg. He didn't interrupt. The old facetious smile flickered but Stan was sincere about his theory. This was the man who'd given Darius a print of the *Pollice Verso* gladiators with a big wink when Darius was still a boy. He wasn't as clueless as Sohaila and Oliver were. It was worth listening.

"And, according to my theory, this is why he had to have flyers, always flyers, from everywhere. Was he looking for a deal? Of course not. No. Nothing to do with that. The question is—why not books, properly issued by the publishing companies? Or newspapers, which madmen especially love? Why not? No. They couldn't be books or newspapers. Nothing from the normal world would work for him. They had to be flyers and handouts, because flyers come from below, from outside the system. You see? He would take the flyers looking for secret, crazy messages from outside."

"And what was he looking for—*d'après toi?*" Darius asked. His discomfort came out as affectation.

"The craziness! It's not obvious? Of course it is. Darius, your father was never permitted to be a human being. He was identical to his money, and money has the lowest entropy of anything. He needed to do things, explode, spread out. Spend! But the only way he saw to do it was by becoming crazy. Where do you think all that money came from?"

"His grandfather."

"Correct. And even before that, there were Dutchmen in Albany doing whatever it is that Dutchmen do with beavers. (Dutchmen have the lowest entropy of any modern people, you know, Darius, except for Finns.) Funny—is it not?—to think your money, ultimately, had its source in the *beaver*. All of us have our source in beaver." He glanced sadly at his mother. "But you—whose money came from beaver—well, you probably came from beaver, too, like the rest of us. But because you're adopted, we can't say this for sure. Not one hundred percent. Is that distasteful? If so, I'm sorry. But, yes, it was the grandfather capitalist who made his gilded age pile of money. By the time Oliver came along, what was there? No beavers, no herds, no railroads, no farms, no factories, nothing but stocks and bonds. Everything had been reduced. Low entropy! So what did poor little rich boy Oliver have in the end? This fantastic potentiality was all he had, all he ever knew. Rich Americans are the saddest of all. His life is waiting to happen, but like all Americans, he must snigger at every unreality except unreal money. He is in a loop! This sniggering, by the way, is true even of nice Christian Americans, because they, with the usual schizo American insanity, have more faith in money than in God! It is why we simpleton Europeans are far more religious! We don't go to church, because it actually matters to us—like children!—that there's no God. But! Darius. As unhappy and—I'm sorry—pathetic as he is, your father is, or was, in a small way, a brilliant man. Because he was a sniggering American, and yet he wanted to turn his money into something through his craziness. This, I'm afraid, was not possible for him. Even though he had this great insight, a truly great insight, it wasn't possible. We are all so weak in the end, no? Even you."

Darius refused to buy into any of this. He tried a smart-alecky retort, but his voice surprised him when it came out, tremulous, almost whining, "All the same, you and Mom seem pretty interested in money. For something you think is unreal. I'm not accusing, but—"

Stan smiled. Barely ironical, certainly not offended. "That's the money in you talking, Darius. You'll have to be very careful,

I think. *Snigger, snigger,* I hear it. You decided to come here to run away from it all, exactly like Oliver trying to go crazy. Maybe it will work in your case. I don't know." He heaved a great sigh and pinched at a leaf fragment the wind had gusted into his water glass. Darius batted a corner of the tablecloth back between his knees. "But sadly, Darius, none of us will last. So even our deepest thoughts are just scribbles. I know this because a bacterium is being genetically engineered, or perhaps it already has been—nanotechnology, you know?—and it will be released, and—it's rather simple—this entire planet will turn to sludge. All this dust made me think of it. I read a book by a great expert, Eric Drexler."

The change of subject was so abrupt, Darius thought Stan was setting up a joke.

But Stan insisted. "Yes, yes, yes. Say, they've finally made the bacterium to eat oil spills, to clean them up, but very soon, what will they eat? All carbon? Poof! Exponential reproduction, and within days the entire biosphere will become like—what?—like ash, phlegm? I don't know. Just a nothingness, no people, no animals, trees, plants, fungi. Poof. It may have started this morning. I'm not sure."

Stan didn't try to make his absurd vision of imminent doom seem plausible, or even arguable. So Darius laughed. "You sound almost like Dad talking about poison gas or something, Stan. Happy Armageddon! I like the concept. We're going to be overrun with man-eating bacteria in a few days." Chuckling, he imagined aloud the headlines, "*Infection Earth! Y2K a blip next to this!*"

"Darius," Stan said rather quietly. Darius didn't notice at once that—stranger and stranger—the Romanian was hurt or angry. "I know you think Bucharest is backwards. And I'm a histrionic Slav. But I'm almost a scientist—nurse. You don't believe my story? Yes, the bacterium is out there. Yes, it will eat up the world. I'm a serious person. I know this."

"*Eat up the world?* Stan, I'm sorry. Listen to yourself."

Sighing, acting very much defeated, Stan took out his credit card. "*Snigger, snigger!* You have no awe."

Darius batted down the tablecloth again, blinking and rubbing his eyes when he was spritzed by dust. He had a slightly wobbly sensation in his chest, which he sometimes got when he thought he may have won an argument but wasn't entirely sure he was right. He was convinced by now that the "serious news" Stan had to impart had never existed. Another of Stan's manipulative fantasies.

Darius felt a wave of pity for the man, watching him help his mother rise with ragged dignity. The only diners remaining were sheltering behind an arcade pier. The table itself lurched and clattered. A waiter hurried over, made their flapping tablecloth into a sack and carried all their dishes away together. Stan's mother held her lapels, her hair, her hem against the wind.

Orienting himself with one pointing arm like a scarecrow, Stan judged his hotel was straight across the park in the direction of Bastille. Halfway into the square's rising windstorm, it occurred to him that he'd forgotten his credit card. He twined his mother's arm around Darius's, squeezed them both and waved them across the park. He said he'd catch up. He had to raise his voice.

The old woman pressed her bosom against Darius for a moment, but as soon as Stan was gone, she disengaged, pointlessly dusted her suit, shielded her eyes and tottered forward, her palms warding Darius off as they had before.

The wind was so strong now, Darius was alarmed for her. Occasional gusts gave him a hint of weightlessness. Gigantic whorl after whorl of dust rose into a yellowish fog, all the more impenetrable because it was dark now. Only the floodlit mansards of the Pavillon de la Reine—or was it du Roi?—were visible above the layer of dust. And a few wan stars remained at the sky's zenith. Darius kept having to shut his eyes against the dust. Head lowered, the old woman staggered off at her own azimuth. His eyes reopening with a fluttering squint, Darius realized Stan's mother had disappeared.

His heart pounded. He hurried a step or two forward. He scanned the ground all around in case she'd fallen. The first figure he made out in the cloud was gangly Stan. The dust clogged his beard, so he looked red-haired like Odysseus. He had to shout to be heard above the wind. "What, have you lost my mother?"

Darius yelled *No* but started calling, "*Madame Constantinescu!*"

Stan hit him on the shoulder. "Don't be an idiot," he yelled, pointing at his ear. "This is like a sandstorm," he complained, trying to stay calm. "Why did you let go of her? She isn't well." Stan was turning his head, and Darius saw, or imagined he saw, not fear, but wild love. Something he hadn't expected from Stan.

It was a relief to Darius that he spotted her first. She was sitting on the edge of the fountain, looking like a statue, her suit reddening to the color of sandstone. Her jacket was pulled up over her hair, and her hand was making its only gesture, not warding them off but the opposite, this time.

Not long after rescuing her, Darius waited downstairs in an unpleasantly cozy hotel lobby while Stan got his mother settled in bed. The lobby was really too small for the meticulous clerk to ignore Darius politely, but he did so anyway. Darius examined a huge engraving of *The Tennis Court Oath* (the unclothed version). The wind hurled bits of this and that against the windows. Curtains resembling old candlewick bedspreads had been pulled closed.

Stan loped in and apologized, sounding more natural than he had all night. "I'm sorry about her. She's not well. Before, it was blood cancer, now the start of pancreatic cancer, I'm afraid. So, yes, what can we—? I know it was tedious. I really did want to see you and not just to be carrying a message." His stare took on a touch of his usual Slavic irony. "I have no dislike at all for your lifestyle, you know."

"I know, Stan."

The room was so small that once Stan took a seat, he could easily drum his fingers on Darius's knees. He actually did this as a sort of flirtatious prelude to business. He then leaned back and crumpled his dusty beard into his shirtfront. "It's not quite an emergency. He's fine. Well, I think he's not exactly fine—I mean, other than the mind, which is obviously not fine. I think he may have—I'm not sure what. No more than bruises probably. That's all beside the point."

"He was in an accident."

"No," Stan said crisply. "Let's say, for him, he's fine. Which is—he's back in that disgusting hole he lives in downtown."

"But it's a huge place. I thought it seemed clean enough. And safe, I guess."

Stan eyed him skeptically. "Darius, did you notice he's blacked out the windows?"

Darius tried to remember. "I think the shutters were closed. He hasn't *blacked them out*."

"Darius, what is it—oilcloth? Or what photographers used to use. I don't know. He's blacked them out."

"You were there?"

"Ah yes. That's why I have to talk with you. This is the news. Your father got into very serious trouble. He was arrested. And before you—" his hand made a blessing to silence the boy. "You weren't told, because we didn't know until the whole thing was over. So why have a phone call? I was coming over to visit, and blah, blah, blah."

His breath shuddering, Darius said, "OK. You say he's fine."

"Fine. Yes. Here is what happened. Your father—this is interesting—it seems he did leave his apartment every so often. Maybe to conduct business. Who knew? I've figured out that he can take the C or the A train to Penn and then Amtrak to Philadelphia where the family bank moved. Easy, so who knows? Anyway, after making one of his mysterious trips, he is returning on the C or A train to his hole. I can't remember which line it was. C, perhaps. About his mysterious business, I make no comment." He shrugged, dropping a long, meaningful look. "He is coming home on the C train, let us say. And there is a young woman standing next to him, wearing tights, I believe, and some Tarzan/Jane bit of suede that passes for a skirt. So the madman—I'm sorry—but the madman Oliver is sitting here below her." Stan's head tipped to the left, his chin still resting on his shirtfront. His eyes rolled up to the paired tulip-glass shades of a sconce on the wall over Darius' head. "And God knows what's in that man's mind! He reaches out and grabs her—very aggressively, I understand—between the legs. This—in his defense—I can almost understand, because if one is heterosexual, you understand, this area, this little mound with vulva is insanely ergonomic for the hand. And yet, obviously, it's forbidden. The girl, dressed like that—not to be anti-feminist—is not at all shy about screeching and making such a commotion that the brute stockbrokers on all sides assault Oliver and drag him from the car at the next stop. Which is City Hall or very close. And from there, police headquarters. And from there—I don't know—the Tombs, probably, also very close down there. You see?"

"He was in jail?" Darius closed his eyes.

"He was in jail. The whole intake procedure. One of them even makes the famous one phone call *for* him. Lucky for Oliver he has a very evil lawyer friend who jumps on top of them and is able to get him home the next day. All during this fiasco, incidentally, I think no one realized what they had in Oliver—a mysterious WASP zillionaire with his nutty subway trips on unknown business."

"First of all, if it's who I think it is, his lawyer isn't evil. He's great. He's loyal and he's a very decent—"

Stan's gaze finally fell. "Perhaps. I thought he was utterly heartless—"

"Stan. He's not. He was great to me."

"Whatever. I think you have too boundless a liking for men, maybe. I thought him a skunk, false, grinning. But he performed his machinations very well indeed, and the affronted woman dropped charges. I'm certain a lot of money was involved. Also certain that she had very weak lawyers on her side for them not to discover who Oliver was and go after him in court seeking much, much more. If it had come to a trial, the whole thing—also for your mother—would have broken open, because I'm fairly sure the issue of competence would have come up. This is something the divorced wife cannot think about. Though the son, perhaps—"

"You think I should try to get him declared incompetent?"

"No. I don't say. He *is* incompetent, this we all know. But to be declared? I don't say. I'm not at all sure, for one thing, if that would solve the problem for Sohaila. Would it be retroactive to the time of the divorce or before? I don't think so. It could make things harder for her."

"Do you think she's ready to sue on her own account?"

"No. She's only nervous and sad. I would like it, as you know."

"Jesus. What are you suggesting I do?"

"Darius." He smiled. "I'm not. I'm the messenger. You have to be told about this. I don't know what your interests are, so I couldn't say."

Darius wasn't prepared for Stan not to be manipulative. "Just off the top of your head. Really. What do you think?"

"You could go home. You could—do the opposite, vanish, go off on your own. Ignore us all. You could—" Stan's expression of thought turned into a shrug. "I don't know." He shook his head.

"Are you avoiding recommending anything because of some legal—I don't know—caution about the future? *Your* future?" Darius couldn't believe how harsh he sounded. He hadn't meant anything so accusatory to come out. The look of suspicion, almost fear, he could feel on his face, made it seem his most primitive nature had risen to the surface—as if he were just waking up again, enraged, after his night with the *Marquis*.

Stan couldn't help but smile gently. "No, Darius. No, Darius. Think of *your* future. You're steeped—*steeped*—in this idea of money."

Even angrier, his voice rising unselfconsciously, Darius blurted out, "Stan, you're the one who's been fighting for it! What have I done? I'm telling you, I've never given a shit about all that." He almost panted. "Seriously. Practically. What would you do?"

"I'm not playing a game, Darius. I'm not like you. What I would do in your place—what does it matter? You're not me. I'm not you."

"Just tell me."

"No," Stan clucked with perfect poise. Again, not unkindly. "No."

To Rolf, they had become a couple. More or less. To Darius, not quite. He was conscious of sheltering with Rolf from everything the *Marquis* or Oliver represented. Rolf wanted to move to

New York, but he also wanted to be near Darius, and for a long time he'd put his life on pause. He sometimes raised the possibility of them going together. His friend, Severine, had a Manhattan apartment she was willing to sublet to them. Soon after his evening with Stan, Darius finally consented. That is, he consented in his heart. He said nothing to Rolf at first, but the decision had been made, instantaneously and in perfect secrecy. He would go back to New York. For several days he seemed to hold Rolf's future in his hands, a power that should have filled him with guilt, whether or not it was the future Rolf most desired.

The millennium New Year came a few months later. It seemed like it should be celebrated in a particularly memorable way. Rolf invited Darius, his roommates, Severine and two of her sporty American girlfriends to spend the holiday in Switzerland at his family *rustico*, which turned out to be several of them—old stone shepherds' huts—on the narrow terraces of the country's wild but ultra-cultivated crags. The huts had been joined together and remodeled in the fifties. A pool had been put in. Far below, Lago Maggiore twisted out of sight between other tremendous mountains, which condensed into existence every morning and dissipated every night.

The place had its own, odd high-altitude season of hot, almost microwave, sunlight and frigid shadow. While it was warm enough to eat outside bundled in a sweater, under the table your hands went numb. The daytime gibbous moon was an icy filigree, its *maria* the same pale blue-gray as the sky.

On December twenty-ninth, they were snowbound. The dizzying mountain switchbacks were impassable under several feet of snow. Even the Swiss would be hard-pressed to clear it for a day or two. In high spirits, a group of them headed down the mountain in the morning and returned at dusk with food and a magnum of Champagne bearing the festive label, "*Édition Deux Mille.*"

Roger-Pôl's friend, Moktar, though he was barely twenty, was an important figure in Mauritanian exile politics. He had to answer his cell phone constantly, coughing out the inevitable invocation to Allah before settling down to political conspiracy. Darius enjoyed the atmosphere of intrigue.

On the second snowbound day, the Mauritanian made them tea with elaborate ceremony. He confessed his goals: to abolish slavery in his country, to establish true democracy there, to become the president. With lovely, unnecessary motion, his slender fingers fussed over little juice glasses of tea. This Saharan tea ceremony was taking place in Heidi's own inglenook in the Alps, while on the terrace outside, next to the tarped, kidney-shaped pool, Severine and her two girlfriends shrieked as they built a sexually explicit snowman. The futuristic jumble of people and cultures felt melancholy like a Sade song.

Despite his straightness, Moktar barely deigned to notice the girls. Perhaps he'd had problems with women ever since his father, the king, had introduced him to sex with a slave when he was twelve years old.

Even the tea ceremony was interrupted by a phone call. Moktar had been waiting all weekend to hear from Doha for a live interview with *Al Jazeera*. Those elegant fingers propped the cell phone to his ear: "*Wa ʿalaykumu s-salam.*" He bowed to the tea drinkers, withdrawing to another room.

Darius, although his *Qajar* connection was imaginary, was giddy with all the aristocracy bouncing around the *rustico*. He looked a little dreamy after Prince Moktar had gone. He smiled at Count Rudolfus, who frowned back suspiciously but maintained his perfect, impenetrable manners.

When the German talked politics or had his late morning Bloody Mary, he could become exuberant, overbearing even, until the flicker of manners came over him. Then, a sad or frustrated caution showed in his eyes. Darius wondered whether the inhibition was just post-1945 Germanness. Like a lot of Germans of his generation, Rolf claimed he wasn't very German at all. But he had a streak of the national literal-mindedness, a Teutonic slowness to grasp silly fun (which is as tender when it's tender as it is scary when it's scary).

Darius decided it was being an aristocrat that caused Rolf's restraint. If such a thing as good breeding could last from the Crusades to now and still matter, still be noticeable, however faintly, it almost made you believe in eternity. Always a welcome belief for Darius. The most welcome one.

When the Count smiled drily, as he did when Prince Moktar bowed to them, the sharp corners of his wide mouth curled up in an expression that was—though you didn't recognize it at once because Rolf didn't *have* those traits—arrogant, even cruel. Perhaps the traits were fossilized in him. Part of the allure of his kindliness was an ancestral capability to become a monster.

Darius and Rolf had decided to feed the apple scraps from last night's *tarte tatin* to a neighbor's dwarf goats in a barn several terraces down. When they got there, they had to elbow aside an aggressive alpaca so the bleating, shaggy dwarves trotting in excited circles could get their fair share of brown apple skins. Rolf hugged the alpaca, immobilizing it while the dwarves finished eating. With a Count's hard-to-recognize bashfulness—it looked like severity toward the alpaca—Rolf brought up the issue of his future. He admitted, "I have this slight *Departure from Cythera* depression about it, but—" He released the animal and straightened.

"Meaning Cythera is like childishness, childish things?"

"I don't think I've been childish during my time in Paris," Rolf countered with dignity.

"I'm probably thinking more of my own case," Darius appeased—honestly, as it happened.

"But I don't think I want to hold off leaving any longer."

"I get it. Even for me, I see how this is the perfect moment. All of our information is going to get erased, right? Y2K," he added with weak irony. "A fresh start."

"You might be finished here yourself, then? You would go back?" Hardly breathing, Rolf tacked on, "I wonder?"

"My father—"

With repressed eagerness Rolf interrupted. He mentioned Severine's news about the Manhattan loft. She was now being sued by the landlord, who wanted to get rid of all the tenants and renovate the building. But New York had loft laws. A *pro bono* artist's attorney had tied the whole thing up for a year at least. After that, going to New York wouldn't be as easy. And a U.N. opportunity Rolf's father had lined up wouldn't last forever. So perhaps as a temporary arrangement? Darius smiled and reached up to touch Rolf's shoulder. He had already decided, of course. He knew Severine's loft was a mere few blocks from Oliver's "hole" on Cedar Street.

On December thirty-first, a neighbor's son came to plough the drive, tires jangling with chains, Eminem blasting from the cab. That night they broke out the magnum of champagne. In sweaters, overcoats, holding flutes in gloved hands, they waited for midnight on the terrace, drunkenly warm, eyes weeping from the cold. At the all-important millennium, fireworks piddled from several spots in the mountains and along the black lake, which reflected the glittering, languorously collapsing trails of sparks.

Church bells started ringing along the valley in glorious relay. This was as spectacular as the fireworks had been sad. The obvious accents of eternity, not faith, exactly, but the gesture of it, could be heard in the broken, wiry-sounding notes and in the imagined creak of timber leaping through the icy air before the laggard bass tones came rolling on. At the brink of heaven up there, at the ragged margin of the world amid romantic crags, everything seemed lovely and eternal to Darius. But part of his weeping pleasure—this was clear even to him—was in not being alone, or in being as close as he could get to not being alone. The mountain and the bells were poignantly beautiful, and—He shivered under his heavy coat.

PART THREE

25

JEANETTE PAUL WORE a point-hemmed black smock top and black stretch pants. She clickety-clicked auburn-painted nails on the fake stick shift. She recognized her beast of an emotion through the behavior of other drivers. After getting on the New Jersey Turnpike, she was thrown into a nervous rage by the flashy lane-changing of drug dealers or party-bound off-duty lawyers or whoever they were, speeding toward the Holland Tunnel and Manhattan on a Saturday afternoon. She slowed on purpose, forcing faster cars to pass. Annoyed heads turned when they passed her. Her dog-in-the-manger pokiness didn't seem to fit with the character of her car, which was black with a large spoiler and a huge red bird of prey painted on the hood.

Jeanette could make out the jets lined up to land at Newark. Loosely strung diamonds, they wavered in the hot air sheeting from below. The queue shelved north and ever higher over a ground-hugging pumpkin haze. Only the closest diamonds were visibly jets, ghostly except for their quavering lights, which became double, quadruple as they neared. They seemed too tiny and transitory to be carrying passengers inside, passengers craning their necks, nervously flexing their thighs at the jolting of screw gears, chewing gum, putting sneakers back on, wishing they'd peed. Least of all could Jeanette connect her son, Barry, to one of these serene celestial flickers. As he had last time, Barry would hitch up his yokel backpack and come clomping out of the gate as if popping out of immateriality. No drama of absence. Simply expecting her to be there as if this was the first day of kindergarten. No awareness that she may have wanted to get picked up at the airport herself once or twice during the years he'd been out West.

She argued this way in her mind for the sake of argument, because in truth, she didn't want Barry returning at all just now. She didn't make that point, however. Even in her own mind, she didn't want to sound like an unworthy mother.

Making an effort to put herself in a better frame of mind, she allowed she was curious to see what Barry looked like since the last time, almost three years ago. Her own look had changed recently. Her hair was cropped in a cresting brush that trailed down the nape of her neck—shades of "glam punk" her hairdresser had—she hoped—joked. And she'd let her hair color evolve from blonde toward ash.

The vast terminal was teeming, but Jeanette's eyes were drawn to her son at once. He couldn't have been on any of the planes she'd seen. He'd been waiting here for a while, feet propped up on the same grubby yellow backpack he'd had three years ago. The sudden meeting, almost involuntary, made gates and flight numbers and arrival times look like over-cautious protocols. Fate got the job done with a shrug. A good thing, too, since Jeanette had obviously gotten the arrival time wrong.

Barry wore a green knit skull cap and a choker of what looked, to Jeanette, like a lizard's vertebrae. He made an easy-going karate chop of a wave. His feet rose, and he bucked out of the chair. Their facial muscles tweaked uncertainly.

"What's this look?" Jeanette asked, annoyed by her nerves.

"Me?"

"Yeah, yeah, all this," her hand butterflied around him—old, tissue paper T-shirt, the choker, the skull cap.

"I don't know. Just clothes. A look." He shrugged, smiling, looking at her just as intently.

She noticed unclean pores, a messy smattering of whiskers, a few fine wrinkles already. "Do you have any hair under that?" she demanded.

"Nope." He tipped it up for her to see the stubble.

"Well, I guess I know why you did that. Afraid I was going to drag you off to Philippe first thing." Philippe was her old colorist. "I'm sure everything I did when you were a kid traumatized you. Anyway, *Hello.*" She hugged him gingerly.

"I haven't had hair for a long time. Yours looks good, though. Sort of a wild look for you. Like Bowie."

Jeanette clasped her hands tightly to keep herself from touching the ash blonde brush in self-consciousness. "Mm," she said, instead of *Thank you.*

The car made Barry laugh. "Very wild, Mom! I'm impressed. You're driving a Firebird. You're going to end up turning into a biker chick, I bet."

She had to laugh with him. "It's what they had. Some kid was in love with it and couldn't get the money together. For me, it was cheap. I figure I saved his life."

"Can I drive it?"

"No, you can't. Ever heard of insurance?"

He could tell she was nervous, because she launched into her plans right away. She warned him the house was a mess. She hadn't had time to make up his old room. Even the bed had been disassembled. They could stop now for a quick bite, but as far as dinner was concerned, he was on his own. She was busy with something that evening. Neither of them mentioned Lynn. They'd get to that later.

The conversation stalled. Jeanette was going to mention the heat, abating that day, but the weather cliché felt too pathetic. "Is this some ghetto Muslim thing you're into with the no hair and the hat?" she asked instead.

"I hadn't thought about it that way." He'd taken an old tobacco pouch from his pocket. He stripped a rubber band from it, which he cat's-cradled on one hand. Dirty nails. He opened the pouch on his lap. His forefinger nuzzled what appeared to be twigs and trinkets inside. He removed something from the collection and palmed it. He plucked out his dog-eared boarding pass and tossed it on the dashboard. He gave the bag of baubles another stir before double-banding it again. His monkey-like self-preoccupation irritated Jeanette, but she forced herself not to ask what he was doing.

Furthermore, Jeanette noticed that she didn't want to hear what Barry was doing in a larger sense—girlfriend, place of residence, job, if any, travel. She had to wonder if that was envy, a despicable thing in a mother. But how could she take pride in a life she was hardly allowed into?

They pulled off the highway at the Cheesequake rest stop for a quick bite. "You mind?" Barry dangled his tobacco pouch after they got out of the car. With ill grace, Jeanette opened the trunk so he could secrete the bag in his yellow backpack.

The trunk thudded shut. "Barry!"

He cocked his head at the sighing pulse of traffic or at the hot murmur of insects. He had a beatific grunginess about him. "Weird to be back here again," he commented. Over the years he'd started to sound a little Western. He spoke with a snowboarder's drawl, childish, enunciation whispery, the quizzical vowels prolonged.

"Barry!" Jeanette repeated. "I can't stand your belt that way. Could you possibly change it? And yes, I know this place is awful. For a nature boy like you." She flipped her hand at the characterless Cheesequake rest stop and parking lots. In a burst of resentment, she narrowed her eyes. "And don't think I'm some suburban New Jersey vulgarian. I know what this place is like. It's just easy."

"This is fine."

Jeanette looked around her sourly as if the place really wasn't fine. Not at all. It goes without saying the rest stop looked poorly maintained and cheap. Jeanette felt she was staring at the manipulative corporate mind behind it all, not at the blah design or the décor. The sickly landscaping had an air of stinginess and inattention.

Barry wasn't sensitive in the same way. He indulged his mother patiently. "What's wrong with my belt?"

"Barry, you've got it threaded under the label thingy, and you missed a loop, too. But mainly I hate that look—the belt running under the Levi's label. It's nerdy."

"What do you want me to do?"

"Maybe you could take it off and do it right."

"Here?" He shrugged. He unbuckled the belt and whipped it off. Butt turned toward Jeanette so she could supervise, he put the belt back on.

"Thank you, thank you," she said, greatly relieved. As they entered the rest stop, she muttered, "When I used to be in charge of dressing you, you always looked so nice and neat. But I got palpitations every time we stopped here and you wanted to pee—because of all the fags loitering outside the—my God, they're still here!"

Booth-like fast food outlets and souvenir shops encircled a pen of tables. A colossal chattering and clinking and cash register noise filled the space. Jeanette and Barry carried trays to the one empty table. Even Barry felt a little defeated by mass marketing. Jeanette told her son that eating fast food always made her fall asleep, so if she dozed and crashed and died and he was left crippled, she wanted to be sure he sued Burger King.

"All right, let's get something straight," she began a little later, looking past Barry's shoulder, still shaking her head at the hoi polloi, at America. "You don't really know the situation here. You fly in, and I'm sure you're thinking I'm not giving dear old dad all the loving kindness he deserves as he fades into the sunset. It's a cute way of thinking about it, but it's not what's going on. Lynn—which people never, *ever*, see—is a true prick. He's always been more like a cat than a husband. He sits in the sun doing not a thing and God only knows what's on his mind. That was even before he turned into a drunk. And now that he's quit drinking, it's even worse, believe it or not." She turned over the cunning cardboard "large fries" sleeve in one hand, wondering at the design super-mind behind it. "I mean, I don't even know why you bothered to come. It's not like now is a particularly dire moment. Although—" She smiled. "You know, I *do* know why. I bet you think I wouldn't tell you when the time came. But that's your own fault. If I had a sure way of getting in touch with you. As it is, at present, I'm worried you're going to get in the way more than anything."

"I wanted to see him. Spend a little time with him."

"What was it, three years ago?—you were here for two weeks, then *poof*!" Her auburn nails flicked at several unused, double-barreled salt packets. One of them skated off the table into Barry's lap.

Putting the salt packet back on the table, he said, "We weren't getting along."

Jeanette noticed that Barry had placed a lustrous black pebble on the table. This was the object he'd taken from his tobacco pouch. She looked at it a moment, making no comment. Then she said, "You can't just hang around the house. I promise you, it's not me. It's him. He likes it to be as quiet as the grave. He's got this perfectly deadly routine. Anything upsets it, and he starts to whine to me. Which he always has, but it's much worse. You never got that. No one did except me. I was always the garbage bin for his self-pity. I almost wish he *would* start drinking again."

"Mom. But I'll help."

"Right. Right. Whatever. All right. How long were you thinking of staying?"

"A long time this time. Right through. Probably as long as—you know. That's what I thought."

"Yeah, that's what you were threatening when you called. But, you know, you're going to have to find a place. And a job, too. There's absolutely no money."

"OK," he said.

He said it so readily she snorted. "You have no idea."

"Maybe it could be cool for you too, Mom. Think of that? Like, lighten the load."

"Yeah, that would be cool. Twenty years ago, it would be cool. The thing I can't figure out is what the hell you're going to do. Job-wise."

"I can always find something. Tree surgeon."

She laughed and mouthed, "You idiot," and he grinned back at her.

"You'll see. You'll be happy somebody's around," he said. "I can tell you haven't talked to anybody all day. You don't probably talk to anybody ever."

"There, you're wrong. I do happen to have somebody. I know I need support—of course I do—and I've found it."

"A guy?" Barry asked matter-of-factly.

The question made Jeanette pause. Not for the reason you'd expect. She suppressed her instantaneous reaction in order to think for a moment. She appeared to be weighing *Yes* and *No* as answers, regardless of which one was true—the way a storyteller might. But she also wondered whether Barry's question was just condescending twenty-six-year-old flattery, as if she couldn't really find a man. Less scornfully than she might have, she said, "No. It's not a man. It's sort of a group. But I'd rather not get into it right away."

"OK. Sounds cool, though."

During this exchange, Jeanette had been fussing with the garbage on the table. Aligning the diminutive orange trays, unsticking the paper placemats glued to the trays with blots of Coke, riffling a wad of napkins, feeding a spiral of drinking straw wrapper into a crispy chicken sandwich clamshell. Mainly she seemed to be adjusting things so she could jostle the black pebble without it appearing obvious. Moving the clamshell caused the pebble to wobble. Yanking the stuck placemat caused it to revolve once. The pebble then disappeared entirely under the wad of napkins. It reappeared, wobbling, when Barry took the napkins off and stuffed them into an empty bag. "Is there anything I should particularly know?" he wondered. "Special news or—or information?"

"What about?"

"About Dad."

"What do you mean? About his medical condition? What's there to know? He's got cancer. You might stick a finger up your own butt when the time comes."

"That's not what I meant. More like results and—prognosis and stuff. I guess you're right. I don't know how this works. It just makes me sad."

"Hmmmm," Jeanette vocalized. The humming was meant to obliterate Barry's too naked remark. Eyes screwed almost closed at the pebble, lips compressed like a twist of candy wrapper, she said, "Of course, it *is* sad. But it's not romantic sad like you're probably thinking. That's a very common mistake. People are actually mean and disgraceful and badly behaved when they're, you know, near the end. What I should really do—" By a subtle degree her tone became lighter. "What I should really do is poison him. Don't you think? I fix all his food. I could do it little by little, so it wouldn't look any different from the drugs they've got him on. He really doesn't need to live any longer. How much sitting in the sun does one person need to do? It would certainly be convenient for me. I think there's some minuscule old insurance policy. That would really be more than he's ever done for me."

Barry believed she was joking, but he said somberly, "I don't think you should do that. Could be bad for the soul even to talk about it."

"But Barry," she said, more broadly now. "This is obviously why I don't want you rattling around the house, getting underfoot. You might come across my stash of lye. So I won't get my chance to pour it down the bastard's throat in peace."

"Mom."

"Oh, Barry." She waved him off.

"What's your stash of lies?"

"Lye, Barry, lye. It's a poison. Like arsenic or Drano or something." The whole story bored her now. Her mouth lost color as it puckered into a twist again. "What *is* that thing?" she snapped. Pinning the black pebble with a fingertip, she pulled it along the lip of his tray. "Do we really need this?"

"Oh, yeah. It's sort of important."

"What is it?" When he opened his mouth, she added, "I mean, apart from the obvious. It's a black rock."

"I found it in the Colorado River this one time. By Gypsum. We were all thinking it soaked up negative energy."

She looked at him, feeling pride, almost, at how poised he was in his daftness. She knew the daftness hadn't come from her. Certainly not Lynn. (He'd contributed a big, fat nothing.) But wherever it came from—and she did have an idea—she thought she could at least take credit for his presence of mind, his tremendous presence of mind in the face of ridicule. She'd trained him well. "I see. So it's a spiritual pebble. Do you think it's working?"

"Could be. Usually it does."

"And all that—crap in your little baggie—that was more amulets or whatever?"

"Right. Good medicine." He grinned. "Top notch. I find these things. They sort of come to me, I guess."

"Are you telling me, Barry, that you've become a medicine man?" He grinned with contented amusement, fondness, even. But he wiped his grin away when she asked, "Are you planning on doing anything weird to Lynn? Psychic surgery?"

"Of course not. I wish I knew something to do."

"Because I wouldn't mind at all," Jeanette said affectionately. "If we had a really big one of these we could bash his head in with it."

"He can't be that bad. He's a quiet guy, Mom. And this has got to be intense."

"You know, loud, articulate, aggressive people can also be smarter and deeper than they seem," Jeanette barked resentfully. "Nobody knows your father. Not even you. The man's been half-alive his whole life. Who knows why God wasted his time shuffling him into a mortal coil? He belongs in limbo. He could never get it up to speak of, and there wasn't any Viagra back when it mattered." She flushed and stumbled. This was an outrageous and off-color thing to say, and she was unexpectedly exacting about what she would and wouldn't say. Recovering with a shrug, she simpered at a slovenly, much-bobby-pinned girl who'd come to pick up their trays. "Monique," if you tipped your head left. Monique took Jeanette's tray. Then the girl froze, staring at the black pebble on Barry's. She gave it a stagey, disdainful look. Barry had piled refuse on his tray and missed the stone behind it all. When Monique eyed him uneasily—the beanie, the choker—he smiled. He offered her the tray. She looked back at the pebble as if its slight unseemliness were so enormous she couldn't touch, much less take, Barry's tray.

"It's a fucking pebble, OK?" Jeanette said. "Big deal! Just take them, will you?" She plucked the stone from Barry's tray.

"Well, and *bitch* to you too," Monique muttered in Jeanette's face, before sweeping off with the trays. A yellow burger wrapper pirouetted on one tray. And a folded napkin jack-knifed to the floor in her wake.

Like a naughty child, Jeanette bowed her head. "I'm sorry," she offered. She asked Barry, "Was I a bitch first, or was she? I can never tell."

"That's a tough call," her son said thoughtfully.

Jeanette's mouth was turned down in regretful displeasure. Squarish red patches had appeared on her cheeks. Her hands, which had vanished contritely under the table, reappeared holding the pebble. "I don't think this works." She touched her face with it, a little bit all over, as if it were a powder puff. "Or I need an extra strong dose. No surprise there, I guess, huh?"

The parish room at The Little Church of the Transfiguration, universally known as "The Chapel," was the meeting place for Jeanette's support group. The church had been built by well-heeled local Episcopalians in the twenties in a clubby burst of religiosity. Now a good fraction of the church's income came from couples paying to be married in so quaint a setting: a cozy, wisteria-covered stone church by a broad stream, swallows scrabbling and shitting under the steeple eaves, sanctuary itself a beautiful golden haze of shellacked pine and old stained glass—all in amazingly good taste, because to the extremely fancy congregants, the mystery of taste was exactly like God's, a bit more vivid, even.

The rector, Addie Mueller, started a support group the year before for anyone in trouble, and it attracted the remains of the local gentry—the sobered-up fly fisherman with an interest in cooking, the unbeautiful heiress studying veterinary science, the too-countrified descendants, nurse and contractor. Jeanette was drawn to the group like a moth to flame, partly because joining it made her look bad. Everyone assumed that she was social climbing. In fact, she was a person in trouble. She knew it. She was alone with Lynn, drinking herself now, miserable. Sincerely, indeed with a very Christian abjectness, she joined the group, but she still hoped the world would think she was awful.

She was disappointed by God, or by God's agents. While the rest of the group unburdened themselves Saturday after Saturday, Jeanette said little. She found herself observing Bea Sayles mostly—a garden club type, steely, meek, short-nailed, a golfer. Jeanette knew all about the woman's aristocratic family in Noroton. And how the glamorous old friends she'd been raised among pitied her ending up here in New Jersey with a Don Juan of a husband. It was pure chance that Bea was in the group—no one would have guessed her religious. It happened that Jeanette had made a study of Bea over the years—when Jeanette briefly belonged to the Westerbrook Club, when she and Bea both had kids in the same botany/ornithology program, "Jimmy Pedersen's Woodland Weekends." Jeanette had her reasons.

It was strange to see Bea open up when they all sat in a circle in the parish room. Bea didn't talk about her philandering husband but about seeing, maybe—she whispered and gazed at the floor—an angel one night. Afterward, there was a long, reverent silence. Bea looked uncomfortable. Crickets sawed outside. You heard them through the screens of the open windows. Bea flicked at an imaginary mosquito on her calf and at last broke the silence herself, in her less shy, golfer persona: "Who knows what it was, really?" Her sheer eyebrows frowned in boyish consternation, and she looked imploringly at Addie. Jeanette wondered whether this angel vision was a sort of love-offering to the minister on whom Bea seemed to have a crush.

Jeanette had about given up on the group and meant to quit. She needed to try something else for consolation, since martyring her reputation here turned out to be only a stopgap. Not long after Barry returned, however, a little plan came to her which made her stick with the group several more weeks. She needed to engineer a private word with Bea. This was difficult because the other woman was breezy and active. After one Saturday session, Jeanette loitered in an octagonal vestibule under the belfry. A red rope came through a hole in the ceiling and was secured to a davit on the wall. Jeanette eyed the names and dates lettered in faded fountain pen under old blessing-the-hounds photographs lining the walls. Soon enough, Bea came out of the dimly lit sanctuary hefting two christogrammed silver vases. She'd return them Sunday morning full of her garden's flowers. Interception successful, Jeanette engaged Bea in a little back and forth. After-session hilarity curlicued outdoors, and a car door hushed the crickets for a moment, before they restarted and tires on pebbles joined them. Much more roundabout than she needed to be, Jeanette slyly clapped a hand to her cheek. "Oh, I'm going to have to run, Bea. I've just remembered about Barry.

Believe it or not, I've got the lout home again. And he's running me ragged. Cook, clean, chauffeur."

Bea laughed easily, thinking, *What an awkward woman!*

Having gotten that far, Jeanette decided to go to church the following morning and close the deal. Or not. On Sunday, Bea's peach iris blazed in the silver vases. Actually, they were the color that used to be called flesh, nicely symbolic when communion came around, but people noticed only the sun-struck beauty of the flowers. Bea Sayles's leggy youngest daughter, Eleanor, examined the vases intently with a deep, private sense of contrition. She'd committed sacrilege with one of the vases earlier that morning. The sacrilege wasn't too serious, easily made up for with an uptick of fervency now. The pretty cycle of sin and repentance, even this minor one, made God seem realer to her than her ordinary blamelessness did. She looked from the vases to her mother to the radiant Jesus in stained glass.

Though Eleanor was getting on well with God, she was still angry with her mother. Bea had snapped at her in the sudden, spooky way she had. She'd poured Eleanor's broth of pennies out of the vase in a cold fury, talking about scratches, not sacrilege, and what's the point of washing coins, and, no one would care if there was gunk on them—they were money. Eleanor suspected her mother was a hypocrite.

On the organ, Mrs. Nash's son, back from the Peace Corps, tooted through a recessional, and then some. The crowd spilled out onto the pebbled drive and the lawn. Bea fawned over Addie's sermon, which caused people to back up. Addie rubbed Bea's shoulder and firmly shifted her eyes to the next in line, a stooped former banker, now birder.

Plummeting out of the bright sky, a flock of starlings shied from the chittering crowd. The flock warped like a blown veil over lilacs and hedgerow and settled on a stubble field beyond. Eleanor found a girlfriend. The two waited until they weren't being watched, then picked their way through the high weeds into the brush behind the lilacs. The spot was rank with wild grape and otherworldly forces. The emanations attracted the two girls. Also the rumors of a long ago Mafia burial there.

Abandoning her jealous attentions to Addie, Bea stepped off the chapel stoop and couldn't find Eleanor. No one else had seen her. She strolled around the back of the building. Jeanette Paul made her move. She came out of the parish room where she'd gotten a cup of coffee. She put her lips to the rim of the cup as if she were perching on it. "Here we are again," Bea greeted her with a laugh. "I seem to have misplaced my daughter."

Jeanette smiled tightly and sipped. She attached herself to Bea. Reminding herself she had no gift for *pleasant* small talk, she was silent. They walked toward the stream, broad but as shallow as a puddle, glistening over a bed of shale. Kids loved stepping into it—the water almost hot, the velvety layer of silt under bare feet, the sudden tranquil pandemonium of thornlike minnows.

Bridging the watery silence, Bea began, "Seems like my daughter's a bit wayward. Not *literally* wayward!" she caught herself. "I mean—be thankful you don't have a daughter, Jeanette. Really, Flossy—that's what we call Ross in the family—is much more accommodating—which goes against what people say—about boys and girls."

"Bea," Jeanette spoke into her coffee. The stream gurgled and cooed.

Bea was attentive to a special tone of Jeanette's.

"I have an idea that I think might—*might*—work out for both of us. You want some coffee?" she interrupted herself obsequiously. Bea didn't drink coffee. "Listen, I'm sure you know all about what's happened with Lynn."

"Oh, I *know*, Jeanette!" Bea's sympathy was so emphatic, Jeanette thought for a second it must be false. Or it was just richly stylized. Bea wore an expression of sublime sorrow. She turned it on Jeanette with terrific force. "So hard for you!"

The blast of commiseration made it difficult for Jeanette to go on without lowering her eyes. Using the toe of her shoe, she stroked a thick tuft of grass atop the stream's eroding bank.

"Careful you don't fall," Bea mothered, ever-vigilant.

Jeanette thought, *How can anyone love a woman who makes one feel so small?—but they all do, they adore her*. Aloud, she began,

"Having Barry at home—well, I'm afraid it's driving Lynn up the wall. To say nothing of—this is embarrassing, but—the expenses have gotten just—"

"Oh, of course, Jeanette. Of *course*!"

"You used to talk about there being a garage apartment over at your place. And how you'd hire somebody sometimes to take care of the property—lawn work and—"

"But—"

"I know you've got somebody in there, now."

"Dean. We do, I'm afraid."

"Well, it so happens Dean is an old friend of Barry's from Lawrence. I know this is getting pushy of me, but didn't you mention Dean wasn't doing as much as you'd hoped?"

"Well—"

"Not because he isn't a wonderful guy, but because he's so busy. What is he, a mortgage broker?"

"No, now he's into some insurance thing. And I suppose it's true. He hasn't had as much time to work around the place, which was how we set the thing up originally—him staying there."

"There. I was just wondering if maybe—possibly—if Dean and Barry could work something out between the two of them. Both of them stay in the garage. That way you'd get your yard work done, and—that outdoors stuff is right in Barry's line. He's spent years tramping around out West, not exactly a forest ranger, but close enough."

"Right. Well, I'm not sure. Maybe if the boys themselves came to some sort of agreement. I couldn't promise anything. The fact is, he's not taking care of things as well as we'd like. I could test the waters with Preston at home and see. See if he wouldn't mind paying someone. Just see."

A screech came from over by the lilacs. Bea walked to the side of the church. Beyond the hedgerow, the flock of starlings broke for the sky with the sound of hail pelting an awning. A second screech was less spontaneous, more willful, a happy simulacrum of horror. Eleanor came loping out of the brush. She was breathless. The back of her hand hit her forehead in mock faintness. "Oh, you're here! You're here! Thank God!" she cried to her mother, not quite seriously. Her panting was a kind of laughter.

Coltish limbs trembled with exertion or amusement. She bent forward, planted her hands on her knees. All her joints went soft for a moment, then stiffened with a jerk. "She scared me so badly, Mom," Eleanor said. "We rented *Halloween 20* last week, which was fairly weird and terrifying, and she just did a huge *Michael Myers* on me. So creepy!" She straightened and patted her heart for a while. "And like, she did it to me over there." She pointed to the hedgerow, where saplings started to move.

"Sounds dreadful," Bea said, not joining in the humor yet. She'd heard the story about the Mafia burial and hated it. She didn't like horror movies, either.

The other girl, abashed, appeared among the saplings. Eleanor squealed, "It's Michael!" She grabbed Bea's arm and mock-cringed by her side. "Keep him away from me!"

Bea was won over. "Oh come on!" she roared humorously. She turned back to Jeanette Paul, but the other woman had lingered unsociably by the sparkling stream. She was too far away to speak to, so Bea made a big shrug and shook her head. *Children*! And Jeanette toasted her with the coffee cup.

26

BEA'S HUSBAND, PRESTON, General Counsel of Flexalt Corporation of Teterboro, New Jersey, sat in a restaurant in Manhattan's Meat Packing district. He watched his son Ross, called Flossy, walk away from their table. Blithe was popular with film people, Flossy had *sotto-voced* over *risotto*. Only Flossy could have dragged Preston to a place like this. Single ears of wheat bristled from perforated plywood. A great, spot lit *arte povera* heap of millet sprigs sat in the middle of the polished concrete floor. Departing, Flossy stepped around the pile without the least inhibited caution, not even looking down. Shoulders square, he gave no one in particular a nod and breezed past the doorman into the pink glow of the awning outside. Before the doors eased shut on lush hinges, Preston could see Flossy looking immensely contented with himself.

Flossy must have inherited his grand manners from his mother's side of the family, the Noroton crowd, even though Bea herself had none of it. But Preston didn't think the boy's pride was entirely innate. Flossy enjoyed it too much for that. He had a touch of social ambition. That could only be a good thing in this city, in this day and age. He was the soundest of the three kids—three, leaving out Eleanor, who was too young to decide about. Yet wasn't there also something dense about Flossy? A happy money-grubber and blinkered. It's always the servants who are the clear-eyed ones, and parents are the servants of their heirs.

Preston disliked Blithe and would have left with Flossy after their two o'clock lunch. He stayed and had another drink just because he liked the hostess who'd led them to their table. She noticed his interest. Seeing him abandoned, she came over to fuss for a moment. A serene beauty, she looked like a California vintner's wife, Preston decided. Her defenseless, almost infantile, friendliness was a kind only ever glimpsed in the cloisters of luxury. On the way out, he paused by her dainty lectern to flirt a little more. Bluff, harmless, he showed her the book he'd picked up, and she laughed.

Her gentility was particularly sweet, because Preston felt like a Cossack. He'd dealt with an ethically unpleasant case in meetings all morning. This unease with his profession came over him at regular intervals, a hound's breath at the back of his neck. The power he'd spent his life accumulating as a lawyer had no decent uses at all, really. Having drunk too much, he decided to go straight home instead of to the office in Teterboro.

President Clinton happened to be in town, and traffic had come to a standstill around Penn Station. Preston got out of the cab to walk the last blocks in sweltering heat. His too-starchy shirt chafed at his belly, which was solid and squared-off like a bag of potting soil. He was in time for a 4:49. Quirky, train schedule time. He paused for a vodka tonic at a commuter bar in the station. A feint of Fourth of July exuberance in the décor did nothing to disguise the dismal functionality of the place. Preston hurried his dose and left.

At the last moment, just as the doors were pinging, a young woman with a baby got into Preston's car, alone but with all the bustle of a horde. Convinced she was being looked at critically by everyone, she flounced into the seat facing Preston, crossly hefted a grubby-cheeked baby in a paisley sling, and drew her Tibetan saddlebag—or whatever it was—close to her hip. In the saddlebag she found a tub of mashed lentils and began feeding the baby. She took alternate spoonfuls herself.

She wasn't truly dirty. Her skin and hair, the paisley and the saddlebag, the thin skirt and the blue jeans underneath—that had to be hot—all had a well-thumbed softness. Maybe she was some university president's daughter with a weakness for India.

Resentment and dysentery hadn't destroyed her looks, but they gave her a beetling, vengeful attractiveness. Severe, prematurely aged, she looked like a coed made up to play Medea. She also appeared ready to blow up in anger at any moment.

Preston did watch her, but not critically. He didn't mind the way she sucked up attention, something many people find annoying. He wanted to speak to her, in fact, partly as a distraction, partly out of curiosity. A delicate job, clearly. She'd probably turned her back on a father a lot like Preston to go on her penurious pilgrimage to India or Myanmar or Sri Lanka.

Preston had always been one of those people who strike up conversations with strangers. It wasn't an inveterate loner's meek abandon. Nor the twitchy monologist's incurious sociability. It was interest and seduction. He did it by reflex. He knew through experience that this girl wasn't as unlikely a prospect as she seemed. He displayed his book invitingly, so she could read the title, *Dogs That Know When Their Owners Are Coming Home*. She never glanced at it.

He took the book up and riffled its pages in a subject-broaching sort of consternation, working his lips. Full of unnecessary movement, he fished a pen from his pocket. He opened the book and began sketching rapidly on the flyleaf. Not drawing her, of course, but the saddlebag. After a moment his work got a frown from her, and he instantly murmured, "Amazing motif." He didn't look up.

"What are you, a designer?" she asked sourly.

Preston made a meaningless, deprecating sound.

The car's fluorescent lights winked out. Their sudden disappearance revealed a *mise-en-scène* for terror lying under the surface of things. The tunnel's bare bulbs strobed noirishly. The silence of the passengers felt more like doomed foolishness than unconcern. Preston kept sketching.

The girl waved the spoon through a drifting cleaver of light to see whether the baby had gummed it clean. "Ripping off traditional design?" she wise-cracked.

"I'm not a designer. Far from it. What's the bag, though? Tibet? Burma?"

The girl said nothing. She gripped the spoon in her mouth and shifted the saddlebag so Preston couldn't see it.

Obligingly, he closed his book. He lied, "I work for an oil company. Agip, but here in the States."

"Oh, God!" she groaned, making the spoon's handle flicker like a silver tongue before she pulled it out.

"They're Italian. We are. Maybe a little less rapacious." He chuckled.

"I doubt it."

"You must be—not to assume—but maybe you're—anti-globalization—what have you—all that."

The girl said nothing. Then she mocked, "All that."

"If so—I don't want to take you from your baby—but I'd adore asking you a business question. Advice."

The lights came on. The girl had pinched her nostrils unpleasantly. She turned her head to read the title of Preston's book.

"I had a terrible morning," Preston continued. "Meetings and meetings with a gaggle of advertising types. We're opening up an oil field over in Kazakhstan. Kashagan by the Caspian Sea." Preston had no idea where this elaborate lie was leading. Flexalt had consulted with a company called Mercator on the project, but that was it, and he'd had nothing to do with it himself. "We're—uh—trying to figure a way to spin it. Not for the locals. We could spill all the oil in the world. They couldn't care less. Couldn't get worse in that country than it is now—after the Soviets. But it's people like you who monitor every move we make."

"You're asking *me* how you can get away with such a—such a—?"

"Am I?" Preston wondered innocently. "I guess I am. You seem to know your mind."

She spoke over him. "Stay out. That's my advice. Leave them alone for once. Not that you will."

Preston appeared satisfied with her answer. His finger scribbled idly over the dog pictured on the cover of his book. When the train broke out of the tunnel, sunlight blazed on his hand. The heads of the passengers made wakeful turnings, greeting the sun in New Jersey. Everywhere in the broad, motionless industrial landscape, shining patches of river, chrome bumper and airplane fuselage revolved with the motion of the train—as if noticing its arrival.

"That's what my son and daughter would say—the older two. The younger two don't care, but Anna and Philip, they're more like you. They've gone off. She's in Asia, and he's in Central America." That much was true. "They're both environmentalists of a sort. The thing is, the environment there—this is in Kazakhstan—it's already been trashed. In our plan we put a little aside for restoration, so ironically, it might be better for the environment if we do go over there. I'm not saying it definitely would be, but it could."

"Exxon Valdez. Heard it all before," she chirped bitterly.

"Are you an activist? A traveler obviously."

"Traveler, I guess, in a way. Activist, no. But I care. Like a lot of people do. Whatever it is you're planning on getting into over there, I hope you fail. I really do."

She didn't say a word more to him and got off at one of the first New Jersey stops. Preston nodded vaguely. He wasn't offended. In fact, a sparkling pleasure had replaced the worries about the law and children that had been preoccupying him all day. It was a pity his good mood came at the price, in a sense, of this wanderer-mother's misery. That was the very problem with Anna and Philip. Both had an incurable longing. The source of it, he'd long ago decided, was in Bea's family.

He'd picked up on it right after marriage. Afternoons with his wife's family in Noroton had been strangely spiritless. He hadn't expected the sharp-elbowed disorder of his own New Jersey upbringing, but maybe a touch more awareness—the occasional wink. It never came. Never a drunken fight, never the slightest messy hoopla. They were one of those loftily self-effacing WASP families with no talent for celebration, if not exactly a horror. Unavoidable big occasions, like weddings, came out pallid successes. To them, the mother-in-law's seventy-fifth birthday, Bea's own marriage to him, were almost unpleasantly ostentatious. They preferred living under the radar. When Preston cottoned on to this, he realized that he loved it. He wasn't like them, but he loved it, and he could afford to love it because he wasn't like them.

In their obscure conviction of unlimited self-worth, they may have been trying to use the back entrance to eternity. Rather than mark time with turning points and big parties and accomplishments—rather than sink their claws into the passing flank of history—they preferred not to engage. Letting time remain undifferentiated made it look a bit like "forever." This had seemed the perfect setting for his life, an eternal human coziness, and he'd relished their polite serenity. There was a kind of power in their unworldliness which he certainly didn't possess himself.

Over time he grasped that their method didn't work. The longing came out. The university president's daughter fucked her way to India. Sooner or later it came to them, maybe not that they were unhappy, but that they didn't even know what happiness tasted like. Their lives had been spoken in a tone that undermined the meaning entirely—like irony, but irony that was neither funny nor mean. To get the accent right, you had to learn it as a child. Bea had. So had Anna and Philip. Flossy had been spared because he loved money. But Preston worried that he ought to have done more for the rest of his children.

Sitting in his car at the station, gloom returning, he thought of adding one more to the two women he'd desired today—make a sort of bouquet of three different types. Scrolling through the names saved on his cell phone, he came to Claire M., a colleague at Flexalt, Claire Malouf. "Claire, I'm not going back to the office today. I'll stop by. It'll be around six. If you get this or you're in, wonderful. If not, no worries." She was in. A little after six, they were in her cozy bedroom thrashing on top of her cozy bed.

Claire murmured something, spouted a laugh, and he pulled out. She'd made concluding noises, weary or wanting to be considerate, or possibly both. To pause, in any case, suited Preston. "I'm so dry, I think I have to use a *crème*," she said. Cute *pudor* made her Frenchify the word. "We can go on—"

"Oh, I thought you'd—"

"If you want, we can—"

"No, I'm right as rain."

"So I can see, Jupiter-Daddy," she said with a fond slap. "Sure you don't want to—"

"I'm a bit sore myself. Seems to have rubbed at the skin a little—what we were doing. Haven't always rolled around so much. And with the rubbing—"

"My teeth may have done it."

"Don't think so. It's more like Indian burn. Just rubbing."

She lay there, arms flung back, Andromache chained to her rock. She pouted, eyelids fell closed. She writhed, partly pretending to struggle, partly just stretching. Grunting, Preston half-tumbled off the bed. His blood shifted like a falls. He stood for a moment recovering from spotted faintness, looking down over his belly to watch himself wind down: tick, tick, tick, tick. Claire skipped out of the room and reappeared in a *peignoir* as she liked to do.

Claire plugged in a laptop to check her email from work. Among her many playful fantasies, she liked to mix business with love.

Preston settled on a girly upholstered chaise without dressing. He knew he looked gross, more Silenus than Jupiter, but he'd learned Claire appreciated a touch of boorishness. Besides, he was woozy, tired. No longer gloomy, at any rate. The blinds were lowered, which made for spindly, tropical light in the room, though the air conditioner was blasting.

Claire made a little noise over one of her emails, inviting Preston to ask about it. He didn't want to. When she made a second effort, whispering, "Christ!" to herself, he tried diverting her. "Kitten—" He was slow to think of something to say. "Kitten," he said. "That was memorable."

"Why, thank you, Preston. Now, you would not believe the note I got here from that funny creature who does the motor pool and all that. Winkie-something. Do you know him?"

"Not sure. I don't think so."

She scrolled. "Winckelmann. Well, he's an officious creature, and I can't honestly say I like him, but here he's done something about an issue—something I asked him about. On your behalf, I might add. See, how I look out for you? Even when it might could come back and bite us, though I hope not."

"What's he say? What's it about?"

"Well, this is all about a car. Car you rented when you went down to Trenton. Hear anything about it? 'Cause I did. Seems like there was a ding and a ticket on it."

"What?"

"Yeah, a ding and a ticket, and not even from Trenton, but from Asbury Park. How do you like that? You ever go there? I didn't think so. Now, look—who's that—?" She scrolled. "Well, it's that boy that lives with you. I know it is. Dean, isn't that right?"

"Christ. Are you kidding? He lives in the garage. Garage apartment."

"Right. I didn't mean lives *with* you."

"I must've left the car in the drive one night. He's a loose cannon. Bea's fed up with him. He chipped her glass door—the sliding glass door she put in in the kitchen. He's a bow hunter, and he shot the thing right at the house, took a big divot out of it—tempered glass, too. He said he got turned around in the woods. But this is worse."

"See, it is a problem. I wanted it quiet, so I asked Winkie to email me."

"He was also supposed to be clearing brush for us, taking care of the property. It's why we let him stay in the apartment for free, but it hasn't worked out at all. Place looks awfully shabby. Maybe I'll throw him out."

"See, I didn't know exactly what the relationship was. If he was a family connection or—"

"Hardly."

"I wonder what he was doing in Asbury Park to get a ding and a ticket?" She pouted extremely.

"He's a kid."

"You've got more important things to think about. You got Vijesh, I guess, working on the ATCA case?"

"Yes. He drove me into the city this afternoon. I had lunch with Flossy." Preston's hand slid thoughtfully over the heap of his belly—down to the silky, sparse pubic hair on its own little bulge below.

"Well, you're taken up with that case and quite rightly, so why should you have to worry about this troublemaker? That's what I thought. It is trouble, too, see, because Winkie says cars rented on the company dime—blah, blah—something like this happens and—blah, blah—*could jeopardize our insurance agreements*."

"Fuck. I'll ask him about it."

"Now, don't tell Vijesh—or even Winkie—that I passed it along. Though that'll be pretty obvious. I know a touch about in-house politics from Georgia when Nicky was at Delta. And corporate types—I say it myself—are not always the most savory people in the world."

"Worried about Vijesh? Don't bother. And this isn't bad. Just awkward. Was your Nicky the same as Vijesh—Indian?" Her husband, a commercial pilot, had died in a car accident years before.

"Oh, no, no, no. Nicky was Lebanese. And not hardly even that. He went to Ole Miss, and he was KA—that's Kappa Alpha. He was one of those old, old Lebanese families that always had the general store. You might could go to any town in the south with 'Welcome to—' on the water tower, it used to be the Lebanese made all the money at the store. They had pots of money, Nicky's family did, at one time." She swung back and forth on the shammed stool at her dressing table.

When she stood to pace, he could see the desktop image on her laptop, a travel brochure picture of a woman in a white *après-bain* lying on an empty beach. Glowing as it was, this picture made all the rest of the dim, real bedroom look like drab frame, like the cartonnage interior of a telescope aimed squarely at fantasy. A champagne flute had tipped from the woman's hand, so she was dozing—or dead—and the ocean was so stark that luxury looked like devouring nullity.

"Isn't it just divine?" she asked, seeing him eye the picture. "I put it on last winter when I was all—cabin-fever-y with the cold. It's Cay St. Georges. I need to get somebody to take me next year. I tried a resort in Jamaica on my own one time, but that was terrifying. This place'll be more peaceful, only I don't want to go alone. It's kind of a be-seen place."

"Any prospects?"

"Alas, no. You take up all my time, Preston. You're irresistible. I've gotten into this horrible groove of being the tramp on the side." She laughed gaily.

"We don't often think about where we're headed—" he made the gallant invitation to talk, since he was conscious of having just used her like a faucet.

As expected, she frowned slightly with glassy pleasantness. Mention relationships, adultery, widowhood in anything close to a direct way, and she froze up for several seconds. Does not compute. She actually gave her head a brisk little shake of coming to. Preston had wondered at first whether the way she zoned out like that wasn't a technique—a specialty of southern womanhood—for driving men wild with uncertainty. But more likely her future needed to be as pretty as Cay St. Georges to bear even thinking about. He'd been shocked once to find her padded denim photo album full of pictures of himself, some clipped from company brochures. "Kitten, let me ask your advice."

She flung herself on the bed, twisting up on one elbow, tucking the peignoir around her.

"I met a young woman on the train."

"Uh-oh."

"No, nothing like that. She reminded me of my daughter, Anna."

"Uh-oh."

"No, no. But I've been a bit worried about my kids, lately. In a big, general way. How they're disaffected—let me start over—I have this book I left in the car. Silly thing about dogs that have ESP. I saw it in a window and picked it up because I had a tiny experience I thought might be a bit like that."

"ESP? Like a dog?"

"Right. Except about my kids, not my owner, which is how the dogs get it. They sense when their owner's about to come home."

"How eerie! I'm so surprised at you, Preston! Your kids are coming home?"

"That's what I thought, but it turned out to be something different. There was this woman. I won't say who. Quite a long time ago."

"Uh-oh. This, I'm *not* surprised about. Lothario!"

"Right. She had a kid. And she's made it plain to me over the years, without causing any problems or anything—but she's made it plain to me she thinks the kid is mine. He—the kid is a boy—went out of town a long time ago, but he comes back now and then for a visit. And almost every time, this woman manages to talk to me—not putting pressure on, exactly, but just so she knows I know the thing is still hanging over me."

"And you had a sense this boy was coming back."

"Exactly that. And it turns out he did. His father—his real father—and maybe it *is* his real father, since—"

"They've got tests now, you know."

"Oh, I know. But we never got to that—"

"Not about money, even?"

"She never cared. So she said. But now the boy's father is sick with cancer. Dying, I think. And I'm starting to think about my responsibility. If I have any. And even though there was never any test, this ESP twinge made me think, *Maybe.* I haven't talked to her, though—the woman."

"Oh, boy, honey. This is hard. I don't know if I can help."

27

PRESTON LOOKED AT the conical divot in the sliding glass door, which the arrowhead, striking the outside, had punched away on the *inside.* It was Sunday, and he had the house to himself. He bent forward, legs hurting, and touched the divot in the glass. *Yup, inside.* Tucked behind a potted ficus next to the door he noticed a small blue plastic tub. Inside it was a slurry of coins, pennies mostly. The water had partially evaporated. Only an inch or two was left. He thought he recognized the coins from a cracked red lacquer rice bowl he kept on his dresser for loose change, a hoard he'd given Eleanor last Sunday. She had to be washing them.

Preston opened the refrigerator and, bending over, legs hurting, he pulled a bottle of ReaLemon juice from the door. He emptied this into the blue tub. Satisfied—but a little worried by the soreness in his legs—he went back to the refrigerator and poured himself some tomato juice, which he spiked from the freezer's fingertip-scalding bottle of vodka.

The soreness in his legs was worse since yesterday. A little like the time he'd pinched a sciatic nerve. But he was afraid it was a flare-up of herpes, which he'd gotten a million years ago and which had driven an enraged Bea to go on a long natural history cruise to the Galapagos. The bane of dirty teenagers hadn't fit with who he was, or seemed to be. Supposedly, an epic course of Acyclovir had done away with it. But the soreness in his hamstrings felt familiar. And his recent work and family anxieties made it all but diagnostic—herpetic stress.

Unhappily, he returned to last week's worry. Lifelong fealty to the harsh and lofty good sense of the adversarial system looked like cynicism. It was clear to him this morning that life was all about tracing and retracing the story we've mistaken for our life. Time came in repetitive layers rather than longitudinal extension. Today, he wanted to ignore his lack of progress. His tender lemon-juice service to Eleanor couldn't atone for much. He ought to be drinking water. Maybe water could dilute the herpes—were they spirochetes, as well? Little screws that punished a little bit of screwing. Heaven help him if Claire Malouf got it.

In the library, he spun a lavish four-foot enamel and silver-gilt globe to Mongolia and shuffled together the blasted pieces of the *Sunday Times*. Hamstrings twinged when he straightened. He dumped the glanced-through mess of newspaper into a brass bucket holding one spindly log from last winter. He thought he might enjoy getting angry with Dean. So he gave the layabed a warning phone call, saying only that he was coming over to put the garage storage room in order today, a likely pretext.

Barefoot, he padded out onto the asphalt loop of the drive. Bea must have had the sprinklers on earlier. A leggy black gloss spread down the slope of the sun-heated matte drive. A barefooted childhood memory came to him, vague but keen—a new memory, never thumbed-to, as fresh as experience. He smiled with pleasure and watched Flossy's car coming up the drive.

The pleasure of memory turned into speculation—mostly jocular—about whether he may have *sensed* Flossy was about to arrive and had come out to the drive to wait for him. Flossy parked. Preston greeted him with a routine *how-d'ye-do* warning that the boy's decrepit Saab was burning oil. Flossy placed fancy restaurants ahead of cars, a priority Preston couldn't countenance.

Flossy was wearing a tank top and long baggy shorts. Preston thought he recognized gay fashion. He also thought with approval that it didn't come off too much that way on Flossy. Perhaps because the boy was relatively square-built and unfussy. Flossy even got away with those ankleless little socks women used to wear for tennis. In fact, the faggiest thing his son wore was the bead choker, Preston's recent gift to him. Seeing it—a tender service he'd forgotten—pleased Preston in a motherly way.

The choker was strung with turquoise glass trade beads from the sixteenth or seventeenth century. Preston found it while shopping for an antique gewgaw for Claire Malouf. Though he had no idea whether the beads had been scratched from the dirt in Indonesia or the Mississippi delta, Preston swore up and down to Flossy, as the seller had sworn to him, that the little blue cylinders and batonnets had been made at the same Spanish manufactory that produced the strings of beads Peter Minuit used to pay for Mannahatta. A perfect charm for Flossy, whether or not it was gay. Or too gay.

"Is everything burning up out here?" Flossy asked about the garden. He was carrying a manila envelope with an old-fashioned red string clasp. He started doing isometrics with the envelope.

"Not too bad." Preston shrugged. "You out for a few days now, Rosso?"

"Yessir, I think so. But I was hoping to go over this list with you today." The envelope started nodding at Preston, isometrics turning into a kind of *Namaste* greeting. "Cause the auction's on Monday, and I'll have to drive out pretty early."

"We'll take care of it. Now, who was I telling? What was the name of that place? Blithe. I told someone at the office, *My son's started living like Donald Trump*. What's your net worth?"

"Not to brag, but I think I have a lot more class than he does," Flossy smiled.

"Uh-huh. And how's your fortune?"

Flossy smiled. He told no one—no one—that he was up to three hundred and forty-eight thousand dollars now—at age twenty. "I'm doing all right."

"Not telling me?"

"No, sir." Flossy had picked up the habit of littering his remarks with *sir* from Preston, who'd picked it up from the World War Two generation at Flexalt.

"OK, Floss, we'll do your Simon Legree bit," Preston nodded at the envelope. "But let me get my shoes on, and help me with a chore first. You mind?" Rosso didn't mind. He could have been the son in a fable or a bible story, loving and obedient. Bea actually had trouble trusting in the boy's too-golden character. Even Preston used to think there was something wrong with him. Sadness, trouble—the gay business at seventeen, for instance—came over him with the naturalness of storms, then cleared entirely. Not like Anna and Philip. And unlike them, Ross was untalkative, considered a bad sign nowadays.

Flossy stretched hugely and announced on the exhalation, "I joined a gym for the first time. So I'm sore in all these weird places."

"It gets worse," Preston indulged himself with the wry woe of the aged. "What did you do? You mean weightlifting?"

"A little, I guess," Flossy admitted with a shy frown. "It's boring, though. I'd rather do real things. The gym's just—" He pumped his biceps limply. "—boring."

"I thought you looked a little pumped up."

"Nice try. I've been maybe five times." But his biceps looked as plump as a sofa cushion, with a thick vein as neat as piping.

As yet another tender service—for he knew Flossy was all but in love with him—Preston forced out, "Well, you're looking good." Awkward as it made him feel, saying this to his gay son, dutiful love must have been magical, because he was instantly cured of herpes. It dawned on him that his hamstrings were sore because he'd also pumped up—pumped down, that is, on Claire Malouf. He had sore muscles from an old man's energetic fucking, not herpes. "Good thing you like real. This chore's all muscle work." And Flossy nodded, a contented laborer.

They knocked on the garage apartment door. Dean Quinn appeared in pin-striped boxers and a UPenn T-shirt. Inside, the shaded, weakly air-conditioned apartment had a germinating dankness. The tousle-headed tenant chortled, "Sorry. Heavy night last night, guys." He grabbed coin-ballasted khakis from a broken spindle-backed chair by the door.

Without even looking, Preston caught a subtle shock of desire from his right side, from Flossy. It made his own anger more satisfying somehow. "Go ahead up, will you, Floss?" he rumbled.

Flossy took the stairs two at a time. Preston made a passing face at Dean's fug. Interesting, since in the outside world, Dean always looked as crisply put-together as a Mormon on a mission.

The flowery scent of beer hovered in the background. "I don't know what you want me to do," Flossy called from the door to the storage room.

"Start making a pile of things we can throw out." Even as Flossy thumped across the floor upstairs, Preston started crowding Dean. One leg in his khakis, the boy had to hop backwards, jingling. Giving him no time to collect his thoughts, Preston started in with menacing joviality. "What the hell do you do in Asbury Park?" The belt buckle thudded when Dean dropped his pants. He grabbed them up. "Dean-o, I've got to ask you, what's this crazy story about a car that got banged up in Asbury Park?"

"Not—"

"Did I get that right? Was that you?"

"Not banged up!"

"Did you steal my fucking rental car?"

"I'm so sorry, so sorry, Prez. That wasn't banged up. That was like a—like a dent. They can punch 'em out with a ball-peen hammer. You never even noticed the next day, right? Did you? I'm so sorry, man."

"You stole my car! You little prick. What'd you think I wasn't going to hear? Company's not going to tell me some dickhead got a ticket on my car?"

"I'm sorry. Really sorry. The distributor's been screwed up on my car, so it doesn't even start a lot of times. I had to go out with Pia. I knew it was wrong." He looked pathetic, near tears almost. It made the thing less enjoyable for Preston. "I was sorry. I was actually sorry—I swear—when I saw you left the keys in it. Why'd you do that? You can't do that, man."

"The keys are in the car, so you—you're a dickhead. You have no self-control. Why the fuck didn't you just ask?"

"I know, man. I'm so sorry." With a tragic look over his shoulder at his lair, he asked, "Is this going to mean—"

"No," Preston said judiciously. "I wanted to get the story from you. It'll probably cost you, though. We'll see. You ever fuck with my stuff again—"

When Preston went upstairs, Flossy stood with his eyebrows raised eloquently. He was silently asking what that was all about. Preston shrugged, shook his head a little, and held up a finger to mean, *I'll tell you later*. It hadn't been as satisfying as he'd hoped. He looked around him with a sigh. A 1988 renovation had come to nothing. A kitchenette along one wall had never been used. The label in the basin of a stainless sink had only ever been wetted enough to wrinkle. The space under it was packed with wallpaper rolls and mini-buckets holding pucks of dried caulk. Over the years the room had filled with junk. Broken, paint-caked lengths of molding bristled with nails. Another spindle-backed chair was as gray as driftwood. "Let's throw everything the fuck away. Everything," Preston said. Promptly, Flossy unpegged the loose back of the chair. Preston helped in a token way, but Flossy soon told him it would be just as easy to do the whole thing himself.

After Flossy had thrown everything out a window, gathered it all in contractor bags and made a heap of them by the garbage, he went hunting for his father in the library. Preston was grateful and happy to go through Flossy's list. Flossy unspun the red string from the disc on the envelope. Noticing his hands were dirty from work, he wiped the pigment of rust onto his shorts and began, "We'll just do the ones I was thinking of taking. Should be about five minutes."

"You take whatever lien you want? I thought it was an auction."

"It's this little group of old guys. Maybe six in all. When I first did it, I didn't get their system. But what we do is we sort of talk ahead of time and divide it up, so we aren't bidding against each other." He smiled when he saw Preston raise his eyebrows.

"You saying you've got it rigged?"

"No sir." He stopped smiling. "It's only a few of us. And we don't keep anybody out. They never tried to keep me out. Like they do in New York, supposedly. But let's just go." As usual, after a rumbling of ethical thunder, Flossy was all blue sky.

The lists in his manila envelope were of properties in several Monmouth County towns—names, addresses and property values. Other columns noted details like lot number, acreage, building type and the annual tax assessment. The key column came last: total taxes in arrears. The county was auctioning off the taxes to private investors at attractive interest rates. The government got ready cash, and the investors profited behind the scenes—less if the delinquents paid off right away, more if they couldn't and were subject to mounting interest, fines and, ultimately, foreclosure. Although, as Flossy explained it, the system benefited the delinquents by postponing foreclosure, he must have had a vague qualm, because he wanted to make sure he never bought the taxes of anyone the family knew.

"The first ones are peanuts. Don't know if it's even worth it. *Gates, Londra E. 6208 Fairhope Drive. Condo.*"

"Nope."

"Davenport, Guy and Louanne. 14 Teakettle Lane. Townhome."

"No."

"Oberdorfer, Harry. 1280 Plainview...Fanelli, Frances. 923 Maple...Testaverde, Anthony and Gail. 717 Garfield...Vijay and Sanjay Inc. 1300 Woodmere..."

"What was that one, Vijesh?"

"Vijay. I think it's a business."

"OK. No, then. No for all of them."

"Lester and Gross, partners. 48 Olde Towne Road..."

"Architects, I think. Don't know them."

"Van Nest, Sohail—"

"Ho-ho!"

"Shit, you know him? That's a big one."

"*Her*. It's just her name on the listing?"

"Yeah."

"No. I don't really know them. Or her. It's strange, though. Her husband is supposed to be a very rich guy. Old money. Or so they said. They're divorced now. Everyone also said he was crazy."

"What are you saying? Maybe it's just a cash flow problem for her? She'll pay it right off? That would be less interesting."

"Listen to you."

"No. I'm sorry. It's just—any information helps."

"I'll tell you I'm very surprised the name is there. Maybe she's a screw-up with money."

"That would be better."

The list went on and on. Preston's energy flagged, and he stopped teasing his son about the odor of the thing. But the list, intoned with an inquisitorial lack of inflection, was sad. Preston was sensitive today. Imagining all these people were cheats or low-lifes made the summary of failure more bearable. But Preston wasn't innocent enough to believe it.

"Flossy wants to rent the globe," he mentioned to Bea that evening. She was sitting in a pink-slip-covered chair by the little fireplace in their bedroom. An explosion of dried flowers between the fire dogs was cobwebbed and dropping litter. The old air-conditioner buzzed with faint, flying saucer oscillations. Preston lay in bed, sketching the flower arrangement on the blank pages of a book.

"Rent the globe!"

"Your dad's globe in the library."

"Oh. I thought you meant rent the *world*."

"Ha. No, he's got some pal works in the movie business, set decorator. And the guy said he'd pay two thousand to rent the globe for a couple of days. Move it themselves. Flossy said he'd give us half. Rapacious commission, now I think about it." He chuckled.

"I don't know, Preston. It's such a nice old thing. Moving it around—movie people moving it—couldn't it get damaged? I bet it could."

"That's what I told him you'd say. Anything that came from Noroton is sacred. No touchee." He snapped to a new page in the book and continued drawing.

"Come off it, Preston. You always say that, and it's not true. I'm much more relaxed than you think I am." She draped the accordioned directions for a bible quotation gizmo across her lap and gazed at him. "Are you mad?"

"Not a bit. Why? Oh. No, I'm just playing here." He snapped to another page.

"When did you start drawing?"

He shrugged. "Why did you say it was kismet that me and Flossy cleaned up over in the apartment? Actually, Flossy did all the work. I just jaw-boned like—an old guy on a pickle barrel." He wiggled his toes and flexed his legs to worry the soreness.

"Ah. It was fate, because of Jeanette Paul."

Suddenly very dainty with the pages, Preston leafed back to the first drawing. The twinging in his hamstrings became an all-over *frisson*.

"She's been at church an awful lot lately and asked me a favor," Bea explained. "Which is not really a favor, but might be a good idea for us. But first, tell me if this is a good time. She asked me a while ago, and I've held off, because I know you have an awful lot on your plate just at the moment. Work."

"What? The ATCA thing? That's always there. I don't know if it's a good time."

"Her son Barry's come back into town from out West, and it turns out he's a perfect sort of a yard guy."

Preston said nothing for a while, canceling his drawing with hash marks. "You know, we can't just throw Dean out."

"I'd like to, as a matter of fact. He's useless for anything but shooting up my windows with his silly arrows. But the point is, he and Barry are old friends. Apparently they'd be fine together if Barry took the upstairs. There's enough room for two over there."

"Pay him, you mean? Who can afford somebody new?" Without looking up, he asked pointedly, "Jeanette Paul asked you this? *Can my son live at your place?*"

"Yes. Not in those words. But it's because of Lynn, don't you see? I know she's a strange woman, but you were friends with Lynn."

"I was never friends with Lynn. Never had two words with him."

"All right. But you were both at Lawrence together."

"Never had anything to do with him. Nobody did. Nobody wanted to touch him. He had that—I don't know what it is—a repulsive quality. Perfectly OK up to a point, but if he got too close, he made you cringe."

"Who cares what he *was* like? The poor man's dying of cancer. You'd think we could help a little. I'm surprised. I always thought I was the more hard-hearted one. What is it, sweetheart?" Her voice changed instantly as she looked toward their bedroom door. Preston hadn't even heard the mousey knocking.

The door creaked open. Eleanor walked in. She held something in her fist. She walked in a strange way. She pressed herself flat against the wall Egyptian style. She gave Preston a glance, but she was evidently keeping as far from him as she possibly could. Sidling along the wall like a jumper on a parapet, she hurried stiffly, with bizarre shyness, to Bea's chair and crumpled, half on her mother's lap, half on the floor. Spilling directions and bible computer, Bea leaned forward to hear a secret and caressed the girl's hair. Like cruelty, Bea's love thrived on the helplessness of its objects.

They whispered for a while. Eleanor opened her fist covertly. Preston could hear Bea's half of the exchange. "I don't think so, but who knows? Sometimes a chemical reaction—and even if it was, it's a nice thing, nothing to worry about. Your hand smells like lemon. Did you put juice in with them?"

Preston's drawing had turned into a cross-hatched darkness. He downed the puddle of limed meltwater in his old-fashioned glass.

Bea kissed the crown of Eleanor's head. Even her love was a well-punctuated emotion. On her way out, Eleanor flattened herself against the wall again. Again, she sidled past Preston, as far from him as she could get. *What was he, an ogre?* Giving him the briefest glance, she whispered, "Night, Daddy."

Searching the crevices of the pink chair for her bible computer, Bea chortled.

"What's with her? Am I an ogre suddenly?"

"She's adorable! No. She was just playing. She wanted to show me. Last Sunday she washed a bunch of coins in one of the Chapel vases. I was so pissed with her about it! Anyway, she just found them where I guess they'd been sitting all week, and they'd gotten shiny. They *were* shiny, too. But that can happen if they soak a while—ionization or something—can't it? Maybe lemon juice got on them. That's an acid, right?"

"Mm. I'm worried about her."

"What are you talking about?"

"She shouldn't be so shy."

"What do you mean? She was just embarrassed, Preston. She probably thought you'd tease her."

"But that walk! That twisty, tense way she moves. That bodes ill. Like she'll end up some nutty Emily Dickinson in the attic. Probably be obvious what's wrong, if we weren't her parents."

"What's gotten into you, Preston? There's nothing wrong with Eleanor. She's lovely and shy."

"Bea, they're a mess. All of them. The naturalness and—the life's been squeezed out of all the kids, except maybe Flossy. They don't know how to act for themselves. God knows how they'll get on in the world!" Blandly, he play-acted this hysteria. At the same time, he wondered whether everything he said wasn't the absolute truth.

"Preston," Bea scoffed. "Your daughter was wondering if I thought it was a miracle. A tiny miracle. It was sweet. Of course she didn't want you to make fun—and tromp—over everything."

At work Preston felt dyspeptic and groggy. The Flexalt headquarters was a bronzed, mirrored cube. It sat in a great lawn surrounded by a grassy dike. The dike had been built to baffle the noise from Teterboro Airport across Airport Road. Preston's office faced the hangars and tarmac, and he could often watch, as he did now, the MetLife blimp slowly revolving down to its berth. Cocoa mulch had been freshly spread on the Flexalt flowerbeds. The incongruous smell of chocolate, intense outside, somehow got in through the seams of the glass cube, and a young lawyer, Vijesh Talwani, said it was making him hungry.

Vijesh felt a need to chew over their case. He'd swung a great pile of papers onto Preston's desk when he came in. The pile included a log of company emails for which they were claiming attorney-client privilege. Vijesh rolled a small bottle of water between the palms of clay-colored hands and paced with puppyish energy. "In one sense it may be good for us that they killed Azil in such a disgusting way. And right in front of his kid brother. Because on the narrow issue of what we can *reasonably* have expected—how can anyone *reasonably* expect crimes that are psychopathic? They're unreasonable by their nature, right?"

"But if you employ psychopaths, you have to expect—reasonably expect—" Preston advocated for the devil, or for the other side, rather. The case hinged on Flexalt's partnership with a Mexican company. As security, the company had employed paramilitary thugs, who happily invited members of the Sinaloa cartel to join them in murdering a bothersome trade union organizer who, they claimed, was somehow informing on the drug traffickers. The victim's mother, in New York now, was suing Flexalt for damages under the Alien Tort Claims Act in U.S. District Court.

"But these were ex-military. Who's going to expect them to be nuts? They've got a sort of government imprimatur," Vijesh argued.

"Anyone who knew anything about the military in Mexico should've—" Preston tried. "No. If they were ex-military, what about post-traumatic stress? Employer could've looked into that before hiring."

"OK, OK, OK, I still think it's a promising line. I haven't worked it all out." Jittery junior debater, he sounded a touch condescending to Preston, his senior by almost thirty years. "We can't let our guard down, just because Doe v. Unocal was dismissed," he instructed his boss, rhythmically patting his water bottle. "The court's language is sympathetic to plaintiff. We'll have to see what happens on appeal. And I don't think it's a good parallel with our situation, anyway. The Coca-Cola one'll be more interesting when it comes up. It isn't Coke they say committed the crimes but a local, independent bottler. Much more like us. And Coke'll argue there's no chain of liability. Flexalt could have a tiny problem making the same argument, though, because of that email to the board." Naturally, he'd memorized it: "*...ironic they want to take the* ATCA *route* (He's talking about the widow's lawyers) *because we had our eye on Unocal even before that case was filed in '97, and our Mexican partnership was configured with the developing* ATCA *risk in mind.* That's an email I wish I could lose. We fucked up not getting it on the privilege log. We can hope they don't find it, but if they get it on disc, all they have to do is press *Search: ATCA*."

"He's saying we anticipated the argument we're making now."

"Right. But if he says the partnership was originally configured—before the murder—in expectation of an Alien Tort Claims Act suit, then we'll have to explain why. They'll say it was because Flexalt thought it likely a crime would be committed and was trying to insulate itself. It isn't like a domestic regulatory thing—you can't just comply with a set of rules and get airtight liability protection. Corporate *mens rea* is going to come up. So what *was* our state of mind? The law is in flux here. If we had the ATCA risk in mind we're basically saying we expected something bad to happen in Mexico and didn't want to be held liable."

Preston's phone rang. He was happy to be interrupted. Until he took the call. He looked up as if he might ask Vijesh to leave, then he didn't. Extremely cautious, he spoke without betraying any information. This made Vijesh listen all the more carefully, though he retreated to the far side of the room and idly beat his water bottle on a bare bookshelf.

"She and I did talk yesterday evening—Yes, I think I can say I was a little surprised. Which is why I wanted to—I'd prefer face to face—That doesn't come into it, of course. I have no reason not to assume, uh, everlasting good faith on, uh, both our parts—Please—Yes, we are a bit in the middle of things here—As soon as possible. Lunch, preferably—Or after work—She was amenable, and even I might be willing to go along, though there's the issue of comfort—Well, isn't that something to be dealt with?—Yes, face to face—I don't know it, a RiteAid? Over by Short Hills Mall?—That's not how I usually go. I take the exit after that—That's fine. So we'll say six?—Watermelons. OK." He never cracked a smile, even after this last bit. When he hung up the phone, he breathed, "Miserable thing."

Vijesh knew he shouldn't comment, but he did. From across the room, he said in a strangely avuncular tone, crossing his arms, "Preston, old man, I think I know who that was." When Preston didn't say anything and didn't look angry, Vijesh continued, "I'm not the kind of guy who brings up things like this, but—" He rushed, "Listen, I have a feeling that was Claire Malouf and—" Still Preston said nothing. Vijesh's perfectly black eyes looked compassionate. "I'll only say I think you should give her a wide berth. Really wide. She's been talking to some people about you—and drinking."

"She's drinking?"

"No. You. Supposedly."

"Ah. Always had a nice working relationship with her, I thought."

"I'm not sure she feels the same way, Preston." Both of them looked out the window. Trailing Gulliver-like ropes from front and back, the MetLife blimp dipped its nose.

Preston looked at his clock and decided an hourglass was a better model for time than the constant electric gliding of a second hand. Time ran, came to a stop, then all was inverted, shaken up like now, before it commenced seething forward again.

During the phone call, Jeanette Paul (*not* Claire) had proposed meeting Preston at a supermarket. She said she'd only have five minutes after Lynn's sponge bath and before his dinner. Preston guessed she wanted him to fall in with her routine, act the supplicant. When he found her by the appointed pyramid of watermelons, she didn't appear to be in a rush at all. Her cart was empty. A redhead with a tray was offering her a sample of cheese. Jeanette took a tiny mallet of sweating cheddar on a toothpick. She made the woman wait till Preston came over. Preston demurred twice, white extra-sharp and yellow.

Drily, Jeanette judged her sample "better than it looks."

The redhead smiled and couldn't have cared less. She galleoned off along a misting bank of lettuce.

Without preamble, Jeanette told Preston, "I'm not doing anything weird. Just so you know. You're the one who wanted to see me. Which I understand—keeping tabs on my frame of mind. As far as I'm concerned, there's no need. Nothing's changed."

That was a promising start. Relaxed. Preston was equally careful to appear casual. Stepping around a smattering of crushed champagne grapes, they drifted from the crowded fruits and vegetables to a quieter aisle, pausing by cake mixes. Jeanette backtracked to introductory small talk, which soon became banter. With anyone else Preston would have shrugged off the teasing. With Jeanette, teasing had a dark cast, implied a secret and tragic virtuousness like the unhappy, painful-looking, creases of her face. Not unlike the university president's daughter twenty-five years on.

"You understand why I wondered, though," Preston told her with a confiding smile.

Jeanette parried with an unexpected question, "You never liked Lynn, did you?" Preston's silence was close enough to assent, so she went on. "Yeah. In your case I used to think it was—you know, when you really wrong someone, wrong them terribly, and then you can't stand having anything to do with them? I thought it was that way with you and him."

"Go ahead and shop, if you need to," Preston offered. She didn't take her eyes off him. He told her, "I'm sorry about Lynn. Truly sad about it. I've known him a long time. And it's rotten for you, Jeanette, it really is."

"But I decided nobody liked Lynn. Nor had they ever. Nor had I maybe. Maybe he was a convenience when I decided I wanted to get married. He'd have leapt at anything, and I like my men to leap. But isn't it terrifying—if that's your fate—to be the sort nobody cares for? And it's not how he was brought up or anything he did or anything that happened to him. You know I'm right. You know it's true. In his case, it's like autism or something. It's in his skin and always has been. I'm not claiming that means there's anything so all-fired saintly about me taking care of him—"

"Why couldn't there be? What do you get out of it, Jeanette? Always making yourself seem so sinister?" Tardily, Preston smiled to make that comment seem light.

But Jeanette gave him a nettled, haughty, "Is that what I'm doing?"

"About Barry," he said, changing the subject. Then he thought to apologize, "No. That's not what you're doing: pretending to be bad. I'm sorry. But about Barry—"

"Money comes into this not at all, Preston. So you can relax. If you can pay him a bit, fine. If not, not."

It made him nervous that the thought of money was so close to the surface. "Well, of course, I can do that, but I'm a little in the dark why you never want to settle the issue once and for all. What I mean to say is, it's been your pleasure to keep this thing in doubt for an awfully long time."

"*Pleasure?*" she repeated grandly. "I'd hardly call it that. *The thing*—my son—always was in doubt. I told you that from the beginning. I've never known for sure. But it was also never a pleasure. You know perfectly well, for years I dyed the poor kid's hair. You know that. I guess I was frantic someone might notice. Wasn't that a pretty desperate, unhappy... not a pleasure anyway! I'm sure everyone thought I was an idiot. Or a monster."

"Jeanette, resemblance was never the issue you seemed to think it was," Preston cajoled. He didn't want to come off condescending. At the same time, he tried to sound more positive than he felt. He didn't really know—nor had he ever—what Barry Paul looked like. For a few years, Barry had been a blond boy pointed out across the pool at Westerbrook or fishing lost golf balls from a water trap on the course. Then he vanished.

"No? You never thought so? I'm not saying I necessarily think so myself. Now. But I notice your kids never went to Lawrence, even though you did. No class pictures."

"Come on, Jeanette! That had nothing to do with it. Bea decided all that. Schools."

"Really? I seem to remember you and I having a talk at some point."

"No. Where I said the kids wouldn't go to Lawrence? I don't think so."

"I told you I was sending Barry there."

"I don't remember that. They were all at the club together with Barry often enough during the summers."

"Only when Lynn and I belonged. Not a long time at all. But why get into all that?" She put a stop to it, so he couldn't. "Look, if you feel you have to know, know absolutely, before you throw him a shekel, then by all means, let's do the DNA test like some—some ghetto couple. I feel not the slightest need myself. But if you do, let's be done with it. Who knew at the time there'd ever be this magic test?" The wildness of her threat warped her vowels. She was speaking in a low-pitched, laughter-like tone of voice. Neither of them could help looking up and down the aisle.

This was her line. Preston was certain of it. To perpetuate doubt forever. Since no demands had ever been made, she could think of herself as pure, untouched by vulgar self-interest. Whatever the cost to her, her life became a thing of beauty, as if it were art she was making with the thousand moral pigments of her frustrated existence. She'd come to him forever, whispering, *I'm not doing anything.*

"Let's stop pussyfooting, Preston," she said. "I know you don't believe it, but I'm not coming after you. I'm not! I'm not!"

"Why don't you want the kid at home to help you with Lynn, then?"

She smiled. She shrugged. "I need peace and quiet to poison the bastard, don't I?"

28

WEARING RUBBER BOOTS, Barry Paul and Dean walked through a field on Preston Sayles's property, their strides tangled, stringy, snapping. They were making their way back to the house. They'd just come out of the woods, and their flushed temples and pallid forearms were spangled with bright scratches and black specs. Boulders trucked in from a road-building project had been heaped picturesquely in the field. Dean leapt up on the largest one. He tottered.

Barry uncinched the long gauntlets of yellow gloves. Careful of the invisible poison, he plucked them off. He rubbed the stubble of his scalp.

From the boulder, Dean explained, "Just wanted to see if Preston's car was in."

"Too early."

"I know, but—" Dean was touchy with Barry, trying to be friends in a different way than in their schoolboy past. He enjoyed towering over Barry on the boulder. He also felt stupid, like he'd been trying to cut ahead of Barry in line all day. Not that Barry did anything but shrug affably. Even clearing brush in the woods. Dean had inserted himself in a task he'd left undone for months just because Barry was going to do it. And the bragging way he told Barry about his little intimacies with Preston felt desperate. Still, he couldn't stop. He'd been talking about the time Preston ran for Congress.

"So anyway, they videotaped him bullshitting with Ford, so they could make a TV commercial. He has a copy still, but he won't let anybody see it. He told me it's too embarrassing. He talked the whole time, and Ford just sits there nodding—*uh-huh, uh-huh*—and maybe once he says, *You're completely right about that, Preston.*"

Barry smiled, wondering if Ford had really sounded so stupid and if the job of president could really be so humiliating. "Why didn't he try again after he lost?"

"Claims he didn't like it. I think it might be that he liked screwing around too much. It would have been too dicey, too many skeletons in the closet. Never tell Bea, obviously. But it's pretty well known what he's like."

"Didn't seem to hurt Clinton that much."

"This was the old days. And, incidentally, he hates Clinton, and I think that's partly why. No, everybody wanted him to be a candidate when he was young. He told me they even took him to the White House once when Nixon was president. They go into the Oval Office, and he actually has the balls to ask if he can sit in the president's chair. Nixon wasn't there or anything. You got to get him to tell you. It's fucking hysterical." Dean took off his own gloves. He had allergies and tried blowing his nose but only got a nostril to burble thickly. His wire rims were smeared with sweat. His old scars itched. When Barry started walking again, he jumped down from the boulder and fell in with him.

Up by the sprawling house, the sunlight looked thick enough to fall in cords like honey. The trees around the house—golden already—shifted in a rogue gust of wind making Barry think, *girls under a shower*. Though they didn't see her at first, Bea's raucously friendly voice came from somewhere, "Pretty warm for October! You boys must be burning up" There she was, in a full-length aqua housedress. She was filling birdfeeders. A great plastic bag was at her feet, and a tin scoop shone in her hand.

It didn't register with either boy how peculiar the aqua outfit was for Garden Club Bea. Rather suddenly she'd given up her dainty sapphire guard rings and tiny gold sand dollar earrings. Since Addie Mueller had come to the chapel Bea had started opting for hunks of jade and amber and a big Celtic gold cross. The menopausal shift to clunky jewelry and garish colors, as mysterious as finding religion, had happened quickly in her case. Some of the new jewels tumbled into the gold-embroidered *décolleté* of her screaming housedress. If the boys didn't notice her clothes, they did notice that Bea was more harshly friendly than ever, even for a golfer. Her neat gray hair was coming apart. "Aren't you nice! Aren't you nice!" she railed. "I don't know how to thank you."

Dean rushed to speak first. "There's still a lot down there, Bea. It'll take two more days, maybe."

Something about his authoritative tone made Bea give him a brief stare that looked like it might turn into laughter.

Barry enthused, "We found this one incredibly huge one. Hundred years old maybe. Like a tree trunk." He made a ring with his hands.

"I've never heard of poison ivy growing like that!" Bea exclaimed. She couldn't not be as loud and happy-sounding as possible just now. Her oldest son, Philip, had managed a phone call from Nicaragua—long, accusing, irrelevant. Barry and Dean assumed puffy, reddened eyes were ordinary for a woman her age, not a sign of crying.

"The thing was awesome," Barry smiled at her. "Chthonic!"

"Well! I don't know how to thank you. For even just starting to get it out of there. No, Dean!" He'd bent forward to help drag the bag of seed to the next group of feeders. She didn't want his help and stopped him almost crossly.

Philip had said to her, "Now you're doing it to me. Don't you see how we, as a class, are cruel, power-mad? The niceness is a blind. The underclass is right. The only thing they don't get, because they can't conceive of it, is that we have total conviction. We really do think we're nice. And you can't fight faith." His voice had sounded villainous, no other word, its tone a cross between scalpel and oracle. So what could she—not the most dialectical person in the world—do but snort in contempt and shout, "Goddamn it! Class! What planet are you on, Philip?"

With a cheery "whoof!" she hefted the seed bag and got it propped against the green pole of the next birdfeeder. Its weight caused the squirrel guard to tip. *De-draingy-dang-dang*. "No, if the girls had ridden over from camp and gotten all poison-ivied on the trails—well, they'd think something awful about us. So thank you, boys! Thank you! Thank you!"

It wasn't Philip's cruelty to her. Children often tell you your life was a waste, your marriage a stinker, and *me*—I'm a ruin, thanks to you. But his terrible suffering! As a woman, Bea couldn't help but imagine it had its origin in her—at a level deeper than psychiatry is able to articulate. As if he'd come out as animated crystals of uric acid when all she'd meant to do was create life. In the way of God, she'd *more* than allowed the possibility of sin. Crazily, Philip had gone on: "And this great training in falsehood is exactly why there are so few interesting or accomplished people from privileged backgrounds, in spite of having all the time in the world, and—" She'd had to shrill back at him, "Philip! What on earth are you raving about? Anyone can do anything, if they put their mind to it!"

"It's actually nice for us the Riding Camp girls use the trails," Bea told Barry. "Helps keep them open. You should try some time. I bet they'd let you. If you did any riding out west."

"I can't afford to right now," Barry said. "Oh, that reminds me, I have to talk to Preston about something," he added guilelessly.

Dean nosed in, "Preston isn't back yet? I guess we saw his car wasn't in. Actually I've got to see him about something, too, at some point."

"Well! No, Dean. Preston won't be back till six-thirty or seven. He's visiting his sister at Hazelwood." Preston had a much older sister in a nursing home.

Another gust of wind came along. The many blotches of sunlight on the grass around their feet seemed to wobble on stems. The way nature broke in upon their attention, waving its arms, made human affairs seem puny.

With the particular sensitivity of strong emotion repressed, face to face with what she momentarily perceived to be the godless underlying boredom of the world, Bea made an incredible, tight-lipped expression of warrior sternness. At the wind's second gusting, she used the scoop to hold her gray locks in place. She surveyed the field, the boulders. If God was temporarily absent from the world, she would find Him. She blushed when she noticed Barry's generous face grinning at her in—she thought—admiration. With her usual fostering sweetness, a small voice, she said, "Well. You're both—you must be covered with poison ivy. Why don't you run and change. I'll tell Preston you want to see him, Barry. You, too, Dean."

There were two entrances to the garage apartment, the main door from the outside and another from the big four-bay garage. Barry and Dean went in through the garage, pungent of gasoline and mown grass. They left their rubber boots and gloves on the oil-stained concrete floor. Each took a shower, and afterward Dean heard the indecipherable thumps and knockings Barry often made overhead.

The noise came from Barry's largely made-up version of Tai Chi. With his poor sense of balance, he wasn't any more adept at this than he had been at skateboarding. But he kept trying, hoping it would help him take off a few pounds and get in touch with his body. Dressed only in red sweats, one foot in the air, his hands met in prayer over the dimples of a young man's slight paunch, and his expression was sublimely peaceful. Until he tottered and the raised foot thudded down. He ignored the squawk of the phone from the floor below and began again.

Downstairs, still in his towel, Dean eyed the caller ID before seizing the phone. "Lloyd, you fuckhead!" he answered amiably. "How we doing?"

Lloyd ran their little insurance business, aspired to be a Republican party flack in Trenton and affected to skip greetings. "Ask me if I care if that Swiss Re holier-than-thou motherfucker thought I was an asshole running around after little jackshit insurance commissions! I sold a fucking three-million-dollar policy to the old guy in Brick. How you doing? You talk with Prez-man over there yet?"

"Not yet. I can't bring it up yet. Because of the car still. I've got to let it cool off some more."

"For fuck's sake. Man. That was months, months, fucking months ago. What are you doing for me? Either get me Sayles or get me some other fucking leads over there. Shit." Not sounding overly upset, he rang off after adding, "Gotta go."

Dean's hand covered a gold-toned plastic figure of an archer—more Robin Hood than bow hunter—third place. An erection started to tent the kilted terrycloth of his towel, and he reached under and toyed with it idly for a moment. Still holding the phone, he thumbed his girlfriend Pia's number. As it rang, he slipped his hand under his armpit, drew it out and felt the new sweat on his fingertips, almost as evanescent as alcohol.

"Nah. Nah, I got to go out with Lloyd tonight. He just called," Dean said to Pia. She had mixed feelings about Lloyd. She once called him a *no-goodnik*. Dean offered, "You want me to blow him off?"

"No," Pia sighed. "What's that noise?"

"Barry beating off upstairs."

"Ha ha. No way. Why don't you go into business with him instead of Lloyd?"

After getting off the phone, Dean turned, wondering if he felt like cleaning up the place, and caught sight of himself in the mirror. Although he affected to downplay his good looks with glasses, he was vain, vain in a miserly way. He dropped the towel and turned so he could see his butt in the mirror. After masturbating perfunctorily in the bathroom, he threw on a T-shirt and shorts and pounded on the wall at the foot of the stairs. When Barry answered, Dean called up, "Wondering if you wanted to watch some TV is all. See the debate later, maybe. Not that anybody cares. I have to go out with Pia after."

They'd hardly said a word in the woods, and they hardly said a word now. Both of them sprawled on the couch in the subaqueous dimness of Dean's room. Ghost armies of empty beer bottles lined the counters and sills. On a laminate coffee table were a beat-up copy of *Foreign Affairs*, a plastic bottle cap used as the ashtray for a single half-smoked joint, and more beer bottles.

Elbows flapping, Dean rubbed his eyes. He scratched his ankle with both hands. After he made a series of throaty snuffles, he told Barry he hated nature and wanted to move back to the city with Pia. Barry, who hadn't spent much time down here, was eyeing a rubber plant in the corner of the room. The plant's leaves had all been hacked off and a machete was stuck in the soil of the pot. "That's anxiety," Dean explained to him. "That's my psychiatrist. Preston and Bea gave it to me at some point. But I'm not good with plants. Fuck me if this is a cold and not allergies."

He got a bottle of DayQuil from the bathroom and started taking tiny, pursed-mouth sips straight from the bottle, between bigger sips of beer. He kept mistakenly grabbing an empty bottle from the coffee table. He rolled it out of the way under the couch and reached for the right one, heavy, cool, sweating. They were glued to the evening news, but they didn't seem to be watching.

Without taking his eyes off the screen, Dean asked, "You're going to ask Prez for little extra—" His hand gestured *cash*.

"That obvious?" Barry laughed.

"No. But maybe you want to talk to Bea. She decides a lot of that. A lot of their money comes from her family. I know she's a pain to talk to."

"You think so?"

"For me anyway. I think she likes you. The thing is, I've got to try to sell Preston a big policy. A nice piece of property. But if we both go after him at the same time... Also it might not be such a good time for Prez. There's this huge lawsuit at Flexalt—and his sister—that costs a lot keeping his sister in that place."

"They're pretty rich," Barry observed, not petulantly.

"In a way. In a way, though, rich people don't think about it like that. They have all those kids, the house. What do you need more money for?"

"It's sort of to do with my dad."

"Shit. Right."

"Yeah, I keep having to ask my mom and dad for money they can't spare."

"Right. It sucks. How's he doing?"

"Not great. They're always finding more—you know—cancer."

Dean seemed to concentrate on the TV news for a while. He didn't have any comforting vocabulary. With an adolescent show of tough honesty, he observed, "Your dad always seemed—kind of a sad guy." Glancing at Barry, he saw that wasn't a good line. He started over. "For money, there's a couple of things you might try, though. Like you could ask your dad if he has a life insurance policy lying around. A lot of guys like him probably would."

"I don't know." Barry shrugged.

"The thing is, you can sell it. Like other people will invest in it. It got popular when all those guys were dying of AIDS and needed money. People would sort of bet the guy was going to die in a year or two. They'd pay like ninety cents on the dollar for the policy. Then when the guy did die, the people who bought it would get the whole dollar. It was good for the AIDS guy, too, because he got all this money to spend before he kicked. That could be your dad's situation. I don't know for sure, because I don't know all the details of his—or even if he has—"

"That's so sick," Barry said. He didn't sound appalled or outraged, more fascinated. "I think he does have a policy, though. My mom may have said something."

Sounding more crafty than even-handed, Dean frowned at the TV. "On the other hand, it might be less of a good thing for you in the long run. If you and your mom were beneficiaries, say, when he died you wouldn't get the payoff. So it might be less good in a—you know—in a selfish sense. Up to you whether you want to get into it."

"I don't know if it would matter to me. To my mom maybe."

"Or you could try for the real jackpot."

"What's that?"

"Well, that would be sue what's-her-name—Ms. B. The one you fucked."

Barry could tell Dean was, at least a little bit, serious, but he chuckled, and soon they both laughed. With a fanfare of tympani, the TV flashed back to a news anchor strolling through the as yet empty presidential debate set.

Dean made as if to drop the subject of money. He impatiently left before the debates even started, however, lying that he was off to see Pia as he'd lied to her that he was off to see Lloyd. He was headed to Asbury Park aiming for one of his compulsive fuck-boy pick-ups. On his way out he reminded Barry, "Seriously, about that insurance thing. If you ever decide. My man Lloyd does it all the time. He's got these little tricks. You could talk to him. Also think about this—maybe you could help me out with selling Prez on a policy. He loves you. If you took the commission, or most of it, that would be some money for you, too. We should talk about it. You'd be a good salesman."

After Hazelwood, Preston drove to the Clipper Room at the Radisson for a drink. From there he drove home on instruments, not trusting himself. He kept his Lexus speedometer needle from budging a millimeter. The dotted yellow line appeared to rise through the bottom of the car. Into him, he imagined. It flickered in his heart. He zippered together patches of woodland, horse farms, tracts of expensive houses. Whenever he pulled up at a stop sign, a heavenly silence descended on the crossroads. He could hear a single leaf skitter across the road. Drunkenness was a way of looking at things like any other. Through it, he was becoming a little hopeful.

A car with a ski rack followed him somnolently. He made the last turn, catching the berm. He straightened the car with a jerk as he would a suit jacket. The Lexus interior exploded with light. Heart racing, Preston thought reproachfully, "Now *that's* dangerous."

Lurid red, white, and blue swirled over his hands, his cheeks, the dashboard, clinging and flowing like oil. It hurt his eyes to glance directly at the flashing ski rack in the rear view mirror. He judged his pulling over a model of the art under the circumstances.

The police officer left his lights mutely yipping at the woods. He came up and stood a prudent distance from Preston's window. Preston smiled. He raised his eyebrows politely. The policeman switched on a flashlight. Sweeping Preston's lap and the front seat of the car, he slurred, or Preston heard him slur, "See your license, please!" or "Sir! License, please!"

"Of course." Preston handed it to him, adding, "I haven't seen you around."

"Nose her." The officer walked back to his car. After a long moment he switched off the flashing lights. When he returned, he said, "You live right here." His shoulders swiveled somewhat, but he continued rereading Preston's license with the flashlight.

"That's correct," Preston said in too pedagogic a tone. "Right there." He pointed. The moon beat lividly on the roof.

The officer glanced up from the license into Preston's eyes, a look that would have been bashful were it not so serious. Cautiously, Preston prompted him. "There was a problem?"

"Sort of crossed the line coming out of the turn," he said. He mumbled, "Missed the road, too."

"Live here so long, you start driving like you own the road. Which is dangerous," Preston said contritely. His drunkenness had burned down to a headachy flush by now. He eyed the young man's mustache, an ideal wave about to break over those silent lips.

"Arrive carefully," the policeman slurred, handing Preston his license. More likely, "Drive carefully."

Bea and Eleanor were in the kitchen when Preston came in. Preston gave Bea a rundown on his sister and her friends at Hazelwood, and he mentioned the cop. That got him a look. Bea told him the boys had started clearing brush and poison ivy from the woods. Eleanor was splitting Goldfish crackers with her incisors.

With innocuous-sounding cheerfulness, Bea suddenly exclaimed, "I'm in a mood to shake things up!" Her chin rose as she tried to think of a for-instance. Preston guessed she'd talked to either Philip or Anna. "Finally take care of this window, maybe." Bea didn't sound like she thought that was such a fun example of a shake-up. She didn't even glance at Dean's arrow's divot in the tempered glass. She seemed to be trying to think of something better.

"How's basketball, El-meister?" Preston asked.

"Fine."

"You want to shake things up, too? With me and your mom?"

"Sure. If we can *please* have horses, Daddy." She'd decorated her wrist with a cabochon Goldfish, which she now licked off.

"I'm not taking care of them," Bea laughed. A touch wildly.

"No, really. I'm serious, you guys. I think it would be totally normal to get a pony."

Preston bluffed. "You want a penny? Here you go. Let me—" He fished in his pocket.

"Not a penny. A *po-o-ony*, Daddy!"

"Right here. A shiny new penny!"

"Po-o-o-o-o-o-o-o-o-ony!!"

"What's that you say? Eh?"

"Preston." Bea put an end to the teasing.

"She just thinks she ought to want a pony, because that's what the general theory of little girl-ness says."

"Preston!" Bea said more sharply than was called for. As if Preston were tempting Eleanor with a cursed apple of knowledge, if a very small one.

Bewildered by the joke, Eleanor also stared at her father, not sure whether she was being made fun of. She insisted, "I *do* want a pony."

"Oh, damn," Bea remarked. "El, will you run out to the garage for some vegetables? Pick whatever you like. Us guys don't care, do we?" In the unused fourth bay of the garage they kept a freezer full of vegetables and Lean Cuisine packages and a butchered side of beef.

In the silence after Eleanor had gone, Bea and Preston could hear a pissy-sounding talking head from the TV blasting in the library: "Gore saw Clinton as damaged goods, because of the Monica Lewinsky imbroglio. Was it a miscalculation?"

With Eleanor out of the room for a moment, privacy created a slight awkwardness between Bea and her husband. Chin jutting, Bea brushed it aside. "That reminds me. Both Barry and Dean want to talk to you. And I have a feeling both of them—*both* of them—are going to ask you for money."

The flat of Preston's hand came down on the kitchen table. "Look—"

"Hey! Don't do that to me. I'm just telling you what they said. Well, maybe they didn't say anything about money, but I'll bet you..." She trailed off. She muttered, "I really do want to shake things up."

"Why now?"

Her voice rose as if he'd challenged her. "Maybe now's the time. I'm sorry. I know you're tired and worried about work. But maybe I'm tired and worried, too. You know, I quit with Dr. Berman. I'm not going to see him anymore."

"What brought that on? I didn't even know that was on the table. Why now, Bea? Did you talk with Anna or Philip today?"

"Maybe I did. Philip. Big deal. That has nothing to do with Dr. Berman. I've been thinking about that for a long time. Half the fun was having lunch with Cassie Vail every time, and now she can't because she's gotten so grand. I don't mean that the way it sounds. I mean, good for her! She's busy with her gallery. Doing something."

"You always said Berman was a big help."

"Of course he was. But there're other ways to change—to get out of being so—maybe, I'd like to try going to seminary! Is that so out of left field? Who knows?" She'd gotten a touch shrill. "I'm not at all sure you realize, Preston, how discovering God in my life has been—very important," she avowed doggedly.

"I know, Bea. Of course, I know," he said gently.

"I have to say I admire Cassie in so many ways. And Addie Mueller, too. Do you realize, that woman has a chance of becoming a bishop? Not that that's what it's all about. But—listen, you and I have worked pretty well together. And I'm glad of it, of course. But—but—" Unable to get something out, she turned accusing in frustration. "What do you mean, we're messed up? Why don't you think any of our kids can get along in the world? What about your part in it? Ever think of your responsibility?"

"Bea."

"I'm serious. I don't want you teasing El for being a fake little girl or me for being fakely nice or fake whatever else you think I am, when—when maybe that was exactly what you always expected of us!"

"Fake? I don't get this."

Bea took a moment, calmed herself and looked at him, now feeling forgiving as well as sweetly estranged from him. "You don't, of course, Preston. I don't think you *can* get it."

In the dark garage, Eleanor could hear Barry Paul spilling his tools in front of Dean's TV. He was going to work on his bicycle while he watched the debate. Eleanor kept shuttling a frosty carton of frozen peas between her hands so it wouldn't burn too much. Keeping to the darkness, she crept, stepping on rubber boots and gloves, until she got a view through the door's glass window. Barry had inverted his bicycle and was examining the chain for the master link. An American flag rippled on the TV screen. Eleanor could hear a trumpet flourish.

She could see the scar-like white scuffs in Barry's stubbly scalp, as if he'd been in a war. Why was he a thousand times more appealing than Dean, who was beautiful but not even attractive? She imagined Barry and herself running through a war zone together. Their happiness would be entombed by some disaster. If she survived, she'd cry her life away. Squeezing the softening box of frozen peas, she heard the sound of the collapsing rubble that, perhaps, would kill him. Or her. She felt the arousing glory of it in her gut. She nuzzled an edge of the wet, warming, softened carton of peas between her legs. It took a second, then the cold flashed through her forest green tights and cotton panties and flooded her with tingling from the puckered apex of her thighs to her shoulder blades. It was semi-painful, semi-wonderful, the most romantic wound. She took the package away only when it started dripping. Boldly, she used the box for a sly knock on the window.

She wasn't sure he heard. She squeezed the black stone he'd given her from its secret pocket behind the waistband of her skirt. She knocked with the stone, and he heard her this time. Plucking at the front of his red sweatpants, he stood. He padded over. By the time he opened the door, she'd run to hide behind her father's Lexus.

She could see him. He crouched. He reached out into the garage and righted the pairs of rubber boots. He smeared possible poison from them on the thighs of his sweats. He sat on his haunches, smiling gently as if he knew Eleanor was out there in the garage. Still on his haunches, he pretended to be blind, a performance just for her. His hands, streaked with bicycle grease, waved blindly through the doorway. He almost lost his balance and had to grab the doorframe. Still, he played, eyes closed, smiling as his head moved about like a blind worm coming up out of its hole. It was all a performance for her. "Where was she?" he played. "Where was Eleanor?" She let him hear her giggle once before she ran out of the garage with the peas.

29

PRESTON WASN'T ABLE to set up a meeting with Barry until almost a month had passed. He told himself it was the demands of the Azil case, but he was also intimidated by the idea of a fully developed person rather than merely scared of the time bomb in swaddling Jeanette had taunted him with all these years. With close study, Preston thought, he'd be able to distinguish himself from Lynn in the boy's—what was it?—phenotype. He felt the algebraist's curiosity to solve for an unknown. Apart from the biology and the math, his muddy emotions bemused him. His slight excitement would have been spoiled had Barry known whom, or the possible whom, he was going to meet. Jeanette had always assured Preston that Barry had no clue. So Preston had the psychological elbow room to examine this alternate history in the form of a person.

Preston assumed, at least for the purposes of the meeting, that Jeanette's story was true. He'd liked Barry, the property care worker, instantly. Both Bea and Eleanor adored him. Did that mean anything? In fantasy, Preston imagined bestowing a real job or a college education on his putative offspring. He'd be a good, industrious son, more like Flossy than poor Philip, who was too smart for his own good.

For his part Barry expected a quick chat and nothing more. Perhaps standing together on the drive in New Jersey. When Preston suggested a trip into the city and a long lunch at someplace really nice, like Blithe, Barry, who almost never went into the city, said *No*. What he wanted to talk about wasn't anywhere near that important.

But Preston insisted on making an event of it. He decided to try reproducing a long-ago lunch, when Bea's father had driven in from Noroton and entertained his future son-in-law at the University Club. Preston remembered being awed by the place. He was curious to see Barry's reaction.

November was cold in the city. Snow fell a full week and a half before Thanksgiving. The plowed heaps were soon reduced to exhaust-blackened remnants, more like pumice rocks at a Hula Pele than the background for Christmas carols. Meltwater slicked the sidewalks around the University Club. The sandstone façade of the building had been ruined by a cleaning in the seventies. The blurry, dark brown structure looked like it had just stepped out of the sea.

When Preston saw how Barry was turned out, he realized the boy wasn't the same kind of ambitious New Jersey asshole he himself had been when trying to impress Bea's father. This wasn't diagnostic of non-relatedness, of course. Philip, unquestionably his, was even less like him. Barry wore work boots with an ill-fitting blazer and tie obviously borrowed from Dean. He'd left his knitted beanie at home, but his shaved head and his default drowsy contentment came off a little *rent boy*. His choker of vertebrae, or whatever they were, peeked over a threadbare button-down yellow collar. To Preston the choker betokened a possible brotherly likeness to Flossy, who now never removed his own choker of blue trade beads.

A funny property of the mind is lag. Every moment that comes along is the same size. It takes a little while for psychology to blow up the big events and discard the superfluous ones. As they occur, boiling water for pasta and burying a parent take place on a uniform scale and at exactly the same steady beat. Even if Preston was having lunch with a long-lost son, the title character of an opera full of rubato and wild crescendos and diminuendos, in the moment things felt perfectly ordinary, easy, pleasant. Preston had to work to make the lunch feel as momentous as it ought to have been.

Barry laughed when he was given a menu without any prices on it. "It's pretty easy to guess." The white-jacketed Black waiters made him think he'd stumbled into a thirties movie. The dining room, while grand, showed an institutional decay worse than the blurred sandstone. Yellowed plastic runners lay over the carpet in front of the kitchen, and a carton of roach traps had been stashed indiscreetly under a sideboard with peeling veneer. A thousand-year-old employee strolled about holding a tablecloth and a single German silver fork, either in dementia or in a pretense of work.

"People who don't know expect it to be impeccable in here. Like a restaurant," Preston said, guessing Barry's thoughts. "But we like it run down. A renovation wouldn't do. That wouldn't convey the right note of aristocratic weariness." He looked at Barry to see if he understood Preston was mocking this paradoxical form of snobbery.

Twisted bundles of wires crusty with old paint hugged the moldings. They led to defunct phone jacks and window alarms. The wires circled the room at the baseboard and ran up the walls here and there to disappear into clumsy holes that leaked plaster dust. He did understand Preston's delicate humor, but to him the décor called to mind inertia.

Preston continued. "Too bad it's not spring. Shad roe's the one thing worth coming for. All the rest—" His hand tipped back and forth, meaning, *mediocre*. "I do like the pea soup sometimes—mushrooms and mint, which is avant-garde for them. Most of the menu's out of fashion. They were serving jellied *consommé* and *pêche melba* till the day before yesterday." He kept watching Barry. The boy was surprisingly alert to Preston's gastronomic shadings. He wasn't the oaf Jeanette talked about.

A bloated wreck of an old man, who looked famous to Barry, greeted Preston familiarly. Preston made a little joke. The famous-seeming man brayed and gripped Preston's shoulders from behind. His yellow-toothed laughter came off as stylish and ghastly at the same time. He gave Barry a high-caliber wink before moving off. Preston explained that the man wasn't really famous. His father had amassed the world's largest collection of

English hammered pennies, and his mother used to go parachuting on Long Island.

Preston's mouth stuck in kissing position as he consulted the menu. His fingertips, the very tips, touched the padded edge of the table in front of him as if he were about to start typing. This was his dainty imitation of Bea's father. He waved off a somnolent waiter twice while they sipped cocktails.

Preston shared a creaky joke about one of the grandiose but boring landscape paintings on the walls. "The huge jungle one with a volcano in the background used to be called *A Portrait of Miss Mary Cavour*. You can read the little label on the frame. She was an actress the turn-of-the-*last*-century crowd thought was *hot stuff*. So it was: volcano equals *Mary*, *ha-ha*. Yeah."

"Pretty daring," Barry smiled.

"And the one that looks like Antarctica has always been called *Frankenstein*. Unofficially. I'm not sure why. Was there a big snow scene in *Frankenstein*?"

"Never saw it," Barry shrugged. "Nice frame, though. Wow!" Soon he was starting to feel drunk. Politely, he kept up with Preston, though he'd mentioned that he hardly ever drank. This slight recklessness (two drinks so far) appealed to Preston. "My mom thinks I'm a nature boy. I've got to tell her I had an actual three-martini-lunch. She'll love that."

"Oh, yeah?"

"Yeah, she's more the social-climber type than me. I don't mean that in a bad way. She's just a lot more aware, you know? She hates it that I'm doing lawn and garden stuff. But I like it. Less responsibility. Of course, it means I'll be kind of grubby all my life." Barry announced this with unexpectedly sophisticated irony, a chip off the old block tone of voice that delighted Preston. "So she'll be relieved if I'm turning into a businessman," Barry looked into his drink while pumping his eyebrows like a strip club tout.

"The martinis on the rocks?"

"No. Not only them."

Preston copied an expression of elegant inquiry he thought he remembered Bea's father giving him.

Barry planted an elbow confidingly on the table between them. His torso slanted, making his whole demeanor a little arch. "I've got to tell you my plan. I've got a plan for today, Preston. You probably knew that. Today I really am a businessman."

Preston encouraged silently. Barry wasn't handling his glass or his sips like someone who never drank.

"Yeah. Before we get up from this table, I'm gonna get you to buy a big life insurance policy. Five million, at least. A very nice piece of property, too. If I say so myself. Or that's what I'm told and fully believe," he finished slyly.

This was a new Barry. If the bleary-eyed performance was supposed to represent *accidental* drunkenness, it was a clever way to conjure up intimacy. Preston stared, not displeased.

The corners of Barry's mouth drooped and indented crossly. He pushed his glass away and murmured, "Better not get too drunk."

"Dean's got you working his insurance racket now?"

"Sort of a funny deal, Preston. They want you to put down your address as Georgia when you buy the policy." Barry grinned. "Which you will."

"Because?"

"They figure I'll wrap you around my little finger."

This wasn't exactly a sales pitch. Why would he be telling tales on his partners? Preston wondered casually, "Why do they figure that?"

"I don't know. I think Dean thinks you're in love with me (which I know you're not). But I'm supposed to be bait. The truth is, I think he's the one in love. I mean, I think he said it about me, but really *he's* the one who's in love. With *you*."

"Love?"

"You know what I mean. Not *love* love. Idolizes. You should see his rubber plant."

"This doesn't sound like a sales pitch. What would you be getting out of it?"

"He hacked it. With his machete."

"What?"

"The rubber plant. I know that doesn't sound like *idolizes*, but I kind of think that's what it means. Like obsessed. He wants to be a politician. Like you were."

"Not quite. But tell me. Are you making a sales pitch or what? You sound like you don't care that much. What's in it for you?"

"They say I'll get half the commission. To be honest, it's money I could use. The thing is, I was going to ask you for a loan straight out, but they have a gimmick figured out that's good for everybody. Supposedly. Everybody gets something. I'll get half the commission on your policy, and my dad will get the viatical whatever-it-is on his old one." Barry smiled and winked big, an imitation of the penny-collector's son. Preston was sure Barry was using this hint of drunkenness partly to sell, partly to ask for advice, partly to ask for money.

Preston sized him up again with—almost—pride. "They?"

"Dean and that guy Lloyd he works with."

"And I'm supposed to give a false address?"

"They thought you probably knew somebody down in Atlanta. According to their scheme, it makes the thing more profitable. The rules are different in Georgia. I'm just the front man. Because you make Dean nervous. Not as much as Bea does, but still."

"But he loves me?"

"Sure. Don't you get nervous when you love somebody?"

"Oh. Maybe a long time ago. I don't think so anymore. If I even did back then." Preston actually thought about this for a second and concluded, "Strange not to remember how it felt."

Barry exaggerated a pouty expression of commiseration or deep thought, putting his palm to his stubbly scalp as if to adjust his head in space.

Barry's skin was smooth, Preston noticed, not like his own large-pored coarseness. Its color tended to gold, not to his own burst capillary pink. Smooth and gold were traits of Jeanette's. He couldn't remember any of Lynn's for the life of him. Only the man's general ickiness, and Barry had none of that.

Preston's retreat from the moment ended. "I'm enjoying this," he said. "But let's go over it. You're on spec for Dean and what's-his-name. You're the salesman. Why aren't you trying to be more convincing? I suspect you know what you're doing."

"Well, I don't know the whole story. For instance, I know selling my dad's policy and you buying yours aren't connected, but they almost wanted me to think so. They were subtle about it, but they were also hoping I got confused. Maybe I am. I think they just wanted me to do the work for them. I figure my best chance with you is to lay it out the way it really is. Buyers like real, huh? So it's almost a technique. Once you—you, Preston—know what the policy is really worth, maybe you'll understand what's going on and be able to tell for yourself if it's a good deal like they say. You'll put the facts together better than I can."

"You're not really drunk. Let me ask you, Barry, you need money, right? Partly on account of your father. Right. Living expenses, I guess. Whatever. Your mom have anything to do with us meeting?"

"My mom?" Barry reached for the drink he'd pushed away.

"Just wondering if you talked to her about this—intricate deal. Or about me, ever?"

"I guess," Barry shrugged, but his answer, to Preston's unstated question, was clearly *No.*

"Don't have anything to do with those boys, Barry. To me, it sounds like a scam. Or close to it. I'll check it out with Dean, though. He's an ass. And not honest. About the money—let me ask you, you ever get your BA when you were out West?"

"I never finished."

"Maybe that's something we could look into."

Barry drew back his head in surprise. "What are you talking about? I'm all on hold. I'm not doing anything, because of my dad."

"I get that."

"And college must be ten grand a year. Or I'd have to stay in Jersey for twelve months to qualify for a public one. I thought about it, but I'm not sure I'd want to stay that long—especially if I was suddenly—at liberty, you know?"

"Sure, sure. Let's put all that aside for a minute. I'll loan you a couple of thousand on top of the yard stuff. Pay it back whenever. But don't tell Dean. I'll follow up with him about the rest of it. Honestly, there's more I wanted to talk to you about. Other stuff, I mean."

"I thought I wanted to talk to you," Barry corrected.

"Yeah, well, I did too."

They smiled, and the conversation came to an abrupt halt as if they realized they were starting to flirt. Luckily, their meals arrived. Cutlery and glasses were rearranged. Crumbs from the bread Barry had been eating to soak up alcohol (he really was drunk) were scraped deftly from the mattress-thick tablecloth. After the two covered plates were set in front of them, the waiter wearily, without a hint of flourish, lifted German silver cloches from them. Holding these high like cymbals, he departed. Barry laughed. "I didn't know anybody really used those dome thingys. I've never seen one before. Except in a cartoons."

"Yeah. I know. I know. And *Miss Mary Cavour*. And the no prices. The whole place is an old-timey cartoon," Preston agreed. "To tell the truth, I didn't think it would be this bad. I guess I wanted to make an impression, and it's been too long since I've been here. It's not right for you and me. Flossy used to like it." Preston looked at his hand flat on the tablecloth. Barry's hand happened to be resting near it, easy to compare. It was less red, less puffy, more golden, but the thickness and straightness of the fingers, the unemphatic knuckles, the thin-looking, deep set nails, were similar. Preston sometimes had to pry clippers under the ingrowing ends of his own nails. Was he already too close to Barry to judge?

Barry withdrew his hand. "Why would you want to make an impression on me? And what other stuff?"

"Huh?"

"You said you wanted to talk about other stuff."

"Yeah. OK. Let's see. Well—you ever had any supernatural experiences?"

Barry laughed in surprise. "I guess I've got my little amulets—medicine stuff from when I was out West," Barry admitted. "Yeah, I'm a believer. Were you talking to Bea?"

"No."

"Sure you're not setting me up?"

"No," Preston promised.

"What do you mean then? You mean like coincidences or ghosts?"

"Could be those. Or ESP," Preston said.

"I guess I've had that sometimes. Or I think I have. What's this about? When I was a kid my best friend and me played around at summoning ghosts. His schtick mostly. I was telling Bea about it, and she told me—she's a very spiritual woman, as you know—she told me that she saw an angel once. I could believe Eleanor has a touch of ESP, too, or whatever. Maybe it runs in your family. You ever have any experiences?"

"Oh," Preston shrugged. "I'm an old dog. No sensitivities. An angel! That's news to me. She must think I'm too rational and—jeering to tell me anything about it."

"I can believe that," Barry said.

"I'm not. Not really. I don't mean to be anyway. Here's another thing. You have a girlfriend?"

Barry smiled curiously at the interrogation. "Hmm. Last one dumped me. No hard feelings. She was kind of controlling and she thought I was a slacker." He rubbed his thumb and fingertips, *money*. "Like my mom, I guess. A lot of them are like that."

"Women?"

"No. My girlfriends."

"So you've had a lot of them."

Barry frowned and smiled, not wanting to say *Yes*. "I've heard you—"

"No, no! You're answering the questions," Preston laughed. "Don't start asking me or I'll get in trouble."

Barry slid his hands under his thighs and nodded obediently. "I guess I've had a few girlfriends but not a lot of regular friends. Almost no guy friends. I don't know why. Not since my friend growing up, but he was practically in love with me. Not idolized. Real love, I think. And he was gay it turned out."

"That's awkward," Preston said evenly. Despite Flossy, a piggish comment had come to mind.

"No. I don't think he knew it at the time. To be honest I kind of got a kick out of it. It can be cool in a sick way as long as the person is too nervous to touch you. You're powerful. Which I guess I didn't mind at the time. Though it couldn't have been that nice for him. We were young, you know? It was almost the age before you're aware. When did you have sex the first time?"

Preston delicately put his palm to his forehead, as if checking for stray hairs or sweat. Really, he was feeling a wave of nostalgia at the boyishness of this question, of the whole conversation. He motioned for more drinks.

"Is that dumb? No questions allowed?" Barry asked with a challenging lack of embarrassment.

Preston stared across the table: eye color, earlobes, hairline. He'd been expecting a subtle but obvious all over resemblance, or lack of it. Now he thought it could go either way. "Probably a lot younger than you think. She was so young I could've gotten into big trouble if I hadn't been the same age. I'm sure I would have, today."

"My first time was with my teacher. I was twelve-and-a-half. I don't know what she was. Thirties?"

"Jeez! Precocious. Was that—?" Preston stopped himself. "That was at Lawrence!"

"Oh." Barry winced in regret. "I forgot you knew I was there. Dean and me both went. You went too, right? With my dad? Shit! Listen—" He scratched his stubble hairline with a forefinger nail. His expression was troubled. "Don't say anything about it and—don't even try to guess who, because—"

"Relax. I was there a hundred years before you. I wouldn't know anybody. Besides—not that I don't care but—I've got to say, it doesn't seem to have fucked you up."

"No. I mean, I wasn't fucked up. But it also wasn't what you think. Or what people think. It was extremely confusing for a long time. I'd definitely say not good in the end."

"Ah." Preston looked down. "In my case, both of us were fourteen. That's a lot better."

"That best friend I was talking about was from Lawrence, too. Darius Van Nest. Did you know them? You probably knew his dad. I could see him being a member here."

"I knew *of* him, but I didn't know him. The father. He was older. In a different class. He was—quite well known for someone who was never there."

"He was crazy."

"Right. He was famous for that. And an amazingly beautiful wife. Just lovely. But they were divorced."

"Uh-huh. Also, Preston, don't say I told you Darius was gay. I don't even know it for sure. I just assume."

"I don't have anyone to tell. Anyway, I'm discreet. I'm a lawyer." He made a sour expression about the word. "Oddly enough, his family came up the other day. Or the wife did. She has some exotic name."

"Sohaila."

"Mm. Someone told me she has money troubles. But that didn't sound right."

"I don't think so. They were the richest people I ever knew. Except for you, possibly," Barry added out of politeness. "In fact, Darius used to loan *me* money. Or he did once." He cocked his head and looked off "Wow. So I guess I owe him. I shouldn't have let that slide. And I guess I shouldn't have let it slip out now that I forgot to pay him back!" He sipped and blushed, or he was simply flushed at this point. "If you do loan me a few thousand, whatever, I promise I'll pay you back."

Preston laughed. "Now it's a few? Relax. It's open-ended."

"I remember he loaned me money for a girlfriend problem I had a long time ago. I was basically a kid. I still feel bad about it, though. She needed to have—" He pretended to brush something from his lap. "—something taken care of. You know what I mean?" Barry let silence turn this question into something much more direct.

"Yeah, I've had that problem."

Barry smiled gratefully. "It kind of makes you feel bad, even if you're the guy. Not that I'm anti- or anything."

Preston's finger ran back and forth, erasing an arc of white light on the rim of his glass.

30

DARIUS WAS WALKING as fast as he could short of running. Even so, his long strides were only a little more hurried than usual. He was headed down lower Broadway on Thanksgiving night. Office buildings echoed his footfalls in a higher register like the sound of a rockhound's hammer. The deserted streets made for a dramatic contrast with his hurtling, chaotic emotions. He was panicking over his father.

Something about the acoustics and the tomb-like urban backdrop conjured up his old invisible companion, the marquis from Le Trap. But that had been a stroll. He'd been the victim. Tonight he hurried to play, he guessed, the savior, rescuer at least. The eerie, soot-dark defiles were filled with light like weak broth.

He'd taken this exact route, Warren Street to Cedar Street, many times since coming back from Paris. He was always scouting Oliver's apartment. Despite a few trivial phone calls, he hadn't once crossed the apartment threshold or seen his father. He'd tried the street door buzzer a number of times, always retreating from the building with an ultra-self-conscious pantomime: *oh, I must have the wrong time or the wrong address for my appointment*. Presumably the playacting was for the benefit of passersby. It was odd that being ignored by his father was also intense, unwanted attention, or felt like it. One time he'd taped a note to the buzzer panel explaining who he was and how to reach him in case of an emergency. Tonight, long after he'd forgotten about this message in a bottle, the building super or some neighbor—Darius wasn't clear which—finally called.

The incredible fact that Darius had been living in Severine's loft with Rolf blocks from his father for almost a year and hadn't yet seen the man—that incredible fact could so enrage Darius that thought of it made him squeeze his eyes shut. His fingers swanned, his lips disappeared, and he went speechless with emotion. Rolf watched this fit with a look of horror.

Then the tension relaxed, and Darius could claim, in all honesty it seemed, that the situation didn't bother him so much. Smiling, he shrugged at Rolf's concern. "My father's an odd guy," he said. Or he joked, as he had tonight after hanging up the phone, "Looks like I've got a father emergency."

Darius turned right at the foot of City Hall Park where a Staples had just gone in. Overhead the white pinstriped World Trade Center gave off no pathos of foreknowledge. The paired towers were all out of scale to the too narrow streets and couldn't be seen whole from any angle. Observed in passing, they looked out-of-date, ratty, provincial. Huge but not great. Oddly enough, Darius routinely imagined them falling. He did so now when he noticed them from the sidewalk. The dream-image of disaster lasted an instant, and unlike the future reality, the towers fell as timber does. This vision was almost a tic, like replaying Colin Vail's hanging every time he walked into the New Jersey house. On Cedar Street, a man stood propping an industrial door open. Without even a name check, he nodded at Darius, ushering him inside and upstairs.

For a long time Oliver Van Nest had been prey to a strange hallucination—a little more vivid than the falling towers were for Darius and more or less continuous. He thought he could increase or slow the rate time passed for him, while it passed at the usual rate for the world and everything around him. Since he never went out, you'd think it wouldn't matter if a hundred seconds passed for him, while only one did for the faucet or the chair. The effect of seeing everything in extreme slow motion didn't matter if nothing moved.

Oliver had discovered this wasn't the case. When time passed quickly for him and slowly for the things around him, and when he looked hard, he perceived fluttering gray images lined up behind every object, and even, faintly, the walls. The first dozen might be discernible as images of, say, the chair, but after that, the infinite regression of images had the aspect of a phantom tail. These tails shifted about slightly as Oliver moved around the loft. He understood that each of the images forming the long tail was the chair at an indivisible moment of its long existence in time. Each of the images had an infinitesimal being associated with it because, unlike the real chair, they were alive and even had rudimentary, pet-like personalities. Indeed Oliver called the images *infinitesimal beings*. Only the chair of the present was mute, dead. When Oliver sped up, he found he wasn't alone but in the company of multitudes, many multitudes, many infinities, in fact, of tiny personalities. One or another of them sometimes raised its voice, no more articulate than a mosquito's whine.

In order to hear the voice clearly, Oliver attended to the fantastical amplification of what he called a *whispering device*, the tiny slit metal bell at the end of a long lamp chain hanging from a lamp near his usual chair. Sometimes he peered into the minute brass maw as he listened. Frequently, he wrote down what he heard in cheap, spiral-bound notebooks. Though he wasn't aware of it, what he wrote was a looping scribble, not even letters, unless they were long strings of *e*'s and *l*'s. Every few pages the scribble resolved itself into a word like "fuck," or occasionally into something with a disturbing hint of clarity like, "you do not feel well." He could sit writing, or scribbling, for an hour at a stretch. He kept notebooks he'd filled in a suitcase along with a vial of mercury (the type sold illegally for Santería), clipped articles about bizarre accidents, papers relating to his finances, a large hunk of red glass, travel brochures collected in the fifties mostly by his mother and, finally, old family cards and letters, including a diminutive envelope dating back to the eighteenth century. He often moved the suitcase from here to there in the apartment, going for the most secure placement.

His acceleration in time wasn't entirely under his control. It came over him like drunkenness or flashbacks. It had an addictive quality. Though he wasn't always certain when he was moving faster in time and when he wasn't, he did think he was doing it more often and for longer periods. He suspected this put him in danger. As if he were using up the allotted moments of his life too quickly.

The wah-wah of time highlighted for him the terrible contingency of his heartbeat and breathing. Lately, premonitions of dying had gotten the better of him. That Thanksgiving night (pure chance it was Thanksgiving), fear caused him to open his apartment door, leaving it ajar in case someone had to come in and revive him or save him. A neighbor was disturbed by the open door and by a humid stink wafting from inside. She called the super who peered in and tried talking to a mostly non-responsive Oliver. The man went to his ground floor apartment for the note from Darius, which he'd thumbtacked to the wall in his kitchen. As he'd been meaning to for months, he called.

Oliver had the experience of coming to. He could hear the infinitesimal beings, but he couldn't see them. So he was in doubt about the rate at which he was coming to—fast or slow. He was seated next to the whispering device. The lampshade was tilted toward him as if he'd been reading. His suitcase was there in a safe shadow along one wall of the vast room.

The truth was, Oliver wasn't well. Even setting aside delusions and hallucinations, he wasn't well. He had a lingering infection in his throat, which caused him difficulty swallowing. Arthritis made movement painful, though he'd analyzed it as a shearing effect of time on his body. His skin was as delicate as tissue paper and very slow to heal. If he scratched at a tickle or a mite's bite, his skin often bled, and a coagulated scum of blood had accumulated under his nails. All over his bald calves blue veins made twisted heaps like earthworm castings.

He usually only cut the nails of his right hand to write. His thin fringe of hair, for ages unwashed, was sore at the roots. When scratched, his scalp bled, too. An amber smear of blood had gotten on one of the smudged lenses of his glasses. His bathrobe, in constant use, was foul-smelling and stiff in many places. The store tag had long ago fallen off but not its pricking plastic loop.

Hungry, straining to understand the infinitesimal beings, Oliver shuffled into the kitchen and made his usual meal of saltines and tuna fish. As always, he ate standing at the kitchen counter. With fanatical deliberation, he gathered every stray saltine crumb with a licked fingertip. He ate the crackers with one hand cupped under his lower lip. When he was done, he gently raked his beard over the hand, which he then licked clean like a cat's paw. He also licked the empty tuna fish can as best he could without cutting his tongue too much. His mouth was chalky, full of the specks of his meal. He sipped from the running kitchen faucet three or four times. His neck cracked and hurt when he straightened up.

He wiped the tuna fish can dry with a paper towel before stacking it in a cupboard full of empties. Then he carried the towel to his unplugged refrigerator where he stored the refuse he'd judged (a while ago, when he was still judicious) would attract bugs. This time when he opened the refrigerator door, the packed mass of crumpled, discolored paper towels spilled out quietly on the kitchen floor. Old flecks of tuna fish dropped everywhere. This wasn't a small mishap for Oliver. He'd have to get on his hands and knees to clean up the mess. The chore would be painful and might take a full short-of-breath fifteen minutes or half an hour. Which would bring him half an hour, or a hundred hours, closer to his death. He was too nervous to work. Anxiously, he left the towels and hobbled out of the loft.

To Darius, standing in the hall, nervous himself, his father looked awful but probably not as awful as he really was. The old man's mumbled remarks sounded more or less coherent. Darius was even able to guide his father back into the apartment and close the door. The super had lingered at the far end of the hall, and Darius felt a deep shame about his father's neglected appearance and the unpleasant, warm, sweetish smell, sharply demarcated several yards beyond the door. These were an injury against decency. And the injury had been caused by a son's remoteness.

Inside, Darius tried to get Oliver to change. He found clothes in a closet, which the loft's original owner had cobbled together with plywood. When Oliver resisted, child-like except for his furious expression, Darius abandoned the smelly "fresh" clothes and tried to get him to come back to Severine's dressed as he was. Oliver refused in a sibilant muttering. In a hoarse voice he managed a few lucid, depressing sentences, "I'm not completely in my right mind at the moment. I'm just going to stay here and rest, boy. That's what I need to do."

So Darius went to a deli and bought what supplies he could. He found the mess in the kitchen and put the paper towels into a garbage bag along with the towers of empty tuna fish cans from the cupboard. He straightened the bathroom. He extracted a promise—rather, he informed Oliver that he was coming back the next day for further serious discussion.

Holding the garbage bag, which still exhaled that humiliating, sweet, Oliver's-apartment smell, Darius begged a key from the super. The super narrowed his eyes. He couldn't keep a sour stubbornness from showing. But he relented—with provisos Darius paid no attention to. On the street going home it occurred to Darius that maybe the super wasn't so awful. He only needed to be given some money the next day.

At Severine's loft, Darius found Rolf sitting in a window embrasure smoking a cigarette. Beside him, the remains of their Thanksgiving dinner—just the two of them—were tickled by guttering candlelight. Rolf couldn't hide his eagerness to hear everything. Darius stared, feeling a winded blankness, and put him off. He phoned Stan and Sohaila in Bermuda. He over-described and under-described Oliver's condition to his mother, sounding alternately alarming and reassuring. The indefinite result of his description frustrated him. Rolf looked at the floor, eavesdropping gravely. After letting the sound of a foreign siren interrupt her, Sohaila started talking about money. She sounded shrill and worried. Though Darius hadn't meant to upset her so much, she confessed for the first time, that no matter how a trip to Bermuda looked, she was this far—*this far*—from having to sell the New Jersey house.

When he got off the phone, Darius was exhausted. He submitted to Rolf's hug, which ebbed to a hand rubbing his back, to it resting his shoulder, to nothing. They were alike in how they avoided physical intimacy outside of sex. This bleak likeness in itself was a tiny bit comforting.

The morning after this disastrous Thanksgiving, Darius realized he was going to have to consult someone. Someone experienced with older people who run off the rails. He had to do something about his father. The burden felt so heavy and strange to him that he feared paralysis. He was in tears admitting that he'd nothing but indulge himself over the course of his entire pre-paid life.

"I know you hate to be clear about things," Rolf insisted in the Americanizing way he'd adopted. "I know you think I'm pushy, and I know you have important practical things you have to do right now. But when you can, please step back. I truly think this *crise* could be salutary for you in the end." Rolf was dissatisfied with how that sounded as encouragement. "Listen, I want to help. I'll do anything." But Rolf had to go uptown to the UN job his father had arranged.

Stunned in a way that looked, to Rolf, vulnerably open, Darius weakly closed the apartment door after him. As soon as he was on his own, Darius felt a bit more capable. Unfortunately, even with a key, he was unable to get back into his father's apartment. The place had a Fox Police Lock, circa 1930. A steel rod ran from a cast iron box on the back of the door to a slot in the floor. Firefighters, who had axes and rams after all, said it was the best, and occasionally deadliest, way of securing a New York apartment.

The super extolled the lock in a thick accent when Darius hunted him down. When the super finished his disquisition on the Fox Police Lock, Darius suppressed—barely—a spoiled rich boy's whimper of frustration. The super looked at him without sympathy. He barely nodded when Darius pressed a hundred dollars in folded twenties into the man's hand.

His father was alive, at least, because he'd spoken through the door: quite normal-sounding, inflexible and brusque. The tone of voice undermined Darius's sense of emergency. The super warned him that a note under the door would do nothing. He'd tried it himself. Groceries left in the hall would be stolen. The man's unsmiling discouragement was comprehensive. Darius xenophobically decided he must be Russian. (He was Maltese.) Still, Darius remembered to thank him lavishly and, despite the warning, left a box of groceries by the door. Gatorade, dusty, pull-tab cans of corn and beans and beets and Viennese sausages, as well as a few other items available at a twenty-four-hour deli and packaged for end times.

Nothing changed over several days. Darius shuttled between Warren and Cedar, his mind spinning, even during unrestful sleep. The box of groceries was untouched until the third day, when it was gone. Oliver wouldn't admit to taking it in. He gave Darius his short-tempered, formulaic, "I'm fine. I just want to be by myself today." Darius suspected his father only talked through the door because he was wary of a rescue break-in. But after making his daily announcement several times—*leave me alone*—he stopped responding.

Darius needed to talk to someone. Oliver's old lawyer friend would have been perfect, but neither Stan nor Sohaila knew his name. Darius thought of Cassie Vail, who, according to Stan, was quite prominent now. He guessed she would know the lawyer or another likely adviser.

Since getting back from Paris, Darius had seen little of old acquaintances. He read Alan Wilkinson's arch book reviews in the *Wall Street Journal*, but he hadn't called. The Paris Vail show, much enlarged, was due to be mounted at Cassie Vail's gallery. If he went to the opening, he would see Cassie, of course. He also than Alan might be there, though probably not with Tom. He knew his old French tutor David Caperini was in New York and, because they used to talk about Vail together, Darius guessed he too might show up.

According to his program for this evening of old friends, Darius would be amusing and suave. He would tell Cassie her brother's drawings were fake. (It never occurred to him that Cassie might not appreciate a bombshell like that in the middle of her opening.) Then—oh, yes—there's something about Oliver. He'd mention that. Did she happen to know how he could contact Oliver's lawyer friend or some renowned psychiatrist? The best in the city, please.

Darius brought Rolf along for support, but they separated early. The gallery was crowded. Darius was immediately thrown off his program, because Cassie, though very friendly, wasn't as uncertain as she had been when he visited from Choate with Oliver. She had the same alarming El Greco thinness, but up close she was much older. She'd caked on what looked like opera stage make-up, perhaps as an outlandish *fuck you* to her Miss Porter's past. "Darius!" she cried the moment she saw him. She raised her ornamented claws as if to seize his cheeks but didn't touch him. "Darius!"

Cassie was trying to conduct two conversations at once. She'd been regaling a group of collectors with her shocking opinions, and on the side, speaking to an attractive young man who looked about the same age as Darius. She interrupted both conversations. "Oh, Darius, Darius! How in God's name is your father?"

Darius wasn't prepared for her to bring up Oliver right off. He deflected with a weak, suburban *Oh, all is well. All is well.* He cursed his traitor nerves but what else could he say?

The thunder of chat filling the room seemed to oscillate subtly, as if crowd noise were a property of the universe, not something generated by thoughts and remarks. The gallery walls had been given a fresh coat of chalky white paint. The room's brilliant whiteness made for a sore throb in the eyes. Darius realized he wouldn't be able to find friends or have a worthwhile conversation about anything here.

"This young man's father is the uniquely *nutty* Oliver Van Nest! Whom I love!" Cassie crowed, her gaze sweeping the circle of collectors. She realized the name meant nothing to them. So she turned to the attractive young man, "Well, your parents—did they ever know Oliver and Sohaila in Noroton? I suppose the *and* isn't current," she added with a wry look at Darius. "Not for ages. I knew that."

The young man lifted a clear plastic cup of wine in a shrug, or else he was trying to avoid being jostled by someone. "We're in New Jersey, actually," he corrected.

"That's what I meant. Noroton—that's the olden days. Darius! This is—I wanted my darling, darling school friend Bea Sayles to come, and this is her son who showed up!" She sounded both wildly enthusiastic and not entirely pleased. She blundered over the young man's soft interjection reminding her his name was *Flossy*. "Which I'm *very* happy about! Yes, *Flossy*."

To Darius the young man looked more like a Caleb than a Flossy. Nobody was a Flossy. Cassie went on in a rush. "Yes, this is Flossy Sayles. I went to school with his mother. And this is the brilliant—world traveler—Darius Van Nest. My two very favorite boys." She wanted to get back to the circle of collectors, who were all pretending to listen with eager pleasantness as if they were much younger and cared about two more young men.

Flossy and Darius turned to each other, separating themselves off from the larger group. "We'll talk later, Darius!" Cassie shouted confidentially. Her hand, both feathery and hard like live coral, squeezed the back of his neck.

Face to face, smiling, Flossy and Darius spent a silent moment gauging whether they had anything in common. They seemed to settle on *No*. Flossy was too sporty and healthy-minded. Darius was appealing but in a hostile or unhappy way. He broke the silence anxiously, "I was hoping to find my friend Alan here."

Flossy said nothing but his expression modulated. *Am I supposed to know him?* He studied the puddle of wine in his plastic cup, swirled it. "You a fan of the artist?"

"Yes. Actually, I slept in—yes." Darius scanned the crowd so as not to look at Flossy.

Flossy asked him, "How do you know Cassie? She's my godmother. I think. Though I'm not sure she remembers me."

"Really? She dated my father a million years ago. I remember she dazzled me."

Flossy nodded, somehow both warm and uninterested.

The possible faint rejection made Darius narrow his eyes. He decided to run. "I guess I'll get something to drink."

Flossy toasted him on his way.

They turned separately into the crowd. Darius could see Rolf across the room bending forward, crouching almost, to examine the Vail drawings. Rolf was unbothered by the throng. Darius recognized no old friends. Caught in the mob's undertow, he began to feel quite helpless. He bobbed from room to room. His prepared remarks about his father kept coming to him. They sounded all wrong. His father's situation was incommunicable in the circumstances, like news of a giant asteroid due to hit in four days. Darius blamed himself for serving Oliver poorly, for getting brushed off like that by Cassie.

He was beginning to float over toward Rolf when he did see someone, but that too felt all wrong. David Caperini stood in a corner. Perhaps it was the brilliant warmth of the lighting, but something was a touch heightened about the ex-tutor's disheveled appearance. His clothes, his splotchy skin, the stray ear hairs, the bitten nails, the flaky scalp—they were all oddly beautiful in the glorious light. David was talking to an older man in leather and chains, who looked ill, perhaps drug-addicted. His yellowish skin with bluish shadows seemed enameled. Darius positioned himself directly in front of his old tutor. David returned a long, unfriendly stare.

Fear-like recognition scrambled David's expression. He babbled. After a squeal of greeting, he immediately started recapitulating his conversation with the old addict. They'd been talking about how upset they were, because an ordinary but legendary East Village coffee shop was being renovated and ruined. "So many names were scratched into the leaves of their dusty old rubber plant! But Darius! Darius!" David gasped with a joyful artificiality like Cassie's. After taking a huge breath and clamping his lips closed, he gave Darius an aggressive poke in the shoulder. "*Sssssss!* You've gotten so hot—so hot, Darius!" He blew on his fingertip to cool it off. "You were in Paris or somewhere?"

Darius had no idea how badly his sudden appearance spooked David. Once David had recovered, he talked even faster, even more incoherently. He didn't wait for Darius to answer his questions. He laughed self-consciously about his jitters. "*Ah, Darius*, I have terrible ADD. Diagnosed! But only after I left you. I can barely afford the Adderall. Not to sound *pathetic and penurious*! Actually, I'm well. Being creative! But I thought you were in Paris! Do you remember talking Vail for hours on end in the old days, and *en Francais, n'est-ce pas?*"

"*Candi Fury* was on a rubber leaf," the drug addict recalled bafflingly.

David continued, "You know, Vail has been an incredible influence on me. That year at your house—imagine." He turned to the old addict. "Darius lives in Vail's old house! Or used to."

Darius looked at the drug addict warmly, waiting for an introduction. For a moment the man stared back at Darius, or at his lips or the bridge of his nose. His aim was off. With an almost inaudible *uh-huh* he left them. David whispered, "Don't worry about him. But seriously. For years now—all by my lonesome—I've been slaving over a graphic novel about the life of *Piero Cannata—not* the filmmaker."

"I don't—"

"No, of course not. No one knows him. This one attacked Michelangelo's *David* with a hammer. Broke the toe off. 1991. Then as soon as he got out of a psychiatric hospital, he attacked a Filippo Lippi with black magic marker! At the cathedral in *Prato*! And that wasn't the end of it. But—yes, I somehow tried to build on the—on Vail's self-consciousness about his own work. Did you see the drawings? Do you know them?"

"I saw them in Paris as a matter of fact. I don't think they're authentic. But, *Shh!* I haven't told Cassie."

"What? Not autograph works? Incredible! Are you sure? I quite liked them. I even wondered whether they hadn't come through you somehow," he steered close to the truth. "From the house or from your father. Of course, Cassie won't care one way or the other. I happen to know they were sold in a lot to another gallerist, Arthur Greenblatt, but he's in Zurich."

David had used Cassie's first name in the familiar way Americans talk about someone famous. In passing, Darius thought it odd that David knew about the disposition of the drawings. Without suspicion he admitted, "I do think there's a chance they were taken from our house a long time ago."

David was silent. His expression was like a dragonfly landing.

"Maybe by some workman Mom hired or who knows?"

After a long pause David asked, "Why would there be fakes in your house?"

"That part I haven't exactly figured out. I'm pretty sure they were there, though."

"Well, that's—*whoof*—*wow*!"

"David," Darius began. "There's actually something important I'd love to ask you about."

David made an indulgent moue. He brushed long thinning hair over an inflamed corner of his forehead. He had a serious tremor in his fingers. It was particularly noticeable when his hand came near his face, brushing his hair out of the way, as now, or rubbing at a fugitive itch or touching his nose when he lied. Darius had always thought David nervous and vulnerable partly because of this tremor. Appealing to David now felt strange, because he had to abandon his old condescension toward adults. "I'm not sure I understand," David began after Darius had broached the subject of Oliver. "He was always—"

"He's really been going downhill. The whole time I was in Paris. It started even before that. Seven years, maybe. And it's serious. He's not like he used to be. Like when you knew him. He's turned into—almost—one of those germophobe shut-ins. None of us can get in to see him. And frankly, he could drop dead, and none of us would know. I'm sure he's got high cholesterol and high blood pressure and he's definitely not taking anything."

"How is this your responsibility? I mean, if he's been able to function—and I guess he can function now in some minimal way? A lot of people don't go to see the doctor when they should—"

"No. I'm not really asking your opinion. Sorry, David. I'm wondering if you know anybody who's dealt with the same thing."

"I have an aunt with dem—"

"I mean in a professional way."

"Like a shrink?"

"Uh—yeah, I guess," Darius squirmed. This wasn't going well. He'd somehow imagined a glamorous profession existed that exactly suited his father's desperate need. A solution was going to have to involve love and understanding, amateur qualities. He worried because no one could love Oliver.

"Hmm. I want to help," David said as if about to continue with a *but*. Compassionately he said, "Let me put on my thinking cap. Hm. Hm. Hm."

"Oh, don't worry. I can always try Cassie," Darius waved aside his own plea. "They sort of—almost—went out for a while a long time ago." He sounded disconsolate.

"Well, I can think of one person, but I don't know if he's right. Do you remember the teacher of yours who came to the house once? You brought her to dinner."

"Ms. B?"

"Yes, Jane. Right."

"You remember her?"

"We met up again here in the city and got friendly for a bit. Very briefly. I haven't talked to her for ages now."

"But David, she wouldn't know anything about this. In fact, I'm pretty sure she hated Oliver."

"She did," David said with his first natural smile. "But I'm not talking about her. Last I heard she was living with a doctor or—I think—a kind of specialist geriatric psychiatrist. The guy himself is actually very young." With a token lowering of his voice, he gossiped, "She likes young. You know, when I met her she was hooking up with a hunky Hispanic waiter—or dish-washer! And it was obviously all about you know what." Returning to the problem at hand, David wondered, "I'm pretty sure the new guy is a psychiatrist, and not a regular doctor. I'm positive about the geriatric part, because that was funny to me. Ironic."

"Wait! Wait! I'm trying to imagine Ms. B with a dishwasher!" Darius shook his head.

"Yeah. But now she's moved in with this Doctor Nathan Something. And if he isn't the right person, he'll know of some-one. Of course, Cassie probably has a better idea."

"I'm finding it hard to imagine Ms. B having sex at all." Da-rius said clinging to his jokey shock, an unfelt emotion that felt natural to him."

"But she's a very sexual creature," David said knowingly. "She was your—special favorite, right? Your favorite teacher?" David asked, causing Darius to blush. "She doesn't teach anymore. She took care of a PhD dissertation and ended up with a job at the Ford Foundation. Congolese child soldiers. Something like that." David remembered to add, "Young—see?"

To have Jane Brzostovsky drop into all of this was disorient-ing. In truth, Darius hadn't thought much about her over the years. His infatuation with her had cooled long before she left Lawrence. Or so Darius remembered it.

Thinking about the past, however, just because it was past, filled Darius with melancholy. More so, perhaps, because David's advice made Darius feel keenly what a clueless childhood he'd had. He couldn't imagine finding a solution to his father problem by examining the years of his own preposterous immaturity, and he wasn't sure how he felt about approaching Jane at all. David gave him the number and finished breezily, wickedly, "If it's awkward calling her, feel free to try the common-law boy doctor directly. I'm sure he's listed. He's moderately well known."

When the opening began to sputter and the gorgeous assistants were gathering cups and napkins, Cassie led Darius into a sterile, under-furnished office, not at all what he'd imagined. She posed herself on the red pad of a cheap wire chair and offered him the same. Uncomfortable. She was clearly exhausted. Things felt awkward between them now they were in private. "How in God's name is Oliver?" Cassie repeated a touch robotically. Her lack of intonation suggested she was at the limit of her energy. Darius was reluctant to burden her. At the same time, he understood she was a thousand times more capable than he was even in a reduced state.

"He's not doing very well, to be honest," Darius said.

Cassie sighed with fatigue or *weltschmerz*. She stared through the office's single window, all bright reflection of the office interior, except for a faint brick wall showing through their own silhouettes, an airshaft. "You know, I haven't seen him in I don't know how long," she began.

"I know," Darius said guiltily. "I wanted you to know. That's all. I didn't think you'd be able to do anything." This was untrue, of course. Feeling thwarted, he leaned back, and the cruel steel chair knuckled his spine.

"That's right, but maybe I could get the word out among his old friends. If he really is so—"

"He is. That would be a huge help," Darius said without hope. Neither of them could immediately call to mind any old friends of Oliver's.

"You know, I said *nutty*, but that was just a tease," Cassie said. Darius looked confused. "I called him a nut, because—well, he's an eccentric in the grand old tradition, isn't he?"

"We don't really have that tradition in America. But I wasn't offended. *Nutty* is fair to be honest. I'm stuck because I can't think who—well, are there any old guys from Lawrence who knew him?"

"That's possible. I'm afraid I never knew that crowd. I was always here in the city. And prep schools—" Nor did she know the lawyer Darius tried to describe.

One of her assistants put her head through the door with poised submission.

"What?" Cassie snapped. Without waiting for an answer, she ordered, "Yes, go! Tell Adam to wait. Everybody else can go." Noticing that Darius was a little taken aback by her harshness, she said, "They're NYU students. We all hire them. Or someone's daughter. They're ultra-privileged, and people like to pretend they're dumb, or just prestige ornaments for the gallery. They actually work incredibly hard. They've all been crushed underfoot by rich parents. Especially the girls." Cassie eyed Darius and recrossed her arms and legs with a faint jingling. "This isn't the best ambience for a discussion, is it?"

"I know. I know." Darius made a move to get up.

"Darius! Hold on, will you?" She jingled loudly. "I'm saying maybe I should arrange something else. It's quiet out on Long Island at this time of year. Bleak. But that wouldn't bother you, would it? You used to be all in for mournfulness and—tragedy." Cassie said this without irony.

Darius admitted it was true. He added the missing hint of irony to his tone.

She returned a flicker of a smile. "What did you think of that boy who was here?"

"Your godson?"

Cassie frowned.

"He told me he was your godson."

"He is. I was just thinking—godson sounds so quaint. Is it even a thing anymore? I don't think I ever did anything for him. Maybe a present when he was a baby."

"I don't have any godparents."

"You wouldn't. Oliver was—well, your mother was Muslim, wasn't she?"

"And I was adopted."

"That doesn't matter for godparents, does it?"

Darius shrugged. He wasn't above trying to use his adoption as a kind of special pleading. "Mom used to say the Prophet was an orphan boy, too, so—"

"Poor baby!" Cassie deftly cut him off.

Darius responded with silly laughter. Her impatience amused him.

"My friend Bea," Cassie went on. "That boy's mother says all he cares about is money. He's gay. Did you get that?"

"No. I didn't. At all. But we barely talked."

"Would you be interested in going out to Long Island for a day or so if I arranged it? My Carl—my man friend—stays out all winter. He's terribly old and vague, but he might have an idea or two about our problem. He's the same generation as Oliver. I'd try to make it—not too boring."

31

LIGHTLY IT SNOWED. Late afternoon looked like evening. In the haloes of early streetlight, discrete, soundless, peach-colored flurries jerked and streaked. The motes vanished the instant they touched the street, but little drifts like swept sugar formed on the sidewalks and on the windshields of parked cars. Darius stood with his hands clasped in front of him. He did nothing to protect himself against the snow except hunch. The snow motes stuck to his lashes. An icy zing tickled his scalp, another his decolletage, another an inaccessible spot inside his ear canal. The last made him shudder. And at last she came.

Together Jane and Darius entered an overheated coffee shop at the cocktail hour. The time and the place were both off-kilter. The dusty orange-yellow snow hit the plate glass windows with a whispery clicketting. Quaintly mismatched tables and chairs were vacant. Walls of black-painted brick were hung all over with mirrors, giving the place an air of night's storeroom stacked with lustrous extra ingots of darkness. Jane had suggested the place just because it was in her neighborhood. She hardly felt obliged to travel to see Darius. She wore an unteacherly scalloped bustier. At work, a jacket had covered it, but it was hot in here. One of Darius's fingers pinned her soaked napkin to the table-top, so she could lift a large paper coffee cup clear. Slightly soupy breasts rose in pallid swells when she took a steadying breath. Her puckered lips sipped gingerly at the rim of the cup. Her lips were thin and dry, the top one scored by vertical hash marks.

There was more than the usual awkwardness between them at first. Once again, Jane found Darius a type of young man she just didn't get along with—gay, she assumed. Without her former awesome authority she now struck Darius as a much more specific person, and surprisingly fragile. They both struggled to smile and make small talk. Both veered wildly from bland politeness to mechanical recollection of their shared past. After winding through news about David Caperini and Jane's new Doctor Nathan and Darius's Rolf, they'd gotten onto the subject of marriage. "I always dreaded it," Jane said firmly. "I still do undoubtedly." She backtracked. "No. I suppose some of my friends have decent marriages." She laughed. To think she was having this typically American confessional conversation with little Darius Van Nest, the peculiar, insufferable one.

To Jane's surprise, he quickly agreed. "I don't know any yet—any marriages. Or even any long-term relationships. The inwardness. It sends shivers down my spine. I can't think of a single case where the friends aren't dropped like leaves. Always a kind of *folie à deux*. Like my mom and Stan. Though, I guess they need each other."

"*Folie à deux*," Jane echoed. Her stare was blank, neither friendly nor unfriendly. "One does begin to think being alone—well, in a certain way—is preferable. Don't know what it's like in your case, but I've never felt the pressure some women do. The baby clock. I don't know why. You do think about it. But I was never driven like—well, that's not anyone you know. None of this is really anything we need to talk about." Jane shook her head at her lap. "Are you finding this as odd as I am?"

"A little," Darius admitted.

Jane folded her arms. She repeated it more firmly, "I owe you ten thousand dollars." The drawings had been the first thing she mentioned. She hadn't shifted blame to David, but she let Darius understand the facts. She had sold the drawings, but they came to her from David and before that, as she understood it, from Darius's own New Jersey basement. "And that's just if we consider the small percentage I received. You helped pay for my graduate degree."

"That's not really the issue with me. Not now. I—" Talk of money would make this conversation much harder.

Jane warned parenthetically, "We're going to have to talk about the money at some point, Darius." Then she returned to marriage. "You know," she admitted brightly. "Maybe I *am* thinking of marriage. Even at this late date. I guess, with Nathan—"

"I often feel sorry for straight people. They have to deal with all those expectations. You're sure it's not that? None of my business, I know." He shrugged. "Why not get married, if you want to?"

"What about you and your friend? Ralph?" she asked with surgical care.

"Rolf. He's German. But marriage?" Darius shuddered primly. "We're not really together like that. And anyway, I think I'm too young. I hope I am."

"Obviously, you are. Obviously! I can't help prying. I'm sorry. But if anything ever does happen with him, I suggest you make sure it's on your own terms. Well, not *on your terms*. With another person there's always compromise. But—well, you hardly need my advice about that! I can't shake the bossy teacher thing with you." Not entirely friendly laughter flooded out of her like silver coins. "I'm not your teacher anymore," she reminded herself. A forefinger with a short, neatly glazed nail stopped a drop of coffee in the center of her lower lip.

"Did you mean I might be too compromising or not compromising enough?"

More coins spilled. Jane hunted in her purse. "I can't advise. I don't think we're alike. Enough about all that. Why am I asking about your love life? Awful way of putting it, huh? *Love life.* Why would I assume you had any at all?" She took lipstick from her purse. A few last coins of laughter tinkled, and she apologized. "I'm sorry, Darius! That sounded rude. Of course, you have a love life."

"No. Don't worry. I don't. No love life."

An expression of revulsion crossed her face almost too quickly to register. "No one?" she wondered blandly, trying to gauge the color of the lipstick in the darkness. "I remember you used to spend all your time with that boy? That was a sort of childhood crush, wasn't it? Barry? You ever see him now? Or know what he's up to? No?"

A slightly uncomfortable silence fell, during which she reached for the table's votive candle and held it near the butt of the lipstick tube, which read, *PassionFrost.* Darius quietly dropped, "I did like him a lot."

"Hunh!" She raised her eyebrows.

"No big surprise, maybe? That I liked him?"

"No, not really. Somebody told me he came back into town because his father was sick. I never hear from old students. I don't think I was the popular type. Plus, I only taught a few years. I'm a much better fit at the Foundation." Jane twiddled the lipstick, which she hadn't put on yet. She brought it down on the table with a little rap of order. "Listen, when our annoying friend David Caperini called, he told me you wanted to ask Nathan something. Something about your father?"

"Yes—"

"Mm?"

"Yes, it's about my father. I was over there—on Thanksgiving—"

A hint of a mocking drawl audible, she said, "I can imagine holiday dinners with your family—"

"No, no. No, my dad lives alone now. Downtown. A lot has changed. When I saw him, it was the first time in years. Literally years. He's got some psychological problems, and they're much, much more serious than when you came over for dinner that time." Darius was starting to feel something worse than bashfulness. Grief maybe. It was rising suddenly the way emotion sometimes did when he disinterred little pieces of his story. it mostly happened with Rolf, who—thank God—was scheduled to rescue him from this immobile maelstrom of nostalgia. Indeed, Darius didn't have much time left.

Jane was as attentive as he could wish now. With appropriate gravity, she asked whether something had happened to change Oliver's state of mind. Or was it age?

Darius continued determinedly, "It's mostly age I think. But considering where he started off... It's actually good you met him. You have an idea of how he was, how he already had a lot of issues back then. But if you imagine turning the dial up on what you remember. Not to ten. Eight, maybe? I mean three or four higher. But eight or nine in all."

She asked for specifics. She nodded for him to go on when he couldn't speak for a second.

"He's sort of—not clean." She didn't respond, so he added, "I think he's blacked out the windows."

She looked askance. "Newspapers?" She caught herself adding gently, "This happens."

"No. No newspapers. Well, paper towels—I don't know. I know he almost never goes out. Also some people have called me and told me that he wasn't in his right mind. Which, of course, I knew, but now—"

"Who called?"

"A guy Ali I used to know. A fundraising guy. Some of the calls I have no idea who it is."

"Anonymous! You've gotten anonymous calls? More than one? Are you kidding? Darius!" she exclaimed in a windy whisper.

"I think it was someone from his building. I've met the super. He's at least aware of what's going on. But this might have been a neighbor. I'm guessing. And a couple of calls had area codes from out of state. That may have been somebody Stan hired. Stan kept trying to get an investigator to look into my dad's business. For mom. We thought Oliver might have secret business in Philadelphia or somewhere." Darius snorted about the overwrought complexity of things and at the scattershot way he was trying to explain. He'd never been able to tidy things into a story. "Basically, I think I have to do something about him. Oliver. I have to."

"What about your mom?"

"Well, you know. They're divorced. A long time ago."

"But still."

"I think I may be the only legal—"

"Darius! Are you talking about having him declared incompetent?"

"No," he whispered reflexively. He was almost breathless with shock. Is it what he'd been leading up to? The coffee shop barista stacked unsold plastic-wrapped sandwiches and slices of cheesecake in a fridge. He emptied the display counter of oval dishes and dropped them into a sink along with parts of an espresso machine and empty coffee pots. "They close early," Darius fretted. "They probably want us out of here." He turned, searching for Rolf. The barista looked up from the dishes and waved a soapy hand for them to stay.

Jane asked, "I wonder who it was? This anonymous investigator guy? That's so—"

"Please. I was just hoping you could talk to your—to Nathan. To see if he has any ideas."

"It sounds like you need a lawyer. I mean, needless to say, I'll talk to Nathan."

Though Darius, he minimized the job. "I only need to know what he would recommend in a case where someone is older and shut off and refuses to see people and just—refuses all help." Like a child Darius was secretly asking for everything to be taken care of.

"I'll ask, Darius. Of course, I'll ask. This is right up his alley. That's perfectly true. It's a joke of ours. He handles the oldsters and I deal with the kids—meaning my work at the Ford Foundation, not teaching. Darius, do you remember—? This almost reminds me. Do you remember—you couldn't have been more than twelve? Before you left Lawrence for Choate. Maybe the year you had me over for dinner. You kept coming to me to ask about legal emancipation. You were obsessed with it for months!"

Darius responded to this with chills. Luxurious and slow at first, they ran along his inner arms and the backs of his thighs. He had no memory of what Jane was talking about.

She continued, "Well, you were obviously much too young. I had no idea how seriously I should—in the end, I just remember thinking it was—it was—" Even now she was having a hard time showing compassion for the boy, as if that entailed a loss for her. She'd meant to say she remembered thinking his request was sad. But she finished, "—that it was really unfortunate."

Soon Rolf came. They all stumbled outside, hunching and pulling up collars. Voluble Rolf greeted Jane with his usual friendly animation and without teasing Darius too much. He obviously liked her. He chatted about his UN job, and she talked about a Ford Foundation study on art therapy for ex-child soldiers. They shared their outrage over an American diplomat who'd recently claimed on TV that Africa had bigger problems than mental illness. Without exactly being jealous, Darius observed Rolf and Jane, two distant parts of his life, interacting. He walked quietly on their wing, hands clasped behind his back, occasionally lifting a shoulder to rub at a ticklish snowflake on his neck. When he looked at Jane's profile for a long time, trying to see her as the new person Rolf was meeting, she sensed his stare. She looked at him, and for a second, it seemed, they recognized each other the way rivals sometimes do, not with mutual dislike but with a pitiless fondness.

32

CARS MAKE SUBURBAN extra-marital affairs difficult. A doctor neighbor's little red Volvo parked in a strange drive was like a flashing sign, *The Adulterer Is In.* In this case the neighbor became quite artful about parking at a distance or squeezing the car behind a screen of hedges. Even so, everybody caught on. Bea listened to Cassie's story with slight discomfort. "You can't call the glamorous Hamptons *suburban*!" She sounded complaining.

Cassie trumpeted, "That's exactly what they are. I'm telling you *the Hamptons*, as we have to call them, are wonderfully vulgar. I like it. There's nothing stuffy here like Noroton used to be. It's all show-offy ambition. Shrinks and bankers. TV people. Carl bought this place back when Henry Geldzahler and Jerry Robbins and that whole gay crew were swanning around Southampton. It was kind of expected if you had a big gallery. And Carl was being gay back then anyway. Crossdressing, even. Crossdressing was a huge seventies thing. You remember?"

Bea did not. She smiled, ever more uncomfortable. Crossly, she thought Cassie's conversation sounded pat and inattentive. Her friend was hauling stories out of one bin and tossing them into another, like separating whites. A chore. Their old girl friendliness felt irrecoverable.

They were in a large beach house in Bridgehampton, where Carl Hagen, Cassie's long time going-to-benefits companion, sat out winter weekends. The blankness on the landward side, potato fields and empty houses rimed pale, balanced blankness on the thundering seaward side. The occasional wanderer on the

December beach looked like he or she had no qualities at all in the existential ur-landscape. The plaintive gleam of a ship in the Atlantic offing was the epitome of solitude.

Cassie had invited Bea and her son Flossy to stay the weekend, thinking she would have a chance to catch up with a neglected friend at the same time she took the edge off a visit from Oliver's son Darius. The two boys were about the same age and gay and Carl adored having young men in the house. Mounded like a toad in his wheelchair, he could only follow them around with his eyes.

Carl's nurse, a cook/housekeeper and another young assistant lounged and chatted with the guests. Status was blurred. Everyone went around shoeless in heavy socks, wearing jeans or sweatpants, cable knits or slinky cashmere sweaters. Visitors could play a kind of parlor game, guessing who was a guest and who was paid for their time. Bea divined that the ones who really knew their way around the house were employees.

The cook/housekeeper answered Cassie's nod by strolling over to the open kitchen. Pensively she started putting sandwiches together on the vast white counters. "I often think this is the nicest season," she announced as she set out tubs of washed romaine and watercress.

In an immense living room, the nurse was contemplating a half-completed wooden puzzle on a low table. Flossy knelt near her though he'd stopped fingering pieces and pretending to help. He turned to look at the Atlantic over his shoulder. The sphynx cat was lounging by a heating register in front of the wall of windows. It raised its head alertly and stared at him. Without thinking, Flossy said, "Uch. Steel gray."

"You don't see something subtle in all this?" Cassie wondered, gesturing as she returned from confidential murmurs in the kitchen.

"Of course, I do. I'm sorry! That sounded churlish."

"It has been gray for a long time," the nurse commented. Cassie stared down at a sketchpad and a nest of charcoal pencils on the off-white living room rug. She looked like she might want them off the rug. The third employee, the assistant, who was coming back from the bathroom, noticed Cassie frown and promptly collected the pencils and pad for her. She set them on a white side table and called down a nearby spiral stair, "Darius? This art stuff is yours, right?"

From downstairs, Darius cried, "Oh, I'll get it—yeah, I'm still working—I'll take care of it."

Cassie shrugged. With a thumb and forefinger, she held her watch on its limp diamond bracelet against her skeletal wrist. "I have a telephone call at four. I don't know if you're still working on the computer in the study. I need to make it in there."

"I had to stop," the assistant sighed. "I was feeling faint because I haven't eaten anything, and that awful computer light! It's like Occupational Affective Disorder. OAD."

"Why don't we all have sandwiches out here?"

The assistant protested, "I can easily make a sandwich for myself."

"I've got them," the cook/housekeeper called sweetly from the kitchen. Her various elegant sandwiches involved roasted peppers and artichoke hearts (not marinated), country pate, cornichons, cold salmon, butter, various greens, crusty sourdough and focaccia. Without much visible effort the sandwiches were set out with wine and bottled water and white cloth napkins. Even the nurse got up from her puzzle to help.

Flossy had to hold his sandwich away from the sphynx. Darius skipped up the steel spiral stair, which made a twangy rumble. His eyes hunted for his pencils and pad. He politely exclaimed over the sandwiches.

Bea was watching her son. "With that choker, you and Barry are twins," she observed.

"Ow," Flossy warned the cat and poured it from the crook of his elbow. He held his sandwich aloft.

Before taking a sandwich himself, Darius crossed the room to stand in front of the wall of windows.

Eyeing his back and, beyond him, the Atlantic, Flossy announced, "You're right, Aunt Cass. It is subtle. It's beautiful."

Darius turned from the permanent winter twilight, from the cold beach, cold water, cold sky to look down at Flossy. "I think they call scenes like this sublime, not beautiful. Not to be a know-it-all."

"Kant!" Bea ejaculated. The almost involuntary cry, so improbable that everyone stared, had come out when she remembered a survey course she'd taken at Smith years ago. "That's Kant, Flossy. But that's all I remember. The beautiful and the sublime."

Flossy murmured, vague, not mocking, "Wow. Cool."

Eating nothing, Cassie swept a strangely predatory gaze over the group. She decided visibly not to join the conversation for now.

"All *I* remember was he died a virgin," Darius said.

Flossy raised his eyebrows, now skeptical of Kant.

"Or was Nietzsche the virgin?" the assistant wondered.

"Both of them, for all I know," Darius said. "Thinking so much probably makes it hard to deal with people."

"I'd find it depressing. I don't want to sit around," Bea said. "I want to be free, get out there!"

Cassie smiled faintly. In a hiatus of conversation, the landscape outside felt momentarily heavier and more insistent.

"Philosophizing's not for me either, Mom," Flossy said, picking crumbs from the carpet around him.

"You couldn't possibly die a virgin, Flossy," Darius said. He blushed in case what he'd just said without thinking sounded hostile somehow.

All of them were quietly absorbed through the afternoon. The nurse with her puzzle. Bea reading a thriller. Flossy walking on the beach with the assistant. Darius trying to draw them in the lineless foggy style of a Seurat charcoal. The cook/housekeeper napped after straightening up the kitchen. Cassie disappeared into the study. Carl, who hadn't appeared for lunch, was supposedly working on the catalogue for an American Folk Art Museum show of non-representational outsider art. But that's what guests were always told. Free time, leisure, old age, all had a bad reputation in that famous summer colony of work-crazed New Yorkers. The house was as silent as a library, except for the repetitive sound of the waves—like the muted collapse of bookshelf after bookshelf.

Carl finally made his start and stop entrance when they all sat down to dinner at a huge round table. He let Cassie adjust the placement of his wheelchair. Its joystick couldn't manage fine motion. The cook/housekeeper and the assistant ferried dishes from the kitchen, but for once they didn't join the party.

The all-day twilight had finally expired. The ashen sea thundered almost invisibly beyond candlelit, prosciutto-hued reflections of their hands and faces. Flossy settled his eyes on a blip of yellow light, a container ship coasting Long Island on its way to, perhaps, Rotterdam. This happy fantasy of trade didn't make the ship appear any less forlorn to him.

Flossy wasn't enjoying the weekend much, but he made a dutiful effort at dinner. He told a curious anecdote about an arrow delivered to him at his college dorm. "I think it was meant to be a cupid's arrow. Love offering." He shrugged. "But some people tell me they think there's something threatening about it. I mean, it is sort of a stalker's gift, isn't it?"

"Decadent," Darius commented. He was charmed by the idea. "The kind of thing some *poète maudite* would—"

"I didn't like it a bit," Bea said.

"But who on earth sent it?" Cassie asked. "Not anonymous I hope."

"Oh, just some TA. Nothing came of it. It was still a lot better than the guy in a bar once who came up and gave me a penny and then said, *Now you owe me something.*"

Everybody made faces and clucked in disapproval.

"That's insulting," Darius said. "Who'd want to respond to something like that? The arrow may be creepy, but it's a lot more—elegant. You have a lot of suitors?" He sounded nakedly interested.

With perfect pleasantness, Flossy didn't answer.

"Carl!" Cassie raised her voice, leaning forward. Carl's head swiveled. He squinted and raised a beaming face more or less in Cassie's direction. "Carl, do you remember the first thing I ever bought from you? *Trompe l'Oeil* dollar bills or something. Americana. Well, I gave it to Oliver Van Nest, who is this boy's father! I've told you about him."

Carl rumbled something at length. Not a word could be made out, but he seemed satisfied with the comment. At least the tone of it was unmistakable: a drily humorous aside. Cheerily, Carl turned his head. Everyone at the table smiled, even chuckled, at the incomprehensible witticism.

Cassie laughed hardest of all, finally translating, "He says he ripped me off. But it was a positive thing, because he's never been able to love anyone he hasn't cheated first." More polite laughter. "But Carl do you remember everything I told you about Oliver? Darius has come partly—" She looked to Darius for permission, and he nodded, even whispering to Flossy next to him, *My dad needs some really serious help*. "He wants to talk about his father. So, do you remember when Oliver was around in the old days? It seems like he's closed himself off more than is good for him, or anyone."

"Oh, Darius!" Bea said. "But that's upsetting to hear. Preston and I never really knew your parents, but they were—I just hate it when things like that happen as people get older. It's such a trial."

Carl rumbled something briefer than the earlier joke but not much more serious. After giving him a frosty look of disapproval, Cassie translated, "He says capitalizing the *Van* in your name is an American vulgarization. Sorry," she said crossly, though Darius was laughing. "That's a big help, Carl," Cassie huffed.

The cook/housekeeper came to set more dishes on the table, imposing a silence. "What were you drawing today?" she asked Darius.

"Lotte is a painter. A fine one," Cassie glossed, smiling at her cook/housekeeper.

"Oh! Him actually." Darius nodded at Flossy. "Down on the beach. But he's just a smudge. And I'm sort of a *dilletante*, I guess."

"Just doing it is the main thing," Lotte said.

"I tried to get your necklace, though," Darius told Flossy. "I love the color. Unfortunately, I only had charcoal and graphite."

"Supposedly they're antique trade beads," Flossy said.

"It's new," Bea put in. "Our gardener has one just like. I guess boys all wear chokers nowadays."

"Mine isn't like Barry's, Mom," Flossy complained.

"Not Barry Paul," Darius said.

Bea looked astonished. "Yes, as a matter of fact. Barry Paul. You know him from Lawrence?"

Darius said, "I heard he came back to New Jersey because his father was sick."

"Why are fathers such burdens?" Cassie muttered. She chuckled when Carl mangled a word. "*Only post-insemination*, he says," she translated.

Bea continued in excitement, "You know, another old Lawrence boy is living in our garage apartment. Did you ever know a boy named Dean?"

Darius shook his head. "No. But I knew Barry. We were best friends for a while."

"We all have a big crush on him," Flossy said. "Even my father. Even me."

Darius flushed. Wildly, he thought for a second that this ungay-seeming gay person had somehow managed to seduce his old friend. His mind reeled with jealousy, though he remained perfectly poised. "He's another of your suitors?" he let slip, a touch sourly.

Flossy laughed. "Barry! No! I'm sure he's not—well, actually I don't know. I haven't seen him with any girls." A pondering expression cleared. "Oh, yeah, he *is* straight. Definitely. Dean told me he had sex with one of his teachers when he was twelve. A woman."

"Good God!" Bea clapped her hands to her bosom.

Cassie laughed. "Bea!" The group allowed room for Darius to make some comment, since he'd said he knew Barry so well. But Darius looked quite stupid, and his flush redoubled.

Cassie had been frustrated during dinner. She was annoyed when she tried to say something, and her verbal memory ratcheted a bit too slowly for her to jump in and out of rapid conversation. She held her hands up. "Wait a minute. I have to get Carl to be serious for just a second." But at that moment the cook/housekeeper/painter Lotte came back to the table and started picking up plates. Cassie shrugged, and the corners of her mouth screwed tight.

Obliviously, Lotte asked, "Has anybody seen Becca Stern's gargantuan watercolors? A couple of them are up at the Parrish show. They're kind of hideous."

"That should cheer you up, at any rate." Cassie smiled, lifting a plate for her on weak wrists.

"Why on earth?" Lotte asked.

"I'm sorry. I always thought you were a little jealous of Becca. The way people kowtow to her. And her family has that huge house. Fantastic art collection. Her father's an even bigger cheese than me."

"I'm not jealous of Becca."

"Anyway, we have to get back to Darius." Cassie played at pounding the table. "I promised Darius that Carl and I would try to—"

"I may have some slight, healthy degree of envy. But that's what spurs you on in life," Lotte said. "The only reason I said I didn't like Becca's family was they were Bush supporters, which I can't conceive. And her mother had that extreme face-lift. I mean, who wouldn't feel a little low looking at someone whose face is so—*up*?"

"Cassie," Darius said. "I did finally get a chance to talk to Nathan Kimmelstine about Oliver." Everyone looked attentive. The name prompted no recognition. "Isn't he kind of famous in New York? I thought so. He's a geriatric psychiatrist. He had an article in the *New York Review of Books*." Faces remained blank.

"Was he able to help?" Cassie asked. "Carl, listen. I wanted you to think back if there was anyone around who used to know Oliver Van Nest. All of us, let's bring the hive mind to bear."

A few whispers or snuffles came from Carl. Bea threaded her napkin through the napkin ring repeatedly, vaguely magical.

"I'm sorry to drop this on everybody," Darius said. "Cassie's been incredibly nice. She's trying to help me with my madman father."

"Don't be cruel about him," Cassie said tepidly. She remembered Oliver was the cruel one.

"It's true," Darius protested. "He's more or less insane. You saw what he was like in the old days. And now he's worse. He lives like a hermit. Won't—he won't see anyone. Literally."

"Was the geriatric psychiatrist able to tell you anything?" Flossy asked, sounding truly concerned in a way that caused Darius an extraneous shiver.

"Can you imagine?" Darius exclaimed. "You live in the same city, and your father refuses to see you? People aren't insane like that anymore, are they? I was hoping it was something that would clear up if he started taking one of those drugs. SSRIs. But Nathan says that won't happen. He did try to help, I guess." Darius sounded grudging. "He gave me plenty of names. For nurses and stuff. He looks younger than me. Like Doogie Howser."

"He knew what he was talking about?" Flossy asked.

"I guess," Darius drawled.

"Darius thinks the situation can't go on," Cassie explained. "Oliver never goes out. The place is completely shut up. Anything could happen. I've been asking around, but what do you do when an old person holes up like that? It must happen sometimes."

"As long as someone can get in," Flossy tried. "The family. And it sounded like you're still able to get in? Or not?"

"Only sometimes," Darius said unhappily. "I think it's worse than just the old person who doesn't go out. I wasn't being cruel about the insane part. I really think something organic might be wrong. But Nathan said he'd have to be able to make it to his office. Which I know my father won't do, or can't."

"You can't get through to him at all? Oh, Darius," Bea commiserated.

"Basically, Nathan told me when someone really can't take care of themselves, the first thing you do is contact a geriatric social worker or a geriatric nurse. See whether they can get in. And I will do that. Kimmelstine can't do it himself." Darius tartly demoted the doctor from first names. "Some geriatric psychiatrists will make a house call, but not him. I asked. He said it can be dangerous. I don't think he wanted to get involved." He snorted in feeble amusement. "I told him Oliver is hardly dangerous."

Cassie made a face. "I hate this, but Darius may be right. That it's more than just an old person being a recluse. I knew Oliver, and he was always—off. I'm sorry, Darius. By now, who knows?

Maybe insane isn't too strong a word. Not that that helps us at all."

Darius stuck out his lower lip thoughtfully. "People just keep giving me names. Nathan said that if he gets truly disoriented or belligerent, I have to call 911. They're actually trained to deal with people like that."

"They break in?" Bea asked in discomfort.

"That's what I heard, yes, they break in. They have a rule of thumb. *If person is a danger to themselves or to others,*" Darius sing-songed.

"What?" Flossy demanded. He immediately softened the question. "I mean, if they're a danger, then what?"

"What?" Darius echoed, wondering himself. "It must mean that if they're a danger in some way, then you can do what you want and you don't have to worry about what they want any-more. Or their opinions."

33

"TOO BAD IT'S not a more beautiful day," Rolf said. His elbows were on the table, and a forearm as long as a child's leg teetered toward the sweeping windows. He was radiant in a silky shirt and unseasonable white jeans. Blotches of sunlight raced across the carpet of the Delegates Dining Room and out onto the dingy East River, fading and brightening the whole time, as if an imp were playing with the dimmer switch. The water took on a faint brownish hue when the sun appeared. Then all faded to black and gray again, and the thronging platelets of ice in the river continued to shift without really flowing anywhere.

Rolf's companions for lunch weren't bothering with the view, yet they had a hard time looking at each other. Rolf scanned the room contentedly. "It's impressive, though, isn't it?"

"I'm impressed," Flossy smiled. He was enjoying Rolf's almost impenetrable niceness. The din of cultured accents and unknown languages sounded oddly uniform. Despite an effort at national dress here and there, the UN functionaries all looked like iterations of the same polite person. Not unlike the collectible dolls in the gift shop. Darius was achingly silent. He discarded the nervous jokes that appeared in his thoughts. Next to him, Barry Paul was equally silent. Flossy continued to his new acquaintance, "The actual delegates—do they ever eat here?"

"Not often. *Parfois, quand même,*" Rolf said, in case Flossy was disparaging the place. "It's mostly the view. And the architecture. Though the building's in terrible shape. Partly the US arrears."

"I always forget about that," Flossy said. To him sluggish bill-paying was a normal business practice.

"We don't. It's most of our budget. And really not a huge amount. It's just a stupid xenophobic statement. Not that I'm some huge Wilsonian *queen*. But with the billions you spend, I mean, really, who cares?"

Rolf's fluent and campy *queen* was more strongly accented than usual. *Quveen*. Darius felt an old, closeted reflex to glance at Barry when Rolf came out with it. Barry looked reserved but serene. "The country's rotten," Darius grumped.

"Well, I hope we pay up soon, so you can stay in New York." Imitating Rolf's politeness, Flossy sounded almost flirtatious.

"These jobs aren't permanent. It's for the resume. That's the way of things," Rolf said without a smile. He admitted, "It's funny about your ambitions. I used to be incredibly political. Even ambitious for a while after I was at the Beaux Arts. But that seemed to fade. Then the other day, I realized all I wanted was a job and money, a lot of money. It's sort of disappointing."

"Don't say that!" Flossy laughed. "That's my dream."

"Money? You're probably just starting your career. The U.N. is almost like student life, and student life is different. Maybe if I looked for a real job, it would reenergize me. Who knows? The truth is, I would like to stay in New York."

Under Rolf's relaxed gaze, Flossy looked away. Catching sight of Barry, he snickered, "Whenever I look at you, now, Barry, I have to laugh. The whole time we drove in, I was laughing."

Barry seemed to be in on the joke and smiled pleasantly.

"He looks normal to me," Rolf said.

"Right, but we're twins," Flossy began.

Darius gave Barry a careful once over for the first time since sitting down. Tentatively, he guessed, "Is this about what your mother said on Long Island!"

"Exactly," Flossy said. He turned to ask Rolf, "You see why?" "Because of the necklaces?"

"Ah," Rolf said vaguely

"Right," Flossy went on. "He's brown and I'm blue. It looks a little matchy-matchy. My mom was so cute. Because of us, she thinks all boys wear puka beads now. She also thinks it's gender-bending. Which it may be in my case, but not yours, Barry," he said.

Barry shrugged.

"You do look a bit alike," Darius said.

"He made me change twice," Barry said.

"I did," Flossy admitted. "At first we were both wearing almost exactly this shirt." He plucked at his blue button-down. "We couldn't possibly go around looking like that. Like a boy band. So I told him to change into something completely different. But the first time he comes out, he's wearing practically the same shirt again, maybe half a shade lighter."

"I don't have a lot of dress clothes," Barry said.

"Anyway, yellow looks good on you. You're tanned," Flossy said.

Darius didn't think it was the subject of fashion, but he decided Flossy seemed gay this time. Meeting Rolf had energized the young businessman. Darius stole a glance at Barry.

With exquisite politeness, Rolf tried engaging the straight outlier. "Barry? Darius said you went out West after school. Are you thinking of staying here now?"

"I'm not sure. I don't really have a plan. I just came to help out my mom because my father is sick." Rolf made a murmur of compassion to which Barry returned a shrug. "Cancer. It is what it is."

"Such a weird expression," Darius noted. "What does that mean? *It is what it is*. Everybody's started using it. Where'd it come from? It always reminds me of *Iago—I am not what I am*."

Barry gave Darius a remote, admiring smile, probably about the Shakespeare quotation. Darius felt the admiration was so undeserved he frowned.

"But do you have a—say, a career plan?" Rolf wondered.

"Jesus!" Darius stopped him. "You sound so American. I thought you guys were better than us. You're asking about career plans?"

Barry made it clear he wasn't bothered. "I'm sort of the gardener for his family." He nodded at Flossy. He added, "Which I'm really liking." The others gazed at him expectantly. It didn't occur to them not to wait for more. Barry finally continued with a smile. "And I'm getting into financial crime. According to Preston—his dad."

Flossy buried his face in a palm. "That's so fucked up. None of us had any idea."

Barry quickly reassured Darius, "It's not that serious. You remember Dean?" Darius shook his head, *No*. "He was a friend of mine, too. And he's down there at Flossy's parents' house. It turns out he was into some kind of insurance scam, and he tried to get me involved. But Preston figured it all out. It was some low-life friend that got Dean involved. And it was big talk more than anything. Dean's an OK guy."

Flossy raised his eyebrows skeptically. "I think it's more serious than you're making it sound. Dean may just get a slap on the wrist, but people remember that stuff. Now every time he tries to do business with anybody in the area, anybody who knows, that's the first thing they'll think about. His reputation is kind of ruined." Flossy explained to Rolf, "This person we're talking about is a total bro. One of those guys with a big hot shot attitude."

"Hot shot!" Barry said dismissively. "More like nervous."

Flossy shrugged.

"I hope it doesn't go too badly for Dean," Barry said. "His girlfriend already dumped him. He wanted to marry her."

"*Ouf*," Rolf said. He was reverent about relationships.

"Uch!" Darius said. He disliked them.

"Darius is phobic about commitments," Rolf noted possessively. He planted one hand on the table between them. It looked gargantuan, even threatening, emerging from its too short cuff. Though it wasn't very close to him, Darius felt crowded by it. The sun pinkened the still hand wanly in passing.

Darius told Barry, "This has been old home week for me. Or month. Besides you, I also saw David Caperini a little while back. And—" he almost mentioned Jane. "You remember, he was the weird, nervous guy my parents got to teach me French."

"Ah, yeah," Barry said, smiling at the memory.

"He's still a cipher, maybe a tiny bit bitter now. He got married for two minutes. Which I can't fathom. I always thought he was semi-gay. And I think I heard there was some baby involved. He was too young for that."

"That's what happened to me," Rolf said.

"Your parents got married too young?" Flossy asked.

"No, me."

"You weren't married!" Darius asserted.

"Darius, I'm sure I told you," Rolf said brusquely. He was embarrassed to realize that, despite the radical American openness he aspired to, he'd left this item out of his resume. "It was a very brief thing. A *mariage blanc.* She was from Turkey, and she'd come to Paris to the Beaux Arts. She needed EU papers. That's the whole story. A few months. Then we divorced. She lives in California now."

"Rolf!" Darius exclaimed. He didn't know why this information delighted him. "You have secrets!"

"My parents were furious. They were worried about money."

"A whole secret life," Darius said. "But was it—I mean—amicable? Do you see her?"

"Of course, it was friendly. It wasn't real. And no, we're not in touch. It was just for papers. Even so, we were too young."

Flossy had to wonder, "That's so different from me! I don't think I could ever do that. Even to help out a friend. Besides being gay."

"I'm just as gay. And that doesn't matter. We can get married now," Rolf trumped him. "In fact, I wonder if I don't romanticize the domestic life in a way. Because my parents were diplomats and had to move around so much when I was growing up. On the other hand, my parents are the ones who have the—antiquated dynastic ideas. When my brother got married two years ago, the girl had to sign a prenuptial agreement."

"A morganatic marriage? Because of the title?" Darius pressed with pleasure. Naturally, he'd told everyone that Rolf was a count in the course of phone calls setting up this lunch.

"No. Because of money." Rolf gave Darius a stare like a poke. "Strictly speaking, there is no title. Legally, in Germany, it's just part of your name. Like Mr. Count."

Flossy started laughing. "Mr. Count! Oh, so the woman becomes Mrs. Count, not Countess whatever. That's too bad. I mean, obviously, it's *right*, but—"

"That's the theory anyway," Rolf said. "The priest still calls my father *Excellency*, which isn't even the right term. We just roll our eyes."

"Married and divorced. God, and when we met, I thought you were immature—" Darius produced a stagey cough of laughter. "Sorry, I mean, more, innocent. You've always seemed innocent to me!"

Rolf grinned, insulted but not displeased.

After this uncharacteristic teasing, Darius went quiet. His mind was clouded by a lady-like inwardness. He gazed at his plate. He shifted an uneaten orange Tandoori rubble with his knife. At the buffet, a woman in a sari rang the lid of a steel chafing dish closed. "You get married, and I get raped. You know, that makes sense," he said brightly.

Rolf's expression went black. His chin rose, his lips compressed and he gazed out the windows. A mass of cloud, gray on gray, sped, unbudging, over Queens like a flat on rollers. The others were naturally stunned, but Rolf had heard this before. He hated the bizarre, airy tone Darius invariably used when he mentioned rape.

Barry and Flossy both looked down as if dust had gotten into their eyes. Barry asked, "Are you for real, buddy?"

"I'm sorry. I shouldn't have said that," Darius said too assertively. "It was a date rape drug situation. A long time ago and I really have no memory. Not that I should make light—"

"Shut up, Darius," Rolf said. His mouth formed a tighter seam. He caught the others' eyes. He shook his head at the outlandishness of his friend. No matter how often Darius insisted, he couldn't possibly be as blasé about this as he pretended.

After lunch Rolf offered to show Flossy the U.N. building. Without any particular goal in mind Darius and Barry walked west along Forty-Fifth Street together. They felt a sort of duty as old friends to talk privately, though neither knew what to say at first. Because it was blustery, they kept half-looking to stop in a diner or Starbucks. Sizing up various places as they walked created awkward interruptions in the conversation.

First off, clumsy and delicate, Barry went back to the lunchtime revelation. Darius snapped, "Of course, it's true. Why would I make up something like that? It's actually Rolf who annoys me. He wants me to be all mournful. Why do I have to act like that?" His better nature rolled in like a wave. "Listen, Rolf is lovely. Don't get me wrong. It's just—I'm much more worried about my father now. Like you are, too, right?"

"Ah. Yeah," Barry agreed. "Flossy told me what's going on with Oliver. But also, right. Both of us."

Darius could hardly believe Barry's gentleness was failing to have the effect he wanted. His old friend's personality was showing strange gaps, like thoughts or qualities politely withheld. This wasn't exactly the Barry he remembered, and it might be a new person entirely. Darius himself felt too revealed. And in his case, there was no doubt about it. He was unpleasantly different from the boy he used to be. "Freezing," he muttered unhappily. "Honestly, that one looks a little—roach-infested to me. Sad, but I almost need a plasticky chain place to make me comfortable." After a considering pause, they continued walking/searching. Darius said, "You seem a lot more—grounded. More than I am anyway. I mean, you look good."

"Thanks. You, too."

"I guess problem fathers aren't making us—uh—lose our looks or anything," Darius finished the sentence almost at random and looked dissatisfied with how it came out. He laughed suddenly. "I remember I used to stare in the mirror as a kid and think, *Jesus, I've been alive for so long and I'm* still *so young!*" Darius waited for a response. None came. "Then my face turned into Bloody Mary after a while. Of course."

As in the old days, Barry was pleased with his friend's slight insensitivity.

"Have you met anyone?" Darius asked. "I know Rolf kind of gives the impression we're—but it's not at all clear between us, really."

"I was seeing somebody out West. She dumped me. Right before I came back."

Darius said, "I can tell you're lying. Somehow you dumped her. Don't hide your infinitesimal ruthlessness from me. You're already so decent you make me want to kill myself. You always have."

"Shut up." Barry grinned. He didn't mind Darius catching him in a self-deprecating lie. "*Kill yourself!*" he repeated in a whisper, savoring the old familiar extravagance. He gestured at another restaurant in front of which they were automatically slowing. "I'm OK with this one. I think it's fast food, though."

"You're right. We can do better." They kept walking.

"No, I want to get on with my life," Barry said. "But I'm not in any rush to shack up with somebody. I don't have any outsider stake in the ideal relationship—the way gay people do. Not you maybe, but—I don't want to just stumble into something. That would make me feel—I wouldn't like it. I'm happy enough at Preston's for now. The whole family is pretty cool."

"How's it been seeing your dad?"

"Harder seeing my mom." Barry smiled.

"But you two always got along in a weird way."

"Yeah."

"Everything I'm saying sounds harsh. Or snarky. I don't know why. I'm usually all—" Darius made a wide-eyed, comically sweet face. "That's how I used to be, right?"

"Not really," Barry said.

"At lunch I hope we didn't make you feel like not having some stupid New York career made you inadequate. And can you believe you were the only straight guy? That's not fair."

"No." Barry laughed, then pondered. "I guess I don't want to be *only* a lawn care guy forever. My mom would probably kill me."

Darius couldn't feel his own wild nerves, but he started to rave. "You should become my imam. I'd follow you anywhere. I'd blow myself up for you." Barry waited for this burst of eccentricity to fade. Darius finished, "Sorry." He looked around them. "This block is dead."

Barry suggested a pizza shop, but Darius didn't want to stand at a high top talking in front of bicycle messengers and lawyers on the run.

They spoke up at the same time. Each had remembered something he needed to talk about. Darius went first. "There was this odd story I heard. Not even a story. Actually, that guy Flossy mentioned it when I was in the Hamptons with him. I guess he heard about it from his family? I don't know. They said you had sex with a teacher when you were a kid."

Barry kept his gaze on the sidewalk and tried repressing a smile, not an amused one. More like a grimace.

"Wow," Darius said. "That explains why she always disliked me so much. That's—I'm assuming. It totally pulls the rug out. I really liked her. I was always convinced she liked me, too. Until—until Paris, I guess. I must've thought I was irresistible. You know, I saw her recently. I thought she might have some ideas about Oliver. I told you it's been like old home week. We weren't—I'm sorry. Have you seen her at all? You know she's in the city, right?"

Barry eyed Darius. "Yeah. No, I haven't seen her. I thought maybe I'd try at some point."

"I can give you her phone number," Darius began. His upbeat helpfulness came to a hard stop. After a long time, he tried, "That must've been—well, I don't have any idea. Weird?"

"Yeah. It was a little sick. A lot of pressure not to tell anybody. That fucks with you. Of course, at the time I thought I was totally into it—"

"Uch," Darius said helplessly.

"It wasn't about looks at all. Even though—"

"Looks? Oh, cause she was old? But nobody ever knew? Who figured it out? Did you ever tell anyone?"

Uncomfortable, Barry made a face. He didn't feel like answering a barrage of questions. Darius saw this at once and held back. When Barry finally spoke, he changed the subject. "It sounds like shit, the stuff you've been dealing with with Oliver."

Darius felt Barry's hand come to ghostly rest on his shoulder blade. Involuntarily he pulled his shoulder forward, breaking contact. At once laughter erupted from deep in his chest. "Ha! My God!" In the cold air, his innermost breath steamed out like smoke. "Did you just see that? Like I couldn't stand being touched by you. That's like Oliver, actually."

Barry's mouth twitched. Mutual self-consciousness was an irritating distraction. Both he and Darius were wondering whether Darius shying like that, like a little bird, wasn't really a flash of old jealousy over Jane Brzostovsky. Barry decided it couldn't be.

Darius was about to say that it probably was—a swirl of memory and love—and turn it into another stark, confessional joke—*I used to love you*—but he didn't. His good behavior acted as a chill between them. Without saying it aloud, they both decided to skip the coffee shop. They turned and headed back toward the garage where Flossy had left his car. The wind blew their hair in the opposite direction.

Darius interrupted a last attempt of Barry's to say something, "There wasn't any place decent around here anyway. We can sit down and talk another time if you want." This sounded a little—omniscient narrator.

"Actually," Barry persevered. "I have something for you."

A silly excitement sparked in Darius. It burned out at once when Barry took the smudged something from his pocket.

"I completely forgot," Barry said. "I'm usually pretty good about things, but this was so long ago. And it was really a crazy time for me." Barry squeezed a pad of folded bills in his fist.

"You're giving me money?"

"No. It's yours. I borrowed it—I remembered the other day."

"But I don't remember. I don't even remember how much it was. No."

"This is five hundred. Four-ninety, actually. It was probably a lot more."

"This was for the abortion? Barry, no. It's old and—just, no."

"Let me do it, Dare. I took this out for you. Come on. It makes me feel good. I don't want to owe you."

The bills didn't look like they could have come from any machine. The soiled dollar green made them look organic in Barry's pale gardener's fist. "No," Darius said almost stridently. "No." He took a step back and held his hands up so they couldn't possibly touch the money. He tried to make this pantomime good-humored, but he wasn't feeling it at all. Just the opposite. He was embarrassed, angry.

Barry played at being good-humored, as well. Held out slightly, his fist wavered like a pet hoping to nuzzle. He didn't appear pleased by the refusal.

34

BARRY WASN'T SAYING much. Dim familiarity with his teacher from the distant past towed his present self like an empty skiff. For her part, Jane mistrusted the sequence of events since they'd finished lunch at a pink-and-chartreuse place in a cute commuter town. In fact, she couldn't remember why she drove him home or decided to drop in or fastidiously climbed the narrow stairs to see where he lived now—over some New Jersey millionaire's garage, it seemed.

All afternoon she kept noticing a kind of worry afloat behind Barry's brown-eyed, lopsided-smiling sweetness, something she had no memory of. She supposed it was adulthood. During their first phone conversation, Barry had mentioned wanting to ask her something. A passing terror came over her that he would be completely different. That she'd destroyed him, and he was coming after her, his wizened soul in his palm to shame her. Penitently, she met him anyway. At a glance, more than a decade's fear dropped away. He wasn't after her. There was only that odd worry in his eyes, something private-seeming for a boy she remembered being utterly transparent.

The impersonal effects of time triggered faint grief, which distracted Jane from the narrow business of meeting Barry after so long. His slight pudginess. Unmanicured threads of beard on his neck. Little flaws and scars and nascent wrinkles and maybe even thinning hair. Her short-term memory shortened even further to pure observation. She was fascinated by Barry's heavy-pawed masculinity. Not only was it grown up, but also completely unlike Nathan's gentlemanly primness.

As she expected, the apartment had hardly any furniture except a bed, neatly draped with a duvet but not exactly made. They sat on it, Barry leaning back on his elbows, Jane leaning forward over crossed knees. They sat there quite a while, expressions nervously explicit from time to time, fingers quirking on the surface of the duvet. Barry purred or groaned at the back of his throat, an against-my-better-judgment noise. Neither of them resorted to words, which paradoxically seemed liable to gum up everything. Barry's palms drummed at his sides. When one of his hands stopped, tensed, Jane's fingers slipped under it, forcing themselves between a callused palm and the bedspread.

Barry smirked vaguely when she was naked. She frowned. Even his silken penis with its flaring, hat-like, mauve-tinged tip—even it—had aged fascinatingly, acquired a saltiness and a scribble of thick veins. He didn't have much hope of punching past her tonsils, but slowly, deliberately, he tried, playing at inconsideration—a streak of hostility, perhaps, which he was basically too cheerful to notice in himself.

Jane threw herself backward on the duvet, but Barry disregarded her vulnerable wrists or simply didn't pick up the hint. This in itself was sexy. It wasn't a winking game for him. Inept, rough and very strong despite their unbaked pallor, his hands ran over her, kneading a little, possessive but aimless, unsure of the point of it all. His face went slack in concentration. Jane could already feel the depression to follow, fugitive as a ghost and, for the moment, outrun by pleasure. It was going to hit the second they were finished. And sure enough, the depression was right there in the room, all but laughing at them the instant they came to themselves.

They caught their breath. "That was a mistake," Jane said the obvious. "Nice, but a mistake. Probably."

Barry had to clear his throat several times. He chuckled weakly. He tried to shrug but couldn't quite since he was lying on his back.

"Of course, it was," Jane agreed with herself.

Finally, he admitted, "But I'm not all that surprised." He frowned at the ceiling. A word or two began and died on his lips. Each caught the other's eye a few times. They settled on not looking. Barry stared through the never painted bathroom door, wishing he were in the shower already.

Trying to season the unhappiness, Jane drily complimented him on having a big dick, which made him snort.

"I've never been told," he lied.

"What? Do you only see virgins?" This came out harsh, instead of ironical.

"No. Not at all." Answering the virgins crack made him sound flat-footed, he thought. A cross frown appeared for a second, unusual for him. "No. I haven't been with anybody for a long time."

"Of course, you're not the type: all virgins all the time." Jane squeezed her eyes shut at her involuntary *virginity* talk.

He made a dismissive sound, rude about his own attitude not about hers. Surely, you knew what would happen—that much was clear, Jane thought. "Oh, Barry," she said. "So maybe it was stupid. But so what? It's not the end of the world."

They used the bathroom one after another. Their present personalities had come back, as thick as wax on preserves, and they made a grown-up effort to forget their unhappiness, which nevertheless didn't decrease.

"I'm surprised you're not with someone, Barry. You're a wonderful guy, and you have that same gift you always had—making people feel good."

"I was seeing somebody," He countered childishly. He didn't want to talk to her, but, as a sop, he commented, "Maybe it would surprise you, but I'm actually pretty happy where I'm at in my life." He looked at her so seriously he *might* have been comparing now to the past. She wasn't sure.

Feeling guilty about extinguishing his earlier good mood, she tried, "You were always wiser and more—grown-up. Probably why we got into trouble in the first place." She corrected herself, tapping her sternum and mouthing, *Why I did.* Between their present selves—even them—what had happened was extremely awkward to mention. "There was never anybody when you were away? Or out West?"

"Yes, I just told you," he said.

"Right-right!" she whispered. His hint of self-pity, so at odds with his personality, so at odds with the note of happy contempt in sex, was just the sort of concealed weakness that saddened Jane about men. "Have you seen our little Darius Van Nest since coming back?" she asked just to change the tone of things. "Of course you did. You told me. He gave you my number."

"Darius knows them out here, I think," Barry chucked his head in Preston and Bea's direction. "Or used to. Or his family did or something."

"Well, and I guess you've heard. Our favorite rich kid's father—" Jane immediately corrected what sounded like a sneer. "Darius, I'm afraid his father is... Of course, you know. But that's why he and I got together. He wanted to consult my friend Nathan." She mentioned the name without a flutter, a minor but perfect deception. "Also, I owed him money, but that's another story," she slipped in wryly. She used the past tense.

Barry asked in astonishment, "Why did you owe him money?"

"I didn't, really. It was that very affected French tutor he had. I happened to meet him in the city years later. I was the go-between for a money problem between him and Darius. All very complicated." Another smooth lie, though she wondered why she'd bothered to confess in the first place.

"You never liked him much."

"Who? David?"

"No, Darius."

"I don't know. He was just another student." That didn't sound true. "He probably made me feel like a crude Polack. I imagined his family were all vile, weary aristocrats. That was a turn-off."

"But we were kids, him and me. He was just acting pretentious."

"You were kids," she echoed forlornly. "And even though he was a little gay boy, he probably never came on to you," she added.

"That's right, he never really did. And I loved him. I probably would've messed around with him, too. It wasn't that unusual." He grinned in a Barry-like way.

"He didn't. I did," she sighed.

"You don't have to sound so tragic," he told her.

"What did you want to ask me?"

"You know, you didn't fuck me up. I'm not stuck on this one thing that happened in my life." He jumped up and clapped his hands energetically. He returned to the bathroom. "Quick shower!" he ordered himself. "OK, if I'm first?"

"But what did you want to ask?" she called. Her frown felt pettish.

Barry called through the door, "Oh—I guess, I wanted to know—" He laughed at his own naivete. "Since I can't remember for me, I wanted to know if—back then—if you were in love with me. Or thought you were." He didn't sound as if he still wondered or cared.

"It was depressing," Jane said to Rolf. She had to tell someone, and they had quickly become friends. But she only talked about this time in the garage apartment, not about the original sin. "Like something you do in high school." That particular word choice made her drop her face into her palm for a second. She kept cutting it close with Rolf. "And not made up for by the sexiness at all. At all. Which is depressing in itself. Maybe that's it, in fact. You realize you're getting old—not you, but someone my age—and you're too weak not to protect yourself—not to *not* do that wonderful, idiotic thing. Of course, he wasn't any happier about it than I was. Miserable, I think. With him it wasn't guilt, though, but maybe some buried resentment. Like he's forever under my power. Because I was his teacher, I mean. But he kept trying not to seem young, to be exaggeratedly *not* that way. He actually said *Thank you.* Which I despise. It gives me the creeps. Like women give up something."

"Don't they?"

"Of course not," she said scornfully. "Rolf, that's so primitive of you!"

"I can't believe you slept with an ex-student!" He sounded admiring.

"Mm–"

"You're unstoppable. More women should be like that. Dare to be the aggressor with men. Unless–well, it wasn't that you thought you'd missed the boat and wanted to catch up with this guy?"

"With a student? Ex-student? God, no! First of all, I feel like never seeing him again. The thought makes me–"

He smiled. "The post-coital black mood. Anti-sex really, and it's like–like love–like the inverse of love!"

"You would know about inverted emotions." That was a bit too harsh to be funny. "Or Darius would."

"Homophobe!" Rolf exclaimed happily. But the mention of Darius made his face fall after a moment.

Jane insisted, "And in no way have I missed the boat sexually. Just for your information."

"Maybe, I was thinking more about me," Rolf admitted.

Jane looked around Severine's apartment. "Why is Darius living here with you? I though he was rich." She sounded irritable all of a sudden.

"He's here because his father's place is right around the corner."

"Oliver's down here? How strange. Not exactly the neighborhood you'd expect. You've never met him, have you? Awful, awful man. Partly because of him, I always wished I could've been–more compassionate with Darius, but I had such a hard time. Has he mentioned his school days much? Or talked about me?"

"You mean other than you being his teacher?"

"Maybe. I felt we had a little trouble connecting when he was a boy. Frankly, I should never have been teaching. I mean, I liked it, but–"

"He hasn't talked much. If anything, he said you were his favorite, I think."

"Promise not to tell him, but that former student I was just telling you about, he and Darius were friends back then. Good friends, even."

"Wow. That is young." Rolf's manners slipped for once. He had no idea.

"Thanks!" She slapped his enormous knee. "But really don't mention it, unless—unless you have to for some reason. Not that it's important. Lawrence was another world. In fact, I find myself much more—tolerant of this new, grown-up Darius. *Tolerant* is a snooty way of putting it, isn't it? And you love him. I'm sorry."

"I do love him. God knows why? But I certainly understand how someone could find him maddening. As a matter of fact, even I'm getting to the point where—well, he's been elusive with me for a long time. Let's leave it at that. And now this apartment is wrapping up, so—you don't know his friend, Flossy, do you? More like a family acquaintance."

"Flossy? A girl?"

"No, very much a boy. Gay."

"Is that some kind of drag name?"

Rolf howled. "I never thought of that. It does almost sound that way. But no, I think it's—it must be a childhood name or a nickname."

"Well, I wouldn't know him. You're the only friend of Darius's I've ever met. Since school, anyway. Has he ever mentioned a school friend called Barry?"

Rolf shrugged, not even recalling Barry's name from the UN lunch. "I don't remember. He's talked about some friend he felt the classic longing for, the gay boy longing for his straight best friend. But all of us have felt that at some point."

"I suppose it could've been Barry. Or any number of boys, really." Jane smiled blandly.

"But what was he like as a boy? Darius? He said he was artistic in a way. But he's so self-deprecating."

"I suppose he was a little arty," Jane said grudgingly. "I was English, not Art, so I never saw anything." In truth, Darius had loaded her like a parent with his fond creations, all disposed of long ago.

"Was he happy?" Rolf asked.

"No," Jane drawled. "He had his manic episodes. That looked like happiness. And he had a gruesome streak. He loved the Borgias."

"And according to him, he had—" Rolf continued avidly. "He had an almost mystical relationship with the artist who killed himself in their house. Colin Vail. He still knows his sister. She's incredibly grand, but ancient now."

"I don't know anything about that," Jane rat-a-tatted. "Well, that's not true. I do. It's interesting. I do know about the Vail person, the artist, and I think I've heard some of his story. Suicide—all that. Darius never actually knew him."

"But he grew up sleeping in the man's bed," Rolf said empathetically. "Can you imagine?"

"Darius hasn't mentioned me in connection with this Vail artist?"

With a blank look, Rolf showed her he was entirely in the dark.

Jane explained, "There's a very weird, winding story about a series of Vail drawings, and I'm tangentially involved."

"I know those drawings! I don't know the story, but Darius and I have talked about them. As art. He thinks they're fakes."

"Who knows?" Jane shrugged. "What they really are—and Darius knows all of this—he probably didn't tell you out of consideration—but what they are is stolen. By the old French tutor—"

"My God, I met him at the show! The Vail show."

"Right. David. A slightly oleaginous, downward-spiraling guy."

Rolf looked aghast at Jane's cruelty.

She smiled to put a patch on his shock. "Anyway, I met him here in the city, and he convinced me to sell these drawings for him. I didn't know he'd stolen them. Well, I suspected, but... Anyway it's old news and hugely embarrassing. I have nothing to do with David now. But of course, I owe Darius money from the sale. I've been meaning to—"

Hurt, Rolf murmured, "I can't believe he didn't tell me this. We've talked a lot about those drawings. We both thought there was something off about them."

"Have you ever owed somebody something—money—and it's not that you can't get it—that's no problem—but you just can't bring yourself to pay it back?"

Rolf laughed. "Have I been reluctant to part with money? Of course. You don't want to pay Darius for the drawings?"

Jane made a face. She hadn't meant to be quite that transparent. She'd wanted to be like brother and older sister with Rolf. She'd planned to subtly guide this ethical dialogue with her own gentle hand. Suddenly Rolf didn't seem like such a tame companion, much less sibling. She hadn't realized how much it meant to her to be liked by this sophisticated young German. She ignored a pang of disappointment. "Of course, I'm paying him! I have to borrow the money from Nathan temporarily. Which is awkward in a very minor way. That's all."

"But he's your husband."

"No, Nathan and I aren't married. Yes, we might as well be. I just don't like to—well, I hate dealing with money. Simple as that." Jane rolled her eyes hoping to lighten the mood by seeming ditzy. She grabbed one of Rolf's Nepalese pillows, an elaborate brocade glinting with sequins and bits of mirror. She held it tight to her belly. Its edges hidden by her upper arms, she looked, for just an instant, like a jewel-bedizened goddess of love. The tall windows behind her were just high enough for an open rooftop view stretching to the river and beyond into the next borough. In the afternoon gloom, the broad, anonymous-looking cityscape, cubic and drably colored, appeared perfectly motionless, like a boring panoramic photograph, until your eye caught the near-secret trickle of traffic, the lengthening smoke from venting boilers. It was real.

Darius got into the Cedar Street apartment with groceries for Oliver. Gratitude about the unbolted door was shadowed by self-pity that he should feel, of all things, gratitude to be allowed to bring groceries to his father. Maybe the door's mysterious binary state—sometimes bolted, sometimes not—betrayed rationality on Oliver's part. He seemed aware that he needed food sometimes, and he had the wit to let it into his privacy. Darius never had the impression he was wanted for himself or for company. But the brutal functionality of their relationship was comfortable. It had none of the anxious *perhaps* that love always did.

On the far side of the dim room, Oliver was lying, like a knight's effigy, on his single bed. Every so often, his hand waved at a pestering nothing then came back to rest with the slowness of a jeweler tweezing a diamond into place. His hands had no dexterity. Frozen, root-like, they found their place atop the hem of the sheet crossing Oliver's chest. They stopped. From where he lay, Oliver watched Darius enter the loft but said nothing. Darius bustled into the kitchen with the bags, hoping to conjure an air of normalcy. He passed close enough to hear his father test a few word-sounds in a raspy voice.

"Thank you," Oliver said belatedly. His mouth quietly smacked at the taste of his voice. He probably hadn't spoken since the last time Darius had gotten in. His stiff hands came into motion again, making crippled gestures as if to fling his sheet away.

While unpacking the groceries, Darius surveyed the kitchen. New paper towels had been stuffed in the refrigerator. Oliver had been using a coffee cup with a bullseye mineral deposit on the bottom. Not for coffee. There was nothing to drink but tap water. Oliver was two tuna fish cans from starvation.

The kitchen had a small window, narrow as a loophole, covered by an old-fashioned parchment shade. As he did every time, Darius pulled the shade away with his finger. Behind it, opaque black cloth had been duct-taped across the glass. He touched the waxy cloth. Close up, it didn't suggest madness, but Darius checked on the black cloth every time, in case the reality of the situation became incontrovertible to him. It never did.

His visits to his father were untethered from the normal world. The moment he walked in, a fog of uncertainty overcame him. He knew he ought to take an afternoon to sound out Rolf or Cassie or Nathan Kimmelstine, or now, even Barry. The truth of his father's condition could only be established through talk, the simple social back-and-forth he and Oliver were both incapable of. Nevertheless, Darius felt at home in the loft's dense atmosphere of make-believe. It made sense to him in the same way Oliver's brutal emotionlessness did. No one was here to argue. No one was here to propose or dissuade. Decisions were unnecessary in the home-like stupor.

Darius didn't want it to remain this way. He tried to bring the world in with him. He had plans he clung to. Hidden in his pocket, his fingers made arpeggios against his thigh, muscular and silent. The sequence of fingertips represented his to-do list. Food. Clean. Health check. Disable bolt. Arrange geriatric nurse visits. Coming out of the kitchen was like stepping on stage. He crossed the scrappy, narrow nineteenth-century floorboards, earth-colored with age. The floor was startlingly vocal, creaking. The strange animal whines stopped when Darius stood over his father's bed.

Oliver was almost sitting up now, an odd, half-reclining posture. "One thing," Darius began, curling a sweaty forefinger in his pocket. "I keep wondering if it isn't time for a—sort of a maid or assistant to come over here. A few times a week? At least. In my opinion it definitely is time."

That got nothing. Shifting, Oliver sighed or huffed. Darius realized his father was trying to sit up fully. His feet had snagged in the sheet. Darius lifted his arm to pull the sheet away, but he saw Oliver brace for a tug-of-war. Root-like hands clamped on the threadbare cotton. Apparently Oliver wanted to sit up but he also wanted to remain entirely draped in the unclean sheet. Darius helped him accomplish this.

In hand the uncleanness of the sheet was obvious and unpleasant. The mealy bedclothes also reeked of sweat or ferment. A metallic tang of urine ran through the fug. Darius recalled the muddy-colored bums of his childhood years, the men who'd huddled at gratings, in abandoned doorways, on the grimy marble of Grand Central.

"Tired?" Darius asked. "It looks like you have some weird something under your eye."

Again, no response. Oliver's hands let go of the sheet to twiddle at a non-existent something. His sudden movement, full of nervous precision, made his general immobility look less like feebleness than like a yogi's eerie self-mastery. The silence between father and son felt like *something*, too, a coiled stillness. Not for the first time, Darius feared he'd put things off too long. The fear drifted from him almost lazily, another misty uncertainty. His father watched him like a listening dog.

"For some reason, I was just remembering the time we came to the city together. The time I was at Choate, and you were seeing Cassie Vail. That was a good trip. That was the only time we went anywhere together. I told you about the show Cassie put on, right? And afterward I went out to her place for the weekend. She always asks about you. There was also a woman named Sayles who claimed to know you. Actually a lot has gone on since last time." Darius didn't usually bother to chat like this when Oliver was unresponsive. "One thing I've really got to do—this was something Cassie told me to do—and everyone, really—I have to make another set of keys, so we can give one to the nurse person or whatever. That way they'll be able to get in here. Whatever person we settle on. I was thinking maybe every day for an hour would be good? I don't know if that's how it works. I'll keep asking around. When you do the research, you find out these people have all got a system. You have to conform. I guess to yourself your problems look really particular, but to everybody else, they just fit their system."

The dog spoke! Something about his son's soliloquy must have jogged Oliver, who said, "Perfectly fine." He then turned his head to the side with a mild expression like, *Who said that?*

"Good!" Darius exclaimed instantly. After that, the silence coiled up again. Darius tried a few more *Goods,* each one smaller. The loft felt like nature, a desert landscape, and the coyote had barked or rocks had tumbled, indicating, somewhere, a living presence.

"You liked his stuff," Oliver croaked. It could have been a question or just a memory. His tone, for a change, had a touch of the old, healthy unpleasantness. "The art shit."

Darius figured out he meant Colin Vail. "I do like it. Always did. You probably remember I do." The room seethed. Darius doubted whether his father could sustain an exchange of remarks for long. He reached out for the sheet. "Let me take that. There's a good one somewhere, I bet." He was worried Oliver had wet himself under the sheet. But the old man remained rigid, and Darius couldn't just drag the sheet away from him. "Well, I'm glad you're OK about the person coming. Don't bolt the door. And I'll be here, too, the first few times at least."

At length Oliver interrupted another long, desert-like hush. "You got any money?"

Because the old man said *money* out loud—the first time he'd mentioned it since his immurement here—Darius grabbed at the opportunity. He was blunt. "Actually that's an issue. You talked about it a long time ago and made it sound like I was supposed to get something, but I have to tell you—something I've tried to talk to you about before—that mom is in desperate shape as far as money goes. She's about to give up the house. Stan is also still talking about suing. He doesn't trust how you set things up for us, Mom and me. You probably don't realize how hard you've been to approach about—"

"Oh, I do."

"You do?"

Darius had to pull Oliver's next words from a whispery thicket of sound. "I understand everything microscopically."

With complementary precision, Darius answered, "I don't know what you're thinking of."

"You think I'm dying?"

"No," Darius said automatically. Haste made it sound like a lie. "No."

With agonizing slowness, Oliver raised his forefinger to the red sore Darius had noticed earlier under his eye. He grazed it several times too feebly for normal skin even to sense the touch. Oliver's skin was unearthly white. Darius had thought about this pallor on and off for a long time. He assumed at first it was the natural result of never getting any sun. But Oliver's skin had turned paper white, opaque white. It didn't look natural, and close up it looked unreal, even impossible. A few blue veins showed in Oliver's forearms and temple, like serpents frozen in thick ice.

Whenever Darius registered a novel detail connected to his father's decline—the strange whiteness, in this case—his heart raced and he flushed with fear. Anxiety about Oliver's death crested. Then it quickly receded when the loft's bizarre, altered normality reasserted itself. Oliver calmly breathed and blinked. Darius felt his heart rate return to normal and the flush burn off. An existential boredom rushed in. "I don't know what that is under your eye. But now maybe somebody can look at it."

Oliver swung his legs out with three kicking motions. He pushed himself up to a sitting position. Very unsteadily, he stood. He kept the sheet wrapped around him like a child playing king. "You're able to walk and get around all right?" Darius asked. He stood back, his hands raised at his father's precarious balance.

Oliver gave him a withering look so slowed down it was almost unreadable. He shuffled toward the kitchen. "I used to have a lot of multidimensional activity going on in here," Oliver mumbled. Such a long sentence seemed to cause him pain. He had to stop walking and raised squinting, watery eyes to the pressed tin ceiling. "I can barely piss. A few drops."

"What about the money?" Darius asked.

"I need a cracker."

"What about money for mom?

With a ghostly form of his old severity, Oliver croaked, "Everything was arranged a long time ago. I don't remember. I honestly don't remember." He passed into the kitchen.

"Is there anything in Philadelphia? Stan says there's an investment company somewhere."

"I don't remember." Oliver hacked. A cracker sounded like the last thing he needed.

While his father was in the kitchen, Darius took a tiny metal plate the super had provided him and a tube of polyurethane glue from his pocket. He opened the apartment door in stealth. He smeared the metal square with glue and after using his fingertip to brush clean an opening in the doorjamb, he pressed the plate inside the hole. The thickness of the plate would shrink the size of the hole enough to keep the bolt from sliding into it. At the same time, if Oliver examined the bolt, the hole would appear relatively normal. Visually, the edge of the inserted piece might look like part of the metal strike plate that covered the whole doorjamb.

After saying goodbye to his father and dropping many more casual reminders about the visitors coming soon, Darius closed the door. He thanked the super on his way out. Spiking the bolt had been the Maltese's idea. His pot-bellied gravity, the unfriendly kindness of his dark, expressionless eyes made Darius feel trivial when he shook the man's hand. His thanks were ornamental, his own assistance to Oliver obviously inadequate. His delay, nerves, affectations, fine distinctions, attention to detail—all of these were a structure as frail and merely suggestive as one of Colin Vail's paper villas or a Vail/Van Nest drawing—one the mysterious fake collaborations now dispersed to oddball art collectors. The keys to his father's apartment weighted Darius's front shirt pocket like a steel teat. At the hardware store, new keys with a strawberry sheen shrieked as their fangs were ground.

Afterward, Darius stood on lower Broadway for a long time in stunned inaction. Annoying as they were, the crowds struck a chord with Darius. All strangers seemed dear. He'd heard that overflowing tenderness like this sometimes affected people who were dying, perhaps because the dying know they have to hand off consciousness any minute to whatever fools happen to be around, so why not love them? Standing cow-like, Darius saw a particular stranger in the crowd, a very nice-looking boy laden with bulky Century 21 bags. This turned out to be Flossy Sayles. The last person he wanted to see. Darius almost hid, almost turned away, but he didn't have the alertness to do either. Passively he let Flossy's sticky glance turn into recognition.

From a few yards and very far away, Darius watched the other boy, not unhappy or excited, merely curious now. Flossy had been on a clothing shopping spree. That much was obvious. And he could tell Flossy was pleasantly surprised to see him. Darius was too exhausted to be flattered by the strange enthusiasm. But it intrigued him. He thought of Flossy as cool, appealing but not overly nice. Flossy charmingly deprecated his shopaholism, raising the bags as evidence. Did his materialism embarrass him? But nothing would especially embarrass Flossy in front of Darius.

Of course, Flossy hadn't bought Sohaila's taxes in the end, but knowing that Darius' mother was in arrears created an illusion of intimacy for him. He meant to take advantage of it.

At Flossy's suggestion, they wandered from Chambers Street across the sun-stuffy skyway to the Winter Garden, where free concerts took place at that time of day. Today, surprisingly, it was Patti Smith at the beginning of a comeback. To Darius, the stroll, the concert, even Patti Smith, had a dream-like civility. When he commented on this—some babble about a genteel universe parallel to this grim real one—Flossy smiled uncomprehendingly. Thinking Darius was talking about the palm-colonnaded Winter Garden, or about the city in general, Flossy said his older sister and brother, Anna and Philip, pretended to hate the way New York had gotten. "They would say this is *police state.* Or Vienna. Boring. But I'm like you. I like it."

"I have to say it's causing me a kind of cognitive dissonance to see her in this place." Darius nodded at Patti Smith and her little mob of black leather devotees in the sun just outside. New York harbor sparkled like a children's book illustration behind the stage.

As they chatted, Darius didn't think anything was going on at first. Flossy cheerfully selected and repositioned chairs for them. He arranged his bags in front of them with an air of satisfaction. He even unstapled a few of the bags to show Darius a sweater he'd bought, several shirts and a not-jeans pair of pants. In passing, he mentioned his best color was green. And that he thought Darius was a man-in-black type. "But not like them." He gestured at the retro Patti Smith audience. He asked about the keys Darius had been toying with this whole time.

Darius used them to catch the afternoon light in a stuttering, bloody rhythm. "They're not the keys to happiness," he said wryly.

Flossy shrugged. He philosophized, "My key is *I don't care.* I've always figured if I ever do anything too embarrassing or painful, I can just kill myself." Darius thought this was a strange remark coming from an inhabitant of the parallel universe of civility and palm trees and nice clothes—and one who seemed so healthy-minded at that. "I wanted to ask you about the man we all had lunch with—your roommate or—?"

Darius frowned into his palms. "Rolf? He's a count."

"So you said." Flossy smiled drolly. "I thought he was great. Most of the people I know are airheads. Business types like me, I guess. I couldn't tell if you and he—"

"I don't think you're an airhead," Darius said automatically. "Oh." He suddenly realized this was a particular kind of conversation he'd never had. A charming movie plot point he'd never experienced in life. Love had never struck him as subject to a plan or decision, or people subject to claims. "Oh, oh, oh. No. We're friends. Feel free! We had a brief something in Paris, maybe, but—and as a matter of fact I think he said he found you—you know—appealing. I know him incredibly well. And he's—"

Flossy put a stop to Darius's writhing. He'd found out what he wanted. "I definitely didn't mean I'm an airhead. I care about appearances. A lot. My Dad would say *too much*."

"*Kill yourself!*" Darius repeated, waggling the keys on their wire ring.

"No," Flossy reassured him.

"And isn't that backward? With your dad? Isn't the parent supposed to care more about appearances than the kid?"

Flossy made a showy two-handed gesture at his bags of new clothing. "Not in my case."

Darius smiled weakly at the hint of camp, and Flossy wondered whether he was that particular type, the ultra-stiff, slightly homophobic gay person. Ex-military almost. (Office-worker military, not the macho kind.) Darius said, "They're to my father's place, these keys. I'm sorry. I was just over there, and that's why I probably seem distracted. He's a very difficult guy. I find it depressing."

The party was on a Sunday night. They were calling it a dewarming party, because it was the end of all housewarming. The management of Severine's loft, irritated by the chore of suing its own tenants, hadn't been fussy about maintaining the boiler or anything else. The apartments were indeed cold. They were also all empty now except for Severine's. After moody transatlantic consultations with Rolf, she, like the rest of the tenants, was finally going to accept ten thousand dollars to abandon her lease. Rolf and Darius would have to move out.

They spent the day together. Darius had the fantasy to make their farewell party glamorous. That was impossible, of course, given their futons and frat house red plastic cups. But Darius bought quail's eggs and exotic radishes in Chinatown and planned to serve them with little dishes of salt from Khewra, Pakistan.

After shopping the streets for a while, they found themselves in a glitzy mall. Except for herbalists, a not too clean noodle shop and sparsely provisioned jewelers, most of the storefronts were empty, which gave the place an air of financial speculation gone wrong. Darius was conscious of being solemnly eyed by idle patrons, as if he'd interrupted a game of dice or worse. The mall punctured his mood. When he teased Rolf about Flossy's possible interest in him, hoping to lighten things up, Rolf reacted angrily. They returned to the loft, both unhappy. They readied everything for the party, hardly talking at all.

After an awkward and mostly distracted conversation with two early birds, Rolf started welcoming guests who arrived in cheerful knots. They talked, formed groups, exhibited personalities and behaved independently. This ordinary spectacle pleased Rolf, as if something he'd built with his own hands worked the way it was supposed to. A pompous young sage from the U.N. held forth on the Balkans and had to endure someone's raillerous boyfriend, who said he was sick of Balkan nativism and was sorry they hadn't all killed each other off. A French girl made an illuminating comparison to Africa, and Rolf, letting Darius handle the door for a while, invited Jane to make a Ford Foundation-related comment. Jane had come alone and was noticeably the oldest person there.

Darius found his way to a corner and pretended to arrange the radishes and hard-boiled quail's eggs. The crowd struck him as a little boring, glib, but he admitted to himself that he was out of sorts. The only person he looked forward to seeing was Barry Paul.

Dean Quinn, a completely unexpected apparition, had come in from New Jersey with Flossy. Dean stood in the middle of the room, apparently at ease but talking to no one. A smirk made him look unapproachable. Elbow out, he raised his red plastic cup of whiskey-and-soda to his lips at long, relaxed intervals.

Drawn by the blond arrogance, Darius approached him and joked confidentially, "You have a look of Satanic pride standing here." They introduced themselves and made the Lawrence Academy/Barry/Flossy connection rapidly without undue excitement. Darius talked to Dean in the sourly ironic tone that got him into trouble with Rolf. With Dean, it was a good fit. Dean's smile became more and more natural.

"Not that I meant you looked evil at all," Darius said, ingratiatingly or maybe not. In any case, it wasn't true.

"I don't know this crowd," Dean said.

"They're interesting. Friends of my friend Rolf, mostly," Darius commented blandly.

"Seem sort of intellectual. I'm used to business types."

"You were doing some insurance thing? I remember now. Someone was talking about you and mentioned insurance. Flossy, maybe."

Dean looked at him narrowly. "I'm between careers."

"Ah," Darius said, not sure how to respond to Dean's defiance.

Pumping defiance into pure aggression, Dean then said, "I just got back from Hawaii. My fiancée and I broke up. For the second time."

"I hope—I hope it was amicable."

Dean hitched his wire rims with an ugly contortion of his beautiful face and seemed to enjoy Darius's discomfort. He said, "To be honest, it wasn't something I particularly wanted. But I was having some troubles. Now she wants me dead." He smiled.

Darius scratched his chin. Oliver had taught him to be unafraid of getting mauled in conversation. He said, "That reminds me of a time—also at a cocktail party—some guy told me he just found out he had Lyme disease. I think he wanted me to go away."

"No," Dean touched his forearm. "Don't worry. I'm a little sensitive is all."

Before he could stop himself, Darius made a cutesy remark. "I like you. Maybe you're nice underneath?"

Dean laughed and repeated *Nice*. It wasn't a word anyone would use to describe him. It made Darius seem appeasing and false, which felt surprisingly good to Dean.

Embarrassed by the weird declaration, Darius voided it, asking when Dean thought Barry was coming. Dean said he doubted Barry would show up at all. He looked significantly at Jane across the room and murmured, "Because of—obviously—" He added, "You know what I'm talking about?"

"Yes," Darius said. He was cool to Dean for the first time, too subtly for Dean to notice.

"I think they hooked up again, believe it or not."

Again, Darius repeated, as Dean had repeated *Nice*.

"Like now. Weeks ago. When they met." Dean raised his eyebrows.

"But he won't come tonight, even so?"

"That's probably why he won't. I'm only here cause Flossy has a crush on the guy who lives here. Flossy can't do anything alone." Dean tilted his head and said unexpectedly, "You seem smart. Maybe you can tell me how I fucked up with Pia."

Darius shook his head. *No*.

Dean barreled on, "I tried to make up with her by buying these earrings. I took them down to Hawaii. A total fucking waste. She never threw anything before. She never got mad at me like that, until this time."

"What'd she throw?"

"The earrings. One of the stones broke. It actually broke. I thought she was just mad about the money." He chuckled incongruously as though this were party chat. "It all happened because there was this—there's some business pressure I've been under. Flossy's family knows about it—cause I'm living out there with Barry—like I said before," he explained incoherently. "Anyway, she isn't going to forgive me for some decisions I made. Like ever."

"Maybe you're better off. I don't know." Darius thought of ending the conversation. "I know sometimes a couple can get stuck and then it's hard—forgiveness."

"You don't understand. She's Asian. They never forgive."

"You're positive Barry's not coming?"

Dean looked at the crowd contemptuously. "He won't come."

"Well, I'm sorry about your girlfriend."

"She's a bitch. Luckily I'm bi." Dean said this with a flash of giddy hostility. Naturally, it stopped Darius from going away, but he couldn't think of anything to say in response. He bobbled three useless thoughts in mind. Dean was not coming on to him, because the confession was purely hostile. Dean was the least gay-seeming person in the world, so maybe he was joking? Could Dean be the kind of aggressive, closeted guy who was actually a total, almost masochistic, bottom?

As Darius eyed Dean, becoming a little more sure that he wasn't joking, he decided the last idea was closest to the truth. Dean stared back with unpleasant defiance. Darius asked, "Did she find out? I mean if you've been—the whole time—?"

"*On the down low?*" Dean snarked.

"And didn't you say she was your fiancée?"

"I did say fiancée. So what? It's not weird. Every so often you sneak off to Asbury Park and fuck some guy. Big deal. That doesn't have to affect your real relationship."

Darius snorted and shook his head. "I don't know. Maybe because I'm gay—and you knew that, right?"

Dean made a broad do-I-look-like-an-idiot expression. Darius felt the usual twinge of irritation, which he blamed more on himself than on Dean's constant, unfriendly playfulness. Darius was also wounded, because—to be honest—he found the handsome blond wildly attractive. It was a chore suppressing even this passing, party desire, like the straight schlub cowed by a model. It reminded him of being with Oliver, though Oliver was the opposite of physically attractive. It almost made him wish for the *Marquis*, a man who'd hardly been there at all.

Darius and Dean made a vague promise to get together. Darius ducked over to the table littered with bits of eggshell and radishes scored by front teeth. He'd insisted indoor smoking be allowed and someone had stubbed a cigarette out in the salt. He surveyed the tabletop as if doing something.

Jane left early, after Rolf had sequestered himself in a long smiling-touching conversation with Flossy. Dean woodenly ended that, shepherding his driver out. Later but not truly late, Rolf tried to rouse the clay-footed stragglers. An hour earlier, someone had turned the music higher hoping to get everyone to dance. It hadn't worked. After Flossy had gone, Rolf's genial host act wore thin. He stalked over to a little screen running iTunes. He frowned at it with a hint of German censoriousness as his oversized fingers pecked the volume down. He started carrying things to the steel counters of the galley kitchen. Darius disapproved of this on principle, but he was too indifferent to ask Rolf to stop the unfestive chores.

"Don't clean up," Darius ordered when they were finally alone. "It's awful in the morning, but it's much better now," he said with the authority of a socialite. "Maybe just whatever'll be really gross."

Rolf spread his arms for a celebratory hug. Picking up the radish and salt dishes, Darius managed to get past him with half a hug, patting his back skittishly.

"You tell me what'll be really gross," Rolf called after him.

"Oh, any creamy, saucey things. Cups and bottles are OK to leave." He came back and flounced into a chair facing the loft's anonymous city view.

Rolf continued straightening up. "I think that was a big success."

"You do?" Darius said doubtfully. "Some people didn't come. You think everyone had fun? They left so early."

"It's almost midnight. Who didn't come?"

"Barry Paul."

"I think everyone had fun. Everyone I talked to did."

"That's nice." Darius was sitting with his back to the room and listened to the peaceful clatter behind him as Rolf carried things to the kitchen. For a minute, eyes full of tears like lenses, he toyed with his vision. He blinked at the glinting Nepalese pillow. The tears disappeared to the nowhere they'd just come from—maybe his eyes absorbed the excess. "You had a good talk with Flossy?"

"Mm."

"Did you see the beautiful blond guy who came with him?"

"Yeah."

"He told me he's bi. I didn't think he looked it at all. Did you?" Darius still sounded supremely indifferent.

Rolf came around and knelt by his chair. He looked at his friend so intently Darius had to close his eyes for a second. Rolf didn't touch him, but he steadied his hand on the arm of the chair against which Darius had tucked up his knees. Darius had to force himself not to move his knees to the other side. "Have you called the home health care people?"

"Not yet," Darius answered. "I think I drank more than I realized. I don't want to leave this place."

"*Moi non plus.*"

Later on, Darius was unable to sleep. Once he rose stealthily to masturbate with the most delicate attention to silence. Metabolizing alcohol and Dean and thoughts about Barry and Oliver and Rolf and Jane combined in a faint nausea of love behind his sternum.

35

GUILTILY, DARIUS SKIPPED a visit to Oliver the day after the de-warming party. He'd woken in the powder blue dawn and, needing more sleep, polished off the remainders of several bottles of wine standing amid a scatter of cigarette butts and withered radishes and slumping cheese. Next time he woke, he felt vaguely ill and decided to stay in. The following day, at about eleven, he made it to the Cedar Street apartment bearing a cheap set of sheets he'd picked up at a dollar store along the way. The spiked bolt remained spiked, unlocked. The hall outside the apartment smelled of distant poison, which, as soon as the door opened, resolved into inflammatory fumes of bleach. He always recognized that smell from the basement laundry room growing up. Something was off about the stillness in the apartment.

Darius dropped the flimsy plastic bag containing the sheet set and left the door ajar. He walked into the apartment with a ticklish spine. His knees felt a little spongy.

Oliver's bed was unmade and empty. The old suitcase was on its side, open and also empty. Its boulder of red glass was on the floor along with the old beading tray and several strange wafers and pearls of dusty mercury. The mercury quivered against the floorboards when he walked over to see what it was. The papers and letters from the suitcase were all missing, along with the many notebooks of l's and e's. Oliver had brought his demented work on the notebooks to a close quite a long time ago, when he'd somehow been able to achieve a more perfect monotony.

This appeared saner at least. But he'd carefully preserved the old notebooks.

Darius called his father's name as sternly as he could. He heard a pretty, startled tinkling of liquid from the bathroom. It sounded like the showerhead had dribbled, or someone soaking in the bathtub had lifted an arm.

Giving the door a wide berth, Darius came around to look into the original owner's slapdash attempt at a super-sexy bathroom. Brown sedimentary stains caked the aged basins of a black tub and sink.

On a tingling wave of nerves the inevitable fantasies came to Darius—discovering a body in there, someone cut into pieces, someone hiding and liable to spring out. The dizzying stench of bleach intensified the closer he came.

Oliver couldn't really kneel anymore. His chest and arms rested awkwardly over the edge of the bathtub, while the lower half of his body was propped against the closed toilet. He looked almost like he'd fallen partway into the gap between toilet and tub, but he was full of desperate energy. Evidently in a hurry since hearing his name called, he clawed fistfuls of papers from the tile floor with both hands and plunged them into the bathtub. The splashing was violent. The old man kept forcing the papers to the bottom of the tub. He'd pushed back the sleeves of his filthy dressing gown. The sleeves were soaked black to his shoulders, and the silk stuck to his meatless biceps. His forearms were burned bright red from the bleach. Oliver turned his face away from the fumes and splashes as best he could, but his chest and his crumpled lips were already wet. He tried to dry his cheek with a wet shoulder of the dressing gown.

When Darius could finally speak, his question sounded bizarrely ordinary. "What's up, Dad? Can I help?" His heart raced. His sense of responsibility skated toward panic.

Oliver squinted open an eye, a crazed look on his face. Darius could now see his father's cheeks and chin were also inflamed. Red spilled-liquid shapes marked the pallor. His arms rose from the tub trailing water. He felt around his hip for an empty plastic bleach bottle, which he threw through the door at Darius. Taking the last of the papers in his fists, he submerged them. He kneaded the documents against the deglazed bottom of the tub. Blue-green-black water sloshed drunkenly from side to side and onto the bathroom floor, and the smell of bleach came out in waves. Oliver worked the wet paper like a laundress. All that remained on the bathroom floor was a heap of stretched spiral wires, the confetti of torn perforations and the odd scrap of a glossy travel brochure.

"OK!" Darius called. He wanted to sound stentorian, to shock Oliver into attention. He strode into the bathroom. He stood over his father in uncertainty. His sinuses burned and ran with thin mucus, so he tried breathing the poison through his mouth. Oliver's arms kept moving in the tub with the same washerwoman stirring and kneading. Darius took hold of his father's frail upper arm, which kept moving like a tie rod. Oliver shook the hand off again and again. In what looked like a pantomime of drunkenness Darius started missing his father's arm with his slow-moving hand, or his father easily jerked his arm free from the gentle grasp. When Darius held on at last, a ridiculous yanking back and forth started.

After several grunting attempts, Darius got a purchase under both his father's arms and began pulling him to his feet. Oliver screamed. The scream was feeble, a high-pitched, loudly spoken, *Aaaahhhh, Aaaahhhh!* Oliver repeated it like a siren. He interrupted himself only to move on to a nasal keening, a sound of pain or physical effort. He struggled as Darius walked him out of the bathroom toward his bed, across the puddled mercury which divided and scattered and glinted as they shuffled through it.

Darius found his father's gaunt body surprisingly heavy. At least his struggling was feeble. He heaved Oliver like a sack the last two feet to sit him on the bed. Oliver kept screaming.

Where his own hands had gotten damp and where he'd rubbed under his nose, Darius could already feel his skin burning. His few patches of redness were nothing compared to Oliver, who looked as entirely red now. Head bowed, a haggard, waifish figure, Oliver sat on the edge of the bed and screamed, stinking of bleach.

Oddly, Darius wasn't overly worried at first. He let Oliver scream the repetitive *mezzo-forte* scream but felt certain he had plenty of time. His real anxiety was historical. All those letters. He went back to check on the papers in the bathtub.

Most were already ruined. The ink of the old letters had become weird blotches and swirls on ghostly sheets suspended in the electric-colored water. The sheets moved like sea grass under the still wobbling surface, mercuric flashes slowing. Anything that still showed lettering, Darius gingerly pulled from the water. He held his breath to keep the fumes out. His fingers burned. He ran intact sheets out to the loft and lay them on the floor. The bleach made his hands feel hot to the core and raw and, somehow, mealy when he dried them on his thighs.

After several trips in and out of the bathroom, he noticed the writing on the pages he'd laid out on the floor continued to vanish. Likewise for pages he'd draped over the shower curtain rod or the lip of the sink. He'd have to rinse the bleach out of the soaked pages. He opened the faucet.

He transferred wet sheet after sheet into the basin of pure water. Like a photographer working against the arrow of time, his lines and shadows kept disappearing in his bath of fixer. Many of the papers tore. Many collapsed into a wet hank of whiteness. The work was futile, really, but Darius became absorbed in it. His race against time so played on his nerves that when an empty truck passed outside with the usual clangor of pothole and steel, he jumped violently, ruining the damp pages from one of Oliver's scribbled journals. He drained the tub of its poisonous liquid. When the gulping stopped, all that was left was a mass of pulp from which Darius could no longer separate single pages. He filled the tub with clean water in a last effort to save something, but the force of the running water made a mess of what was left. Fragments of paper swirled like vortices of leaking egg white in boiling water. The handful of letters he'd been able to rescue, keep intact and lay flat outside the bathroom to dry, were now blank.

All this time, Oliver screamed. Darius barely registered the screams or the voices rising, he thought, from around the big pothole outside. On one relay, he looked over at Oliver, noticing instantly that the screaming wasn't petulant eccentricity but real pain, agony even. Without a break in his desperate pace, Darius changed jobs. Now he bunched hand towels in the sink basin, destroying the last of the paper floating in it. He ferried the soaking towels to Oliver, runs that sent whips and drips of water and mercury flying everywhere. He tried to wash Oliver's hands and forearms. Any rubbing against the bright red skin, however, any pressure at all, increased the volume of the screams. The noise rose and fell, nearly mechanically, as Darius manipulated the towels as gently as he could. He wrung them over Oliver's lap and head, trying to rinse him in spiraling gouts of water.

After several trips, Darius came out of the bathroom to find other people were inside the apartment. One must have kicked his plastic bag of sheets from the door into the room. Imprinted with a pinkish *I Heart New York* heart, it sat near Oliver's empty suitcase, deflated and wrinkly. These were the voices Darius had thought were coming from outside. One stranger, a neighbor probably, knelt by Oliver. Another was just hurrying back into the hall. The door had been propped open. The super hovered outside. Darius handed a towel to the kneeling neighbor without thinking, and she suggested, too calmly given the noise Oliver was making, "Why don't you fill a big pot with water. Like a spaghetti pot. This was bleach, I guess? Did he fall?" In a few places, blisters were already forming on his father's skin. Oliver's mild screaming ceased completely when his first heart attack started. His eyes squeezed shut and opened in shock. The color of his cheeks deepened. His chest spasmed with silent gasping. His body didn't appear physically capable of what looked like wracking motor seizures. Nor did the color of his congested expression of surprise seem at all realistic.

Contrary to Oliver's old promise, nothing had been arranged. Sohaila waited in vain for the trustees of Mather Capital to get in touch with her. For over a month, Stan made furtive, sometimes enraged, phone calls to his investigator. He couldn't afford to restart the investigation. Worse, the glib investigator now seemed unsure of most of the information he'd given Stan the first time around. He'd merely *talked* to trust companies and investment firms in Philadelphia but had never discovered a solid connection to Oliver, the one Stan remembered so clearly. Stan began to suspect the sleuth had scammed him. He couldn't find any papers referencing the discovery of Mather Capital. Ali was called. He dug out his charity's records. The checks he'd thought had come from Mather Capital had come from an ordinary Capital One bank account, and in the space for notes was the scrawl *Mather* or, just as likely, *Mother*.

The three of them walking around made the floorboards squeak and chitter. This was the first time they'd returned to the Cedar Street apartment. Like a crime scene, the rooms remained exactly as they had been the day of Oliver's initial heart attack. But paper towels, cans of tuna in the kitchen, the mineral-stained coffee cup on the counter were all drained of personal significance. Some light-fingered neighbor or EMT may have taken the hunk of red glass and the beading tray. They were nowhere to be seen. A number of yellow and blue plastic bits, the broken tabs from medical *somethings*, had been dropped here and there. The EMTs had tackled Oliver's heart attack first. The chemical burns were slow to develop, so the medics hadn't registered how severe they were for quite a while. Nevertheless, the floor was also strewn with crumpled pieces of gauze, fresh and soiled, some of which had been used to dress the worst of Oliver's excruciating burns.

He suffered two more attacks later in the hospital, where he lingered for a month, mostly in blessed unconsciousness as the doctors struggled to treat his heart and the second degree burns covering his body, to say nothing of toxic levels of methyl mercury from his all-tuna diet. Oliver's mercury levels were so high it was suspected he'd been swallowing doses of straight mercury from his *Santería* vials.

An explosive *pop pop pop pop pop* came from the kitchen, followed by the noise of something falling. A sudden ugly brightness poured through the kitchen door. Stan had succeeded in tearing the black cloth from the window frames and that had also caused the shades to collapse.

Sohaila touched her neck in alarm, but a shout from Stan calmed her. She walked over to the kitchen and peered in. She produced a whimpering sound of disgust and pity at the state of the kitchen in sunlight. She'd been making the identical sound, a nervous repetition, ever since they'd entered the place.

The smell of bleach had volatilized completely. The sickly sweet Oliver scent had returned. It seemed strange that such a stagnant, intimate odor could fill the whole loft space. Stan strode from the kitchen. "I'm opening the windows," he announced. He reached behind the shades in the main room and started tugging at the black cloth covering those.

Darius eyed the open suitcase in the main room. The mercury was also gone. Where? It wouldn't have evaporated or been consumed by insects or dribbled through cracks in the floorboards. No trace of it remained. Strange. He continued his exploratory stroll.

In the bathroom, under the sink, a white hand towel and a washcloth sat in dried swirls like cowpats. The terrycloth ridges had turned a sickly yellow, which made them look like they'd been there for years. Spiral notebook wires and paper fragments, fewer than Darius remembered, had been swept aside into a corner. Had he done it himself that day?

Kneeling by the black tub, he got his first whiff of bleach. In such a weak concentration that it smelled like cleanness. On the stained bottom of the tub sat a heap of paper pulp, thoroughly dried like the towels. Darius picked away at the mass. The pile was dry to its very center. Certain folds of this *papier maché* were starting to yellow like the terrycloth and to exactly the same hue. No print or handwriting or images remained, not even faint traces of the photos from the glossy travel brochures.

"What was that crazy person yelling at us when we came in?" Stan called.

Darius heard his mother's keening whimper from the far end of the apartment. Her heels tock-tock-tock-tocked across the floor in his direction. Stan's footsteps made a soft *cree-cree-cree*.

"He was just being a clown," Darius answered Stan loudly. "He wanted money."

"Did you find anything?" Sohaila asked her son from the bathroom doorway. Darius shook his head. *No.*

"Yes, but what was it he said?" Stan insisted. He was by the kitchen again. The whole loft was now lighted, pathetic in color, all the windows stripped of black cloth. "It was something funny. I'll give him a dollar on our way out if he's still there."

Darius called from the bathroom, "He said, *I was born with no sense of smell, no tonsils, and no tailbone.*"

"Right!" Stan started laughing.

"Stop yelling, both of you," Sohaila hissed.

Stan, who couldn't hear her, called, "That's so peculiar a thing to say. It's probably true. He was probably a friend of Oliver's. Maybe his banker."

They'd tried to come at a time when the neighborhood would be deserted, a Sunday. But they had to cross the street to avoid a homeless man dancing by himself. He stopped dancing, bowed his head and side-eyed them as he shuffled along the opposite sidewalk. He wore a showy pout of resentment, as if to demonstrate how their rejection crushed him. From across the street he then yelled in a seemingly happy shift of mood, "I was born with no sense of smell, no tonsils and no tailbone!"

Coming out of the bathroom Darius answered Stan in a normal tone of voice so as not to annoy Sohaila. "That's a lot of odd stuff to be born without. But you're right, it doesn't really sound like, *poor me, I was born with no hands, give me money!* Maybe it's true."

"Yes, it was his true autobiography," Stan agreed.

"I don't see anything." Sohaila came over to join them. "I don't want anything here." Her voice was a touch thick with emotion, which she expelled in another whimper. She clapped symbolic dust from her hands.

Her emotion made Darius notice his own lack of any. He wasn't displeased. If anything, he was happy that he might be turning into an untouchable monster. Like the sharks of his childish imagination, whose only lovable quality was their perfection and the fact they couldn't be harmed by anything.

"Could there be any secret hiding places here?" Stan wondered.

"Stan!" Sohaila chided him for the fantasy.

Looking around him Darius shrugged, meaning he thought it would be hopeless to search a place like this for anything hidden. Aloud he said, "I'm not sure I would ever tell people about the intimate me. Like my tailbone or my nose. Why would they need to know? Even if it was for money."

ABOUT THE AUTHOR

DAVID *McCONNELL* is the author of *American Honor Killings: Desire and Rage Among Men* (Akashic, 2013), which won the 2014 American Library Association Award for Non-Fiction. His other novels include *The Firebrat* (Attagirl, 2003), *The Silver Hearted* (Alyson, 2010). His short fiction and journalism have appeared widely in magazines and anthologies, including *Granta* and *Between Men*. He lives in New York City.

BOOKS BY ITNA

Urban Gothic: The Complete Stories
Bruce Benderson

Crashing Cathedrals: Edmund White by the Book
Tom Cardamone

Settlers Landing
Travis Jeppesen

Bruno's Conversion
Tsipi Keller

The Virtuous Ones
Christopher Stoddard

After David
Catherine Texier

Mermelada de Estrellas
Las cinco noches

MERMELADA DE ESTRELLAS

1

LAS CINCO NOCHES

RENÉ VALDEZ RAMOS

Ilustraciones del autor

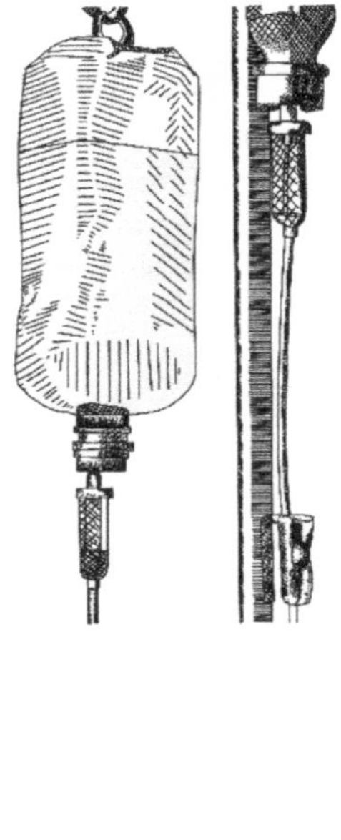

1ª edición, diciembre de 2019

Comentarios y sugerencias:
mermeladadeestrellas@outlook.com
Facebook: Mermelada de Estrellas
Instagram: @renevalram
Twitter: @Renevr9

Mermelada de Estrellas: Las cinco noches

ISBN: 9781651869123
Independently published

Fotografía: Rene Moroyoqui Loceña

SOBRE EL AUTOR

René Valdez Ramos nació en Sonora, México, en 1993. Se licenció en educación secundaria con especialidad en español y posteriormente se dedicó a impartir clases y escribir obras de ficción para el público joven. Actualmente, trabaja en la saga *Mermelada de Estrellas.*

Esta dedicatoria se compone
de cuatro partes elementales:

Para mis padres, que me guiaron
siempre por el buen camino;

para aquellos excelentes profesores
que me ilustraron a lo largo de la vida;

para mi hermana Yolita, con
quien empecé a contar historias;

y para Rene, que me alentó a desarrollar
sin límites esta intrépida aventura.

"Había una vez, un joven narrador de historias que se volvió cazador, con tal de salvar a su hermana de convertirse en cristal".

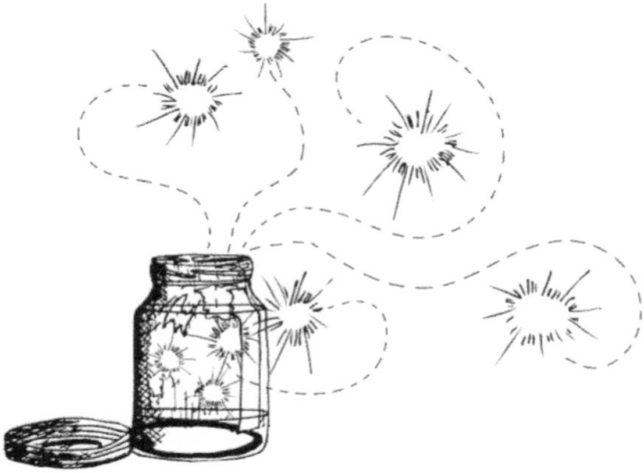

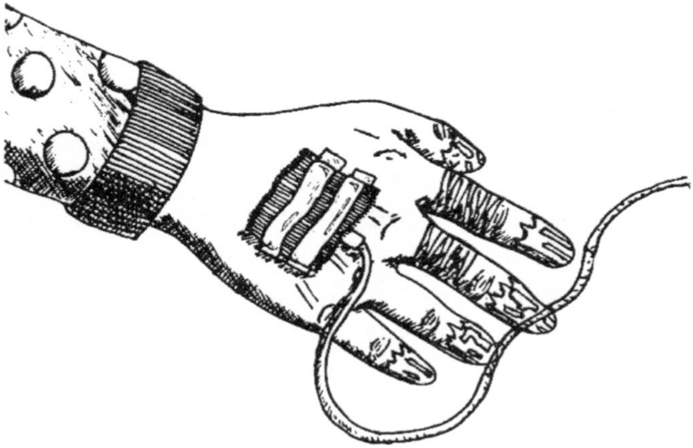

Capítulo 1
Dedos de cristal

Aquel domingo de diciembre, Ariel Castillo Rivas, de trece años de edad, fue testigo de algo extraordinario y, al mismo tiempo, terrible: la primicia de una fase de «cristalización humana». Para su mala suerte, el de la persona más allegada a él: Alondra, su hermana menor. Por supuesto que en ese momento Ariel desconoció el nombre de la enfermedad, y también ignoró que el cristal avanzaría por el cuerpo de la niña como un veneno a cuentagotas.

Previo al incidente, Ariel le puso a Alondrita sábanas limpias con olor a lavanda y sustituyó su unidad de suero vacía por una nueva. Era algo que hacía con frecuencia por las noches, antes de dar apertura a su sagrada reunión de hermanos: el Club de los Cuentos de las Sombras.

Ella dormía tranquila, pese a los imprudentes pitidos originados por el viejo aparato electrónico que les

donaron del hospital, encontrado en la cabecera de la cama. El suero que conectó Ariel pronto avanzó por el tubo de plástico en una carrera irrefrenable, hasta colarse por el puente de la aguja y desembocar en la mano de la niña de siete años.

Entonces, de forma repentina, el suceso ocurrió.

Las puntas de sus pequeños dedos se tornaron claros como el agua y frágiles cuales pétalos de una flor. Perplejo, Ariel tuvo que pestañear tres veces para convencerse de que estaba despierto.

«Lo debo estar imaginando», se dijo, con el corazón en la mano.

Caminó, vacilante, al costado de la cama. Tras inclinarse un poco pudo ver, literalmente, a través de los dedos de Alondrita, como si asomara los ojos por pequeñas ventanas de vidrio. Horrorizado, aún sin asimilar lo que acontecía, Ariel corrió a la oficina del señor Villalobos, su padrastro. Lo único que pudo expresarle fue la siguiente cabalgata apresurada de palabras: señor, algo, malo, pasa, manos, Alondrita.

—¿Qué le sucede? —interrogó el impaciente señor Villalobos. Entró a la habitación ejecutando largas zancadas, seguido de Ariel. Inspeccionó los signos vitales en los monitores (Todo está bien por aquí, susurró) y recorrió con la mirada cada uno de los cables que zigzagueaban por el cuarto asemejando serpientes amazónicas—. ¿Moviste un cable? ¿Conectaste mal el suero? ¿Tiene fiebre?

Boquiabierto, el muchacho negó con la cabeza y señaló las manos. De seguro su padrastro no tardaría más de un segundo en advertir los dedos translúcidos y llamar al doctor Haro…

Justo en ese instante, de modo inesperado, irrumpió la señora Rivas —madre de los dos chicos— en el cuarto. Llevaba su delantal de tela verde con un nudo

mal amarrado a la espalda. Agitaba un paño sucio aferrado en su mano, igual que una monja retiene su rosario bendito. Por su abatida mirada, podía comprobarse que se hallaba terriblemente cansada.

—¿Qué está pasando? —preguntó.

Como nadie le respondió, recargó su cabeza en el marco de la puerta. Volteó los ojos de Ariel a Alondrita, y de Alondrita a su marido, con el entrecejo fruncido, tratando de descifrar el misterio por ella misma.

—Explícame lo que viste, muchacho. ¡Ahora! —demandó el señor Villalobos, casi gritando—. ¿Qué le ocurre a tu «media» hermana? —Hizo hincapié en la palabra.

En seguida, el hombre se aproximó a la cama y le palpó a su hija de sangre la cabeza, el pecho y los brazos.

—Allí, señor..., sus manos. Mire los dedos de sus manos —respondió Ariel.

Estaba demasiado impresionado como para ordenar, de forma correcta, las oraciones que brotaban de su boca.

—¿Se fracturaron? —presagió el padrastro, estudiando la manita que tenía más próxima.

Era obvio que no. De ser cierto, Alondrita estaría llorando a causa de un dolor enloquecedor. Ya se había roto los dedos.

—¿Qué descubriste, Ariel? —cuestionó la señora Rivas a su vez, en un tono débil.

Se paró detrás de su marido, todavía con la frente arrugada. Luego descansó las palmas abiertas en sus caderas. Incluso para ella resultaba embarazoso no poder ubicar el problema.

«¿De qué están hablando?», se preguntó Ariel.

Los dedos de cristal estaban ahí, delante de sus narices. ¿Por qué no podían apreciarlos? Acaso...

«¿Será que ellos no logran notarlos? —advirtió, llevándose ambas manos a las sienes. La cabeza empezó a punzarle y sintió que le estallaría—. No me puede estar pasando esto de nuevo.»

—Se hicieron transparentes —aclaró él mismo, para que lo entendieran.

Pero no estaba tan seguro de cómo se lo tomarían, principalmente el señor Villalobos. Aquel lo miró con fiereza, sin embargo, Ariel esquivó su mirada de acero y reveló al fin:

—Los dedos de Alondrita son de cristal.

Y la pequeña despertó en ese intermedio. Dio un fuerte estornudo y sus extremidades tintinearon igual que campanillas de Navidad. El sonido fue musical, bello y angustiante a la par.

—¿Qué pasa? ¿Qué hacen aquí? —preguntó adormilada, con sus ojos pequeños como cuentas.

—Nada, niña de mi corazón. Todo se encuentra bien —musitó el señor Villalobos. Sacó un pañuelo desechable de la caja sobre la cómoda y la ayudó a sonarse la nariz. A renglón seguido, le dijo—: Vuelve a descansar, mi vida. Ariel y yo requerimos hablar de hombre a hombre.

El fulminante vistazo que le dirigió a Ariel fue dominador. La señora Rivas, en cambio, se relegó en la esquina de la habitación con ambas manos almacenadas en el pecho, promoviendo un respiro. Se tranquilizó al comprobar que había sido una falsa alarma.

—No juegues con estas cosas, Ariel —mencionó mortificada, limpiándose el sudor de la frente con el antebrazo—. Sabes que puedes contarle historias a tu hermana, pero mezclar tu imaginación con la vida real... Eso no es para nada correcto. Nos diste un buen susto.

La madre de Ariel estaba acostumbrada a tratar con

sus caprichosos pensamientos. No era el caso del señor Villalobos, que reprobaba con absoluta claridad cualquier derivado de la «fantasía». No obstante, más que eso, odiaba por sobre todas las cosas a su hijastro.

«Tengo que convencerlos de que digo la verdad. No soy un mentiroso», precisó Ariel para sí.

—Alondrita, mira tus manos —ordenó, evitando los sombríos y marcados ojos de su padrastro, quien seguía observándolo como si quisiera estrangularlo con lentitud—. Míralas y quiero que me digas lo que ves —reclamó.

Ella levantó sus extremidades y las situó delante de su cara. Pero al parecer tampoco pudo ver las extrañas y magníficas puntas de cristal, que se abrían y cerraban como alas de mariposa.

—Veo mis uñas, mis deditos, mis manos...

—No puede ser —negó Ariel, desesperado (¿Me estaré volviendo loco?)—. Fíjate bien. Obsérvalas más de cerca y dime si notas algo diferente...

—Es suficiente, Ariel. Basta —impuso el señor Villalobos, alzando la voz a fin de que Ariel dejara de interpretar la misma cantaleta. Plegó los labios en una fina línea recta. Acto consecutivo, le susurró a Alondrita con una empalagosa voz de ruiseñor—: Tú vuelve a dormir, hijita mía, nosotros ya nos íbamos. Lamento que te hayamos despertado por nada. Buenas noches.

Y le plantó un tronado beso en la frente.

Para ese entonces, la señora Rivas había sido la primera en abandonar la habitación, con tal de seguir sacudiendo los muebles de la sala con su trapo viejo.

El señor Villalobos agarró a Ariel por el cuello de su piyama y lo arrastró de pies hasta que alcanzaron el pasillo.

—¡Estoy harto de tus tonterías! —Golpeó la pared de madera.

Como secuela, cayó al suelo una fotografía enmarcada que retrataba a Ariel y a la señora Rivas abrazados en el zoológico.

—Te advertí que dejaras esas niñerías en el pasado, pero parece que no lo quieres entender. ¡Acabas de cumplir trece endemoniados años! ¡TRECE! —reiteró trastornado, con un vozarrón—. Pero tienes la mentalidad de un niño de siete: inmaduro y... «soñador» (dijo esa palabra como si le causara urticaria). Te exigí que fueras más realista. Realista, ¡maldita sea! ¿Cuántas veces tengo que repetírtelo para que lo entiendas?

—Señor —repuso Ariel en voz muy baja—, es que si prestara más atención a las manos de mi hermana...

—Tu «media» hermana —corrigió.

—Sí. Mi «media» hermana —restableció—. Podrá darse cuenta de que el cristal está allí. No estoy inventándolo, se lo juro...

—¡Por favor! —expresó en tono sarcástico, con un excelso volumen de voz—. ¿No se te ocurrió elaborar una mejor broma? Tu pobre «media» hermana —machacó otra vez— sufre de *osteogénesis imperfecta*, un trastorno genético que también llamamos *enfermedad de los huesos de cristal*. ¿Y pretendes convencerme de que, mediante un truco de magia, irónicamente se volvió de vidrio? Qué... —Inspiró y exhaló hondo, haciendo palpitar las aletas de su nariz—. ¡Qué tontería! Es un insulto, una majadería. No cabe la menor duda de que careces de madurez. Si hubieras sido mi hijo... —Se golpeó reacio el pecho con el índice (a Ariel se le antojó que se hubiera hecho un hoyo profundo)—, desde un inicio te habría educado como debe de ser; con los pies bien plantados sobre la Tierra. —Y agregó—: con las mejores calificaciones en la escuela, haciendo rutinas de ejercicio para desaparecer esa bola de grasa que escondes bajo tus sudaderas talla extra grande;

hubieras sido un ávido lector de obras matemáticas y físicas que en verdad valen la pena, y te habría comprado un ejemplar de revistas de divulgación científica cada mes del año. Por fortuna me deshice de las mugrosas novelas «fantásticas» que trajo tu madre. Esa imbécil fue la mayor culpable de tu deteriorado estado mental.

Ariel comprimió la quijada. A él, su padrastro podía escupirle, humillarlo y gritarle todo cuanto quisiera, pero aborrecía que se metiera con la persona que le dio la vida. El adulto sonrió luego de verificar el semblante afectado del chico. Comentó con una risa lo que le sigue de desagradable:

—No te gustó lo que dije, ¿eh? A qué no.

—Con ella no se meta —desafió Ariel.

Pero un bofetón imprevisto, con el revés de la mano del ruin señor Villalobos, hizo que se le torciera el cuello a Ariel noventa grados. Su mejilla enrojeció y percibió el sabor metálico de la sangre.

—Ya no toleraré tus faltas de respeto, muchacho insolente. ¡Cuán harto me tienes! Es la última vez que te burlas así de mí —ladró—. ¡Y lárgate a tu habitación! —sentenció, tronando los dedos—. No me cedes otra opción más que dejarte sin cenar hoy. Así tendrás tiempo de sobra para reflexionar acerca de la intolerable actuación que diste esta noche.

El señor Villalobos levantó la fotografía del suelo y la miró de soslayo. El cristal se había cuarteado. El rostro de la señora Rivas quedó irreconocible bajo grietas blancas.

—Con esta lección —prosiguió—, confío en que te quedarán menos ganas de hacerte el payaso con estúpidos cuentos de hadas.

Ariel se mordió la lengua, incapaz de mencionar algo más y se resignó a aceptar su derrota. Se enclaus-

tró en su habitación, sin fijarse que su padrastro contemplaba el retrato del zoológico con un examen impropio.

—¡Y no estrelles la puerta de esa manera, muchacho torpe! O te obligaré a reparar el resto de las que hay en esta casa —amenazó.

Colgó el cuadro dañado en la pared. A continuación...

—¡Papááá! —chilló Alondrita.

El sonriente señor Villalobos entró al aposento de la niña aligerando el paso.

—¿Qué ocurre, luz de mis ojos? —preguntó con afecto.

—Papi, ¿ya te fijaste? —dijo la niña, entremezclando un tono de fascinación y terror—. Mira mis manos. Creo que mis deditos... se hicieron de cristal.

Capítulo 2
Un encuentro inesperado

Ariel vivía en el número 72 de la calle Monteseaur, lo cual era «extraño». Extraño, por el hecho de que resultaba ser el único hijo varón en todo lo largo y ancho de esa vía pública. Monteseaur era, en primer lugar, reconocida por sus jovencitas rubias y presumidas, de mejillas sonrosadas y regordetas. No era raro mirarlas sonriendo con coquetería, como muñequitas de porcelana. Gracias a ese detalle, nació el primer chiste que se contó de Ariel en la escuela.

—¡Miren quién viene llegando! *Lady Arielita*, bendita entre todas las mujeres —canturreó Brandon Portillo el primer día de clases.

Y sus compañeros, sin haberlo conocido todavía, se rieron de Ariel con cinismo y establecieron la regla de llamarlo de tal manera. Por desgracia, las cosas no mejoraron conforme cursaba la secundaria. Después lo apodaron *Pelota*, *Apestoso*, *Tripas*, *Pez globo*, *Panzón*,

Cerdoman, *Puerquín*, *Bola de grasa*, *Cebo* y cientos de sobrenombres diferentes. No obstante, todos sus problemas pasarían a segundo término, porque la noche misteriosa de viento helado y cielo tachonado, en la que Alondrita comenzó a tornarse de vidrio, su vida daría un giro inesperado. Se convertiría, ni más ni menos, que en un cazador de estrellas.

Sucedió a las doce de la noche, una hora que la mayoría de las personas aprovecha para dormir. Pero esa ocasión especial, había algo en Ariel que lo reprimía a cerrar sus ojos. No podía dejar de pensar en otra cosa más que en los dedos de su hermana. ¿Fue real? ¿En verdad había ocurrido? O tal como le había enunciado su padrastro, pensó Ariel, tenía un estado mental de locura a causa de leer y contar tantas historias mágicas.

El rugido que profirió su estómago en ese momento fue el encargado en responderle. Este hizo que sus pensamientos aterrizaran de nuevo a la realidad. La verdad es que Ariel tenía muchísima hambre. Y lástima que iba a serle imposible complacer su apetito. Para empezar, el estricto señor Villalobos (a propósito de dejarlo sin cenar) obstruyó el refrigerador y la despensa a cal y canto con pesadas cadenas de hierro, suponiendo que de esta forma su hijastro no quebrantaría el castigo.

Además, ya se sumaban dos días en que aquel individuo tenía confiscadas sus golosinas en el tarro que se encontraba en lo más alto de la alacena. Ariel jamás había logrado llegar hasta allá. De hecho, lo intentó más de una vez en la última hora, parándose de puntitas sobre una silla de la cocina. Pero solo el padrastro, con aquella colosal estatura de dos metros, era el único que podía prolongar sus extremidades lo suficiente para alcanzar el lugar. Ariel era muy bajito, y apenas

podía aventajar ciertas cosas con el brazo estirado.

Se lamió los labios, imaginándose el sabor de los dulces que colmaban el tarro, y de pronto escuchó que fuera de casa…

¡TRAZ!

… un nervioso metal colisionó contra algo.

¿Qué habrá sido eso?

«Un robot. —Fue lo primero que le cruzó por la mente. Dejó a un lado los imaginarios caramelos con sus envolturas brillantes, que giraban apetitosos en el techo, y siguió pensando—: Un robot que se escapó de la fábrica donde lo construyeron porque se negó a vivir la triste y monótona vida que le fue destinada. Después de tanto correr, perseguido por los agentes de la «PFR» (Policía Federal Robótica), se refugió en el jardín de mi casa, bajo la copa de un árbol. Y ahora está solo, necesitado de compañía.»

Ariel clausuró sus pensamientos y sacudió la cabeza en señal de negación. Cerró los ojos, poniendo en pausa la imagen del hombre mecánico. Recordó las palabras que le expresó el acertado de su padrastro esa misma tarde, cuando lo descubrió dibujando un caballero medieval que lanzaba flechas a cierto dragón lanzallamas:

—¿Por qué no eres más sensato? —había dicho el señor Villalobos, arrancándole la hoja de las manos.

Hizo trizas el dibujo y lo echó a la basura de inmediato. Ariel miró cabizbajo la forma en que llovían los trozos de papel en una somnolienta nevisca, mientras seguía oyendo en silencio la fastidiosa cháchara del adulto.

—Estoy haciéndote un favor. Abandona esas historias absurdas que te cruzan por la cabeza y enfócate en la realidad —refunfuñó. Después anexó—: Lo que trato de decir es que deberías distraerte haciendo algo pro-

vechoso; otro tipo de actividades. Puedes iniciar, por ejemplo, leyendo algunas enciclopedias de mi oficina. Construirías nuevos conocimientos en ese cerebrito de pájaro que tienes alojado en el cráneo. —Asentó una sonrisa torva en su rostro—. Con el pasar de los años, hijastro, entenderás que las ridículas fantasías que tu madre te inculcó no sirven para nada cuando uno se vuelve mayor. ¡Sé *realista*!

Siempre aprovechaba la oportunidad de mencionar esa palabra en sus conversaciones:

«Realista.»

A Ariel no le agradaba mucho que digamos, era pesada y dramática. Pero, al final de cuentas, quien la pronunciaba era él: un adulto, su padrastro. Y por esa sencilla razón, Ariel creyó que debía tomarla en cuenta, así le gustara o no.

Las severas reglas del señor Villalobos eran totales verdugos de la imaginación. Si Ariel no se esforzaba por ser un poquito más realista, las cosas podían ponerse realmente feas en el hogar. Así que...

Abrió los ojos, renunciando a la historia del robot solitario (que pudo haber sido un excelente relato para narrarle a Alondrita en la próxima sesión del Club de los Cuentos de las Sombras).

Intentó pensar de manera *realista*.

«Metal chocando contra algo, ¿qué podrá ser? —se volvió a preguntar, observando el cielo centelleante de estrellas por la ventana—. Quizás, un hombre cruzó la calle tomándose una soda —predijo—. Cuando acabó con la bebida, arrojó la lata al contenedor de basura, ocasionando ese impacto...»

¡Bah! La contestación fue tan desabrida y madura que le supo a una sopa sin sal.

«Qué aburrido es pensar como adulto, carece de emoción y aventura. Mi padrastro es un...», comentó

para sí una expresión malsonante.

Él prefería seguir pensando como hacía todos los días: inventando palabras, personas, disparates y ciudades que no existen; forjando odiseas que lo separan de la realidad; continuar siendo él mismo: Ariel Castillo Rivas. De modo que, un ruido de latón estrellándose... ¿Qué sería...?

«Un robot que se esconde en el jardín», reafirmó, con la solidez de un sargento.

Casi pudo oír aquellos pasos dejando huellas lodosas. A veces, resultaba difícil acatar las órdenes razonables del señor Villalobos; más cuando la poderosa imaginación de Ariel estaba de por medio.

Decidido, abrió la ventana y sacó la cabeza a la intemperie, esperando encontrarse una enorme cara de hojalata y un par de ojos con vista de rayos X. Se confió. ¡Cuánto deseaba que un personaje ficticio viniera por él y se lo llevara lejos, muy lejos, a un lugar maravilloso, donde no tuviera que vivir con los conflictos cotidianos del mundo! Así como les sucedía, casualmente, a los jóvenes solitarios en los libros que tenía escondidos bajo su cama.

Por un sagrado segundo, tuvo la inocente idea de que el robot iba a ser real, que aquel le devolvería una sonrisa afectuosa, saludándolo con un amable y mecánico «¡Hola!». Mas cuando se encontró frente a frente con el exterior, apoyando sus manos en el alféizar de la ventana, no hubo nada de lo que sospechó. Ni hombre mecánico, ni tampoco una aburrida lata de gaseosa.

Un gato negro estaba siendo perseguido por otro de su especie, y allá delante, atravesando el estropeado jardín de su casa, descubrió la fuente del sonido.

Por su travesía, los escurridizos mininos habían derribado el depósito de basura, trayendo como consecuencia que se desparramaran los desperdicios de una

semana por la acera. Ariel sonrió por tremenda travesura felina. Se puso sus pantuflas blancas de borreguito y dio un salto al exterior.

De no haber salido a la calle a tales horas, esa noche no habría tropezado con el anciano. El detalle estaba en que desde luego lo hizo. No quiso encargarse de limpiar a la mañana siguiente, cuando los perros hubieran hecho un desastre con la basura y el señor Villalobos lo estuviera obligando a barrer la calle de principio a fin.

Sin tener remota idea de lo que ocurriría después, Ariel se aproximó, de vez en vez, a su extraordinario destino.

La noche era oscura, atrevida, hospedaba el misterio de una caverna inexplorada. No era bueno salir a esas horas. ¿Qué le había dicho su madre el otro día?

—No todas las personas son buenas afuera. Recuerda que el mundo es un pantano lleno de cocodrilos, por eso procura que tus pasos sean cautelosos. No confíes en nadie y presta mucha atención a tu alrededor.

A pesar de la advertencia, Ariel reflexionó en esos momentos que andando cerca —siempre y cuando su hogar estuviera a la vista—, estaría seguro dentro de esa zona. Creía, en su infantilismo, en la existencia de una tiza invisible dibujada en el suelo, que separaba el territorio «seguro» del «peligroso». Si sacaba un pie de la calle Monteseaur, entonces sí que le pasaría algo, como que lo atacara un puñado de monstruos de tres ojos o (si pensaba de forma realista), que lo raptara un equipo de secuestradores con el designio de vender sus órganos al mercado negro.

Glup.

Tragó saliva al visualizar el contenido gráfico de esa hipótesis.

Atravesó el triste jardín, que había sido bello, prós-

pero y envidia de contados vecinos de la cuadra; y que, con todo, tras un largo año de desatenciones, hoy por hoy, se hallaba más marchito que el desfallecimiento de un rosal en otoño. En él ya no moraban flores coloridas sino hierbas largas y espinosas. Le otorgaban un aspecto lamentable.

Ariel llegó a la acera, levantó el barril y lo acomodó en su sitio. Luego se dedicó a meter las bolsas plásticas al interior. Mientras lo hacía, buscó sin triunfo a los gatos causantes del episodio, que tal vez se recluyeron en algún callejón. Instaló la tapa de latón cuando terminó y se sacudió las manos. Dio media vuelta para volver por donde llegó y echarse a la cama. Dormiría de una buena vez por todas.

Antes de mover los pies, sin embargo, aquello lo «atrapó». No a él, en sentido literal, porque no fue el famoso secuestrador del que murmuraban todos desde el pasado mes de noviembre; el del costal y las manos grandes: el *Robaniños*. No. Fue algo que atrapó su vista. Una imagen muy rara y, a la vez, consoladora.

En la negrura del parque abandonado, a unos cuantos domicilios, aparecieron dos ojos pálidos, como de caricatura animada. Uno de ellos le guiñó con encanto. Aquella era una invitación para que se acercara. Y tan pronto como aparecieron, se esfumaron en un par de filamentos de vapor.

«¿Qué fue eso?», se preguntó Ariel, con los brazos rígidos.

Era el segundo evento insólito que notaba ese día. De inicio, los dedos de cristal de Alondrita; al presente, unos globos oculares blancos que lo llamaban, flotando en medio de la oscuridad.

Ariel estaba paralizado, aferrándose a la idea de que eran imaginaciones suyas, como parecía estarle sucediendo últimamente.

«Me pregunto... —pensaba—, ¿y si voy a averiguarlo?

Después de todo, el parque recreativo estaba cerca de su vivienda, se respondió. En la zona segura, antes de la tiza invisible de la calle Monteseaur.

Sin darle vueltas más veces, se alejó del buzón rojo con el número 72 y echó a andar, mirando los alrededores igual que un ratón fuera de su agujero. Las casas semejaban rostros adormecidos de una fila de gigantes. Las ventanas eran sus miradas y las puertas sus bocas. El miedo más robusto de Ariel era que despertaran y se lo comieran de un bocado, motivo por el que sus pasos fueron l-e-n-t-o-s y *sigilosos*, como los de un ladrón entrando de puntillas a la bóveda de un banco...

Allí estaba su imaginación, afanando sin descanso. Ser realista, como le pedía el señor Villalobos, iba a costarle la vida entera.

Alcanzó el término de su recorrido. En la entrada del área descubrió un letrero enmohecido que rezaba:

Parque de Juegos Monteseaur

"Los mejores aprendizajes de
la vida se hacen jugando"
Francesco Tonucci

Detrás de este, se abría un amplio terreno de césped desaliñado que, en opinión de Ariel, tenía aires de la alborotada melena de un león. El lugar se encontraba con falta de iluminación y llevaba incontables años siendo un museo de cacharros viejos. Sus ruinas eran pasamanos, columpios y toboganes que los niños usaban para divertirse en una época precedente a la aparición de las consolas de videojuegos, teléfonos inteligentes y tabletas electrónicas.

Piezas de automóviles estancadas en el suelo y tu-

bos izados igual que banderas nacionales formaban parte de la decoración; también existían arbustos elaborados con alambre de púas, botellas de vidrio empañadas y una incalculable cantidad de llantas amontonadas en altas columnas, partidas a la mitad, como si un tiburón hubiera pretendido comérselas y al final no resultaron tan apetitosas como había esperado.

«Cof. Cof», oyó Ariel cerca de él. Fue tan quedito que en ese momento no le prestó la atención debida. La noche poseía muchos ruidos que confundían el oído de la gente: chicharras, sapos, el maullido del viento, el canto de los grillos...

Miró en derredor, tratando de encontrar los ojos de caricatura que lo llamaron. No consiguió entrever otra cosa que cachivaches estropeados y abundante herbaje verde que se fundía con la imperturbable oscuridad... ¡Oh! Y también había un par de columpios sobrevivientes al otro lado, bailando al compás del viento, con la pintura descarapelada y las cadenas oxidadas. Fuera de eso, no yacía algo más sorprendente en aquel lugar abandonado por la mirada de Dios.

Ariel interpretó que la luz que lo «atrajo» pudo haber sido una ilusión óptica —como le explicó el señor Villalobos un día— que le jugó su vista en la oscuridad. Como cuando miraba retratos de su familia por las noches, antes de acostarse y, entre esa penumbra, las bocas de sus protagonistas parecían moverse con lentitud, queriéndole susurrar cosas.

Otro motivo realista por el que pudieron aparecer los ojos blancos, debió tratarse de alguna simpleza de la naturaleza, tal como el reflejo de la luna contra una de las innumerables botellas de vidrio que rodeaban el área.

«Sí, fue eso», se dijo Ariel.

Mas falló al encontrarle sensatez a su hipótesis,

puesto que no había ningún objeto limpio que cumpliera con la característica de reflejar luz. Se entendía, de raíz, que el parque estaba conquistado por mugre y el olvido.

«¡Cof! ¡Cof!», se escuchó más fuerte, Ariel volvió a ignorarlo...

De todas maneras, él no tenía sueño, así que podía pasar un par de minutos más fuera de casa. Se sentó en el pasto sucio con las piernas entrecruzadas y lanzó la cabeza hacia atrás, con el rostro direccionando al sublime techo del mundo. Sus fantasías pronto se avivaron. Especuló ideas maravillosas que lo separaron del mundo real.

Se imaginó nadando arriba.

Recreó en el cielo una piscina matizada con colores purpúreos; vasta y profunda, en la que pudo sumergirse y flotar con brazos y piernas abiertas, en la posición de la estrella. Jugó con la luna; la lanzó lejos y esta rebotó en las plomizas calles de la Tierra, para luego volver a sus manos...

«¡COF! ¡COF!», esta vez fue imposible pasarlo por alto.

Se desvió Ariel, pasmado, de su aventura nocturna y supo de tajo, como si le hubieran golpeado la cabeza con un mazo, lo que era ese indispuesto sonsonete. Era una tos, muy parecida a la de un enfermo de tuberculosis, que figuraba el crujir del pan tostado. Cuando desenganchó la mirada del cielo se topó con un anciano de barbas desvaídas, asentado en un columpio.

Capítulo 3
El trato a la medianoche

Tenía la espalda encorvada, a causa de una enorme joroba que imitaba un monte irlandés. Su atuendo, un abrigo pardo que le quedaba muy holgado, apestaba a calcetines sucios. En sus delgadas y artríticas manos sostenía un bastón para andar, pero parecía más una varita mágica, ya que poseía un bello diseño de espirales en el mango. Sin embargo, lo que más llamó la atención de ese anciano mal vestido eran sus ojos; inmaculados y brillantes, semejantes a dos bombillas de luz que recién fueron apagadas. En medio de ellos existían un par de misteriosas pupilas negras cuales pozos sin fondo, del tamaño de una aguja.

«Está ciego», pensó Ariel.

Supo pronto que estaba equivocado, porque descubrió que aquellos puntitos azabaches se fijaron en él.

Se levantó rápido Ariel del suelo, sin dejar de contemplar al extraño. Desanduvo con un caminar de can-

grejo. El corazón le latió deprisa.

«¿De dónde salió? ¿Será el famoso Robaniños?», se preguntó.

¿Cómo es posible que no hubiera reparado en su presencia, ni que sintiera aquella mirada pesada analizándolo desde quién sabe cuándo? Y, sobre todo, ¿cómo pudo cometer la sandez de asistir al parque a la medianoche? Actualmente estaría en su dormitorio, arropado de pies a cabeza. A salvo.

—Ya era hora de que me vieras —habló el anciano con maneras de impaciencia.

Tosió una vez más y golpeó el suelo con su cayado. Cierta fina onda de polvo se extendió hacia todas direcciones.

—Me estaba cansando de toser tanto —dijo el señor, acaso respingando. Carraspeó—: *Éjem, éjem…* ¡Hola! ¿Qué estás haciendo aquí, jovencito? Deberías tener más cuidado, esta es la hora en la que el Robaniños hace de las suyas. ¿Que no te advirtieron tus padres lo peligroso que es salir de tarde?

Ariel se limitó a responder.

«No hables con extraños», era otro consejo de los adultos, y no quería incumplir otra regla.

Con todo, el viejo de repente insistió con una voz quebrada y lastimera que recordaba el chocar de las olas del mar:

—No quise asustarte —expresó abatido—. Mmm, puedes irte si quieres. Pretendía tener una buena charla contigo. A veces me siento tan… —Robó aire—, pero tan solo. ¡Fíjate en la expresión que tienes! Tu cara de repulsión demuestra lo que soy para ti: una arcaica aberración de la naturaleza, benemérita de la soledad.

—Eso no es cierto —replicó Ariel, recobrándose del susto—. Me sorprendí porque…, porque no sabía que

había alguien más aquí.

—Oh, por supuesto que no —rebatió el otro—. Es porque soy horroroso, ¿verdad? Lleno de segmentos pellejudos colgando de mi cuerpo como tela vieja; un saco de huesos quejumbroso y adolorido que ya no sirve para nada; un despreocupado ermitaño; un adefesio de la naturaleza que usa ropa de segunda mano exhumada de la basura; el puntito negro en el arroz.

—Escuche, señor —emitió el tímido Ariel—, tranquilícese. No diga cosas tan negativas de usted. Ya le expliqué que solo me asombré cuando lo vi en el colum…

—¡No discutas conmigo, mocoso maleducado! —gritó el tipo, hecho una furia—. Soy un adulto y por eso tienen razón todo lo que pronuncian estos labios. He dicho que soy un adefesio de la naturaleza y punto. ¿Quedó claro?

El agresivo veterano quedó con un tic nervioso en el ojo izquierdo. Ariel asintió, sobrecogido. Ni siquiera se percató del inaudible «ajám» que evaporaron sus labios. El anciano, arrepentido de su conducta, acarició su amplia frente y se acomodó una greña rebelde detrás de la oreja. Cuando volvió a hablar, esta vez, lo hizo con mansedumbre:

—*Éjem, éjem*. —Volvió a aclararse la garganta—. Me disculpo, jovencito, estoy avergonzado. Me cuesta trabajo mitigar mis nervios. La excentricidad es buena amiga de la vejez, te lo dice la voz de la experiencia. —Acompañó lo dicho con una risita—. Pero siendo honesto contigo, comprendo tu impresión: es bastante normal que te hayas espantado al verme. Como imaginarás, estoy acostumbrado al rechazo y a las brutales humillaciones de la sociedad. Los viejos damos miedo, repugnancia o causamos lástima, sobre todo si pertenecemos a la calle. —Tosió y arrojó una flema verdosa

al centro de una llanta que tenía a más de cinco metros de distancia. Ariel acabó impresionado por el truco—. Y también enfermamos —continuó diciendo el indigente—. Por el contrario, los jóvenes brindan esperanza y están llenos de alegría. Daría lo que fuera para retroceder las manecillas del reloj y gozar de tu edad una vez más. ¿Cuántos años tienes? ¿Once? ¿Doce?

—Trece —respondió Ariel en voz baja.

—¡Trece años! —repitió asombrado—. La adolescencia es una edad maravillosa, ¿no lo crees?

Se frotó los ojos con su mano mugrienta. En efecto, estaba llorando, y sus lentas lágrimas surcaron por las carreteras de sus arrugas. Ariel se imaginó a un sinnúmero de personitas navegando encima de ellas, remando hábiles de derecha a izquierda sobre ordenados kayaks. Sintió tanta compasión por el veterano callejero, que su miedo se dispersó igual que un termómetro a bajas temperaturas. En el segundo por venir Ariel se sentó junto a él, en el columpio de al lado, con la confianza que un nieto le profesa a su abuelo. Desde allí, pudo percibir más el aroma a rancio. Para sus adentros, quiso adivinar cuántos días llevaba el indigente sin bañarse.

—Yo daría lo que fuera para que mi hermana se curara —confesó el sereno Ariel, aferrándose a la cadena oxidada del columpio.

Recordó a Alondrita intubada en la cama, rodeada de una medusa de cables y aparatos médicos... Y las puntas de sus dedos hechas de cristal.

El desconocido arqueó las cejas y sonrió de oreja a oreja, postergando la tristeza que exhibió en un empiece por distraída felicidad. Acababa de cambiar repentinamente una emoción por otra, igual que su enojo encarnado minutos atrás.

Ariel reflexionó que el tipo tenía graves problemas

de bipolaridad. Olvidándose por entero de las aflicciones de su edad, aquel se enjugó las lágrimas con las anchas mangas de su abrigo y aplaudió, diciendo:

—Bueno, eso es algo en lo que soy «muy bueno» —subrayó—. Verás, yo me dedico a remediar las enfermedades de las personas —explicó alegre, acomodando con orgullo ambas manos en la curvatura acaracolada de su vara.

—¿En serio lo hace? —La noticia le compró una sonrisa al muchacho.

Había escuchado Ariel de ancianos curanderos y chamanes que aliviaban con métodos naturistas a la gente, pero jamás había visto a uno en persona. Quien tenía a un lado, por sí o por no, se trataba de uno de ellos.

—¡Claro que lo hago! ¿Crees que un vejestorio como yo te mentiría?

—Supongo que no. Quiere decir, señor, que... ¿intentará curar a Alondrita? —preguntó Ariel en un tono jubiloso—. Si lo hace, se resolverían muchas cosas.

Se representó en su cerebro, sin embargo, el recuerdo de los dedos de vidrio, tintineando equivalentes a la cadencia de un xilófono. Con certeza supo que, al igual que en el caso de la señora Rivas y el señor Villalobos, aquel merodeador no creería en su palabra. Por lo que Ariel aseguró, ahora, sin ánimo:

—Pero no podrá ayudarla. Le está ocurriendo algo demasiado extraño.

—Si no me dices qué la aflige, no podré sanarla —objetó el pordiosero—. ¿Por qué no empiezas describiéndome su enfermedad?

—Pues... —inició Ariel—, Alondrita nació con osteogénesis imperfecta (OI) —explicó, vacilando.

—Osteogénesis imperfecta —coreó el anciano, moviendo sus ojos pálidos de un lado a otro, como si estu-

viera leyendo un catálogo fantasma. Luego tronó los dedos y exclamó despabilado—: ¡Oh, claro! La enfermedad de los huesos de cristal, tengo experiencia en eso.

—Pero la OI no lo es todo —defirió el chico, determinado a declarar el verdadero problema—: Mi hermana, bueno, esta noche, después de que le cambiara su suero, los dedos de sus manos se hicieron... (experimentó un escalofrío antes de pronunciarlo) transparentes.

Supuso que el veterano lo echaría del parque con una fuerte amonestación, arguyendo que era un mocoso embustero que quería tomarle el pelo y burlarse de su latosa vejez.

Mas en vez de eso...

—¿Transparentes? Hum, ya veo —murmuró—. Por allí hubieras arrancado, muchacho. Está claro que tu hermana padece un insólito caso de *cristalización humana* —señaló.

—¿Entonces sí existe? ¿Usted me cree? ¿Me cree de verdad? —preguntó Ariel a la velocidad del relámpago.

—Indudablemente —reconoció el erudito andante, afirmando con la cabeza—. La «CH» Es una aflicción bastante infrecuente, que florece en una persona de cada millardo.

—¿Millardo? —remachó aturdido.

—Mil millones —explicó—. Se extiende poco a poco por el organismo y va dejando paralizadas a sus víctimas. Obstaculiza cualquier movimiento. Si me aseveras que hoy comenzó, para mañana el vidrio habrá invadido sus muñecas y también sus pies. La *cristalización humana* procede de las extremidades del sujeto afectado, hasta arraigarse, a última hora, en su corazón. En los días posteriores, tu hermana tendrá cubiertas las piernas, sus brazos, el torso... Y así, la enfermedad seguirá arrestándola hasta su muerte (Ariel

sintió una navaja clavándose en su pecho cuando oyó eso último). Es muy poco conocida y no podrás encontrar ningún artículo médico que te hable sobre ella, porque son escasas las personas que consiguen verla. Solo aquellos soñadores de corazón puro son capaces de atestiguar una fase de *cristalización humana*. Y por lo que me acabas de contar, perteneces a uno de ellos. —Lo apuntó con su dedo artrítico—. Afortunado, chico. Eres muy afortunado.

—¿Quiere decir que puedo detenerla? —quiso saber Ariel, intrigado.

—En realidad no. Puedes mirar, mas no remediar. Eres, digamos, un simple espectador.

—Pues no entiendo cuál es la fortuna en todo esto —comentó defraudado—. Es todo lo opuesto: una maldición.

El viejo rio.

—No comprendiste, chico —sonó optimista—. Yo me encargaré de curarla. ¿Que no pusiste atención cuando te dije que me responsabilizo de remediar las enfermedades? A eso me dedico. —Después de hacer una larga pausa, el longevo adoptó un semblante serio y concretó—. Pero, a cambio deberás ayudarme antes con algo.

La expresión de media sonrisa de Ariel se desdibujó.

—¡Oh, vamos! ¿Qué pensabas? —alborotó el peregrino—. Los favores no se hacen gratis, muchacho. Por más sencillos que sean, uno los tiene que saldar a su socio en determinado momento —murmuró ventajoso.

—¿Y con qué quiere que lo ayude? —inquirió, impulsándose con los pies a fin de mecerse en el columpio con suavidad. Las cadenas chirriaron como un par de ardillas rabiosas rivalizando por una bellota—. Yo casi no tengo dinero.

El anciano respondió con voz persuasiva:

—No quiero dinero, jovencito, sino otra cosa; algo que conseguirás para mí. Será una tarea muy fácil. Estoy seguro de que la harás bien. Y te lo explicaré en su debido momento. Lo primordial que debes hacer justo ahora es aceptar el trato. —Le tendió su mano abierta—. ¿Qué dices? Cumpliré tu petición de sanar a... ¿cómo se llamaba? ¿Susanita?

—Alondrita.

—Oh, claro, claro, discúlpame; gracias por recordármelo. Como verás, soy bastante olvidadizo (se lo debo a las propinas de la edad) —delató. Más tarde ratificó en un grito alegre—: ¡Alondrita! La sanaré a cambio de que tú, muchacho, me devuelvas la «juventud».

«¿Quééé! ¿De devolverle qué? ¿Su juventud?», estalló Ariel en su cabeza, confuso.

El aparente curandero, en realidad se trataba de un loco de remate. Ariel, no obstante, ya había levantado un poco su mano y cuando menos pensó, esta fue estrechada con aquella de piel gastada.

—¡Perfecto! ¡Es más que perfecto! —escandalizaba el anciano con entusiasmo, moviendo de arriba abajo el brazo derecho de Ariel, como si fuera un interruptor de electricidad—. Acabas de convertirte en mi cazador.

Ariel quiso soltarse y negarse, pero era desatinadamente tarde. Había sellado el trato.

—Espere... Yo, si le soy franco, no estoy seguro de... ¿Acaba de decir en su cazador? —interpeló.

El viejo sacó de su abrigo un frasco vacío de vidrio y se lo entregó. Ariel estaba más aturdido por su nuevo nombramiento que por la idea de que ayudaría a alguien a restituirle su juventud. ¿Qué es lo que tendría que capturar en ese pequeño tazón? ¿Escarabajos? ¿Mariposas?

Inmortalizó cuando solía coleccionar arácnidos. Cuatro años de eso. Su excéntrica afición terminó, con

todo, en el momento que un ejemplar venenoso lo mordió en el dedo gordo del pie y lo mandó a una camilla de hospital. Experimentó arcadas espontáneas, vómitos con espumarajos y espasmos musculares.

Otra persona que se entretenía coleccionando formas valiosas, por raro que pareciera, era el señor Villalobos. Un gran buscador de monedas antiguas con historias seductoras. Guardaba celosamente, por ejemplo, la que gastó Porfirio Díaz cuando se compró un traje de gala para su última presentación como presidente de la República Mexicana; también aquella de oro que usaba todos los días la segunda emperatriz de México, Carlota de Bélgica, como amuleto de la buena suerte, luego de volverse chiflada; y también reunía algo más en su misteriosa «caja secreta», que siempre mantenía oculta bajo el escritorio de su oficina, reforzada con candados y trinquetes. Ariel jamás la había visto abierta y no se atrevía a preguntarle a su padrastro qué cosa guardaba en su interior porque, en parte, temía recibir la peor de las respuestas. Una vez llegó a imaginarse que sus entrañas amparaban una colección de cabezas humanas encogidas, provenientes de una tribu africana; y en otra circunstancia, que en ella su padrastro gestionaba elementos para efectuar rituales de magia negra: muñecos vudú y cosas por el estilo.

Con una sonrisa todavía más amplia, el veterano ilustró:

—A lo largo de cinco noches, inaugurando con esta, tendrás que reunir algo muy importante para mí. De ese modo, lograrás retornar la lozanía que tanto anhelo y, a cambio, tu hermanita será la niña más saludable que exista en el planeta. Te doy mi palabra de que no sufrirá ninguna clase de padecimientos —dijo con una mano en el pecho, cual testigo que jura solemnemente decir la verdad ante la corte—. Crecerá, envejecerá y

morirá como pocos afortunados lo hacen: de causas naturales... ¡Oh! Pero antes de continuar... —Alzó el dedo. Sus uñas eran amarillas y porosas—, deberás prometerme que esto no se lo contarás a nadie, ¿eh, muchacho? O no habrá trato.

—Hecho —aceptó Ariel, dubitativo.

Lo que le pedían era pan comido. No tenía amigos, para empezar.

—Esa norma también incluye a Alondrita —añadió el anciano.

Pero allí acababa de surgir un inconveniente. ¿No contárselo a su hermana? Eso sí que iba a ser una tarea algo difícil. Tras pensárselo unos segundos, tuvo que conformarse y aceptar la regla de silencio. A final de cuentas, lo haría para mejorar su salud, ¿no?

Aunque estaba aquello de devolverle la juventud al menesteroso.

—Está bien, no se lo diré —convino el valiente Ariel—. Ahora, dígame... ¿qué es lo que debo cazar para usted? —preguntó, al punto que giraba el recipiente en sus manos, descubriendo que no había nada especial en él.

«Solo es un frasco vacío de mermelada», se dijo.

El viejo emitió una cortante carcajada, originaria de su tos flemosa. Celebró antes de explicarse:

—Estrellas, obvio, ¿qué otra cosa si no? Ve para allá y comienza atrapando unas cuantas —apeló—. Cuando llenes el frasco me lo traes de vuelta.

Vio al anciano con un repaso expectante. Su boca estuvo a un pelo de caer al suelo, dispuesta a atragantarse con un cúmulo de tierra. Casi caía en el juego y por poco le creía que sanaría a Alondrita de su *cristalización humana*. Primero «devolverle su juventud». ¿Ahora atrapar estrellas? Estaba desquiciado, seguro que sí. Ariel volteó al cielo despojado de nubes y divisó

un centenar de lucecitas, que se visualizaban como flamas de veladoras eternas. ¿Cómo iba a ser posible que alguien le pidiera que se convirtiera en un cazador de estrellas? Era ridículo, un insulto, una tontería mayúscula. ¿Qué le hubiera dicho el sensato de su padrastro en esos momentos?

«Sé realista», sin duda.

El acuerdo del viejo, en definitiva, no tenía pinta de ser una negociación cuerda. Tal vez, se trataba de un fugitivo del centro psiquiátrico. Sería lógico, valoró Ariel, porque dicha residencia no se hallaba muy lejos de la calle Monteseaur y...

¡Cielos! ¿Y si era el Robaniños? Quizás intentaba engañarlo para después, en el segundo menos esperado, meterlo en su saco y llevárselo a una cabaña arrinconada en el bosque. Si eso ocurriera, ¿lo cocinaría entero en un caldero especial para adolescentes? ¿O lo desmembraría con un hacha a fin de adornar el perímetro de su casa? Un jardín hecho con partes humanas. ¡Qué horror! Lo que debía hacer Ariel, en el acto, era tirarle el frasco en la cara y escapar lo más pronto posible de ahí, antes de que los tenebrosos gigantes de las viviendas de la calle Monteseaur despertaran y lo persiguieran hasta el número 72.

Ninguno de esos pensamientos era realista. Bueno, lo del Robaniños sí. A lo mejor un poco.

«¡Aaarg! ¿Por qué es tan difícil ser realista, incluso en las situaciones más peligrosas?», protestó el muchacho consigo.

—¿Qué estás esperando, chico? La noche no durará toda la vida. Si amanece habrás desperdiciado tu primera encomienda y el trato habrá sido en vano. Yo pensé que querías salvar a tu hermana —mencionó en un tono inteligente, abriendo más de lo normal sus ojos blancos.

Esa fue la única meditación que retuvo a Ariel de pie allí, en el parque abandonado.

¿Y si lo que le decía el vagabundo era verídico?

—Señor, ¿cree que puedo atrapar estrellas? —interrogó, confiado.

Era de esperarse que su ilusión lo hizo dudar. Las cosas irreales siempre lo habían atraído como una mosca yendo hacia una irresistible trampa de miel.

«¡SÉ REALISTA, ARIEL!!», alardeó la voz del señor Villalobos dentro de su cabeza.

—¡Qué pregunta es esa! —bramó el anciano, alzándose de hombros—. Eres el soñador de corazón puro que pudo visualizar la *cristalización humana* de su hermana; un *cazador de estrellas* que me devolverá la juventud hurtando los luceros del cielo. Claro que puedes atraparlos, no seas ridículo.

—¿No estará... —Dudó antes de pronunciar lo siguiente—: mal de la cabeza?

—¡Pero qué muchacho tan irrespetuoso! «¡Mal de la cabeza!» —repitió encorajinado. Golpeó la punta de su bastón contra los columpios. Acto seguido, dijo en tono engreído—: Así pasaran mil años, jamás perdería la cordura. Déjame contarte algo, jovenzuelo: tendré un aspecto andrajoso, pero poseo un juicio sano como ningún otro. —Se paseó una mano por su barba hirsuta, que semejaba un nido de aves, e indicó—: Ni Einstein se compara con mi sabiduría e inteligencia, pese a mis achaques de la vejez y emociones alternas. De entre muchos de mis atributos, uno que me diferencia de los demás adultos es que yo sé la verdad de las cosas, sin necesidad de andar a diestra y siniestra, estudiando saberes de la ciencia. No me preocupo por pretender ser «realista».

Ariel fue tomado por sorpresa cuando oyó la palabra que concluyó aquel discurso. Le resultaba extraño que

fuera señalada por alguien que no fuera su padrastro.

—Lo siento, no quise ofenderlo —se disculpó con espontaneidad, acallando la vocecita del señor Villalobos que de nuevo le gritaba enloquecida que se fuera de allí.

—Bueno ¡Ya basta de tanta palabrería absurda! —ultimó el desesperado indigente, poniéndose en pie—. Es hora de que comiences con tus tareas solicitadas. Ponte a atrapar estrellas de una buena vez. Vamos. Ve, ve, ve...

Ariel se incorporó y el anciano le dio empujones con su báculo, encaminándolo al centro del parque. El joven miró los ojos albos del viejo, donde sus diminutas pupilas, cuales puntos detonantes de un texto, lo enfocaban sin discreción.

¿Habrán sido esos los ojos que aparecieron en la oscuridad, cuando Ariel echaba las bolsas al contenedor de basura?

Antes de responderse, avanzó con aquellas dudas aflorando en su razón.

Penetró en el sector donde el zacate descuidado era más alto que él. Ya que estuvo en medio, le quitó la tapa al frasco. Lo alzó lo más que pudo, parado de puntitas. Se sintió ridículo, como cuando estuvo en primaria y lo obligaron a hacer el papel del conejo saltarín en la obra de primavera, lanzando confeti al público y comiendo zanahorias de cartón. ¡Qué humillación! Lo peor fue que Brandon Portillo también estuvo allí, riéndose de él. Y por supuesto, aquel había sido el principal de la representación: el valiente príncipe que salvaba a la princesa del temible hechicero.

Esperó un minuto entero con los párpados sellados, haciendo memoria de aquella parte de su vida que le apetecía borrar, y llegó el momento en el que los pies le hormiguearon. Bajó el recipiente y asomó un ojo por

la abertura. Descubrió, como era de esperarse, un fondo vacío.

«Es inútil —comentó para sí—. No puedo ser un cazador de estrellas, es imposible. Esto es ser irrealista de sobra.»

Entonces oyó pasos detrás de él.

¡Alerta roja!

Desde luego, ese era el instante en que el anciano lo atrapaba en su costal y se lo llevaba a la cabaña del bosque. Por ingenuo, Ariel siguió sus necias instrucciones, creyendo en el cuento de que sanaría a Alondrita. Se convertiría en la próxima víctima del Robaniños. Su foto aparecería pegada en los postes eléctricos de la ciudad, en los cartones de leche y periódicos locales. Gustavo Pompa, el famoso conductor del noticiero nocturno hablaría de él. Jamás lo encontrarían, ni vivo ni muerto, así como les ocurrió a los cinco adolescentes extraviados del pasado mes de noviembre, que se fueron sin dejar rastro.

Ariel se dio la vuelta y…

—¡No! ¡No! ¡No! ¡Así no! —El anciano no lo echó a un costal, venturosamente. Sin más, protestó por detrás, golpeando la punta de su cayado contra el suelo, haciendo saltar piedrecitas, tornillos y resortes estropeados—. ¡Lo estás haciendo muy mal! No te compliques tanto la vida, jovencito, e intenta efectuarlo mejor. Si no sabes cazar estrellas, puedo cambiarte por cualquier otro adolescente ordinario, que seguro lo hará en menos de un segundo.

Ariel apretó el envase, furioso por la provocación. Quizá, pensándoselo mejor, el anciano hablaba en serio y no se trataba de un loco salido del psiquiátrico (o del Robaniños, recapacitó). Todavía había posibilidades de evitar que su hermana se convirtiera en un adorno de exhibición para soñadores de corazón noble

en el museo de arte de Lorenzo Cortines, ubicado en el centro de la ciudad. El impedimento estaba en que no sabía de qué manera atrapar estrellas. ¿Cómo se realizaba tal cosa? Que él supiera, no existía un manual que hablara de cómo ejercer dicho cargo, ni mucho menos tutoriales en línea que atañeran el tema.

«Necesito una pista del siguiente paso. Que el anciano me diga de qué manera empezar», habló por dentro.

—Intento hacerlo lo mejor que puedo —murmuró Ariel, justificándose—. ¿Podría darme una instrucción? —exhortó.

—No —rechazó el viejo—. Tienes que hacerlo por tu cuenta. Por eso aceptaste ser cazador.

«Pero ¿cómo? —pensaba—. ¿Cómo?»

De anticipo, Ariel inmortalizó las historias que le contaba a Alondrita, esas que siempre le narraba todas las noches en el Club de los Cuentos de las Sombras, antes de irse a dormir. En ellas siempre aparecían personajes valientes que cobijaban esperanzas, incluso en las situaciones más escabrosas. Sí. Eso era lo que precisaba, un poco de lo que estaban hechos los heroicos protagonistas que instituía en sus cuentos:

«Fe.»

Creer que se convertiría en un cazador de estrellas. Si era auténtico lo de los soñadores de corazón noble, era verosímil, del mismo modo, que tendría éxito.

Volvió a levantar el frasco, esta vez con mucha determinación, susurrando desde lo más hondo de su alma:

—Por favor, bajen —imploró a los cuerpos celestes—. Alondrita tiene que aliviarse y la única forma de lograrlo es que se metan al frasco. Vamos. Si lo deseo con fuerza voy a conseguirlo. Nada es imposible, solo tengo que confiar en mí. Puedo hacerlo. Soy un cazador

de estrellas. Puedo hacerlo. —Y luego lo repitió, silabeando—: Soy-un-ca-za-dor-de-es-tre-llas.

Todo transcurrió muy rápido y no hubo tiempo para advertir lo que había sobrevenido. Allá arriba, un puntito azul se sacudió en un escalofrío, se separó del cielo y descendió zumbando como una abeja, dando giros en el aire hasta estacionarse dentro del envase.

Ariel sintió el golpe a través del vidrio. Sin demora bajó el frasco, se lo pegó en la nariz. Estupefacto, sin creerse que aquello estuviera aconteciendo de verdad, escudriñó la estrella. ¿De verdad estaba sucediendo? ¿Acababa de obligarla a que bajara del firmamento? Quién lo diría, Ariel Castillo Rivas era un auténtico cazador de estrellas. Allí tenía su primer astro, una esferita resplandeciente y titilante, que semejaba un solecito flotando en el frasco de mermelada.

—¡No es suficiente! —vociferó el anciano con desagrado. Se notaba un brillo de maldad en su mirada, si bien, también de alegría—. Requiero más. Atrapa todas las que puedas.

Ariel miró el cielo más entusiasmado que nunca y alzó los brazos. Su corazón pataleaba como una liebre alborozada en primavera, corriendo con absoluta libertad por verdes campos. En esta, su siguiente oportunidad, no le suplicó al cielo que cumpliera sus fervientes deseos, porque al final creyó en sí mismo.

Una treintena de deslumbrantes luceros se despegaron de su manto oscuro y se dejaron caer en espiral, mediante un abstracto remolino. Se colaron por la abertura del recipiente y acordaron en bailar pacíficos en su interior. Su brillo se volvió uno solo. El parque recreativo quedó copiosamente iluminado por el potente farol que Ariel sostenía con el apoyo de ambas manos. La luz fue radiante y color azul claro, como las aguas de un mar en calma.

El anciano pronto estalló en risas sonoras y murmuró entusiasmado:

—¡Sabía que esto iba a funcionar! ¡Lo encontré! ¡Lo encontré! ¡Encontré al cazador de estrellas! Después de buscar y buscar a tantos muchachos durante siglos... al fin lo encontré. —Y le arrebató a Ariel el objeto con todo y tapadera—. Tienen que encerrarse en cuanto caen del «Reino Astral» porque no duran mucho fuera de él —explicó, como si lo supiera todo respecto al tema.

Dicho esto, obstruyó el envase y las estrellas siguieron traveseando dentro como un vivaracho banco de luciérnagas. Mirarlas era algo maravilloso, no había palabras para describirlo. Su luminaria resultaba tan diferente a cualquier otra que residiera en el mundo, que opacaba la propia existencia de luz con su belleza. Ariel no era digno, siquiera, de pestañear...

—¿Qué crees que haces, muchacho? Voltéate hacia otro lado —apremió el viejo, cubriendo el recipiente con las mangas de su abrigo. Vigiló a Ariel con irritación, acaso teniendo celos de que contemplara a los astros (Es decir, *sus* astros). Después, aquel manifestó—: Mirar a una estrella de cerca, por más de cinco segundos, altera a las personas hasta dejarlas desequilibradas. Provocan la extraña obsesión de que quieras observarlas durante toda tu vida. Los luceros hacen que uno se olvide de comer, de hacer sus actividades diarias, ¡incluso de dormir! Pensarías en ellos hasta el día de tu muerte.

—Eso es decepcionante —comentó Ariel y cambió su enfoque, cuanto antes, hacia un enorme álamo.

—Pues ya lo sabes. Así que las próximas cuatro veces, cuando tengas estrellas delante de ti, tendrás que mantenerte alerta para no volverte loco. Solo imagínatelo, tu hermanita se convertiría en un maniquí de

cristal y yo moriría de viejo, incapaz de curarla. Espero que lo hayas comprendido.

Ariel lo reflexionó. Sonaba absurdo y, de la misma manera, espantoso. Se prometió que no contemplaría un solo astro más de cinco segundos.

—¿Y qué hará con ellas? ¿Las va a coleccionar? —preguntó—. ¿Sabe? Yo antes solía recolectar arañas —informó inmodesto—. También las encerraba en frascos. Hasta que una me mordió y…

El anciano interrumpió la anécdota gruñendo.

—¿Para qué desperdiciaría mi valiosa vida coleccionando estrellas? ¡Darles de comer! Ja. Se nota que no tienes ni idea —resopló y tosió, como si sus razones fueran muy obvias—. Y tampoco me haré una mascarilla facial que quita las arrugas, por si llegaste a pensar eso.

Rio con su voz resquebrajada.

—¿Entonces? ¿Para qué las quiere? Cuéntemelo —pidió.

—Me las voy a comer.

En contestación, Ariel torció la cara de horror.

El veterano caminó, apoyándose de su bastón, y se sentó en el columpio de antes. Estando allí, de un inesperado segundo a otro, soltó su báculo y revolvió el frasco. Ariel presenció la forma en que la danza del enjambre de estrellas llegaba a su desenlace. Su existencia se convirtió en una espesa y brillante masa glutinosa.

«¡Desagradable!», pensó Ariel.

El vagabundo quitó la tapa y la dejó caer al suelo; extrajo un azucarero de su chamarra hedionda y espolvoreó harto contenido al interior del recipiente. Hurgó en las bolsas deshilachadas de su abrigo y desenterró una cuchara oxidada, doblada a la mitad, que enderezó a la fuerza. La utilizó como herramienta para zam-

parse los luceros cual exquisito manjar, cuya consistencia igualaba a la de la jalea. Aquello era, sin lugar a dudas, una mermelada de estrellas. Y la forma en que la disfrutaba, daba a entender que resultaba deliciosa.

No desperdició nada. Cuando la cuchara ya no le sirvió para acumular el aperitivo resplandeciente, metió uno de sus dedos desgarbados al interior y talló el fondo. La última gota quedó brillando, tras un segundo, en la cumbre de su uña. Por último, la succionó con arrebato.

—¡Inigualable! Ya no recordaba su magnífico sabor —mascullió, lamiéndose la comisura de los labios, igual que un perro satisfecho después consumir su retazo de carne. Se incorporó, quejándose de sus dolores de espalda y, levantando su adornada vara del suelo, comunicó—: Tu misión de esta noche ha culminado con éxito. Vuelve mañana a la misma hora y procura no tardarte tanto. Me fastidia la gente impuntual.

Arrojó el frasco a la melena de león, donde se perdió de vista. El callado Ariel miró al individuo, esperando ser testigo de algo fenomenal, cuando... detectó algo impresionante que le recordó los dedos de cristal de Alondrita. Las manos envejecidas del viejo ¡estaban transformándose! Sus uñas largas y amarillas fueron recortadas por sí solas, tornándose de un color rosado; aquellos, sus prominentes nudillos, quedaron suprimidos junto con sus arrugas por una capa de piel tersa y suave; sus falanges torcidas se encarrilaron, originando un nauseabundo tronido de huesos; y sus muñecas adquirieron mayor volumen. Ya no eran más las delgadas manos de un adulto prehistórico, sino las de un jovencito.

«¡Entonces todo es cierto! Si las estrellas lo rejuvenecen, quiere decir que... ¡También sanará a Alon-

drita!»

Ariel casi bailaba de alegría.

—¿Estás sordo, muchacho? ¿Por qué sonríes como idiota? *¡Chus!*, vete de aquí. Tienes que cargar energías suficientes para la siguiente misión. Lo que acabas de hacer hoy fue lo más fácil del contrato. Mañana es cuando la cacería se vuelve un riesgo considerable.

Con su palo empujó a Ariel por la espalda y lo sacó del parque.

—¿Qué hay con lo de Alondrita? ¿Cómo la curará? —preguntó el adolescente, ansioso por descubrirlo.

—¡Bah! Eso lo haré después, cuando cumplas con tu parte del arreglo —dijo, agitando una palma en el aire como si espantara moscas—. Creo que te lo dejé bien claro al principio.

Ariel, manteniéndose en sus trece, inició su marcha de regreso por la calle Monteseaur.

—Hasta pronto entonces —dijo, encogiéndose de hombros, pero todavía anonadado.

Al no recibir respuesta a su despedida se giró, descubriendo así que el anciano había desaparecido. Simplemente los columpios se zarandeaban, prueba de que dos personas estuvieron sentadas en ellos. Y más atrás, donde la hierba crecía tanto como el carrizo, entre el montón de fierros viejos y llantas apiladas, los bigotes de la larga melena de león bailaron con las corrientes del aire invernal.

Volvió al número 72 en silencio, esquivando con la mirada los rostros de los gigantes dormidos. Cerró la ventana de su habitación y corrió las cortinas. Se desplomó en la cama, haciendo gemir los resortes. Más tarde oteó las manchas de humedad que convivían en el techo. Ni siquiera pudo pensar en los rugidos hambrientos de su estómago. Estaba ilusionado. Feliz. Nunca había experimentado emociones tan impetuo-

sas de dicha y esperanza. Segundo tras segundo, escuchando el tic tac del reloj colgado en la pared (un gato Félix muy sonriente), se quedó dormido.

Tuvo una horrible pesadilla, que también se le presentaría después, pero con superlativa intensidad. En ella corría en medio de una oscuridad amenazante. Era perseguido por algo monstruoso y terrible. Entonces, cuando *aquello* casi lo alcanzaba, surgió un destello de la nada. Cinco luces giraron alrededor de Ariel, iluminando el entorno. Quiso desvelar el rostro de la criatura que acechaba sus pasos, no obstante, antes de lograrlo... Despertó impregnado de sudor.

Pasaría un buen margen de días para que se enterara del significado de esa revelación. En aquel momento, por lo pronto, desconoció la magnitud, relación y claridad que esta poseería para la misión más grande de su vida. La olvidaría en la brevedad de la mañana.

—¡Levántate, holgazán! —exigió el señor Villalobos. Abrió la puerta de la habitación arrojando gritos y asomó su desagradable rostro—. Anoche los perros hicieron un desastre con la basura. Límpialo ahora si no quieres llegar tarde a la escuela, porque pobre de ti me presentes bajas calificaciones al final del trimestre.

Se marchó sin cerrar la puerta.

El precipitado Ariel se levantó y separó las cortinas. Para su desconcierto, un ramillete de desperdicios y alforjas plásticas agujereadas adornaban parte de la calle y la acera.

Sin refunfuñar fue por la escoba.

Capítulo 4
Hablando entre sueños

—¿Adónde crees que vas, Cerdonio? —gritó Brandon Portillo cuando Ariel iba rumbo a la clase de Historia.

El afectado escuchó la burla en silencio, con las orejas enrojecidas y la vista enfocando el suelo. Por el rabillo del ojo entrevió las descaradas sonrisas del racimo de estudiantes que lo rodeaba. Algunos lo apuntaron con el dedo, cantándole: «*Cerdonio, Cerdonio…*», hasta que sus bocas se cansaron de pronunciar el apodo y Ariel de escucharlo.

Sin más que explicar, aquel fue el primer sobrenombre del día. Este le dio partida a una larga y contundente procesión de burlas crueles, que esperarían tras la puerta como soldaditos de plomo, ansiosas por encañonar su rifle y ser disparadas.

Portillo jaloneó a Ariel de su camisa blanca y lo metió al baño de varones con ayuda de Olegario Rocha, un chico con cara de rata que hacía todo lo que aquel le

ordenaba.

El profesor Méndez, de Formación Cívica y Ética, vio la escena mientras metía la llave a la puerta de su aula. Pero en vez de entrar a los aseos y evitar una pelea entre los alumnos, prefirió responder los convenientes mensajes que en ese espacio llegaron a su celular. Entró al salón moviendo sus piernas de pingüino, fingiendo no haber visto nada.

Ya estando en los lavabos, Brandon empujó a Ariel, haciéndolo estrellar de espaldas contra las baldosas aperladas de la pared. Había dos testigos más, niños de primer grado, que cerraron los grifos de los lavamanos con la misma prisa de una caricatura animada. Ambos se encogieron de hombros, mirando al bravucón con sonrisas trémulas. Temían, con obvia razón, convertirse en sus próximos mártires. Y todo por haber estado en el lugar y a la hora menos indicados para acudir al retrete.

—Veo que ya se está borrando el recuerdito que te dejé la última vez —susurró Portillo, acariciando el labio partido de Ariel—. ¿Qué te parece si te doy uno nuevo, pero en otro lugar?

—Sí, Brandon. En la mejilla, dale un golpe en la mejilla —sugirió Olegario, con los ojos saciados de regocijo, pegado a la espalda de Portillo como una sanguijuela.

El par de niños de primer grado se afianzaron al borde de la histeria. Uno de ellos se mordió las uñas, sobre todo porque de pronto ocurrió algo que nadie se esperaba...

«Soy un cazador de estrellas —se dijo Ariel, pero como si hablara con Brandon en voz alta. Lo miró a los ojos. En ocasiones solía llamarlo *Baladrón*. Ese era su alias ideal de villano desalmado—. Soy un cazador de estrellas —repitió Ariel para sí—. Y tú, Brandon el Ba-

ladrón, no vales nada. No tienes nada especial, salvo tu fuerza bruta en el arte de molestar a los otros. Solo eres un...»

—Cabeza hueca —musitaron sus labios.

En aquel agravante silencio, el insulto su escuchó igual que el grito de una quimera.

Olegario y los demás convinieron en permanecer petrificados. Con los ojos desorbitados, aguardaron lo que pasaría a continuación. En la difusa historia de la humanidad, era la primera vez que alguien insultaba de tal forma a Brandon Portillo.

—¿Cómo me llamaste, *Cerdonio*? —preguntó entre dientes.

Sus mugrosas uñas lo atenazaron del brazo.

Era tarde para disculparse. ¿Qué le decía siempre el señor Villalobos a Ariel como consejo si se encontraba en una situación parecida a aquella? Que fuera valiente, ¿no es así? Pues era hora de asumir ese papel, o por lo menos intentarlo.

—Lo que oíste —replicó el desafiante Ariel, con los ojos húmedos a causa de la humillación. Sentía que su hombro se exprimía en aumento, entre las fuertes manos de Portillo. Aun así, lo repitió—: Te acabo de llamar «cabeza hueca».

Aparentemente, no supo de dónde le salió decirle eso. Fue como si algo dentro de su ser lo hubiera obligado a pronunciarlo. A lo mejor, haberse convertido en un cazador de estrellas lo hizo más valiente (o quizá más idiota, recapituló). Los niños de primer año, por su parte, se llevaron una mano a la boca y no soportaron tal turbación. Se acobardaron ante la furiosa cara enrojecida del Baladrón y desaparecieron tras la puerta que daba al pasillo principal, dejándola bailar en vaivén como una chica plantada en el baile de graduación.

—Pégale Brandon. ¿Oíste cómo te llamó? Te dijo «cabeza hueca», amigo. ¡Qué agallas de este gordinflón! Acábalo de una buena vez. Vamos, castígalo. Castígalo —farfulló Olegario con impulso, como si el insulto hubiera sido para él.

¡RING!

El timbre de entrada sonó por obra del mismísimo destino. Ariel se dio el privilegio de pellizcar un suspiro.

—Te salvó la campana —susurró Brandon—. Pero tendrás tu merecido a la hora de salida. Nadie me insulta y logra salir con vida. Juro que esta vez no te la vas a acabar. —Sonrió con tal perversidad, que Ariel experimentó escalofríos—. Por cierto, te dejo un adelanto de lo que te espera más tarde.

Portillo empuñó la mano, la alzó en el aire, apuntó al ojo derecho de Ariel y...

¡PUM!

Cinco minutos después, la profesora Cuevas comenzaba la clase de Historia con su habitual pase de lista. Ariel entró al aula a mitad del proceso.

Se sembró el silencio.

La meticulosa maestra alzó la mirada y lo analizó.

—¡Castillo! —gritó— ¡Llegas diez minutos tarde! Es la quinta ocasión este mes. Y eso contando el hecho de que vamos iniciando diciembre. Anexaré otro reporte a tu historial académico.

La profesora Cuevas inclinó la cabeza y prosiguió nombrando los apellidos de cada integrante del grupo. Mientras tanto, los demás colegiales contemplaron el ojo morado de Ariel con sus bocas abiertas de asombro.

Brandon se cruzó de brazos, orgulloso de su obra de arte. Le regaló al recién llegado una sonrisa desde su escritorio. A su lado, Olegario liberó una risa chillona, despuntando sus pronunciados dientes.

Ariel se sentó en su pupitre, al final de la última fila, y se quitó su mochila roja. Sacó cuaderno y lápiz. Abrió el primero y se empeñó a dibujar seres fantásticos y garabatos en las últimas páginas.

Cuando la maestra finiquitó el pase de asistencia, Ariel todavía sentía los ojos de sus compañeros clavados en él, como astillas.

Los concluyentes acosos de la jornada tuvieron lugar en la clase de Español, donde una estudiante llamada Rebecca creó una imagen caricaturizada de Ariel. Dibujó, en cierta hoja color pergamino, un cerdo de ojos amoratados que usaba el uniforme de la institución: pantalón pardo y camisa blanca. Del burlesco personaje emigraba una flecha que apuntaba un recuadro. En este último, la muchacha registró con mala ortografía la palabra «Serdonio». El grupo rio en voz baja, pasándose el papel de mano en mano, a la vez que la profesora Nogueda anotaba una tabla en su pizarrón blanco, cuyo tema era: *Los diferentes tipos de nexos que se pueden emplear en la redacción de un ensayo literario.* La última persona que recibió la viñeta fue el mismísimo Ariel, quien observó el dibujo con las cejas entrecruzadas y musitó desinteresado:

—Es pésimo, yo lo hubiera hecho mejor.

Y en ese instante todos rieron a carcajadas.

La profesora Nogueda soltó el rotulador azul con el que escribía en la pizarra y dio media vuelta rápidamente (como si hubiera creído que la burla era para ella). Sus ojos bailaron sobre sus cuencas, buscando entre aquella estampida de carcajadas el punto clave del alboroto.

No tardó mucho en descubrir el pupitre de la esquina.

—¿Se encuentra todo bien, Ariel? —preguntó ella misma.

Se ajustó las gafas moradas sobre el puente de su nariz. Estas le daban el aspecto de un felino muy inteligente. A la profesora Nogueda le encantaban los gatos, y prefería convivir más tiempo con ellos que con miembros pertenecientes de su misma especie.

Brandon el Baladrón se encargó en responder:

—Se rio de usted —mintió, negando con la cabeza.

—Brandon tiene razón, maestra —lo coadyuvó Rebecca, la propia autora de la caricatura—. Ariel hizo caras y gestos para que nos burláramos de sus anteojos. Y también nos susurró que usted parecía una gata callejera.

Otra ola de risas.

La maestra, que ese día llevaba una blusa blanca adornada de gatos negros, demandó que guardaran silencio.

—¿Es eso cierto, Ariel? —inquirió serena, mirando con paciencia al acusado—. ¿Tú has dicho semejante cosa de mí? ¿Puedes explicarme qué pasó?

—Qué importa —susurró Ariel.

—Dilo más fuerte, para poder entenderte —solicitó la amable mujer.

—¡HE DICHO QUE ME DA IGUAL! —gritó Ariel, cosa que nunca había hecho. Hasta él se sorprendió de haber sacado ese potente rugido de su garganta.

Quizá la madurez comenzaba a formar parte de él. ¿Esa llamarada que lo quemaba por dentro, era lo que experimentaban los adolescentes cuando se encaminaban al sendero de la adultez?

Como caída del cielo, la campana lo salvó nuevamente de una situación incómoda, recortando el amargo silencio. Hubo un rumor de plumas y cuadernos siendo guardados en mochilas y pasos inquietos

que se dirigían a la salida.

La profesora les deseó una bonita tarde a sus alumnos y les pidió que salieran todos del aula. Todos, menos Ariel, por supuesto.

Antes de desaparecer tras la puerta, Brandon le hizo señas amenazantes a Ariel, deslizando un meñique de izquierda a derecha por su cuello. El mensaje era claro: si lo delataba con la maestra, le iría muy mal. Además, agregó el bravucón a su pantomima marcando un reloj invisible en su muñeca, haría antesala en la puerta principal por él para añadirle el tatuaje prometido.

—¿Qué está ocurriendo contigo? —preguntó la profesora Nogueda con voz comprensiva.

Ella jamás lo reprendía, sea cual fuera el motivo. Era como si Ariel, con su simple presencia, evocara en la maestra la memoria de un ser querido. Aquella ocupó el asiento de enseguida y le dijo:

—Puedes confiar en mí.

Aguardó a que el pupilo expresara algo. Como no fue el caso, continuó hablando flexible:

—Sé que la estás pasando muy mal con la situación de tu hermana. Me enteré, hasta hace poco, que las cosas no salieron del todo bien como esperábamos. Lo siento mucho.

¿Lo siente? ¿Qué es lo que sentía la profesora?, se preguntaba Ariel. ¿Qué sabía ella de tener a una hermana con esa horrible enfermedad? Y, sobre todo, de estarse convirtiendo en una niña de cristal. De lo único que debía preocuparse era de sus amados y preciados gatos.

Sin percatarse que le retiraban el papel arrugado de las manos, pensó Ariel en su pobre madre. ¿Qué le diría ella de verlo en esa situación tan humillante? Siendo la burla de sus compañeros, viviendo como el

típico muchacho de la escuela que sobrelleva infortunios familiares; el estudiante marginado del que maestros sienten lástima.

La docente alisó la hoja y contempló con tristeza el personaje de *Serdonio*. Volteó con Ariel.

—¿Quién lo hizo? —cuestionó.

Ariel se encogió de hombros, a lo que ella expiró con un sonido de «hum».

—En el receso tuve la oportunidad de hablar con un maestro, el profesor Méndez —dijo—. Me parece que lo conoces. Creyó haberte visto entrar esta mañana al baño de varones, acompañado de Brandon Portillo y Olegario Rocha. Pero testificó no estar seguro del todo. Imagino que ellos, Olegario y Brandon te... —La profesora se aclaró la garganta, fijando su sentido en el lastimado ojo de Ariel—. ¿Te golpearon? Puedes contármelo con confianza. Lo reportaré a la directora para citar a sus padres mañana a primera hora.

Ariel negó con la cabeza. No sería la primera vez que reportaban al Baladrón. A los desventurados chicos que abrían la boca (con omisión de que los tacharan de «soplones») les esperaba una violenta venganza surtida de sangre.

—Esto me lo hice antes..., en casa —falseó.

—Quieres decir que tu padrastro, el señor Villalobos... —insinuó la profesora.

—No —se apresuró a responder Ariel, antes de que la educadora malinterpretara las cosas—. Me lo hice yo solo. Me resbalé, estando en la ducha.

—Por favor, Ariel. No hagas esto. Mentirme —dijo—. Sabes que a mí no puedes engañarme. Soy tu maestra, te conozco como a mis «hijos». —Con sus hijos se refería a sus gatos. Todo el mundo sabía que no tenía niños—. Me preocupo por ti. Hay muchos adolescentes que, a lo largo de mi carrera como mentora,

ayudé a sacar de problemas muy graves. ¿Ya te había dicho que tengo un doctorado en psicología? ¿Sí? Bueno. Puedes confiar en mí. Quiero zanjar cada caso de acoso escolar en este plantel. Si deseas apoyo, conmigo lo tienes. —Lo asió de una mano—. Así como aquella vez que conversamos acerca de tu mamá. ¿Te acuerdas?

Ariel lo perpetuaba a la perfección. Dicho capítulo fue uno de los peores de su vida, y no era un paréntesis que ambicionaba desenterrar de sus recuerdos. Él prefería que esa, junto con otras remembranzas tristes, se quedara allí, en una esquinita. No reparar en su existencia. Mencionar el tema de la señora Rivas, su madre, era algo incómodo y doloroso. Además, ¿en qué podía ayudarlo su profesora? En nada, pensó. Absolutamente en nada. ¿Acaso tenía un antídoto para curar la *cristalización humana* de Alondrita? ¿Sabía de algún método especial que lo ayudara a cazar estrellas? ¿Poseía una varita mágica que ablandara el corazón del señor Villalobos? O que Brandon el Baladrón dejara de molestarlo. La respuesta a esas interrogantes era un rotundo «no».

Como Ariel persistió con sus labios sellados, la maestra no tuvo más remedio que dejarlo ir.

—Bueno, a la fuerza hasta el agua es mala —alcanzó a escuchar Ariel que le decía la profesora, mientras él cerraba la puerta con lentitud—. Pero tarde o temprano tendrás que desahogarte —ultimó.

Salió Ariel por el patio trasero como un fugitivo que escapa de prisión, para no toparse con Portillo en el acceso principal. Corrió lo más rápido que pudo. Por suerte, ese día no llevó su bicicleta. De otro modo, habría tenido que ir a la entrada, donde la encadenaba en un cicloparqueadero. Era el lugar preferido del Baladrón cuando se trataba de peleas.

De haber tenido un buen compañero, quién sabe si las cosas hubieran sido distintas para Ariel. Por lo que él había leído en los estimados libros que guardaba en su recámara, los verdaderos amigos ayudaban en situaciones difíciles a sus colegas. Lástima que no conocía ese sentimiento de contar con el apoyo de un aliado. Y lo más probable, a cómo iban las cosas, era que moriría sin saberlo.

Pero Ariel contaba con un secreto. El primero de dos...

Continuó corriendo como alma que lleva el diablo, sin mirar atrás, porque a sus espaldas Brandon lo seguiría con el niño rata, quien a pesar de que Portillo se burlara de sus enormes dientes y cara de roedor, era su seguidor más fiel.

Anduvo el pulverizado Ariel por la calle Monteseaur jadeando y sudando, a la máxima velocidad que podían concederle su par de jamones. Esquivó los postes de electricidad que apadrinaban fotografías de los cinco muchachos desaparecidos el mes anterior. Todos ellos varones. Se presumía que habían sido raptados por el «Robaniños», o eso es lo que se rumoraba.

Cruzó la zona segura de la «tiza invisible» y ese hecho le dio seguridad. Cuando llegó al buzón rojo con el número 72 y pisó el consumido jardín de su casa, volteó para atrás. Se sintió a salvo. Nadie lo había seguido.

Terminó con la camisa empapada y sucia. Una de las mangas le sirvió para secarse la cara chorreada. Se dejó caer y sus rodillas concibieron dos cráteres en la tierra lodosa. Tomó muchas bocanadas de aire antes de entrar a la vivienda. Todavía faltaba para que terminara la guerra civil.

Se quitó la mochila con dificultad, haciendo muecas a causa del hombro magullado que le apostó Portillo con sus uñas, y sacó su gorra favorita. En un principio

había sido amarilla, pero la usaba tanto que, en la actualidad, ya parecía la deslucida prenda de un mecánico. Era color mostaza pálido y recluía en su visera una colección de manchas oscuras, semejantes a un compuesto de lágrimas de gasolina. Por esta ocasión, la utilizó para encubrir el abultado cardenal que su ojo ponía de manifiesto.

Abrió la puerta. Cerró mansamente y caminó reservado por el recibidor, con la tentativa de no ser descubierto. Su ingreso triunfal pretendiendo ser prudente, sin embargo, no le sirvió de nada, puesto que su padrastro, quien ya había terminado su jornada de trabajo (impartía clases de Química Avanzada en la preparatoria), inspeccionaba el interior de su «caja secreta» en el estudio, con la puerta entreabierta. Cerró el cofre al dar cuenta de su hijastro y lo miró con recelo.

—¿Qué demonios es eso? —bramó.

Ariel sintió que su sangre se coagulaba dentro de sus venas. Justo eso era lo que no quería: encontrarse con él.

El señor Villalobos puso el candado a su baúl misterioso, lo escondió debajo del escritorio y se levantó de su silla de cuero. Caminó a largas zancadas por el corto pasillo. Al encallar en el vestíbulo le quitó la gorra al muchacho con un movimiento brusco, haciéndole volar los pelos.

—¡Otra vez! —gruñó, llevándose el índice y el pulgar a las sienes, como si tuviera migraña. Lo miró severo—. Tu falta de valentía me deja pasmado, hijastro. Desearía que fueras un hombre de verdad y no la vergüenza afeminada que forjó tu madre. No necesitas decirme quién ha sido. Brandon otra vez, ¿tengo razón? Lo sabía. ¡Ya viene siendo hora de que defiendas tu dignidad, idiota! ¿Dónde queda tu honor? Tu lugar. —Entornó los ojos—. Confiesa: ¿Alzaste las manos? ¿Te

mantuviste a raya con ese malnacido?

—No, señor.

—Tal como lo imaginé. La próxima vez que te encuentres en una situación parecida, atéstale un puntapié en la espinilla a ese majadero. Por lo menos así te evitarás andar con el ojo morado y recibir un golpe como el que estoy por darte...

Molió la nuca de Ariel con sus nudillos.

—¡Deténgase, señor! ¡Por favor! —rogó Ariel, llevándose las manos a la cabeza—. Yo..., yo lo llamé cabeza hueca —informó, sobándose la zona del aplastamiento.

—¿Lo llamaste «cabeza hueca»? —repitió, sonriendo—. ¿Y eso qué? Una vil nenita, eso es lo que eres. ¡Ponte a hacer los malditos deberes! La comida estará dentro de poco.

Dejó caer la gorra amarilla al suelo y se marchó a su oficina. La sigilosa señora Rivas asomó media parte de su cuerpo por el corredor que daba a la cocina. Saludó a su hijo agitando la mano. Ostentaba una sonrisa triste y cansada.

—¿Cómo te fue hoy en la escuela? —preguntó.

—No muy bien, mira —respondió cortante, exhibiendo el lado malo de su cara.

—Ven, voy a ponerte hielo.

Desapareció tras el arco y él la siguió. Su madre nunca participaba en las discusiones entre él y su padrastro, ni tampoco lo salvaba de los remoquetes. Pero era tan buena persona y tan pacífica que, en ocasiones, Ariel pensaba que llegaría a convertirse en santa, como esas mujeres que solía escuchar en sus clases de catecismo. Claro que eso fue antes de que su padrastro le negara la salida a la Iglesia. Intentó convencer a Ariel de que aquello no era más que una «pérdida de tiempo».

—Se lo suplico, señor Villalobos, Arielito está a punto de hacer su primera comunión. Le resta muy poco —imploró la madre Hortensia por teléfono, su catequista, después de que el señor Villalobos avisara que su hijastro no seguiría escuchando aquellas «doctrinas de la ignorancia y la sumisión»—. Concédale el regalo de la eucaristía —insistía la monja—. Solo le faltan dos meses. Además, es un chico tan bueno y cortés. Ojalá los demás jovencitos de su edad tuvieran un corazón tan humilde y noble como el suyo...

—No me interesa que sea bueno. Quiero que sea fuerte, inteligente... Un hombre de verdad —bufó el caballero, casi escupiendo al teléfono—. Creer en Dios no es más que un disparate de toda su gente para hacer a las personas más estúpidas de lo que ya están. ¿Tengo razón? De esa forma pueden controlar el mundo a su antojo. Ariel no volverá a meter un pie allí, beata. ¿Me entendió? Es mi última palabra.

Y colgó.

La hermana Hortensia llamó otras veinte veces durante los siguientes días. Al final, se dio por vencida.

En un principio, que Ariel asistiera al catecismo fue idea de su mamá. Pero desde que se volvió sumisa y callada, el señor Villalobos ya no la tomaba en cuenta para sus decisiones. Era él quien agarraba las riendas de la familia. Y la señora Rivas, al igual que Ariel y Alondrita, tenía que doblegarse y aceptar sus reglas escrupulosas.

Lo que más le entristeció en ese momento a Ariel, con todo, fue que él y la dulce de su mamá ahora tenían algo en común: un ojo amoratado.

¡Ah! Y el primer secreto de Ariel...

Era un adolescente demasiado soñador como para comprender las dificultades de los adultos; uno de esos chicos despistados que viven imaginándose en cientos

de aventuras fantásticas, y que cuando lo reprenden, como en esa última discusión con su padrastro, o si un maestro le enuncia un discurso por «no estar prestando atención durante la clase», se refugia en las paredes de su imaginación, y mentaliza un cohete espacial ascendiendo al centro del universo. Ese era su primer secreto (el segundo era todavía más preponderante): desterrarse de la realidad para vivir en un mundo surreal. Una facultad más intensa y concreta que cualquier superhéroe de película.

Cruzó por un lado de la señora Rivas, mientras aquella abría la nevera y sacaba unos cubitos de hielo. Los metió en una bolsa hermética que, posteriormente de sellarla, la colocó a su hijo en la zona malherida.

¡Vaya! Qué agradable fue sentir el frío amainando el dolor de su cara. La mujer le besó la frente y le sonrió.

—Mi buen muchacho —le dijo en voz baja, entregándole el bulto—. Me duele que estés pasando por esto. No es justo para ti.

—Sabes, mamá, a veces quisiera desaparecer para siempre. O quedarme dormido y no despertar —confesó.

—Pero ¡qué dices! —chilló—. No quiero escucharte hablar así otra vez, ¿oíste? Yo te amo, me partiría el corazón si te ocurriera algo —dijo de forma prudente. Lanzó miradas al pasillo, temiendo que entrara el señor Villalobos por sorpresa. Miró a Ariel con cariño por última vez, antes de dedicarse a sacudir la mesa con su pañuelo—. ¿Por qué no vas a ver a tu hermana? Lleva extrañándote toda la mañana.

—Claro.

Ariel presionó la bolsa en su cara y esperó a que se le adormeciera el dolor. El hielo, empezando a derretirse dentro del envoltorio, ejerció a que el hule trans-

pirara y lo complaciera.

Abandonó la cocina y entró sonriente a la habitación de Alondrita. Ella le pediría una explicación de lo que había ocurrido. «¿Qué te pasó en la cara?», preguntaría. Él le contaría que, de camino a casa, un león estuvo a punto de comérselo vivo. El animal le dio un zarpazo en el rostro con una de sus garras, logrando dañarlo, pero Ariel, gracias a su inteligencia humana, le lanzó a la bestia la tapa de un contenedor de basura, igual que un *Frisbee*. Le dio justo en la cabeza, dejándola que admirara estrellitas...

No obstante, Alondrita no le pidió explicación alguna. Ariel la encontró durmiendo. Temblaba y ardía en fiebre. Había recaído en la intolerable gripe, enfermedad que recién venció en noviembre. Salvo que, con mayor rigor, como un mal crónico. Los medicamentos parecían prestar el menor efecto posible a sus defensas y el doctor Haro, en cada visita semanal, valoraba menos esperanzas en su pronta recuperación. Ariel desplumó un pañuelo de la cajita encima del mueble y limpió el sudor que le cubría la frente a su hermana. En respuesta al tacto, aquella movió sus labios.

«Está hablando dormida», razonó Ariel.

Preguntándose qué estaría enunciando, acercó su oreja.

—*No confíes en el anciano, Ariel* —musitó—. *No es lo que parece. No es quien dice ser...*

Ariel se alzó de inmediato y se mantuvo atónito.

—Cómo... —musitó.

¿Cómo se habría enterado Alondrita del anciano? Y más elemental todavía: ¿por qué lo prevenía de aquel?

La niña se movió y sacó las manos de las sábanas. Ariel sofocó un grito. Fue por el rápido avance de la *cristalización humana* que, tal como había predicho el viejo del parque, en ese momento abarcaba los límites

por encima de sus muñecas. Las manos de la infanta eran transparentes. Sus articulaciones hacían un sonido de *clic clac* cuando se movían. El mortificado Ariel se animó a acariciarlas y las sintió lisas, cuales piedras pulidas. Caminó al otro extremo, a la base de la cama, y alzó las cobijas. Como se lo temía, los pies también se habían vuelto de cristal, a la altura de los tobillos. Lo que simbolizaba que su apremiante función como cazador de estrellas debía acabar cuanto antes.

Pero ¿por qué Alondrita habría dicho aquello del anciano?

«¿Qué es lo que sabe ella de él?», se dijo.

En el intervalo que trató de responderse, su hermana entreabrió los párpados y lo vio.

—¿Qué te ocurrió en el ojo? —preguntó en voz baja.

Ariel cubrió los pies de cristal con ligereza y olvidó contarle su ficticia aventura con el rey de la selva.

—Alondrita, respóndeme algo —requirió serio—. ¿Por qué estabas diciendo que no confiara en el anciano? ¿Cómo te enteraste de él?

Ella arrugó el ceño.

—¿Anciano? ¿De qué anciano hablas, hermano? Yo no recuerdo haber mencionado algo parecido.

—De tu sueño. Lo que estabas soñando antes de despertar. ¿Lo recuerdas?

Alondrita negó con la cabeza, contrariada por no entender de lo que estaban hablando.

«Ella de verdad no lo sabe —comentó Ariel para sí, sin encontrarle pies ni cabeza a lo que acababa de presenciar—. Sin embargo, es demasiada casualidad...»

—Olvídalo —emitió por último—. Sigue descansando. Te visitaré cuando sea hora del Club de los Cuentos de las Sombras.

Le dio un beso en la frente y se ordenó a la puerta.

—Espera, Ariel. Creo que... sí me acuerdo de algo

—anunció Alondrita, con voz ronca y mormada—. Estaba soñando con un hada. Era pequeñita... y muy graciosa. Me estaba pidiendo que te diera un mensaje.

—¿Y qué decía el mensaje? —preguntó Ariel, dándose la vuelta.

Miró a su hermana con intriga.

—Que no fueras esta noche al «Parque de Juegos Monteseaur». ¿Significa algo para ti?

Los vellos de la nuca se le erizaron y su boca conservó un aliento intranquilo y pesado.

—No —contestó con celeridad—. Nos vemos —barbotó—, nos vemos en un rato.

Y salió.

Capítulo 5
El Club de los Cuentos de las Sombras

Esa misma tarde llegó el doctor Haro para llevar a cabo el chequeo semanal de Alondrita. Era un anciano cascarrabias, de piernas temblorosas, que se comunicaba como si alguien lo estuviera correteando.

—Tendremos que administrar otra dosis de medicamentos para la OI de su hija —indicó como el vuelo.

El señor Villalobos, la señora Rivas y el doctor Haro se hallaban en la salita de estar del 72. Ariel no estaba presente con ellos, pero podía escuchar la conversación desde el pasillo, arrebujado tras la delgada pared de madera.

—¿Eso qué significa? ¡Que tengo que gastar otra tanda de dinero? Esas son canalladas suyas —alegó el furioso señor Villalobos—. El mes pasado dijo que mejoraría con las píldoras de calcio que conseguí, y no tengo suficiente dinero para darme el lujo de comprar más medicinas. La última vez que se rompió el brazo

renté aquel dispositivo eléctrico para su piel, ¿lo recuerda?

—Sí. La estimulación eléctrica transcutánea del nervio —replicó el médico.

El señor Villalobos se percibió molesto ante la respuesta. Miraba con malos ojos a quien le corregía y resultaba más instruido que él.

—Ya lo sé —dijo, aún más ceñudo que antes—. También pagué sesiones de acuapresión —mencionó altivo, procurando demostrar que no era ningún estúpido y sabía del tema—, porque mi niña no soportaba el dolor por las noches. ¡Caray! Ni siquiera tengo lo necesario para solventar los gastos de la casa y conseguirme un fisioterapeuta. —Elevó la voz—. Y para empeorar las cosas, tiene gripe. ¿Se entera? ¡Gripe otra vez!

Al acabar su discurso, Ariel lo estimó fatigado.

—Siempre hay otras opciones, señor Villalobos. No se altere. Puede pedir un préstamo al banco, o visitar una casa de empeño...

—¡Váyase al diablo!

Esta vez, fue el doctor quien se molestó.

—Si no se tranquiliza me veré obligado a retirarme de su morada sin llegar a darle mi respuesta médica —amenazó el decidido doctor Haro.

—Bien. Bien. Me relajaré. —Hizo una pausa, lanzando un resoplido parecido al de un toro en brama—. Entonces, ¿qué sugiere que haga? Sin necesidad de vender y empeñar mis cosas.

—Ya se lo comenté la última ocasión que nos vimos —contestó—, pero se lo recalco otra vez, por si no le quedó claro del todo: «Íbamos a probar novedosos medicamentos para ver si su hija mostraba mejoría y prolongaba, de cierta forma, su calidad de vida». Acuérdese que el tipo de osteogénesis imperfecta de Alondra

es muy extraño, único en su tipo, y mucho más delicado del que hemos tratado los expertos. El pamidronato que le aplicamos por vía intravenosa retarda la destrucción del hueso, para promover la construcción de este y fomentar el desarrollo del calcio. Pero también estuvimos al tanto de que era un proceso que demoraría bastante. Aparte, hay otra cosa que está dejando de lado, señor Villalobos. Ya le había explicado que, en la situación en la que se halla su hija..., bueno, no hay mucha probabilidad de que sobrepase este tratamiento con éxito. —Respiró—. Sus defensas se encuentran muy bajas y, tal como usted lo mencionó, la gripe diagnosticada es un reloj de arena para su organismo vulnerable. Necesitaría un milagro para... Ya sabe usted a lo que me refiero.

—Le entiendo. —Asintió el señor Villalobos—. Requiero que me diga lo que ocurriría si dejo de darle la medicación. No hablo de la gripe, sino del tratamiento de la OI.

—Me temo que acortaría más el período que le queda de vida.

—¿De cuánto estamos hablando?

El doctor Haro se tomó unos segundos reflexivos para responder.

—Un par de días, quizá dure una semana.

Se creó un pesado silencio que nadie quiso rasgar.

Ariel corrió a su habitación.

«No sucederá. No lo permitiré», convino.

La mayor parte de su vida, Alondrita estaba recostada en su cama, puesto que, si transitaba o se recargaba sobre sus piernas durante largos períodos, corría el riesgo de que sus huesos se partieran como lápices. Su esqueleto, en general, era tan frágil que podía compa-

rarse con los adornos de porcelana que las mamás instalan en las salas de sus casas: quebradizos e irreparables. La buena niña no podía correr por las aceras como otros de su edad, tampoco salir a dar una caminata al parque, bailar en fiestas infantiles, saltar la cuerda, ni lanzarse a la piscina para darse un buen chapuzón. De hecho, si llegaban a salir en familia al cine o al zoológico (cosa que no pasaba desde hacía un año), ella tenía que ir en su sillita de ruedas. Y si asumía el antojo de caminar un trecho por sentir los muslos agarrotados y la espalda magullada, a causa de permanecer tantas horas apresada en el colchón y en su vía de transporte, se comprometía a hacerlo breves minutos en su habitación, de paredes acojinadas y suelo cubierto con fibra de algodón; pero con ayuda de un soporte rodante, llevar puesto un collarín (este detalle no había que olvidarlo, pues una vez se lesionó las vértebras cervicales por dejarlo pasar), y tener los codos y las rodillas salvaguardados con almohadillas.

La última ocasión que sufrió una fractura realmente fea fue cuando intentó imitar en su recámara el baile de Aurora, la *Bella Durmiente*. Mientras miraba dicha película animada, experimentó un mareo, y sin tomar las precauciones necesarias apoyó su brazo en la pared. El peso de su cuerpo al recaer sobre este, produjo un chasquido parecido a cuando se mastican tostadas de maíz. Tardó meses en recuperarse. Los lamentos de aquellas noches seguían refugiados en los agujeros de las paredes, esperando volver tras acontecer otra fractura.

A pesar de sus desdichados percances, Alondrita veía su vida como sinónimo de absoluta felicidad. Amaba oír música, dibujar bocetos en cartulinas con gis al pastel, entretenerse con juegos de mesa y escuchar las atrayentes historias de su hermano (sobre

todo eso último). ¡Qué sería de ella de no dar oídos de los maravillosos cuentos que Ariel le contaba todas las noches? Era su parte favorita del día, igual que la de él.

Ariel llegaba a su dormitorio, a eso de las diez u once de la noche, y la saludaba con un célebre beso en la frente. Después, le acomodaba los almohadones de respaldo y la ayudaba a reclinar su delicada espina dorsal en el soporte. Finalmente, Ariel dejaba la habitación como boca de lobo cuando apagaba las luces, se arrellanaba al lado de Alondrita y encendía su linterna, con el propósito de proyectar una perfecta circunferencia amarilla en la pared, en medio de la oscuridad.

—Érase una vez, un hada pequeña (¡Qué digo pequeña! Minúscula, con la delgadez de un alfiler) en un bosque muy lejano... —contó Ariel, un par de años atrás, innovando sombras de árboles con sus manos.

—¿Y era bonita? —preguntó Alondrita, con su distinguida voz aguda.

—La más hermosa de todas, aunque no más linda que tú —le respondió.

La chiquilla, cautivada por las amables palabras de su hermano, miró embelesada las figuras del muro. La trama emprendió con un hada que vivía en los límites de cierto bosque encantado. Obsequiaba una semilla de diente de león a los niños bien portados.

—Pero no eran semillas comunes y corrientes —indicó Ariel—. Iban cargadas de deseos. Si se les soplaba lo bastante fuerte y estas se iban volando alto, muy alto, hasta desaparecer en el cielo, el deseo podía cumplirse...

Fue cuando por primera vez, la inquieta imaginación de ambos se las arregló para que la historia, en rigor, cobrara vida.

Alondrita fue la primera en notar aquella maravilla.

Observó que, dentro de la rueda de luz proyectada por la linterna de Ariel, las sombras se transformaron en un bosque; mismo que fue llenándose de ramificaciones, arbustos y hojarasca. De inmediato, una mujer tímida con alas de libélula y vestido corto se alzó y estiró los brazos, como despertando de un placentero sueño. Empezó a volar en círculos. Detrás de ella, se dibujó la silueta de una ciudadela. En seguida aparecieron calles, moradas, torres y habitantes. Estos últimos eran personas que platicaban y se saludaban entre sí, como si ese espectáculo de manchas fuera lo más normal del mundo. Ariel y Alondrita quedaron boquiabiertos.

Los personajes, quienes existían gracias a las palabras de Ariel, ejecutaban al pie de la letra las acciones que este narraba. La manera en que contaba las historias: variando las entonaciones, exagerando las expresiones más destacadas de los protagonistas, haciendo comentarios irónicos en las escenas graciosas, e incluso evacuando un mar de lágrimas en las partes sentimentales, el muchacho otorgaba vida a un maravilloso mundo en blanco y negro (o amarillo y negro, en este caso). Sus cuentos prometían a Alondrita experimentar los sentimientos más sinceros y emotivos que una niña de su edad pudiera gozar.

Y por más cansado que se encontrara, cada noche, con supremo entusiasmo, Ariel tenía una aventura diferente para narrar que acababa siendo más entretenida y venerada que la anterior. A veces las declamaba, con rimas y exquisitos versos; o las cantaba, como un juglar en sus épocas de gloria. Componía tramas llenas de aventuras, héroes simbólicos, monstruos espantosos, villanos aborrecibles y batallas épicas. Era espectacular. No existía una palabra en el diccionario que describiera dicho prodigio. Sin embargo, hubo algo que consideraron chocante en su descubrimiento: reco-

nocieron que solo ellos dos eran capaces de avizorar las siluetas actorales. Cierta vez, intentaron enseñarles a sus padres el evento. Aquello terminó siendo un rotundo fracaso.

Ariel los había invitado a que se sentaran en la cama de Alondrita. Algo nervioso, porque el señor Villalobos jamás lo había escuchado contar historias, Ariel entabló su narración. Las apariencias oscuras se transfiguraron en dos caballeros de armadura y espada andando sobre caballos pura sangre, a punto de enfrentarse a un dragón escupehielo.

—¡Allí están! —gritó Alondrita, apuntando a la pared—. ¿Los ven?

Ambos adultos se voltearon a ver, embarazados. Si no vislumbraron al vigoroso dragón que batía sus alas, mucho menos pudieron apreciar cuando este escupió una tormenta de saetas de escarcha a los caballeros del cuento. Los ojos del señor Villalobos y la señora Rivas, ciegos de imaginación y ocupados de realidad, no lograron entrever más allá de una descalza burbuja amarilla en el muro. Acaso sus fantasías los desabrigaron distantes años atrás, junto con su inocencia, al volverse mayores. Y habían perdido la capacidad de imaginar. El equipo de hermanos tardó mucho en entender ese pormenor, e intentaron de mil y una maneras demostrar las acciones que efectuaban las sombras: seres pequeñitos y graciosos que agitaban sus manos y saltaban desesperados de un lado a otro, con la intención de ser vistos por los señores.

Alondrita chillaba cuando surgían apariciones insospechadas, como la resurrección de un ogro entre los escombros de un castillo; profería sonidos de admiración si las sombras adquirían la forma de una persecución de animales salvajes que corrían en estampida por la sabana. En el último de sus intentos, Ariel arrancó

la rama de un árbol del jardín y con ella apuntó las proyecciones. Aun así, seguía siendo inútil. La madurez vendaba las miradas de su madre y su padrastro; no les permitía revelar la verdad.

Alondrita y Ariel acabaron dándose por vencidos tras tantas estrategias fallidas. Pese a ello, al punto de la noche, acordaron en reunirse regularmente para vivir nuevos relatos. A esos particulares encuentros Alondrita los bautizó como el «Club de los Cuentos de las Sombras». En veces —si es que el argumento de la historia merecía tal galardón—, pedía a su hermano que se la contara otra vez. Y el bueno de aquel, súbdito de la característica nobleza de su niña, accedía a las peticiones sin soltar una queja. Por otro lado, las sombras corrían apresuradas por el escenario a fin de ocupar sus puestos.

Capítulo 6
La travesía de Aura

Por la noche, después de acabar con la tarea, Ariel entró al cuarto de su hermana y amoldó los cojines de respaldo.

—¿Me dirás qué te pasó en el ojo, hermanito? —preguntó Alondrita, con la nariz constipada.

—Después —contestó. Tenía la mente en otro lado—. Primero necesito saber cómo estás tú. ¿Te sientes bien?

Más pálida que de costumbre, Alondrita le mostró sus manos de cristal como respuesta.

—¿Te duelen? —quiso saber él, atraído por la transparencia.

—No, pero en ocasiones, cuando quiero mover los dedos, se quedan quietos… ¡Mira! —escandalizó en el instante—. ¿Los ves?

Las puntas de su mano derecha quedaron paralizadas, imitando los rígidos mástiles de una embarcación.

Luego de unos segundos, como si hubieran sido deshechizadas, dieron autorización de movimiento.

—Igual que en el Club de los Cuentos de las Sombras, solo tú y yo podemos ver el cristal —confirmó ella—. Ariel, ¿crees que si el cristal me cubre toda me romperé en pedazos?

—No, princesita. Eso no pasará —dijo—. Antes de que el vidrio llegue a tu corazón, yo lo detendré. Haré hasta lo imposible por evitarlo.

Acto seguido de cambiarle el suero, se acomodó a su lado. El apresurado Ariel encendió su linterna. Con ella apuntó hacia la pared y sintió que los dedos delicados de Alondrita le acariciaron el antebrazo.

—¿Estás lista para una nueva aventura? —preguntó, relegando sus pensamientos.

Cuando contaba historias, Ariel se despojaba de todo lo demás y vivía ese momento.

—Siempre —avisó ella. A continuación, estornudó—. Pero antes pásame un pañuelo, por favor.

Ariel cogió uno de la cajita verde. Tras ayudarla a sonarse, se adecuó de nuevo en las almohadas y dio inicio la velada.

—Había una vez, una princesa que cayó gravemente enferma.

Ariel narró en un tono cambiante, solemne. Con una voz que siempre había considerado que le pertenecía a otra persona. A un verdadero narrador de cuentos que vivía en su cabeza. Alondrita trasladó ambas manos al rostro y fundó una letra O con sus labios.

—¿Y qué le pasó? —preguntó, después de estornudar otra vez y limpiarse los orificios nasales con el pañuelo que le ofreció su hermano.

En la rueda de luz apareció una joven que caminaba desconsolada.

—Todos dijeron que moriría —denunció Ariel.

Comenzaron a surgir más personitas y manchas en la escena, que se cuchicheaban cosas al oído, cubriéndose la boca con una mano.

—Se corrió el rumor de que existía, muy lejos de su reino, una bruja que tenía resguardada una poderosa pócima —informó el narrador.

Los personajes desaparecieron en un remolino y surgió una bruja sonriente, de sombrero puntiagudo, que llevaba un frasco en la mano. Le dio vueltas al recipiente y la sustancia espesa se agitó de un lado a otro, como la cambiante marea del océano.

—¿Qué tenía esa poción? —cuestionó Alondrita con ansias.

—Decían que sanaba cualquier tipo de enfermedad —explicó—. Con todo, solo era una antigua leyenda. Una que muchos no creían porque se oía demasiado fantasiosa como para ser verdad. Algo que no parecía «realista».

La bruja se esfumó y en su lugar apareció un grupo de aldeanos que negó con la cabeza.

—Qué tontos —protestó Alondrita—. Todos saben que si no tienes fe no puede existir la magia. Pero si crees con el corazón, como me enseñaste, es posible que se haga realidad, ¿no? Por eso solo tú y yo podemos ver a las sombras vivientes. Y también que me hago de cristal. ¿Verdad, Ariel?

—Así es, mi inteligente hermana. Las personas de ese reino, al igual que nuestros padres y los demás adultos de este mundo, no podían creer en la existencia de la magia. Por lo tanto, el rey y la reina, sin albergar esperanzas de que su hija Aura fuera a sobrevivir, prepararon un baile de despedida en su honor, para que esta no muriera sin antes haberle dicho el adiós a sus amigos y familiares.

En la superficie del muro, las siluetas se entretejie-

ron, igual que los hilos de una bufanda, y erigieron un salón impresionante.

—Al dar alcance la noche de la ceremonia —refirió Ariel—, la Familia Real se percató de que habían acudido más invitados de los que habían previsto. No fue ninguna inconveniencia para el rey. Pronto envió órdenes al cocinero en jefe de que triplicara la cantidad de platillos previstos. Asistieron gentes que la doncella ni siquiera conocía. Esto se debió a que la noticia se corrió por el reino como la pólvora. Todos quisieron conocer (en parte por curiosidad) a la famosa princesa del momento; la de cuya vida expiraría pronto…

Apareció Aura en la pared con un vestido despampanante, abierto de los costados cual rosa; bailando y despidiéndose de un centenar de individuos en el majestuoso salón.

—Qué bonito, ¿no es así Ariel? —interpeló Alondrita con ojos soñadores—. Me gustaría estar allí…

—¿Bonito? No. Me parece horrible —rebatió él, de manera inesperada—. Le estaban diciendo adiós sin haber intentado salvarla.

La niña contempló a su hermano arrepentida de haber hecho su comentario y volteó con la princesa, que continuaba recibiendo abrazos y un sinfín de regalos de todas las personas que se le aproximaban. Obsequios que quizá no tendría oportunidad de abrir, pues eran bastantes.

—Aura, en realidad se sentía muy desilusionada —denunció Ariel—, porque confiaba en la leyenda. Muy lejos de aquí, pensaba ella, existe la sagrada pócima de la sanación. Cuando solicitó que emprendieran un viaje en su búsqueda, días previos a la fiesta, ningún caballero quiso arrancar dicha travesía por considerarla imposible.

»—No, hija mía —negó rotundamente el rey—. Me

estás pidiendo que mande a mis mejores hombres a localizar una patraña inventada por viejas charlatanas del pueblo. A veces, la gente suele pregonar fantasías baratas para ganar dinero y dar falsas esperanzas. Solo eso, mi niña. —Resopló—. Aura, querida, es hora de que te resignes a aceptar tu..., tu inevitable final.»

—¿Entonces qué hizo Aura? —cuestionó Alondrita.

Estaba deslumbrada por los bellos adornos que cubrían las paredes del palacio y de la vestimenta anticuada de los personajes, quienes convertían ese baile en una escena de ensueño.

—Bueno, antes de adelantarme a los hechos, pasó algo durante la fiesta que no se le iba a olvidar nunca a la doncella. Aquello la marcó. Un gallardo caballero, reconocido por sus heroicas hazañas en batalla, le obsequió un hermoso collar de perlas. Ella lo aceptó con aprecio. El joven le situó el amuleto en el cuello y bailaron juntos casi toda la noche. Resultó ser un príncipe. Se sintieron muy apenados cuando la música acabó, ya que de ese encuentro resultaron enamorados el uno del otro. Fue un amor poético, medieval, trágico, imposible, platónico —enlistó Ariel—. Los dos eran conscientes de que su relación no duraría más de esa noche. Antes de despedirse, a pesar de todo, Aura le prometió al príncipe que se volverían a ver. El muchacho no la comprendió. Esto era porque ella contaba con un plan...

—¿Cuál? —interrogó la agitada Alondrita.

Los actores de la escena se retiraron y la princesa fue realizando, mediante una ráfaga de imágenes alternativas, las acciones que Ariel iba especificando con entusiasmo:

—Esa misma noche, mientras todos dormían, echó en un morral tres hogazas de pan, un cuarto de queso, dos peras y una cantimplora hasta el tope de agua.

Bajó las escaleras del palacio usando una túnica oscura, para camuflarse en las sombras y no ser descubierta. Evadió con talento a los guardias de las puertas principales y a los que rondaban por los pasillos del castillo. Sin demora, la arriesgada Aura entró a las caballerizas. Ahí dentro, eligió a un caballo para abordar su aventura. Salvo que no lo seleccionó al azar —dijo Ariel, sembrando una mueca seria—. Aura observó a los corceles y dijo:

»—Necesito la ayuda de uno de ustedes. Buscaré a la bruja de la que tanto se habla, con el fin de arrebatarle su brebaje mágico y, de esta forma, salvar mi vida de la cruel enfermedad que la atormenta.»

—¡Qué valiente! —Suspiró Alondrita.

—La doncella aguardó a que los animales respondieran. Ninguno suscitó ruido alguno. Pero allá al final, en la esquina de la cuadra, donde casi no llegaba la luz de las antorchas, se oyó un relinchido. La princesa sonrió plácida y se paró frente al valiente corcel que hizo el honor de ofrecerse. De esta forma, descubrió que aquel era viejo y feo. Estaba delgado, la carne se le enterraba en las costillas y tenía la piel tan llena de cicatrices, a causa de las innumerables batallas a las que sirvió durante temporadas de guerra, que figuró un antiguo pergamino de piel de oveja. Para colmo de males, sus patas traseras temblaban ridículamente.

»—Entonces tú serás mi compañero», mencionó Aura.

»Y echaron a correr a toda velocidad. Bueno, lo más rápido que podía galopar el pobre caballo, porque sus gastadas patas ya no eran tan fuertes como en su juventud, cuando valerosos y fuertes caballeros cabalgaron sobre él. Se proscribieron de las tierras del reino, con la esperanza de que encontrarían lo que buscaban.

—La princesa no debió haber hecho eso —contrarió de pronto Alondrita, en un tono testarudo—. Yo hubiera elegido a otro caballo. Uno fuerte, joven y bonito, que la llevara más rápido a su destino.

En el muro, la muchacha intérprete del cuento se hallaba inclinada sobre el viejo corcel, con su cabello despeinándose a causa del viento. Marchaban a cámara rápida. Las nubes cruzaban por su lado como fotografías surrealistas.

—Quizás su corcel era débil, pero el poder de su esperanza era más fuerte que la de diez hombres juntos —concretó Ariel—. Recuerda que ese caballo enclenque fue el único en todo el reino que quiso ayudarla. Eso, a mi parecer, es más que suficiente para embarcarse en una aventura.

—Si tú lo dices. ¿Adónde fueron, entonces?

—A todos lados y, al mismo tiempo, a ninguno.

—¿Cómo? —inquirió.

—Se contó la leyenda de la pócima, mas nunca se divulgó su paradero. En ocasiones corrieron al norte y otras veces por el este. Y cuando Aura no estaba muy convencida del lugar al que se dirigían, daban la vuelta y avanzaban hacia el sur.

—¡No puede ser! —exclamó Alondrita, al punto de arrancarse el cabello—. ¿Y si van por el camino equivocado, Ariel? ¿Cómo encontrará Aura a esa bruja si no sabe qué dirección tomar?

—Con ayuda de su fe —respondió—. Aguarda un momento y lo sabrás. Los días pasaron, la comida y el agua escaseó —prosiguió con la trama—, la joven se sintió inferior por el hambre y la enfermedad, la marcha redujo su velocidad. Después, la exhausta Aura se fue dormida a espaldas del caballo, permitiéndole a él tomar el rumbo. Para esos momentos, habían pasado tantas horas juntos que terminaron convirtiéndose en

amigos entrañables.

—No lo entiendo. ¿Por qué se hicieron amigos si el caballo no puede hablar? —preguntó Alondrita con las cejas casi pegadas.

Preguntas infantiles que Ariel, gustoso, explicaba con paciencia a su hermana.

—Porque cuando nace un verdadero sentimiento de amor entre dos seres vivos, todo lo demás es complementario —respondió sabiamente—. Las razas, el habla, la vista, el tacto; son elementos que pasan desapercibidos en el lenguaje del amor. Por ejemplo, ¿recuerdas a la señora Orquídea?

—¿La vecina sorda?

—Sí. Ella no puede escuchar, se comunica con la lengua de signos. Y, aun así, tiene un esposo que la ama muchísimo. Lo que importa es tu espíritu, tu forma de ser y tus acciones las que invitan a que otros te quieran, así sean personas o animales. ¿Qué ocurrió cuando adoptamos a *Mimo*, nuestro perro? Nunca pudo decirnos una sola palabra. Aullaba, ladraba o lloraba. Al principio nos tuvo miedo, se alejaba y se escondía en el rincón, ¿te acuerdas? Pero cuando le dimos comida y le brindamos confianza, no se quería despegar de nosotros. Nos quiso y fue un excelente amigo.

—Sí. Me acuerdo de sus enormes ojos prestándome atención, esperando que bajara mi manita de la cama para rascarle detrás de las orejas. Yo quería a Mimo y él me quería a mí. Tienes razón, Ariel. Lástima que Mimo huyó de casa. ¿Crees que se encuentre bien?

—Por supuesto que sí. En estos momentos ya formó una familia en el bosque y estará contándoles a sus cachorritos, en lenguaje canino, que tuvo una adorable dueña llamada Alondrita —inventó.

La verdad (una que Ariel jamás pensaba contársela, pues le rompería el corazón) era que Mimo se había

puesto malo de salud. El señor Villalobos, sin poder costear un veterinario, se vio en la necesidad de arreglar el problema rápido, con su rifle de caza. Mimo estaba enterrado en el jardín.

Alondrita sonrió entusiasmada, comprendiendo el tema del amor y la amistad, y Ariel siguió contando su relato.

—La princesa estaba débil, le costaba mantenerse de pie, las piernas le flaqueaban. Pasaron días (semanas quizás), Aura había perdido la noción del calendario. No obstante, jamás malgastó la esperanza de que hallaría la pócima.

En las sombras, el corcel se arrodilló para ayudarle a la doncella a que se subiera a su lomo, luego de que esta llenara su cantimplora en un hermoso lago.

—¿Y al final encontró lo que buscaba?

—Cierta tarde, halló un poblado abandonado que amparaba un imponente castillo en medio. Sus ladrillos centelleaban de forma extraordinaria con la luz del sol. Lo insólito de ese dominio era que sus viviendas tenían las ventanas y las puertas abiertas, exhibiendo sus cocinas con la comida recién servida en las mesas. Los platos humeaban; copas desbordadas de vino fuerte y cerveza artesanal le daban la invitación a Aura de que se acercara y las bebiera; quesos de cabra y panes calientes reposaban en canastas y trapos; y lo más extraño de todo fue que Aura encontró ropa adornando las calles solitarias. Había vestiduras desoladas de mujeres y hombres, de desfavorecidos, de ricos y niños. Como si sus propietarios se hubieran convertido en polvo.

—Qué miedo —mascculló Alondrita.

En la representación, la princesa se bajó del caballo mirando las casas con curiosidad. Con la punta de los dedos levantó un pantalón deshilachado del suelo.

—¡Y vaya que le dio miedo a la doncella! —exclamó Ariel—. No había explicación alguna para entender por qué desaparecerían los habitantes de una ciudad tan grande como aquella. Con todo, era tanta el hambre que tenía, que entró a la casa que le quedaba más próxima y comió duraznos y pescado frito; dio cuenta de una copa de vino y dos panes. Al acabar el almuerzo, sintió el estómago del tamaño de una sandía. Pero no creas que fue la única que se dio un festín para recuperar fuerzas —le comentó en tono gracioso—. El debilucho corcel tampoco se quedó atrás. Él aprovechó para embucharse un cesto entero de manzanas.

La niña rio cuando el hábil equino en la pared pateó la canasta y la lanzó al aire. Las manzanas volaron. Al caer, el animal las atrapó con la boca.

—Después de eso, se dirigieron al castillo.

—¿Al castillo de la bruja? —preguntó Alondrita, embelesada.

—Al castillo, quizás era el de una bruja, o puede que no —rectificó Ariel—. Pero algo le dijo a Aura que en ese lugar encontraría algo beneficioso —susurró.

Dada esa pequeña pausa, el señor Villalobos entró a la habitación interrumpiendo la historia en su parte más emocionante.

—Es hora de dormir —anunció con voz tajante.

Las sombras se cruzaron de brazos quejumbrosas (incluido el caballo), porque fueron conscientes de que no continuarían con su aventura hasta la próxima reunión. Se despidieron de los niños agitando manos (y patas, en el caso del corcel), sin antes sacarle la lengua al señor Villalobos, cosa que hizo reír a Alondrita.

Ariel apagó la linterna y se ofreció en ayudarle a su padrastro a ponerle los «escudos nocturnos» a su hermana; una solicitud que aquel rechazó porque prefirió hacerlo él solo. El muchacho solo tenía autorización de

cambiar el suero.

Los escudos nocturnos, como le gustaba llamarlos Ariel, eran las toallas y mangas elásticas especiales que se le ajustaban a Alondrita antes de dormir. Los paños, que le envolvían las piernas, servían para que no corriera el riesgo de partirse la tibia, el peroné o las rodillas en un movimiento involuntario. En los brazos se le introducían mangas elásticas, que igual funcionaban para que los codos no se le fragmentaran. Y en último lugar, le era implantada una prenda especial, parecida a una camisa de fuerza, donde quedaban sus brazos apresados en el interior. En conjunto, estos protectores del esqueleto evitaban que sufriera una secuela. Aunque ello no quitaba el hecho de que parecía una momia. Ariel opinaba que las noches de su hermana debían de ser bastante incómodas.

Al terminar su labor, el señor Villalobos encendió la lamparita de la cómoda y le ordenó a su hijastro que recogiera los pañuelos sucios dispersados por el suelo. Por último, le expresó un cálido «buenas noches» a su hija y se marchó, sin emitirle una sola palabra a él.

Ariel esperó quedarse a solas con Alondrita y le susurró al oído:

—Prometo que no dejaré que te transformes en cristal, ¿de acuerdo?

Le otorgó un beso en la frente y se retiró en silencio.

—Hasta mañana, Ariel —susurró Alondrita.

El cazador de estrellas entró a su recámara, sacó el piyama del armario, se quitó el uniforme y lo echó al cesto de la ropa sucia. Ya tenía uno limpio para el día siguiente, por lo que no ocupó darse una vuelta por el lavadero. Ariel era el encargado de lavarse su propia ropa a mano. El uso de la lavadora estaba descartado. El señor Villalobos decía que el aparato gastaba exceso de electricidad.

La señora Rivas apareció en el acceso. Ariel y ella se sonrieron.

—Buenas noches, mamá.

—Que descanses, mi niño.

Su madre le tiró un beso en el aire, antes de emparejar la puerta.

Acostado en la cama, con el piyama puesto, el paciente Ariel miró los astros a través de la ventana, aguardando a que las manecillas de Félix, el reloj, marcaran las doce en punto.

«Falta poco —dijo para sus adentros—. Ya falta muy poco. Solo serán unas cuantas noches.»

Llegada la hora de cazar estrellas, se incorporó con el corazón taquicárdico.

Capítulo 7
La anécdota del vagabundo

Metió los pies en sus pantuflas de borreguito, cogió su frazada azul, alojada entre las almohadas, y abrió la ventana. Un viento gélido entró a trompicones, haciendo bailar las cortinas. Antes de sentarse en el alféizar para dar un salto se puso su vieja gorra amarilla, que le dio un toque de personalidad y, para las razones irrealistas de Ariel, valentía. Se impulsó hacia delante y terminó en el jardín, feo como de costumbre. Si no hubiera vivido en esa casa, habría conjeturado que en ella vivía una familia de hechiceros perversos.

Echó a andar por Monteseaur y se alejó del buzón rojo. Aquella noche el frío era penetrante y molesto, le entumeció las puntas de las manos y los dedos de los pies. Tras dar varias inhalaciones, sospechó que en cualquier momento le saldría un picacho de hielo por cada orificio de la nariz, hasta aparentar una morsa. Se envolvió a sí mismo con su manta y aprovechó el

aire tibio que manaba de su boca para calentarse las extremidades.

Aparecieron, de pronto, dos luces en el doblez de la calle. Lento, como un escarabajo, se acercó un automóvil pequeño. Ariel erró a la acera por sentido común y se le encogieron las tripas cuando descubrió quién conducía. Era la señora Corrales, la viuda que vivía enfrente, y quien tenía cortísima relación con los vecinos de la cuadra. Aquella metió su vehículo al garaje, en una maniobra igual de acompasada que su manera de conducir y apagó las luces.

«¿Será posible que me haya visto?», se preguntó, sin dejar de contemplar la vivienda color durazno con un dorado 73.

Eso solo significaría una cosa: malas noticias. La señora Corrales era peligrosa. Se trataba de esas vecinas chismosas y entrometidas que deseaban saberlo y comunicarlo todo. Y pobre de aquel que cometiera una imprudencia en su presencia, porque ella se encargaba de notificarlo a los oídos del vagabundo más distraído de la ciudad. Qué mejor manera de terminar su día, que con el cotilleo de última hora:

—Comadrita, el pobrecito niño de Ariel, con tantos problemas en casa y andando a solas por la calle a la medianoche. ¿Puedes creerlo, comadrita? ¿Crees que esté involucrado en esa banda de jóvenes ocultistas que matan animales en el cementerio?

Ya imaginaba Ariel su voz de urraca contándoselo a las esposas de los vecinos.

En el más extremo de los casos, la mujer llegaría corriendo a su habitación a velocidad de guepardo (muy contradictoria a su manera de conducir) y marcaría un número de teléfono. A la par, se asomaría por la ventana, escondida tras las cortinas, aguardando que las luces del 72 se encendieran. El señor Villalobos

atendería la llamada, furioso por haber sido interrumpido de su sueño. Allí recibiría la inaudita noticia de que su hijastro acababa de ser visto en la calle.

—Oh, sí, señor Villalobos. Arielito paseaba solo y sin rumbo fijo —diría la señora Corrales con fingido tormento—. ¿Adónde irá? ¿Lo sabe usted? ¿No está enterado que el Robaniños hizo desaparecer a otro adolescente, más o menos de su edad, la semana pasada? Un hecho terrible, señor Villalobos. ¡Terrible!...

Si esa película proyectada en la mente de Ariel ocurriera, su segunda noche como cazador de estrellas no terminaría con un final feliz; más bien como una tragedia al estilo griego. Todavía tenía la oportunidad de volver corriendo, cerrar la ventana y echarse a la cama hecho bola, en lo calentito. De este modo, cuando su padrastro entrara frenético a la habitación, con el cinto de cuero en la mano, comprobaría que la historia que le contó su vecina había sido otra de sus calumnias.

«Pero si regreso, habré quebrantado el pacto del anciano y Alondrita terminará haciéndose de cristal —caviló Ariel. Le dio vuelta a su gorra, de modo que la visera apuntó al sur, y se dijo—: Tendré que afrontar el riesgo. Al final, me lo agradecerán.»

Reanudó su marcha, pretendiendo pensar en otra cosa que no fuera su padrastro o la señora Corrales. Se fijó en la calle desierta, que esa noche parecía una cueva de paredes y techos vaporosos. En el firmamento desfilaba una peregrinación de nubes, que ponían en duda si llovería en cualquier momen...

Los pensamientos de Ariel fueron interrumpidos, porque de la nada, una de las cortinas del número 46, que constaba a su lado, se agitó.

Experimentó Ariel lúcidos escalofríos. La carne se le puso de gallina. ¡Los gigantes, después de dormir tantos años, despertaron! Ya se levantarían, carca-

jeándose. Sus paredes se separarían del suelo, haciendo un ruido estrambótico; sus techos anaranjados se resquebrajarían. Temerarias pisadas de ladrillo lo perseguirían a brincos, dejando huecos en el hormigón. Ariel se cubrió con su frazada hasta la cabeza, imitando un fantasma de sábanas, y corrió ahuyentado.

Llegó jadeando al Parque de Juegos Monteseaur, con el corazón en el pescuezo y arrojando arroyos de vaho por la boca. Parecía una locomotora de vapor. Se detuvo y viró en redondo, de cintura para arriba. Por dicha se encontró con una calle desierta cual pintura al óleo, tenuemente iluminada con sus altos alumbrados.

«Ya pasó, cálmate Ariel. Estás comportándote como un paranoico», se tranquilizó.

Detrás de recobrar el ritmo de la respiración, fue momento de buscar al anciano. Incrustó el joven su vista en los columpios, donde esperaba encontrárselo igual que la noche anterior: balanceándose con su bastón de espirales.

No fue así.

Tampoco lo halló de pie, tras la hierba alta.

«¿Dónde estará metido? —se preguntó, girando sobre su propio eje, buscando en los rincones más lóbregos del terreno—. ¿Se habrá buscado a otro cazador? Uno más valiente y fuerte que yo... Uno que fuera más parecido a Brandon el Baladrón.»

—¡HOLA! —Escuchó una voz vibratoria tras él.

Al segundo, una mano se cerró en su hombro cual tenaza de escorpión.

—¡Ah! —gritó Ariel.

Dio tal salto de alarma, que la manta se le escapó de las manos y cayó extendida sobre el césped desaseado, figurando una alfombra mal acomodada.

—¡Qué buena estuvo esa entrada! —señaló el an-

ciano, partiéndose de risa—. Hubieras visto tu cara.

—¿Por qué lo hizo? ¿Por qué? —remachó el chico—. Pude haber sufrido un paro cardiaco. No tiene idea de lo que acabo de sufrir.

Sintió que las venas del cuello lo ahorcaban.

—No me lo digas —repuso el veterano, alzando un juicioso dedo índice. Apagó su humor de tajo—: Viste a la chismosa de tu vecina. Pensaste que le marcaría a tu padrastro por teléfono cuando llegara a su casa, para comunicarle que te miró en medio de la calle a las 12 am. Y después, creíste que unos *terribles gigantes* —escandalizó— te perseguían hasta acá, con tal de aplastarte como a una cucaracha. «*¡Ayúdenme! ¡Socorro!*» —Hizo la voz de una damisela en peligro, que le salió perfecta.

—Para empezar, yo no hablo así —musitó Ariel, malhumorado.

Pero estaba impresionado. ¿Cómo se enteraría el viejo de todas esas cosas?

«¿Podrá leer pensamientos?», se llegó a cuestionar.

El viejo rio un poquito más. Tuvo que desistir de sus carcajadas, porque fue aporreado por un ataque de tos.

—¿Cómo supo lo de la señora Corrales? —preguntó Ariel, recogiendo su frazada de la tierra.

La sacudió y se protegió con ella. La temperatura descendió durante el último minuto. Los columpios se escarcharon y el césped quedó empapado de un rocío congelado. Fue raro que al anciano no le afectara el enfriamiento. Y Ariel no había prestado suficiente atención antes, pero hoy se percató que su acompañante no llevaba pantalones puestos, sino unos shorts rojos demasiado cortos, que hacían lucir unas piernas delgadas y lampiñas, y rodillas protuberantes cuales bolas de tenis.

—Ya te lo dije, tengo una mente extraordinaria. No

se compara con la de Albert Einstein o la de Stephen Hawking, quienes, por cierto, ya murieron —murmuró—. La muerte es un tema tremebundo —expresó con disgusto—. Ah, sé muchísimas cosas tuyas en este momento, Ariel Castillo Rivas —nombró—. Cosas que ni siquiera conoces de ti mismo.

—Imposible —mencionó Ariel con impacto—. ¿Cómo puede saber algo de mí que ni siquiera yo conozco?

De cualquier forma, lo dudó:

—A ver, ¿podría mencionarme una de ellas?

Especuló que aquel conocía su segundo secreto. Un intenso efecto de cobardía se apoderó de Ariel, pues lo observaron las aterradoras pupilas del vagabundo (que parecían distinguir más de lo que un ojo normal podía ver).

«Fácil se nota que allí reside su poder de la adivinación» —dedujo Ariel.

Le llegó al cerebro, de pronto, la impresión de que al otro lado de esos globos oculares blancos alguien más lo observaba.

—¡Bah! Solo te estaba tomando el pelo, muchacho. Es bueno divertirse un rato inventando cosas. Es propio de nosotros los ancianos, y propio también de los soñadores de corazón noble, como tú. Atiende mi siguiente pregunta: ¿Has inventado cosas alguna vez? —cuestionó en un improvisado tono de interés.

Meditó Ariel la interrogante.

—Claro que sí. Cuentos —declaró—. Siendo honesto, contar historias es lo que más me gusta hacer en el mundo. Pero solo se las refiero a mi hermana ¿eh? —puntualizó con firmeza. Lo que menos quería era que le pidieran dramatizar un cuento en el parque abandonado, frente a un total desconocido. Sobrada mala experiencia sufrió con su madre y su padrastro—. ¿Sabe?

A mí me sonó muy cierto lo que me dijo —fijó—. Acertó en todas sus suposiciones. Además, ahora que lo pienso, creo que sí sabe algo de mí de lo que no estoy enterado —expresó convencido. Entonces, se le vino otra cosa a la cabeza, con lo que expresó, casi gritando—: ¡Un segundo! ¡Hace unos momentos me llamó Ariel Castillo Rivas! Yo jamás le dije mi nombre. ¿Cómo lo supo?

El astuto merodeador entrecerró los ojos.

—Lo leí en tu gorra, chico tonto —replicó irascible.

«Aaaah...», murmuró Ariel en voz alta, quitándose la gorra.

Leyó su nombre y apellidos cosidos en la parte trasera y se la volvió a poner.

—Aun así, sigo sin entender —dijo—. ¿Cómo supo que imaginé a los gigantes y lo de la señora Corrales? —insistió—. No me estará siguiendo, ¿verdad?

Su voz se oyó convulsa.

—¿De dónde sacas semejante barbaridad? ¡*Yo*, siguiéndote? —rugió.

—Pero...

—¡Silencio! —Colocó el dedo índice en sus labios y en seguida dijo, empleando una voz roñosa—: Quiero que me expliques cómo te hiciste ese bombazo en el ojo.

Había olvidado Ariel por completo la contusión que le confeccionó Portillo en la cara.

El mendigo apoyó sus manos rejuvenecidas en el bastón y movió los labios de arriba abajo, imitando un elevador descompuesto. Ariel se tocó el párpado con la punta de los dedos. Ya no le dolía tanto como hacía unas horas, pero lo sentía del tamaño de una naranja.

—Me golpeé contra un poste —mintió, a lo que el anciano se destornilló de la risa.

—Eres incalificable manejando mentiras —dijo burlesco—. «Me golpeé contra un poste» (imitó). Esa farsa

no me la creería aun presenciándola. A mí no me engañas, cazador de estrellas. Un compañero de la escuela te golpeó hoy, ¿no es así?

Ariel evadió la vista de hielo. Asintió.

—¡Bah! ¿Lo ves? ¿Qué te costaba ser sincero conmigo? —protestó.

—Como si le importara —replicó Ariel.

Y el buen humor del longevo se pulverizó en un parpadeo.

—No me importa, en eso tienes razón —confirmó irritado—. Es más, siendo franco, me despreocupa en lo más mínimo lo que llegara a ocurrirte. A excepción, claro está, de las noches en las que me servirás como cazador. Yo también debería importarte, adolescente desentendido, porque en tu última misión sanaré de su cristalización humana a Susanita.

—Alondrita —corrigió con malestar.

—Da lo mismo su nombre. El punto es que el único interés que tenemos en común es que termines con tu parte del trato. Y nada más.

—Yo deseo lo mismo —susurró Ariel.

Pero en eso fue embustero, porque se moría de curiosidad por saber lo que le pasaría al anciano cuando recuperara su juventud. ¿Qué tantos años se quitaría de encima? ¿Se transformaría en un muchacho de su edad o en un recién nacido? ¿Qué haría después de lograrlo?

—Te contaré una anécdota, cazador de estrellas —dijo el viejo.

Se inscribió en un columpio. Las cadenas de este se quejaron y expulsaron lagañas de hielo, las cuales se tumbaron en la tierra escarchada. Ariel siguió al vagabundo, como un perrito obediente, y se acomodó a su lado. El asiento congelado en sus posaderas lo hizo tiritar de frío, sin embargo, le encantaban las historias;

eran su debilidad. Por eso mismo, evitó quejarse. Se arropó con su manta hasta las orejas y escuchó con atención lo que estaban por relatarle:

—Cuando yo era más joven —emprendió el longevo—, en el lugar de donde vengo había alguien que se creía la gran cosa. En ocasiones se burlaba de mí y hacía comentarios altaneros sobre mi aspecto y manera de pensar. Los otros se reían. ¡Huy! ¡Cómo detestaba a ese tal...! —Iba a pronunciar un nombre, pero se arrepintió en el último segundo y continuó relatando la anécdota—: Hum, alababan sus absurdas actuaciones de baratija, así fueran ridículas. Se encargaba de manejarlos a todos como marionetas.

El atento Ariel lo miró magnetizado. Eso era, precisamente, lo que ocurría entre él y Brandon Portillo. Aquel era el rey, los estudiantes sus marionetas y Ariel su bufón.

—¿Qué le pasó después? —preguntó, con los oídos hambrientos de palabras.

—En un principio, nada. Soporté por muchos años su egocéntrica idiotez. Yo, a pesar de tener inteligencia y gran sabiduría, nunca brillaba en la comunidad. Solo era, como llaman por aquí, un don Nadie. Y te lo digo sin exagerar, fui alguien sin prestigio del que todos se reían. —Concibió un silencio oportuno, haciendo memoria de los hechos. Prosiguió—: Hasta que llegó un momento en que no lo toleré más y estallé.

—Pero ¿qué hizo con él? Con el que le hacía la vida de cuadritos —interpeló Ariel.

—Ya te lo dije, muchacho. Exploté. ¡Bum! ¡Taz! ¡Catapum! Fin de esa etapa de mi vida. Desde aquella ocasión nunca más volvieron a reírse de mí. Pero eso sí, a causa de ello me quedé solo. —Miró embelesado el cielo y concluyó—: Dado lo del incidente, no tuve ninguna compañía. Aunque eso es lo de menos. Vale más impo-

ner miedo que ser un don Nadie, ¿no crees?

Ariel no creyó estar muy de acuerdo en eso. Era un final deprimente. Con razón el veterano estaba desamparado.

«A lo mejor desea rejuvenecer para corregir los errores que cometió en su pasado —imaginó Ariel—, y cuando pasen los años, esta vez tendrá la posibilidad de ser feliz, trabajar en algo que le guste, estar rodeado de una esposa, hijos maravillosos y nietos traviesos.»

Pero todavía estaba aquello que no le quedaba del todo claro. ¿A qué se habría referido aquel cuando dijo que había *explotado*? ¿Acaso se enfrentó, a base de trompadas, al sujeto que lo molestó? Lo dejaría humillado frente a la sociedad, tal como le sugería el señor Villalobos que hiciera Ariel con Brandon Portillo cuando lo molestara.

«¡Defiende tu honor, hijastro!»

Si así fueron las cosas, ¿por qué el anciano se quedó solo en el mundo? Si lo único que hizo fue darle al tipo su merecido. La historia debió haber terminado al revés.

«¿O lo asesinó?», se le cruzó la hipótesis a deshora.

—Basta de tanto parloteo —dijo el pordiosero, poniéndose en pie—. Es hora de poner manos a la obra y continuar el plan. Esta noche echarás a andar una de mis mayores creaciones. ¿No te dije que también era inventor? —preguntó petulante.

Metió sus manos juveniles al abrigo.

—No lo había mencionado.

—Hum —gruñó—. Pues ahora lo sabes.

Buscó algo en el fondo de su chamarra y sacó un par de zapatos deteriorados. Se los ofreció a Ariel, quien arrugó la nariz en cuanto los tuvo enfrente. Eran viejos y su interior despedía un olor a queso rancio que promovía ganas de vomitar.

—Tienes que ponértelos —ordenó el viejo, agitando los calzados de un lado a otro—. Tómalos.

Capítulo 8
¡Brinca!

—¿Para qué son? —quiso saber Ariel.

Los recibió con la punta de los dedos y aprovechó la otra mano para taparse la nariz.

—¿Pensaste que atraparías estrellas igual que la noche pasada? —preguntó el mayor, de forma socarrona—. No muchacho. Te lo dije claramente antes de que te marcharas ayer a tu casa: hoy es cuando empieza lo complicado. Verás, cada ocasión que atrapas luceros debe ser diferente a la anterior. Las estrellas podrían darse cuenta si se les engaña una vez. Por lo antes dicho, la técnica de caza debe variar. Ese es el secreto que convierte a uno en buen cazador.

—¿Y de qué manera me ayudarán estos anticuados zapatos a cazar estrellas? Se ve que no sirven. Mire, hasta tienen agujeros —anunció, acercándole las suelas abiertas.

El jorobado hizo sonar la punta de su bastón en el

suelo.

—¡Haces tantos comentarios quejosos que desesperas mi razón! —refunfuñó, encogiendo el ceño—. Emplázalos a tus pies, después te daré explicaciones.

Aquellos ojos pálidos hicieron que Ariel no tuviera ganas de volver a preguntar. Dobló su frazada y la dejó sobre el columpio de al lado. Se quitó sus pantuflas de borreguito y metió los pies en aquellos apestosos objetos.

—Necesitan estar bien ajustados para que no se te desmonten —demandó el sujeto.

El joven actuó conforme a las recomendaciones. A pesar de apretar los cordones lo más que pudo, con todo, los botines le quedaron un poco flojos. Eran, al tanteo, tres números más grandes que los de su talla normal. Aunque para su sorpresa, resultaron cómodos. Ariel formalizó un paso al frente para probárselos.

—¡Detente! —ladró el anciano—. ¿Qué crees que haces, inútil? ¡No muevas un solo músculo!

Ariel permaneció quieto y asustado.

«¿Qué hice mal?», se dijo.

El mendigo murmuró cosas en voz baja, mirándolo de la cabeza a los pies, como un médico analizando a su paciente. De aquel cuchicheo impreciso, Ariel pudo rescatar las siguientes oraciones:

—La técnica... Los ángulos son correctos... Su peso es más del que planeaste... No seas ridículo... Pero es muy gordo, de eso no cabe la menor duda... ¿Tendrá el tiempo oportuno para llenarla? —Acarició las mechas de su barba erizada—. ¡Bah! Pero qué tonterías estoy diciendo, funcionará a la perfección. —Elevó la voz—. Todo está listo, muchacho. Ahora coge esto.

Volvió a hurgar en las bolsas.

«¡Caramba! —discurrió Ariel—. Ese abrigo sí que puede esconder muchas cosas.»

Sin tardanza, el adulto extrajo una pequeña aspiradora manual, de aquellas que ocupan baterías para funcionar. Inseguro, Ariel agarró la pieza y miró a su acompañante, intentando descifrar aquella mirada lechosa. Preguntándose qué debía hacer ahora.

Los labios del anciano se curvaron en una mustia sonrisa de luna menguante. Casi nunca se le veía sonreír.

—Cuando llegue el momento indicado, encenderás la aspiradora que sostienen tus manos —dijo disciplinado.

—¿Y cómo sabré qué momento es ese?

—Ya estarás al corriente. No puedo decírtelo todo yo, para eso eres cazador, ¿no? Solo es cuestión de que prestes mucha atención y mantengas ojos y oídos abiertos. Deberás atrapar tooodas las estrellas que puedas, hasta que la capacidad de almacenaje del aparato llegue a su límite. —Luego preguntó—: ¿Entendido? Oye, bribón, no te quedes callado. Estoy proporcionándote las instrucciones. Dime si entendiste. Asiente o niega con la cabeza, por lo menos.

Ariel confirmó, todavía confuso. ¿De qué manera atraparía estrellas? ¿Correría con los zapatos viejos por el parque, llevando la aspiradora encendida sobre su cabeza?

—Hay algo más que debes saber.

El anciano dejó su agrietado rostro frente al del chico, con el objetivo de que no olvidara la siguiente instrucción. Su aliento maloliente lo abofeteó. Ariel pudo visualizar sus retorcidos molares amarillos y llenos de caries.

—Tendrás que ser lo más rápido que puedas, porque el salto dura pocos segundos —dijo.

—¿Salto? —repitió Ariel, aturdido. Su pensamiento de ir corriendo por la congelada melena de león se difu-

minó—: ¿A qué se refiere con eso? No estará hablando de llegar al cielo… por medio de un salto, ¿no? —Volteó hacia arriba. Su voz sonó decepcionada—. Es imposible.

El añejo individuo golpeó los columpios con el bastón. De sus ojos saltaron chispas.

—¡Kfgbrnr! —gritó.

Ariel se le quedó mirando. Aquella expresión sonó como un gorgoteo bajo el agua, junto con el crepitar del fuego de una chimenea. Un ruido que no parecía humano. Mas le hizo recordar algo de su niñez temprana. No supo a qué con seguridad.

—¡Es posible! De eso estoy seguro —bramó el veterano. Al contado, habló como un científico loco al que acababan de humillar en una conferencia—: Los botines que traes puestos en realidad se llaman «saltines», ¿escuchaste bien? Saltines. Yo mismo los he fabricado. El problema está en que solo tienen un salto de capacidad, por eso debes aprovecharlos al máximo cuando llegues al firmamento. Hum. Y ya está de más aconsejarte que si no quieres perder el juicio y volverte loco —recalcó, alzando una ceja—, respeta el límite de tiempo.

—Claro, no observar a las estrellas más de cinco segundos —susurró Ariel.

—Cuando vengas de vuelta, aterriza en aquel árbol. —Apuntó a un álamo con su cayado.

Ariel volvió a desnivelar la cabeza. En lugar de prestar atención a su punto de aterrizaje, se miró los zapatos. No notó algo especial en ellos. Por lo general, en las historias legendarias, como *El mago de Oz*, los calzados mágicos eran coloridos y relucientes. Y los que llevaba puestos esa noche, en cambio, eran feos y lo opuesto a la palabra maravilloso. Todo indicaba que su misión número dos, siendo cazador de estrellas, acaba-

ría bastante mal.

Recordó pues, al corcel de su cuento; aquel huesudo animal que decidió ayudar a la princesa Aura en su osada búsqueda de la pócima sanadora. Igual que los saltines, aquel caballo era viejo y no tenía muchos atributos especiales. Pero fue el único del reino que tuvo la gallardía de ayudar a la princesa.

«El poder de su esperanza era más fuerte que la de diez hombres juntos (...). Eso, a mi parecer, es más que suficiente para embarcarse en una aventura», fue lo que le había dicho Ariel a su hermana.

Acaso si corría con la misma suerte que Aura, los saltines podrían ayudarlo a cazar estrellas. Por supuesto que sí. Tener confianza era el punto. Sin ella, para empezar, jamás hubiera logrado atrapar luceros la noche anterior.

—¿Estás listo? —cuestionó el anciano.

—Sí —respondió ilusionado, abrazando la aspiradora.

Visualizó el corcel de Aura.

—¡Ah! Una última cosa. Es vital que la obedezcas. —Habló en susurros arbitrarios—. En el Reino Astral no debes hacer ni un solo ruido, ¿quedó claro? Ni un lamento, queja, llanto, exclamación o murmullo. Es más, ten cuidado hasta con tu propia respiración; no te agites demasiado. Allá, el sonido no es bienvenido. Un suspiro en falso y las estrellas despertarán, te rodearán y en lo que deletreas la palabra «socorro» te raptarán y llevarán a su castillo.

—¿Las estrellas tienen un castillo? ¿En serio? —interpeló Ariel, con los ojos desorbitados.

—Bueno, lo que quiero decir, es que no sería un final bonito para nadie —se apresuró a agregar el viejo, antes de hablar más de la cuenta.

Al recibir aquella información, Ariel descubrió que

el veterano escondía demasiados secretos. Y su intención no era compartirlos con él precisamente.

—¡Sin más preámbulo, llegó la hora! —gritó el vagabundo.

El corazón de Ariel empezó a latir más rápido (¿Por qué se aferraba al presentimiento de que aquello no terminaría nada bien?). Contempló el océano de lamparillas en el cielo, disimuladas por largos brazos de nubes cenizas. Le aterró la inmensidad del espacio, la idea de perderse en él y dar vueltas en la eternidad.

«Un momento, ¿que no la gente muere asfixiada si no lleva traje espacial? ¿Por qué el anciano no me facilitó uno?», reflexionó Ariel, con el estómago oprimido.

Pero ya era muy tarde para cambiar de opinión.

«Tal vez pueda aguantar la respiración, lo conveniente como para llenar la aspiradora», se alentó para sus adentros.

—¡Brinca, muchacho! ¡Brinca lo más alto que puedas! —aulló el anciano a todo pulmón, poniendo su vara en alto.

Ariel tragó saliva y ajustó su moteada gorra amarilla, con la visera insinuándose al frente. Las orejas se le pusieron heladas, como un par de cubitos de hielo.

Entonces saltó.

Y volteó a su alrededor. Pero las cosas siguieron igual.

«Qué raro», se dijo.

Brincó otra vez, y volvió a esperar…

No ocurrió nada. No voló, ni tampoco realizó el brinco magnífico que le mencionó el anciano. Ariel proseguía con los pies tocando el suelo, abrazando una ridícula aspiradora manual como si fuera su alma.

—¡Por las mil centellas! Algo debió haber salido mal —protestó el viejo.

Se aproximó al frustrado Ariel y se deshizo del bas-

tón, arrojándolo a los columpios. Cayó de rodillas y lanzó un quejido de dolor. Dio a pensar que se las había fracturado, con lo frágiles y delgadas que eran...

—¿Está convencido de que los saltines funcionarán, señor? —interpeló Ariel.

—¡Calla ahora, sinvergüenza! —rugió el jorobado. Al rato, mientras palpaba los botines, masculló lo siguiente—: ¿Qué les pasa a estas porquerías? No entiendo por qué razón... ¡Oh, ya! ¡Aquí está! —emitió, como si hubiera revelado algo muy obvio—. El eje se encuentra mal puesto. Déjame ver. —Hizo girar un par de broches e informó—: Ya está, jovencito. Prepárate para dar el...

¡Toing!

Ariel no logró terminar de escuchar la expresión, porque el viejo ya no se hallaba presente. Un sonido de rebote se escuchó en sus pies. De las suelas de los calzados nacieron unos resortes. El terreno sucio del parque recreativo, los columpios escarchados, las llantas fraccionadas a la mitad, las botellas empañadas y la congelada melena de león se desvanecieron.

Tuvo una rápida sensación de vértigo en el vientre, igual a cuando soñaba que caía de lugares muy altos. Sus entrañas jugaron a armar un rompecabezas. Vio borroso a su alrededor, como las emplumadas alas de un gavilán. Los pelos se le estamparon en la frente y un largo hilillo de baba desbandó por la comisura de sus labios. Estaba volando por los aires. O, mejor dicho, iba en dirección al cielo; un proyectil atravesando las capas atmosféricas a toda velocidad. Recordó las aventuras que soñaba gracias a su primer secreto: la imaginación. Ya no tenía necesidad de inventarlas, porque hoy vivía la más maravillosa de todas.

¡Cuán equivocados estaban los adultos con sus ideas realistas! (Mayormente el señor Villalobos). Lo irrea-

lista era cierto, palpable, igual que acariciar las páginas de un libro. Ariel pegó su mentón al pecho y averiguó que estaba alejado del suelo. Tanto, que el parque abandonado adquirió las dimensiones de un tablero de ajedrez. Pudo visualizar los rostros de los gigantes dormidos de la calle Monteseaur haciéndose pequeñitos, fingiendo tener las cortinas cerradas, cuando en realidad lo analizaban de reojo. Además, se fijó en el jardín de su casa: un penoso y lúgubre azulejo negro, entre los prósperos jardines verdes del resto de los domicilios.

Divisó el centro de la ciudad y los automóviles circulando por las calles, como apresurados insectos. Edificios de tamaños variados y rascacielos besando las nubes también coordinaron esa magnífica ilustración. En sus altos ventanales, con el formato de puertas, se produjo un espectáculo visual maravilloso. Estos reflejaron las despampanantes luces de las estrellas en un anochecer mágico.

Continuó Ariel apartándose del suelo. El mundo bajo sus pies se limitó a convertirse en un mapa geográfico con los trazos bien definidos a cargo de un pincel de cerdas suaves. Gritó de excitación. El ánimo se esparció por su cuerpo, igual que un virus. Agitó los brazos, imitando el aleteo de un ave. Disfrutó del viaje dando movimientos aleatorios. Hubo un momento, pese a ello, en que el aparato estuvo a punto de caérsele de las manos. Fue allí, cuando decidió enfocarse en su cometido. Apretó el artilugio contra su pecho y miró en derredor.

Le fue imposible quedarse quieto y aguantarse las risas, porque apreciaba una sensación seductora nunca antes vivida. Cuando terminara aquella misión, le contaría a Alondrita, con lujo de detalles, lo que tuvo que pasar a lo largo de cinco noches para salvarla de

su cristalización humana.

Los espectros que eran las nubes empezaron a cruzar por su lado. Los atravesó cual flecha lanzada desde una ballesta. Rompió contra toda ley física que su padrastro le había impuesto. Tuvo la impresión de que rasgaba, con el cuerpo, una muralla de seda delicada, y que atravesaba un campo de niebla que parecía no tener fin. De esta forma, emergió de las nubes y se enteró que no se encontraba más en la Tierra. Ya no entreveía viviendas ni altas edificaciones. Por el contrario, se topó con un mundo de cielo achocolatado y ciudadelas urdidas con algodón.

Listones color violeta giraban en remolinos independientes. En sus centros resplandecían luces blancas que rodeaban un agujero negro. Se enteró que eran galaxias lejanas, había cientos de ellas. Observó asteroides cruzando encima de él, como barcos piratas en busca de tesoros; distinguió a Saturno, presumiendo sus preciosos anillos alrededor del cuerpo; descubrió al imponente Júpiter, con manchas rojas parecidas a las de la viruela; y a lo lejos a un azulado Neptuno, que figuraba una pequeña canica. En seguida, contempló al Sol. Hermoso. Una burbuja amarilla y cálida que suscitaba erupciones de fuego. Asumió la oportunidad, incluso, de tener a la Luna tan cerquita de él, que aquella asemejó un retrato colgado en la pared. Era mucho más pequeña de lo que Ariel se imaginaba: del tamaño de una pelota de baloncesto. Vio varias banderitas descoloridas en su superficie, apostadas por los astronautas que habían puesto su pie en ella. Se le antojó desprenderlas con la punta de los dedos.

En eso quedó deslumbrado. Vio cientos de hermosas esferitas de Navidad desperdigadas. Salvo que no eran tal cosa, sino estrellas que flotaban a modo de medusas brillantes bajo un profundo mar. Resultaban tan feno-

menales, que Ariel no pudo dar crédito de lo que atestiguaron sus ojos. Se ubicaba en el Reino Astral, un espacio merecedor de tal nombre y propio de aparecer en libros de fantasía. No existía una explicación razonable que describiera las maravillas que le arrebataron el aliento. Todo se resumía a que era un lugar...

«Fascinante», concluyó.

Tuvo mucho cuidado con no hablar, como le había sugerido el anciano. En la garganta, si bien, se le insinuaba una nota de voz, y su corazón, suplicante, proclamaba que diera ese grito que tanto deseaba sacar. Así, percibió que podía respirar.

«¡También hay oxígeno aquí!», pensó.

Existía algo más en aquel paraje que lo caracterizaba: un sagrado silencio de biblioteca. Los sonidos de los automóviles y el bullicio de las conversaciones humanas se apagaron en un santiamén. Quedaron atrás, sepultados tras la barrera de nubes. Fue como si los músicos de una orquesta se hubieran cansado de tocar sus instrumentos y pidieran exhaustos al director una pausa con tal de descansar. Ariel se preguntó por qué para la gente las estrellas se hallaban a años luz de la Tierra, en los confines del universo, cuando para él quedaban tan cerca que se podían arrancar con las manos, igual que los frutos de un árbol.

El viaje se detuvo.

Dejó Ariel de sentir la gravedad y sus cabellos flotaron a una manera bajo el agua. La tela de su ropa onduló, otorgándose a sí misma el regalo de la vida, y lo mismo ocurrió con los cordones de los saltines, que se ondeaban igual que un par de gusanos. Puesto que la energía de estos calzados empezaba a agotarse, los pies de Ariel principiaron a bambolearse.

«Es hora», caviló, temeroso de romper el mutismo del Reino Astral.

Tuvo en cuenta las consecuencias expuestas por el anciano: si las estrellas despertaban, aquellas podían lanzarse contra él y trasladarlo a su castillo.

Llevó el dedo pulgar a la aspiradora y, *lentamente*, presionó el botón de **encendido**. El boquete del aparato succionó los astros más cercanos. Era lo mismo que limpiar la alfombra de la sala, pero mucho más asombroso. Sigiloso, separó los luceros en un deslumbrante torbellino. Entonces, le llegó un pensamiento que puso en tela de juicio su labor:

Lo que estaba haciendo, es decir, cazar estrellas a cambio de devolverle su juventud a un anciano y salvar a Alondrita, ¿era lo correcto?

Tragó saliva para asimilar la pregunta.

Claro que era lo correcto. Él no era un ladrón, pero…

«¿Acaso no estás arrebatándole algo al cielo?», replicó una vocecita en su ser.

«Salvaré a mi hermana», rebatió.

«Pero estás hurtándole los astros al firmamento. Eso te transforma en un ladrón.»

Así fue como le llegó la última pregunta:

¿Y qué pasará cuando ya no existan más estrellas en el cielo?

Exacto. ¿Qué ocurrirá después, cuando el quinto día de su misión, los luceros que distinguieron la noche del día, elementos que llevaban adheridos en el éter durante milenios, queden extintos por causa de un simple muchacho? Nadie volvería a admirar las hermosas constelaciones. Los navegantes que todavía usaban astrolabios para viajar, un antiguo instrumento astronómico, se perderían en el océano. ¿Qué habría luego, en aquella oscuridad profunda? Las estrellas se convertirían en un cuento antiguo. Una historia que, con la vereda de los años, se bautizaría como un mito que ocu-

rrió cientos de generaciones atrás. ¿Le enseñarían a la gente del futuro, en sus clases de Historia, que un adolescente de trece años, llamado Ariel Castillo Rivas, robó las estrellas del cielo para curar a su hermana?

«Qué persona tan egoísta», dirían.

Sintió Ariel un piquete de culpabilidad en el alma. Si no efectuaba su papel de cazador de astros, no sería buen hermano, ya que Alondrita moriría. Pero si continuaba desclavando cuerpos celestes de la bóveda nocturna, no obraría como buena persona. Dejaría vacío el universo. Las dos opciones lo posicionaban entre la espada y la pared.

Así que, ¿cuál era la mejor decisión?

La aspiradora llegó a su límite de capacidad. Ariel aplastó el botón de **apagado**. Volteó con la mancha oscura que quedó en el sitio. Sintió pena al considerar el destino que les aguardaba a esos luceros. El artefacto en sus manos vibraba. Las estrellas del interior habían despertado.

A Ariel lo interrumpió un movimiento irregular de los saltines, cuya energía había llegado a su fin. Su baloteo se convirtió en una danza huracanada. Los zapatos lo obligaron a descender y se sumergió en las nubes. Sintió que las tripas se le juntaron en la cabeza. Volvió a desgarrar aquel muro de seda y abandonó los confines del Reino Astral. Los ruidos de la ciudad (automóviles, cláxones, fiestas juveniles y sonidos de la noche) hicieron notar su regreso en la orquesta, que volvía a tocar en el Gran Salón de la Tierra. Era imposible divagar que segundos atrás estuvo en una zona inexplorada por el hombre. El mapa del mundo se ensanchó conforme fue cayendo a la mayor velocidad, sin embargo, ya no iba chispeante de alegría como en un principio.

Examinaba Ariel sus decisiones, cuando de pronto

lo asaltó una indicación que le advirtió el anciano, antes de dar el salto:

«Cuando vengas de vuelta, aterriza en aquel árbol», le había dicho.

—¡Rayos! —exclamó Ariel, con el corazón dando brincos en su pecho.

Se encontraba a corta distancia del suelo. Un miedo espeluznante se apoderó de él. Se vio a sí mismo reventándose como una bolsa de sangre en el asfalto. Entrevió la copa del árbol que le había indicado el jorobado, pero la veía tan lejana, tan imposible, que se enteró que no caería en ella.

Ora agitaba los brazos, ora movía las piernas como remos, recordando los movimientos de los cursos de natación a los que el señor Villalobos lo obligó a asistir durante las vacaciones de verano. Los compañeros de Ariel se rieron de él porque tuvo que quitarse la playera y exhibió su cuerpo semidesnudo. Pero es superficial hablar de ello justo ahora.

Dio piruetas, volteretas y patadas sin sentido que aceleraron más su caída. Su cabello era una batalla campal que le picaba los ojos. En una de esas sacudidas, la aspiradora escapó de sus manos y se separó de él inevitablemente uno... dos... tres metros.

—¡No! —repetía.

Trató de alcanzar el artefacto y, al mismo tiempo, pretendió acertar su descenso en la copa del árbol que tenía más próximo.

Reconoció al anciano mirándole desde abajo, cuyos ojos blancos no publicaron la más mínima preocupación por su vida. En su rostro curtido y severo se moldeó una terrible rabia, como si deseara aniquilarlo. El viejo soltó su bastón y corrió con los brazos abiertos, calculando el sitio donde se desplomaría la aspiradora llena de estrellas.

La caída de Ariel llegó a su fin (por poco acabó disgregado en el suelo). Había alcanzado la copa de un álamo con abundantes hojas que amortiguaron su doloroso desplome. El golpe le arrebató el aliento. Creyó que se había roto las costillas. La aspiradora, por su parte, no corrió con tanta suerte. El anciano no pudo atraparla. Esta colisionó en el suelo y se partió en cuatro partes.

Una luz incandescente inundó el parque. Los bigotes de la verde melena de león palidecieron. Fue una luz comparada con la intensidad del Sol en pleno mediodía. La ropa del viejo, a pesar de estar roída, sucia y remendada, se tornó celeste y limpia. Lo mismo derivó en Ariel, que se vio a sí mismo como una persona hecha de sal. Los árboles semejaron columnas glaciares y los cachivaches del suelo montículos de nieve. Pudo visualizar el muchacho, gracias a su imaginación, un magnífico Polo Norte asentado en el parque recreativo.

Tan repentino como la luz lo cubrió todo, aquella se apagó de inmediato. Las estrellas se fugaron en masa lo más rápido que pudieron, redirigiéndose a su hogar.

El viejo gritó en aquel lenguaje extraño que le resultaba a Ariel particularmente conocido. De su cara enrojecida saltaban gotas de sudor a modo de paracaidistas. Sacó un costal de lona de su chamarra. Encerró al reducido grupo de astros que terminaron atrapados bajo los escombros de la aspiradora, y a los que deambulaban a la redonda, como moscas despistadas incapaces de intuir cómo habían llegado hasta allí.

—¡Eres un inservible! —vociferó el desquiciado adulto, embriagado de una furia que le arrebató la cordura.

Ariel nunca había visto a alguien tan enfurecido, ni siquiera al señor Villalobos. Y cuando se fijó en aquella

rabiosa mirada, tuvo un estremecimiento. Por un instante creyó haber visto los ojos del vagabundo trocarse en dos brillantes rubíes, pero debió haberse equivocado, porque la vista de la gente no cambia de color cuando se enoja.

Logró bajar Ariel de las ramas dando un salto. El cuerpo adolorido. Luego cogió su frazada del columpio y se protegió con ella.

—¡Pudimos haber avanzado mucho! ¡Vaya desperdicio! —protestó el anciano—. Las estrellas que huyeron avisarán a las demás que están siendo cazadas. ¡Eres insensato! A partir de hoy nuestros planes estarán pendiendo de un hilo. Si esta noche fue complejo cazar estrellas, los siguientes días serán una completa odisea. ¡Malograste todo, idiota! Yo no recuperaré mi juventud y tú... —Lo apuntó con el dedo— no salvarás a *Susanita*, o como se llame, de su cristalización humana. Olvídate de la posibilidad de curarla. Acabará siendo presa del cristal y no podrás hacer nada para impedirlo. Morirá. ¡Oh, sí que lo hará!

—Pero usted puede aliviar los malestares de la gente, es bueno en eso —murmuró Ariel.

—¿Que puedo aliviar los malestares de la gente? ¿De dónde sacaste esa bobería? ¡Oh! —exclamó, arrepentido—: Es decir, sí, soy bueno curando a las personas —balbuceó—. Por supuesto que lo hago. Yo no miento —dijo, recuperando su timbre autoritario—. Pero hicimos un trato y lo incumpliste —revalidó—, no actuaste como debiste haberlo hecho y tampoco seguiste mis indicaciones por entero. Ya puedes esfumarte. *Chus.*

—Usted es inventor. Fabrique otros saltines, señor —suplicó Ariel, con los ojos empañados.

—¿Crees que es así de fácil?

Se le aproximó, recogió su bastón del suelo y lo gol-

peó en la cabeza con él.

Ariel se llevó las manos a la frente. Era el tercer porrazo del día.

—No puedo hacer más zapatos que brincan, muchacho. No es temporada de resortes botadores. Solo existían un par de saltines en esta Realidad: los que traes puestos. Y ya no son más que un par de botines ordinarios. No te imaginas todo lo que tardé. —Mordió su lengua—. Décadas de trabajo, tras ir juntando diferentes materiales de la primera región del multiverso. No esperaba que un mocoso inepto como tú desaprovecharía la oportunidad.

—Lo siento —se disculpó, manteniendo las lágrimas en los párpados.

Después razonaría aquello del «multiverso», porque de momento no tenía otra cosa en la cabeza más que averiguar una manera rápida de arreglar el problema.

Una estrella escapó del costal. El parque volvió a iluminarse con una sutil luz azul. El viejo intentó atraparla con la mano que tenía libre, no obstante, aquella se le escurrió de los dedos y se fue zumbando al firmamento.

—Vete —dijo entre dientes—. Veré qué puedo hacer para recuperar las pérdidas que tuvimos hoy.

Volvieron a quedarse a oscuras, salvo el interior del costal, en cuyos orificios escapaban numerosas espinas de luz. El veterano apretó el costal contra su pecho.

—¿No oíste? —gritó—. ¡Vuelve mañana a la misma hora! ¡Lárgate!

—Debe de haber algo —insistió Ariel—. Algo que podamos hacer.

—¡No! ¡No lo hay! ¡He dicho que te fueras! —ultimó.

Ariel retrocedió.

No se había equivocado; los ojos del viejo eran rojos como la sangre. Y la luz que escapaba del costal chocó

contra su cara arrugada y mugrienta, otorgándole un aspecto de cadáver poseído.

No pudo Ariel contenerse más. Llorando corrió a la calle Monteseaur, esquivando los objetos que había regados por el suelo. Ya estando en medio de la calle, sobre la zona de los gigantes dormidos, se dio la vuelta.

Espió al jorobado, a punto de consumir su medicina de la juventud. Aquel separó sus dientes, preparándose para engullir las estrellas. Luego abrió el costal. Mas hubo algo aterrador en aquella escena que provocó que Ariel resultara perplejo. La boca del merodeador se abrió, pero de una forma muy anormal. Su quijada se separó tanto de su cabeza que pareció no tener huesos que la sostuvieran. Imitó la mandíbula desplegada de un caimán. Ariel descubrió que aquel encorajinado, extraño, introvertido y egoísta vagabundo no pertenecía a la raza humana.

Las estrellas cayeron, aún vivas, en el acantilado profundo de su garganta. En breve, el indigno viejo no se molestó en hacerlas mermelada en un tazón. Desenfrenado, se las devoró sin la más mínima sensibilidad. Ninguna logró salvarse, porque se las tragó cual hambrienta fiera. Restituyó el tamaño original a su boca y volvió a la postura de un viejecito indefenso. Se limpió las muelas con la lengua y tragó. Rebuscó en el interior del costal, con sus ojos mezquinos, por si había faltado un astro más. Cuando reveló que no fue así, dobló el saco y lo guardó de nuevo en el abrigo. Acto seguido, cerró la mano en la empuñadura de su báculo de madera y emprendió una lenta caminata hacia la hierba alta.

Para ese entonces Ariel, en medio de la calle, estaba a un pelo del infarto. Si un automóvil hubiera cruzado a toda marcha por allí, lo más seguro es que se lo hubiera llevado de corbata. Tuvo suerte de que no ocu-

rriera así. Y si el chico pensó que ya había acabado todo, nunca estuvo más equivocado. Faltaba por ocurrir lo peor.

El hombre de la tercera edad se dejó abatir y se estampó en el suelo, rompiendo por consecuencia algunas botellas de vidrio. Se retorció de dolor, semejando una anguila eléctrica. Parecía que acababa de ingerir veneno para ratas, porque sufrió una mórbida epilepsia. Tosía y daba extrañas arcadas para vomitar. Expelía espuma por la boca. Era una secuencia traumatizante. ¿Qué estaba pasando?

El acobardado Ariel se enjugó las lágrimas, que le habían llegado hasta la barbilla. Estuvo dispuesto a aproximarse y ayudarlo, con todo, al revelar lo que sucedía cambió de parecer y prefirió quedarse en su lugar, haciendo el papel de una gárgola de catedral.

La joroba en la espalda del viejo se hundió, como si un yunque invisible le hubiera caído encima; sus huesos se alargaron a una acelerada velocidad de bambú. Su esqueleto crecía y crecía sin parar. Parecía la transformación de un hombre lobo a la plateada luz de la luna. Y vaya que lo parecía con una tan llena como la de aquella noche. Gigantesca, resplandeciente, a punto de ser encubierta por una nube oscura.

El viejo se incorporó, pero para mirarlo a la cara Ariel tuvo que levantar la cabeza. El anciano era alto, tan inhumanamente alto que podía alcanzar las copas de los árboles sin tener la necesidad de pararse de puntas. Asimismo, asumía de una delgadez acentuada. Sus piernas, brazos y el resto de su cuerpo eran escuálidos, como patas de asno. Ariel admitió que aquellas rodillas podrían romperse con la punta de un bastoncillo para limpiar orejas. Era una afirmación incorrecta, por supuesto, porque las extremidades del indigente eran más fuertes de lo que aparentaban. A continua-

ción, estas le permitieron movilizarse sin ayuda de ningún bastón.

El vagabundo se percató en la presencia del muchacho y, aprovechando su colosal estatura, lo miró desde arriba con sus ojos otra vez blancos. Estos fulguraban escondidos entre los matorrales de su cabello cano, haciendo alarde de la mirada de un animal intratable, oculto entre los arbustos. Agregó cierta sonrisa torcida a su semblante demacrado y lanzó una carcajada que pudo diagnosticarse maquiavélica.

Con auténtico pavor, Ariel corrió por Monteseaur sin detenerse, con las manos acopiadas en su pecho. Su frazada flameaba con el viento como una especie de capucha que circunvalaba sus hombros. Oyó las fuertes pisadas del gigante. Aquel lo estaba persiguiendo por la calle. No le importaron los rostros de los gigantes dormidos al adolescente, a pesar de que sus cortinas se movían con salvajismo.

¡ZUM! La ventana que tenía más próxima se abrió de súbito.

—¡Eh! ¡Espera, Ariel! —gritó alguien.

Pero no le apetecía al nombrado, ni por asomo, girarse.

Estaba trastornado. Fuera de su juicio.

El anciano promovió un brinco y se encargó de correr por los tejados de las casas. Ariel fue capaz de ver su transformada silueta por el rabillo del ojo, hasta el momento en que aquel tropezó con una chimenea y cayó de bruces en un jardín trasero. El muchacho aprovechó la situación y se mantuvo transitando sin detenerse, escapando del hambriento tirano que se alimentaba de estrellas.

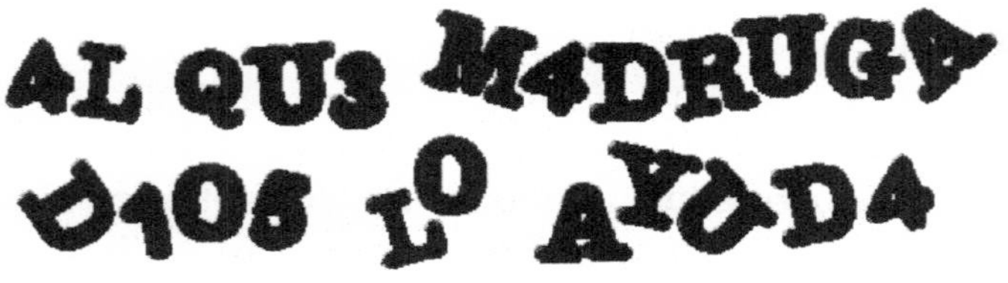

Capítulo 9
Meditaciones en el desayuno

Cometió un salto admirable por la ventana abierta de su habitación, después de la carrera olímpica que ejecutó en la calle Monteseaur. Cerró con rapidez, pasó el seguro, alzó la mitad de la cortina y se arriesgó a pegar su cara al cristal. Corroboró si el enorme anciano había llegado hasta su jardín.

Favorablemente (suspiró) las cosas no fueron así.

«Si eso hubiera ocurrido...», pensó Ariel.

Anticipó que el veterano habría sido capaz de romper el tejado con facilidad y meter sus brazos para raptarlo. ¿Por qué detuvo su marcha, después de tropezar con la chimenea? ¿Resultaría malherido?

«O no pudo avanzar más allá de ese punto —descifró—, por la existencia de la tiza invisible. Como me encontraba en zona segura, el monstruo no pudo acercarse más a mí».

Se desplomó en la cama, haciendo chillar los resortes.

Más tarde se fijó en sus pies.

—¡No puede ser! —se dijo, pegándose en la frente con la palma abierta.

Traía puestos los saltines.

Por lógica no tenía aspiraciones de volver por sus pantuflas olvidadas, a menos hasta que llegara la próxima noche (si es que existe una, infirió). Se llevó ambas manos a la nuca y... ¡Maldición! ¿Dónde estaba su gorra favorita? Ni siquiera se dio cuenta que no la llevaba montada en la cabeza. ¿Habría quedado enzarzada en las ramas del álamo en el que cayó, cuando perdió la aspiradora? O en los columpios...

No. Ya no podía reconsiderar las consecuencias de sus actos. Tenía sueño, su cuerpo le clamaba que se echara a dormir. Se anidó en su cama. Los botines enmugraron las cobijas de lodo seco. Cerró los párpados. Qué delicia fue sentir el colchón dándole la bienvenida y el grueso edredón amparándolo en una cueva que lo apartaba del riesgo. Accedió a que su mente quedara en blanco, guardándose su primer secreto. A secas, Ariel irrumpió en la nación de los sueños.

Con insistencia, se le manifestó aquella terrible pesadilla. Iba corriendo a toda velocidad en la oscuridad, fatigado, perseguido por algo enorme y furioso. ¿Sería el vagabundo del parque? Estaba oscuro. Ariel no podía ver el camino que tenía delante. Tendría suerte si no se estampaba contra un muro de concreto aparecido de la nada.

Cuando la criatura casi lo alcanzaba, surgieron cinco luces que se embarcaron a dar vueltas alrededor de Ariel. Cinco, como la última vez. Así pues, cuando quiso desvelarle el rostro a la bestia...

El gato Félix anunció la hora de recibir la mañana.

—No es verdad —farfulló Ariel.

Calculó que no había pasado ni media hora de haber llegado a casa, con lo que supuso que el reloj estaba averiado. Era imposible que fueran las seis de la mañana. Vamos, no tardó tanto haciendo sus deberes de cazador. Cuando mucho, apenas sería la una de la madrugada. Procuró, en definitiva, ignorar los maullidos del gato Félix que, en determinado segundo, se apagaron. Volvió a cerrar sus ojos.

Entonces, oyó el paso del señor Villalobos, al otro lado de la puerta desvencijada, transportando a Alondrita en su silla de ruedas rumbo al baño, para asearla y vestirla.

—Por favor, no —se quejó Ariel, susurrando con agotamiento.

Alzó las colgaduras de la ventana y asomó medio perfil por el panel de cristal. En efecto, amanecía. El sol aclaraba el cielo en la alborada, encumbrando su corona como un trofeo universal.

—¡Arriba, holgazán! —saludó el señor Villalobos al otro lado del cuarto, con su habitual amabilidad matutina.

Como el castigo había concluido, el inaguantable padrastro retiró las cadenas que atrancaban el refrigerador y la despensa. Ariel fue por una caja de cereal y remató su contenido en un bol. El señor Villalobos aprovechó tal acción para emitir un comentario descalificador sobre la corpulencia de Ariel.

—No eres el único con necesidades nutritivas, gordinflón —insultó—. Echa la mitad de tu plato de vuelta a la caja. Limitando tu alimentación es como empezaremos a ahorrar en este maldito lugar.

El hijastro hizo lo que le ordenaron.

Al estar desayunando, zampándose atestadas cucharadas de hojuelas azucaradas, Ariel miró los imanes del refrigerador. Un año llevaban acomodados de la siguiente manera:

4L QU3 M4DRUGA DI05 LO AYUD4

La señora Rivas era la que ponía mensajes y refranes semanales en la puerta, combinando letras y números; le daba un toque divertido a la cocina. Sin embargo, había perdido el interés en dicho pasatiempo por distracciones relacionadas con la limpieza del hogar.

Vio Ariel a su madre entrar cojeando, con los pies adoloridos e inflamados de tanto trabajar. Aquella cogió su viejo mandil, colgado en la pared, y se lo amarró a la espalda en un nudo flojo.

—Buenos días —dijo, haciéndose sonar un poco alegre.

—Buenos días —respondió Ariel.

El señor Villalobos, que leía el periódico al otro lado de la mesa, arrugó el entrecejo.

—¡Buenos días! —dijo también, pero de mal genio.

Le dio un sorbo a su café y reanudó su lectura.

En la primera plana aparecían fotografías faciales en blanco y negro de los jóvenes que habían desaparecido a manos del Robaniños. Ariel estudió sus rostros. No los conocía, pero dispondrían más o menos su edad. En la nota se les invitaba a los habitantes de la ciudad que participaran en una brigada de búsqueda, con el propósito de explorar los sitios donde se les vio a los adolescentes por última vez: en el centro histórico, en la playa, en un campo de trigo, en la carretera rumbo a Villa Hermosa y en el bosque.

«Esa última fue muy cerca», reconoció Ariel.

La señora Rivas se puso a fregar el suelo con un trapeador viejo. Cuando se aproximó a trapear debajo de la mesa, Ariel levantó los pies. El señor Villalobos, por el contrario, no movió un solo pelo, salvo para darle vuelta a la hoja del periódico. Su mujer tuvo que arrodillarse, quejándose entre gemidos del dolor de várices. Solo así pudo infiltrar el trapeador en el sitio.

«Infeliz», pensó Ariel, examinando a su padrastro.

Sus próximas cucharadas las masticó con mayor fuerza. Recordó la transformación del anciano en un invencible titán de cuatro metros y le vino un escalofrío. ¿Cómo es que no pudo prevenir que algo así pasaría? El poder transformaba a las personas. En este caso, se dijo Ariel, el poder de las estrellas.

Ya no estaba tan seguro de que el vagabundo fuera humano del todo. Había muchas cosas que lo refutaban. Por ejemplo, sus ojos blancos y aumentados; sus dones físicos sobrehumanos; los de adivinación; comentarios extraños que tenían que ver con su edad, como que tardó décadas construyendo los saltines, y que llevaba *siglos* buscando al cazador de estrellas. ¿Cuántos años tendría? ¿Doscientos? ¿Quinientos?

«Jamás ha existido un hombre que haya vivido tanto», reflexionó Ariel, acercándose al final del plato.

Consideró la teoría de los vampiros, en específico que el veterano era descendiente del conde Drácula. Si bien, transmutarse en un gigante de dos pisos y comer lunares del cielo no entraba en el perfil vampírico.

Y otra cosa también. ¿Era posible que las estrellas formaran una alianza para defenderse y comunicarse entre ellas? El tipo puso una cara de preocupación cuando se le escapó divulgárselo.

«¡Y luego tienen un castillo!», pensó Ariel.

Según el señor Villalobos, las estrellas eran una

masa de plasma, compuestas por un gas de helio e hidrógeno. Aunque Ariel ya podía tomar esa información científica como un distraído error, porque también fue su padrastro quien le explicó que, para llegar a la estrella más próxima, bautizada Próxima Centauri, tardaría muchísimos años luz. Tantos, que no bastarían un montón de vidas suyas para culminar dicho viaje. A menos que contara con una nave espacial que anduviera a la velocidad de la luz, igual que en *La guerra de las galaxias*.

«¡Por favor!», se dijo Ariel, encubriendo una sonrisa.

A él le había bastado un pequeño salto para estar al lado, no de uno, sino de todos los cuerpos celestes existentes. «Es un pequeño paso para el hombre, pero un gran salto para la humanidad», fue la frase acertada que utilizó Neil Armstrong, el primer astronauta en caminar por la Luna, cuando transitó por terrenos desconocidos (Ariel rememoró las banderitas de distintos países que yacían en el satélite). Pero esa faena se quedaba corta con lo que había hecho Ariel: el primer ser humano que alcanzó las estrellas.

«Y también el responsable de aniquilarlas», recapacitó después, desdibujando su felicidad.

Hizo sonar el metal entre sus dientes.

—No muerdas la cuchara —regañó el señor Villalobos.

En conclusión, por lo que a Ariel respectaba, todo lo que su padrastro y los científicos deliberaban del universo no era del todo cierto.

Pero volviendo a lo mismo... ¿Para qué el viejo querría tantos luceros? Ariel seguía sin entender la afición que aquel tenía por devorárselos. No obstante, de lo que sí estaba seguro era que los deseaba no solo por adquirir juventud y alargarse excesivamente, sino por algo más. Un secreto que no revelaría tan fácil. Su ver-

dadero objetivo.

Por lo demás, ya no creía Ariel en su lastimera actuación de abuelito infeliz, como la primera vez que lo vio sentado en los columpios, quejándose de sus tormentos. Desde un inicio se comportó de forma extraña, descarada y bipolar.

«Pese a todo —se dijo Ariel—, estoy decidido a continuar con la misión, sin importar los riesgos y desenlaces que esta pueda tener. Espero que mi error de anoche pueda remendarse hoy.»

—Es extraño —comentó de pronto el señor Villalobos, al otro lado de la mesa. Le dio otro trago a su humeante taza de café y leyó—: «Astrónomos reportan que varias estrellas han desaparecido del cielo». —Acto continuo, ofreció su punto de vista—: Lo más probable es que hayan sido estrellas fantasmas, es decir, que murieron hace mucho tiempo y su luz apenas terminó de llegar al planeta hasta estos días —expuso con su acento fanfarrón—. Aunque eso no explica que hayan sido tantas a la vez.

El hijastro se quedó rígido, mientras miraba la imagen espacial en alta resolución que acababa de aparecer ante él. Según el pie de fotografía, fue tomada por un potente telescopio del extranjero.

Percibiendo un remordimiento, Ariel inquirió:

—Señor, ¿cree posible que alguien las haya robado?

Se arrepintió de haber preguntado.

Su padrastro estampó el periódico contra la mesa. Saltaron platos y cubiertos. La taza derramó un poco de café. La señora Rivas se sobresaltó, con el trapeador en mano. Corrió al lavatrastos y abrió el grifo, dejó correr el agua. En seguida, fue al otro extremo de la cocina y miró desafiante a su esposo. Se cruzó de brazos, envolviendo el palo del trapeador.

En ocasiones como esa, cuando el señor Villalobos

se irritaba, la señora Rivas solía hacer cosas raras. De momento, el padrastro observó la delgada corriente que caía a chorros en los platos sucios. Entornó la vista. Caminó al sitio dando pasos precisos. Después de girar la rosca del grifo, volvió a sentarse con rectitud en su silla.

—¿Qué clase de pregunta absurda es esa? —cuestionó—. ¿A qué te refieres con que «alguien se las robó»?

—Lo siento, abrí la boca de más...

—Claro que lo hiciste, siempre es así. ¿No te dije que te olvidaras de las historias de tu madre? No hacen más que volverte tonto.

Ariel miró a la silenciosa señora Rivas, que no articuló una sola palabra. Luego la vio marcharse de la cocina.

—Eso no es cierto, no fue por ninguna de sus historias —confesó Ariel, sin alzar demasiado la voz—. Es algo que se me ocurrió a mí. Ella jamás me contó algo relacionado con las estrellas.

Lo que defendía era incuestionable.

Ya iba más del año que su mamá dejó de leerle novelas y narrarle leyendas antiguas. Recordó Ariel el librero que había en su habitación, saciado de novelas. Meses atrás, el señor Villalobos se encargó de arrojarlos todos a la basura (bueno, casi todos), con la justificación de que era hora de que su hijastro cambiara la lectura infantil por obras científicas y enciclopedias. No contó el padrastro con que Ariel tendría el coraje suficiente para rescatar algunos de ellos, antes de que se los llevara el camión de la basura. El chico los escondió bajo el colchón de su cama. En ocasiones los leía a escondidas, después de entrampar la puerta de su alcoba con una silla.

—Como sea, ya conoces mi respuesta —aseguró el

padrastro—. Eres demasiado raro. Te caería bien la escuela militar de la que te hablé el otro día, podría enderezarte un poco. El Colegio Emilio Echeverría Álvarez. Cada vez estoy más convencido de inscribirte en él. Harto estoy de tu inmadurez. Si por las noches te permito esa tontería del Club de las Sombras con tu «media» hermana, es porque ella se encuentra en malas condiciones y es muy pequeña para comprender ciertas cosas. Pero en cuanto todo acabe, sé consciente de que delante de mí no volverás a pronunciar ninguna narración absurda. ¿Quedó claro?

Fue Ariel a cambiarse y a lavarse los dientes. Estaba enojado con su padrastro y su realística manera de pensar. Enojado por la sumisión de su madre. Enojado porque nadie refugiaba la esperanza de que Alondrita renacería de su enfermedad.

Avanzó a la habitación de esta última. A propósito de estar dormida, la niña sufría la peor fiebre de su vida. Acababan de serle cambiados fomentos de agua tibia en la frente y el abdomen. La señora Rivas estaba allí, acariciándole la cabeza. Sus ojos mantenían el antifaz de un mapache. Tenía la mirada desvelada y desanimada, a causa de sus llantos nocturnos. Llevaba cubierta la mejilla izquierda por un largo flequillo de pelo, en un intento desesperado por ocultar lo más oscuro de su matrimonio.

Le sonrió a Ariel y fue a envolverlo en un abrazo.

—Todo estará bien —le dijo—. No permitiré por nada del mundo que ese hombre te inscriba en el colegio militar.

Le cayó muy bien ese abrazo a Ariel. Respiró el aroma de su madre y la ira que lo quemaba quedó disuelta en un vaso de tranquilidad. Hacía demasiado que no le daban uno de esos, y se sintió fabuloso: la llama de un cirio encendido justo en el centro de su pe-

cho. Podía quedarse toda la vida así, bajo la cálida y amoratada piel de esa buena mujer.

Reveló, con todo, asomándose por encima del hombro de su madre, que Alondrita desplumó sus extremidades de las sábanas. En ese instante, la cristalización humana subió dos centímetros más, como la escala de un piano. Con horror, Ariel se enteró que su hermana fue diáfana hasta los hombros. No pudo conceptuar que la enfermedad haya aprovechado esa noche para cosecharse. Los bracitos de la niña, al flexionarse, indujeron a que el vidrio se arrugara aún con goce de blandura, ocasionando un ruido de cristal agrietándose.

La señora Rivas, ajena de lo que estaba sucediendo, le dio un beso reservado en la mejilla a Ariel y lo desenvolvió. Se marchó de la habitación. Él, por su parte, se aproximó a Alondrita. La niña, acorralada por múltiples cables, apenas pudo abrir los ojos y mirarlo a la cara.

—¿Viste a mamá? —preguntó, con voz débil.

Ariel afirmó, oliendo aquel aroma que todavía reinaba la habitación. Sentía en la espalda las manos de la señora Rivas y el beso en la mejilla.

—Me dio un abrazo, hace mucho que no lo hacía —dio a conocer Ariel.

—Quisiera que las cosas fueran como antes —mencionó ella.

—Yo también. Eso y que te alivies es lo que más deseo en el mundo.

Capítulo 10
La escurridiza espía

Salió Ariel del 72 en su bicicleta azul, cosa que Brandon Portillo aprovechó ese día para contar otro de sus tantos chistes de pacotilla:

—¿Qué es una pelota andando sobre ruedas? Pues Arielita Castillo Rivas en su bicicleta.

Y su cuadrilla de amigos rio de aquella tontería como hienas descerebradas.

—Ya se las verá conmigo —les dijo el Baladrón a sus escuchas—. Ayer, el muy idiota escapó de mí por la puerta trasera de la escuela. No sabe lo que le espera a la salida.

Ariel desertó su vehículo en el estacionamiento de bicicletas del patio principal y entró a la institución, encaminándose al salón de Historia.

Sonó el timbre, que plagió el ruido de una parvada de cuervos graznando. Por el corredor pulularon estudiantes y maestros apresurados, que desaparecían una

vez dentro de sus respectivas aulas. Ariel, en contraste, marchó pesadamente por falta de siesta, con las correas de la mochila enterradas en sus hombros.

No contó con que alguien le tocaría el brazo.

—Hola —lo saludó una sonriente alumna.

Se llamaba Ellie Durán, un nombre demasiado extranjero que levantaba los chistecitos de ciertas alumnas engreídas. Tenía trece, igual que Ariel, y cursaba sus estudios en otro grupo de segundo año. Ariel sabía quién era, no era muy diferente a él: solitaria, se la llevaba escribiendo en un cuaderno que solía aferrar bajo el brazo (justo como en ese momento) y tampoco era agraciada. Su casa, por cierto, quedaba cerca del domicilio de Ariel. Vivía en el número 46, así que, de cierta forma, se armonizaban como vecinos.

Ellie tampoco encajaba con el prototipo de las jovencitas que vivían en la calle Monteseaur: niñas de mejillas sonrosadas y regordetas, que evocaban a muñecas de porcelana. Sus mejillas, para empezar, eran todo menos sonrosadas. Durán era escuálida e insípida. Tenía el pelo encrespado cual arbusto en clima árido; usaba unas horripilantes gafas con extra aumento que hacían lucir sus ojos como dos frijolitos; en su boca predominaba un rosario de dientes chuecos, y poseía las cejas más pobladas que Ariel hubiera visto jamás. Se parecían al bigote del profesor Méndez, el mismo docente que el día anterior miró a Ariel siendo escoltado por Brandon Portillo al baño de varones, y que no hizo nada al respecto.

Ariel la observó hipnotizado. Sin pretensión de exagerar, era la primera vez que otro estudiante de secundaria le dirigía un saludo cortés.

—Te llamé como loca hoy por la madrugada, pero saliste huyendo. ¿Qué estabas haciendo en el parque tan tarde?

El cazador de estrellas meditó en ello.

«¿Cómo acaba de decir? ¿Hoy por la madrugada?», pensó.

¿En qué momento le había dirigido la palabra esa joven? Oh, un segundo. Claro que sí. Volvió la vista hacia atrás y refrescó el grito que lo nombró esa noche en la calle Monteseaur, mientras huía del gigante como un loco:

«¡Eh! ¡Espera, Ariel!».

Se había tratado de esa muchacha abriendo una ventana y llamándolo.

—¿Eres mudo o qué? —inquirió Ellie, malcontenta.

—Hola —respondió Ariel, en voz baja.

La joven sacó el cuaderno que tenía bajo el brazo y lo abrió. Había titulado la portada con marcador permanente de la siguiente manera:

Bitácora de Observación

PROPIEDAD DE

Ellie Durán

—A las 5:53 am saliste del parque abandonado. Parecías asustado, como si alguien te hubiera estado siguiendo —mencionó, repasando con la pluma unas líneas. Estudió la cara de Ariel y luego habló con ligereza—: Hubo una sacudida en mi casa, como un pequeño temblor. Investigué en Internet y no hubo ningún registro del incidente. Pero alcancé a ver una sombra, un animal grande o algo parecido, no estoy segura. Intuyo que eso fue lo que provocó el temblor. Además, la chimenea de la vivienda de al lado resultó destruida. ¿De ese animal escapabas?

Ariel no respondió.

—Por tu mal aspecto puedo deducir que no has dor-

mido nada en dos o tres noches —continuó Ellie—. Y ayer recibiste una buena paliza por parte de Brandon Portillo, según fuentes confiables. Planeas hacer algo importante, o ya lo estás ejecutando. Te he estado observando durante dos días seguidos. ¿Se puede saber cuál es tu secreto?

Ariel se sobresaltó. Pensó que Ellie hablaba de su «segundo secreto». Aquellos ojos pequeñitos, a través del cristal, lo observaron con esmero.

—Tengo que ir a clase —disintió Ariel.

Estaba aterrado. Lo habían estado investigando sin que se diera cuenta.

—Bueno, ¿qué asignatura tienes antes de receso? —preguntó ella, decisiva.

—Creo que Español —contestó, después de haber repasado su horario.

—Te enseña la profesora Nogueda, ¿no es así? Bien. Aula 18. —Lo anotó en su libreta—. Tengo Física con la profesora González a esa hora, pero me las arreglaré para escabullirme de su clase, antes de que suene el timbre. Estaré esperándote afuera del salón de Español. Nos vemos.

Durán se metió la bitácora bajo el brazo y marchó presurosa. Ariel se preguntó si la extrovertida adolescente habría averiguado más de la cuenta.

«Si llega a enterarse que soy el responsable de la desaparición de las estrellas, el anciano no se pondrá nada contento. Jamás curará a Alondrita y mis acciones habrán sido echadas en saco roto. Debo andarme con mucho cuidado», se advirtió.

Metió los pulgares en los tirantes de su mochila y caminó al módulo de Historia. Al llegar, la profesora Cuevas lo reprendió.

—Tres minutos tarde, Ariel.

«En definitiva, la maestra la trae contra mí», aclaró

Ariel consigo.

El día fue rutinario y aburrido. La profesora Cuevas hizo sus tediosas dinámicas de siempre, en las que tenían que reunirse en equipos y colaborar con sus compañeros para construir una línea de tiempo. Como si a Ariel le gustara mucho hacer eso. Siempre quedaba al final de las elecciones porque ninguno de sus compañeros quería hacer equipo con él. La profesora lo metió de relleno al que tenía menos integrantes y esto ocasionó quejas y miradas en blanco.

—Ya estamos completos, profesora. No necesitamos la ayuda de Ariel —discutió Rebecca—. Siempre hace las cosas mal y arruina los trabajos, no sabe prestar atención. Aparte está loco, se la lleva hablando solo.

—¡Guarden silencio! —exclamó la docente, elevando la voz—. Ariel estará trabajando en este equipo y punto. De no ser así, habrá consecuencias para cada uno. ¿Quedó claro?

Rebecca y sus amigos fulminaron a Ariel con la mirada.

—Sí, maestra —respondió la antipática chica.

—Bien —dijo la profesora Cuevas, dándoles la espalda—. ¡Empiecen a trabajar!

Ariel acomodó su escritorio entre los cuatro alumnos que formaban el equipo.

—Gracias, *Cerdoman* —le susurró Rebecca—. Espero que nos sirvas de algo. Ten estos marcadores.

Lo único que llamó la atención de Ariel durante la jornada escolar, cabe destacar, fue cuando la profesora Nogueda, en la clase de Español, leyó el fragmento de una novela. La obra trataba de un grupo de niños que quedó atrapado en una isla tras sufrir un accidente de avión, sin compañía de adultos. Ariel se sintió identificado con un personaje llamado Piggy. Cuando la maestra leyó la escena violenta donde los demás asesinan al

antedicho, lanzándole una piedra desde un risco, los ojos de Ariel vertieron lágrimas. Meditó que era una historia desgarradora, cruel, pero inmensamente acertada si se comparaba con la naturaleza humana. Si los treinta alumnos de su clase estuvieran viviendo la misma situación que en *El señor de las moscas*, Brandon Portillo, Olegario Rocha y Rebecca Solís habrían acabado, en menos de veinticuatro horas, con las vidas de la mitad de los estudiantes.

El timbre anunció la hora de descanso y los alumnos salieron con caras aburridas. Nadie saboreaba tanto la hora de lectura como lo hacía Ariel.

—Pensé que no ibas a salir nunca —le dijo Ellie en cuanto emergió aquel del salón.

Tenía la espalda recargada en la pared adyacente al aula 18. Ariel avanzó sin prestarle atención. Ella lo siguió y abrió su libreta.

—Ariel Castillo Rivas —leyó Ellie en voz alta, siguiendo las notas que había escrito en las últimas páginas—. Un chico extraño que no tiene amigos. Durante los recesos conversa consigo mismo y mira la lejanía pensando cosas. Pero la cuestión es... —Lo volteó a ver—: ¿En qué tanto piensas? ¿Tienes un problema? Puedes contármelo, prometo no burlarme de ti.

Ariel se detuvo y la contempló. Ya recordaba algunos de los apodos que le decían a esa chica: *Cuatro Ojos*, *Dientes de Castor* y *Cejas de Chewbaca*, aunque estaba también el más antiguo de todos: la *Lombriz Solitaria*, porque era muy delgada y siempre escribía en soledad.

—Yo pienso en mis asuntos, en mis historias —respondió el tajante, con el objeto de que Ellie perdiera el interés en él.

—Vaya. ¿Inventas cuentos?

—Sí.

—¿Me permites leerlos? —pidió.

—Los digo en voz alta, no los escribo.

—Entonces, ¿podrías narrarme uno?

—No. Solo se los confío a mi hermana.

«¿Cómo podré quitármela de encima?», pensó.

—Deberías anotar tus historias en una libreta, así podrás guardarlas por siempre. Te puedo asegurar que escribir es uno de los actos más apasionantes que existen en el mundo. Mi psicóloga, la señora Kim, es excelente consejera. Ella fue quien me recomendó tener un diario conmigo en todo momento, para registrar los datos que atestiguo durante el día. De esa forma, nació mi deseo de convertirme en detective. Cuando tenga la mayoría de edad y acabe mis estudios universitarios, seré reconocida por muchísima gente gracias a resolver casos difíciles, como los que se relatan en los libros de Sherlock Holmes.

—Sí, creo haber escuchado el nombre de Sherlock en algún lugar —dijo Ariel.

—¡Qué? ¿Estás tomándome el pelo? ¿Crees haber escuchado su nombre? —rugió, como si le hubieran faltado el respeto—. Claro que lo has oído. Es Sherlock Holmes, el caballero que resuelve crímenes que la policía no puede solucionar. Me habría encantado ser su compañera de trabajo. Claro, si el señor Holmes hubiera existido de verdad.

Llegaron al comedor, un patio amplio refugiado bajo altos techos de lámina, donde los demás estudiantes corrían y jugaban frescos. Otros consumían sus alimentos en las mesas del comedor, frente a la cooperativa, e intercambiaban el almuerzo con sus amistades. Ariel detuvo su marcha y observó a su acompañante.

—Mira, Ellie, fue un gusto conocerte, y me da pena decirte esto, pero estoy mejor solo. Como lo anotaste en tu diario: «No me agrada mucho la compañía», igual

que a ti, supongo. Somos ermitaños —anexó.

Ella lo analizó en silencio. No le sentó para nada bien el último comentario.

—Si estoy sola es porque trabajo en mi futuro —repelió—. Tú, en cambio... Nadie tiene idea de lo que haces.

—Lo siento.

—Bueno, por lo menos lo intenté —dijo ella, cerrando su cuaderno con tristeza—. Pensé que podía conocerte mejor y así revelar tu secreto.

—¿Cuál secreto? ¿De qué estás hablando? —interpeló Ariel, desconfiado.

—Lo que haces por las noches en el Parque de Juegos Monteseaur. ¿Qué otra cosa si no?

Ariel se cruzó de brazos.

—No puedo decir nada.

Miró Ariel a los alumnos que jugaban pateando el balón, en la cancha que se localizaba al otro lado del comedor. Luego se fijó que de una mesa a otra se lanzaban avioncitos de papel con mensajes secretos. Vio a los adolescentes tan despreocupados y alegres, que inclusive le dio un poco de envidia pensar en sus perfectas vidas. Como ellos no tenían a nadie en casa sufriendo de una cristalización humana...

—De acuerdo —mencionó Ellie malhumorada—. Pero te aviso que lo descubriré de todas formas. Continuaré investigándote.

Y se marchó rechinando los dientes, con todos los colores subidos al rostro.

Corrían las dos de la tarde, treinta minutos después de la hora de salida. Ariel se ubicaba en uno de los compartimentos del baño de varones, refugiándose de Portillo. No deseaba que el Baladrón le pusiera el otro ojo

morado, ni que el señor Villalobos lo tachara una vez más de cobarde. Inmóvil y silencioso, se colgó su mochila del hombro y se aventuró a abrir la puerta. Los alumnos del turno vespertino ya se encontraban en clases. Salió de los aseos con cautela y avanzó por un estrecho pasillo conectado al corredor principal. Daba la apariencia de una T. Ariel dobló por la izquierda y se topó con la profesora Nogueda, que cerraba su aula. Sobre el dintel del acceso se exponía el número 18, y debajo de este, con pulida fuente de Broadway, la palabra **ESPAÑOL**.

La docente llevaba un pilar de trabajos en su brazo izquierdo, en el otro, bolsas de plástico. Portaba en el hombro su conocido maletín de imitación de piel de tigre. Odiaba los artículos y ropa de piel de animales, pues siempre los consideró una barbarie de la humanidad. Como de costumbre, tenía el maletín tan atiborrado de carpetas que se veía a punto de reventar.

La profesora dio vuelta a la llave y el edificio de papeles que cargaba alzó el vuelo. Las hojas cayeron disgustadas y se mantuvieron agonizando en el suelo.

—¡Oh! —musitó la profesora Nogueda. Después detectó a Ariel en el pasillo—. Ariel. ¿Qué haces aquí? —expresó, cogida por sorpresa—. Hace más de media hora que salieron los estudiantes. —Al no recibir respuesta, dijo—: ¿Podrías ayudarme con esto?

Ariel accedió y rejuntó los papeles. Sin musitar palabra alguna, acompañó a la profesora hasta su automóvil, un *Saturn* color plomizo. Pese a que ella insistió en sacarle conversación, el chico respondió con oraciones concisas y movimientos de cabeza. Juntos metieron las cosas en el maletero. Al terminar con la tarea, Ariel volteó en dirección al cicloparqueadero. Quiso romper en llanto, mas contuvo las lágrimas por hallarse en presencia de una docente.

Su medio de transporte, que encadenó por la mañana, se hallaba en un estado penoso. Tenía las llantas desinfladas, la cadena rota y el manubrio chueco. Pero lo que más le dolió a Ariel fue el hecho de que aquella bicicleta había sido un obsequio de su madre. La señora Rivas había trabajado en una lavandería durante un mes, a escondidas del señor Villalobos, y con el sudor de su frente logró comprarla. Inventó a su marido que la había encontrado, por casualidad, en un bazar a un precio accesible.

—No puedo creerlo, Ariel. Los muchachos no tienen límites. Se lo diré a la directora —comentó la irritada profesora Nogueda. Cerró la puerta de la cajuela—. ¿Tienes idea de quién pudo haber sido?

Ariel lo sabía. Claro que lo sabía. Aquella atrocidad era producto de Brandon el Baladrón.

—No tengo idea —mintió.

La cara le ardió de rabia y tristeza.

—Si quieres puedo darte un aventón a tu casa y así aprovecho para platicar del tema con tu padrastro —sugirió.

El despechado Ariel se negó, sacudiendo la cabeza. Aquella visita de su maestra en casa solo empeoraría las cosas. Miró el suelo, desencadenó su vehículo y huyó como una bala.

—¡Aguarda! No te vayas —gritó la profesora.

Pero él ya iba demasiado lejos, intentando hacer girar las lesionadas llantas de aquella inservible cosa. La profesora Nogueda lo miró desaparecer en el doblez de la calle.

—*Lady Arielita*, ¿adónde crees que vas? —escuchó Ariel que dijeron a sus espaldas.

Portillo había seguido sus pasos, escoltado de Olegario Rocha y dos chicos de tercer año. Sus nombres eran Octavio Valenzuela y Raúl Quijano, un par de sus

secuaces. El bravucón se detuvo frente a Ariel y más tarde de apuntar la bicicleta con su dedo, lanzó una carcajada desagradable. Los acompañantes ensayaron la acción y constituyeron un coro de risas.

—¿Qué le ocurrió a tu bicicleta? —preguntó Brandon—. ¿Es que comiste tanto que la apachurraste con tu trasero de vaca?

Más risas. El rostro de Ariel se ruborizó. Sus lágrimas, ahora secas, le perfilaron dos carreteras.

—¿Dónde estuviste metido? —interrogó Olegario.

—¡Calla, *Niño rata*! Yo soy el que hace las preguntas aquí —dijo Portillo. Luego repitió—: ¿Dónde estuviste metido, *Cerdonio*?

Ariel se mordió la carne interior de los cachetes. Temblaba de enojo. Lo que el tirano de Brandon había hecho ese día fue una verdadera villanía. Estaba harto de él y de Olegario. ¿Por qué no era valiente? ¿Por qué si podía llegar al cielo y robar las estrellas, salir victorioso en la persecución de un horrible gigante por la madrugada, y soportar los problemas de casa, no era capaz de oponerse a él?

Volteó Ariel hacia un lado y su sentido chocó, casualmente, con la entrada del parque abandonado. Los cacharros viejos, vistos a la luz del día, parecían esculturas cobrizas de una civilización antigua.

«Qué alivio», se dijo.

Concibió que estaba en los límites de la zona segura, en la calle Monteseaur, por lo que Brandon no podía hacerle daño.

—*Puerquín*, te acabo de hacer una pregunta. ¿Dónde estabas? —presionó Portillo.

—Escondiéndome de ti —respondió, sin pretensión de publicarse valiente.

Los amigos de Brandon volvieron a reír.

—¿En dónde? —sonsacó aquel.

—En los baños —reveló.

—Sabes que esconderte de mí —le decía el bravucón, acercándose— te da la oportunidad de recibir un golpe extra, ¿verdad? Creo que te expliqué a la perfección las reglas de mi jueguecito.

Olegario asintió con la cabeza.

—Sí, se lo dejaste bien clarito desde el principio —lo apoyó—. Se merece un castigo.

—Ya no eres tan valiente como cuando me llamaste «cabeza hueca» el otro día, ¿no es así, *Sucia-bola-de-grasa*? —enunció—. Se te acabó el teatrito.

Hizo su intimidante posición de boxeador, reconocida por el cuerpo estudiantil del instituto, y comenzó a saltar de un lado a otro, rodeando a Ariel. Le lanzó un golpe en el hombro, aquel lo esquivó. Olegario y los muchachos sonrieron emocionados, soltando otra tanda de carcajadas. Lo que ellos querían presenciar era sangre y dientes volando a cámara lenta. Ariel se cuestionó por qué les enardecía vigilar esa clase de espectáculos violentos.

—Déjame recordarte mis condiciones —dijo Portillo—. Ya van dos días que te escabulles de mí. Eso me regala dos golpes complementarios. Entonces, contemos: el golpe de ayer, otro de hoy, más los dos extras son uno, dos, tres y...

—Suman Cuatro —intervino Olegario—. Cuatro golpes.

—Sí. —Sonrió Brandon estúpidamente—. Cuatro trancazos. ¿Estás listo?

Ariel se estremeció. Dudó si la tiza invisible de la calle Monteseaur funcionaría de verdad. Debía hacerlo, se dijo. La tiza lo salvó del monstruo en la madrugada, no pudo ser casualidad. Tenía que salvarlo una vez más.

Brandon apuntó a su cara y...

Lamentó Ariel que la zona segura fuera otro producto de su imaginación, como los gigantes dormidos. Y todo, como especificaba el señor Villalobos, por no ser realista. Sus labios se reventaron entre aquellos fornidos nudillos, perdió el equilibrio y soltó el manubrio de la bicicleta. El vehículo cayó al suelo; la cadena se deslindó de la llanta trasera. Entrevió el chico a Portillo con los ojos de un cervatillo al que recién le fue clavada una flecha en el bosque.

El bravucón continuó con su pose de atleta: puños en alto y pies danzando.

Faltaban tres lesiones.

Ariel intuyó que venía el próximo trompazo y levantó los brazos en defensa propia. La fuerza del siguiente golpe se descargó sobre su ancho hombro. Olegario y los otros chicos vitorearon con entusiasmo.

—¡Miren nada más! *Arielita* sí que tiene agallas —se burló el Baladrón, al percatarse de que Ariel aspiró a darle cara en la batalla con sus puños en alto—. Veamos qué tan bueno eres peleando.

A Ariel se le agarrotaron los músculos de las piernas, sin embargo, usó la única pizca de valentía que corría dentro de él en esos momentos. Despidió su primer puñetazo y Brandon lo esquivó fácilmente. Sus acólitos aplaudieron.

—¿Es todo lo que puedes dar? ¡Qué patético eres! —humilló Portillo.

Y atacó, esta vez remitiéndole un trancazo a Ariel en las costillas. Un dolor agonizante hizo que la víctima se retorciera. Se le fue el aire de los pulmones y tuvo que bajar la retaguardia. Especuló que no volvería a respirar y moriría asfixiado. Brandon aprovechó su estado de indisposición para atestarle el tercer porrazo en la sien, casi en la oreja. El atarantado Ariel miró, una fracción de segundos, sombras rojas y ama-

rillas. No pudo mantenerse mucho más tiempo en pie. El suelo le abrió paso para recibirlo de frente y se dejó caer. No le suplicó a su atacante que parara. Jamás lo hacía. Lo único que le quedó por hacer fue echar un vistazo, con la cara ensangrentada, a la tupida hierba del Parque de Juegos Monteseaur. Se preguntó si el anciano estaría oculto tras ella, siendo espectador de la pelea. Disfrutándola a lo grande porque Ariel arruinó la segunda misión y esta sería una clase de venganza. Se lo imaginó comiendo palomitas de maíz y dándole sorbos a una bebida gaseosa congelada.

«Ayúdeme», le suplicó Ariel.

Brandon se aproximó y le propinó el último golpe: una patada en el abdomen.

Ariel expulsó un sonido de «¡hug!» y se dobló de sufrimiento, abrazándose a sí mismo. Albergó la esperanza de que el viejo aparecería, dando un espectáculo con su cuerpo descomunal. Aquella manada de peleoneros no se volvería a meter con él jamás.

«¡Ayúdeme!», clamó Ariel otra vez.

Brandon, Olegario, Octavio y Raúl lo aprehendieron de sus cuatro extremidades, siguiendo instrucciones del primero, y lo arrebataron del suelo.

—¡Uf! Cómo pesa —protestó Olegario.

—¿Qué esperabas? Es una vaca —bromeó Raúl.

Lo trasladaron hasta un depósito de basura. Brandon desatascó la cubierta. Después de olfatear el interior, ostentó una cara de triunfo.

—Arrojémoslo dentro.

Lo echaron juntos a la porquería, sobre un montón de desperdicios diarios. Al instante, Ariel respiró un asqueroso aroma a carne podrida.

—Nos vemos mañana en la escuela, *Puerquín* —cantó Brandon. Lanzó dentro la mochila roja del atormentado y cerró el contenedor—. Si es que alguien te

libera de aquí antes.

El cazador de estrellas observó a sus enemigos por una rendija. Reían y contaban a modo de chiste lo que acababa de pasar. Experimentó arcadas, a causa de la rabiosa peste. Creyó haber tocado los huesos de un pollo y el cadáver agusanado de un gato. Aguardó a que el bravucón y su equipo de lacayos se hubieran marchado. Cuando ya no recibió sus machacantes voces, alzó los brazos para empujar la tapa de la prisión. Pero Portillo se encargó de no dejarle una salida difícil. Había atrancado la tapa. Ariel respiró por la boca, no obstante, no pudo sobrellevarlo más. Se vomitó encima, embarrándose la camisa blanca con los cereales del desayuno y unas papitas con queso que se engulló durante el receso, luego de su discusión con Ellie Durán.

Se dedicó a gritar.

Nadie atendió su socorro. De hecho, no lo escucharon hasta dos horas más tarde, ya que su nariz se acostumbró, en parte, a la hediondez. Escuchó pasos aproximándose y pidió ayuda a alaridos. El depósito fue abierto al minuto y dio un salto al exterior con la mochila aferrada. Cayó de bruces.

A la vez que aprovechaba el aire limpio y fresco, agradeció a su rescatista.

—Gracias —dijo, con la boca adolorida.

—No tienes por qué agradecérmelo, solo vine a tirar la basura de mi casa. Tenía que hacerlo —respondió Ellie Durán, echando un par de bolsas al contenedor.

No parecía asombrada, ni mucho menos preocupada. Todavía se entreveía molesta porque Ariel no le confesó lo que hacía por las noches en el parque recreativo. Pero la miró diferente. Algo había cambiado en ella. Tenía el mismo pelo ensortijado, cejas pobladas, los mismos lentes y dientes chuecos, pero ¿por qué Ariel, al presente, la miraba tan... interesante?

Tal vez, caviló, porque acababa de salvarlo y se convirtió en su heroína.

—Prometo que te lo contaré, todo sobre mi secreto —le dijo, poniéndose de pie—. Pero no es el mejor momento —susurró, lanzando un vistazo al parque.

—Tienes razón —concordó ella, tapándose la nariz—. Primero necesitas darte un buen baño. ¡Hueles a cadáver! ¿Eso es vómito? —preguntó.

Se miraron a los ojos. Hubo algo extraño. Ariel sintió una presión en la entrepierna, debajo del pantalón. Sintió vergüenza de que Ellie lo notara. Nunca le había ocurrido semejante cosa. La encontraba tan atractiva, tan diferente...

Se dio la vuelta para sitiar su embarazoso problemilla. Al mismo tiempo, comprobó que su desfigurada bicicleta continuaba en el mismo lugar donde la desatendió.

—¿Nos vemos mañana en la escuela? —preguntó él, indeciso.

—Claro —replicó Ellie, con un estado de ánimo discordante al que tenía antes de que Ariel le diera la buena noticia.

El muchacho la juzgó satisfecha y caminó con su bicicleta por la calle Monteseaur, dejando un celaje vaporoso de pestilencia por donde cruzaba. Cuando casi llegaba a su casa, advirtió que la entrometida señora Corrales lo espiaba desde una ventana, simulando que sacudía con una escobilla sus horribles cortinas, que parecía haberlas conseguido de un sofá antiguo. La ignoró y metió el vehículo en la cochera. Cubrió la bicicleta con una manta vieja. Quizá podría arreglarla antes de que el señor Villalobos la echara en falta.

Lo primero que hizo al entrar a la vivienda fue quitarse la ropa y darse un baño a conciencia. Se secó con la toalla y se miró los golpes en el espejo. Su gemelo

tenía la mitad de la cara hinchada y los labios partidos. Un moretón había surgido en su abdomen.

Se cambió y visitó a Alondrita, quien ya había zanjado lo peor de la fiebre. Como aquella estaba durmiendo, Ariel solo se acercó y le dio un beso en la frente. Contempló sus brazos de cristal, que en ese momento cambiaron de posición, resonando.

Se marchó al patio trasero y preparó un balde con suavizante de ropa. Se dispuso a lavar su uniforme con jabón en el lavadero.

—¿Qué te pasó en la cara? —le preguntó su mamá, que pintaba de blanco las tablas del cerco.

Dejó la brocha y la cubeta. Se le acercó. Lo tomó de la barbilla, obligándolo a observarla.

—Tu hermoso rostro —dijo—. Cada día que llegas de la escuela tienes peor aspecto. Me tienes muy preocupada. ¿Fue Brandon, otra vez?

—No quiero hablar de eso, mamá —musitó.

—Esto no se va a quedar así. Mañana mismo pondré a ese abusivo en su lugar.

—Yo prefiero que no. —Talló la mancha ambarina de vómito con el cepillo.

—¿Y por qué no? —quiso saber la señora Rivas con tenacidad, una actitud rara en ella—. Soy tu madre.

—Porque yo mismo debo resolver mis problemas.

—Parece que estoy escuchando la viva voz de tu padrastro —comentó desilusionada—. No puedo creerlo.

—Y yo no puedo creer que te hayas casado con ese hombre tan horrible.

El gesto enojado de la señora Rivas cambió a una mueca de vergüenza.

—Bueno..., eran otros tiempos —balbuceó—, yo era muy joven. Solo te tenía a ti, estaba sola, había mucha necesidad por aquellos días. El hambre es un sufrimiento terrible.

—¿Me puedes hablar de mi verdadero padre? —preguntó Ariel, poniendo en pausa su tarea.

—Sabes que no me gusta hablar de eso.

—Si me dijeras una sola cosa de él, no te lo volvería a preguntar.

—¿Qué más quieres saber, Ariel? Nos abandonó —respondió, en tono resentido—. Nos dejó de patitas en la calle en el peor momento de nuestras vidas y nunca se preocupó por nosotros. Jamás nos quiso. Fin de la conversación.

La señora Rivas dio media vuelta, cogió la brocha de la cubeta y siguió pintando la valla.

No volvieron a mencionarse una sola palabra el resto del día.

Capítulo 11
El interior del castillo

El cuidadoso Ariel reapareció en la habitación de Alondrita a las once en punto, sin promover un solo ruido. Había estado evitando encontrarse con el señor Villalobos a lo largo de la tarde. Halló a su hermana dormida, con sudor en la frente. La calentura había retornado a las ocho. Alondrita tenía la piel lívida, como maniquí de cera. Esta abrió los ojos al sentir la presencia de su hermano mayor y esbozó una sonrisa.

—Hola.

—¿Cómo te sientes? —preguntó él, tomando su manita de cristal, que era delgada igual que el tallo de una planta.

—No muy bien —respondió en voz baja, después de toser. Sus dedos repiquetearon dentro de sus escudos nocturnos—. Ariel, ya está mejorando tu ojo, pero ¿por qué hoy tienes la cabeza hinchada? —Abrió más la mirada, con la voluntad de revisarlo—. ¡Y mira tu boca!

Está partida. ¿Me puedes explicar cómo te haces esos golpes?

Ariel se tocó la cara, sin saber qué manifestarle. Antes de responderle, colocó un suero nuevo en el atril de acero inoxidable, hizo los ajustes necesarios, revisó el electrocardiógrafo, apartó el ejército de cables de la cama y se reclinó a un costado de Alondrita. Al final, lo único que le confesó fue:

—Falta de valentía.

—¡Qué va! Si eres la persona más valiente que conozco. De otra forma, los personajes de tus cuentos no serían valientes, ¿qué no? —reconoció ella—: A veces quisiera ser más como tú.

—No sabes ni lo que dices, princesita —repuso riendo—. Y no te preocupes, ya se me quitarán estos moretones —explicó, ruborizándose. No quiso seguir hablando del tema, por lo que sacó la linterna del Club de los Cuentos de las Sombras—. ¿Estás lista para reanudar la historia de la princesa que enfermó? —preguntó.

Ella susurró un «sí» muy quedito y Ariel cayó en cuenta de su agotamiento, enmascarado por la emoción de una niña feliz que hace todo lo posible por mantenerse despierta. Apagó Ariel la lamparita de la cómoda y se ajustaron a oscuras. Accionó la luz de la linterna. Pronto, las mismas siluetas actorales de la otra vez se dibujaron frente a un imponente castillo. La princesa Aura agitó una mano en el aire para saludar a su público. El corcel inclinó la cabeza. Alondrita los recibió con una cordial y discreta bienvenida.

—Al llegar a las afueras del castillo —empezó Ariel—, la princesa Aura amarró su caballo en una cerca de hierro. Los animales, como bien sabes, no pueden introducirse a los grandes palacios. Antes de subir por las escaleras exteriores, se percató la doncella de

que había un sinnúmero de hormigas caminando por el suelo. Corrían hasta su lugar y alzaban las patitas delanteras. Le pareció a Aura un comportamiento extraño en ese tipo de insectos, pero nunca se le cruzó por la cabeza que procuraban comunicarse con ella. Las ignoró y continuó su marcha.

En el muro, la damisela subió la larga escalinata del palacio con la espalda arqueada, agotada por su enfermedad, a la vez que en cada escalón un grupo de hormigas intentaba llamar su atención.

—Al abrir la enorme puerta de entrada entrevió un vestíbulo lujoso con pinturas colgadas en las paredes, muebles valiosos avecinados a los alrededores y alfombras rojas revistiendo el suelo. En cada esquina había armaduras de acero que, o eran adornos para la decoración del lugar, o fueron utilizadas por alguno de los caballeros del pueblo antes de desaparecer, porque se miraban muy sospechosas, como si alguien estuviera morando en su interior. Sobre sus yelmos, una pirámide de hormigas se las arregló para no desmoronarse. Formaron las letras A, Y, U y D. Pero Aura no se esmeró en aplaudir su espectáculo cirquero. Estaba más preocupada en coincidir con un humano, que por divertirse con insectos acróbatas.

»Transitó por varios corredores que se interconectaban entre sí. Dos veces allegó a un pasillo por el que en ya había pasado, con lo que deliberó que aquella era una trampa laberíntica para confundir a los visitantes. De improviso, la asaltó una idea.

—¿Qué cosa? —preguntó Alondrita.

—¿Recuerdas aquel collar de perlas que le regaló el príncipe del que se enamoró? El que conoció en el baile de despedida que organizaron sus padres.

—Sí, me acuerdo —respondió dichosa por saberse la respuesta.

—Pues ese mismo collar —decía Ariel—, se lo quitó y acordó en desbaratarlo. En cada sala por la que cruzaba, dejaba una esfera en medio. De modo que, si en su recorrido volvía a toparse con esa bolita, interpretaría que no debía cruzar por allí.

—¡Qué inteligente!

—Aprovechando su táctica, pudo dar con un acceso.

—¡No puede ser, Ariel! ¿Se encontró a la bruja?

Ariel alzó las cejas en señal de suspenso.

—La doncella empujó una puerta grande y pesada —refirió—, y autorizó su paso a una habitación de alguien perteneciente a la realeza. Había obras religiosas colgadas en los muros, una cama con cortinas azules, cierto juego de ajedrez empezado encima de una mesita y un armario con sus puertas abiertas, lleno de vestidos (con este último dato fue evidente que se trataba del dormitorio de una mujer). La pared del otro extremo constaba con una amplia ventana panorámica por la que podía mirarse el pueblo abandonado. Aura dio pasos cortos y reveló que había alguien en ese sitio.

Alondrita, lo que le sigue de emocionada, no perdió las palabras de su hermano.

—Una mujer de mediana edad la miró boquiabierta —reveló el narrador—. La desconocida se levantó del borde de la ventana echando lágrimas. Fue a abrazar a la princesa y le dijo:

»—¿Cómo lograste pasar el laberinto hechizado? ¡Gracias a Dios que llegó alguien!

»—De manera que era un laberinto encantado —observó Aura—. Ya decía yo que no eran pasillos comunes y corrientes. ¿Me puede explicar qué pasó aquí? ¿Dónde están todos?

»—Una horrible e impulsiva bruja —decía la extraña— maldijo este pueblo. Hizo que la gente se convirtiera en hormigas... Y a mí, que soy la reina, me dejó

aprisionada en mi alcoba con una barrera invisible que me impide salir.

—¡Ariel! —voceó Alondrita—. Ya entiendo por qué había tantas hormigas. Eran los habitantes del reino, queriéndole pedir ayuda a la princesa. Menos mal que Aura no pisó a ninguna.

—Acertaste —ratificó Ariel—. Aura también lo entendió después de la explicación de Su Majestad. Y la esencia de bondad que formaba parte de ella, la hizo sentir pena por la reina y le preguntó:

»—¿Cómo puedo ayudarle?

»—Tienes que encontrar a la bruja y arrebatarle el brazalete que lleva puesto en la mano derecha, allí es donde resguarda su poder —contestó—; es lo que la mantiene viva. Solo así nos liberarás a todos de esta agresiva condena. Justo ahora se encuentra descansando en la última torre del castillo. Pero deberás apresurarte, muchacha, porque la maligna duerme durante el día y... —Echó un vistazo rápido a la ventana— la noche está por caer. Si despierta y te encuentra aquí conmigo..., ¡huy! No sé de lo que será capaz.

»La princesa, de buen corazón y sin pensar en su necesidad, accedió en ayudarla.

»—Con los pasillos del castillo embrujados, no tengo ni la menor idea de dónde podría ubicarse la torre —reconoció la reina—. Solo me queda desearte buena suerte.

»Armándose de valor, Aura salió de la habitación e ingresó de vuelta al laberinto, que se tornó más difícil a partir ese punto. Ahora caminaba por pasillos rotos, llenos de agujeros, en cuyos fondos se entreveía una oscuridad aterradora; pasillos donde el techo y el suelo intercambiaban de puestos, mediante un distorsionado caracol, y la gravedad se alteraba. En esas situaciones, Aura presentía que el techo la traicionaría y la dejaría

caer sin previo aviso al otro lado, rompiéndole los huesos.

» Siguió empleando su estrategia de dejar una perla en los corredores. Hubo un pasillo por el que de plano no consiguió seguir avanzando, ya que sus pies resultaron estáticos, sujetados por algo invisible. Y por más que intentaba, no lograba hacerlos funcionar. Más tarde descubrió que si marchaba en reversa, sus extremidades se movían, pero al lado contrario. Es decir, cuando Aura caminaba hacia atrás, sus piernas rebeldes hacían lo opuesto a sus órdenes y recorrían la zona avanzando de frente. Jamás se había sentido tan confusa en toda su vida. Entre desplomes y quejidos, pudo salir del pasillo con éxito, aunque con heridas menores y algo mareada.

»Cuando metió la mano por última vez a la bolsa del vestido, descubrió que estas se terminaban. No tuvo más refugio que empezar a memorizar, mediante un mapa imaginario, sus próximas rutas.

»Se asomó por una ventana. Alcanzó a comprobar que el crepúsculo estaba a punto de desfallecer. Debía apresurarse. Tenía pocos minutos antes de que el cielo se enfundara con el velo de la noche.

»El siguiente pasillo fue más difícil de cruzar —informó Ariel, frunciendo los labios—. No era como los demás, carecía de alfombras y adornos, pero tenía mosaicos irregulares en el suelo (grandes, pequeños y de figuras geométricas diversas), que le daban la apariencia de una obra de arte. La trastornada princesa avanzó, pero cuando uno de sus pies tocó el diseño más próximo, que era del tamaño de un libro, todo a su alrededor se evaporó y se vio apareciendo al inicio del corredor. Asustada, eligió otro mosaico, uno apropiado en el que cupieron ambos pies; sin embargo, corrió con la misma suerte y reapareció en el sitio de antes. Que-

ría decir que, si deseaba llegar al otro lado del pasillo, debía apisonar las figuras del suelo en un orden específico.

»Decenas de veces cruzó por mosaicos incorrectos que la llevaron al empiece. Tardó cerca de media hora en superar aquella tediosa prueba, sumando más errores que fortunas. La respuesta acertada estuvo en formar una Z gigante que tocaba las cuatro esquinas de la habitación. Cuando escapó del pasillo, desesperada y con las piernas adoloridas, asomó su rostro por una ventana circular. Vislumbró que el disco anaranjado del Sol se ocultaba, casi por completo, tras una colina. Matices rosados entre las nubes eran las últimas señales que quedaban del día. Dando a entender que la bruja de la torre pronto se recobraría de su sueño.

»Aura dobló hacia la izquierda, por el corredor contiguo, y descubrió un agujero en la pared en forma de arco que marcaba el final del laberinto. Al otro lado, había unas escaleras que subían en círculo. «Este debe ser el camino hacia la torre más alta», pensó Aura.

»Subió los peldaños de piedra (que fueron demasiados) y entró a una habitación oscura y mohosa, de una sola ventana, donde dominaban el olor a humedad y a cebolla podrida.

»Había una cama con cortinas de velo blanco. Podía verse, a través de ellas, a alguien durmiendo. Aura se acercó y reveló a una vieja de nariz ganchuda y pelo suelto, que roncaba largo y tendido. Sintió pavor cuando descubrió que aquella descansaba con sus ojos abiertos, puesto que no tenía párpados. La princesa descarrió la mirada. Al prestar más atención al cuerpo de la anciana, se fijó que esta llevaba en su muñeca la pulsera que mencionó la reina. Sus dedos eran larguiruchos, con uñas afiladas. Aura acercó sus temblorosas manos a las de ella, y contempló los ojos vidriosos, que

parecían bolas de golf. Se dedicó a desabrocharle el brazalete.

»Fue en ese momento cuando se oyeron las aturdidoras campanas de la iglesia, que advirtieron el anochecer. No había campanero disponible que se hiciera cargo del trabajo (ya que también estaba convertido en hormiga), por lo que con seguridad la bruja se encargó de lanzar un maleficio a las campanas, a fin de que sonaran solas tras la puesta del Sol.

»El «ding dong» se repitió en la cabeza de Aura cual sinfonía de muerte, quien alzó la vista y sintió que una colonia de murciélagos le atravesó el pecho. La anciana se había despertado. Y lo supo porque sus enormes ojos de avestruz la estaban mirando.

»La hechicera lanzó un grito agudo y penetrante, que helaba la piel. Una escoba arruinada entró volando por la ventana lanzando despojos por donde pasaba. Derribó a la princesa, pero esta por nada del mundo soltó el brazo de la bruja.

»—¡Suéltame! —exclamó la vieja con voz chillona.

»Atenazó a Aura con su otra mano, clavándole las uñas. Aura permaneció firme, pese al miedo. Desabrochó el amuleto y ocurrió algo impresionante…

—¿Qué pasó, Ariel? ¡Dilo ya! —exigió Alondrita.

—Una onda potente reventó las ventanas del castillo, haciendo saltar cristales de colores en todas direcciones. La magia de la bruja, que estaba resguardada en el objeto, abandonó a su dueña. Su piel arrugada empezó a desvanecerse en un humo purpúreo, hasta que quedaron sus huesos protegidos por sus ropajes negros. La escoba mágica renunció a dar vueltas por el techo de la habitación y cayó al suelo. Ya no sería usada con otros fines más que hacer la limpieza.

»No pudo creer la doncella que había vencido a una poderosa hechicera. Soltó la pulsera sobre el colchón y

experimentó una pesada angustia en seguida de apreciar el esqueleto en la cama, cuyas cuencas vacías parecían estarla observando. Aura descubrió un bulto en las vestiduras de la bruja. Una forma sólida oculta. Alzó la tela. Rebuscó con la mano y encontró un frasquito del tamaño de un dedo pulgar...

A Alondrita se le iluminó el rostro por un momento. Su emoción, sin embargo, desapareció en cuestión de segundos y fue suplantado por un ceño fruncido.

—Hermanito, haz una pausa. Me duele mucho la cabeza.

—¿Quieres que le hable al señor Villalobos? —preguntó el preocupado Ariel.

—No, solo cerraré los ojitos un momento para descansar —resolvió—. Pensaré en cosas bonitas para que el dolor se vaya poquito a poquito. Quiero que sepas que la imaginación que me hiciste tener sirve más que todas las medicinas del mundo.

—Bueno, dejaremos la historia para otra reunión del Club de los Cuentos de las Sombras.

Ariel apagó la linterna.

Ninguno de los dos se percató en la despedida graciosa que hizo la sombra de la princesa Aura en la pared, meneando el brazo del esqueleto de la bruja. Ariel le dio un beso en la frente a su hermana y se levantó. Después acomodó los cables de la cama. Advirtió que la cristalización humana, justo en aquel momento, se afianzó al cuello de Alondrita.

—Nos vemos pronto, princesita.

—Buenas noches, Ariel.

Caminó a la salida y, siguiendo una de las reglas del señor Villalobos, dejó la puerta abierta.

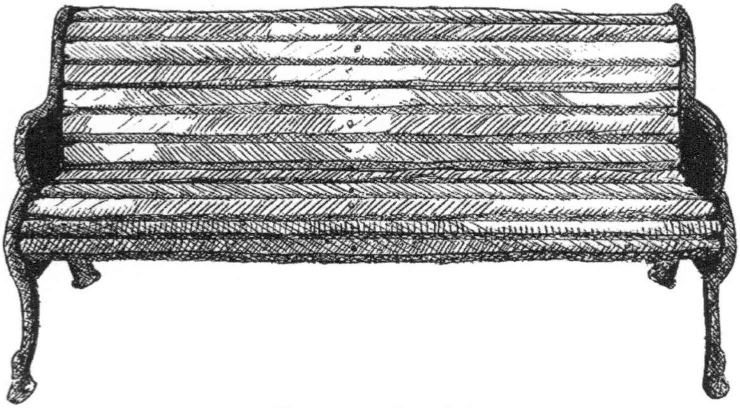

Capítulo 12
Diosa Venus

Ya en su habitación, el gato Félix le anunció a Ariel que faltaba media hora para que dieran las doce en punto. Sobraban minutos para encontrarse con el viejo. Lo que más quería el cazador de estrellas era acabar con su misión de una vez por todas, con tal de que Alondrita no siguiera sufriendo. Cogió su frazada azul y metió los pies a los saltines, que en realidad ya no eran tal cosa mágica, sino unos botines ordinarios, faltos de resortes.

Abrió la ventana. Lo primero que se le ocurrió fue, por alguna extraña razón, ir a la casa de Ellie Durán. ¿A qué? No lo sabía con seguridad. Pero no había dejado de pensar en su flameante cabello ensortijado.

Salió al exterior y caminó por la calle. Se cubrió con su manta. Cada día hacía más frío que el anterior. Cuando llegó a la vivienda 46, agarró cierta piedra pequeña del jardín y la arrojó contra una ventana (la que

vio abrirse por la madrugada). Las cortinas fueron corridas y salió una cara terriblemente molesta. El vidrio se deslizó.

—¿Qué crees que haces? Vas a romperme el vidrio —dijo Ellie en un tono poco amistoso, acomodándose las gafas.

Estaba despeinada, pero Ariel consideró que se miraba como la diosa Venus.

—¿Te gustaría hablar? —preguntó él mismo, casi balbuceando.

—¿Justo ahora? —Ellie miró un reloj que tenía a sus espaldas y exclamó—: ¡Son las once y media de la noche, Ariel! —anunció, como si fuera el fin del mundo. Luego de meditarlo un rato, musitó—: Pero está bien. Espérame. Primero tengo que ver si mi mamá y *su novio* ya no están en la sala —Puso la mirada en blanco.

—Muy bien. Yo *espero te* aquí —tartamudeó—. Perdón, quise decir aquí te espero.

Pasados cinco minutos, Ellie salió de puntillas con una bata de dormir puesta.

—¡Cielos! Qué frío está haciendo —comentó. Se sentó junto a Ariel en el jardín, sobre una banca proporcionada para dos personas—. ¿Y bien? ¿De qué quieres hablar?

Ariel no había pensado en ello y se sintió como un tonto.

—Pues... ¿Estabas dormida?

—La verdad no —respondió Ellie, como si estuviera preparada para esa pregunta—. Llevo noches que no concilio el sueño. Y te preguntarás por qué. Bueno, pues la última conversación que tuve con mamá me dejó pensando en muchas cosas. Oye, ¿puedo confiar en ti?

Ellie era muy elocuente, Ariel acababa de percatarse en ello. La chica era capaz de hablar de cualquier

tema de forma rápida y concisa, sin haber tenido tiempo de preparar un discurso.

—Claro —respondió Ariel. Y nunca había hablado tan en serio.

—No sé si aceptaré a Horacio, su novio, después del divorció con papá —confesó—. No lo he superado. A pesar de que Horacio parece buen tipo, no me agrada la idea de que tenga sus gestos cariñosos hacia ella, que se abracen, que se den besos. ¡Me provoca asco!

—¿Y él es buena persona? ¿Horacio? —preguntó Ariel, con honesto interés.

Su nueva amiga profundizó la pregunta.

—¿Buena persona? Erm... Parece que sí. Ya lo había pensado, sin embargo... —reflexionó unos segundos—. Mira, te platicaré algo chocante que me pasó hoy. Mamá insistió en que Horacio, ella y yo fuéramos al cine a ver una película. Quise portarme sangrona con él, pero después de conocerlo un poco confieso que es divertido. Hace rato compró pizza para los tres y jugamos lotería.

—Quiere decir que tu mamá es feliz con él, ¿verdad?

—Lo sé —reconoció, un tanto tensa—. Nunca antes la había visto tan contenta, ni siquiera cuando ella y papá estaban juntos. Eso es lo que me pone de mal humor: confirmar que jamás fueron felices y que estuvieron enlazados tantos años por compromiso. Por haberme tenido a mí.

—¿Y cómo es tu relación con él? Con tu papá —examinó Ariel.

Por un momento había olvidado que estaba congelándose. Lo único en lo que podía pensar, justo ahora, era en la situación de Ellie.

—En la tarde hablé con él por teléfono —replicó—. Dijo que vendría este fin de semana, pero (suspiró desilusionada) igual que la semana pasada y la otra, y la

otra, sacó la vieja excusa de que surgió «una reunión superior en la oficina, mi niña. No puedo faltar» —dijo Ellie—. En conclusión, cada vez creo menos en sus promesas y entiendo a mamá en ciertas cosas. No digo que no lo quiero, lo amo muchísimo. Pero me hallo en el dilema de aprobar o no a Horacio como padrastro. —Entonces, Ellie volteó al cielo y comentó de la nada—: Eh, es extraño lo que ha estado ocurriendo en el cielo, ¿no, Ariel? Las estrellas desaparecen sin más.

Ariel no estaba preparado para aquel comentario tan repentino.

—¿Qué? —dijo.

Desvió los ojos de Ellie y vio hacia arriba. Ya era bien sabido por la gente del globo terráqueo que el espacio exterior empezaba a negociarse desnudo. Prueba de ello estaba en el periódico que leía el señor Villalobos por la mañana.

—¿Qué te ocurre? —musitó Ellie, arrugando la frente—. ¿Por qué de pronto te comportas como si te hubieran sentenciado a una cadena perpetua? ¿Sabes lo que le está ocurriendo al cielo?

De los labios de Ariel brotaron sílabas absurdas.

Ellie se incorporó y lo apuntó con el dedo.

—Lo de las estrellas tiene que ver con lo que haces en el Parque de Juegos Monteseaur, ¿no es así?

—No... sé de qué hablas. —Se puso en pie.

—¿Me creerías si te digo que alcancé a ver una luz resplandeciente la otra noche, antes de que te fueras a tu casa? ¡Cómo me hubiera gustado grabarlo! El parque se iluminó como si hubieran estallado fuegos artificiales. Fue hermoso, como algo mágico. Luego de eso se fue volando un banco de luciérnagas. Sentí que estaba viviendo una escena de cuento de hadas.

—Creo que ya me voy. No fue buena idea venir aquí —dijo Ariel, tomando distancia.

—Y allá vamos otra vez —refunfuñó Ellie. Agarró una esquina de la frazada de Ariel y lo detuvo—. Esto no puede continuar así. ¿Vas a decirme tu secreto?

Ellie lo encaró lo suficiente como para que se vieran frente a frente.

—¿Y por qué llevas esos zapatos tan anticuados? —inquirió—. ¿Dónde están las pantuflas blancas que llevabas puestas ayer? No creas que no me di cuenta.

Era muy intuitiva, Ariel tenía que reconocerlo. Estaba Ellie enterada de cada uno de los movimientos que ejecutaba, y no daría su brazo a torcer tan fácil. Significaba que el cazador de estrellas se hallaba al borde de la cuerda floja. Si le contaba lo de su misión secreta a su primer amor platónico, lo perdería todo. Absolutamente todo.

—Lo siento, Ellie, tengo que irme.

—No intentes escapar. Voy a seguirte —desafió.

—No —rogó él—. Es muy peligroso.

Se percató, con todo, que Ellie se estremeció, como si hubiera visto algo aterrador en la oscuridad.

—¿Qué te ocurre? —inquirió el alarmado Ariel.

—Acabo de mirar algo raro —le contestó—. Estaba moviéndose en los árboles…

Ellie entrecerró sus ojos pequeñitos y los enfocó en dirección al parque abandonado.

—Quizá fue una ilusión óptica —explicó Ariel.

«¿Y si es el anciano? —pensó—. ¿Y si está oyendo nuestra conversación?».

Ariel no deseaba, por nada del mundo, que Durán atara los cabos sueltos y pusiera patas arriba su misión. Y tampoco quería que saliera herida.

—Mmm, una ilusión óptica, podría ser lo más lógico —opinó Ellie—. Aunque nada de esto lo es. ¡Oye! No quieras cambiarme de tema. Te acompañaré hasta el parque y me lo explicarás todo.

—Tú no lo entiendes —Alzo la voz, haciendo que Ellie se sobresaltara. Tuvo que esforzarse por domar sus nervios—. Correrías un riesgo si vas conmigo. Mira, prometo que te lo contaré, pero hasta dentro de unos días. Este no es el momento más apropiado.

—Entonces admites que tienes algo que ver con la desaparición de las estrellas.

No quiso responderle Ariel. Deseó negarse ante todo y abandonarla. Era posible que el viejo los estuviera acechando justo en ese segundo entre los árboles. Lo correcto era quedarse callado y mantenerse al margen. Mas cuando Ariel analizó los gestos faciales de Ellie y sus ojitos atentos, aguardando una respuesta, sus labios actuaron por sí solos.

—Sí. —Asintió, hablando lo más bajito posible—. No puedes decírselo a nadie. Una vida está de por medio. Entra a tu casa y finge que no te dije nada. Actúa con normalidad...

Ellie se llevó ambas manos a la nuca, anonadada.

—¿Estamos siendo observados, justo ahora, Ariel? ¿Nos están espiando? —susurró.

—Es lo más probable.

—Oh. ¿En qué lío te metiste?

—Haz lo que te dije: entra y disimula. Nos vemos mañana.

—Claro. Claro.

Se separaron y Ariel se marchó a toda prisa envuelto en su frazada, sin darse la vuelta. En medio del follaje de los árboles creyó haber visto una cabeza gigantesca.

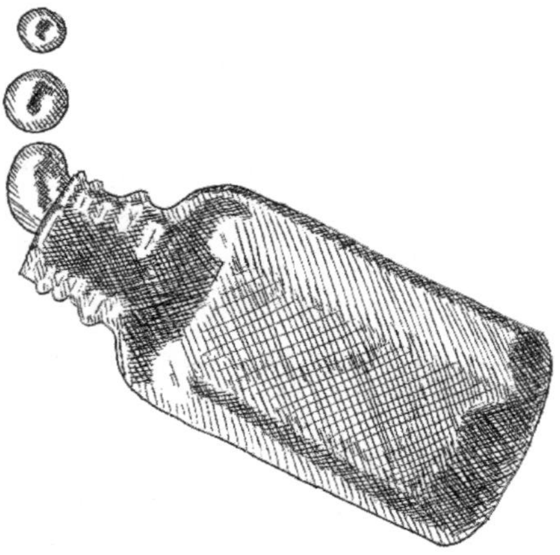

Capítulo 13
Pegaluz y antigrav

—Esta vez te será bastante difícil —dijo una voz imponente, que hizo un eco, antes de que el muchacho llegara al Parque de Juegos Monteseaur.

Mientras se aproximaba, Ariel advirtió que empezaba a nevar. Pero, al voltearse a la calle Monteseaur, averiguó que allá no había pizca de blancura. Singularmente en la zona del parque (y en ningún otro lado) caían copos en perfecta armonía.

—Guau —se dijo Ariel, absorto.

Del letrero de entrada colgaban carámbanos de hielo, los árboles parecían pelucas del siglo XVIII y la larga melena de león imitaba, entretanto, el pelaje de un oso polar. Las cadenas de los columpios yacían congeladas y en sus quietos asientos descansaban cerros inmaculados. Los pies del pacífico Ariel desampararon huellas en la nieve. Conforme avanzó, aquellas huellas

pronto se convirtieron en agujeros, y de agujeros a túneles abismales. Terminó hundiéndose hasta las rodillas. Y en ese punto, el frío se volvió tan insoportable que su manta no le sirvió de protección. Tiritando y con los dientes castañeando estudió los alrededores. Distinguió un par de pilares delgados que se movieron en la espesura. ¿O eran dos troncos cambiando de locación? Advirtió que, sin duda, eran las piernas del anciano, acercándose.

«Eso es lo que vimos Ellie y yo —comentó Ariel para sus adentros—. El vagabundo estaba espiándonos —confirmó—. Solo espero que no haya escuchado nuestra conversación.»

El veterano se paró frente a él. Conservaba su barba tiesa a causa del mal clima, aunque no se quejaba de las temperaturas extremas. Inclinó la cabeza con la quijada prensada y amoldó las manos a su cintura. Al parecer, seguía disgustado por la noche anterior. Y para afirmar esta teoría, sus ojos resentidos intimidaron al chico.

—Hoy acatarás mis reglas sin soltar una queja, cazador de estrellas —dijo aquel.

El suelo tembló con su voz, que sonó áspera y estruendosa, como si poseyera tambores en lugar de cuerdas vocales. Con las fuertes ondas de sonido, las ramas de algunos árboles se desligaron, dichosas, de la nieve pesada que las humillaba. El aterrado Ariel contempló al viejo con la nuca en la espalda.

—¿Qué te pasa? ¿Te comió la lengua el ratón? —preguntó el de arriba.

El gigante flexionó sus piernas en una sentadilla y acercó su cabeza (que sin exagerar era del tamaño de un sofá individual) al pequeño y regordete cuerpo de Ariel. Su altura era impresionante. Los brazos le colgaban del armazón cuales cuellos largos de jirafa.

—¿Te doy miedo? —preguntó el vagabundo.

Ariel asintió, con el labio inferior temblando más de pánico que por el frío.

—Muy bien. —Rio el insolente viejo—. Si te atemorizo tendrás una fuerte motivación para no equivocarte en la misión. Porque si cometes un error, por más minúsculo que sea, esta ocasión te voy a comer vivo, muchacho. Aunque podemos arreglar mi altura por ahora.

El sujeto comenzó a encogerse junto con su abrigo y adquirió las proporciones de una persona alta.

—¿Así está mejor? —cuestionó, llevándose las manos a la espalda—. Cada vez me siento con mayor fuerza, chico. Ya adquiero tamaño extra, si bien, por el momento tengo un límite de altura. Con las estrellas de esta noche conseguirás hacerme colosal como una montaña, y cuando me las coma todas, en las cacerías venideras, seré tan alto y tan ancho que ni te lo podrías imaginar. Además, tendré juventud y belleza, claro —anexó, sin darle mucha urgencia al último tema.

Ariel se atragantó con su propia saliva. ¿Para qué querría aquel indigente ser enorme, además de joven?

—¿Es un brujo? —osó preguntarle Ariel.

—¡Vaya! Miren nada más, el niño habla —expresó sarcástico—. Por supuesto que no soy un brujo. Me he encontrado a muchos de esa calaña. Son feos y tontos, siempre hacen las cosas mal. A excepción —corrigió—, de una hechicera que conocí cierta ocasión. La más inteligente, calculadora y poderosa de todas… Hum, pero eso no tiene ninguna relevancia al día de hoy.

Ariel inmortalizó a la bruja sin párpados del cuento que le estaba narrando a Alondrita. Misma que fue derrotada por la princesa Aura cuando le desabrochó su brazalete archivado de poder.

—Entonces, ¿qué cosa es usted? —preguntó.

—Mejor que no lo sepas.

—Pero humano no, ¿verdad?

—Lo obvio no tiene por qué ser explicado, jovencito —expresó impaciente—. Y tampoco tengo la intención de darte detalles de algo que jamás comprenderías. No serías capaz de retenerlo.

—Puede intentarlo.

—Ja, no lo creo —refunfuñó.

—Bueno... ¿Por lo menos puede decirme su nombre? Llevo tres noches trabajando para usted y... la verdad es que jamás me lo ha mencionado.

El anciano abrió sus ojos por entero y lo vio con desagrado. Aun así, el muchacho siguió:

—Opino que sería lo justo, porque usted conoce el mío.

—¿Distingues que yo pregunto cosas sobre tu miserable vida? ¡No! —gritó el mendigo, golpeándose los muslos—, ¿o de cómo no te defendiste cuando estuviste frente aquellos insolentes muchachos y te echaron al contenedor de basura? ¡No! Porque no me interesas. Si sé información acerca ti es porque abres tu gran bocota sin que yo te lo haya solicitado, o porque descubro cosas por corazonadas mías. Lógica. Y también por contemplarlo todo desde aquí. —Sonrió—. De esa manera te vi con la muchachita de aquella casa. A propósito, ¿de qué tanto estaban platicando? Los percibí muy susurradores.

«¡Está confirmado! ¡Sí nos estaba espiando!», se dijo Ariel.

No quiso meter a Ellie en la conversación. Sabía que su amiga correría grave peligro si el anciano se enteraba de su terquedad en investigar lo que él (Ariel) hacía en el Parque de Juegos Monteseaur. Por lo que dijo, con fingida inocencia:

—No hablábamos de nada. Solo de..., ya sabe, cosas de adolescentes —aseguró, desviando el asunto. Luego

enunció otra cosa, aturdido—: Oiga, ¿quiere decir que vio a Brandon Portillo cuando me estaba matando a golpes y usted no hizo nada al respecto?

—*Ja, ja.* ¿Querías que *yo* peleara por ti? —Se tocó el pecho con ambas manos—. Por supuesto que no. Tú eres quien debe enfrentar sus propios duelos, muchacho. Jamás aprenderás a ser valiente si dejas que los demás luchen las batallas que te pertenecen a ti. Al final, el único que se lleva la satisfacción eres tú, nadie más.

—Yo lo hubiera hecho por usted —susurró Ariel.

—¿Qué has dicho? —preguntó—. Pensé que a ti tampoco te importaba mi vida, o esa es la afirmación que me juraste ayer. Dime, Ariel Castillo Rivas: ¿te importo?

El oyente no respondió. Se talló los brazos, que empezaban a encalambrársele de frío, debajo de la frazada.

—En fin, chico. Esta noche me encuentro de buen humor y te diré mi nombre, aunque no sirva de nada —murmuró—. Me llamo *Arngfz Knifux Ýjal.*

—¡QUÉÉÉ? ¿De verdad ese es su nombre? —preguntó Ariel, sin podérselo creer—. No puedo pronunciarlo. Parece una mezcla de ruso, alemán y francés.

—¿Lo ves? Es en vano explicar cosas que jamás entendería un *humano* tan inútil como tú... Quiero decir..., un *chico* como tú —reformó.

—Entonces, lo llamaré Arngfz.

—Como sea —dijo. Volteó a los pies de Ariel y sonrió—. Veo que preferiste quedarte con los saltines que tanto detestabas, antes que tus pantuflas fachosas.

Y Ariel se miró los botines, viejos y grandes. Se le veían igual que ridículos zapatos de payaso.

—No es que me hayan gustado. Olvidé mis pantuflas aquí anoche, antes de que...

—De que lo arruinaras. —No permitió que Ariel terminara la oración. Más tarde, apuntó hacia los columpios—. Allá están. Podrás ponértelas en cuanto hayas concluido la tercera misión.

Ariel echó una ojeada al lugar indicado. Sus pantuflas descansaban sobre el segundo asiento, cubiertas de nieve.

—Esta noche mantendrás activos tus cinco sentidos y darás tu mayor esfuerzo —dijo Arngfz—. No solo vas a cazar la cantidad de estrellas que tenía pronosticadas para este plazo, sino que también recuperarás las que dejaste huir ayer. No pierdas en cuenta que de esta empresa depende salvar a Susanita de su cristalización humana.

«No puedo creer que siga sin aprenderse bien su nombre», gruñó Ariel para sí.

Dicho esto, el anciano transitó con sus manos de atleta depositadas tras su espalda sin joroba. Iba erguido, como un catrín, sin ayuda de ningún bastón. Se dirigió a los columpios con la cabeza alzada, exhibiendo los pelos inmóviles de su barba. Sus piernas raquíticas salían de sus shorts semejando astas. De repente, el vagabundo abrió su boca y, originando una especie de arcada, extrajo de ella el extremo de una cuerda.

—Increíble —soltó Ariel— ¿Cómo hizo eso?

Arngfz no despejó su duda.

A una velocidad súbita, el indigente pescó el cabo de la soga y se concentró en halar de esta sin parar, imitando ese antiguo truco de magia en el que el mago saca un sinfín de pañuelos coloridos de su boca, y todos los espectadores observan deslumbrados el acto, preguntándose hasta qué punto los pañuelos dejarán de salir. Mediaron cinco minutos y la cuerda continuó sin tener acabose. Aquella recubrió el terreno como un espagueti. A última hora, ya que Ariel empezaba a abu-

rrirse, el remate de la cuerda salió por fin.

—Toma —urgió el anciano, jadeando—. Hay que empezar. Uf. Eso sí que fue agotador —se quejó.

Ariel aceptó el extremo del objeto entre manos. Estaba cubierto de saliva negra. Analizó su longitud. ¿Cuánto mediría?

«Unos cuantos kilómetros, eso es seguro», calculó Ariel.

—Arngfz —nombró—. ¿de qué manera me ayudará la cuerda? —preguntó, sacudiéndose unos copos de nieve de la cabeza.

El individuo dibujó, fastidiado por tantas preguntas, un arco con sus pupilas misteriosas (derecha-arriba-izquierda) y luego se mordió la punta de la lengua.

—Amárratela en uno de los pies ¿es que no puedes pensar un poco? No sé qué les enseñan en la escuela a estos ingratos —refunfuñó para sí.

Ariel improvisó un fuerte nudo entre su tobillo y la pierna. Miró al viejo con incertidumbre. La pregunta que en ese momento saltó con signos de interrogación sobre su cabeza fue: ¿qué situación extraordinaria ocurriría ahora?

—¿Seguro que estás bien atado? —inquirió Arngfz, tirando de la soga con fuerza—. Bien, bien. Ese nudo está perfecto. Ahora necesito que te tomes esto.

Le entregó una botella color ámbar con un relleno espeso y brillante, parecido al metal líquido. Ariel observó el envase. Existían algunas desconfianzas enganchadas en su cabeza, pese a ello quitó el corcho y bebió el contenido. En cuanto su lengua percibió el sabor de aquel brebaje hizo una mueca de aborrecimiento. Se le revolvió el estómago.

«No vomites otra vez», se riñó asqueado, trayendo a su memoria el contenedor de basura en el que fue en-

cerrado por la tarde.

El menjurje de Arngfz supo a extracto de sábila con vinagre. Ariel escupió y deseó haber llevado, por lo menos, uno de los tantos dulces que continuaban apresados en el tarro de la alacena. La saliva de Ariel, en vez de caer al suelo, se elevó y se perdió en las alturas.

—Nadie dijo que sabría a chocolate —dijo el anciano, apoderándose del frasco.

Lo arrojó a la calle y alcanzó a oírse un lejano chasquido cuando se rompió en pedazos.

—¿Y ahora? —preguntó Ariel.

—¡Qué importuno eres! Sobrepasas una confianza entre los dos que no existe —se quejó el frenético Arngfz—. Espera a que la poción surta efecto. Deja de ser un muchacho tan preguntón y aguarda. Yo te daré las indicaciones cuando sea adecuado. Mientras tanto ¡cállate! —chilló.

Ariel escupió otra vez, todavía con ese sabor a bilis en la boca. Su escupitajo se encaminó a las nubes. El chico se lamió los labios, puesto que sus heridas ardieron, como si se hubiera pasado un limón sobre ellas.

«¿Me habrá envenenado?», pensó.

Y pronto experimentó en carne propia los primeros síntomas de un envenenamiento: dolor de cabeza, de estómago, mareos, vértigo, sudoración (pese a la nevisca), hormigueo en manos y pies y pulsaciones aceleradas.

«Voy a morir», se dijo.

Pero eructó.

Para cuando volvió la cabeza al frente, su vista chocó con el vagabundo, quien tenía un costal metido en la axila. Fue el mismo que este utilizó la noche anterior para atrapar las estrellas que escaparon de los restos de la aspiradora. En la mano llevaba sujetadas unas pinzas para sacar cejas y se las ofreció a Ariel. El

cazador las cogió sin pronunciar pío, sobrellevando aún las ganas de vomitar. Todo le daba vueltas. Recibió el costal y apretó ambas formas con la pasión de un soldado al que le ofrendaron las armas para defender su patria. Esa noche no fallaría.

—Por tu ineptitud de ayer, las estrellas se adhirieron a los techos del Reino Astral con su majadero «pegaluz» —avisó el merodeador—. Es su primera etapa preventiva cuando se sienten amenazadas.

—¿Pegaluz? —repitió Ariel, tocándose el estómago.

—Estás cansándome con tus interrogaciones, hablo en serio —enjuició Arngfz. Pero de todas formas, se lo explicó—: El pegaluz es una sustancia que se les otorga a las estrellas en situaciones de peligro. Se sujetan con mayor fuerza al firmamento.

—Pero ¿quién les da ese pegaluz? ¿Hay alguien que las protege? —mencionó Ariel, más tranquilo.

Las sensaciones del presunto envenenamiento se redujeron. Divagó Ariel en sus meditaciones. Imaginó que las estrellas eran animales inteligentes, así como las abejas, y que tenían a una soberana grandota y enojona que les daba órdenes. Se le vino a la mente el grito de la Reina de Corazones: «¡Qué le corten la cabeza!», de *Alicia en el país de las maravillas.*

—Y ¿cómo es que usted sabe tanto de las estrellas? No creo que lo haya leído en un libro.

—¡Ah, qué necedad la tuya! No atenderé ninguna duda más, ya lo dije. Solo te sugiero que seas muy cuidadoso cuando te encuentres allá arriba. Las estrellas ya saben que hay alguien merodeando por su zona, haciendo desaparecer a las de su especie. Y si encuentran a ese cazador (o sea, a ti), te atraparán y te llevarán lejos, sobradamente lejos. —Estiró el brazo lo más que pudo, unos seis metros, haciendo aplicación de su magia.

—Pero ¿adónde? ¿A su castillo? No lo entiendo.

—Y no tienes por qué entenderlo. Solo haz tu trabajo y punto. Sin saber. Sin preguntar. Sin razonar. Sin hablar. Actuando como debes actuar: ser un cazador silencioso que sigue mis órdenes. ¿Queda entendido?

Ariel iba a afirmar juntando el mentón a su pecho, mas algo se lo impidió. Distinguió un estremecimiento en el cuerpo. Cambió su percepción del entorno, a lo mejor se debía a la sustancia platinada que ingirió. Sintió, de repente, estar zambulléndose en una piscina.

Se miró los pies y (¡No puede ser cierto!, pensó) estaban separados del suelo. La manta azul se le escapó de las manos y cayó entre las secciones de la cuerda.

—¡Estoy volando! ¡Mire Arngfz, estoy volando! —gritó Ariel, sacudiendo las piernas en el aire, dejando de lado el hecho de que ya no tenía con qué protegerse del frío.

—En realidad flotas. La sustancia que bebiste es «antigrav», una anestesia que adormece tu capacidad de ser afectado por la fuerza de gravedad. Solo dura unos minutos —añadió el anciano.

—Con razón me siento extraño. Anestesia —repitió Ariel—. ¿Quiere decir que no peso nada?

—¡Claro que pesas! Piensa un poquito —dijo. Después volvió a su postura discreta y argumentó—: De hecho, posees el mismo peso de siempre. No ha cambiado nada en ti. Como lo acabo de señalar, el antigrav solo durmió tu impresión de la gravedad por un lapso breve.

—¡Es genial! —convino Ariel, sintiendo que la sangre se le acumulaba en la cabeza—. Le apuesto que Brandon el Baladrón, el que me echó a la basura, se quedaría impresionado si me viera en este momento.

—Ya lo creo que sí. —El otro soltó parte de la cuerda que llevaba en sus manos.

Ariel ascendió y se apartó del parque recreativo.

—¡Vamos allá! —gritó el muchacho, alzando los brazos, pretendiendo ser igual de rápido que una bala.

—Un momento, señorito —repuso Arngfz.

Un fuerte tirón en el tobillo. La marcha de Ariel se detuvo. Viró la cabeza hacia abajo y chocó con el rostro del anciano convertido en gigante. Ambos quedaron frente a frente. Aquellos ojos, con las proporciones de un espejo, hicieron que Ariel se llevara un susto de muerte. La enorme mano de Arngfz lo apuntó con un dedo.

—Más te vale no fallarme como ayer, si no yo tampoco cumpliré con mi parte del trato. Te comeré vivo, recuérdalo —amenazó.

Indicado esto, desajustó la soga y Ariel subió de súbito.

Imaginó que era un globo de helio. Notó el aire gélido partiéndose en su cabeza, deslizándose por los codos y escapando por sus piernas, mientras se perdía en las alturas de la bóveda nocturna. Por su travesía, una bandada de patos pasó junto a él. Agitadas las aves por adentrarse en una zona de nevisca, se vieron indispuestas. Ariel pretendió acariciar una de ellas, pero la criatura escandalosa retrocedió aleteando sus alas, parpando, antes de ser ultrajada por manos humanas.

Ariel expulsó una carcajada inmarchitable y se llevó los brazos a los costados, una acción que le otorgó mayor velocidad de propulsión.

La nieve seguía cayendo en la zona del parque abandonado. Ni un centímetro más, ni un centímetro menos. El ardor que corría por las venas del electrizado Ariel era más fuerte que la sensación de frío que lo torturaba. El mundo se miraba hermoso desde esa distan-

cia, a través de la cascada de nieve que caía en cámara lenta.

«La mejor perspectiva que cualquiera pudiera desear», pensó.

Jugueteó con las corrientes de aire y las rasgó con sus extremidades, antojándosele que fueran de crema. Pescó nieve, le dio forma de una pelota de béisbol y la soltó. La bola cayó en picada y terminó, de modo accidental, en el rostro de Arngfz, quien irritado enseñó sus dientes.

—¡Concéntrate y déjate de juegos! —gritó, quitándose los residuos de la frente.

—Lo siento —se disculpó Ariel.

Pero se cubrió la boca para reírse a escondidas. Después giró en un baile lento. Deseó con todas sus fuerzas que aquello no acabara jamás. Se alejó lo bastante como para surcar por las nubes y prestar atención a la curvatura del planeta; ese doblez que aclaraba que la Tierra no era plana, como deducían en la antigüedad.

Atravesó las capas atmosféricas y laceró con su cuerpo la membrana que dividía su mundo del Reino Astral. Los ruidos se sofocaron, quedando lejos y a la vez tan cerca. Los resplandores del cielo se hallaron salpicados por todas partes, como las manchas de un dálmata. El frío cesó y una atmósfera templada acobijó a Ariel. La nieve que forraba su pelo consintió en derretirse y le mojó los hombros y el cuello. Otra parte del agua, en cambio, permaneció flotando a modo de burbujas que se alejaron tímidas.

Tan pronto como se infiltró en el territorio de los astros, la cuerda que tenía atada al pie se tensó. Arngfz la sujetó fuerte desde el globo terráqueo, para que Ariel no superara los límites del espacio. Vista desde un segundo plano, la soga que salía de las nubes y se conectaba a las manos del anciano era una firme antena de

radio que vinculaba los áticos del universo con los campos del planeta. Ariel dio un suspiro lento y aferró las pinzas entre el índice y el pulgar.

Era hora de promover la cacería.

Abrió el costal y acercó las pinzas abiertas a la estrella que tenía más cercana. Capturarla resultó más fácil de lo que imaginó. Fue equivalente a arrancar el cabello de una cabeza. Al principio, el lucero se sintió fijo y duro, no obstante, al hacer un pequeño esfuerzo jalándolo hacia atrás, se produjo un sonidito de «*ting*» y lo despegó del cielo. Más tarde, Ariel lo guardó en el fardo. Se cuidó de no mirar los resplandores más de cinco segundos, tal como se lo recomendó Arngfz. Lo que menos quería era volverse loco a esas horas del partido.

Estuvo, quizá, más de quince minutos ejecutando su acción: despegando y guardando solecitos en el costal. Se avecinó, sin embargo, el período en el que el saco quedó repleto de astros. Este se agitó de derecha a izquierda, como resguardando un huracán en el fondo. Las estrellas se revolvieron dentro, atolondradas, conscientes de su captura. Pretendieron huir por cualquier orificio. El impaciente Ariel se vio obligado a sacudirlas para inmovilizarlas. Fue allí cuando notó algo que lo cautivó y lo dejó rígido:

Una estrella, muy diferente a las otras. Amarilla, con las cumbres definidas cuales espinas de un rosal. Frágil. Bella.

«No debes mirarlas más de cinco segundos o te volverás loco», se recordó a sí mismo.

No obstante, su despampanante brillo y belleza lo llamaban. El lucero tenía un imán que atraía los ojos humanos.

«Uno», contó Ariel.

Aquel resplandor era una imitación incomparable

de la rosa de los vientos. Acercó el cazador las pinzas a la estrella, mas no pudo capturarla. Tuvo miedo de acabar con su lindura, que su luz dejara de proyectarse.

«Dos.»

¿Qué ocurriría si contaba hasta el número cinco? ¿De veras se arriesgaría a llegar al final, a pesar de que Alondrita se haría de cristal?

«Tres.»

Tenía que dejar de ver y aferrar esa cosa entre las pinzas. Solo era un lucero, uno de tantos que ya había cazado para el anciano.

Pero era tan hermoso. No le había tocado ver uno tan resplandeciente. ¿Por qué era dorado, como el Sol?

«Cuatro.»

Si no cerraba los ojos se volvería loco...

«Cin...»

No pudo terminar de contar.

Un fuerte jalón lo arrastró por el mar de nubes, hacia abajo. Al atravesar la neblina y rasgar la película de seda (lo que ya había considerado como la puerta oficial del Reino Astral), descubrió a Arngfz en el parque abandonado, pasándose la soga de mano en mano, haciéndolo descender en un ritmo casi musical.

Se reprodujeron los ruidos nocturnos. Las bajas temperaturas estremecieron a Ariel. Volvieron a verse los copos de nieve despeñándose.

«¿Cómo pude ser tan tonto? —se dijo—. Estuve a punto de echarlo todo a perder. De no ser por la intervención de Arngfz, estaría en este momento con la boca abierta, escurriendo baba, sin pensar en otra cosa que no fuera en las estrellas; en quererlas contemplar siempre, con el mismo amor con el que se ama a una persona.»

Se le vino a la cabeza el rostro de Ellie, en el se-

gundo que pensó la palabra «amor».

—¿Listo? —dijo Arngfz, cuando Ariel tocó tierra.

El chico repitió la experiencia de mareos, hormigueo en la punta de las extremidades y ganas de vomitar.

—El antigrav perdió su efecto. Ya puedes caminar con libertad —señaló el veterano—. ¿Cómo te fue?

¿Tan rápido había llegado? Ariel ni siquiera disfrutó el viaje de regreso.

Arngfz, que tenía su figura de cíclope, volvió a adquirir la simetría de una persona normal.

—Me fue perfecto —respondió Ariel—. Aquí tiene sus estrellas.

Le consagró el saco, que no paraba de agitarse. No le apetecía ser regañado, así que no mencionó lo que por poco ocurría allá arriba. Al fin y al cabo, no contó hasta el número cinco.

El anciano abrió los ojos de emoción y abrazó el costal con la pasión de un amante. Ariel, mientras tanto, fue a sentarse en un columpio, no sin antes echar abajo el montículo de nieve que aquel poseía encima. Se puso sus pantuflas blancas de borreguito y desertó los saltines en el asiento de al lado. A continuación, fue por su manta, que había quedado sepultada entre la nieve y la soga. La sacudió y se envolvió en ella como un burrito de carne. Su pelo pegado en la frente se escarchó. Sin demora, rebuscó algo en los alrededores.

—¿De casualidad no ha visto mi gorra? —le preguntó a Arngfz.

No obtuvo contestación.

Se volvió de frente y halló al gozoso vagabundo tragándose las estrellas de la bolsa. De su boca abierta extrajo una larga lengua de color azul pálido, que se desplegó cual liga elástica, rebuscando los luceros que intentaban escapar de su destino. El veterano simuló a un sapo que atrapaba bichos alados en un pantano.

El observador Ariel se sobrecogió por presenciar escena tan desagradable. Después de acabar con su cena, Arngfz se tiró al suelo igual que la noche anterior. Convulsionó. Al mismo tiempo, ocurrió algo insólito con su cuerpo. Su cabello cano empezó a rizarse y a teñirse de un tono tropical dorado, su larga barba albina de mago Merlín se introdujo en su piel y desnudó un perfecto mentón partido, propio del género masculino. Sus brazos demacrados y piernas se ensancharon, poseyendo ahora los músculos de un héroe. Y la piel que antes le colgaba flácida, se tonificó en una capa perfecta de juventud.

Los luceros le arrancaron varios inviernos al vagabundo. Dejaron ante sí a un hombre con la edad aproximada del señor Villalobos. Ahora Arngfz era fuerte, terrible y poderoso.

Y aprovechó ese momento para explotar su naciente poder. Esta vez, su organismo se amplificó sin detenerse. La estatura fue inimaginable, un edificio departamental de diez pisos. Pero la cosa aún no acababa allí. Arngfz se alargó más, y todavía más, hasta que Ariel tuvo que echar a correr para no ser machacado por sus pies. El talón del mendigo aplastó los columpios, sus dedos se enredaron en la cuerda prolongada. Algunas torres de neumáticos salieron volando a toda olla y tres árboles se partieron a la mitad.

Al acabar con la transformación, Ariel pudo distinguir un rostro en la distancia. Era la punta de un rascacielos. En dicha lejanía, entrevió unos endemoniados ojos blancos que lo apuntaron. Dos faroles en medio del mar.

—Ahora vete y prepárate para mañana, muchacho. El Sol está por salir —dijo Arngfz con una voz corpulenta, digna de un monstruo escalofriante. Esta hizo temblar el suelo y derrumbar lomas de nieve en peque-

ñas avalanchas—. En cuanto a tu vieja gorra amarilla, no la he visto. Quién sabe dónde la habrás dejado, sé más precavido con tus objetos personales.

Ariel deseó que se lo tragara la tierra y lo escupiera en su habitación. No podía seguir mirando. Era horrible. Nauseabundo.

«Pero ya falta poco para que acabe esta pesadilla —se animó—. Esto llegará a su fin dentro de dos noches más.»

A pesar de sentir las piernas de goma, a raíz del miedo, Ariel se atrevió a preguntar:

—¿Cómo es que amanecerá pronto? Ayer pasó lo mismo.

El gigante se apresuró a encogerse (Ariel suspiró de alivio por ello) para responderle.

—Si te diste cuenta, el tiempo transcurre diferente aquí abajo que en el Reino Astral —dijo Arngfz—. En pocos minutos que pasas arriba, en la Tierra se suman horas. —Su voz gruesa, conforme iba acortando su estatura, fue haciéndose soportable. Terminó hablando en un tono intuitivo y varonil, sin traba de tos—. ¿Por qué crees que las estrellas han durado tanto vivas? —preguntó—. Envejecen lentamente. Han sido las testigos de la evolución del hombre a lo largo de la historia. Viendo a cámara rápida la construcción de sus ciudades, cómo acaban con los bosques para su supervivencia, la manera en que se reproducen año tras año, como repugnantes bacterias celulares, y también atestiguan la forma en que agotan los recursos naturales para su beneficio.

El parque de juegos quedó hecho un desastre. Había arboles despedazados, llantas por doquier, la soga infinita enredándolo todo, juegos recreativos hechos trizas (o aplanados). ¡Por Dios! El sitio aparentó la consecuencia de una contienda de espadas.

—Eso... —musitó Ariel—. Eso lo explica todo. Gracias, entonces ya me voy. Buenas noches.

Pero Arngfz no respondió a la despedida. Nunca lo hacía.

Cuando Ariel volteó hacia atrás, ya no vio a nadie allí. Lo que sí pudo revelar, no obstante, fue que detrás de los columpios triturados, la melena de león se agitó impetuosa. Y la nieve que antes la cubría cayó desenfrenada. El anciano (bueno, ya no era un anciano, sino un adulto joven, reflexionó Ariel) se fue corriendo por ahí a la velocidad de una gacela.

Capítulo 14
La hoguera

Ariel emergió del parque y dejó de percibir aquel frío salvaje. En la calle Monteseaur no helaba tanto como al otro lado de la acera, en el parque recreativo. Los copos de nieve que escapaban de la cascada no tocaban el hormigón. Antes de emigrar de su territorio, estos se desintegraban en un microscópico polvo blanco al empalmarse con el aire del exterior. En el acto dejaban de existir.

«¡Sorprendente!», exclamó Ariel.

Caminó de vuelta al número 72. Se topó con los lánguidos rostros de las casas. Los gigantes aún dormían y lo más seguro era que no despertarían jamás, porque vivían en su imaginación, igual que la absurda «zona segura» dibujada en la calle. Cruzó por la casa de Ellie y no halló su silueta al otro lado de la ventana.

«Estará dormida —caviló—. Seguramente se mira hermosa mientras duerme...»

Procedió en ahuyentar sus ilógicos pensamientos y miró el cielo, que confinó unas nubes aborregadas. La noche previa no se notó tanto, pero al presente, en el firmamento yacía un manchón oscuro donde antes habitaban estrellas. Ariel estuvo seguro que la imagen angustiaría, a más no poder, a cualquier espectador que repasara el firmamento en esa ocasión. La mancha se había ensanchado tanto desde la última vez, que era imposible no darse cuenta de la extinción de luceros.

Los cuerpos celestes que se salvaron esa misión seguían aferrados al Reino Astral con pegaluz. Y su imagen enviaba a la memoria el perfil de las montañas del Himalaya. Contemplar aquel terrible boquete con el color de la pez, estimuló que un escalofrío se intercalara por los discos de la médula espinal de Ariel, semejando a un chorro de lejía que le recorría la espalda; mismo que pronto se convirtió en un arroyo malsano que lo zarandeó de cabo a rabo. Halló otra figura en la sombra de las alturas. Las fauces de un tiburón. Con sus dientes afilados y sonrisa valerosa.

Ariel bloqueó sus accesos de aire por el susto, se le complicó respirar.

Para ese entonces llegó al buzón con el número 72. Atravesó el jardín maltratado, con anhelos de entrar por la ventana de su habitación y tumbarse en la cama, enrollado en el edredón. Olvidarse de todo. Le escocían los ojos, los párpados le pesaban. Por fin descansaría...

Pero algo impredecible le arrebató, de nueva cuenta, el aliento.

La puerta de su casa fue abierta con un golpe fuerte.

—¡Oh! —expresó el amedrantado Ariel.

El arisco señor Villalobos, con sus ojos resaltados y ennegrecidos, observó a su hijastro como si de carne fresca se tratara. De su nariz derivaron dos chorros de vaho, armonizados con su atropellada forma de respi-

rar. Caminó a largas zancadas por el barro hasta el joven, lo asió de la muñeca y lo obligó a entrar al vestíbulo.

Antes de que el hombre cerrara la puerta de una patada, Ariel alcanzó a ver de reojo un movimiento de cortinas en la casa de enfrente. Un rostro victorioso.

«¡Fue ella! —pensó—. La señora Corrales se lo contó todo.»

—¿Dónde te habías metido? —preguntó el huraño señor Villalobos—. Y... ¿Y qué le pasó a tu rostro? Dejaste que Brandon se metiera contigo de nuevo, ¿verdad? —Su cara estaba enrojecida—. ¿Te defendiste esta vez?

—Procuré hacerlo —replicó Ariel, encogido de hombros—. Pero eran cuatro... ¡Cuatro contra uno, señor! No fue una pelea justa. Estaba solo, no pude hacer mucho.

—¿No pudiste o *no* quisiste? Deja de poner excusas en tu boca, muchacho. —Enterró sus escuálidos dedos en las greñas alborotadas de su cabeza, mirando a Ariel con altísimo desprecio. Como si estuviera avergonzado de ser su padrastro—. Aunque ese no es el punto ahora —prosiguió—. Quiero que me expliques, en este preciso instante, lo que haces afuera. ¿Vagabundeas como un callejero? Van dos noches seguidas que la señora Corrales me llama por teléfono para contarme que te ve caminando por la calle. La primera vez no le creí porque no pensé que fueras tan estúpido como para hacerlo y preferí quedarme en la cama. En muchas ocasiones tu madre y yo te exigimos que jamás cometieras semejante cosa. «¡NUNCA SALGAS DE NOCHE!», te dijimos. Y cuando recibí la segunda llamada de aquella vieja chismosa, hoy en la madrugada, supe que ocurría algo. Entré a tu habitación y ¿cuál fue mi sorpresa? —Aplaudió para darle dramatismo a su

perorata—. No estabas ahí. Te esperé una, dos, tres, cuatro, ¡más de cinco horas! —Contó con los dedos de las manos—. ¡Y mira! Acaban de dar las seis en punto de la mañana. —Apuntó al reloj de la cocina—. Quiero saber en dónde estabas metido. ¿Qué demonios hacías? ¡CONTÉSTAME!

La garganta de Ariel se cerró de pura agonía. ¿Qué le diría? No podía contarle de Arngfz, ni que era un cazador de estrellas. Para empezar, no le creería. Aunque tampoco era probable mentirle. El señor Villalobos tenía un don olfateando las mentiras.

Se dio cuenta Ariel de que la señora Rivas también estaba ahí, congregada en el acceso del pasillo, negando con la cabeza y acariciando su desnudo cuello de cisne.

—¿Por qué lo hiciste, mi buen muchacho? —preguntó ella—. Nos tenías alarmados.

Miró a su hijo con sus tristes y amoratados ojos. Ariel sintió que la vergüenza lo derribaba. A su madre no podía mentirle.

—Estaba en el parque —confesó.

La señora Rivas asintió con la cabeza. El momento de tensión había pasado, si bien, no del todo.

—¿El Parque de Juegos Monteseaur? ¿El sitio abandonado al final de la calle? —vociferó el señor Villalobos—. ¿Qué hacías allí?

Ariel negó con la cabeza.

—¿CON QUIÉN ESTABAS? —siguió el padrastro.

—No puedo decírselo. Es un secreto que prometí guardar. Pero confíe en mí, señor, por favor. Las cosas se van a arreglar.

—¡DÍMELO! ¿CON QUIÉN ANDABAS?

—No.

—Conque no vas a desembuchar.

El hombre encerró los dedos de la mano y atestó un

golpe en el ojo sano de Ariel. La señora Rivas lanzó un escandaloso chillido y se desmoronó.

—¡Detente! —escandalizó.

Su marido tomó otro impulso y empujó a Ariel por los hombros, quien por secuela cayó al suelo como una arpilla de manzanas. El muchacho se cubrió la cara, adolorido. Lo siguiente que sintió fue una patada en el estómago.

—¡Vas a matarlo! —gritó la señora Rivas, arañando el suelo—. Déjalo y maltrátame a mí, te lo suplico, pero ya no le pegues a mi hijo. ¡A él déjalo en paz!

—¡LEVÁNTATE! —le ordenó el señor Villalobos a Ariel—. Quiero que veas lo que estuve preparando con ansias para ti, mientras llegabas. ¿Sabes lo que es una «hoguera»?

Ariel apenas se pudo mover y comprender lo que le decían. El dolor lo tenía doblegado. De su boca brotaba sangre.

—¡HE DICHO QUE TE PUSIERAS DE PIE! —ladró el señor Villalobos.

Encolerizado, cogió una de las extremidades de su hijastro y lo arrastró por el suelo. Ariel, estando bocarriba, entrevió la oficina del señor Villalobos. Encima del escritorio, iluminado por una lamparita de mercurio, reposaba su «caja secreta». ¡Se hallaba abierta! Ariel siempre había tenido curiosidad de revelar lo que custodiaba en su interior. Pero el cofre estaba demasiado lejos y él demasiado aturdido como para pensar en ello.

Atravesaron la cocina. Por la puerta salieron al patio trasero. La señora Rivas los siguió, suplicándole a su esposo que se detuviera.

—¡Deja a Ariel! Permite que yo platique con él. No es necesario que hagas esto —clamó.

Alondrita despertó. Desde su habitación unió su voz

al coro de llantos inquietantes y griteríos del 72.

—Gracias a que estuve esperándote en tu recámara, descubrí que tenías esto —puntualizó el señor Villalobos.

¿De qué estaría hablando?, se cuestionó el indefenso Ariel. ¿Qué encontró? Cuando pudo incorporarse, en medio de quejidos y dolores bajo las costillas, estudió el terreno cuadrangular con la mirada. El nuevo ojo hinchado le dolió al desplazar la pupila. Localizó, en cierne, su uniforme colgado con un par de ganchos en el tendedero. Persistió paseando su centro de visión por el patiecito y fue atraído a la ubicación de su padrastro.

—¡No! —Ariel expulsó un grito ahogado.

Todos sus libros, los de fantásticas historias que leía por las noches a escondidas; aquellos vehículos que lo transportaban a otros mundos para vivir cientos de aventuras; los únicos compañeros que disfrutó durante los días más difíciles de su vida, mayormente en el trote del último año; las reliquias que salvó, cierta vez, de aquel hombre cruel que tenía por padrastro; salvavidas que lo protegieron y lo aconsejaron de no caer en un abismo umbrío de soledad y desesperación; los que tenía escondidos como tesoros irremplazables, bajo el colchón de su cama; sus codiciadas joyas de entrañables personajes y tramas hechizantes, con pastas maltrechas pero con elogiada prosa, versos suculentos y dibujos sublimes. *Las aventuras de Tom Sawyer, Un mundo feliz, El mago de Oz, Aura, La historia interminable, Peter Pan, El principito, Don Quijote de la Mancha, Fahrenheit 451, Harry Potter y el prisionero de Azkabán, Demian, Los viajes de Gulliver, 1984,* por no mencionar otros de sus venerados libros; todos ellos, yacían apilados sobre un asador de carne como innobles prisioneros, esperando una injusta pena de

muerte por un crimen que no cometieron.

Ariel comprendió entonces por qué el señor Villalobos había referido con tanta bravura la palabra «hoguera».

—Jamás imaginaste que los encontraría, ¿verdad? —mencionó el adulto infame, rodeando el asador—. Ahora conozco el motivo de tu infantilismo. ¿Sabes por qué no puedes plantar bien los pies sobre la Tierra? ¿Sabes por qué no eres realista? —El señor Villalobos levantó algo del suelo mientras hablaba. Sostuvo en su mano un garrafón blanco. Se dedicó a bañar el lote de libros. El líquido se vertió sobre sus lomos y portadas; se escurrió por entre sus páginas y tomó camino propio para adueñarse de las obras que estaban debajo—. No eres realista porque no te despojé totalmente de esta inmundicia —continuó diciendo—. Me engañaste, haciéndome creer que los deseché. Pero no hiciste un buen trabajo ocultándolos bajo la cama. Tarde o temprano los iba a encontrar.

Gastó más combustible y arrojó el garrafón, medio vacío, a la esquina del cerco que pintó la señora Rivas por la tarde. El objeto dejó su huella en las tablas y las salpicó de gasolina. Apareció una cerilla en la mano del señor Villalobos. Luego de frotarla con la punta de sus dedos ásperos, se creó una ansiosa lengüeta de fuego, que danzó de forma peligrosa cerca del asador.

—Por favor, no lo haga —imploró Ariel, mirando aterrorizado la pequeña flama.

Sintió los brazos de su madre rodeándolo por la espalda.

—Esto te lo ganaste a pulso —dijo el señor Villalobos.

Y arrojó el fósforo.

El fuego se extendió por los libros en un poderoso destello. Las portadas, con hermosas ilustraciones y ti-

tulos impresos en relieve, fueron devoradas por la lumbre, junto con sus páginas amarillentas. Las llamas se alzaron metro y medio y el patio residió iluminado por una sutil y vibrante luz anaranjada, que hacía bailar sombras siniestras.

—Mete tu uniforme —decretó el padrastro—, o de lo contrario apestarás a humo en la escuela.

Dicho esto, el individuo abandonó el patio.

Ariel no acató su orden.

La señora Rivas se arrodilló para estar a la altura de su hijo y lo abrazó.

—Lo siento mucho, hijo. Lo siento mucho.

Tenía riachuelos de lágrimas. De ese modo permanecieron largo rato. Juntos y en silencio. Hasta que el fuego se sofocó a los minutos. En el asador prevaleció una colina de tristes cenizas que, aún encendidas, expulsaban un manto fúnebre. Alondrita ya no clamaba ni lloraba, el señor Villalobos se habría encargado de consolarla. Ariel contempló la cortina de humo de la parrilla y su instinto trabajó en hallar figuras consoladoras en ella. Lo único que obtuvo, sin embargo, fueron rostros maléficos de sonrisas dementes.

Aquel era un triste adiós para sus libros. Y sintió turbación en el cuerpo, como un ataque de ansiedad. Dolor, agonía, rabia, las costillas comprimiéndole el corazón, desesperanza, impotencia, nostalgia.

Tuvo ganas de no seguir existiendo.

Era la misma conmoción que experimentó un año atrás, la fecha donde ocurrió aquello que lo cambió completamente todo.

Su segundo secreto.

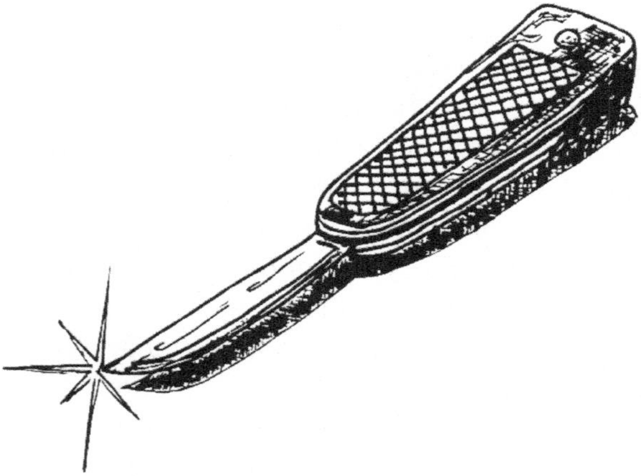

Capítulo 15
La navaja suiza

Ellie Durán salió apresurada de su casa cuando miró a Ariel de pasada. Lo estuvo esperando tras la puerta, asomando un ojo por los cristales de colores de la puerta.

—¡Adiós, mamá! ¡Ya me voy a la escuela! —gritó.

—¡Qué tengas buen día, mi cielo!

Ellie cerró la puerta del 46 a toda prisa y se avecinó a Ariel.

—Buenos días —saludó, con su bitácora bajo el brazo.

La chica llevaba cierto gorro extravagante que hacía juego con una bufanda de franjas grises y rojas, enrollada a su cuello. Usar atuendos con los colores decembrinos se había convertido en la moda más avivada entre la gente, sobre todo en los jóvenes. Justo esa mañana, los vecinos encabezaron la tarea de adornar sus casas con soberbias lucecitas navideñas, camillas de

nochebuenas en los jardines, ostentosos renos mecánicos, trineos superpuestos en los tejados cargados de enormes fardeles, inflables con figuras de muñecos de nieve, rostros de Santa Claus dando la bienvenida en las puertas de entrada y no pudo faltar el más importante de todos: el árbol de Navidad. Preñado de esferas de distintos tamaños y cercado de luminaria excesiva, con tal de darle una apariencia espectacular.

—Hola —le respondió el triste Ariel a Ellie.

Una pilastra de vaho emergió de su boca a causa del mal clima. El tiempo empeoraba conforme avanzaba el último período del año, y lo más probable, es que no mejoraría.

Vientos glaciales cogieron el cabello de Ellie y la fastidiaron haciéndole pasear las puntas del pelo por la cara.

—¡Qué frío hace! —comentó la muchacha.

—Bastante —corroboró Ariel.

Se estiró las mangas del suéter y metió los puños para resguardar sus manos de las bajas temperaturas. Mas tarde, se cruzó de brazos.

—Bueno, ¿vas a contarme lo que haces en el parque? —inquirió Ellie, de rebato, apartándose las greñas del rostro.

—Jamás te darás por vencida, ¿no?

—Ya sabes la respuesta.

—Ojalá pudiera, Ellie. Todavía no es el momento. Como te mencioné anoche, tienes que esperar un par de días más. Y precisamente —dijo por lo bajito—, «no podemos hablar de esto justo ahora».

—Hay alguien que nos espía, ¿no? —susurró.

—*Sí*. Así que hablemos de otra cosa.

Pasaron por el parque recreativo. Durán volteó hacia la izquierda y se percató del rostro mutilado de Ariel.

—¡Dios mío! ¿Qué te pasó en la cara? —interrogó impactada.

En seguida, hizo anotaciones en su libreta.

—Tuve una fuerte discusión con mi padrastro —explicó Ariel, pretendiendo leer de reojo lo que Ellie escribía de él.

—¿Estás diciéndome que el señor Villalobos te hizo eso? —dijo Ellie, entrecerrando los ojos—. No te creo.

—Solo puedo decir que entre él y Brandon juegan competencias para ver quién me mata primero.

—Ariel, quiere decir que, aparte de los abusos de Brandon Portillo en la escuela, ¿sufres de violencia intrafamiliar? ¡Qué injusticia! Deberíamos hacer algo para detenerlos...

—No, no, no. Es mejor dejar las cosas así —objetó de pronto, arrepentido de habérselo contado.

—Pues a mí no me lo parece. Para empezar, lo que está cometiendo ese hombre, tu padrastro, es un crimen atroz —sentenció malhumorada, en un tono pertinaz—. Podríamos hablar de ello al Sistema Nacional para el Desarrollo Integral de la Familia.

—¿Al DIF? —nombró—. ¿Y que separen a Alondrita de mí? Ni de chiste. Es lo último que haría.

Caminaron en silencio. Ellie cerró su bitácora y volvió a confinarla bajo el brazo. Acto seguido, olisqueó una pestilencia en el aire y acercó su nariz al pecho de Ariel. A este se le aceleraron las pulsaciones cuando la tuvo así de cerca, sobre él. Deseó poder abrazarla, llorar sobre su hombro, acariciar su pelo... Sintió una cosa diferente, aunque placentera, en el centro del estómago. Similar a cuando se bebió el antigrav. Quizá, serían los efectos secundarios de dicho brebaje horas detrás, o las patadas que le propinaron sus dos peores enemistades. Si bien, conceptuó que aquella sensación estaba más ligada con la presencia de Ellie que por el

antigrav y los trancazos de sus golpeadores.

Respiró Ariel del cabello ensortijado de la chica (olía a champú de fresas).

—Ariel, ¿qué es ese tufo? ¿Por qué hueles a humo?

Volvió en sí y se apenó de su situación. Durán era la primera persona, después de su madre o Alondrita, de quien sentía que en verdad se preocupaba por él. Cuando menos pensó, le detalló que su padrastro había hecho una hoguera con todos sus libros para que fuera «realista». Y que debía darle las gracias a la entrometida de la señora Corrales por haberlo llamado.

Ellie sacudió la cabeza de un lado a otro.

—Tu padrastro es un monstruo —señaló, decepcionada—. Estoy anonadada por lo que acabas de contarme, Ariel. Todos piensan en la colonia que es un hombre amable y respetable, que cuida bien de sus dos hijos. Hasta los vecinos sienten compasión por él, ya sabes, por lo que sufrieron el año pasado.

Ariel la miró conmovido al auscultar eso último, a lo que ella le comunicó con afecto:

—Acabo de meter la pata por hablar de eso, ¿no? Lo siento —se disculpó—. Pero no te preocupes, evitaré tocar el tema. Soy una completa tonta. Es algo incómodo de sacar a la luz. Bueno, para mí lo sería —admitió, abochornada—. Volviendo a lo que te estaba diciendo: de la señora Corrales puedo esperarme cualquier cosa. Es una mujer que no sabe otra cosa más que chismorrear asuntos de los demás. ¡Cómo me gustaría hallar un defecto en ella y divulgarlo ante la cuadra para que se le quite ese odioso comportamiento! Apenas así aprendería a no volver a hablar mal de las personas. Sería como darle una cucharada de su propia medicina. Sin embargo, si lo piensas, de eso a quemar tus libros en un asador de carne, creo que el premio de la locura se lo ganó el señor Villalobos. ¿Cuál es su pro-

blema? ¿Qué diablos se le cruzó por la cabeza?

—Me odia —respondió.

—Ninguna persona en su sano juicio haría cosas así. ¿Y por qué debería de odiarte? Si tú no le has hecho nada.

—Ni idea, pero de algo estoy cien por ciento seguro.

—¿De qué?

—Que no soy realista.

—Oh, Ariel, por favor. No vayas a hacer caso a eso.

Ariel discurrió en el tema que Ellie sacó en la conversación momentos atrás. Lo de hacía un año. El martirio que marcó históricamente a su familia. Más tarde que temprano, se obligó a rechazarlo de sus pensamientos.

—Por cierto —expresó Ellie—, si algún día quieres leer, te puedo prestar un libro. Eso sí, mantenlo alejado de la vista de tu padrastro. No queremos una segunda cacería de brujas.

Continuaron transitando y doblaron por la calle Altamirano. Unos metros más adelante, ingresaron a la secundaria.

—¿Nos vemos en receso? —le dijo Ellie a Ariel, cuando iban caminando por el pasillo principal.

Ariel la notó sospechosa. Preocupada.

—¿Te ocurre algo? —preguntó.

Ellie encubría algo en la punta de la lengua que no se animaba a soltarle tan a la ligera.

—Sí —reveló—. Hay algo que tengo que contarte (¡Lo sabía!, se dijo Ariel). Y esta vez, necesito que me des una explicación honesta.

«¿De qué estará hablando? ¿Se habrá dado cuenta de mis verdaderos sentimientos hacia ella? ¿O sabrá de mi segundo secreto?», se preguntó Ariel, acongojado.

—Está bien, nos vemos en el receso —farfulló—. ¿En qué lugar?

—¿Qué te parece en el comedor? —propuso Ellie.

—Me parece *comedor bien*. Quise decir: me parece bien en el comedor.

«Estoy hablando como un tonto.»

Ellie le sonrió y se marchó, ondeando su larga bufanda de rayas tras la espalda.

«¿Y por qué se va sonriendo? ¿Se ríe de mí?»

Jamás se sintió tan turbado por la opinión que tendría de él una chica. La cara se le puso del color de un tomate y marchó intranquilo. Vio a Brandon Portillo contándoles a sus amigos cómo había encerrado a *Cerdonio* en la basura, con ayuda de sus secuaces. Un estallido de carcajadas atronó por el corredor. En el segundo que Ariel pasó enfrente de ellos, fue apuntado por decenas de dedos.

—El depósito olía a estiércol —continuaba diciendo el Baladrón, fanfarroneando sus memorables episodios del día anterior. Agregó, con una mueca maliciosa—: Pensé que era un sitio ideal para él. —Luego le gritó al susodicho—: ¡Eh! ¿Dónde está tu bici, *Lady Arielita*? ¿Por qué no viniste en ella?

Brandon se separó de sus amigos y, acompañado de Olegario, le cerró el paso a Ariel. Portillo le dio un empujón en el hombro y le dijo algo. El acosado cerró los ojos y tarareó una canción, imaginándose a Ellie Duran tomándolo de la mano.

—No me ignores, *Bola de grasa* —gritó el bravucón. Lo abofeteó suavemente cerca del ojo que tenía más hinchado—. Oye, un momento, no recuerdo haberte hecho esa marca. —Arrugó la frente—. ¿Hay alguien más haciendo mis deberes? —preguntó entre dientes.

Ariel negó con la cabeza.

—¿Cómo te hiciste eso, entonces?

El cazador de estrellas emitió algo en voz baja.

—¿Qué? No te oí —espetó Brandon—. Habla más

fuerte.

—Cuando me arrojaste a la basura mi cara se estrelló contra una pared del depósito —mintió Ariel.

—Bien dicho. Sabes que solo yo tengo derecho a pegarte. —Lo miró—. ¡Y guácala! ¿Qué es esa peste? No me digas que en tu casa quisieron hacer chicharrones contigo.

Olegario rio y se mordió el labio inferior con sus dientes de castor.

—Es un cerdo asado, ¿a que sí, Brandon?

—Sí. Es momento para ponerle un nuevo apodo —indicó Brandon—. ¿Qué te parece *Cenipuerco*? También me gusta *Cara Cortada.*

—*Frankenstein* —sugirió Olegario, interrumpiendo su discurso.

—¿Por qué no te callas, *Niño rata*? —vociferó—. Ese ya existe.

—Pues *Cara Cortada* también —desafió—. Creo que es una película de terror.

Al recibir la mirada de Portillo, Rocha quedó con la cola entre las patas.

—*Cara Cortada* es perfecto. Me encanta *Cara Cortada* —se corrigió.

Portillo dejó de darle cuantía a Rocha y regresó a sus asuntos.

—¿Te gustaría conocer una nueva amiguita? —le susurró a Ariel en un tono malévolo.

Se metió la mano al bolsillo del suéter y sacó una navaja suiza.

—¡Órale! —expresó Olegario—. ¡Qué chulada! ¿De dónde la sacaste, Brandon?

—Se la quité a mi padre. Tiene otras cuatro en casa, así que ni se dará cuenta de que la tomé.

En aquel instante, entró la profesora Nogueda por la puerta principal. Brandon, en un abrir y cerrar de

ojos, escondió el arma en su bolsillo y contempló a su mártir.

—No olvides nuestra cita a la hora de salida. ¡Ah! Y pobre de ti le cuentas a alguien que traigo esta «preciosidad» conmigo. Nadie debe enterarse.

Le dio unas macizas palmadas en la espalda, antes de desaparecer con Olegario en la marea de estudiantes. La profesora Nogueda le sonrió a Ariel. Él no le devolvió el gesto. Estaba helado, impresionado, sin poderse creer todavía que Brandon llevara un arma a la escuela y que lo hubiera amenazado. Significaba que su nivel de maldad iba en aumento. Si Ariel no le ponía un alto, es decir, si no lo enfrentaba con valentía, la villanía de Portillo no tendría límites. ¿Aquel sería capaz de asesinarlo a sangre fría, antes de cumplir con las cinco noches de su contrato?

Sería un destino infortunado para todos.

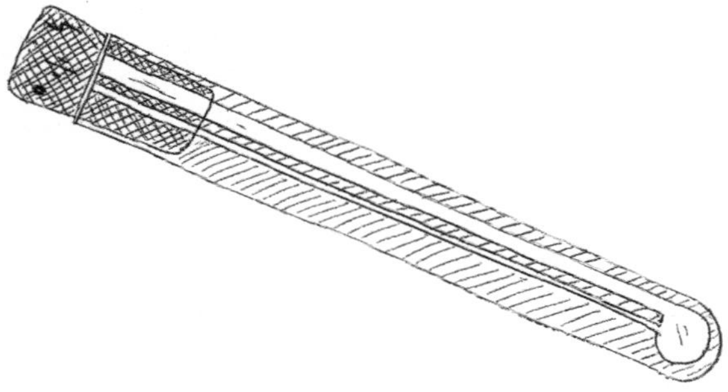

Capítulo 16
Delator

La primera clase del día fue Historia, con la profesora Cuevas. De actividad, solicitó a sus alumnos que redactaran un resumen de quinientas palabras. El escrito debía tratar sobre la vida de algún personaje histórico de México. El cansado Ariel acomodó el libro abierto frente a su rostro y aprovechó para apresar sus ojos.

Entonces lo soñó otra vez. Iba corriendo. Estaba siendo perseguido por algo. Las piernas le dolían, en origen de la velocidad a la que iba. Cuando pensó que llegaba su fin, ocurrió un chispazo y aparecieron las cinco luces. Entendió en ese momento lo que eran. Por supuesto que sí. Después de cazar muchas de ellas durante las últimas noches, ¿cómo no iba a saberlo? Eran estrellas. Cinco estrellas que giraban enloquecidas a su alrededor, tratando de decirle algo, como advirtiéndolo. Pero ¿de qué? ¿Del monstruo? ¿Qué querían comunicarle? La bestia llegó a él, y cuando se volteó para

advertir su rostro...

Vio a la profesora Cuevas de pie, a su lado, con el entrecejo arrugado. Ya no merodeaba Ariel en los oscuros territorios de su sueño. Había despertado y se ubicaba en el salón de Historia, acorralado de sonrisas. El libro de texto había caído en su regazo, exponiendo su semblante adormecido.

—Ariel Castillo Rivas —enunció la profesora—. ¿Quieres que te traiga un chocolate caliente y una cobija? ¿Crees que estoy aquí para tolerar alumnos que se duermen en mi clase? ¡Sal ahora mismo del aula! Para mañana quiero que me presentes tu redacción a mano, y no de quinientas palabras, como lo harán tus demás compañeros, sino de dos mil.

Se oyeron murmullos entontecidos y risitas roñosas. Ariel guardó el libro de Historia, se colgó la mochila de un hombro y salió a toda prisa.

En las clases consecutivas fueron frecuentes algunas preguntas de ciertos maestros, que tenían que ver con su rostro golpeado y el ahogante olor de su ropa.

—¡Abran las ventanas, por favor! —dio la orden la profesora González, de Física, mientras se cubría la nariz con un pañuelo perfumado—. Hay que ventilar el aula. ¡Deprisa! ¡Deprisa!

Acto seguido, la docente roció el salón con aromatizante ambiental. En especial, echó una bienoliente llovizna en la zona donde se localizaba Ariel.

Solo la profesora Nogueda intentó sonsacarle al muchacho si estaba todo bien en casa. Él le respondió que sí, y se sintió más incómodo cuando, después de que el timbre anunciara el receso y todos hubieran salido, la maestra prolongó su interrogatorio.

—Cuéntame, ¿estás acostándote tarde?

—Sí... pero solo por estas noches —respondió áspero, guardando sus cosas.

—¿Solo por estas noches? —repitió ella con dulce voz—. ¿Y eso a qué se debe?

—Profesora, no quiero sonar grosero, pero tengo que hacer algo importante y debo marcharme.

La profesora Nogueda deseaba ayudarlo. Él lo sabía. Pero…

—Ariel, como ya te lo he dicho, si tienes problemas en casa puedes hablarlo conmigo, o con la orientadora del segundo piso. Ambas brindamos buenos consejos.

—Lo tomaré en cuenta, gracias —dijo resuelto.

Se ajustó la mochila y caminó a la puerta de salida. La profesora lo siguió con la mirada, detrás de sus gafas. Y frunció sus delgados labios pintados de negro.

Ariel se desvió al comedor. Durante su travesía advirtió que Olegario constaba en la esquina del pasillo principal, rodeado de un grupo de estudiantes rebeldes. Era virtuoso abordando una charla animada. Hablaba con un volumen de voz muy bajito, casi en secreto.

—Sí, te lo juro —decía eufórico—, Brandon trae una navaja chulísima.

—¿De verdad? —habló otro—. Qué valiente. Brandon es el tipo más genial que conozco.

«Un momento —pensó Ariel—. Brandon dijo que *nadie* de la escuela debía enterarse que llevaba un arma, ¿no?»

Pues Olegario, su discípulo más fiel, acababa de traicionarlo.

Aceleró el paso Ariel y salió al comedor. Una corriente de aire le voló el copete. Eran pocos los alumnos que paseaban por allí, al aire libre, soportando el clima helado. La mayoría prefirió quedarse dentro de los hospitalarios corredores del edificio, charlando de temas mundanos y actividades escolares.

—¿Vamos al salón de Dramaturgia?

Ariel se volvió. Quien formuló la pregunta fue Ellie, que apareció a su lado.

—Es un lugar seguro para platicar —siguió hablando ella—, y mucho más acogedor que aquí afuera. Muero de frío.

Se abrazó a sí misma. Ariel asintió. Mirarla otra vez le elevó los ánimos. No pudo articular ninguna palabra hasta que llegaron al auditorio.

—¿Qué querías decirme? —preguntó él, nervioso.

Los ensayos de teatro eran de lunes a miércoles. Los jueves, como ese día, el aula se afincó exenta de alumnos. Ellie lo invitó a que se sentaran bajo lo que parecía, en opinión de Ariel, un enorme oso de cartón con cola de serpiente en proceso de construcción.

—¿Un oso? —repitió Ellie, risueña—. Es el toro de *Lazarillo de Tormes*, bobo —advirtió—. Los de primer año están adaptando obras del Renacimiento para presentarlas a finales de enero.

Se escondieron bajo la figura y se hizo el silencio. Quizás, ella también estaba sintiendo lo mismo que él y le pediría que se dieran un beso tierno bajo el toro. O puede que, rectificó Ariel, Durán le confesara que no deseaba volver a verlo porque notaba extrañas actitudes en él: el tartamudeo, su cobardía ante Brandon Portillo y las humillaciones del señor Villalobos.

El sencillo pensamiento lo hizo apreciar un malestar de remordimiento. Ellie acomodó su libreta entre las piernas, luego se quitó su bufanda y exhibió su cuello. La chica metió una mano a la mochila y sacó un celular. Lo desbloqueó, buscó un archivo en la galería de imágenes y volteó la pantalla con tal de que su acompañante pudiera ver cierta grabación. Apareció ante Ariel una imagen de noche (¡La calle Monteseaur!, acertó). En el video se hizo un acercamiento violento de cámara y entrevió algo blanco cayendo del

cielo. ¡Era la cascada de nieve que se despeñó en el parque recreativo!

—En el canal meteorológico no se reportaron nevadas en ninguna zona de la ciudad —explicó Ellie—. ¿Cuándo has visto nevar por aquí? Jamás. Busqué como loca por Internet y nada. La nevisca solo cayó allí, Ariel, en el parque abandonado. Y lo mejor es que lo tengo todo grabado.

Ariel no supo qué responderle. Ella contaba con evidencias sólidas. Se estaba acercando a la verdad. No dilataba el minuto en que intuyera que era un cazador de astros.

«¿Podré seguir escondiéndolo por más tiempo?»

—Es momento de que me expliques por qué visitas ese lugar por las noches. No en unos días, no la semana que entra. Quiero que lo hagas ya mismo —demandó Ellie—. Ya hasta me acabé las uñas mientras sacaba conjeturas por la mañana. Estoy muriéndome de la curiosidad. Es lo peor que le puede pasar a un detective: poseer pistas y no tener idea de qué ocurre.

¿Qué debía hacer Ariel? ¿Irse corriendo en actitud de gallina y perderla para siempre? O contárselo todo, con la condición de que prometiera guardar el secreto como una tumba. La grabación finalizó y la joven guardó el móvil en su mochila.

—No tenemos todo el día —urgió Ellie—. ¿Vas a contármelo o no?

La pregunta era sencilla. Ariel debía tomar una decisión.

—Debes jurarme que no se lo dirás a nadie —sentenció.

—¡Claro que no! ¿Quién te crees que soy?

La muchacha sonrió animada y sus ojitos se hicieron todavía más pequeños de lo normal.

—Te lo juro —expresó con una sonrisa radiante, alzando el dedo pequeño de su mano.

Ariel alzó el suyo y terminó el pacto. Era lo más cerca que había estado de Ellie. Al momento de estrechar sus meñiques, sintió que se le agitaba el corazón. La sensación de mariposas en el estómago volvió. Empezó a sudar y su respiración dejó de tener el ritmo de siempre. Cuando se soltaron, todavía percibió su dedo aferrado al de ella.

Como si la conociera de toda la vida, se lo contó. Desde el descubrimiento de la cristalización humana de Alondrita, hasta sus increíbles aventuras en el Reino Astral. Ellie no consideró verídica su descabellada historia. De hecho, ni al desarrollo ni al final de esta le creyó una sola palabra. Creyó que le estaba tomando el pelo. Discutieron de la autenticidad de los capítulos del cazador de estrellas, hasta que la campana timbró para finalizar el receso. Su amiga rechazó la existencia de Arngfz, de los saltines, del pegaluz, del antigrav y la teoría de que las estrellas podían tocarse y desprenderse del cielo cuales lentejuelas de un vestido.

—Piénsalo Ariel —le decía, anotando apresurada en su diario—. Si todo lo que me dices es cierto, alguien ya lo hubiera descubierto antes. Digo, no puedes ser la primera persona, en la vasta historia de nuestra especie, que haya encontrado el Reino Astral que me acabas de contar, ¿verdad?

—Pues es cierto. He vivido un sinfín de cosas durante las últimas noches y ya voy a mitad del camino. Ese es el secreto que no podía contarte: el trato que acepté para salvar a mi hermana.

—¿No habrá sido un sueño? He leído de muchas personas que sufren sonambulismo.

—¡Por favor, Ellie! ¿Notaste que estaba sonámbulo

cuando anoche fui a tu casa? —debatió—. ¿Recuerdas la intensa luz que viste la otra noche?

—Ajám.

—Fue cuando la aspiradora se estrelló en el suelo. ¿Lo ves? Tiene lógica. Además, ¿cómo explicas los informes en los periódicos y noticieros de que las estrellas desaparecen del firmamento? Todo el mundo está enterado. Mi historia concuerda.

Ellie abrió la boca, dudosa, sin expresar nada, y luego la cerró. Ariel ganó esa disputa. Se oyeron los pasos de los estudiantes encaminándose a sus aulas.

—En ese punto tienes razón. Tu historia concuerda —comentó ella—. Pero, supongamos que el testimonio es cierto. ¿Estarías dispuesto a extinguir las estrellas del cielo? ¿No te sentirías culpable, Ariel?

—Claro que sí. Me lo he preguntado cientos de veces. No he dejado de pensar, desde que me convertí en cazador de estrellas, en las consecuencias de mis actos.

Ellie lo estudió con los lentes recargados en el puente de su nariz.

—Es una situación muy complicada —opinó en modo de suspiro. Se rascó la cabeza con la pluma—. ¿No has pensado mejor en, no lo sé, dejar que las cosas pasen? Que la situación continúe con su rumbo natural.

—¿Estás pidiéndome que deje *morir* a mi hermanita?

—Dicho como tú lo acabas de expresar, suena terrible. Pero sí, es lo que quiero decir.

—Sé que en mi lugar cualquiera haría lo mismo —mencionó en verdadero tono de desconsuelo—. Así sea robar el cielo, las olas del mar o el Sol. Confiésame, Ellie, de tener la posibilidad en tus manos ¿tú no harías lo necesario si la vida de tu madre corriera riesgo?

Ellie sacó la pluma de su cabello y con ella tambori-

leó en su libreta.

—Cierto. Discúlpame de todo corazón. Es que no me había metido de lleno en tus zapatos. Acabas de cambiar, de forma radical, mi manera objetiva de pensar —concluyó. Echó un vistazo a la puerta—. Eh, debo ir a mi clase de Ciencias. Pero mira, haremos algo: te acompañaré esta noche al Parque de Juegos Monteseaur, cuidándome de que «Arngfz» (o como se llame), no repare en mí.

—¡Estás loca? —se apresuró a refutar Ariel. La definición de miedo se reflejó en su cara—. Arngfz nos tragaría vivos a los dos. Le juré que no se lo contaría a nadie...

—Estaré bien oculta.

—No, ni se te ocurra. Jamás. Jamás.

—Vaya, sabía que te negarías —farfulló—. Ten esto entonces...

Se metió una mano al bolsillo del suéter y sacó un tubo de ensayo, sellado con un corcho. Ariel se hizo con el objeto.

—¿De dónde sacaste esto? —le preguntó.

—En casa tengo muchos juegos de laboratorio —aclaró—. Si mi meta es convertirme en una gran detective, igual que Sherlock Holmes, debo estar preparada las veinticuatro horas del día para recibir cualquier prueba, ¿no?

—Me impresionas —mencionó.

Ellie se abochornó por el comentario.

—Okay, el tubo de ensayo servirá para corroborar tu historia y estudiar más a fondo estos cuerpos celestes. Eres un cazador de estrellas, ¿no es así? —susurró—. Atrapa un lucero y mételo ahí. Juntos descifraremos la verdad. Quizá me convierta en la joven inspectora que descubrió el secreto más célebre del universo. Con tu ayuda, por supuesto. —Volteó a los re-

flectores del techo con aire soñador. Luego, expresó—: Tráelo mañana a la escuela y nos veremos en el laboratorio de Ciencias 3 durante el receso. Los de segundo no tenemos acceso a él, sin embargo, tengo entendido que el profesor López, quien es el dirigente del área, asiste a la sala de maestros cuando se llegan los veinte minutos de descanso, con la excusa de que va a tomarse una taza de café. Según mis averiguaciones, el profesor López está detrás de la señorita Nogueda, aunque ella prefiere hacerse de oídos sordos... ¡Ay, pero eso ya es harina de otro costal! Estando en el laboratorio, analizaremos la estrella con un microscopio.

—¿Y si quedamos apresados bajo la maldición? No volveremos a ser nosotros mismos.

—Calmémonos, ¿sí? No podemos asegurar que eso vaya a ocurrir. Arngfz parece ser un mentiroso compulsivo. Te oculta información importante. Y yo seré la primera que mire por el microscopio.

—No quiero que te pase algo malo —refutó Ariel—. Nunca me lo perdonaría.

—¿No me oíste? Según lo que me contaste del anciano, estoy convencida de que ha estado jugando contigo. Confío en que no me pasará nada.

—Pero...

—Nada de peros, no acepto un «no» por respuesta.

—Eres muy persistente —murmuró Ariel.

—¿Y? —inquirió, alzando ambas cejas—. ¿Lo harás?

—Hecho —dijo Ariel, no muy satisfecho, aunque encandilado por la valentía de Ellie—. Igual yo quería pedirte un favor. ¿Podrías seguir la pista del significado «multiverso»? Y también averiguar qué clase de criatura podría ser Arngfz. Claro, si tienes tiempo.

—Por supuesto —declaró complacida.

Lo anotó en su libreta.

—Gracias —musitó Ariel.

Su mirada quedó clavada en aquella mano zarandeando la pluma.

Se dividieron al resurgir del aula de Dramaturgia. Él quería seguir pasando más minutos con ella, pero era consciente de que por el momento no era posible. Ellie escogió el camino de la derecha y Ariel fue por el de la izquierda. A esa hora tenía Matemáticas con la profesora Lechuga, una mujer triste y de cuello rollizo. Dobló en el pasillo principal y desveló, por la puerta abierta de las oficinas escolares, la dirección. Esta se pactaba rodeada por delgadas ventanas de cristal que daban la impresión de no estar allí. Razón suficiente para que consiguiera avistar lo que ocurría dentro.

Un obeso padre de familia discutía de mala gana con la directora. Aquel tenía un bigote grueso y oscuro y vestía como un motociclista rebelde. Ariel no oyó lo que controvertían, pero por la cara del hombre estuvo seguro de que nada bueno. La rectora Oralia apuntó en repetidas ocasiones al estudiante protagonista de aquella visita. Era Brandon el Baladrón, llorando a moco tendido. Aquel hombre robusto de mal genio sería su padre. El señor Portillo le gritó sofocado a su hijo, mostrando una navaja suiza ante su rostro (la misma con la que Ariel fue amenazado por la mañana). El señor Portillo, que asumía la esencia de una persona desagradable, lanzaba gestos amenazadores a Brandon. La profesora Oralia declinó la discusión segundos más tarde. Se dieron la mano y el visitante salió de la oficina en compañía de su hijo, dirigiéndose al pasillo. Ariel recobró el sentido de la realidad, asombrado por su impertinente presencia ahí, y se hizo a un lado.

Los Portillo cruzaron delante de él.

—¿Estás satisfecho? —le susurró Brandon—. Sé que tú fuiste el soplón. Me las vas a pagar, *Cara Cortada*.

Ariel se desorientó. ¿Escuchó bien? ¿Brandon lo acusó de haber pasado por alto su advertencia matutina y delatarlo? Eso no era cierto. No se lo contó ni siquiera a Ellie Durán durante su conversación del receso. El Baladrón estaba desequilibrado, tenía delirios... ¡Un segundo! Pero Ariel sí que sabía quién habló de más: Olegario Rocha. Este quiso hacerse el destacado del día, contándole a media escuela que su mejor amigo, su gran héroe, portaba una navaja suiza.

—¡Ven ahora mismo, Brandon! —gritó el señor Portillo—. Robarle a tu padre una de sus armas. ¡Imbécil! Dale gracias a la directora que solo fueron tres días de suspensión y no una expulsión definitiva. En otros lugares no habrían sido tan tolerantes contigo. Ya verás cuando lleguemos a la casa.

Brandon se talló las lágrimas, acribilló a Ariel con la mirada una última vez y alcanzó a su padre sin desclavar una palabra de su boca.

Capítulo 17
Diáfana

Ariel reparó en que la cristalización humana de Alondrita conquistó sus clavículas pronunciadas. La pequeña, influida por el progreso de la enfermedad, que le oprimía el pecho y las vías respiratorias, respiró con dificultad. Sus infiltraciones de aire se inclinaban al ronroneo de un gato: rumorosas, agónicas y, en cada plazo, más lentas.

—Hola, hermanito —expresó forzada.

La afectada Alondrita miraba caricaturas en la televisión. Ejercía un rostro decepcionado. Quizá porque el control remoto se ubicó atrapado en su mano endurecida.

—¿Cómo te encuentras hoy? —le preguntó Ariel.

—Quiero, cambiar, de canal —se comunicó entre pausas—. Pero, no puedo. Mis, deditos…

—Déjame ayudarte.

Se le arrimó Ariel y le abrió con cuidado, uno por

uno, las puntas de vidrio. Al hacerse con el control, preguntó:

—¿Qué canal te gustaría ver?

—El que, viene, después de, este.

Ariel presionó el botón triangular del remoto y la imagen de la pantalla cambió. Se escuchó el tema principal de una serie infantil de moda.

—Perfecto, va, empezando —susurró Alondrita—. Pensé, que me, la iba, a perder. Gracias, Ariel.

—¿Has visto al señor Villalobos? —inquirió él.

—Se fue, hace unos, minutos.

—¿Te dijo adónde?

—No —replicó ella.

—¿Quieres que te cocine algo?

—No tengo, hambre. Gracias.

—¿Segura?

—Sí.

—Entonces te dejo. Iré a la cocina.

—Hermanito, ¿por qué, hueles, a quemado?

Se lo habían preguntado tanto a Ariel en la escuela, que no le sorprendió.

—Una larga historia, princesita.

—¿Me la vas, a contar?

—Algún día.

Ariel asistió a la cocina y chocó con una nota en el refrigerador escrita a pulso por el señor Villalobos. Comunicaba el siguiente mensaje:

Hoy llegaré tarde. No olvides
cambiarle el suero a tu media hermana.

Se cocinó tres huevos revueltos con tocino. Luego de comer, lavó los cubiertos sucios. Se dirigió a su habitación. Atravesó el pasillo y halló a Alondrita balbuceando otra vez en sueños. Su programa de dibujos ani-

mados había terminado y estaba en la parte de los créditos. Le apagó Ariel la televisión y se enfiló a la puerta. Esta vez no se aproximó para escucharla. Estaba demasiado cansado. Durmió toda la tarde con el uniforme ahumado puesto. Le dio pereza quitarse el suéter, desabotonarse la camisa, sacarse el pantalón, los zapatos, darse un baño y después alcanzar unos pants del armario (dio un resoplido solo de pensarlo).

Se recobró del sueño cuando la noche alzó su templete negro, revestido de nubes inclementes. En la calle, alcanzó a ver por la ventana, el estreno de los alumbrados y adornos mecánicos de Navidad de los vecinos. La señora Corrales, por ejemplo, amuralló cada centímetro de su morada con lucecitas que reproducían melodías conocidas. Unificado a esto, la vecina entrometida instaló un nacimiento del niño Jesús que dilapidaba los límites de la exageración; representado por personajes de tamaño real en una escenografía esmerada de establo.

«Seguro se lleva el trofeo a la vivienda mejor adornada de la colonia», pensó Ariel.

El número 72 sería el único domicilio que no estaría preparado para las fiestas de fin de año. Al señor Villalobos no le agradaba celebrar la Navidad.

Miró a Félix en la pared. Eran las ocho en punto. Todavía le restaban cuatro horas para encontrarse con Arngfz. Tomó un baño rápido y se empotró en su piyama. Empezó la extensa redacción que le encargó la profesora Cuevas. Eligió al emblemático Emiliano Zapata como su personaje principal. Se apoyó con un libro de Historia que el señor Villalobos tenía en su oficina. La curiosidad lo apremió a voltear debajo del escritorio.

La caja secreta no estaba.

Al acabar el texto, Ariel lo guardó en la mochila.

Más tarde, fue a lavar su uniforme. Colgó la ropa en el tendedero y miró con pesimismo el asador de carne. Todavía subsistían cenizas en él, la mayor porción de estas fue llevada por el viento.

De regreso a su cuarto, se topó con su madre y el señor Villalobos (quien acababa de llegar a casa) sentados en el viejo sillón de la sala. Miraban el noticiero nocturno. Gustavo Pompa explicaba el «extraño fenómeno» que sacudía al mundo entero: el ocaso de estrellas (como lo llamaron los astrónomos). Mencionó que, hasta ese momento, seguía desconociéndose la naturaleza de dicho acontecimiento.

—No quiero asustarlos, queridos televidentes —decía Pompa, con voz melosa—, pero les recomiendo que durante estas noches permanezcan apreciando el firmamento en familia. Disfruten de las estrellas, porque se prevé que muy pronto estas desaparecerán para siempre. —Encuadró un silencio suspensivo de tres segundos y después volvió a hablar, sonando un poco más achispado—: Y en otras noticias, hoy se cumple una semana de que no se obtienen nuevos informes sobre el Robaniños, el presunto secuestrador de menores al que se le adjudica la privación de su libertad a cinco jóvenes de entre doce y quince años de edad. Lo que nos hace formularnos una interrogante: ¿Continuará la temporada de delitos del Robaniños? O el culpable tendrá miedo que sus planes sean descubiertos por las autoridades. Los cinco adolescentes que se observan en pantalla: Manuel N., Pedro N., Fernando N., Alberto N. y Germán N. siguen desaparecidos. Sus familiares y las brigadas de búsqueda continúan registrando las zonas de la ciudad donde se les vio por última vez. Para apoyar el caso, la policía recibió las características físicas del sospechoso, gracias a un testigo presencial. Se trata de un niño procedente de la Colonia Americana,

quien presume haber sido entrevistado a la medianoche por un hombre jorobado de la tercera edad...

La voz del conductor fue bajando su volumen conforme Ariel se alejaba.

—Buena noches —saludó a Alondrita cuando entró a su habitación.

Emparejó la puerta. En cuanto quitó los cables de la cama, se recostó a su lado. Su hermana movió un brazo laboriosamente, a causa de la parálisis.

—Hola —respondió ella, sonriéndole.

Quedó azorado Ariel por lo rápido que avanzaba la enfermedad. El limpio cristal, que ahora lamía la barbilla de Alondrita, insinuaba que su cabeza flotaba en el aire. Ariel alzó la cobija. Sus piernas eran totalmente translúcidas. Descansaban quietas, como maderos. Se sintió preocupado. ¿Y si no terminaba a tiempo con su encomienda y la vida de su hermana llegaba a su fin?

—Ya casi, no percibo, dolor —musitó Alondrita, de pronto—. ¿Crees que me, vaya, a morir?

—No vuelvas a decir eso —amonestó Ariel, con la garganta cerrada—. Nunca. Estoy haciendo todo lo posible por aliviarte.

—Empieza, a gustarme —dijo ella en tono optimista, mirándose—. No siento, frío, ni calor. Y me encanta, el sonido, que hago con, mis deditos, cuando puedo, moverlos. Escucha.

En ejercicios retardados, Alondrita bajó la cobija a la altura de su cintura y levantó parte del suéter que llevaba puesto. Consintió en relucir su abdomen y ombligo apenas visible. Con las puntas de sus manos repicó en su estómago. Aquella melodía correspondió al arpa de un ángel. No obstante, al cabo de un minuto, sus extremidades volvieron a congelarse.

—¡Qué lástima! —mencionó ella—. Llevaba, practi-

cando, toda la mañana, para, enseñarte —explicó, decepcionada.

—Pues me pareció maravilloso.

Ariel se fijó en que los dientes de su hermana se habían teñido de color maíz, y sus ojos se volvieron pequeñitos, cuales granos de arroz. La ayudó a bajarse su suéter, acomodó sus extremidades a los costados y la arropó. Inmediatamente de cambiarle la unidad de suero, volvió a arrellanarse a su lado, la ciñó con un brazo y le prodigó un beso en la frente. En seguida, encendió la linterna. Las sombras se desperezaron y saludaron a sus espectadores.

—¿Recuerdas en qué nos quedamos? —le preguntó Ariel a la niña.

Alondrita pestañeó como si le pesaran los parpados. Respondió en voz baja:

—En la parte, donde la princesa, vence a la bruja, y encuentra, una pócima.

—¡Perfecto! Me complace que me lo recuerdes. Yo la verdad tengo muy mala memoria.

La chiquilla sonrió y prestó su atención a la rueda de luz.

—La princesa Aura, después de derrotar a la bruja sin párpados, bajó las escaleras con las pocas fuerzas que le quedaban —empezó a contar Ariel.

En el muro, los personajes y escenarios aparecieron en una animación coordinada.

—No le quedaba mucho para sobrevivir —recalcó Ariel—. Para su alivio descubrió, después de cruzar el agujero en forma de arco al final de las escaleras, que los corredores se privaron de estar maldecidos. No quedó rastro del laberinto mágico de antes.

»Aura halló las perlas que disgregó de su collar reunidas en un solo lugar, sobre una alfombra. Las recogió y se las guardó en el bolsillo del vestido. A conti-

nuación, regresó a la recámara de la reina. Aquella la recibió envolviéndola en un fuerte abrazo. Lágrimas de agradecimiento ahogaban su rostro. La soberana reconoció el heroico acto de la doncella y la invitó a asomarse por la ventana. Aura quedó sorprendida al enterarse de que los habitantes del pueblo estaban convertidos en personas, poniéndose sus ropajes. Aplaudían animados desde abajo. La princesa pudo ver también a su viejo corcel asegurado en las rejas del castillo, siendo el punto de caricias de un grupo de niños semidesnudos.

»—Serás recordada por nuestra gente —expresó la reina, llena de alegría—. ¿Te gustaría concederme el honor de realizar un baile y agradecer tu hazaña? Asistirá cada habitante del reino, tenlo por seguro. Todos querrán conocer a su salvadora.

»Aura sonrió. ¡Claro que aceptaba celebrar dicha noticia con un baile inmemorial! Por lo demás, ahora tenía en sus manos la pócima que la salvaría de la desgracia. Bailaría con cada invitado hasta sentirse cansada. Y a la mañana siguiente, cabalgaría con su viejo potro de vuelta a su reino. Les contaría a sus padres, con abundante alegría, la buena nueva. Abrazó el frasco, arrullándolo como a un recién nacido. La reina pronto detectó la existencia de este.

»—¡Qué dicha más grande! —exclamó—. Además de acabar con nuestra maldición, encontraremos la morada donde vivía la bruja infame, con la bebida que llevas en tu regazo.

»Aura arrugó el ceño, por no comprender lo que acababa de decir la soberana.

»—¿Acaso no es esta la pócima que me salvará de mi enfermedad? —preguntó.

—¡Oh, querida! ¿Tú también te hayas en busca de la poción sanadora? Pobre niña. Lo siento desde lo más

hondo de mi corazón —expresó atolondrada—. Me temo que lo que conservas en tus manos no es más que un «hallador».

»La joven miró el frasco. ¿Un hallador? Tras asimilarlo, se compadeció de sí misma. Había perdido la batalla. Se sintió terrible por el hecho de que desperdició incontables semanas de búsqueda; días que pudo aprovechar para despedirse de sus seres queridos y llenar de abrazos y besos a sus padres, a quienes acababa de fallarles una última vez. Tiempo que debió aprovechar para convivir con el amor de su vida, el príncipe. ¿Cómo es que imaginó que existía el brebaje de la sanación? Tal como el padre de Aura aseguró, la pócima milagrosa había sido un invento de las ancianas embusteras del pueblo, ingeniado con el afán de obsequiar falsas esperanzas a los desmejorados. La reina acompañó a la princesa y se sentaron juntas en la cama. Su Majestad principió en contarle algo:

»—Tengo una hija que sobrelleva un padecimiento muy raro —confesó—. Y es una enfermedad tan chocante, que creería imposible que otra persona tuviera la aflicción que mi pobre Diáfana. Me enteré, al igual que tú, de una pócima que sanaba cualquier tipo de enfermedad a quien la ingiriera. Eso me dio la esperanza de acabar con el sufrimiento de la princesa. Contraté a los mejores caballeros de mi reino para que buscaran a la bruja que se mencionaba en la leyenda. Les decreté que acabaran con ella a toda costa e hicieran llegar su poción a mis manos. Sin embargo, esa arpía de la magia negra se enteró de mis planes y vino volando en su escoba mágica hasta el palacio. Su poder era tan grande, que exterminó a mi ejército con mover un solo dedo. Logró entrar a mi aposento y me obligó a mirar por la ventana. Recuerdo lo que me dijo: «Por tu osadía e impertinencia, cada súbdito de tus dominios será

convertido en una hormiga obrera. Y para ti, mi queridísima reina, tengo un maleficio especial. Tú y Diáfana, la adorada hija que tienes, quedarán atrapadas en sus habitaciones el resto de la eternidad, sin albergar esperanzas de volverse a ver. Ligado a esto —continuó diciéndome—, aquellos que se atrevan a ayudarte, se verán atrapados en un difícil laberinto que tengo preparado para sus desamparadas almas». La hechicera agitó su mano y lanzó una carcajada maléfica. Todo lo que pronunciaron sus labios se hizo realidad. A la gente le salieron antenas del rostro, lo vi todo desde aquí. Sus ojos se tornaron negros, patas oscuras y fibrosas brotaron de sus costillas, sus manos se transformaron en tenazas y sus cuerpos se hicieron tan pequeñitos que, desde esta altura, no los pude seguir mirando. La bruja salió de mi habitación tan pronto como efectuó su encantamiento y emigró a la torre más alta para descansar. Quedó debilitada. Horas más tarde llegaste tú y nos salvaste. ¡Qué afortunados fuimos al ser parte de tu destino! Las coincidencias no existen.

»—Pero ¿qué es un hallador? ¿Por qué la bruja lo traía en su bolsillo? —quiso saber Aura, quien después de escuchar la anécdota de la reina, se sintió un poco mejor.

»Salvar a una persona era bueno. Salvar un reino, prodigioso.

»—Ese hallador puede ser nuestra salvación —explicó Su Majestad—. Verás, joven liberadora, muchas brujas temen que las encuentren. Razón suficiente para ocultarse de los curiosos. Hacen que sus casas cambien de sitio a cada momento, sin previo aviso. Pueden vivir en campos desolados o bosques sombríos, apartadas de la civilización. Sin embargo, cuando se ven amenazadas se encargan, mediante un conjuro, de

que sus moradas viajen a un rincón diferente. Al desierto impenetrable o a la montaña más alta. Mientras más alejadas de ojos humanos estén, es mucho mejor. Como las brujas son viejas y despistadas, y se la llevan viajando en sus escobas voladoras por el mundo, a veces olvidan en qué lugar dejaron su vivienda. Es por ello que crean pócimas que las ayudan a encontrarlas: el hallador. Quien lo beba podrá vislumbrar un camino que para los demás será invisible, cuya trayectoria lo dirigirá a la casa de la bruja. Y esa, heroica muchacha, es nuestra salvación. Porque puede que al lugar donde nos lleve ese frasquito que llevas en tu amparo, esté el brebaje que sana cualquier enfermedad.

»Aura observó la pieza y avizoró su rostro enfermo reflejado en él. Pese a reconocer que hizo algo extraordinario: salvar la vida de cientos, se sintió mal consigo misma. No le quedaba tanto tiempo. Se vio inconsolable varios minutos. ¿Otra búsqueda imposible?, pensaba. ¿Barrer más distancias? Su cuerpo no podría hacer cara a nuevas aventuras.

»—Lo entiendo —dijo Aura.

Sin más drama, se talló las lágrimas y decidió disfrutar los últimos momentos que le restaban de vida. Aceptó asistir al baile. La reina salió del aposento y volvió con un par de criados que, no sin antes agradecer a la princesa por haberlos desembrujado, le entregaron un hermoso vestido verde con lentejuelas. Era un obsequio de Diáfana, la hija de la reina (a quien Aura todavía no conocía).

»Antes de que la ceremonia se abordara, Aura escribió una carta de disculpas y despedida. Pidió de favor a un mensajero que se la hiciera llegar a sus padres. En seguida, visitó Aura al corcel que la acompañó hasta ese reino. Los encargados de las caballerizas trataron al animal como todo un ídolo. Lo asearon y hala-

garon, lo peinaron y perfumaron, le quitaron sus herraduras viejas por unas nuevas y, asimismo, le facilitaron abundante comida. La mirada de la bestia traslució gratitud. Allí se quedaría lo que le restaba de vida. La historia de cómo fue elegido aquella noche, por una princesa de nombre Aura, se hizo leyenda.

»En menos de lo que canta un gallo advino la hora de la celebración. La hija de la reina no asistió al convivio. Aura imaginó que estaba tan enferma que no se le concedía salir de sus aposentos. Profundizo que tal vez se la presentarían más tarde, en el transcurso de la noche. Dejó de pensar en ello y se puso a saludar a cada ciudadano que le presentaba la reina, y a todos los que se avecinaban. Aura lució su despampanante vestido verde limón. Con bordados de oro y lentejuelas brillantes. En los pies llevaba puestas unas zapatillas de plata irreales. El orfebre del poblado se encargó de arreglar su collar de perlas, a fin de que lo luciera esa noche. Aura bailó hasta que los pies le dolieron y sus pulmones se fatigaron. Se deleitó del momento. Y conforme los minutos avanzaban, la llama de su corazón iba extinguiéndose, latido tras latido...

Ariel detuvo su narración y las sombras en la pared voltearon al frente, alteradas por la inesperada interrupción. Alondrita lloraba a mares. Se llevó sus frágiles manitas a la cara empapada.

—Pobrecita —dijo entre gemidos, con sus particulares pausas respiratorias—. Todo lo que, la pobre princesa, pasó: semanas, buscando, la pócima; atravesó un, laberinto hechizado; venció a una, bruja sin, párpados... Para que, al final, todo resultara, en vano.

Su llanto fue tan enternecedor que Ariel, contagiado por su aflicción, tuvo un nudo en la garganta. Hubiera preferido tener un cuento más emotivo, más cálido y menos miserable. Pero ¿de qué manera le explicaba

que él no creaba esas historias, sino que eran ellas las que se entretejían por sí solas, antes de brotar de sus labios? Alondrita era muy pequeña, no tenía edad para entenderlo. Él tampoco querría que ninguno de sus personajes viviese tragedias, no era culpa suya que esto sobreviniera. Aquellas invenciones se contaban por aquella voz, que siempre había dicho que le pertenecía a alguien más, al narrador de cuentos que vivía en su cabeza. Ariel no podía, por nada del mundo, intervenir en la trama.

—La historia no ha terminado, hermanita. Estoy seguro de que ocurrirá un milagro —susurró, dándole un gramo de esperanza.

—¿Me prometes, que la princesa, no morirá? —preguntó Alondrita con su inocencia a flor de piel.

Ariel se fijó en sus pequeños y enrojecidos ojos, que apenas podían abrirse. Le partía el alma mirarla así, tan enferma y tan... de cristal.

—Eso no puedo asegurártelo —respondió.

La tomó de la mano, que le pareció más dura y fría que la última vez. Tuvo cuidado de no rompérsela. Habló con su mejor voz tranquilizadora:

—Recuerda que debemos tener fe. La esperanza es lo último que muere.

Alondrita asintió y volvió a posicionar su mirada en el círculo, donde las sombras se alzaron de hombros, preguntándose a qué hora se reanudaría el cuento. Habían llegado al punto de taconear el suelo. Se morían de ganas por seguir actuando en la gran festividad descrita por Ariel.

—Mientras bailaba, la princesa escuchó algo —relató Ariel. Dando un corto suspiro, las sombras danzaron simultáneamente—. Oyó una hermosa voz parecida a la de las sirenas, tarareando una melodía poco conocida. Era exquisita, un rebelde placer al oído. Aura

se mantuvo quieta, oyendo aquella canción, y el muchacho que la acompañaba quedó frustrado. Ella se disculpó y se separó de él. Algo dolido, el joven tuvo que buscarse a otra chica para bailar. Aunque más tarde presumiría a sus amigos que fue de los pocos afortunados que bailó con la salvadora.

»Aura sintió que el mundo se paralizaba a su alrededor a causa de la voz. Mas cuando recorrió el salón con la mirada reveló que nadie, salvo ella, podía escucharla. Los aldeanos, que usaban sus mejores vestiduras, siguieron actuando con normalidad: hartándose de vino y cerveza, degustando exquisitos bocadillos servidos en bandejas de oro sobre largas mesas; bailando en parejas al compás de la trova, contando chistes colorados, o compartiendo la experiencia de ser hormigas. Pero ninguno de ellos oyó el hermoso canto.

»"¿Cómo es posible que no escuchen?", se preguntó la doncella.

»Le llegó el absurdo pensamiento de que la voz le pertenecía a la Muerte, quien la llamaba para arrancarle el alma del cuerpo. La conduciría por un túnel hasta reunirla con los antepasados de su familia, y estos la recibirían con una fiesta igual de admirable que aquella. Cerró los ojos y apagó los demás ruidos de la habitación. Todo sonido existente se perdió en contraste con la voz, que dejaba rastros de notas musicales, como pistas, para que Aura diera con su cantora. Armada de valor y con la incertidumbre de si aquel era su final, abandonó la fiesta. Persiguió la canción por los concurridos pasillos del castillo. Mismos que parecían las calles de un mercado a plena luz del día, porque igualaban en cantidad al número de personas que uno podía encontrarse por ahí. Atravesó la mayor parte del palacio y allegó a la cocina, donde fue sorprendida por unos criados, quienes llevaban apresura-

dos más vino y comida al salón de baile. Unos ayudantes de cocina la reconocieron de inmediato. Abandonaron por un instante sus labores culinarias y se dedicaron a darle su eterna gratitud. Aura aceptó un obsequio del cocinero en jefe: un pastelillo relleno de insólitas frutas que, por aquella época, solían crecer en otro continente. Se marchó de allí, muy sonriente, por otra puerta. Le dio una mordida al pan y el azúcar creó una explosión de sabores en su lengua. El postre la hizo añorar su hogar.

»Por los próximos corredores transitó menos gente, razón por la que fueron más fáciles de atravesar. La voz solista todavía se escuchaba, pero Aura tenía miedo de que se apagara de repente. Jóvenes enamorados que abandonaron la ceremonia corrían de un lado a otro, buscando un lugar en el que pudieran aprovechar su intimidad. Aura les sonrió, avergonzada, imaginando si su príncipe y ella se encontrarían algún día viviendo una situación parecida.

»Transitó por otros cinco pasajes y llegó a una puerta vieja que empujó con las palmas abiertas, haciendo todo un esfuerzo con los músculos débiles de sus brazos. Reveló escaleras en espiral que bajaban en dirección a las mazmorras. No se distinguía nada a causa de la oscuridad, de modo que sacó una antorcha del muro más cercano y descendió por los peldaños de piedra, enfilándose con ella. Las notas vocales subieron de volumen y los estribos acabaron. Aura quedó ante una puerta monumental, tallada con rústicos adornos de oro y pintada de un rojo brillante. La melodía venía del otro lado. Si esa voz era la del final (es decir, su final), tenía que descubrirlo. Abrió la madera y ocurrieron dos cosas a la par: la canción dejó de percibirse y una luz cegadora la obligó a cerrar los ojos. Luego soltó la antorcha encendida y esperó a que sucediera lo que tu-

viera que pasar.

No obstante, no percibió cambio alguno: ningún arrebato de su alma y tampoco un abrazo de la Muerte. Seguía sintiéndose enferma y cansada. Abrió los ojos y consintió que sus pupilas se acostumbraran a la luz. Descubrió una habitación grande, que tenía un aroma femenino. Las pulcras paredes del aposento estaban cubiertas por algodón. Había alfombras gruesas que daban la apariencia de un césped rosáceo y las esquinas de los muebles eran protegidas por cojincillos. La misma situación ocurría con los espejos y los marcos de las pinturas colgadas en la pared. Aura calificó extraño este hecho. Era como si la persona que vivía allí, temiera caerse y romperse un hueso. Emplazó Aura la antorcha encendida sobre los escalones de piedra, cerró la puerta con esmero y caminó por la amplia recámara. Era proporcional al salón de baile de la planta de arriba. Le sorprendió que, después de haber atravesado un pasillo tan húmedo y oscuro, localizara un hermoso recinto para descansar. Sin embargo, aún se preguntaba de dónde vino la voz de antes. No miró a nadie más rondando por allí. Se admiró cuando giró a la izquierda, pues justo enfrente yacía un tocador con espejo. Y delante de este halló una pieza peculiar, sentada en una silla acojinada.

Era una muñeca de vidrio. Aura pudo ver el cuarto a través de su cuerpo. Tenía las facciones muy marcadas. Quizá, su artista la erigió a lo largo de muchos años, para perfeccionar los pequeños detalles que la instituían, entre los cuales se destacaban los siguientes: poseía la estatura de una joven promedio; labios definidos; cejas marcadas; cuello prominente y barbilla pequeña; párpados con diminutas pestañas; ojos con sus respectivas pupilas, lagrimales y un par de iris confeccionados; orejas de las que colgaban un par de

aretes de esmeralda; gozaba de manos con marcas en los nudillos y líneas de vida en las palmas; uñas que parecían la mera verdad; de su cabeza brotaban una hilera de imposibles cabellos blancos. La asombrada Aura se le aproximó y los acarició. Al ir pasando los dedos por el pelo, descubrió que estos también eran de vidrio, salvo que de una clase considerablemente delgada. Las fibras cristalinas traquetearon entre sí, generando un son agradable. Le recordó a cuando se copean unas personas con otras, celebrando un brindis. La expresión de la muñeca era sereno y tranquilo, como si fuera una persona real observándose en un espejo. Llevaba puesto un amplio vestido amarillo de encaje que la hacía parecer una gobernanta de hielo.

»—Qué bonita eres —susurró Aura—. Me gusta mucho tu vestido.

»—Lo mismo digo del que traes puesto —expresaron aquellos labios transparentes, con voz de sirena—. Yo misma lo elegí para que mamá te lo hiciera llegar. Era mío, pero a ti te queda espectacular.

»La muñeca sonriente dio una vuelta de cintura para arriba. Sus extraños ojos enfocaron a la princesa Aura, quien casi cayó desvanecida al suelo por tremendo descubrimiento.

»—¿Cómo es que puedes...? —articuló titubeando.

»—¿Hablar? —acabó el cuestionamiento—. Lamento haberte asustado. —Se puso en pie—. Por lo que me doy cuenta, puedes escuchar mi voz. Esa no es una noticia muy grata que digamos.

»Hizo una reverencia elegante, común entre la gente perteneciente a la nobleza. Aura, todavía con la boca abierta, realizó la misma cortesía. "Se puede mirar a través de su cuerpo", concluyó. Con todo, a pesar de su translucidez, era capaz de notar el contorno de las clavículas bajo su garganta y cada uno de los deta-

lles fisionómicos propios de un ser humano.

»—Eras tú quien estaba cantando —dijo Aura—. La voz que tarareaba aquella canción. ¿Por qué solo yo pude escucharla? —preguntó.

»—Es a lo que iba. No todos pueden oírme —dijo la joven—. Es una maldición que cargo desde mi nacimiento. La gente suele ver mis labios moverse, mas no escucha la voz que estos emiten. De hecho, mi madre jamás ha atendido mi voz, y espero que así siga siendo. Para ella he sido una hija muda desde siempre.

»—¿A qué se debe que ciertas personas te oigamos?

»—Joven salvadora, solo me oyen aquellos que van a morir pronto.

»Aura lo comprendió y no preguntó más detalles del argumento. Miró a la joven de cristal y volvió a analizar la habitación. Concibió entonces por qué estaba tapizada con bordes de algodón y cojincillos suaves.

»—Soy la princesa Aura —se presentó, tendiéndole una mano.

»—Lo sé, y me da gusto conocerte —expresó vivaz la frágil doncella—. Mi nombre es Diáfana, y como ya te habrás enterado soy hija de Su Majestad —cantó. Observó la extremidad de Aura con incomodidad e hizo una mueca divertida—. Lo siento, pero no puedo estrechar tu mano. Si lo hago, estaré corriendo el peligro de que se me rompa un dedo.

»—Cierto, no había pensado en eso —musitó avergonzada, bajando el brazo.

»—Pierde cuidado, es algo que ya me ha pasado antes (y con frecuencia) —susurró irónica, riendo de su propia broma—. El dolor no es más que un viejo amigo que regresa cada vez que me extraña. ¿Ves? —Acercó sus miembros, que estaban llenos de cicatrices—. Y bien, tú eres la heroína de la que tanto habló mamá. Tu noble acto será rememorado por la gente de nuestro

reino. Sujetos a quienes conoces mejor que yo.

»—Pero ¡qué dices! Si apenas bailé con ellos un par de horas —repuso Aura.

»—Por eso mismo —expresó la chica de vidrio—. Jamás he estado fuera de estas cuatro paredes. No platico con nadie más que con madre. Bueno, tuve oportunidad de conocer a mi padre y a la abuela también, que en paz descansen —comentó con tristeza—. Ambos escucharon mi voz antes de morir, y por suerte pudimos despedirnos de ellos con antelación. Frecuento a algunos criados del castillo, pero la reina no les permite permanecer demasiado tiempo conmigo porque podrían lastimarme. De modo que tú eres la primera persona que conozco, proveniente del exterior. Como verás, es evidente mi emoción por tenerte de invitada, así como la ilusión que sostengo de encontrar la cura de mi maldición. Cuéntame, princesa Aura, ¿cómo llegaste aquí?

»Y así fue como nació la grande amistad entre las princesas Aura y Diáfana. Charlaron durante horas. Aura le platicó de cuando sufrió los inicios de la enfermedad de su corazón, seguidos de dolores de cabeza, fiebres y resfriados repentinos. El curandero del reino distante en el que ella vivía, delató que su enfermedad era incurable y mortal. De allí le explicó a la joven de cristal el motivo del baile de despedida que le organizaron sus padres. Le describió a Diáfana los sentimientos que tenía por aquel príncipe del que quedó flechada. Diáfana no sabía lo que era sentir el amor. Pero había leído en muchas de sus novelas, de jóvenes que se oponían a sus padres y a la sociedad. Aquellos preferían morir juntos antes que vivir separados el uno del otro. Aura continuó relatándole de la travesía que emprendió con su viejo corcel, de su arribo en la ciudad en la que se situaban y que reveló las calles y sus casas

vacías; narró su aventura en los corredores del laberinto hechizado, de cómo encontró a la reina atrapada en su habitación y la manera en que le arrebató su brazalete a la bruja sin párpados, dando como resultado, que se acabara la época de sus diabólicos maleficios. Aura también mencionó que encontró un «hallador» en las vestiduras de la hechicera. Diáfana se alegró tanto al escuchar esa palabra, pues sabía lo que era. Había leído en un libro de brujería acerca de la utilidad eficaz de un «hallador». Así que se le ocurrió sugerir algo bohemio y peligroso:

»—Aura..., ¿por qué no buscamos juntas la casa de la bruja para dejar atrás nuestras desgracias? Amo a mi madre y lo siento mucho por ella, pero estoy cansada de vivir encerrada en esta jaula. Anhelo con todo el corazón, al igual que tú, experimentar el amor, conocer el mundo y vivir grandes episodios. ¿Qué opinas? ¿Lo hacemos?

»Aura vaciló. Para ella, los segundos de su existencia eran como monedas de oro peligrando en el fondo de un fardo roto de una esquina. Estaba al corriente de que no llegarían oportunamente a la meta establecida. Por otro lado, igual quería hacer algo para ayudar a aquella original muchacha.

»—Por favor, Aura —insistió Diáfana—. No pierdes nada con intentarlo. En cambio, piensa esto: ¿qué ganarías quedándote aquí? Una muerte lenta y agonizante, eso es seguro. Mientras me platicabas tu historia, noté algo que te caracterizaba: valentía, fe. Y eso, querida amiga, parece que lo olvidaste por completo. Vamos, arriesguémonos a salir esta misma noche. ¡Luchemos por nuestra felicidad!

»La otra permaneció callada largo rato. Aura opinaba que se hallaba vaciada de vida. Era muy dura de roer, pero, de alguna manera Diáfana la convenció.

»—Hagámoslo —dijo, conceptuando que aquel viaje era más insensato que el de la primera vez.

»Como Diáfana no tenía permitido salir de su dormitorio, Aura se esmeró en maquillarle la piel con óleo. Todo con tal de que pareciera una persona común y corriente que había asistido a la festividad. En los brazos le fueron colocados unos guantes largos y ligeros, que se le miraban muy elegantes, y su cabello fue teñido de negro, igual que sus pestañas y cejas. Aura le pintó los labios de un ardiente color carmesí, añadió sombras azules a los párpados y aplicó rubor en las mejillas. Con lo que no pudo hacer mucho fue coloreándole los ojos, ya que era imposible efectuar dicho acto. Diáfana se quejaba de dolor cuando los bigotes de la brocha (¡Ay! Ten más cuidado, Aura) le picaban las pupilas. Los ánimos se les vinieron abajo a las doncellas, hasta que de pronto se le ocurrió algo a Aura.

»—¡Puedes ir con el rostro oculto! —propuso—. ¿No tienes un abanico por ahí, entre tus cosas?

»Diáfana se levantó ilusionada y caminó al armario, que se hallaba al otro extremo del aposento.

»"Eso sí que será un problema", se dijo Aura, fijándose en la lenta y precavida forma de caminar de su compañera.

¿Cómo saldrían del castillo si este permanecía tan atiborrado de gente? Un golpe en falso y su amiga podía quedar hecha trizas, pulverizada bajo los pies de un centenar de personas. Diáfana volvió con un abanico que combinaba con su vestido.

»—¡Estoy lista! —exclamó entusiasmada.

»Se miró presurosa al espejo y quedó pasmada por la mujer que la miró del otro lado.

»—No puedo creer que esta sea yo. Desearía verme así después de beber la pócima. Oh, Aura, muchas gracias. No te imaginas lo que esto significa para mí.

»Sus ojos derramaron lágrimas de vidrio, que quedaron como dos diamantes perdidos sobre la alfombra. Sin poder abrazarla, Aura le sonrió apenada y abrió la puerta. Levantó la antorcha (todavía encendida) que dejó en la escalinata. Tardaron más en subir los estribos por la velocidad de andar de Diáfana, que en lo que tardó Aura maquillándola. Al pisar el último peldaño, Aura profesó deseos de retroceder y cancelar el viaje irrealizable. Opinó que estaba siendo la cómplice de un suicidio. Intuía que las personas de la fiesta se empujarían, se darían de codazos y tropezarían unas contra otras.

»—¿Adónde crees que vas? —le preguntó Diáfana, cuando Aura se disponía a regresar por el pasillo que conducía a la cocina—. No podemos ir por allí, podrían descubrirnos. Mamá invitó a todos los del reino, así que sería imposible atravesar el salón de baile sin ser vistas por los guardias.

»—Pero allá se encuentra la salida, ¿no? —replico Aura, algo aturdida.

»—Sí, pero no es la única. Lo leí en los libros de Historia y arquitectura del castillo. Aproveché mi largo encierro para aprenderme los planos de memoria. En ocasiones me imaginaba andando por ellos, ideando salidas furtivas por las noches. Pero la verdad es que nunca me arriesgué a hacerlo, hasta ahora —mencionó encantada—. Sé que existen cuatro salidas. Una de ellas fue bloqueada hace cincuenta años, por lo que, sin contar la que tú conoces (la del Gran Salón de Eventos), nos quedan dos opciones: el pasadizo de los calabozos y el túnel de la torre oeste.

»Aura pensó en ello.

»—Condúcenos a un lugar que no tenga escaleras, por favor —suplicó.

»—En ese caso, partiremos a los calabozos.

»Se colaron inadvertidas por los pasillos. Si escuchaban a alguien acercándose, Diáfana se llevaba el abanico a la altura de sus inmaculados ojos, que semejaban dos madrigueras de conejo, y simulaba estar conversando con su acompañante. Eludieron a un par guardias de aspecto criminal y atravesaron un corredor donde yacía una pareja de jóvenes besándose. Diáfana se les quedó mirando.

»—Jamás había visto un beso. No me lo imaginaba así —musitó decepcionada.

»—¡No te detengas! ¡Vámonos! —urgió Aura—. Después nos daremos el gusto de platicar de estas cosas.

»Los muchachos oyeron voces femeninas y detuvieron sus besos. Con todo, al averiguar que no había nadie más en el pasaje, se volvieron y continuaron en lo suyo.

»Tras recorrer gran porción del castillo, Diáfana se llevó un dedo a la boca, como quien calla a un niño en misa, y cambió de dirección por un corredor desaseado y poco iluminado. La confusa Aura la siguió y deliberó, en determinado momento, que su amiga no sabía muy bien adónde se dirigían. No obstante, al superar el pasillo tropezaron con un estrecho y prometedor túnel de piedra.

»—Es por aquí —anunció Diáfana.

»Penetraron el pasadizo, que las condujo a los calabozos. Un quinteto de presos tras las celdas miró atentó a las damas. Los prisioneros les versearon piropos. A Aura no le pareció nada divertido. En vez de eso, las intenciones de los hombres le resultaron descorteses y vulgares. No fue el caso de Diáfana. Rio como una chiquilla, mientras contaba unas rocas en la pared. Cuando estuvo segura, le pidió a Aura que empujara el muro con seguridad. La otra así lo hizo, aliviada de irse de allí.

»El panel se dividió, desenmascarando una puerta secreta.

»—Llévenos con ustedes, bombones —suplicó uno de los presos.

»Aura puso los ojos en blanco antes de internarse por el hueco.

»—Quizá para otra ocasión, guapo —le dijo Diáfana.

»Le tiró un beso en el aire y el preso se tocó el corazón. El resto de los reclusos rio y aplaudió.

»Las doncellas ahondaron en el pasadizo, que pareció el interior de una mina. Entramparon la puerta del calabozo, dejando tras de sí a los presos. Salieron veinte minutos después por las caballerizas, donde Aura le solicitó al mozo de cuadra que les confiriera, por sobre todas las cosas, un carruaje especial; acolchado por dentro. Le mintió al caballero, arguyendo que le fastidiaban las sacudidas de los viajes cuando los caballos trotaban a galope. Ambas jóvenes entraron dispuestas a la carroza seleccionada.

»Estando allí asentadas, Diáfana decidió que fuera su nueva amiga quien se bebiera el «hallador».

»—¿Y si muero durante el camino? Jamás hallarás la casa de la bruja, Diáfana —controvirtió Aura.

»—Eso no ocurrirá. Tengo fe en que las cosas saldrán más que bien.

»Y Aura se empinó el líquido, no muy segura de que fuera la decisión más congruente. Al principio no ocurrió nada, pero a los sesenta segundos, tuvo un momento de revelación: distinguió una silueta amarilla en el aire, como un resplandeciente hilo dorado que desprendía motitas de luz. El filamento apuntó al horizonte. Aura le explicó al chofer, un joven bastante apuesto, la ruta que este debía tomar para llegar al supuesto reino donde vivía «su amiga Victoria de toda la vida». Los caballos, luego de relinchar, hicieron sonar

sus cascos. Las princesas habían iniciado su aventura juntas.

Alondrita estaba emocionada, tanto, que la coloración de su piel blanca se tornó a un rosado primaveral. Se identificó con el personaje de la princesa Diáfana y quedó atrapada por el coraje al que se aferró aquella, de salir de su recámara para encontrar la pócima salvadora.

La puerta de la habitación se desembarazó y el señor Villalobos entró tambaleándose, como recordando algo. Las criaturas del Club de los Cuentos de las Sombras salieron huyendo despavoridas por tremendo azote y Ariel apagó la linterna de forma anticipada.

«¿Habría estado el señor Villalobos escuchando mi cuento?», se preguntó.

Lo dudó. Se imaginó al padrastro agazapado tras la puerta, poniendo atención a su historia.

«Sería algo demasiado raro», se dijo Ariel.

—¿No te he dicho mil veces que la puerta debe estar abierta? ¡Eres un bruto! —amonestó el padrastro, abandonando sus evocaciones y volviendo a su malhumorada normalidad. Al contado, miró la hora en su reloj de mano—. Son las once y media de la noche. Ya déjala descansar.

El adulto se acercó a Alondrita y tardó menos de un minuto en prepararla para dormir. Hizo unos ajustes rápidos a los aparatos que se hallaban detrás de la cama y le deseó buenas noches luego de otorgarle un beso en la frente. Emergió de la habitación en silencio.

La señora Rivas, como un animal asustado y escurridizo, entró y besó a sus dos hijos, haciendo recepción de su orgullosa dulzura. Tan pronto como lo hizo, persiguió las huellas de su marido hasta la recámara. Para ese entonces, Alondrita ya había cerrado los ojos. Ariel le dio un beso en la frente y dejó la puerta sepa-

rada unos ochenta grados. Avanzó hasta su habitación y se puso las pantuflas blancas de borreguito. Esa ocasión no necesitaría de los anticuados e incómodos saltines para andar.

Miró el gato Félix en la pared, meneando sus ojos con elegancia. Este le anunció que faltaban veinte minutos para que evacuara su casa y se pusiera a cazar estrellas. Consiguió el tubo de ensayo de la mochila y se lo guardó en el bolsillo del piyama. Antes de efectuar su labor, se dijo que visitaría a su amiga Ellie. Se preguntó si habría averiguado algo de lo que le pidió en la escuela.

«¿Y si el señor Villalobos me descubre otra vez fuera de casa?», pensó también.

«Ya no tiene con qué castigarte», manifestó su voz interior.

Después de que su padrastro destruyera sus queridos libros, Ariel ya no tenía nada más que pudieran arrebatarle. A excepción, claro está, de Alondrita.

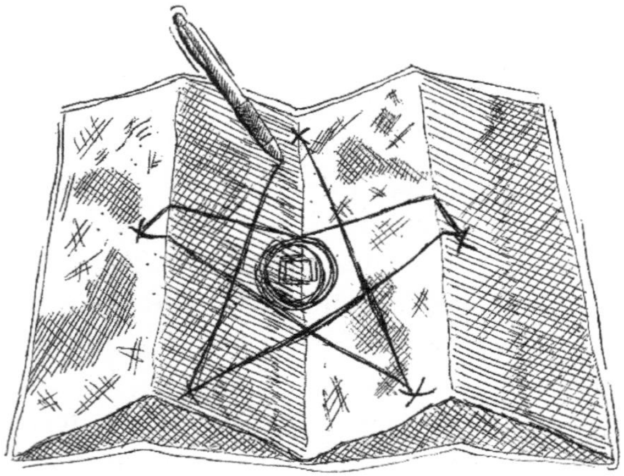

Capítulo 18
El descubrimiento de Ellie

Abrió la ventana. Un aire mucho más frío que las noches anteriores le puso la carne de gallina. En tales condiciones, requirió ponerse un suéter afelpado por dentro y encima de este su frazada azul, con la que se cubrió. Las resistentes corrientes lo empujaron adrede para hacerlo caer. Las ramas de los árboles flanquearon horizontalmente sus copas y los barriles de basura rodaron calle abajo como neumáticos sueltos de un tráiler. El clima se identificó cual huracán categoría 1. Ariel no pecó de ignorancia: la agitación sentaría mucho peor en el Parque de Juegos Monteseaur.

Al llegar a la casa de Ellie, tomó Ariel una piedrecita del jardín con la mano temblando de frío y la arrojó a la ventana. Falló el tino. Cogió otra roca, tanteando el suelo. En seguida apuntó y esta vez acertó. Apareció una sombra al otro lado del vidrio empañado. La silueta talló un círculo con la mano y se asomó. Era el

rostro de Ellie. Por la impaciente expresión de la chica, Ariel comprendió que tenía capturadas varias respuestas. La sombra se esfumó y el vidrió volvió a empañarse en segundos.

Un minuto después, Ellie abrió la puerta del domicilio y le hizo señas a Ariel de que pasara. Ya constando en la vivienda, hermosamente preparada para las fiestas decembrinas, ella lo dirigió en silencio a una favorecedora salita de tres sofás. El tiempo era cálido allí dentro, muy diferente al del número 72. El señor Villalobos decidió ahorrar electricidad ese año, descartando el servicio de calefacción. Ariel sintió más calor aún, cuando Ellie lo tomó de la mano y le susurró cerca del oído, casi besándole la mejilla:

—Espera. Mamá y Horacio acaban de encerrarse en su habitación. ¿Puedes creerlo? Ya duermen juntos.

Meneó la cabeza y se acomodó las gafas.

—En fin, debemos hablar en voz baja. No me agradaría para nada que te vieran aquí conmigo.

Aquel comentario inocente hirió a Ariel. Se sentaron en divanes apartados y fue él quien dio hilo a la conversación.

—¿Encontraste algo? —preguntó.

—Chist, baja más la voz —refunfuñó Ellie—. Sí. Acabo de descubrir algo valioso. Pero dejaré lo mejor para el final. Empezaremos con lo que me pediste que sacara en limpio: el multiverso.

Abrió su libreta, que había retenido bajo el brazo en todo momento. Buscó apuntes en las últimas páginas, orientándose con el índice, y soltó:

—Bien, aquí está. El multiverso —redundó—. Es un término que se usa para definir el conjunto de múltiples universos. En nuestros días, existe una hipótesis que afirma que existen realidades diferentes a la nuestra. Estas, a veces son llamadas universos paralelos,

pero en otros contextos también poseen distintos nombres, como: universos o realidades alternativas, universos cuánticos, dimensiones interpenetrantes y mundos paralelos. De acuerdo con el cosmólogo Max Tegmark, hay una clasificación para los universos existentes, pero él solo tiene una teoría.

—¿Quiere decir que hay más realidades? ¿Y la nuestra es una de cientos? —susurró Ariel, anonadado—. Arngfz mencionó que llevaba bastantes años aquí, ideando su plan. De hecho, una vez se le salió confesar que tenía «siglos» buscando al cazador de estrellas. Ellie, ¿tú crees que este no es el primer universo que visita? ¿Y si existe la posibilidad de que haya acabado con las estrellas de otros mundos y esta sea una de sus muchas paradas?

—Pero difiere con lo que me informé —controvirtió la joven detective—. Según los científicos, las realidades están separadas por una distancia infinita. ¿Sabes lo que eso significa? Que es imposible transferirse de una a la otra. Solo en la fantasía y relatos de ciencia ficción podría ocurrir algo semejante...

—Oh, vamos, Ellie. Dadas las circunstancias y los hechos presentados, ¿no es probable que esos científicos estén equivocados?

Ellie asimiló lo que Ariel altercó y asintió con la cabeza. La lógica no era un argumento sólido en esa plática.

—Supongo que se requiere de mucha energía para lograr saltar a otro universo —conjeturó la muchacha—. Y en cuanto al origen de Arngfz, te debo una disculpa. No he desenterrado nada importante sobre él todavía. Es difícil encontrar información de criaturas que se alimentan de estrellas, a menos que estés hablando del juego de Mario Bros. —anexó, a modo de broma.

—No hay problema —dijo riendo, atendiendo el chiste—. De verdad, muchas gracias por lo que estás haciendo, Ellie.

—A mí no me des las gracias. Yo soy la que debo estar agradecida contigo. ¿Te das cuenta? Estamos inmiscuidos en un caso que gira en torno a uno de los enigmas más complejos del universo. Sin ti, ahora mismo estaría comiendo moscas.

Ariel tomó aquello como un cumplido y le sonrió.

—¿Y cuál es ese tema valioso que guardaste para el final? —inquirió.

Ella puso cara de anhelo cuando escuchó esa pregunta. La había esperado ansiosa durante toda la charla. Se inclinó un poco hacia el frente y habló todavía más bajo.

—Tiene que ver con los cinco jóvenes desaparecidos —declaró.

—¿Hablas del... *Robaniños*? —insinuó Ariel.

Ellie sacó una hoja grande, que estaba metida en su diario, y la extendió. Resultó ser un enorme plano en blanco y negro de la ciudad. Tenía calles y avenidas etiquetadas con notas adhesivas de colores. Ellie quitó unos adornos de la mesa, los depositó en el suelo y por último alisó el mapa sobre la plana superficie.

—Usé estos planos para una exposición de Historia, hace mucho —explicó—. Ahora sirve para un propósito mayor. Te lo mostraré.

Sacó su bolígrafo y marcó un asterisco en una calle.

—Aquí fue visto por última vez Manuel Galaviz, el primer chico que desapareció. Una semana después, Pedro Almada en este sitio. —Marcó otra calle—. Y cuatro días más tarde, Fernando Duarte, mmm..., déjame ver —pensó—. ¡Ajá! ¡Aquí fue! —Rayó el mapa por tercera vez—. Luego de dos días, Alberto Rojas cuando estuvo acá. Y Germán Pimienta, el último en

desvanecerse, se encontraba justo en este punto, la semana pasada.

«La semana pasada —reflexionó él—. Poco antes de convertirme en cazador de estrellas.»

—Sigo sin entender —musitó Ariel—. ¿Qué tienen que ver estos muchachos con nosotros?

—Completamente todo —contestó Ellie—. Mira, ninguna de las desapariciones ocurrió durante el día —dilucidó—. Acontecían entre las once de la noche y la una de la madrugada. Dijiste que a las doce te encontraste con el viejo por primera vez, ¿no? Concuerda con las horas que raptaron a los cinco muchachos. —Metió una mano a su piyama y extrajo de ella una pluma roja. Luego dijo—: Quiero que sigas el recorrido que dibujaré con la pluma. Uniré cada uno de los asteriscos que puse en el mapa y te darás cuenta de algo. Presta mucha atención. Primero Manuel Galaviz..., luego Pedro Almada..., en seguida Fernando Duarte..., después Alberto Rojas y por último Germán Pimienta. Si a este último lo unimos con el primer desaparecido...

—¡Ellie! —expresó Ariel en voz alta, descifrando el misterio—. ¡Es una estrella de cinco lados!

—Chist, no alces tanto la voz. Así es —asintió la chica—. Las líneas forman una estrella, o mejor dicho un pentagrama —aclaró—. Es una figura emblemática de la nigromancia, estuve indagando sobre el asunto. Sirve para hacer ritos de magia negra, brujería y esa clase de cosas. Y no vas a creer esto: según algunas culturas —leyó—, se cree que el pentagrama alberga un poder inimaginable que puede abrir puertas a otros mundos, a cambio de un sacrificio.

—Y el sacrificio, en este caso, fueron los cinco adolescentes —discernió un alarmado Ariel—. Lo pensé la primera vez de Arngfz. Tenía mis sospechas, pero hoy lo confirmo: él es... el vagabundo es... No puede ser,

Ellie. ¡Arngfz es el Robaniños!

—Pero eso no lo es todo —anticipó—. Ve el lugar que queda justo en el centro del patrón que dibujé. ¿Qué hay en medio del pentagrama?

Ariel acercó su rostro y manifestó en voz alta:

—¡Es el Parque de Juegos Monteseaur!

—¡Chist! Baja la voz.

—Discúlpame —susurró. Más tarde, concretó—: Por eso puedo entrar a la guarida de las estrellas —concluyó—. Arngfz hizo todos los preparativos con conocimiento de causa, para que yo abriera la puerta del cielo en el momento preciso. ¿Crees que el Reino Astral se trate de otra dimensión?

—No creo —contestó Ellie—. Se supone que las realidades alternativas no pueden percibirse, a pesar de estar una debajo de la otra. Opino que el Reino Astral es otra cosa, como un paraje disimulado en un bosque espeso. Una vez asistí con mis padres (cuando todavía estaban juntos) al *Museo de lo Increíble*, en Guadalajara —detalló—. En una de las salas había un agujero en la pared por el que podías asomarte. Cuando tocó mi turno, acerqué mi cara y noté que enfrente de mí, justo en la entrada del hoyo, había un anillo dorado. Una inscripción encima del agujero decía que podía llevarse la joya quien pudiera alcanzarla. De modo que metí el brazo para aprehenderla.

—¿Y te la llevaste? —preguntó Ariel.

—No —admitió—. Fue imposible. Por más que metí la mano no di con la argolla. Hasta mi papá lo intentó, y eso que él tiene brazos muy largos.

—¿Cómo es posible eso?

—Porque era una ilusión óptica, Ariel, donde intervenía un juego de espejos. Es a lo que voy. El Reino Astral emplea una especie de ilusión óptica. Está encima del mundo, visible ante la gente, pero nadie

puede acceder a él. Bueno, salvo tú que hallaste la entrada.

—Percibo como si rompiera una telaraña muy delgada, cada vez que entro y salgo de allí.

—¿Lo ves? Es una clase de puerta. Aunque no me queda del todo claro que el hombre haya podido viajar a la Luna y enviar robots y cápsulas espaciales a diferentes partes del sistema solar. Se supone que el universo está en miniatura, ¿no? Tú me lo dijiste.

—Sí —convino Ariel—. En la Luna hay banderitas de los astronautas que pusieron su pie en ella.

—Eso, precisamente, es lo que no entiendo. ¿Cómo funcionarán realmente las medidas y escalas en el cosmos? Es una paradoja, Ariel —Después de un minuto entero de introspecciones, le preguntó a su amigo—: ¿En qué estás pensando?

—Creo que Arngfz pretende viajar a otro universo —respondió—. Y quizá la única manera de lograrlo es consumiéndose la energía de las estrellas del Reino Astral.

—Y como tú eres un soñador de corazón noble —mencionó Ellie—, estás haciéndole el trabajo sucio.

—Tengo que irme —se limitó a decir Ariel—. Debo plantarle cara a Arngfz de una buena vez.

Se puso en pie. Luego detuvo su acción y musitó con tristeza:

—Ellie, ¿crees que haya mentido con lo de Alondrita? —preguntó.

Ella dobló el mapa, lo embutió en su libreta y acomodó los adornos de la mesita.

—No lo sé —respondió con franqueza—. Tendrás que preguntárselo tú. No ha sido totalmente honesto contigo.

Se encaminaron a la salida en silencio. Al abrir la puerta, el viento helado les voló los cabellos. Voltearon

en dirección al Parque de Juegos Monteseaur y distinguieron una terrible tormenta de nieve que caía sin piedad desde las alturas.

—El clima se agrava a las doce de la noche —anunció Ellie, echando una ojeada a su reloj de mano—. Ocurre cada vez que estás por arribar al Reino Astral.

—Es la hora en que el anillo del agujero puede ser capturado —comentó Ariel, haciendo referencia al ejemplo de ilusión óptica que le dio Ellie.

Se despidieron y él le dio la espalda. Promovió Ariel tres pasos y advirtió que lo tomaron de la mano.

—Si el anciano te engañó y no puede curar a tu hermana —decía ella con un matiz de tristeza—, de veras que lo siento mucho, muchísimo. Sin embargo, sea verdad o no, tendrás que detener la cacería de astros y dejar de ayudarlo. Dile que será tu última noche. Ya conseguimos hilar nuestras suposiciones y sabemos que ese sujeto no tiene buenas intenciones con el asunto de las estrellas.

Le suministró un fuerte abrazo a Ariel, quien fue embriagado por su calidez. De alguna forma, lo hizo sentirse un poquito mejor. A la par, notó que la esperanza de que Alondrita sobreviviría lo abandonaba sin retorno.

—Y olvida capturar la estrella en el tubo de ensayo —dijo Ellie, al separarse—. Ya no es necesario.

—Hoy será mi última cacería —le recordó Ariel y mostró el objeto en su bolsillo—. Aprovecharé la situación. Pase lo que pase, mañana analizaremos una estrella.

Y se marchó.

Capítulo 19
El artefacto de da Vinci

En el parque abandonado arreciaba una poderosa tormenta invernal. La nieve caía a modo de mortales guillotinas. El viento soplaba con tanta violencia, que los achatados columpios se blandían delirantes. Ariel esperó de pie en la acera, observando aquella tempestad austral y poniendo en tela de juicio si saldría con vida de esa.

Marchitos algunos segundos, infló sus pulmones. Con su frazada se cubrió la cabeza y caminó de frente. Copos de nieve y fracciones de hielo le aguijonearon la cara. Se vio forzado a entrecerrar los ojos. No pudo mirar a un metro de distancia, puesto que los vientos celaban la zona bajo una capa de gris opaco. Ariel desocupó el aire retenido en sus pulmones. Entretanto consintió en respirar otra vez, el ciclón se apoderó de sus vías respiratorias. Acostumbrándose al mal clima, volvió a inspirar, engulléndose los copos de nieve que

se abalanzaban en su boca. Caminó a tientas, sin aferrarse a la seguridad de estar yendo por la dirección correcta.

—¡Al fin has llegado! —protestó Arngfz, quien por suerte se encontraba en su tamaño humano.

Su voz ya no se escuchaba enferma y entrecortada. Más bien, hablaba como un barítono amaestrado. En cuanto a su aspecto, descontando sus ojos blancos, se miraba distinto: jovial.

—Acércate un poco más para que veas tu próximo equipamiento —dijo aquel, sin necesidad de gritar. Su voz sonaba clara y estridente, pese al alarido de la tormenta.

Se inclinó el vagabundo y trabajó en una máquina excepcional. Ariel quiso adivinar lo que era. Semejaba una especie de cometa con forma de pájaro que apaleaba las siguientes particularidades: dos alas de madera unidas por lingotes metálicos; poleas y fuertes palancas; cables cobrizos y amarres hechos con soga vieja. El invento poseía el tamaño ambicionado para un muchacho de la edad de Ariel. Con un martillo, Arngfz se consagró en hundir largos clavos de seis pulgadas en la base. Ariel examinó mejor el artefacto, que fue diseñado matemáticamente, con ángulos y cortes bien decretados. En resumen, lo avistó perfecto.

Arngfz desertó en el suelo la herramienta que estaba ocupando y sustrajo un destornillador de cierta caja de herramientas congelada a sus pies descalzos. El adulto realizó pequeños ajustes por aquí y por allá en las dos alas y después dijo:

—Este artefacto lo fabriqué gracias a un plano que le hurté a un hombre llamado Leonardo da Vinci. Seguro lo conoces por la pintura de La Gioconda, mejor conocida por esta región como La Mona Lisa. Aparte de pintor, da Vinci también fue un inventor muy inte-

ligente, ¿lo sabías? Fundador de conocimientos dentro de los ámbitos de las matemáticas, física, anatomía humana y de algunas otras aportaciones sustanciales. Pero he de testificar que fue un individuo con el terrible problema del bipolarismo.

—Pues ya veo de quién lo aprendió —dijo Ariel, nada sorprendido.

—¿Qué dijiste?

—Olvídelo.

Arngfz adosó sus pestañas con hostilidad y reanudó su discurso:

—Nadie podía hablar con da Vinci porque no se sabía cuál sería su siguiente estado de ánimo. Un verdadero loco de remate, sí señor. ¡Y un maníaco! —añadió—. Si bien es cierto, en la mayoría de los genios y artistas que destacan en la sociedad, es normal este tipo de trastornos; otros ejemplos de ello fueron Miguel Ángel, Van Gogh, Salvador Dalí, etcétera, etcétera.

Arrojó el destornillador a la caja de herramientas y se puso a tensar los arneses.

—A propósito de robarle algunos de sus planos a da Vinci —prosiguió—, trabajé como su ayudante durante algunos años. Oí los pensamientos que decía en voz alta y puse mucha atención a sus habilidades intelectuales. De esa forma descubrí varios de sus secretos. Tuvo proyectos muy codiciados que no alcanzó a terminar; la mayoría los abandonaba y los dejaba a medias para iniciar con otro. En mi humilde opinión, hice bien en quitarle un ladrillo más de prepotencia a ese arrogante lunático, cuando sustraje de su taller el último plano del pájaro mecánico.

»De habérselo dejado, quizás, el ser humano habría volado desde tiempos inmemoriales. Imagínate cómo hubieran ocurrido los hechos venideros si Leonardo da Vinci demostraba a los demás que podía volar con

ayuda de este pájaro perfeccionado —indicó—. Dicho de otra manera, gracias a *mí* tuvieron que pasar algunas generaciones para que se improvisara el primer aeroplano por los hermanos Wright.

Arngfz extendió una de las alas cual abanico de mano. Estaba conformada por un manojo de plumas preciosas de madera anaranjada.

—La historia habría sido muy diferente —continuó el vagabundo—. Lo más probable es que tú jamás hubieras nacido. Y tampoco estaríamos aquí, teniendo esta conversación.

—¿Qué quiere decir con eso? —gritó Ariel, luchando contra el viento.

—No lo habías pensado, ¿verdad? Es el efecto mariposa, muchacho. Si dejaras caer una moneda en la calle, algún tercero la encontraría y haría algo trascendental con ella; un evento que dicho sujeto no tenía planeado. A lo mejor, comprarse el boleto de la lotería nacional que resulta ser el ganador. Y dicho evento desencadenaría, a modo de ramificaciones, otras acciones que se relacionarían entre sí y afectarían al resto del multiverso, igual que un efecto dominó. Provocarías, en consecuencia de esa hipotética moneda abandonada a medio camino, una baraja de posibilidades: un accidente de tránsito en otra ciudad, un terremoto en China, la decisión de estallar la guerra civil en un país por cierto grupo de independistas; que algún estudiante responda correctamente la última respuesta del examen, o que cierto par de jóvenes se conozcan al tropezar cuando doblaban por una avenida y acaben enamorándose. A estos sucesos se les llama realidades alternativas, muchacho —ultimó.

«¡Acaba de mencionarlo! —pensó Ariel en señal de alarma, evocando el perfil de Ellie—. Acaba de sacar a la luz el tema de las realidades alternativas que des-

cubrió Ellie en su investigación. Quiere decir que es cierto. Todo.»

—De no haber desamparado tu moneda en el suelo, los acontecimientos que acabo de enlistarte, jamás hubieran ocurrido en este mundo, sino en otra realidad alternativa. Por eso te lo dije antes de este discurso breve: «de dejar el plano en manos de Leonardo da Vinci, la historia de la humanidad, a partir del Renacimiento, hubiera sido muy diferente a la que conoces, y el ser humano habría volado desde entonces». Pero bueno, ¡qué sé yo! Ya solté demasiado la lengua. Son cosas que no tienen supremacía ahora. Ven. Te ajustaré estas correas.

—¡Mintió con lo de mi hermana! —vociferó Ariel ante la tempestad, en tono de réplica—. Me engañó. Usted no podrá ayudarla.

—¿De qué estás hablando, pelafustán? —expresó Arngfz, embravecido.

Cogió al chico del brazo, por encima del codo. Ariel se resistió, pero Arngfz, con su fuerza sobrehumana lo depositó a los pies del artefacto fácilmente. Lo despojó de su manta azul, objeto que se fue volando y residió enganchado en las ramas de un árbol. El hombre apresó los brazos de Ariel en las alas de la máquina, con los cintos de cuero que recién había tensado y, acto seguido, le amarró un macizo arnés alrededor de la barriga. En seguida, bajó una palanca.

—Me sorprende la certeza con la que vienes esta noche, cazador —se burló Arngfz, sin sonreír—. Nadie, escúchame bien, mocoso ingenuo, es capaz de salvar la miserable vida de Susanita.

—¡Se llama Alondrita, no Susanita! Estoy cansado de que lo diga mal —rebatió el muchacho—. Sé que me utilizó para llevarse a las estrellas.

—También en eso tienes razón —comentó.

—Es un cínico —habló entre dientes.

—Desde un principio te estuve vigilando. Mucho antes de tu primera cacería —reveló el vagabundo—. Eres un adolescente demasiado fácil de engatusar, Ariel Castillo Rivas. El solitario estudiante de la escuela del que todos se ríen, el narrador de historias fantásticas cuyo padrastro le repite que sea realista, el hermano optimista que le ruega a Dios que su hermanita no se torne de cristal.

—¡Cállese! —repuso. Le ardían los ojos, a pesar del frío—. ¡Cállese ahora mismo!

—No he dicho ninguna mentira, sabes que es así. Cuando saliste a acomodar el barril de basura aquella noche, conjeturé que verías el truco de mis ojos lanzando destellos en la oscuridad.

—¿Truco? —cuestionó.

Arngfz se llevó una mano al rostro y apretó su nariz. De pronto, sus ojos blancos fulguraron como los reflectores de una linterna.

—Los chicos como tú son los que caen, sin ningún esfuerzo, a las trampas —persistió, apagando las luces de su vista—. Seguiste mi pista y llegaste al parque de juegos infantiles. Un adolescente con mínima pizca de inteligencia se habría retirado al verme sentado en los columpios. Pero *tú* te quedaste aquí y confiaste en mí, creyendo que salvaría a tu hermana. ¿No miras las noticias? ¿No escuchaste las advertencias? «Los más jóvenes no deben salir de noche porque el Robaniños está desapareciéndolos». —Hizo una pausa—. Sorpréndete, jovencito, porque he de confesar que soy el autor intelectual de esas desapariciones.

«¡Entonces Ellie y yo tuvimos razón! Él es el Robaniños», confirmó Ariel, perturbado.

—Y te preguntarás por qué razón fueron menores de edad —continuó diciendo Arngfz—. Los adultos son

demasiado realistas y menos fáciles de manejar. Además, no cualquiera puede ser capaz de preparar el acceso al Reino Astral. Las inocentes vidas de aquellos cinco muchachos permitieron arreglar la entrada, dibujando un patrón en la ciudad. Tuve todo fríamente calculado. El último elemento fuiste tú. Quien llama a las estrellas, como ya lo sabes, solo puede ser un soñador de corazón noble que, ante todo, albergue esperanza. Es decir, un chico poco inusual, bueno y necesitado. Y en eso no te mentí. Las estrellas no se pudieron resistir cuando escucharon tus deseos. Gracias a eso, te abrieron la puerta de su colonia.

—¿Qué hizo con los otros?

—¿Los chicos desaparecidos? Pues me los comí. ¿Qué otra cosa iba a hacer con ellos? ¿Un bailable? Ya no existen —confesó, lanzando una desalmada carcajada, aunque sin gesticular una sola mueca en el rostro.

Rebuscó el martillo en la caja de herramientas. Ariel susurró:

—Y si yo no hubiera podido cazar estrellas, usted también me habría...

—Hum, soy muy precavido en cuanto a confeccionar mis planes se trata —replicó—. Era un hecho que me servirías para atrapar astros. Pero si te hace inútilmente feliz que responda a tu pregunta: de descubrir que eras ordinario, sí, te habría comido.

Ariel pensó en los cinco adolescentes: Alberto, Manuel, Pedro, Fernando y Germán. Sintió lástima por ellos, y con toda razón también por sus familias, quienes debían estar en esos precisos momentos sin pegar el ojo en la cama; buscándolos, recordándolos, extrañándolos, aguardando a que ocurriera un milagro y aparecieran sanos y salvos, tocando con los nudillos las puertas de sus casas. Arngfz era más malvado de lo

que Ariel se hubiera imaginado. Carecía de alma.

El antes mencionado localizó el martillo, cogió dos clavos de tres pulgadas y principió a martillarlos cerca de la oreja de Ariel.

—¿Por qué lo hace? ¿Qué gana devorándose las estrellas? ¿Quiere viajar a otra dimensión?

—¡Qué atinado eres! Bien hecho, muchacho. Se nota que hiciste tus deberes. Esta noche vienes acompañado de certeza —lo felicitó con sarcasmo—. Aunque el crédito debería llevárselo tu amiguita de aquella casa. Ella fue quien te ayudó, ¿verdad? La niña ojos de topo, que tiene una libreta llena de secretos.

Ariel dio un brinco de alarma.

Arngfz siguió conversando:

—Yo me entero de todo, mocoso. Nada puede esconderse de mí. Y naturalmente mi propósito es trasladarme a otra dimensión. Verás, el multiverso es infinito, y está compuesto por dimensiones que están unidas entre sí. Si una desapareciera, la que está debajo de ella, por consecuencia, también lo haría. Con todo, hay algo que no hallaron en su tarea tú y la muchacha entrometida; algo de lo que no están enterados los humanos: este mundo pertenece a una de las cinco Realidades Madre, de las que se desprenden el resto de las eternas realidades en cierta unión llamada: Pentaverso. Y si me apodero de las estrellas de sus cinco comarcas, podría atravesar las barreras del espaciotiempo con facilidad y viajar infinitamente a sus dimensiones secundarias. ¡Imagínate lo maravilloso que sería eso!

—¿Quiere decir que, si yo llegara a alimentarme de estrellas, adquiriría la facultad de viajar entre mundos y romper las barreras del tiempo? —pregunto Ariel de repente, tartamudeando.

Hasta ese momento se dio cuenta de que temblaba.

Inauguraba los primeros indicios de la hipotermia.

—Por supuesto que no. Morirías en cuanto tu lengua, harta de inmunda saliva humana, hiciera contacto con el más microscópico de los cuerpos celestes. Estallarías en mil pedazos. Sangre y vísceras revoloteando como insectos estrellándose contra el parabrisas de un coche en marcha. Tu cuerpo no soportaría tanta energía. Así que ni pienses cometer una estupidez.

—Y como usted no es un ser humano... Por eso c-comer astros no le hace d-daño, ¿verdad?

Arngfz hizo un bufido de animal salvaje y respondió con desgano:

—No soy humano. Yo antes era un lucero; una estrella de *Únim*, la primera Realidad Madre... Y parece que esto ya está listo.

Metió una cuerda por el eslabón que se ubicaba en el arnés de Ariel y le hizo un perfecto nudo de marinero. Por fin, tiró de ella para comprobar que se encontraba asegurada. Ariel caviló en lo que le reveló el mendigo. ¿Arngfz había sido una estrella? Entonces, ¿por qué su piel era blanca y fría, desprovista de luz? ¿Apoco los luceros podían adquirir apariencia de gente común y corriente? ¿Una estrella? ¿En serio? ¿Por eso puede vivir tantos años sin morir?

—Esta ocasión encerrarás a tus presas en tres bolsas que te voy a entregar. Cuando una se llene, la amarrarás con un lazo que viene incluido en la abertura y la dejarás caer. Yo me encargaré, desde este punto, de que llegue a su destino.

Sonrió y metió los tres envoltorios en el bolsillo del piyama de Ariel.

—¡A cazar estrellas se ha dicho!

—No lo haré.

—¿Qué has dicho?

—No q-quiero seguir haciendo esto. V-vaya a buscarse otro mugroso c-cazador de estrellas. Me cansé de ser su p-p-patético sirviente.

—Estás jugando con mi paciencia, muchacho. No seas idiota y haz tu trabajo.

—No curará a Alondrita, así que da igual que yo no t-trabajaré para usted. Punto. Desáteme ahora mismo, se lo ordenó. O iré a la p-policía y les contare t-todo.

«Como si me creyeran», agregó Ariel para sí.

—¿Estás seguro de esta decisión? —inquirió Arngfz.

—¡Sí! —respondió—. Libéreme.

Arngfz, entonces, levantó un brazo y lo estiró con repulsión en dirección a la calle Monteseaur. Semejó tenerlo hecho de gelatina; un tentáculo de pulpo. Cuando la extremidad volvió a adquirir su medida tradicional, trajo consigo una caja de pañuelos color verde.

—¿No quieres sonarte? No vaya a darte catarro con este clima —dijo el maligno merodeador.

Ariel sintió que le arrebataban el alma. Aquel objeto de cartón pertenecía a Alondrita. Arngfz había estirado tanto su brazo por la calle Monteseaur, que pudo llegar hasta el número 72, se escabulló por la ventana del cuarto de Ariel, imitando una víbora, recorrió el pasillo caminando con los dedos y se introdujo al aposento de la niña, donde obtuvo con facilidad la caja encima de la cómoda.

—Qué sencillo es llegar a tu casa, ¿no es así, Ariel? —dijo la antigua estrella, haciendo sonar un timbre de amenaza en la voz—. Puedo visitar a Susanita esta misma noche y saludarla. ¿Qué te parece?

—¡D-déjela en paz! ¡Con ella no se m-meta! —gritó Ariel, haciendo temblar el artefacto.

—Si no quieres que vaya a conocer a Susanita en persona, entonces sigue mis instrucciones.

—De acuerdo, lo haré. Lo haré. Pero no vuelva a meter un solo p-pelo en mi casa, ¿oyó? —dijo, titiritando.

Arngfz no replicó ante tal respuesta. Sostuvo un semblante satisfecho, triunfante. Sacó un pañuelo de la caja y se sonó con él. Luego soltó ambos objetos para que fueran arrastrados, en ese mismo segundo, por un arroyo de viento. Se incorporó y adoptó su alcance de gigante. Fue como ver un video a cámara rápida donde se aprecia el crecimiento de una planta. Arngfz sostuvo el extremo de la cuerda que sujetaba al pájaro mecánico y emprendió a correr, saltando de calle en calle, esquivando los tejados más altos de las casas. La soga se miraba como un imperceptible hilo de coser, entre sus dedos del tamaño de los muslos de un hombre. Debido a la perversa opacidad de la tormenta, Ariel no pudo entrever nada de esto. Si bien, se percató que, tras momentos próximos, la hebilla de su arnés repicó contra su estómago, paralela al picoteo de un pájaro carpintero. La cuerda se estremeció en movimientos cimbreantes, cual cable de alta tensión, y acabó tensándose igual que un ligamento muscular.

Ariel se despegó del suelo agresivamente. Las alas de madera, en las que llevaba consolidados los brazos, se desplegaron y alquilaron la postura de un halcón en pleno vuelo. El cazador navegó por los aires borrascosos del parque hasta emerger de la tormenta. A continuación, voló por las calles de la ciudad, apartándose de las bárbaras temperaturas bajo cero. El clima del exterior lo recibió con una placentera oleada de aire, más templada que los torrentes del parque recreativo. Su hipotermia se apaciguó. En la lejanía, Ariel divisó a Arngfz, quien superó las cimentaciones de la ciudad. Rebasaba puentes y anchas lagunas como si de insignificantes pedazos de madera y charquitos de agua se tratasen. Brincaba presuroso por las cumbres de altos

cerros. Gracias a dicha acción, el artefacto volador se elevó todavía más, igual que una cometa siendo encauzada a las alturas por obra de un niño a la orilla de la playa. De este modo, Ariel descubrió el funcionamiento de las alas. Las agitó y esto incitó que el viento acudiera a su favor, haciéndolo dar piruetas imposibles y elevaciones repentinas. Subió tanto como pudo, con la adrenalina aleteando por su cuerpo. Las puntas de sus dedos promovieron un hormigueo.

Cruzó por en medio de los rascacielos más altos y vio su propio reflejo proyectado en estrechas ventanas verticales. Luces automáticas de una fiesta juvenil lo enfocaron. Por un injustificado santiamén, sus ojos fueron cegados. Ariel franqueó el inmueble colindante con los párpados cerrados, pero al consumar dicha acción estuvo a un centímetro de estrellarse contra el ventanal de un edificio departamental de treinta pisos. Ariel acabó salvando de puro milagro su pellejo. Detrás del cristal, una mujer que merodeaba la edad de la treintena, observó la hazaña con la boca abierta. Aquella dejó que se hiciera añicos el plato de cereal que estaba a punto de cenar y su perro se aproximó a lamerle los pies mojados de leche.

A los segundos, Ariel distinguió a Arngfz frenando en seco, en los límites de la playa. Aquel tomó una ruta distinta.

—¡Prepárate! —le gritó el gigante cuando estuvo debajo de él.

El chico predijo lo que ocurriría detrás: el pájaro mecánico giró. Tanto el cazador de estrellas como el poderoso gigante que lo dirigía, retornaron al parque recreativo. Solo allí y no en otro lugar, Ariel era la única persona en el mundo capaz de ingresar al Reino Astral. Para esos momentos, ya tenía la práctica necesaria para dominar las alas de la máquina que lo transpor-

taba, por lo que le resultó más sencillo el viaje de venida.

Un poco más tarde, ya ubicado en la calle de su casa, Ariel perforó la tormenta del parque abandonado. Se internó en una campiña de nubes coaguladas. El pájaro mecánico, con su opulento pico férreo, rasgó la película de seda que abría la entrada a la nación de los astros. Ariel accedió al Reino Astral.

Se notó la sepultura del sonido. Lo bordearon a Ariel aquellas armoniosas luces de estrellas y galaxias cercanas. Se benefició de disfrutar a la Luna muy cerca suyo. Inseguro, acarició la superficie del satélite con la yema de los dedos. Resultó ser helado y roñoso. Un par de fragmentos color gris se desmenuzaron entre sus dedos y cayeron en el tálamo de nubes.

A Ariel no le apetecía repetir otra cacería. Con todo, en su cabeza circulaba la amenaza de Arngfz, que tenía que ver con visitar a Alondrita si no hacía lo que le ordenó. Comprendió pues, que no tenía otra opción más que seguir con la persecución de estrellas, la cual era hora de arrancar. Sacó la primera de las tres bolsas de plástico de su piyama y la desdobló suavemente. ¿Por qué se le ocurriría a Arngfz que fueran de plástico? Dicho material era demasiado ruidoso. Y la regla fundamental de permanecer en el Reino Astral era la de evitar el sonido.

«A lo mejor quiere que me atrapen las estrellas y me lleven a su castillo. Así se desharía de mí», pensó Ariel.

Estiró la abertura de la bolsa con ambas manos y avanzó. Las estrellas cayeron por sí solas al interior, sin tener el requisito de desprenderlas con pinzas, como la noche anterior. Mientras estas iban desmoronándose de sus lugares, cuales hojas de un árbol en otoño, Ariel sentía que el hule se meneaba frenético. Los luceros trataban de evadir a toda costa el cautive-

rio. Cuando Ariel percibió que el envoltorio se hallaba atiborrado de presas, lo cerró y lo amarró con el asegurador.

Lo soltó.

El objeto cayó y atravesó la lechosa neblina. Al punto de transcurrir los segundos, Arngfz se encargaría de liquidarlo. El malestar de culpabilidad y opresión en el pecho asfixió al desmoralizado Ariel. Extrajo el segundo plástico de su bolsillo y repitió la misma operación de antes: lo desdobló con lentitud, ahorrándose la ambición de que no se escuchara el lamento del hule; lo estiró, capturó luceros volando igual que una avioneta de guerra, lo amarró con el listón y, en resolución, lo dejó caer. Sin demora, llegó el turno de la última bolsa. Ariel obró lo mismo que con sus dos predecesoras. Solo que, al presente, después de sellarla, se encargó de no soltarla, porque miró delante de él una forma amarilla-crema con salpicaduras marrones y visera encorvada, dando vueltas perezosas en la nada.

«¡Mi gorra! —se dijo con asombro—. Conque la perdí aquí.»

Planeó hasta ella, haciendo oscilar las alas del artefacto alado y la pescó con una mano. Se la ajustó a su cabeza, con el resguardo apuntando en dirección al sur. Estuvo en la disposición de descender a la Tierra, cuando...

Aquella seductora estrella dorada, la misma de la noche anterior, apareció frente a él.

Su fulgor volvió a hechizarlo. Le pareció más radiante que nunca, y por esa misma razón, era la candidata para llevarla ante Ellie Durán y analizarla en el microscopio de la escuela. Desembolsó el tubo de ensayo, lo privó de su corcho y después hizo un movimiento rápido para apoderarse del lucero. Selló el recipiente y contempló el cuerpo durante una fracción de

segundos. Inversamente de estar aprisionado tras el cristal, el astro aún cultivaba su deslumbramiento. Embobecido, Ariel advirtió que la estrella despertó y revoloteó dentro.

—Quédate quieta —le habló en tono de reprimenda, puesto que casi se le cayó de las manos.

La echó al bolsillo y se percató, entonces, del grave error que acababa de incurrir. Ariel «habló», y no lo hizo precisamente en un volumen bajito. Su voz se repitió como si hubiera gritado desde la punta de la montaña más alta del mundo. El eco de su frase se oyó en cada rincón del Reino Astral:

¡Quédate quieta! ¡Quédate quieta! ¡Quédate quieta!...

Sintió que le echaban un balde de agua fría encima. Las estrellas despertaron.

Capítulo 20
Capturado

Las estrellas que andaban sueltas a los alrededores se despegaron de su sitio bañado de pegaluz. Tan pronto como se recobraron, se aproximaron a su enemigo deslizándose en zigzag. Por donde viajaban, dejaban un rastro de polvitos azulados, similares a las chispas que huyen de las luces de una bengala. Rodearon a Ariel y estudiaron su aspecto. Le atestaron golpes en la cara, que el muchacho percibió como minúsculos piquetes de agujas en la piel. Advirtió que los luceros se afianzaron de sus brazos como prendedores de ropa y tiraron de él con todas sus fuerzas, con el objeto de que no escapara de sus dominios. Otro equipo de lugareños trató, a costa de pellizcos, arrebatarle la bolsa y liberar a sus amigos.

Querían llevárselo al misterioso lugar que ni siquiera Arngfz era capaz de describirle a Ariel. Su castillo de cristal. El pánico se sembró por su cuerpo.

—¡Suéltenme! —vociferó.

Y su eco redobló:

¡Suéltenme! ¡Suéltenme! ¡Suéltenme!...

Batió las alas de madera del vehículo aéreo, pero se le pescaron más astros cada segundo. No conseguía volar.

—¡Arngfz, ayúdeme! —gritó, volteando hacia abajo para que aquel pudiera escucharlo.

¡Arngfz, ayúdeme! ¡Arngfz, ayúdeme! ¡Arngfz, ayúdeme!...

Las palabras de Ariel no atravesaron el tapiz de nubes. Se localizaba en un lugar recóndito, donde nada ni nadie podía entrar o salir de él, salvo un soñador de corazón noble.

Las estrellas lo apartaron de la salida.

Ariel siguió luchando y forcejeando. Era inútil combatir contra el sinnúmero de luceros que lo tenían cubierto. Lo arrastraron por galaxias, cinturones de meteoritos, más allá de todos los planetas del sistema solar y de lo acreditado por la humanidad. Entonces, a lo lejos, escondido tras un planeta anillado cien veces más grande que el señorial Júpiter, pudo entrever un enorme palacio con una fortaleza de cinco lados, suspendido por unas nubes arreboladas. Para horror de Ariel, descubrió que las estrellas podían comunicarse entre ellas. Gritaron palabras en un lenguaje extraño. El sonido igualó el zumbido de un mosquito.

Una puerta majestuosa del castillo se abrió y del interior emergieron varias luces azules, que se aproximaron a toda velocidad.

—¡Por favor, perdónenme! —suplicó Ariel, al límite

del llanto.

Había echado la misión en saco roto.

¡Por favor, perdónenme! ¡Por favor, perdónenme! ¡Por favor, perdónenme!...

Los luceros que lo hostigaban, siguieron empeñados en desprenderle el envoltorio del puño, mas Ariel se rehusó a soltarlo. Era su única llave para evitar que Arngfz le echara una vuelta a Alondrita.

Escuchó el cazador, con ahogante tristeza, que los recién llegados le discutieron y enumeraron acaso sus derechos de prisionero.

En aquel momento, mientras las estrellas parloteaban, Ariel sintió un dolor perpetuo en la espalda. El arnés fue tirado con fuerza, y no por sus captores, los luceros, sino por algo más potente. Los astros se desunieron del pájaro mecánico y de Ariel y fueron expulsados en todas direcciones, como las púas de un puercoespín. El joven ni siquiera logró percatarse de lo que pasó. De estar a punto de ser encarcelado en un enorme castillo, al segundo por venir atravesó el cosmos entero.

Tras romper la telaraña de evacuación del Reino Astral, Ariel se ahogó con las densas nubes por las que navegó. Descendió por los cielos a una velocidad improbable. ¡Era insostenible que aquella soltura, que lo lastimaba, perteneciera a Arngfz! Ariel se empeñó en averiguar lo que estaba pasando. Y entonces se percató de que no iba bajando. En realidad, iba planeando en dirección horizontal. Pero, un momento...

«¿En dirección horizontal?»

¿Qué ocurría? Y, sobre todo, ¿quién tiraba tan fuerte de la cuerda? El pobre de Ariel opinó que la correa se encarnaba en su espina dorsal. Tan pronto como esas

preguntas se multiplicaron en su cabeza, enfocó su visión para reconsiderarlas. Reveló pues, que no era un «alguien» lo que halaba de él, sino un «algo».

Un avión, para ser más exactos.

El aeroplano, que curiosamente pasó por encima del Parque de Juegos Monteseaur, justo cuando Ariel iba a ser llevado al palacio de los luceros, se comprometió a que una de sus alas se llevara consigo la soga que estaba al resguardo de Arngfz. Ariel le dio una vuelta entera a la nave (gritando a todo pulmón, evidentemente), hasta dar otra y de próximo otra, hasta que su cuerpo y el pájaro mecánico quedaron apresados en una clase de amarre. El avión aparentó, de lejos, llevar vendada una grave herida de guerra en su flanco izquierdo.

Ariel atendió el potente clamor del aire y las turbinas del vehículo atronando en sus orejas. La bolsa de estrellas, salvada de milagro en su puño, se zarandeó con los bailes de escape que ejecutaban las luciérnagas de su interior. Por suerte, le quedó al adolescente un brazo libre, puesto que el plumaje de una de las alas del artefacto de da Vinci quedó destruido. Se volvió hacia un lado y descubrió a una niña, que tendría la misma edad de Alondrita, mirándolo detrás de una ventana redonda. Azorada, la pequeña abrazó a su osito de peluche con afecto. Sin preverlo siquiera, la gorra vieja que Ariel acababa de recuperar, salió desbocada de su cabeza y quedó reclutada en las astillas anaranjadas del artilugio.

Estando en aquellos incontables pies de altura, ¿quién podría socorrerlo? Nadie, especuló Ariel, ni siquiera Arngfz. A pesar de que aquel lograra agenciar las dimensiones de un verdadero semidiós, estaba muy alto. Si quería salir de ese embrollo, Ariel tenía que hacerlo por su propia cuenta. Siendo valiente y alimen-

tándose de su fe, agachó la mirada y estudió la cuerda rota que sometía el arnés. Aquella danzaba sobre la imagen panorámica de la ciudad. La aeronave debió haber destrozado la soga con su fuerza, sacó Ariel conclusiones, y en las manos de Arngfz no quedó más que una parte seccionada.

En cuestión de segundos, el avión transportó al cazador de estrellas lejos de las casas y edificios de la urbanización. Hoy por hoy, tuvo el inmenso mar en vanguardia. Y si no lograba liberarse de aquel amarre (leyó el nombre del transporte en la cubierta: *Europea*) atravesaría el Océano Atlántico y moriría congelado horas más tarde, antes de aterrizar en el continente europeo.

Volteó a las ventanas, con el pensamiento de solicitarle rescate a alguno de los pasajeros.

Solo reveló que la niña de antes continuaba contemplándolo desde su asiento, como si presenciara una especie de truco. Aquella dejó de ceñir a su osito de peluche con un brazo y tocó el vidrio con su índice, apuntando a cierto lugar. Ariel rastreó la dirección señalada y chocó con una palanca puntiaguda donde antes se anidaban plumas. La pieza era pequeña, pero práctica como para trozar una soga. Ariel desclavó el segmento con la mano que tenía libre y, henchido de brío, picoteó la cuerda. Fue un trabajo que acabó rápido, se liberó casi de manera inmediata. Desabrochó el arnés donde conservaba arrestada su otra mano. Le quedaba abrir el cinturón que le forraba el estómago para dejarse caer. Lo único que lo mantuvo allí arriba fue su fuerza de voluntad. Faltaba algo más por hacer. Atrapó su gorra amarilla, que estuvo a punto de expatriarse en el soporte del viento, y apretó la bolsa de estrellas. Se encontró listo para saltar. Viró con la niña de la ventana, quien agitó su mano para decir adiós. Ariel agradeció

su ayuda con una inclinación de cabeza, desabrochó la correa y se arrojó al vacío.

Gritó mientras cayó. El mar abarcó cada vez más su amplitud. Por lo menos Ariel no se desplomaría en una calle pavimentada o un montón de rocas, pensó, donde su cuerpo se desparramaría a la par que una bolsa de salsa de tomate. Alojó esperanzas de salvarse. Aunque quedaba un dato significativo: jamás certificó su examen de natación. Estando a unos quince metros de separación del océano, casi besando el agua, avecinó sus pestañas, obligándose a aparentar que las cosas no saldrían del todo mal. Aguantó la respiración.

Y en aquel momento su cuerpo se negó a sumergirse en el líquido helado. En vez de eso, oyó el placentero rumor de las olas, que se le antojó lejano, pero cerca. Ariel se había desplomado sobre algo suave y cálido. Apartó las cortinas de su mirada y analizó en derredor. Su atontada vista tropezó con dos garrafales lunas blancas, que en realidad eran los ojos de Arngfz. Aquel ser adquirió un tamaño más imponente de lo habitual —hablando de atributos de gigantes, claro—. Atrapó a Ariel con su impresionante mano, ideal para reducir la mansión Winchester a una simple tortilla. El nivel del mar remontó, a duras penas, a la altura de su ombligo (y eso contando que se encontraban en una zona profunda del mar). Ariel no deseó ni imaginar la implacable longitud de sus piernas. Cuando contempló el rostro del vagabundo, se conservó petrificado y sin hálito. Ya no quedaba rastro del anciano que conoció noches previas, en el parque abandonado. Arngfz era un jovial y apuesto muchacho de rasgos selectos y blancura marfilada; con una exquisita piel sin líneas de expresión. No se sabía, con seguridad, si se encontraba en una actitud arisca o de felicidad, porque presumía de una imperturbabilidad que helaba la sangre. Su estado de

ánimo era un completo misterio. Tanta belleza, ante un ojo humano, resultaba intimidante. Empalagaba. Su cabello dorado era incandescente, lanzaba breves destellos. Y sus ojos, inmaculados diamantes en bruto, se posaron en Ariel, quien acobardado por su divinidad desvió la mirada hacia las olas embravecidas.

—Pensé que no te librarías de esta —emitió el titán.

Ariel se tuvo que cubrir los oídos para que no le detonaran.

—¡Casi muero allá arriba! —gritó Ariel, sintiéndose sordo—. Y todo es por su culpa.

—¡Y un cuerno! —emitió el mendigo, caminando en dirección a la playa.

Al encallar en la orilla, Arngfz descubrió un calamar gigante consolidado en su rodilla. Se lo arrancó campante y su piel quedó manchada de una grasienta tinta oscura. Arrojó al animal de vuelta a su hábitat natural. Después, el vagabundo estampó a Ariel contra una duna de arena.

—Te traje tu frazada. Dame las gracias —dijo Arngfz, echándole encima la manta azul. En seguida, decretó—: Ahora quiero que me des las estrellas que llevas allí.

—No lo haré —desafió Ariel.

Escupió la arena que se le introdujo en la boca.

Se protegió del frío con el satisfactorio objeto que le proporcionaron.

—¡Sí que lo harás, enano! —gruñó Arngfz.

Pese a que Ariel luchó por tener la bolsa consigo, esta le fue arrebatada por la punta de los ciclópeos dedos de Arngfz. El personaje abrió su boca descomunal y se cargó el envoltorio cual sabroso caramelo. Tan pronto como efectuó dicha acción, adquirió su estatura humana. Al instante, dio partida otra de sus peculiares transformaciones. Sus extremidades se tensaron y ad-

quirieron masa muscular. Se ensancharon tanto, que le otorgaron el cuerpo de un temerario fisicoculturista. Su pelo rubio brilló como una campana de oro. Se evaluó cual ángel inmaculado. Era bellísimo, pero Ariel sabía que por dentro su corazón estaría sofocado por la malignidad. Examinó Arngfz a Ariel con su terrible mirada blanca y se estiró quince metros.

—Sujétate —le ordenó.

Levantó al muchacho y se lo echó a su fornido hombro como si fuera un muñeco de trapo. Ariel se acomodó la gorra amarilla y aferró sus manos a la brillante melena de Arngfz, cuyos mechones eran del grosor de cuerdas de guitarra. El merodeador abordó un trote veloz por la orilla, dejando huellas inmensas de sus pies descalzos en la arena. La manta, a espaldas de Ariel, ondeó igual que la capa de un caballero andando sobre su corcel. Alcanzaron un faro encendido. Ariel aprovechó para vislumbrar el largo acantilado que tuvieron debajo.

Arngfz siguió deambulando. Corrió por campos y granjas, hizo estimar que saltar altas colinas fuera tarea fácil. Atravesó las calles, que al margen de unas horas estarían sufriendo un embotellamiento; y destruyó pequeños puentes de piedra que fueron construidos hacía poco.

—¡Tenga-más-cuidado! —gritaba Ariel, al ritmo de los pasos del gigante—. Puede-lastimar-a-alguien.

Pero dio igual que lo hubiera prevenido, porque Arngfz persistió causando estragos y malevolencias por donde cruzaba.

Muy pronto llegaron al número 72 de la calle Monteseaur. Arngfz se quitó al aporreado cazador de estrellas del cuerpo y lo depositó frente a la ventana de su habitación, sobre el jardín deslucido.

—Ya solo nos hace falta una noche, chico. Una no-

che —repitió, con su voz de trueno—. Mañana nos veremos en el mismo lugar y a la misma hora.

Ariel no replicó.

Arngfz se dio la vuelta y anduvo. Pero se detuvo en la casa de Ellie Durán. Ariel juzgó que aquel vio algo por el rabillo del ojo, a través de la ventana. Se preguntó el chico qué asuntos detuvieron al vagabundo justo allí. Luego de un breve rato, Arngfz siguió su marcha y se excluyó en los árboles del parque de juegos sin mirar atrás.

Fiu. Por un momento creyó Ariel lo peor. Se sacudió la arena del cuerpo y entró a su habitación. Antes de dormir, haría otra cosa.

—Te traje una sorpresa —dijo, un tanto feliz, cuando entró a la recámara de Alondrita.

Adormilada, la niña miró a su hermano con los ojos hinchados. La última fase de la cristalización humana estaba por finalizar. El color de su rostro y cabello empezaban a desvanecerse. Sus labios, orejas, dientes, nariz y pómulos, habían dejado de ser de carne y hueso para ser suplantados por vidrio.

Ariel entrampó la puerta, cogió unas ropas del armario de Alondrita y tapó las aberturas y huecos existentes en el cuarto. En seguida, se sentó al lado de su hermana, extrajo el tubo de ensayo del piyama y lo destapó. Un brillo amarillo sofocó la habitación. Del interior emergió un puntito dorado. Este revoloteó por debajo de la cama, saltó por las paredes, dio círculos en el techo y voló sinuoso por encima de sus cabezas.

—¡Es... un... hada! —expresó Alondrita, dichosa.

Ariel cuidó que su compañera no viera al astro más de cinco segundos. Le cubría los ojos con su mano. Fuera de eso, el espectáculo fue un éxito.

En determinado momento, la chiquilla dijo estar agotada y cerró sus ojos. Ariel caminó hacia el lucero,

que se adhirió al cristal de la ventana contemplando el cielo nublado, quizá deseando volver al Reino Astral. Tardó Ariel minutos en capturarlo. Esto se debió a que la luciérnaga se le iba de los dedos y se relegaba, aterrorizada, en un rincón. Al final, Ariel pudo dejarla inmovilizada cuando le arrojó una almohada encima.

Retuvo a la estrella en el tubo de ensayo y se encauzó a su cuarto. Se dejó caer en su cama igual que un bulto. Se cobijó, dio un resoplido que luego se transformó en un prolongado ronquido y se durmió.

La pesadilla compareció otra vez, paralela a una mancha de vino tinto en un mantel blanco, y que va ensanchándose hasta que lo encubre todo en una dominante oscuridad. Una oscuridad absoluta.

La bestia, que respiraba con salvajismo, volvió a alcanzarlo. Las cinco estrellas doradas brotaron del centro de Ariel. Se le heló el corazón.

Ariel se dio la vuelta y...

Félix, el reloj, maulló con todas sus fuerzas.

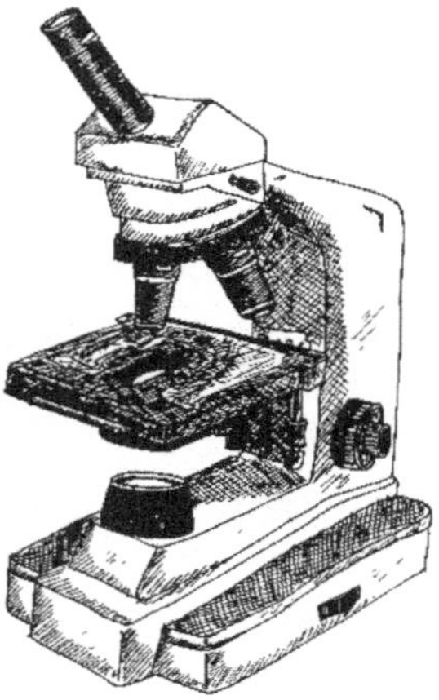

Capítulo 21
Uno, dos, tres, cuatro, cinco

No prestó atención durante la sesión de Segunda Lengua Extranjera: Inglés. La mayor parte del módulo la despilfarró fingiendo que leía un texto que debía traducir al español y reescribirlo en su libreta. El exhausto Ariel en realidad dormía, justo igual que en su última clase de Historia del día anterior (cuando la profesora Cuevas lo descubrió reposando en el pupitre y lo castigó dejándole la larga redacción del personaje histórico de tarea). El profesor Meza, encargado de la asignatura de Inglés, por el contrario de la maestra Cuevas, era un poco despistado. Aquel anotaba oraciones en el pizarrón, ignorando que el alumno de la última fila cabeceaba tras las tapas abiertas de su libro de texto. Ariel abrigaba unas ojeras destacadas, tenía la piel cerúlea y soportaba un cansancio lo que le sigue de terrible. Lo único que lo estimulaba, a intervalos, era la emoción de encontrarse con Ellie y obsequiarle

la estrella. La analizarían juntos en el microscopio.

Ella y él, solos. La idea lo extasió de pies a cabeza.

Se metía la mano al bolsillo de vez en cuando y sentía el tubo de ensayo. El lucero seguía descargando golpecitos. En ocasiones se despertaba Ariel sobresaltado, con el espejismo de que alguien se lo había robado.

Aquella mañana, Ellie no se reunió con Ariel. El señor Villalobos decidió llevar a su hijastro a la escuela en su automóvil. Durante el camino, el padrastro enunció una larga charla acerca de la actual situación política y económica del país. El hijastro aparentó prestarle atención, mientras reflexionaba que Ellie llegaría tarde a la escuela si lo esperaba más de la cuenta en la puerta de su casa.

El timbre de receso se hizo oír y los alborozados estudiantes resurgieron de las aulas como canes persiguiendo su hueso. Era el plazo de la reunión. ¡Ariel le mostraría a Ellie una estrella! Y no cualquiera, sino la más especial de todas, la de doce cúspides. La más brillante. La más preciosa. Paseó por los corredores aprisa, oyendo los dudosos rumores sobre la nueva desaparición de un adolescente y que suspendieron tres días a Brandon Portillo. Llegó Ariel al patio trasero y se detuvo, tal como convocó con Ellie, ante la puerta de acero que velaba el laboratorio de «Ciencias 3». Sin embargo, al transcurrir unos minutos delató que su amiga no llegaba.

«¡Qué raro! Ella no dejaría pasar una oportunidad de esta magnitud», se dijo Ariel, impaciente.

A escasos metros de distancia yacían tumbadas en el césped, aprovechando el sol, un par de adolescentes que conversaban animadas. Ariel reconoció a la que se hallaba más cerca. Pertenecía al grupo de Ellie.

—No vino hoy a la escuela —respondió aquella (cuyo nombre era Denisse), luego de que Ariel se le

acercara y preguntara por su paradero—. ¿Es qué no lo sabes?

Ariel se sorprendió de que se supiera su nombre.

—¿Qué cosa? —preguntó.

—Ellie desapareció esta mañana. Dicen que se la llevó el Robaniños —contestó—. En la escuela no se habla de otra cosa más que de eso y de la suspensión de Brandon Portillo. ¿No lo habías oído?

Ariel, más que sin palabras, se quedó sin voz. De modo que los rumores eran ciertos. Sí que había desaparecido un adolescente, pero jamás se le cruzó por la cabeza que esa persona hubiera sido Ellie. ¿En qué volátil minuto ocurrió aquello? Se sintió afectado por la noticia. Quiso buscarle un fallo al argumento, soltarle a Denisse que no era verdad, que no podía ser posible. Que era incierto que Ellie no estuviera allí. Acababa de verla el día anterior... Pero en seguida recordó que, antes de que el señor Villalobos doblara por la calle contigua de su casa, miró un coche patrulla merodeando por la calle Monteseaur. Existía lógica, pensó Ariel, en la historia de terror que le informó Denisse.

—Dicen que hallaron la ventana de su cuarto abierta, como si alguien la hubiera raptado por allí —agregó la muchacha—. Pero es muy raro que alguien trepe por las paredes y te saque de tu casa sin hacer ruido. Oh, pensé que ya lo sabías, Ariel. Oí que ustedes dos se hicieron muy unidos. Siento que hayas tenido que enterarte de esta forma —concluyó.

La chica curvó sus labios en una contorsión de pena y compasión. Tocó el hombro de Ariel en señal de apoyo. Tras unos segundos incómodos, Denisse se recostó en el zacate con el fin de volver a entablar conversación con su compañera.

Sintió Ariel como si su alma se hubiera fragmentado den dos. Trotando, fue a encerrarse en un comparti-

mento de los baños. Lloró de tristeza, añoranza, rabia; sobre todo de esta última, porque sabía que Arngfz había sido el único responsable. No, Arngfz no. Él mismo por haber metido a Ellie en eso. Ariel golpeó y pateó las mamparas metálicas del compartimento, abovedándolas, hasta cansarse. Sacó el tubo de ensayo y observó, respirando igual que un búfalo, el resplandor. Abrió la puertezuela con los ojos escondidos tras las cejas y se dirigió al laboratorio de «Ciencias 3».

El profesor López no estaba presente, como lo había predicho Ellie un día antes, así que Ariel se infiltró en el aula. Jamás había estado allí dentro. Solo los alumnos de tercer año tenían permitido el acceso a esa estancia para tomar clases de Química. No obstante, eso no le impidió a Ariel acercarse a la estantería que existía detrás del escritorio del docente y tomar un microscopio. Colocó el artilugio en medio de una alargada mesa y se acomodó en una silla. De una vez por todas descubriría qué cosa era una estrella. Se lo debía a Ellie y, en parte, también a él, porque tenía ganas, de todo corazón, de desafiar a Arngfz, quien siempre lo había privado de ponerse al corriente de la verdad.

Revolvió el tubo de ensayo, con el fin de que el lucero quedara inactivo y, sin demora, lo adaptó sobre la platina del microscopio. Accionó el interruptor.

El condensador echó un haz de luz (simple, en comparación con el brillo del astro). Ariel tomó el tubo ocular con una mano y asomó el ojo, mas no hubo nada por avistar. Había una luz dorada, que temblaba como un fantasma nervioso. Le dio un cuarto de vuelta al tornillo micrométrico. No sabía muy bien lo que estaba haciendo.

Giró el revólver y obtuvo el mismo resultado: nada.

Si bien, lo último que le quedaba por hacer era...

—Llegar a los cinco segundos —susurró.

Pegó su pupila al lente, sin parpadear, y emprendió un conteo mental.

«Uno». Tenía que correr el riesgo, así lo establecieron él y Ellie el día previo.

«Dos». Caviló en su madre.

«Tres». Inmortalizó la cristalización humana de Alondrita.

«Cuatro». Allí estaba él, yendo al encuentro del peligro inminente, despavorido, enojado y...

«Cinco». El conteo llegó a su fin.

El timbre en los corredores anunció el término del receso.

Ariel se quedó allí, sin pestañear. Sin embargo, en él no nació el deseo de querer acechar a las estrellas eternamente, como le había señalado Arngfz que ocurriría. Él seguía pensando en su madre, en Alondrita y en Ellie Durán. Se palpó las piernas y el rostro. También era el mismo de siempre. No obstante, sí que hubo un cambió. Pequeño, pero notable. Al regresar su mirada al microscopio, apreció sin tapujos el secreto más íntimo del cielo. Contuvo Ariel su respiración debido a la conmoción.

Lo que la imagen le arrojó era extraño, pese a ello, no imposible. La luz de la estrella dorada se asfixió o, mejor dicho, el ojo de Ariel se acostumbró a ella, como cuando uno permanece mucho tiempo en la oscuridad y entra a una habitación blanca, llena de luz, en la que no se logra distinguir nada. Al aguardar unos segundos, empiezan a distinguirse siluetas, sombras de personas y objetos. Y cuando se espera un poco más, la vista se ajusta al entorno.

La diminuta figura que dormitaba sobre el portaobjetos era un ser vivo. Pero no un bicho, como había intuido Ariel. La vista, a menudo resulta ser uno de los sentidos más sinceros que pueden existir. La estrella

respiraba, y su corazón en miniatura palpitaba frenético. Se trataba de un organismo pequeñito, tanto, que cabía en la uña del dedo meñique. Era un ser de género femenino que poseía la caprichosa complexión de los humanos, y de cuya espalda sobresalían cuatro alas transparentes, equivalentes a las de una mosca. Su piel era de un tono brillante. Su corto cabello, blanco azucarado, era esponjoso y delicado cual diente de león. Daba alusión a los peinados extravagantes que se utilizaban en los años sesenta. Iba vestida con una sencilla prenda color perla y utilizaba zapatillas de oro (aunque le faltaba una de estas). La desdichada mujercita estaba desmayada —si no es que casi muerta, a causa de las súbitas sacudidas que le dio Ariel en el tubo de ensayo—. Alondrita había tenido razón esa madrugada al calificar que aquel travieso puntito de luz, que levantó el vuelo en su habitación, resultó ser algo más o menos parecido a un hada. Lo cual significaba que Ariel, el cazador de estrellas, había sido culpable de que cientos de esas criaturas fantásticas hubieran perecido en la barriga de Arngfz.

Sus sentimientos lo dominaron. Se lamentó por todos y cada uno de los astros que envió al matadero. Tenía las manos manchadas de sangre.

«Soy un asesino. Un ingenuo e ignorante asesino», pensó.

Se enjugó las lágrimas.

—Lo siento mucho, de verdad —le decía a la estrella, sollozando—. Hice mal en confiar en un extraño que me prometió algo imposible. Le vi el lado fácil a las cosas. Siempre lo hago, soy un tonto. Despierte, señorita. No se muera.

Y los párpados de la estrella se separaron, descubriendo así dos abultados ojos purpúreos. Sus alitas se agitaron en movimientos rápidos, hasta que su rostro

dio aviso de un inmenso dolor. Se tocó la espalda con aquellas gráciles manos que parecían raíces celulares. Estaba lastimada.

—No quise hacerle daño a propósito —habló Ariel con clemencia.

La estrella enlazó su mirada con la de su captor.

—No se asuste —suplicó, al fijarse en el pánico del astro—. ¿Puedo hacer algo para sanarla?

La respuesta fue clara de adivinar. La estrella apuntó hacia una ventana.

«Llévame de vuelta», ese era su mensaje.

—Prometo que pronto la devolveré con su familia —dijo el chico.

El profesor López, de pronto, abrió la puerta del laboratorio y miró a Ariel con la frente arrugada.

—Ciencias 3 está clausurado para los de segundo grado —dijo, cerrando la puerta con prontitud.

Luego, aproximándose al escritorio, inquirió:

—¿Puedes decirme qué haces aquí, muchacho?

—Nada —se apresuró a responder el nervioso Ariel.

Buscó el tubo de ensayo en su bolsillo. No estaba allí. Lo encontró en la mesa y se hizo con él, pero no fue suficientemente rápido como para impedir que el maestro lo apartara de la silla y asomara un ojo por el lente del microscopio.

—¡Jesús! ¡No puedo creer lo que veo! —exclamó el profesor—. ¿De dónde sacaste esto?

López manejó hábilmente el artilugio y obtuvo una imagen más nítida. Desde un lado, Ariel contempló a la estrella, que intentaba batir sus alas para escapar. Tal acción lucró que se doblegara de dolor y quedara más malherida.

—Es la segunda vez en mi vida que me toca mirar una roca de este tipo —murmuró el profesor.

«¿Roca? —se preguntó Ariel—. Pues claro, el profe-

sor López es *realista* —descifró a espaldas de unos segundos—. No puede ver a la estrella.»

—¿Es viable que me la dejes unos días para estudiarla más a fondo? Parece fragmento de piedra espacial, es decir, un meteorito —explicó—. Mi hermano, que tiene una manía por coleccionar piezas astronómicas, una vez me mostró un pedazo de meteorito que tenía mil quinientos años de antigüedad. Increíble, ¿no es así? Y te puedo jurar que es idéntico a este.

Extrajo el lucero de la lámina. Lo estudió entre sus ásperos dedos.

—Mira, posee agujeros erosionados. Fulguran una sustancia amarilla —dijo sobrexcitado—. ¿Entonces? ¿Qué opinas de prestármelo unos días?

Hablaba con mucha pasión, como si hubiera querido dedicarse toda su vida a estudiar rocas espaciales, en lugar de ser el encargado del laboratorio de «Ciencias 3».

—No —determinó Ariel.

Y levantó el tubo de ensayo con tal de que el profesor introdujera el astro en su interior.

—Es mía. Devuélvamela, por favor.

—Llamaría a mi hermano. Puedes estar presente cuando la analicemos. Seríamos los tres —dijo el adulto, acercando la mano al boquete del colector—. ¿Estás seguro?

—Muy seguro —declaró el firme Ariel.

El docente soltó la estrella y esta cayó, de súbito, al fondo. Cuando aquella se incorporó, empezó a sacudir su vestido con molestia y se acomodó los bucles de su cabello con delicados movimientos femeninos. Le hizo muecas al profesor y lo apuntó amenazante con el dedo.

—Correcto —dijo con tristeza el caballero—. Si cambias de opinión, que no te quepa duda de que estaré

dispuesto a atenderte, para que investiguemos juntos el origen de esa roca... Te aseguro que tiene una historia muy buena.

Ariel concordó con él en eso último. Se guardó el tubo de ensayo en el bolsillo y se marchó.

Cuando la campana anunció la salida, por esta excusable ocasión, Ariel se unió a la masa de estudiantes que emergían del colegio. Solo que, a diferencia de los demás, aquel viernes él no corrió apresurado para empezar a disfrutar cada segundo del fin de semana, sino para encarar a Arngfz. Bajó las escaleras de entrada a toda prisa y atravesó la calle sin voltear a los lados (lo que provocó que algunos conductores irritados hicieran sonar el claxon de su automóvil). Desfiló sin interrupción y se detuvo en el parque, lugar por el que justo a esa hora corrían vientos amansados.

—¿Dónde está? —gritó Ariel, acercándose a los achatados columpios oxidados—. ¿Dónde es que se esconde, cobarde? ¡Dígame lo qué hizo con Ellie! ¿Dónde la tiene?

El destruido Ariel cayó de rodillas y sintió las piedras encajándose en sus piernas. Con todo, el dolor no le importó en absoluto, porque su sentimiento de rabia fue mucho más potente que él.

Cargaba con una culpa tan grande, que esta se desbordaba como un vaso de agua lleno. El monstruo de Arngfz, reflexionó Ariel, era capaz de cualquier cosa con tal de continuar devorándose las estrellas de los universos. Se detestó a sí mismo por haber sido utilizado; se odió por haber confiado que aquel tenía un remedio para curar a Alondrita; se aborreció por revelar el secreto de las estrellas cuando ya era demasiado tarde. Y maldijo el instante en el que dejó a Ellie des-

protegida, ante la sombra de aquel ser maligno.

—Jamás debí meterla en esto —se dijo—. Nunca debí contarle mi trato con Arngfz.

Chocó con un objeto que se encontraba debajo de un columpio aplastado. Se arrastró Ariel por el suelo y lo tomó. Era el diario de Ellie. Lo abrazó y respiró de él. La libreta mantenía todavía el olor de su propietaria. La hojeó y descubrió que fueron arrancadas las últimas páginas. No aparecía ninguna información relacionada con Ariel, ni nada que tuviera que ver con los acontecimientos de los últimos días. Estuvo seguro de que Arngfz las quitó adrede, acaso porque Ellie divulgaba en ellas cierto contenido que no le convenía que se descubriera.

Ariel se incorporó. Con voz amenazante, denunció:

—No volveré a cazar para usted, ¿escuchó? Quiero que regrese a mi amiga sana y salva.

Dicho esto, se sacudió las rodillas y marchó a un ritmo derrotado por la calle Monteseaur. Se arrimó a la casa número 46, donde vivía Ellie. La ventana de su habitación tenía las cortinas rasgadas. Pudo observar una pared de matiz achocolatado; un color muy peculiar para la recámara de una chica. Se acercó a la vivienda y tocó el timbre.

Lo atendió una mujer de gesto deprimido. Su madre, supuso Ariel. Se parecía tanto a Ellie que, quizá, podía ser su gemela adulta. Aquellos ojos, encubiertos detrás de unos lentes con fondo de botella, igual que los de la hija, exhibieron que había segregado lágrimas en las últimas horas.

—¿Eres amigo de Ellie? —preguntó la entristecida señora. Se fijó en la libreta—. Está claro que sí, traes su bitácora de observación —observó—. Es curioso, ella jamás me permitió echarle un vistazo —susurró. Y luego se tocó el pecho—. Oh, mi pobre niña. ¿Por qué a

ella? ¿Por qué?

Ariel no supo qué decirle, pero la acompañaba en la pena. Le rindió la libreta y la madre la recibió sollozando. Bañó la cubierta de lágrimas. Estrechó después al muchacho.

—Oh, perdóname —se disculpó la madre de Ellie, apartándose de Ariel—. Estoy hecha un desastre. Siento incomodarte. —Se talló la cara y escrutó el cuaderno—. Eres el chico del 72, ¿verdad? Ariel, el hijastro del señor Villalobos.

—Sí —respondió.

—Ellie estuvo hablándonos de ti.

Ariel descubrió a un hombre inquieto hablando por teléfono en la sala (supuso que era Horacio, el novio de la madre de Ellie). Aquel miró al adolescente y lo saludó con una inclinación de cabeza.

—Es bueno saber que tiene un buen amigo —mencionó la señora, en voz baja—. ¿No te dijo haber visto algo sospechoso? ¿Algo que nos pudiera dar una pista de su ubicación?

Ariel negó con la cabeza. Se vio a sí mismo como el mayor mentiroso del mundo.

—Bueno. Espero que de algo nos sirva el diario —dijo ella—. Lo estuvimos buscando como locos cuando llamé a la policía. Ellie anota datos en él. ¿Me permites un segundo? Le diré a Horacio que ya lo encontramos. Se lo entregaremos a la policía como evidencia…

—Hum, señora —musitó Ariel—. ¿Me da permiso de visitar… su cuarto?

—Por supuesto que sí. A lo mejor descubres algo que la policía y nosotros pasamos por alto. Ya lo inspeccionaron y debo decir que no descubrieron relevancias en él. Ni huellas dactilares, ni restos de ADN. El infeliz del secuestrador supo hacer su trabajo —habló entre dientes, impotente—. Bueno, iré con Horacio. Puedes

subir las escaleras. Es la primera habitación a la izquierda.

La mujer se retiró para encontrarse con su novio y darle la noticia. Ariel asistió al segundo piso. La puerta próxima estaba abierta e irrumpió en ella. Se halló en una habitación pequeña y acogedora. Rostros de detectives famosos se estimaban pegados en un muro y había noticias de periódicos enmarcados, en vez de las usuales fotografías familiares. Adherido a la pared, descansaba un librero de madera, integrado de novelas de misterio y thriller psicológico, antologías policíacas y todas las obras de Sherlock Holmes, escritas por Arthur Conan Doyle. Debajo de la repisa, se localizaba una cama con sábanas blancas y enseguida de esta, un escritorio con una computadora encendida. Se acercó a esta última y ocupó la silla. Movió el *ratón*, dio doble clic al explorador de Internet predeterminado y señaló, sin encomendarse a Dios, la pestaña del historial. No era muy de su agrado espiar a la gente, pero, por esa ocasión era preciso hacerlo.

Apareció ante sus ojos la lista de una búsqueda de esa madrugada. Seleccionó el último enlace y esperó a que cargara la página. Cuando leyó el título que aparecía al inicio, se quedó petrificado. Era un artículo astronómico. Releyó el contenido tres veces y supo entonces, el motivo de que Arngfz hubiera raptado a Ellie. Ella descubrió su naturaleza. El apartado proclamaba el siguiente encabezamiento:

"Los monstruos del universo"

Se levantó Ariel del asiento.

Fue a despedirse de la madre de Ellie, quien le ofreció un vaso de limonada. Lo rechazó amablemente y salió de la morada. Llevaba el rostro demacrado.

«Un agujero —se dijo Ariel—. Arngfz es un agujero negro.»

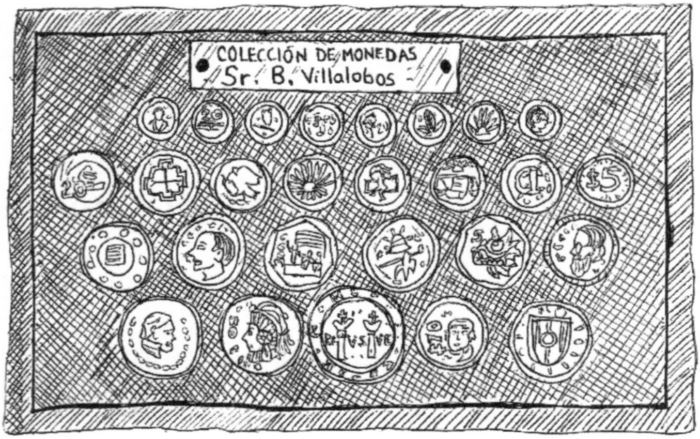

Capítulo 22
El segundo secreto

No se había dado cuenta de que tenía un hambre voraz hasta que llegó a su casa. Lo primero que hizo Ariel fue dejar la mochila en su recámara y después desplazarse a la cocina. Abrió el refrigerador, que estaba más vacío que las entrañas de una calavera. Ingenioso, acomodó un taburete y, parándose de puntillas, alcanzó las últimas cuatro piezas de pan blanco que constaban en una compuerta de la alacena.

Preparó un emparedado y se lo devoró en un dos por tres. Dejó el plato con infortunadas migajas y volteó, aún hambriento, a los dos trozos que sobrevivieron en la bolsa. Ariel pensó que Alondrita también tendría hartas ganas de comer. De manera que preparó un segundo bocadillo y fue hasta el cuarto de aquella, con ambas manos respaldando el plato. Su madre iba saliendo de la habitación con una escoba afianzada en la mano.

—Que buen hermano eres —musitó con una sonrisa vivificante. Le dio un beso en la frente a su hijo y después dijo—: Adelante, aliméntala.

Ariel asintió y se afilió a la recámara.

—Hola, princesita —saludó.

La chiquilla abrió los ojos. Su mirada transparente empezó a buscarlo.

—Hermanito, ¿eres tú? —expresó, en un murmullo—. ¿Dónde, estás?

—¿Cómo que dónde estoy? Me encuentro justo aquí, al lado tuyo —contestó risueño, sentándose en el banquillo.

—Está, muy oscuro. No puedo verte. Enciende la luz. ¿Ya es la hora, de los cuentos?

Ariel la contempló espantado. Observó aquellas pupilas moviéndose con pasividad. Acercó su mano a los ojos translúcidos y la sacudió en el aire. No hubo el más mínimo contacto visual. Era un hecho. Alondrita, que ya se conservaba completamente de vidrio, perdió el sentido de la visión. Ariel versó un calvario de emociones. En silencio, entabló sollozos, mordiéndose la mano para no exhibirse débil ante ella.

—¿Estás triste, Ariel? ¿Por qué lloras? No me gusta, que estés triste —dijo Alondrita.

—No lo estoy —negó, forzando la voz. Tratando de sonar seguro y convincente—. Te traje algo de comer.

—No tengo, hambre. Tampoco frío, o dolor. Eso es bueno, ¿verdad, hermanito? ¿Me estoy, aliviando?

—Por supuesto que sí —contestó después de aclararse la garganta—. Te recuperarás en menos de lo que imaginas, ya verás que sí.

—¿Mamá, estuvo aquí? Creí oírla.

—Sí. Justo acaba de marcharse.

—¿De verdad? —interrogó la niña.

Infló su pecho de vidrio, le costó respirar.

—Dile que regrese. Llámala y, dile que venga. Quiero que, me abrace.

—Te prometo que volverá pronto, pero primero tienes que comer para recuperar fuerzas. No querrás disgustarla.

—Tienes razón —repasó—. Comeré, para no disgustarla.

Ariel le acomodó una almohada para reclinar su cabeza y, acto seguido, le metió pequeñas fracciones de sándwich a la boca. Cuando la comida se escondía tras los labios de Alondrita, esta desaparecía.

—Quisiera, dormir un poco —mencionó Alondrita, tras rechazar el último pedazo—. Ya no quiero.

—Yo igual me siento muy cansado, princesita. Los dos deberíamos dormir.

—Quédate conmigo —suplicó—. No te vayas.

—No me iré a ningún lado. Te lo juro.

Desertó el plato sobre la cama y, postrando su mano en la muñeca de la chiquilla, se quedó dormido, con la mitad del cuerpo encima de la cama.

Despertó un par de horas más tarde, cuando oyó el timbre del teléfono.

—¡Yo contesto! —avisó la señora Rivas, corriendo por el pasillo.

Antes de descolgar el aparato, con todo, el señor Villalobos, que llegaba del empleo e iba emparejando la puerta principal, alcanzó el recibidor antes que su esposa y fue el primero en atrapar el artilugio. Se llevó el auricular a la oreja. Su expresión imparcial, a los minutos se tornó en un gesto de evidente rabia.

—Ajám —decía, en tono avispado—. Bien. Lo arreglaré con él. Muchas gracias.

Ariel sacudió las migas de pan que quedaron sobre la cama de Alondrita y se llevó el plato a la cocina. Por su recorrido, el señor Villalobos lo perforó con la mi-

rada.

—Gracias —ultimó el caballero a la persona del teléfono.

Colgó.

Caminó a su oficina, ejecutando pasos largos. Tras abrir la puerta con torpeza, aulló:

—¡Ariel, ven acá!

El joven quedó aterrorizado. ¿Quién habría hablado con su padrastro por teléfono? Que él supiera, no hizo nada malo. Avanzó con las manos pegadas a los costados. Cuando entró al pequeño estudio, el señor Villalobos hizo ademán con una mano de que Ariel ocupara una de las dos sillas disponibles. La señora Rivas también anunció su entrada, cerrando la puerta pausadamente. Invadió el segundo asiento y le preguntó a su marido:

—¿Quién habló, cariño?

El señor Villalobos se acomodó en el sillón, entrelazó sus dedos y recargó los codos en el escritorio. Ignoró a la señora Rivas. Miró a Ariel.

—¿Me puedes explicar qué pasa contigo?

Ariel se volvió con su madre.

—Acaban de llamarme del Trabajo Social de tu escuela —continuó hablando el padrastro—. Tus profesores reportaron que actúas de forma extraña estos últimos días. Alegan que estás fatigado, que llevas ojeras, que no duermes en casa y que presentas varios golpes todos los días.

—Yo... Bueno, he estado haciendo algunas cosas, señor —respondió.

—¿Qué clase de cosas? Tareas, tan entrada la noche, es obvio que no. —indicó—. Los maestros reportaron que tu desempeño académico bajó. De modo que sé más específico con tu respuesta. ¿Qué haces?

Ariel no sabía si contarle lo de las estrellas. A su

padrastro le parecería estúpido; otra historia fantástica.

—¡Eh! ¡Te estoy hablando! —recriminó el señor Villalobos, golpeando la mesa—. ¡Respóndeme!

La señora Rivas se alzó de la silla, se paró detrás de Ariel y posó las palmas en sus hombros.

—Permite que él nos lo cuente. No lo presiones —pidió con sumisión.

El señor Villalobos se tronó el cuello y los nudillos, con tal de apaciguarse, y entonces aguardó.

—Está bien, señor. Se lo diré —determinó Ariel—. Desde el lunes yo salgo por las noches.

—Sí, la señora Corrales me lo reportó —asintió el hombre—. Y creo que fui bastante claro con mi mensaje para que no lo volvieras a hacer.

—A pesar de eso, yo seguí escapándome a la medianoche —confesó.

—¡Ariel! —chilló la señora Rivas—. ¡Dios mío! Sabes de los peligros que acechan por la ciudad a esas horas. Hay secuestradores, gente mala. ¡El Robaniños, por Dios! Acaban de llevarse a una compañera de tu escuela...

—¿Quieres burlarte de mí, muchacho malcriado? —interrumpió el hombre a su mujer, apuntando a Ariel con el dedo.

Pegó al pupitre con mayor fuerza y los objetos sobre este (bolígrafos, carpetas, libros, y hasta una engrapadora), saltaron medio centímetro.

—¡Te ordené que no volvieras a salir! ¿Qué tanto es lo que haces en la calle? —vociferó.

—Dínoslo, hijo mío —le dijo su madre con afecto—. Estoy aquí contigo, no pasará nada. Dínoslo. Podremos arreglar este problema si lo platicamos con calma. Solo hazlo.

El señor Villalobos miró al adolescente como si viera

al peor esperpento del planeta.

—Estuve cazando estrellas, señor.

—¿Que hiciste qué? —cuestionó incrédulo.

—Iba al parque abandonado porque un vagabundo me prometió evitar que Alondrita se hiciera de cristal. Se lo dije la otra noche, señor, ¿lo recuerda? Cuando descubrí que las puntas de sus dedos comenzaron a volverse transparentes. Pero no me creyó. Y yo tenía razón. Alondrita sufre de cristalización humana, pero solo puede ser vista por soñadores de corazón noble, como yo. El vagabundo juró sanarla y acordamos que también la curaría de la osteogénesis imperfecta, a cambio de que yo le devolviera su juventud. Pero para ello necesitaba estrellas, así que yo me convertí en su cazador, para capturarlas.

Los ojos del señor Villalobos parecían dos papas a punto de prorrumpir de sus órbitas.

—De qué... ¿De qué estás hablando? «Soñador de corazón noble». ¡Te volviste loco!

—Soy sincero con usted —siguió Ariel—. Arngfz (que así se llama el vagabundo), en realidad es un agujero negro y quiere devorarse a los astros. Y no los quiere para recuperar su juventud, como me hizo creer en un principio, sino para conseguir trasladarse a otra dimensión. Y si esta noche consigue lo que se propuso, comenzando mañana, el mundo no volverá a ser el mismo que conocemos. Puede que se apodere del Sol y quedaremos a oscuras. ¿Lo entiende?

—¡Cállate! —Lo interrumpió el señor Villalobos—. No quiero que pronuncies otra palabra más. Estás desquiciado. Alondra está a punto de morir y *tú* te aferras a seguir viviendo en tu imaginación. ¡Sé realista! ¡Se realista! ¡Maldita sea! ¿Cuándo piensas madurar, muchacho imbécil? ¿Cuándo?

—Ya fue suficiente —habló la señora Rivas en voz

baja, pretendiendo tranquilizar la situación—. Yo hablaré firmemente con él en su habitación. Vámonos de aquí, Ariel.

Ariel se puso en pie.

—¡Tu media hermana morirá! —ladró el señor Villalobos—. Cuando eso pase, juro que te arrepentirás con toda el alma.

—Vámonos, mi niño —insistió la señora Rivas, asiéndolo del brazo.

—Ah, ¿sí? ¿Me arrepentiré? —gritó Ariel, surcado de lágrimas—. ¿Así como usted se arrepiente con toda el alma de haber matado a mi madre?

Y su padrastro lo miró, descolorido. No se esperaba que lo atacaran de ese modo. La señora Rivas soltó a Ariel y se avecinó al costado del escritorio, desorientada.

—¿De haberme matado? —inquirió ella, sobresaltada—. Conmigo no bromees así, Ariel.

—¡Tu madre falleció en un accidente de tránsito! —exteriorizó el señor Villalobos—. ¡Y yo no tuve nada que ver con eso!

—Yo no... Están en un error —decía la señora Rivas, enfocándolos a ambos—. Yo no puedo estar muerta. ¿Qué significa esto?

—¡Por supuesto que todo tiene que ver con usted! —protestó Ariel, sintiendo pena de que la señora Rivas se tuviera que enterar de aquella forma—. Mi mamá murió porque intentaba escapar de usted. Se hartó de sus golpes, de sus insultos, de sus gritos... Por eso condujo a toda velocidad aquella noche, después de la última golpiza que le dio.

—Se marchó porque fue su decisión —debatió el enfadado padrastro—. No quieres aceptar la realidad. Los *abandonó* a ti y a tu media hermana porque no los quería. Iban a quedarse huérfanos de madre de cual-

quier forma. Viva o muerta.

—¡Qué alguien me explique lo que está pasando! —insistió la desesperada señora Rivas, con los ojos amortiguados—. ¡Dígamelo alguien!

—Ella jamás nos habría abandonado —repuso Ariel—. ¡Está mintiendo!

—Entonces ¿por qué llevaba las maletas abarrotadas de ropa en el coche? ¿Por qué no iban ustedes en el vehículo? ¿Por qué no la acompañan dos tumbas a cada lado en el cementerio? Admítelo, muchacho. Renunció a ustedes, a sus propios hijos, y los dejó a mi suerte.

—Alondrita y tú son lo más importante en mi vida —gimió la señora Rivas, llevándose las manos a la cabeza, como si le doliera—. Nunca los dejaría solos al cuidado de esta bestia. ¡Él miente! ¡Miente!

—Tiene miedo de que la gente descubra la verdad, ¿no? —recalcó Ariel—. Que se enteren de que, por culpa suya, murió una mujer inocente. Le preocupa que las personas, los vecinos, sepan que los moretones que mi mamá tuvo aquella noche, de hace un año, no fueron consecuencia del choque, sino por obra de su marido.

—Encima de loco, charlatán —incriminó el señor Villalobos—. No sabes el problema en el que te estás metiendo por divulgar esas estupideces. Pero de toda esta situación, por fortuna, acabas de ganarte un premio.

Ariel no quería atenderlo. Aun así, sus oídos se bebieron las amargas palabras de su padrastro con desagrado.

—A partir del lunes estudiarás en el colegio militar Emilio Echeverría Álvarez. Ya está decidido —dictaminó—. Es hora de deshacerme de ti. Justo ahora hablaré con el comandante Arturo Benítez, que es buen amigo mío y director de ese instituto, para comunicarle

que tendrá un nuevo estudiante. Y uno muy difícil, le explicaré. Al cual deberá obligar a plantar los pies sobre la Tierra. Le daré permiso de que emplee el látigo y la vara contigo y te haga sangrar. ¡Oh, sí lo hará! Sangrarás como nunca lo has hecho y yo lo disfrutaré victorioso. Ya está dicho. Te llevaré el domingo, así que prepara tus pertenencias y ve despidiéndote de tu media hermana. Mañana será el último día que pases con ella. En caso de que fallezca, serás el último en enterarte. Tendrás prohibido asistir al entierro.

—¡Eres un monstruo! —gritó la señora Rivas—. Él no irá a ninguna parte. No lo permitiré. —Alzó la voz lo mejor que pudo.

—Mi madre no dejará que se salga con la suya —anunció Ariel—. Una parte de ella permanece aquí, conmigo. Y su recuerdo es tan fuerte que, gracias a la imaginación que usted tanto me obliga a eliminar, le otorgué vida a su espíritu. Y en estos momentos se encuentra justo delante de usted. Ese es mi segundo secreto.

—Tu segundo secreto —repitió—. ¿De qué diablos hablas, imbécil? Su espíritu... En serio que disfrutaré mucho de tu ausencia —expresó, aunque un poco tenso.

El señor Villalobos le temía a todo lo relacionado con lo sobrenatural.

—Ahora razono por qué me ignora cuando le hablo —dijo la señora Rivas, mientras su marido le enumeraba a Ariel lo que haría en cuanto se marchara—. Sé por qué cada vez que limpio la cocina, no levanta los pies al momento de pasar el trapeador. Ya entiendo por qué, por más que limpio esta casa día y noche, el polvo sigue estando allí. Y sé también por qué si pinto la cerca del patio, al instante, la pintura se desvanece. Pensé que estaba perdiendo la cabeza. Ahora lo com-

prendo. Sí, Ariel. Sí, hijo mío. Estoy... muerta.

—¡Mi madre está aquí! —insistió Ariel.

—No lograrás asustarme con cuentos de fantasmas. Y no me interrumpas cuando te estoy hablando —repuso el señor Villalobos. Se levantó y le pegó una fuerte bofetada al hijastro—. He sido muy amable contigo a lo largo de este año...

Pero se quedó hablando a medias, porque un fenómeno inexplicable, le cerró la boca. Un bolígrafo flotó, sobre el escritorio, y luego lo golpeó en la frente. El padrastro se quedó petrificado, contemplando el elemento caído, que terminó emplazado en una esquina. Se fijó en Ariel.

—Cómo... ¿Cómo hiciste eso? —tartamudeó.

—¡No toques a mi hijo! —exclamó la señora Rivas, poniendo su cara frente a la de su pareja, aunque aquel no pudo verla, naturalmente.

—Yo no he hecho nada. Fue mi madre, ya se lo dije. Ella se encuentra justo aquí, conmigo —reincidió.

El señor Villalobos dejó el miedo por un lado y lo invadió una furia incontrolable. Agarró a Ariel del cuello de la camisa y lo sacudió por continuas ocasiones.

—¡No vuelvas a mencionar a tu madre! —ladró—. ¡Te lo prohíbo, muchacho! ¡Cállate de una vez por todas! Porque entonces sí que te mataré a ti.

De pronto, la mesa tembló. El hombre soltó a Ariel y se enderezó con las manos abiertas, atemorizado, mirando aquel evento sobrenatural. La señora Rivas lanzó carpetas al aire, cuyas hojas se esparcieron en todas direcciones; aventó la engrapadora a la ventana, que se hizo añicos; volteó el escritorio de una patada; tiró, uno por uno, los libros enciclopédicos acomodados en la pared, sobre una tabla. El señor Villalobos parecía un niño indefenso que estaba viviendo una de sus peores pesadillas. Su colección de monedas, clavada en

el muro, planeó en el aire hasta estamparse contra la puerta.

—¡Detente! —le exigió el señor Villalobos a Ariel—. ¡Te ordeno que detengas esto, ahora mismo!

Tenía el rostro arrugado de verdadero pavor.

—Ya le dije que no soy yo. Es ella. Su difunta esposa está entre nosotros, vengándose de usted.

—¿Te llevarás a mi hijo al colegio militar? —preguntó la señora Rivas.

—¿Va a llevarme al colegio militar? —repitió Ariel.

—¡No! —gritó el acobardado hombre, con los ojos cúbicos—. ¡No lo haré! No lo haré. Ya lo dije. Haz, por piedad, que esto se detenga. Basta. ¡Basta!

La señora Rivas cogió la caja secreta del señor Villalobos, oculta bajo el escritorio ladeado, y la arrojó con rudeza al suelo. Si esta se abría, sería la primera ocasión que Ariel exploraba lo que residía en su interior. No corrió con tanta suerte. La caja se agrietó de un lado y permaneció cerrada. El señor Villalobos fue corriendo hasta ella, como si de salvar a un recién nacido se tratara.

«¿Adónde se la lleva?», se preguntó Ariel.

El padrastro salió de la oficina, atropellándose con los elementos dispersos que había por el suelo (y esquivando los que seguían cayéndole en la espalda, proyectados por su mujer fantasma). Corrió por el angosto pasillo y cogió, con la mano temblando, las llaves colgadas en la pared del vestíbulo. Emitió chillidos y tardó unos segundos antes de meter la llave correcta en la cerradura del garaje. Al abrir la puerta no se dignó a volverse para mirar a Ariel. Se enterró en el asiento de su viejo vehículo, abrió el portón automático de la cochera, depositó su cofre en el asentamiento del copiloto y se marchó a toda velocidad.

—Mi niño —le dijo la señora Rivas, luego de unos

segundos—. Llegó la hora de que me marche.

—Lo sé, mamá —respondió Ariel, quien odiaba las despedidas.

—Siempre estaré contigo y Alondrita, tenlo presente cada día.

Se fundieron en un abrazo. El triste Ariel volteó con la señora Rivas encharcado de lágrimas. Después de un año engañándose a sí mismo de que su madre seguía viva, nutriendo su fantasma con la imaginación, superó su ausencia y accedió a que las sombras de su pasado lo abandonaran. Tras haberle acariciado la mejilla a su hijo por última vez, la mujer desapareció en un velo blanco, para nunca más volver.

Capítulo 23
La guarida de la bruja

Ariel se coló en la habitación de Alondrita a las 11:24 pm, linterna en mano y su piyama puesta. Aquella sería la última noche en que se celebraba el Club de los Cuentos de las Sombras. Y por esa misma razón, el narrador contaría su desenlace, para clausurar de una vez por todas las aventuras de Aura.

Antes de encabezar la historia, con todo, el muchacho usurpó el tubo de ensayo de su bolsillo y le aseguró con voz queda al lucero:

—Encontraré la forma de regresarla a su hogar, señorita. Lo juro. Pero primero tengo que hallar la manera de impedirle a Arngfz de que acabe con todas las de su especie. Hoy no asistiré al Parque de Juegos Monteseaur, hasta que devuelva a Ellie sana y salva. No habrá más cacerías.

El astro, en seguida de escuchar el nombre de Arngfz, puso una cara desmedida de horror, como si ya

lo hubiera oído antes. Golpeó el cristal con sus diminutos puños. El par de membranas tersas que la hacían volar, por suerte, mejoraron un poco. Ariel la enclaustró debajo de las almohadas de Alondrita. Se dio la tarea de reemplazar la unidad de suero vacía. Fue al armario y se pegó con la sorpresa de que no quedaba ni una sola bolsita.

Sin más compromiso, se recostó desalentado en la cama.

—Ariel, hermanito, ¿eres, tú?

—Sí, aquí estoy princesita. No te asustes. Es hora de terminar la historia.

—¿El cuento, de Aura? —inquirió—. ¿Podrías encender, la luz? No puedo, ver nada. Quiero saludar, a mis amigas, las sombras.

La pregunta lo conmovió. Aquellos párpados de cristal se abrían y cerraban y sus pupilas incoloras buscaban, sin éxito, algo a lo que aferrarse.

—Esta noche será diferente a las demás reuniones —anunció Ariel—. ¿Qué te parece si vivimos el final de la historia de Aura sin luces, ni sombras? —sugirió—. Solo haciendo uso de nuestra imaginación.

Atraída por la propuesta, Alondrita destapó, en parte, sus dientes translúcidos en una sutil sonrisa.

—Me gusta. Buena idea, Ariel —murmuró, arrimando con elevado esfuerzo su cabeza al hombro de su queridísimo hermano.

Las sombras, quienes ya estaban preparadas para la prosecución del relato, agacharon sus cabezas. Esas fieles protagonistas sabían, de buena tinta, acerca de la situación que sufría su estimada espectadora. Permitieron la salida de hartas lágrimas. Le hicieron señas a Ariel de que bajara un poco más la linterna. Así lo hizo, y las sombras corrieron desde la pared al suelo, y del suelo, treparon por las cortinas de la cama. An-

claron sus cuerpos cambiantes al cuello de la niña. Abrazaron el rostro de aquella con afecto y la dispensaron de besos y apapachos. Una de las criaturas, se volvió con Ariel y apuntó hacia él.

«¿Yo?», preguntó este, moviendo sus labios sin emitir ruido.

El resto de los pequeñitos sujetos lo voltearon a ver y asintieron con la cabeza. El chico movió una vez más el enfoque de la lámpara, esta ocasión hacia él, y las sombras tomadas de las manos rodearon su cuello. Bailaron encima de los hombros y pecho de su creador, exhibiendo su gratitud hacia él; despidiéndose del mejor narrador de historias que pudo haber existido jamás. Porque sin él, de ninguna manera ellas hubieran albergado vida. Lo abastecieron de halagos y gentilezas.

—Hasta nunca —les dijo Ariel.

Y en último lugar apagó la linterna.

De inmediato, se sintió extraño. Vacío. Solo. Echaría bastante en falta a las sombras figurantes de sus cuentos. Apostó el objeto iluminador encima de la cómoda y al girarse, con la intención de referir su ficción, las extremidades de Alondrita, brazos y piernas, se arraigaron tiesas. Supo que su hermana no podría, nunca más, flexionar un solo músculo. Su entidad se solidificó. Le dolió saber que, muy pronto, lo mismo ocurriría con su corazón de vidrio. Dejaría de latir.

Le dio un cálido beso en la frente a la niña y comenzó a referir el cuento:

—Las princesas Aura y Diáfana viajaron durante toda la noche… —narró, limpiándose las lágrimas.

—Ariel —susurró Alondrita.

—¿Sí, princesita?

—Te quiero, muchísimo.

—Y yo te adoro como no tienes idea, mi niña —dijo.

—Eres el mejor, hermano que cualquier, niña pu-

diera desear —Aguardó unos segundos para respirar y suplicó—: Por favor, sigue, contando la historia.

—Bueno, allá vamos. —Elevó la voz—. Las princesas Aura y Diáfana viajaron durante toda la noche. Para ese entonces, la reina ya estaba al corriente de la ausencia de su hija de cristal en el castillo. Ordenó a sus mejores caballeros que la localizaran, con la advertencia de que Aura, quien con alevosía y ventaja se aprovechó de su hospitalidad, se obstinó en secuestrar a su Diáfana.

»Por otro lado, llegó un momento de la travesía en que Aura perdió la esperanza de que encontrarían la pócima. Diáfana le aconsejó que no se rindiera, que tuviera fe en que llegarían a la guarida de la hechicera. Para ese entonces, el maquillaje con el que fue disfrazada la doncella de cristal se corrió con el calor. Aura le comentó, con un toque de ironía, que asemejaba un espectro maligno.

»Horas más tarde, en pleno mediodía, pasaron delante de un río. Aprovecharon para pedirle al apuesto chofer de la carroza que se detuviera allí, con la excusa de que requerían de privacidad para sus necesidades corporales. Aura ayudó a Diáfana en quitarle los restos de pintura con el agua del torrente, hasta revelar su cuerpo de vidrio. Cuando volvieron juntas del afluente, el joven que manejaba las riendas del carruaje se molestó muchísimo. Dijo que lo engañaron con íntegro descaro.

»—La reina me matará en cuanto descubra que la traicioné —repuso, asustado.

»Sin embargo, Aura lo convenció de seguir por la dirección que le mencionó, resumiéndole las tristes efemérides de su miserable vida y las de Diáfana, que vivía día y noche corriendo el riesgo de romperse los miembros. Aura remarcó lo importante que era la pó-

cima que estaban buscando. Le prometió al guía que cuando su viaje acabara, sería recompensado con tanto oro, que no volvería a trabajar como chofer en toda su vida. Indeciso, aunque maravillado con la oferta, el muchacho accedió y echó a andar su carruaje.

»Más tarde, se estacionaron frente a un árbol de peras y desayunaron varias de esas frutas exquisitas. El chofer (que se presentó como Bruno), en cierto momento pretendió entablar conversación con Diáfana. Al no escuchar su voz, cayó en cuenta de las habladurías del pueblo. «La voz de la hija de la reina solo puede ser oída por quienes van a fallecer», decían.

»Bastarían unos cuantos libros, quizás una saga de nueve novelas, para describir el total de las peripecias que vivieron estos tres individuos a lo largo de su travesía. Para empezar, la enorme fe que Diáfana le hizo asumir a Aura de que llegarían a su destino, estimuló que conservara más tiempo de vida.

»El conductor, asimismo, abordó sentimientos encontrados por la princesa de cristal. Al inicio la consideró un engendro satánico. Pero revalidó, al cabo de unos días, que estuvo equivocado. Diáfana le resultaba encantadora. Era simpática y bondadosa. Esta coqueteaba con él y le obsequiaba guiños, sonrisas y miradas románticas. De vez en cuanto, le regalaba al caballero figuras de animales hechas con cerdas de su cabello transparente. Se comunicaban mediante señas. Bruno le entendía algunas veces, otras no tanto. Pero al final, el lenguaje del amor fue el distintivo que los unió.

»Aura, con tanto romanticismo de por medio, llegó a preguntarse si su príncipe estaría pensando en ella. Llevó su mano al collar de perlas y acarició cada una de las esferas, como si de este modo mantuviera vivo su recuerdo.

»Una de sus odiseas tuvo desarrollo en el mesón de

un pueblo, donde se hospedaron cierta noche. Aura y Bruno fingieron ser una pareja de jóvenes de una ciudad muy lejana que acababa de fracasar en su empresa de especias. Argumentaron que, en el continente, por algún infrecuente motivo relacionado con la actualización de documentos, los barcos comerciales dejaron de transportar su mercancía. Aura le explicó a la dueña de la posada que en esas fechas su marido y ella se dedicaban a un nuevo, pero delicado negocio, que tenía que ver con la venta de esculturas de vidrio.

»Los curiosos se acercaron con el propósito de admirar a la quieta escultura de cristal que los dos extranjeros (con sumo cuidado) bajaron de su carruaje y metieron a la habitación. El dúo de comerciantes cenó en compañía de muchos aldeanos preguntones. Después, a hurtadillas, le llevaron un cazo a Diáfana con avena.

»El plan hasta el momento iba bien, hasta que un borracho fisgón, un día más tarde, quiso ver de cerca a la famosa modelo de cristal de la que cada ciudadano hablaba, ya que no tuvo oportunidad de verla la primera vez. Situó una cubeta al revés cerca de la ventana del cuarto de los inquilinos. Se subió en ella y asomó la cabeza. Lo que vislumbró fue a una mujer transparente caminando por el aposento. El hombre resbaló del balde. El efecto del alcohol se le bajó de inmediato.

»El ebrio informó a los aldeanos de su hallazgo. Fundamentó que la supuesta pareja de comerciantes los engatusó con historias corrientes de sus viajes por el mundo.

»—En realidad son practicantes de la magia negra —señaló el borracho—. Hechiceros de la peor calaña.

»Su comentario incitó a que se sembrara el caos en la comunidad. La estadía de los tres amigos se volvió una impensada partida. Minutos antes del acorralamiento, una vieja sirvienta entró a la recámara con la

piel lívida, con lo que Diáfana adoptó su postura de pieza de arte. Bruno y Aura habían tejido honestos lazos de amistad con aquella empleada doméstica.

»—¿Qué ocurre, Emilia? —le preguntó Aura, viendo a Diáfana de reojo—. Estás muy pálida. ¿Te sientes bien?

»—¡Ya vienen! ¡Están muy cerca! —decía la longeva, con turbación—. Es mejor que se vayan, antes de que venga la desgracia.

»—¿Quiénes vienen? ¿Y por qué? —inquirió Bruno, que estaba sentado al pie de la cama.

»—Ya no tienen por qué mentir —expresó Emilia, dirigiendo sus ojos a Diáfana—. Lo saben todos los del pueblo. Estás viva, muchacha, no sigas aparentando que eres un objeto inanimado. Lo sospeché desde un inicio. Cuando entré a limpiar durante la mañana y regresé por la escoba, apareciste de pie en otro lugar y en una posición distinta. Me rehusé a decir algo al respecto, porque no soy de las que se meten en los asuntos de los demás.

»Diáfana movió sus brazos insegura y volteó con la anciana. En parte, se sintió cómoda; el jueguecito de hacerse la muñeca cada vez que abrían y cerraban la puerta de la alcoba la tenía trastornada.

»—Quieren mandarlos a juicio —prosiguió la vieja—. Si no se dan prisa, lo último que verán será la soga de la horca entrando por sus cabezas.

»—¿De qué se nos acusa? —preguntó Bruno.

»—Brujería —respondió Emilia.

»Con aquella declaración no hubo nada más que explicar. Ningún sujeto delatado por cargos de hechicería había salido libre de un juicio. Tales acusados eran sentenciados a pena de muerte sin tanto parloteo. Bruno metió sus objetos personales en una alforja. Aura y Diáfana lo imitaron.

»—De paso, aproveché para traerles algo de comida —dijo Emilia.

»En sus manos traía una arpilla con pan, frutas y queso de cabra.

»—Gracias —emitió Bruno, aceptando el obsequio con aprecio—. Que Dios se lo pague, Emilia. —Le dio un beso en la mejilla a la anciana. Abrió la puerta y dijo—: Es hora de irnos, señoritas.

»—Te estamos muy agradecidos, de verdad. Nunca te olvidaremos. —Aura le dio un fuerte abrazo a la veterana y salió del aposento.

»Tocó el turno de Diáfana, quien efectuó una reverencia con la cabeza y caminó hacia la salida.

»—Espera —la detuvo la vieja—. Tengo que revelarte algo sobre tu naturaleza, jovencita. Tú no naciste así. Antes de ser de vidrio, eras de carne y hueso. Fuiste víctima de una maldición al ser una niña. Créeme. Puedo oler un maleficio oscuro a treinta leguas de distancia.

»Diáfana abrió los labios y pronunció palabras que la anciana no pudo escuchar, mas pudo entender a la perfección.

»—Mira, si quieres saber cómo se originó, deberías empezar con preguntárselo a tu madre en persona. Ella te ocultó información muy importante.

»Diáfana asintió. Anhelaba continuar oyendo a Emilia, sin embargo, oyó pasos de un desfile de personas aproximándose al mesón y requirió despedirse con premura.

»—Les daré algo de tiempo —ultimó Emilia—. Tú y tus amigos van a salir a salvo. Solo déjenmelo a mí.

»Acto seguido, alzó las manos, pronunció unas oraciones extrañas que rimaban espléndidamente y la progresión de ciudadanos dejó de escucharse. Diáfana se preguntó qué habría ocurrido y miró al otro lado de

la puerta. Un pichón que bajaba del techo para aprovechar unas migas de pan del suelo, quedó detenido a mitad de su vuelo, con las alas abiertas. Diáfana no tuvo que sacar conclusiones: el tiempo se había estancado. Emilia era una hechicera.

»—Deprisa —urgió Emilia—. Tendrán sesenta segundos de ventaja. Mi magia no es muy poderosa hoy en día.

»Diáfana fue a encontrarse con sus amigos en el patio trasero de la posada.

»—¿Qué está sucediendo? —preguntó Bruno—. Todo está muy callado de repente.

»—Es Emilia, no sé cómo decirlo, ella acaba de parar el tiempo —le notificó Diáfana a Aura.

»—¡Cómo! ¿Emilia es una bruja? Estás tomándome el pelo —le expresó Aura, impactada.

»—No puedo darte explicaciones, nos queda medio minuto para escapar —urgió Diáfana.

»Las dos damiselas entraron a la carroza y Bruno ocupó la silla exterior. Gritó una palabra de dos sílabas para incitar movimiento a sus caballos y emprendieron la carrera. Gracias al noble acto de Emilia, lograron salir puntuales.

»En el intervalo que iban cruzando la salida del pueblo, la parálisis de tiempo fue revocada y el reloj volvió a transcurrir con normalidad. La gente quedó azorada, mirando a los extraños alejándose a toda prisa.

»—¡Se los dije! —vociferó el borracho que vio a Diáfana por la ventana—. Son hechiceros. Si no fuera así, ¿cómo explican que hayan reaparecido en un lugar distinto?

»—Hay que ir por ellos —propuso un valiente, escupiendo en tierra.

»—¡Sí! —lo apoyaron los demás.

»—¡A la horca! ¡A la horca! —ladraron.

Los pueblerinos persiguieron a los forasteros con caballos y ponis, cargados de antorchas, horquillas, cuchillos y machetes. No contaron con que Bruno perpetraría comprometidas maniobras con sus corceles. Sus animales, bien entrenados, trotaban más rápido. Cuando los ciudadanos casi los alcanzaban (por los pelos, cabe aclarar) el chofer se introdujo en un paraje seguro, escondido tras altas murallas de piedra, y aguardaron en silencio.

»El grupo de perseguidores pasó de largo y tomó atajo por una ruta equivocada, perdiéndose de vista. Bruno terminó agotado y bañado de sudor. Sus fatigados caballos, al punto del desmayo. Bajó de su asiento y abrió la portezuela del carruaje, con tal de verificar que las princesas estuvieran a salvo.

»A la primera que vio fue a Aura, quien mostró perfectas condiciones. Diáfana, en desacorde, gimoteó de dolor. Había perdido un dedo anular cuando el carruaje ejecutó la inesperada vuelta en U que formalizó Bruno, antes de penetrar en aquella guarida. Lo buscaron por debajo de los asientos y a los alrededores. La exploración acabó en el instante que Bruno halló la pieza implantada en una rueda del coche. Se la puso a Diáfana y le ató un pedazo de tela, que consiguió desgarrándose un segmento de su camisa. La princesa comentó que, al desfilar unos días, su dedo se recuperaría.

»Para espabilar el efecto de estrés, aguardaron una hora jugando naipes antes de salir del escondite. Diáfana le contó a Aura la revelación que le hizo saber Emilia de su maldición. Le solicitó, de favor, que se lo comunicara a Bruno.

»—De modo que era una bruja —susurró él, después de escucharlo de Aura—. No soy muy devoto de hablar de temas de ocultismo. Me aterran los fantasmas, las

brujas, los demonios… Se me pone la carne de gallina si pienso en esas tres cosas juntas.

»—Sin embargo, Emilia siempre fue muy generosa con nosotros. Era una bruja buena —rebatió Aura.

»—Pues mala o buena, no es de mi santa devoción.

»—¡Ah! —gritó Diáfana, malhumorada, consciente de que Aura era la única capaz de escucharla—. ¡Parece que ninguno de los dos está poniéndome atención! Lo importante aquí es que sufrí un embrujo siendo niña. Mi madre me engañó todos estos años, haciéndome creer que nací de vidrio. Aura, si conseguimos consumar nuestra hazaña, voy a enfrentarla. La reina tendrá que remover parte de su pasado para aclararme muchas cosas.

»Esa misma tarde, un ejército de avasallados de la reina corrió la noticia en el pueblo de que una princesa de cristal había sido secuestrada por una joven que respondía al nombre de Aura. Los aldeanos, comunicaron a los acaudillados de la soberana lo que pasó en el mesón y señalaron la dirección que tomaron los viajeros, antes de perderles el rastro. Así pues, los soldados, como amaestrados perros de caza, siguieron la pista. Aunque cabe aclarar, que jamás lograron dar con ellos.

»En otra ocasión, un grupo de ladrones interceptó el carruaje de los tres aventureros y detuvieron a Bruno. El chofer intranquilo le confesó a aquella pandilla de maleantes que no llevaba nada de valor consigo.

»—Eso lo decidiremos nosotros —dijo el líder en un tono arrogante, amenazándolo con su espada.

»Entonces, al abrir la portezuela, Aura salió dando un brinco, provocando que el bandolero retrocediera. Hacía movimientos y señas ridículas con las manos, pronunciando las primeras palabras que se le venían a la cabeza: «Yuga guaba, lima ruda, cielo rojo, pipa salsa…»

»—¡Es una bruja! —gritó uno de los ladrones.

Y salió huyendo a todo galope en su caballo.

»Los demás se burlaron de la cobardía de su compañero y quedaron de pie ante la princesa Aura, sin creerse el cuento de sus aparentes poderes maléficos.

»—Su amigo hizo bien en huir, porque vaya que soy una hechicera de las más temidas —dijo ella.

»—Compruébalo —decretó el dirigente del escuadrón, con una sonrisa carente de dientes.

»La doncella hizo como que lanzaba un sacrilegio al carruaje y Diáfana salió operando una pantomima de horror, mirándose los brazos y las piernas transparentes.

»—¡La convirtió en vidrio! —anunció aterrorizado uno de los bandoleros.

»—Y también será una estatua por toda la eternidad —agregó Aura, agitando las manos.

»Diáfana se quedó estática, con un gesto agónico en su rostro, y dejó de respirar.

»—Y ahora, si no nos dejan en paz, serán mis siguientes víctimas —sentenció Aura—. Juro que no tendré piedad con ninguno de ustedes.

»Dicho esto, el pánico se propagó entre aquellos machos empedernidos. Se dieron a la fuga a toda velocidad y no volvieron a saber de ellos. ¡Cómo se rieron los tres amigos! Aquella sería una graciosa anécdota que se contaría en familia, durante Navidad, para agregarle partes extraordinarias que quizá nunca ocurrieron, pero que la harían sonar más emocionante.

»Luego estuvo una de las aventuras más increíbles de todas. Ocurrió cuando cruzaban un campo de hierba seca. Percibieron un terremoto. Vieron una montaña a lo lejos que, saltando a ritmo, se acercaba a ellos. Nada más que no era una montaña, sino un gigante de tres piernas. Aquel ser de dimensiones inmoderadas se

paró frente a ellos y dijo con voz rigurosa:

»—¡Alto ahí! Ningún humano pasar de este punto. Ahora yo comerme a ti y a tu carruaje.

»Estos seres, por lo general, tienen un vocabulario precario y son demasiado brutos (le explicó Ariel a Alondrita).

»—No lo hagas —gritó Diáfana, abriendo la portezuela del coche.

»El gigante pudo escuchar su voz, lo que significó que iba a morir pronto.

»—¿Y quién decir eso? —preguntó el gigante.

»Aura salió detrás de su amiga y el gigante se inclinó para verlas mejor. Si existe el amor a primera vista, aquella fue la ocasión perfecta para describirlo. Aquel par de ojos bizcos se fijaron en el transparente material de Diáfana, quien, por efecto del sol, proyectó varios haces de luz. El suelo fue iluminado por un festival de tonalidades de arcoíris.

»El enorme ser, embelesado por el espectáculo visual, acabó enamorándose de ella.

»—¡Qué hermosa tu ser! —le dijo seducido.

»—Si nos dejas ir, yo... Yo te contaré un secreto —mencionó Diáfana, improvisando una treta.

»—¿De qué secreto hablar tú, bella criatura? —preguntó, cruzándose de brazos.

»—Te lo diré, pero primero debes prometerme que nos dejarás marchar.

»—Erm —farfulló el gigante—. ¿No tratar de engañarme?

»—Eso jamás. Estoy siendo sincera.

»—Está bien. Yo prometer —dijo—. Ahora decir tu secreto.

»—Vas a morir pronto —reveló Diáfana.

»En respuesta, el gigante rio a carcajadas. Sacudió el suelo.

»—¡Pero qué graciosa tú ser! Ja, ja. Yo fuerte y grande. No poder morir. Además, yo ser nuevo líder de gigantes. Amigos regalarme vino de dragón.

»Se sacó del pantalón una botella de ron del tamaño de un jabalí adulto y se las mostró.

»—Entonces lo que te entregaron es veneno, porque muy pronto perecerás.

»—¿Cómo saber que veneno es? —inquirió en tono burlón.

»—Compruébalo por ti mismo. Arroja un poco de lo que trae esa botella a la tierra y lo sabrás. Si resulta que estoy equivocada, daremos la vuelta y no volveremos a molestarte. Si tenemos la razón, nos dejarás pasar.

»El gigante le quitó el corcho a la botella, con las cejas entrecruzadas, y vertió un chorrito de vino al suelo.

»—¿Lo ver? Ningún veneno haber —mencionó triunfante.

»Sin embargo, el pasto amarillo se tornó oscuro, y de este emanó una asfixiante columna de humo.

»—¡Deshonestos gigantes! —expresó enfurecido.

»Arrancó un árbol sin hojas del suelo y lo arrojó tan lejos como pudo.

»—Me engañar esos bastardos —dijo—. Ahora ellos saber quién ser yo. El poderoso Rim Bom Bam. Ustedes esperar aquí y no mover un dedo, yo volver pronto.

»Y se fue corriendo y saltando, las dos cosas a la vez, haciendo temblar el suelo. No esperarían Aura, Diáfana y Bruno a que el gigante volviera. Cada quien ocupó sus respectivos lugares en la carroza y echaron a andar, siguiendo la centelleante ruta amarilla que Aura podía ver gracias al efecto del hallador.

»Viajaron el resto del día. Por la noche durmieron en un claro del bosque. Bruno era buen cazador, esa

ocasión consiguió un par de conejos para cenar. Aura se despidió de sus amigos a continuación de alimentarse y se fue a descansar. Tenía que recuperar fuerzas. Se sentía más agotada y enferma que nunca. Diáfana, mientras tanto, aguantó la noche despierta contemplando las estrellas en compañía de quien sería su primer amor. Vio a Bruno a los ojos, acercaron sus cabezas lentamente y se dieron un delicado beso en los labios. En toda su vida, Diáfana jamás se había sentido más emocionada. Las pulsaciones de su corazón de cristal hacían que su cuerpo vibrara.

»A la mañana siguiente, reanudaron su viaje y se intercalaron en lo más profundo del bosque. Por su trayecto, fueron conociendo un mundo fantástico que resultó prohibido y fascinante, lleno de enigmáticas y sorprendentes criaturas. Con obvia razón, el gigante de tres piernas protegía, a viva fuerza, esa zona de entidades humanas. Aura, Diáfana y Bruno libraron en ese lugar batallas homéricas intervenidas por dragones acuáticos, bestias que lanzaban veneno por largas colas; se encontraron con especímenes míticos que aparecían en relatos y leyendas tradicionales de diferentes pueblos de su mundo. Se hicieron enemigos de algunas y amigos de otras, como los *paflinos*: seres de complexión peluda y ojos saltones, que cautivaban a cualquiera que los viera. Estos eran capaces de hablar, sin embargo, solo podían aprenderse una palabra en toda su vida. Al cruzar por un nido de aquellos animalitos, que recién afloraron del cascarón, a Aura se le ocurrió pronunciar en voz alta la palabra «primorosos». En el acto, decenas de pelotitas afelpadas empezaron a saltar felices, articulando el adjetivo que acababan de aprender de su instructora, y que repetirían el resto de su existencia. El carruaje se alejó y sus pasajeros todavía podían oír el coro de festivos paflinos en la distan-

cia, que canturreaban: «primorosos, primorosos, primorosos...».

»Dos días más tarde, llegaron a un páramo cubierto de niebla y suelo fangoso. Árboles alquitranados y sin hojas resurgían del suelo, afines a manos torcidas de un primate viejo. En sus interminables ramas colgaban del cuello muñecos sin rostro, rellenos de aserrín y tejidos con estambre. Parvadas de cuervos observaron a los polizones desde sus nidos, como si les advirtieran que, si continuaban avanzando más allá de ese asentamiento, chocarían con una muerte segura.

»A escasos metros de distancia, los aventureros distinguieron la difuminada silueta de una cabaña de tablón, ocultándose tras aquella espesa bruma que aparentaba estar viva. De su destartalado tejado sobresalía una chimenea torcida de piedra, que insinuaba su capacidad de respirar. Estaba encendida. Pero no exhalaba el humo en dirección al cielo, como lo haría una chimenea ordinaria. Esta escupía su humareda hacia abajo; lo que explicaba aquella chocante neblina.

»Aura notificó que la línea amarilla terminaba justo allí, en la puerta de entrada. ¡Por fin habían dado con la guarida de la bruja!

»Bruno, creyente de los símbolos, embrujos y el mal de ojo, detuvo el carruaje a buen trecho de distancia de la vivienda. Les recomendó a las princesas que se apresuraran. Él no las acompañaría, ni por asomo, al interior de la vivienda.

»—No creas que tengo miedo —le mintió a Diáfana, con la voz oscilando—. No puedo dejar solos a los caballos. Imagina lo que sucedería si llegaran a escapar en la bruma, lo difícil que sería encontrarlos con este mal tiempo. Aparte, me da mala espina amarrarlos en aquellos árboles infestados de cuervos. Si se les presentan dificultades dentro, solo dile a Aura que grite

mi nombre y yo acudiré de inmediato. Estaré aquí en todo momento. ¿De acuerdo?

»Diáfana asintió. Era consciente de que su enamorado sufría de fobia a las cosas sobrenaturales. Se le acercó y le dio un beso (ambos aprendieron de qué manera besarse sin correr el riesgo de lastimar los rebordes de cristal de Diáfana). Con señas, ella prometió volver pronto. Aura, que no quiso interrumpir ese momento íntimo, esperó a su amiga en silencio, dándoles la espalda. Ya que se reunieron las dos, caminaron hacia la cabaña con mucho cuidado, pues los pies se les hundían en aquel lodazal engañoso, que daba la apariencia de arenas movedizas.

»Llegaron al portón de la arcaica morada, que tenía moho en sus tablillas humedecidas. Y la madera seca, sufría de una invasión de termitas. Abrieron la puerta desvencijada, que se lamentó en un quejido largo y desesperado. El olfato de ambas doncellas reconoció la terrible hediondez de vegetales podridos. Tuvieron que cubrirse la nariz para no vomitar las codornices que comieron en mediodía. Las habitaciones parecían equipados (aunque descuidados) invernaderos. Cientos de plantas medicinales, comestibles y venenosas fueron acomodadas en estanterías con sus nombres escritos a mano en pequeños trozos de pergamino. Las jóvenes se internaron en la choza. Era más grande dentro que por fuera, debido a un hechizo de agrandamiento. Avanzaron cautelosas por los corredores estrechos y se internaron en la cocina, lugar que, por cierto, resultó ser un sofisticado laboratorio. Apenas entrando, plantas carnívoras de colores exóticos pretendieron morder a las muchachas y enrollarlas entre sus tallos. No consiguieron alcanzarlas, aunque sí sacarles un grito. Tropezaron con experimentos celebrados a medias, sobre una mesa de piedra, y un caldero en la chimenea que expul-

saba abundante humo blanco.

»—Por eso hay neblina en el páramo —manifestó Diáfana.

»Localizó una tapadera y con ella cubrió el recipiente.

»—Ya comenzará a aclarar afuera —comentó Aura.

»Tuvo razón. La niebla se rindió. Los árboles se hicieron visibles y pudieron ver a Bruno quitándose el barro de sus botas en una llanta de la carroza. Aquel cayó en cuenta de que la niebla se disipaba y miró en torno a él. No tardó en encontrarse con los hipnóticos ojos de Diáfana, que lo miraron tras la ventana. Bruno la saludó agitando su mano en el aire. Ella, antes de girarse y volver a lo suyo, le guiñó un ojo.

»Aura leyó las etiquetas de las estanterías con la finalidad de hallar la pócima de la sanación en ellas. Lo único que traslucía, no obstante, eran frascos que resguardaban sustancias, pociones e ingredientes extraños, tales como: ojos de dragón, patas de sapo, orejas de murciélago, escamas de sirena, virutas de duende disecado y lombrices volcánicas. Diáfana secundó a Aura, repasando una por una, la información de cada contenedor. Pero por más que quisieron, no hallaron el indicado.

»—Al parecer echamos esperanzas en balde, una vez más —susurró Aura, dejándose caer desesperanzada sobre un banco lleno de telarañas.

»Justo cuando su pesó se hundió en el asiento, uno de los anaqueles del laboratorio se hizo a un lado, revelando un pasadizo secreto que encauzaba hacia un lugar bajo tierra.

»—¡Ala! —dijeron al mismo tiempo.

»Se ingeniaron una antorcha con los materiales que hallaron en la cocina y la encendieron con el fuego inacabable de la chimenea. Gracias a la luz, se les fa-

cilitó bajar por aquel túnel oscuro, que desaparecía mediante una inclinada escalinata. Descendieron el último peldaño y entrevieron, a la distancia de treinta pies, metido en la gruta de la pared más retirada, un frasco de color rosa cuya gran etiqueta rezaba:

"*Poción de Sanación*"

»—¡Es esa! —exclamó Aura con algarabía—. Al fin lo hemos conseguido, Diáfana. ¡Lo logramos!

»—Te dije que no debías perder la fe —mencionó Diáfana, satisfecha.

»Antes de volver a caminar, a deshora, descubrieron otro secreto que desmigajó sus ilusiones. Se enteraron que para llegar a la botella, debían bajar otras escaleras y atravesar una piscina infestada de escorpiones rojos, animales letales del desierto de Corín, cuya potente ponzoña era idónea para matar a un elefante en menos de dos minutos.

»—Pasaré yo —se apresuró a plantear Diáfana—. Recuerda que soy de vidrio, y si estos insectos pretenden atacarme, no podrán hacerme ningún daño. Sus aguijones solo repicarán sobre mi piel, como la lluvia contra las ventanas de una catedral.

»Dicho esto, bajó las escalinatas y atravesó el obstáculo con suprema seguridad. Los escorpiones rojos se le encaramaron por las piernas, treparon por sus brazos y se le metieron por los mechones de su cabeza. La acribillaron sin hacerle daño. Cayeron los bichos atormentados al suelo, con sus aguijones partidos a la mitad.

»Diáfana ascendió del otro lado, cruzó el pasillo conclusivo y alcanzó el recipiente. Lo apresó y volvió a la piscina de insectos.

»Tras remontar los escalones de venida, victoriosa, se sacudió los últimos escorpiones que tenía metidos en sus cabellos de vidrio. Subieron emocionadas ella y Aura por el túnel de regreso a la cabaña, festejando y soltando el trapo por su ambicioso logro.

»—¡Lo conseguimos! ¡Lo conseguimos! —canturreó Diáfana eufórica.

»—¡Vamos! ¡Ábrelo! —chilló Aura, mostrando un brillo de ilusión en sus ojos.

»La otra quitó el tapón y... sus sonrisas se desvanecieron en cuanto revelaron el interior.

»—Una gota —dijeron en coro, desconsoladas.

»Era lo único que quedaba en el fondo.

»Y en ese momento les llegó un grito de socorro del exterior. Se asomaron por la ventana (la niebla se había ido) y entrevieron a Bruno en el techo del carruaje, con un trozo de madera en la mano, empleándolo como arma. Golpeaba unas criaturas color marrón anémico que escalaban por el vehículo y querían llegar a él. ¿Qué eran esas cosas?

»—¡Oh, por Dios! —gritó Diáfana, revelando la respuesta.

»Eran los muñecos sin rostro que vieron ahorcados en los árboles. Todos ellos se habían desenroscado de sus hilos y ahora caminaban resueltos, a paso de tortuga, hacia el coche. Eran pequeños cuales niños recién nacidos y, pese a no tener dedos, sus ásperas manos podían adherirse a cualquier superficie. Para empeorar aún más las cosas, los cuervos que descansaban antes en los árboles, inauguraron a desplazarse en círculos, volando encima de Bruno. Los más osados se atrevieron a lanzarse contra su cara, con el objetivo de arrancarle los párpados. Aura cogió un hacha de la cocina y Diáfana un cuchillo para seccionar carne. De las paredes nacieron barreras de hojas y plantas, que las

princesas eliminaron con sus armas. Salieron de la cabaña y corrieron lo mejor que pudieron por el fango (incluso Diáfana, a quien no le importó su delicada morfología).

»Una de las siniestras aves alcanzó a Bruno. Con el pico le arrancó un pedazo del lóbulo de la oreja izquierda. El chofer expulsó un lamento desgarrador y cayó de rodillas en el techo del carruaje, soltando por consecuencia el tronco que llevaba asido en la mano. Los muñecos de estambre llegaron a la capota y tomaron de los brazos y piernas al joven. Lo estiraron. Aura y Diáfana casi llegaban, estaban a solo unos metros de él.

»Y se oyó un chasquido cruel, moribundo. El pie de Diáfana quedó atascado en el lodo. Como secuela, aquel no soportó tanta brusquedad y su pierna, en el nivel de la rodilla, se partió. El cuerpo de la princesa quedó tambaleándose en un solo miembro, como una bailarina rota. En cuestión de segundos, el cuchillo en sus manos salió volando. Para su desgracia, cuando intentó protegerse de la caída con las palmas, sus brazos se desencajaron y se hicieron añicos. Su rostro, que recibió el peor de los impactos, chocó contra el suelo y se despedazó. Antes de que todo se le oscureciera, a Diáfana le vino a la cabeza el recuerdo de Emilia confesándole que estaba bajo un maleficio, y fue consciente, con honda tristeza, que jamás se reencontraría con su madre para exigirle las respuestas que quería escuchar. Nunca sabría la razón de ser maldecida por una hechicera cuando fue niña, ni el motivo de ser oída por personas a punto de morir. De ningún modo sería de carne y hueso; no podría establecer una familia con Bruno, ni tener hijos...

»Aura también sufrió un efecto colateral en su organismo tras echar un vistazo hacia atrás y mirar los res-

tos de su mejor amiga diseminados. Su corazón le falló. Este detuvo y adelantó sus pulsaciones en una dolorosa y quemante arritmia. Se precipitó Aura de rodillas, superada por la enfermedad, y viró la cabeza de un lado a otro, contemplando a sus amistades. Se preguntó qué habían hecho mal y miró el frasco de la pócima sanadora.

»Solo queda una gota, pensó.

»Oyó otro grito. Tres cuervos, encaramados sobre el tórax de Bruno, le rompieron las costillas y le arrancaron el corazón. Riñeron por ver quién se llevaba el órgano a su nido.

»Aura quitó el corcho a la botella.

»—Una gota —dijo, en un murmullo.

»Se llevó el recipiente a la boca. Antes de beber, con todo, un dolor en el costado izquierdo del torso ocasionó que se retorciera en el fango. Había llegado su hora. Aflojó la mano y liberó el frasco. Su corazón, igual que el de sus dos amigos, se rehusó a mantenerse palpitando. La última gota escapó de la botella. Se desvaneció en el lodo.

»El suelo fundó en estremecerse, gracias a la pócima de la sanación, y en la superficie del pantano crecieron plantas de un verde apasionado; de las ramas de los árboles brotaron hojas elegantes y frutas de todo tipo; nacieron jardines de flores coloridas y gran variedad de vegetales. El lugar dejó de ser un horripilante páramo. Los cuervos cayeron muertos, sin explicación alguna, en la intemperie; y los muñecos de tela vieja se volvieron parte del entorno.

»Es por ello que los tres amigos de aquella aventura no habían hecho su viaje en vano. Hicieron algo más importante que encontrar una pócima sanadora. Otorgaron vida, involuntariamente, a aquel sitio aquejado del mundo, convirtiéndolo en un hermoso valle. De la

muerte llegó nueva vida. Muchas veces, hay que dejar que las cosas sigan con su rumbo natural para que el ciclo de la vida cobre sentido. Cada momento y acción en el universo tiene una razón de ser —explicó Ariel.

»La guarida de la bruja sin párpados fue tragada por el fango, la madera vieja se rompió desenfrenada. En su lugar, brotó una laguna de agua dulce. Los caballos de la carroza de Bruno fueron liberados por los brazos de un árbol y cada uno corrió a galope en distintas direcciones. Bruno cayó en la tierra. Alrededor de su cuerpo, el de Aura y Diáfana, surgieron pequeñas raíces que los ampararon bajo tierra. Arriba de ellos crecieron tres árboles, que entrecruzaron sus ramas para crear un ancho tronco, formando así, una edificación natural para quienes lo vieran con ojos de artista, y un hermoso punto de unión para los seres fantásticos trotamundos que cruzaran por ahí.

»Peregrinaron muchos años, siglos, milenios... De aquel árbol nació una inocente flor, misma que producía la sustancia que sanaba cualquier tipo de enfermedad. Del centro de esta se desprendió su néctar, que surcó por las hojas y la corteza del árbol. Una gota atravesó la tierra y, por algún motivo, dio con el esqueleto de Aura. La princesa, tras meses de recuperación celular, salió de la tierra practicando exageradas bocanadas de aire. Había vuelto a nacer...

Ariel volteó con su hermana y se detuvo a mitad del desenlace. Estudió el rostro inmóvil de la niña. Después esperó. Esperó. Y esperó otro poco. Notó que su pecho se privó de moverse.

—¿Alondrita? —llamó Ariel en voz baja—. ¿Princesita mía?

Pero ella no respondió. No sonreía, no lloraba. Sus ojos ya no se meneaban de un lado a otro, como lo hacían minutos previos a iniciar el relato. Sus párpados

no se abrían. Sus pulmones no respiraban. Su corazón (Ariel puso la mano encima de su pecho) no palpitaba. Sintió que el mundo se desmoronó sobre él.

Alondrita se había ido, igual que las sombras y los personajes de aquella historia: Aura, Diáfana y Bruno. Su hermanita había dejado de existir, como su madre lo hizo también un año atrás.

Recordó cada buen momento que pasó junto a ella, los cientos de aventuras que compartieron en el Club de los Cuentos de las Sombras, las salidas al cine y al zoológico, los duetos en el karaoke, los juegos de mesa. ¿Cómo? ¿De qué manera se acostumbraría a vivir solo, sin más cuentos, sin más libros, sin su princesita, sin su imaginación, sin su irrealidad? Permaneció llorando a mares. Y tras hallarse largo rato así, registró una gran mancha de humedad en las sábanas.

Ariel se incorporó, se talló el rostro y contempló el magnífico cuerpo de cristal de su hermana. Le dio un beso en la frente límpida, igual que siempre.

—Yo también te quiero —le susurró—. Te extrañaré mucho.

Tenía la ilusión de que ocurriera un milagro. Que aquellos ojos parpadearan y lo enfocaran. Que sus labios se curvearan en una sonrisa. Que Alondrita volviera a vivir.

Y vaya que ocurrió algo, pero no lo que él esperaba.

De modo contundente, la ventana estalló en mil pedazos. Ariel evacuó un grito de verdadero pánico y se cubrió la cabeza con las manos. Los vidrios salieron disparados como dardos. Una enorme mano, con la envergadura de un automóvil, entró por el agujero que quedó en la pared. La mano pretendió capturarlo. Antes Ariel pudo zafarse de ella golpeándola con los codos y corrió hacia la puerta. Si bien, no fue lo suficientemente rápido. La extremidad estudió la habitación con

la yema de los dedos y percibió las pisadas del joven por la superficie. Volvió a capturarlo, esta vez, sin margen de error.

—Pensaste que escaparías de mí, ¿no es así? —dijo Arngfz, con aquella voz de ultratumba salida de las mismas profundidades marinas.

Sustrajo a Ariel de la morada. Lo observó indiferente.

—¡Oh, pero si allí estás! —expresó con un fingido toque de sarcasmo, sin inmutar su sereno rostro—. Son las doce y cuarto, pensé que habías olvidado nuestra cita.

Enseñó su otra mano. Llevaba una jaula voluminosa, especial para encerrar a cinco monos. Arrojó a Ariel sin piedad al interior y luego cerró la escotilla, convirtiéndolo en su prisionero.

—Bienvenido a tu última noche, cazador de estrellas —dijo el criminal Arngfz.

Y se agenció a circular rumbo al parque abandonado.

Capítulo 24
Imán de estrellas

—**Mi** hermana acaba de fallecer —mencionó el entristecido Ariel.

—Oh, ¿hablas de Susanita? Una lamentable y desafortunada noticia —dijo Arngfz con desaire.

Ariel se movió de adelante hacia atrás, a causa del eslabón en el vértice de la jaula, sujetado imperturbablemente por Arngfz. Las pisadas de aquel agrietaron la calle.

—¿Y dónde está mi amiga? ¿Dónde la tiene secuestrada? —preguntó el chico, temeroso de recibir la peor de las respuestas.

No le apetecía otra mala noticia.

—En un momento lo sabrás —contestó el titán, sosegado.

Arribaron al Parque de Juegos Monteseaur, donde el clima, por extraño que pareciera, no era de corrientes amenazantes ni de poderosas tempestades corrom-

pidas de nieve. Allí no corría viento alguno. De hecho, no se pronosticaba frío, tampoco calor. Los niveles de temperatura se disolvieron en un nivel intermedio, aplacado. Con omisión de la atmósfera desaliñada, Ariel percibió un silencio ronco, que simuló la prudencia acústica del Reino Astral. Volteó a diestra y siniestra y desenmascaró un factor aún más extraño. Las cosas flotaban, congeladas, en el entorno. Como un mágico juego de naipes que alguien aventó al azar y sus cartas quedaron suspendidas en el aire. Intuyó Ariel que el tiempo se había estancado, ya que las botellas empañadas, las llantas de automóviles, los tornillos y demás elementos que configuraban la propiedad, semejaron estar sometidos por hilillos invisibles.

«Tal como en el cuento de Aura —pensó Ariel—, cuando Emilia detuvo el tiempo.»

Arngfz depósito la jaula a un lado de los oxidados columpios aplastados (cuyos deformados asientos cohabitaron separados a medio metro del suelo, con las cadenas arqueadas). El vagabundo comprimió sus dimensiones hasta alcanzar un calibre humano. Era fornido, joven, con la misma belleza, casi venenosa, de la noche anterior. Una perfección que desestimaba la cotización del oro.

Ariel dio vueltas en su cárcel, escarbando indicios de Ellie.

—No la encuentro. ¿Dónde está? —inquirió—. Me dijo que lo iba a saber en un momento. Contésteme.

—No sé de qué me hablas —respondió el antipático Arngfz.

Se encomendó a buscar algo en la marañosa hierba alta.

—No se haga el corto de entendimiento. Estoy hablando de mi amiga: Ellie Durán —precisó Ariel, furioso.

—Oh, cierto —Arngfz detuvo su inspección, extrajo algo de su abrigo y dijo—: Hum, aquí está.

Le entregó a Ariel unos anteojos con fondo de botella que llevaban los cristales agrietados.

«¡Las gafas de Ellie! —adivinó Ariel—. ¡Y están rotas!»

—¿Qué significa esto? —Sus ojos se empañaron de nueva cuenta—. ¿Qué hizo con ella? ¡Dígamelo!

—Erm, ¿qué te digo? ¿La verdad? Bueno, pues allá va: me la comí —admitió.

Ariel desunió sus labios hasta formar una deformada O y se aferró a los ejes metálicos de la jaula.

—¡NOOO! —gritó—. ¡NO ES CIERTO! ESTÁ MINTIENDO.

—¿Por qué armas tanto escándalo, cazador de estrellas? ¿Es que no te das cuenta? Contempla bien esos lentes, porque «una parte de ella permanece aquí, contigo» —expresó, imitando la voz de Ariel cuando este se enfrentó al señor Villalobos en su oficina—. ¿Por qué no empleas tu imaginación para darle vida, como a tu madre?

—¡MALDITO! —gritó el muchacho—. Es un desalmado. No lo ayudaré a cumplir sus propósitos. Esto se acabó. Ya no seré su mugroso cazador de estrellas. Renuncio.

—Hum, de acuerdo, no importa. Porque no tendrás que seguir siéndolo —emitió sin simpatía, regresando a la melena de león.

—Ellie descubrió qué cosa es usted, ¿no? —dijo Ariel.

—Claro, claro —expresó el sereno Arngfz.

—Descubrió que es un agujero negro, ¿cierto? Y quizás, hasta supo la forma de detener su plan. Por eso decidió aniquilarla.

—¡Bah! ¿Tú y ella? Ninguno de los dos representó

ningún peligro para mí —expresó aburrido, casi bostezando—. Solo me asqueó ver que aquella sabionda escribiera en su diario en todo momento, metiendo las narices donde no la llamaban. Le di una buena lección.

Las tres mujeres que Ariel más quería en el mundo: su mamá, Alondrita, Ellie, se habían ido para siempre. Ciñó las rejas de su prisión. El cinismo con el que Arngfz se expresaba de sus crímenes hizo que a Ariel le hirviera la sangre. Estrujó tanto los barrotes que se le atrofiaran los músculos de las manos.

—Y mintió también con lo de las estrellas —farfulló Ariel.

Solo allí, Arngfz entorpeció su actividad. Dio media vuelta y analizó al muchacho con un solo ojo, igual que un pájaro.

—Así que te enteraste de la verdadera naturaleza de las estrellas, ¿eh? —comentó, sin inmutar su rostro—. ¿Cómo lo descubriste?

Ariel invirtió la cabeza hacia un lado. No podía confesarle a Arngfz que se llevó una estrella a la escuela, misma que en esos momentos se hallaba recluida bajo la almohada de su difunta hermana. Tenía que desembuchar una mentira. ¡Diantres! Con lo malo que era mintiendo...

—Lo descubrí ayer —inventó—, cuando volé con el pájaro mecánico... Llegué a los cinco segundos.

Arngfz entornó los ojos.

—¿Por qué sospecho de esa respuesta?

—Pues es la verdad —replicó el adolescente, alzando un poco la voz.

—De cualquier forma, eso ya no importa —susurró Arngfz—. Habría sido un problema si lo descubrías los primeros días. Es obvio que te hubieras negado a ser cazador de estrellas.

Dicho esto, volvió Arngfz con las manos ocupadas:

en una llevaba una cubeta y en la otra una brocha para pintar. Su perfecto cabello amarillo, al caminar, fulguraba como si tuviera luciérnagas bajo el cuero cabelludo. Sumergió la escobilla en el balde y se consagró en pasarla por la fachada de la jaula. Ariel descubrió que no se trataba de pintura. Era una sustancia maloliente e incolora, parecida al barniz. El chico tuvo que pararse en el centro del único cuadrito que tenía de espacio libre, con las manos pegadas a los costados para no engrasarse.

—Estoy al tanto de que sacrificó a cinco jóvenes en un orden específico —glosó Ariel. Respiró por la boca con tal de no olfatear el componente, que lo mareó—. Lo hizo con el objetivo de formar una estrella de cinco picos, ¿no? —expresó—. Y después de dibujar ese pentagrama, pudo preparar el acceso al Reino Astral, para que los astros me despejaran la entrada.

—Y con dicha pauta imaginas que armé una sesión de brujería o un rito prehispánico —repuso Arngfz—. Ya te lo había especificado la otra noche, jovencito: los hechiceros son sujetos incompetentes —subrayó—. Yo nunca quise el pentagrama entero. Lo que pretendí fue aprovecharme del símbolo en medio de este. ¿Sabes cuál es? Un perfecto pentágono —aclaró, dibujando la silueta de cinco lados en el aire con la mano que tenía libre—. Una figura matemática cuya exactitud es imperativa, puesto que a ella le deben su existencia las cinco Realidades Madre.

«Pues claro —razonó Ariel—, un pentágono es una respuesta congruente. Ellie y yo nos equivocamos al pensar que Arngfz quiso activar el portal del Reino Astral con el modelo de una estrella.»

Y de repente Ariel se empinó la melancolía, al evocar la memoria de su amiga. Contempló las gafas en su mano.

—¿Sabes? Ciertas estrellas, al momento de morir —explicaba Arngfz, sin que Ariel se lo preguntara— descargan una poderosa explosión llamada *supernova*. Luego se vuelven agujeros negros y, como ya lo evidenciaste, soy uno de ellos.

—No me interesa saber nada de usted —repuso Ariel, limpiándose las lágrimas que rehusaban a jubilarse de su sentido.

Besó los anteojos de Ellie y se los metió al bolsillo.

—En *Únim*, el lugar del que provengo (y la primera Realidad Madre) —dilucidó Arngfz—, las estrellas vivíamos en la ignorancia. Atesorábamos a nuestras familias, practicábamos las reglas sociales, y por las noches brindábamos luz a los habitantes que coexistían abajo, en el mundo. Aun así, desconocíamos la existencia del Pentaverso —suscitó una pausa—. De lo único que estábamos enterados, era de que la emperatriz, más allá de ser nuestra máxima soberana, poseía la facultad de viajar a *otros* lugares.

—¿Emperatriz? —preguntó Ariel, sorbiéndose la nariz.

—Por de contado —confirmó Arngfz—. Hasta en los Reinos Astrales hay jerarquías, ¿puedes creerlo? Las estrellas tienen a su reina, a sus soldados y a sus reflectores, que son los vigilantes... ¡Oh! Y olvidaba a las despreciables estrellas fugaces, que se la llevan viajando de un lado a otro, llevando comunicados de la emperatriz, con tal de cerciorarse que todo se mantiene ordenado en la comarca del firmamento —explicó—. Bueno, hay una soberana por cada universo. Y son las únicas que, por su naturaleza, pueden atravesar el Pentaverso a su placer.

«Entonces, son cinco emperatrices en total —derivó Ariel, no muy animado—. Una para cada universo.»

—¿Y qué pasó con todas ellas? Con las estrellas de

Únim —titubeó—. ¿Qué les hizo?

—Antes de aclarártelo, te platicaré un poco más sobre mi historia. Ya que tu universo resultará en oscuridad, por lo menos mereces saber la verdad de una vez por todas. Yo era un reflector de Únim. En pocas palabras, un peón sin categoría. Mi trabajo consistía en contemplar la evolución de aquel primer universo y otorgar luz al anochecer. Lo que más anhelaba en la vida, sin embargo, era convertirme en una estrella fugaz; viajar a toda prisa de un lado a otro; sentir el viento agasajando mi cara.

»Cierta ocasión, aprovechando que la emperatriz merodeaba a las afueras del castillo, cerca de mi zona de trabajo, me presenté ante ella y le solicité amablemente un cambio de puesto. La muy estúpida, a modo de réplica, ¿te imaginas lo que me dijo?

»"Tu cargo es imprescindible —habló Arngfz, con voz de mujer—. Cumples con el significativo propósito de contemplar el desarrollo de la vida y ceder luminosidad a los que residen abajo. Qué desconsuelo que no estés conforme ocupando tu puesto en mi reino. Lo siento mucho, pero tengo que negarme a tu petición. Tendrás que aprender a codiciar tu trabajo, así como tus hermanos aman el suyo. Es imposible convertirte en una estrella fugaz. Desde su niñez, todas las estrellas fueron asignadas a sus puestos en el *Instituto de Estrellas de Únim,* para que ejecuten sus labores el resto de su vida. Ya no hay marcha atrás".

»Al acabar su discurso —continuó Arngfz—, los demás se rieron de mí por el atrevimiento de implorar un cambio de plaza a la emperatriz, sobre todo Terso, una estrella fugaz. Cada vez que había oportunidad, aquel acompañaba a la soberana en sus paseos por la región. Ya te había platicado de él, ¿lo recuerdas? Fue aquel fulano que me humillaba siempre —le recordó a

Ariel—. Hacía bromas pesadas y contaba chistes a todos sobre Arngfz Knifux Ýjal a diario. Creo que allí fue cuando la oscuridad empezó a crecer en mí. Y de cierta forma, le tomé provecho.

»Otra noche, escuché una conversación entre la emperatriz y Terso. Hablaban de Realidades Madre, viajes a otros universos y mencionaron, además, la existencia de otras emperatrices y luceros que no correspondían a la comarca de Únim. Muy interesado por el tema, comencé a espiarlos, desatendiendo mis labores. Algunas veces fui regañado y castigado por los soldados en turno, pero nada fuera de lo normal. Los castigos solían ser trabajar un par de días, sin descanso, en las Minas Remotas, donde se obtiene el polvo *zaiko*. Descubrí que, en ciertas épocas del año, la emperatriz desaparecía y retornaba días posteriores. Cuando llegaba, le contaba muy entusiasmada a Terso de sus viajes a través de los mundos y de los prodigios con los que tropezaba. Quedé magnetizado por cada una de sus anécdotas y entonces asumí el desvarío de ya no convertirme en una estrella fugaz, sino en ser capaz de vislumbrar aquellos panoramas. Pero ¿de qué manera lo lograría? Las estrellas obreras no contábamos con la virtud de atravesar espacios temporales ni realidades alternativas; por lo que, de inicio, mi deseo de navegar por diferentes cosmos, se transmutó en un sueño. Más tarde, gracias a mi intelecto, logré dar respuesta a mi pregunta, que dio contestación asimismo a otras valiosas interrogantes:

»¿Quién comandaba la energía de Únim? La emperatriz —respondió él mismo—. ¿Quién la dotaba de toda esa energía? Las estrellas de Únim. ¿Qué debía hacer yo entonces para explorar tierras lejanas?

—Robarle su poder a la emperatriz y las estrellas de Únim —susurró Ariel, asimilándolo.

—Cierto. Ya estás al son de mi canción —dijo festivo, aunque sin sonreír—. Si yo, Arngfz Knifux Ýjal, quería viajar a otra realidad, primero que nada, necesitaba un poder increíble, inimaginable. Ocupaba adquirir *zaiko,* toda la energía existente de Únim, y así viajar más rápido que la velocidad de la luz. Si bien, ello conllevaría sacrificar mi antigua vida. Decidido, envejecí. Es bien sabido que si los astros están bien alimentados pueden controlar el reloj de sus vidas. De ser adultos, tras una buena nutrición, consiguen volverse niños. Cuando envejecen, retornan a rejuvenecer, y así sucesivamente, repitiendo el ciclo de forma inmortal. Pero existen las estrellas jubiladas, que pasan por un proceso de terminación tras haber servido al reino miles de millones de años, y se vuelven agujeros negros controlados, que dan vida a nuevas galaxias.

»*Yo* decidí que mi existencia como lucero llegara a su fin. Me transformé en una raquítica lucecilla que, apenas parpadeaba en el infinito. Ayuné. Y al extinguirse el último destello de mi corazón, exploté. Suscité una ardiente y corrosiva llamarada que lo abarcó todo. Y cuando te digo *todo*, me refiero al Reino Astral letra por letra. Al recobrarme, ya no era el mismo. Experimenté hambre de luz, un apetito de energía. Me había convertido en un agujero negro como ningún otro. Malévolo y lleno de oscuridad. Sin ataduras que me controlaran. Conseguí mi propósito de devorarme a mis enemigas, las estrellas, y acabar con sus miserables vidas —testificó, sin dejar de brochar la jaula—. Cuando fui poderoso, soporté andar durante el día y me consumí su sol. Cada mundo con seres vivos tiene uno. Y si este no existiera, es muy difícil que se desarrollen algunas especies. Seguro lo viste en una de tus visitas al Reino Astral...

Ariel hizo memoria. Así era. El Sol era una esfera

grande de fuego amarillo, imposible de atrapar en un costal o una aspiradora.

—Así pues —continuó Arngfz—, dejé aquel mundo en tinieblas. Y ya cargado de suficiente *zaiko*, obtuve la facultad de saltar entre los confines del Pentaverso hasta llegar a la segunda Realidad Madre: Dual, que es este sitio infestado de humanos imbéciles.

«Quiere decir que es la segunda vez que lo hace», concluyó Ariel.

—Muy pronto, mi hambre se intensificó —prosiguió el devorador de astros—. Fue mi oportunidad de conseguir más luceros. Sin embargo, para errar a mi tercera parada, Trial, ocupaba acabar primero con los astros de este nuevo mundo.

—Y no lo pudo hacer solo —dijo Ariel.

—Al principio creí que sería una tarea fácil —prosiguió—. Pero me percaté de que mi momento de gloria tenía que esperar. No existía ningún acceso libre a este Reino Astral. Intenté más de mil y una formas, en vano, infiltrarme en él, no obstante, había perdido la bondad de mi corazón. Los astros solo abren las compuertas de sus propiedades a seres soñadores de corazón noble, como tú. Por esa razón, tuve que recorrer el mundo entero, durante siglos, descartando a múltiples niños y jóvenes que no resultaron ser los indicados; fabricando artefactos inútiles y otros más que útiles, trabajando para grandes pensadores y patanes; aprendiendo las costumbres de tu especie, ideologías, religiones, cultura, política; inculcándome en el mundo de la Ciencia y las Matemáticas. Viajaba a Únim, de vez en cuando (que es el único sitio que puedo visitar gracias a la energía *zaiko* que obtuve de él), para conseguir sustancias y elementos químicos que aquí no existen, como el antigrav, por ejemplo, o los resortes de impulso que adapté en los saltines que utilizaste la otra noche.

La búsqueda por aquel muchacho, o muchacha, que atravesara las puertas del Reino Astral de Dual, se hizo cada vez más desgastante. Mi cuerpo fue debilitándose. Me convertí en un nómada sin energía. Fui envejeciendo. Los pocos rayos del Sol que caían a la Tierra en el transcurso del día representaron mi única dieta. De esta forma transcurrieron los siglos... Y una noche te sentí, Ariel Castillo Rivas. Había dejado de ser una estrella en Únim, pero mi percepción del alma de la gente nunca me abandonó. Percibí tu bondad, tu inquebrantable fe, tu virtuosa imaginación. Supe en ese bendito segundo, hace ocho años, que eras el indicado para convertirte en mi cazador de estrellas.

—¿Ocho años? ¿Tanto lleva espiándome? —estalló Ariel, sin podérselo creer.

—En ese tiempo estuve confeccionando mi plan, jovencito. Terminé de crear los saltines, preparé el antigrav, armé el artefacto volador de Leonardo da Vinci, elegí a los cinco adolescentes que me servirían para abrir el portal del Reino Astral y me deshice de ciertos obstáculos.

En toda esa conversación, el rostro sin líneas de expresión de Arngfz fue refinado. No manifestó sentir enojo o aflicción en ningún fragmento de su biografía, ni mucho menos remordimiento. Volvió a introducir la brocha en la cubeta y se mantuvo lustrando la prisión con indiferencia.

—Ahora estás por utilizar mi último invento: el «imán de estrellas» —notificó.

Le hormiguearon las manos a Ariel cuando escuchó aquella noticia.

—Y ya está listo —anunció Arngfz. Aventó la cubeta y la brocha a la melena de león. Ambos objetos quedaron compactados en el aire a mitad de su viaje—. No necesitarás esforzarte en hacer nada —dijo—. El com-

ponente que distribuí por el embalaje es un imán para atraer luceros. Las estrellas vendrán hacia ti por sí solas, y quedarán pegadas a las rejas como mariposas en una red. Será imposible que escapen...

—Es un ser descarado.

Había tenido razón Arngfz al decir que Ariel no necesitaba cazar astros para sacar tajada esa noche. Solo requería de su presencia y su corazón soñador, a fin de introducirse al Reino Astral.

—Hum, a propósito, espero que disfrutes viendo a la emperatriz de Dual. Visualizarla es inolvidable, ya te lo diré yo. Es la estrella más admirable del cielo, y por lo general está enclaustrada en su castillo. Casi nunca se le ve fuera —dijo Argnfz—. Disfrutaré contemplando la expresión de pánico de esa mojigata cuando me la esté devorando. No te confundirás al verla. Las soberanas de los Reinos Astrales son las únicas estrellas que poseen un cálido tono dorado.

«¿QUÉ?», reventó Ariel en su cabeza.

¿La estrella dorada que dejó encubierta bajo la almohada de Alondrita se trataba, en realidad, de la emperatriz de Dual? La mandataria de la segunda Realidad Madre.

Antes de que pudiera seguir reflexionando en ello, Arngfz creció a la anchura de una chimenea de una central nuclear, cogió la jaula con su mano lanzadora, concibió un movimiento fulminante con sus atléticos brazos y, en suma, lanzó a Ariel a las alturas como un balón en pleno pase de un partido de futbol americano.

Se integró Ariel a las nubes a la velocidad del sonido. En cuanto rasgó la delgada cortina que dividía ambos lugares, Tierra y Reino Astral, lo encharcó el silencio. Se integró en el firmamento como una saeta y vigiló las pocas estrellas fronterizas a su alrededor. Ya no veía flamas de veladoras perpetuas, igual que las

noches anteriores, sino lo que en realidad eran: diminutas personitas, ajenas del futuro que Arngfz tenía preparado para ellas, con su par de alas puntiagudas en la espalda apuntando hacia abajo. Ariel las encontró despiertas, con espadas y flechas apuntándolo. Esa noche estaban preparadas para la pelea. El cazador de estrellas se puso en pie y, sin pensárselo dos veces, gritó con todas sus fuerzas:

—¡Vuelen! —apremió.

Y escuchó su eco resonante en el ático cósmico.

¡Vuelen! ¡Vuelen! ¡Vuelen!...

Las estrellas lo ignoraron.

—¡Huyan! —prescribió Ariel—. Vayan a refugiarse a su castillo.

¡Huyan! Vayan a refugiarse a su castillo.
¡Huyan! Vayan a refugiarse a su castillo.
¡Huyan! Vayan a refugiarse a su castillo...

Pero los luceros, en lugar de prestar atención a las advertencias de Ariel, en ese momento se lanzaron contra él como pequeños guerreros defendiendo sus propiedades.

—¡No! —gritó, impotente de no tener la capacidad de ahuyentarlas.

Su resonancia coreó:

¡No! ¡No! ¡No!...

Las estrellas que se hallaban más cerca fueron las primeras en ser atraídas hacia los barrotes metálicos de la jaula, tal como la gravedad conquista una entidad para hacerla caer. Los cuerpos celestes incitaron un so-

nidito de *plop* cuando se adhirieron a los refuerzos, y desde allí descargaron golpes y patadas en el aire con tal de liberarse de su cruel tormento.

Plop, plop, plop, cayeron uno a uno, pese a que Ariel les insistía que retrocedieran, que un agujero negro pretendía exterminar a su comarca. Continuaron pegándose a los hierros, y los ecos del muchacho se repitieron incesables. A lo lejos, Ariel divisó unos luceros que se acercaron apresurados, tal vez un ejército de soldados dispuestos a luchar. Quiso indicarles una vez más, con señas, que se retiraran. No funcionó.

En el intervalo por venir, la prisión radicó iluminada igual que un arbolito de Navidad. El universo prevaleció oscuro. Los planetas, la luna, y todo lo que residía en el universo de Dual, resultó en tinieblas. Ariel imaginó que de aquella miserable negrura lo atacaría una garra demoniaca, que le apretaría el cuello para asfixiarlo, inculpándolo de aquella tragedia. Ansió que eso pasara. Arngfz había tenido razón en lo que le dijo cierta ocasión: era un muchacho ingenuo y, sobre todo, tonto. Pudo haber evitado los problemas desde un principio, con la excepción, por supuesto, de que Alondrita se salvara. Se cubrió los ojos. No era su afición mirar aquellas tristes estrellas que le prestaban atención. Estiraban sus bracitos desde los hierros, con sus armas, para jalarlo de las ropas y capturarlo.

—Lo siento, lo siento mucho —les susurraba, anegado en lágrimas.

Recibió flechazos en la cara y las manos, que a Ariel se le antojaron como espinas. La jaula descendió en picada y atravesó las nubes.

Segundos delanteros, Arngfz la atrapó con una mano.

—Misión cumplida —dijo con crudeza.

Adoptó su tamaño característico de gente común y

corriente y abrió la portezuela. Ariel se liberó de un salto y se vieron de frente. La hermosa cara de Arngfz pertenecía a una antigua estatua romana.

—Si quieres, puedes ir a esconderte a tu casa y lamentar a Susanita como se lo merece. Yo me tomaré un buen rato para degustar con placidez este manjar. En unos días, cuando sea capaz de vagar durante el día, me desayunaré al rey de tu cielo, el Sol, y podré saltar a la tercera Realidad Madre. —Hizo lucir sus blanquecinos ojos. Luego, agregó—: Qué adolescente tan infortunado. Si hubieras sido más inteligente, habrías sabido que tras capturar una estrella amarilla uno puede pedirle un deseo.

Le dio la espalda al chico y abrió su exorbitante boca, con el propósito de absorber los luceros uno por uno. Se despegaban de la celda y acababan en aquella inmensa garganta que aparentaba ser el túnel de un tren. Cierta estrella fue tomada de las manos por dos amigas suyas que intervinieron para socorrerla. Al momento de que Arngfz aplicara más fuerza, el conjunto desapareció.

«Entonces no está todo perdido —se alentó Ariel—. Aún tengo oportunidad de enmendar mis errores. El deseo de la emperatriz.»

Dio un giro de ciento ochenta grados y corrió a toda velocidad, dejando atrás el parque recreativo, antes de que Arngfz se diera cuenta de que en la jaula embadurnada del imán de estrellas faltaba la soberana del Reino Astral.

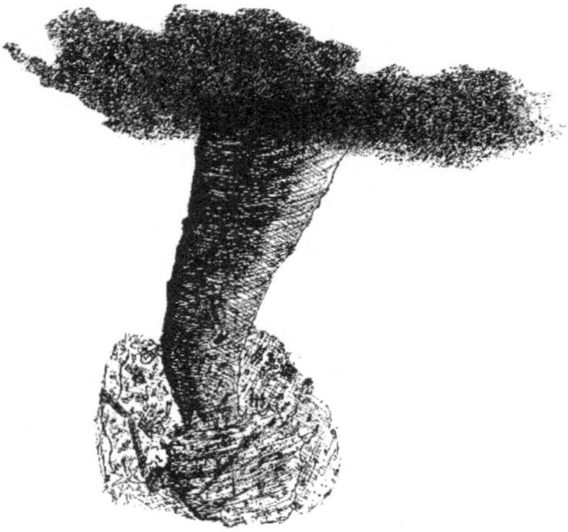

Capítulo 25
El torbellino

Agitó el fatigado Ariel sus enormes muslos acalambrados. Le ardió el pecho. Su corazón se convirtió en una válvula de aire. ¡Qué importaba que estuviera cansado, a punto de desfallecer! Todavía había esperanza. Si era inteligente, en un mismo deseo podía hacer que Alondrita, las estrellas, Ellie, el mundo entero, y hasta quizás, su madre, pudieran salvarse. Casi llegaba a su casa. Unos metros para pisar el decadente jardín.

Treinta metros.

Solo un poco más.

Veinticinco metros.

Iba pensando en su deseo.

Pero recibió un empujón por el dorso y cayó de frente. Su cara se apachurró contra el suelo y sintió un hirviente chorro de sangre brotándole de la nariz. ¿Qué había ocurrido? ¿Quién lo empujó para que se diera contra el suelo?

«Arngfz me descubrió», lo asaltó el pensamiento.

No obstante, estuvo en un error.

—Te tengo, *Lady Arielita.*

Ariel se dio la vuelta y miró a Brandon Portillo de pie, empuñando la navaja suiza. Olegario lo acompañaba, pero más que emocionado, se dio a conocer pálido y nervioso.

—Brandon, amigo, quedamos en que solo íbamos a espantarlo, ¿cierto? —murmuró.

—¡Cállate, *Niño Rata*! Esto es entre él y yo.

Olegario tragó saliva y retrocedió un par de pasos. No le quedaron ganas de oponerse.

—Ponte de pie —le ordenó Portillo a Ariel, apuntándolo con el arma—. ¿No me oíste? Levántate.

Lo pateó en la pantorrilla, Ariel musitó un quejido. Contempló, con ojos muy abiertos, aquel filo metálico que señaló su garganta. ¿Por qué el Baladrón tenía que aparecerse esa noche? ¿Por qué no después de haber salvado al mundo? Otro día.

Se incorporó Ariel, sobándose la pierna, y con el antebrazo se limpió los borbotones que le fluían de la nariz.

—Por favor, deja que me marche. Tengo algo urgente que hacer —suplicó Ariel, jadeando—. Mañana haz lo que quieras conmigo.

Portillo soltó una fingida carcajada e hincó su codo en el pecho de Olegario para que le hiciera coro.

—¿Urgente, dijiste? —dijo furioso—. ¿Qué urgencia puede tener una inútil bola de grasa como tú? ¿Por eso no estabas en tu cuarto? *Rata* y yo ya nos estábamos desesperando. Te tardaste mucho.

—¡No inventes! —exclamó Olegario atolondrado—. ¿Ya viste el cielo, Brandon? No hay estrellas. El hombre de las noticias dijo la verdad. Debimos haber aprovechado esta noche para ver juntos el...

Su amo lo amedrantó con la mirada y Olegario fue bajando el volumen de su voz hasta que emitió un corto bisbiseo.

—Tengo que salvar al mundo —señaló Ariel—. Devolver las estrellas al cielo.

Ariel apreció el moretón que el bravucón llevaba en la frente, uno que le bautizó la mole de su padre.

—Tú vas a ser quien se una a las estrellas esta noche —sentenció Portillo—. Pero cuando te mate.

Se lanzó hacia adelante y atacó.

Ariel se cubrió la cara y sintió el frío metal atravesándole la mano. La herida, que se paseó desde el meñique hasta el dedo pulgar, se abrió cual concha de mar y dejó nacer numerosas perlas de sangre. Lanzó un aullido de dolor y miró con espanto la aproximación de un segundo ataque.

—¿Por qué le contaste a la directora que llevaba la navaja? Te lo advertí —bramó Brandon—. ¿No te cansas de ser un estúpido saco de carne? ¿Te gusta que te destrocen?

Zaz, zaz.

Los siguientes dos cortes fueron rápidos y perfectos. Rasgaron la manga del suéter de Ariel y un par de franjas rojas, como de cebra, le adornaron la piel.

—¡Detente! ¡Yo no fui! —gritaba, retrocediendo—. ¡Yo no lo hice!

—¿Ah no? ¿Entonces quién? Dímelo para picarlo también.

Ariel examinó al verdadero culpable: Olegario, quien le devolvió un miramiento de alarma.

—Brandon, déjalo —insistió aquel—. No vale la pena. Ya le dimos su buen susto.

—¡No! —refutó Brandon.

Olegario escondió la cabeza entre los hombros, igual que una tortuga asustada, y se calló.

—*Cerdonio* debe llevarse su merecido. Tiene que entender que conmigo nadie se mete.

Levantó la navaja suiza para hacer un corte categórico.

—Para —suplicó Ariel, reuniendo las manos en su cuello.

Antes de que pasara lo que tuviera que pasar, se oyó la armonía de mil trompetas. Los tres adolescentes miraron al final de la calle, justo donde se localizaba el parque abandonado.

—¿Qué carajos fue eso? —preguntó Brandon.

—Yo me largo de aquí —exclamó Olegario.

Y echó a correr a toda velocidad, por el lado contrario de la calle.

—¡Cobarde! —lo insultó Brandon—. Ya no quiero que te vuelvas a acercar a mí. No me estés rogando en la escuela que quieres juntarte conmigo, *Niño Rata.*

Ariel conservó la boca abierta, su labio inferior tembló de adentro hacia afuera. El porqué de su compostura fue muy ajeno al hecho de que iba a ser degollado a medio camino por Brandon Portillo. Se enteró Ariel de que ese estallido no fue un conjunto de mil trompetas (como imaginó su atacante). No. Aquello era un grito encolerizado, de rabia, de caos.

Un grito de Arngfz.

—¡LA EMPERATRIZ! ¿DÓNDE ESTÁ? —clamó el gigante.

El par de chicos se cubrió las orejas.

Pum... Pam... Pum... Pam...

Cuatro fueron las pisadas que le bastaron para llegar a la calle Monteseaur.

Los cristales de las ventanas de las casas se rompieron y salieron volando en todas direcciones, los cables de los postes eléctricos concibieron una detonación trastornada de chispas blancas y amarillas; los faroles

que iluminaban la calle se apagaron uno a uno, emitiendo ruidos estáticos; y los coches prendieron sus molestas alarmas. La escena se redujo a la penumbra.

Ariel escuchó la respiración agitada de Portillo, quien, presa del horror, se hallaba a su lado. ¿Qué le estaría cruzando por la cabeza en estos momentos?, se preguntó.

Un automóvil se divisó a lo lejos, que ilustró el supremo cuerpo de Arngfz. Su contorno quedó dibujado en la calle como una silueta. Brandon contorsionó la cara de espanto cuando notó que aquella cosa respiraba y que poseía un par de ojos blancos. El vehículo, por su parte, a pesar de viajar lento como un escarabajo, se estampó contra el formidable talón de la criatura, participando en un aparatoso accidente. El cofre se apachurró y el parabrisas se descuartizó.

«La señora Corrales», acertó Ariel.

Arngfz levantó el auto como si fuera un juguete, miró de frente a la conductora (que empezó a gritar enloquecida) y lo aventó a la lejanía. Por suerte, su caída concluyó sobre un montículo de heno, en una lejana granja porcina. La señora Corrales resultó con heridas menores, aunque con la cara salpicada de estiércol.

Todavía erguido, en medio de Monteseaur, el gigante observó a Ariel.

—¡Te aniquilaré, gusano! —rugió.

Luego, tomando propulsión giró en un solo pie y estiró los brazos, manteniéndolos en una línea recta, sin perder la compostura. Mantuvo el eje central. Su figura se distorsionó, debido a la velocidad con la que giró. Corrientes de viento se elevaron por distintas direcciones. Las hojas de los árboles riñeron unas con otras, nubes de polvo se alzaron como criaturas fantasmagóricas y se oyó un ruido ensordecedor parecido al de una locomotora. Arngfz se había convertido en un

tornado.

Las viviendas estrenaron la ruina cuando sus tejados se desprendieron cuales envolturas de una barra de chocolate. Las vallas de los jardines fueron desapareciendo una tras otra y los árboles se desligaron desde su raíz en un crujido enfurecido. Las cosas giraron en torno a Arngfz. El torbellino se alzó tanto, que se ensambló con el cielo. Su embudo fue sinónimo de cataclismo. Pronto avanzó hacia los dos adolescentes, devorando lo que encontraba a su paso.

—¡Tenemos que irnos de aquí! —le gritó Ariel a Brandon.

Portillo no se movió. Estaba como una estatua, contemplando la catástrofe. Los fuertes vientos le arrebataron la navaja suiza de la mano y la desaparecieron en la tempestad. Eso fue lo que hizo volver a Brandon en sí. Volteó con Ariel y juntos encabezaron una carrera por la vía pública, esquivando por los pelos un ejército de obstáculos que se desplomaban a sus lados desordenadamente, o que cruzaban sobre sus cabezas.

—¡LA ESTRELLA! —bramaba Arngfz—. ¡DAME A LA EMPERATRIZ! TÚ TE LA LLEVASTE.

Llovieron vidrios y fierros oxidados pertenecientes al parque recreativo. Cayeron pasamanos, se veían ramas sueltas y árboles enteros, postes eléctricos, bicicletas, camas y roperos. Ariel y Brandon, oyeron a sus espaldas automóviles que se combaban al estrellarse contra el cemento. Cuchillos y tenedores les pasaron zumbando por las orejas. Algunos vecinos, corrieron presurosos, al otro lado de las ventanas, dentro de sus hogares, buscando refugio. Los dos jóvenes atravesaron el marchito jardín de la casa número 72, cuyo buzón en aquel momento se desgajó de la tierra y se perdió de vista. Entraron al vestíbulo, avanzaron por el estrecho pasillo y se reunieron en la habitación de

Alondrita. El polvo y el viento se colaron murmuradores por el gigantesco agujero en la pared que desertó la mano de Arngfz.

Brandon miró a la niña de cristal tendida sobre la cama.

—¿Y esa cosa qué es?

—Mi hermana. Acaba de morir —respondió.

—No me puede estar ocurriendo esto... —chilló el Baladrón, llevándose las manos a la boca.

Y gritó cuando la pared que tenía delante se resquebrajó. Ariel se vio en la necesidad de ignorarlo. Metió el brazo en la almohada y sacó el tubo de ensayo. El cuarto se ahogó con una luz áurea. Portillo observó, pasmado, la graciosa luciérnaga que había dentro. La estrella vio a su cazador, y hay que recalcar que con bastante molestia.

—¿Puede cumplirme un deseo? —inquirió Ariel, con la ensangrentada mano temblándole de miedo.

La emperatriz lo miró estupefacta, como no creyendo que Ariel fuera tan descarado como para pedirle tal cosa. Se cruzó de brazos y le volteó la cara.

—Vamos. No haga berrinche. Él está por llegar —urgió.

¡Y vaya que tenía razón! El tornado se aproximaba. Los elementos del cuarto comenzaron a fugarse por el hoyo de la recamara. Ariel quitó el corcho al tubo de ensayo y el astro quedó liberado, con su ala curada. De inicio, la emperatriz le administró una bofetada que, a su buen juicio, Ariel se la tenía bien merecida. Luego, aquella volteó al cielo. Expelió un alarido patético cuando reveló la chocante negrura, detrás de las nubes. Encendidos sus ojos de rabia, y sumergidos en lágrimas, le propinó incontables empujones a Ariel, quien apenas pudo percibir los golpecitos en su pecho.

—De veras lo siento mucho, pero es forzoso que ha-

gamos esto de una buena vez, o será demasiado tarde —apremió, sin prestar demasiada atención a los gritos delirantes de Brandon Portillo, que se metió bajo la cama.

El techo de la casa vibró y la estrella reiteró su cruce de brazos.

—Le pido mis más sinceras disculpas, emperatriz de Dual...

Ariel estaba desesperado.

Sus pies se deslizaron por el suelo. Tuvo que aferrarse a una pata de la cama. El lucero sintió también la potestad del viento y se sujetó de las greñas de su captor.

—No existe justificación para lo que les hice —gritaba él—. Eché todo a perder. Exterminé a toda una raza. Fui egoísta. Sin embargo, todavía hay oportunidad de salvar a los Reinos Astrales y a las Realidades del Pentaverso. Se lo suplico, emperatriz, concédame el deseo.

La estrella no pudo responderle, fue atraída por el tornado. Ariel la pescó con su mano libre y un centenar de polvos amarillos salieron de sus alas, revoloteando por la habitación. En ese preciso momento, el tejado levitó y la casa trepidó. Arngfz había llegado. Se hallaba encima de ellos, detrás de los aires plomizos del tornado. Su enorme boca se abrió para atragantarse con la morada. La emperatriz alcanzó el punto del infarto cuando tuvo aquel encolerizado rostro encima de ella.

—¡Rápido! —escandalizó Ariel—. El deseo. Concédamelo.

El astro se llevó ambas manos al corazón, algo mareado, y sacudió la cabeza de arriba abajo.

—Deseo... —dijo Ariel—. Deseo que...

Pero tan pronto como empezó a hablar, Arngfz abrió

más su boca y las paredes de la vivienda desaparecieron. Ariel vislumbró a Brandon girar en el remolino, dando incomprensibles gritos ahogados. Al voltear a la cama, descubrió que Alondrita ya no estaba. La emperatriz se le escurrió de los dedos.

Una ocasión más, había fallado.

Voló, junto con la corriente, siendo molida su cabeza y el cuerpo por los escombros. Y de un segundo a otro, por un golpe en la cabeza, todo se pintó de negro.

Corría otra vez, en aquella adversa oscuridad. La criatura lo perseguía y Ariel no distinguía bien su camino. Luces retoñaron de su cuerpo y giraron alrededor de él. Eran cinco estrellas; las cinco emperatrices pertenecientes a las Realidades Madre. Pero… ¿por qué estaban allí? ¿Acaso ellas lo salvarían de aquel monstruo? Viró en redondo. De una vez por todas, descubriría quién (o qué) lo cazaba. La bestia dio con él y por primera ocasión ambos pudieron plantar cara. Así, Ariel descubrió que esta poseía patas de araña, cuello alargado de cisne y el cuerpo cubierto de vello y plumas oscuras. Aunque, más temible que aquella fisionomía, era su rostro. Era el perfil de una anciana sin párpados. Y le resultó inexplicablemente conocida, sin embargo… ¿en dónde la había visto antes?

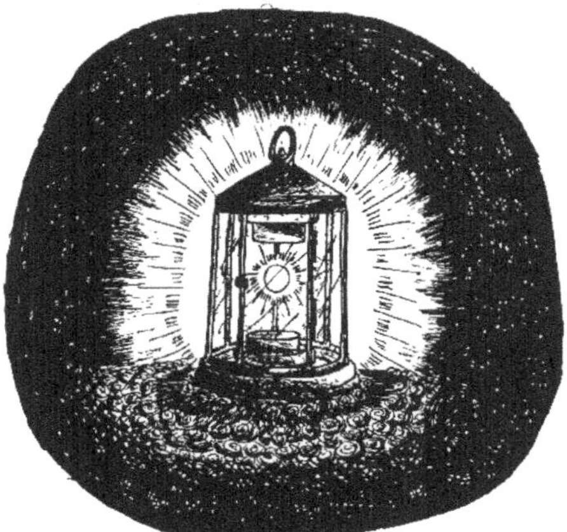

Epílogo
Las dos ancianas

—¡Ay! —Arrojó una fuerte expresión de dolor. Algo le había pinchado las costillas.

—¡Lo que faltaba! Está vivo —se quejó alguien.

—El Arroyo Principal trajo otro muchacho —comentó una segunda persona.

Al momento de despertar, Ariel se percató de que estaba empapado. Sufrió de penetrantes náuseas en el centro del estómago y vomitó una sustancia negra y helada. Más tarde se puso en pie. Cuando se dio tiempo para repasar el entorno, reveló que el mundo se hallaba plenamente en tinieblas. Había un par de ancianas constando a su lado, alumbrándolo con una lámpara.

El adolescente experimentó un repentino escalofrío, pues las dos se parecían a Arngfz.

CONTINUARÁ…

MERMELADA DE ESTRELLAS 2

OSCURIDAD ABSOLUTA

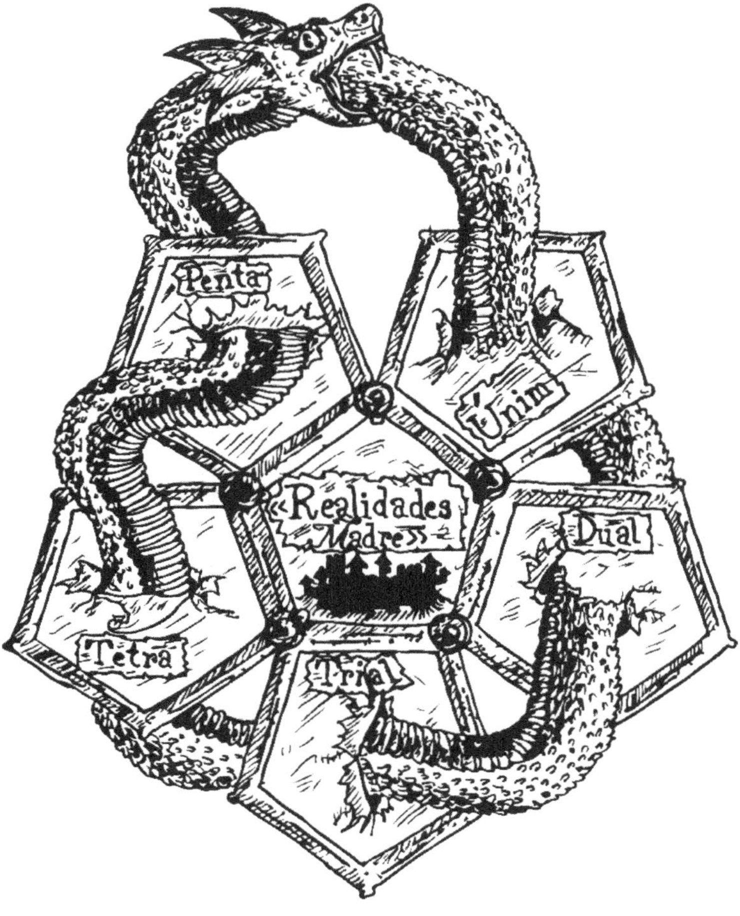
Penta
Únim
«Realidades Madre»
Dual
Tetra
Trial

Mermelada de Estrellas: Las cinco noches

René Valdez Ramos

Made in the USA
Monee, IL
22 April 2023

32248582R00204

Printed in the USA
CPSIA information can be obtained
at www.ICGtesting.com
CBHW012054011024
15217CB00021B/914

9 798988 282952

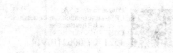